THE ADVENTURES

OF

TALLDORF

AND

SMALL

Book I The Myth

by

Franklin Dunlap & John Perrill

Wilderness Road Books
40050 Wilderness Road
Branscomb, CA 95417
Tel: 707-984-6008

ISBN   0-9626555-0-3

Printed by Kayumanggi Press, Inc.
940 Quezon Ave, Quezon City, Philippines

To my Mother

'Get out of the way with your cobwebs;
wash your windows, I say!'

Thoreau

THE ADVENTURES OF
TALLDORF AND SMALL

TABLE OF CONTENTS

Part One

MAMA'S GONE

Chapter 1

THE GAMBLER'S BOY

Joe 'Pipestems' Talldorf was an upper-story artist and a gambler. It is difficult to say whether Joe's penchant for the horses and the two-dollar window came first or if his antics in the bosun's chair and on the scaffolds, where he risked his life, produced the desire to bet every cent he earned.

Both might have proceeded inversely from his father, C.C. Talldorf, a bricklayer, who built some of the tallest industrial chimneys in Detroit, flinging another wedge of mortar against his fear of heights as the chimney soared skyward.

Neither came from Florence, Joe's mother, who tied her babushka in a loose Irish knot and toted her bucket and her mop with an aim to stay as close to the earth as possible, whether on her knees in church or scrubbing the floors of the Ford Motor Company offices.

At fourteen Joe stood a foot taller than his short, bespeckled father. Joe had his mother's big bones, her delicate high-winded nostrils, her light complexion, with only the fiery brown fanatical eyes of C.C. as proof that he had sprung from his loins.

When Joe was sixteen C.C. got him a job as a chimney sweep with the Plately Sweep & Stoker Company. Joe crawled down the very stacks that C.C. had put up, dangled from a rope as they pulled him to the top coming out between the lightning rods, his teeth black, spitting bits of carbon.

Joe donated most of his earnings to his father's small household. C.C. expected ninety-five percent as paterfamilias. His resentful son, with his voracious appetite, cost him that much in groceries. Joe spent what was left on tobacco and whiskey in emulation of the sweeps who stood smoking on the roof while 'Pipestems' climbed the iron rungs in his shoulder harness, his brushes dangling from his belt.

Red Plately ran the gangs himself. Red stood head and shoulders above the small Irishmen in their greasy coveralls with the large black letters that spelled PLATELY'S SWEEPS which Red provided free and laundered at no charge. Red designed and rigged the pulleys that allowed the small men to drop down the stacks like spiders.

Red was generous and as prolific as any good Irish Catholic. There were six sons at home. All the boys had jobs though none of them worked for Red. Red's daughter Mary went to school, did the cooking and the housework, washed the laundry and darned the socks while Elinore, her mother, manned the office and kept the Plately Company's books.

Joe Talldorf had his own key now and kept his own hours, but it wasn't enough to satisfy his taste for independence. C.C. frowned at him constantly and Florence fussed. C.C. sat in the kitchen in his undershirt popping his bacon and bread under his mustache. "Decent hours!" he said sullenly. "How da ye expect ta give Mr. Plately his money's worth if ya don't get yer rest, I'd like ta know."

Joe bought a rainbow-colored suitcase at Arky's Pawnshop. "Wrap it up fer me." Arky had strummed his suspenders with annoyance but he'd done what Joe had asked. Joe carried his package by the handle which stuck out of the brown paper. It was easy to sneak the suitcase down the hallway past C.C.'s snoring into his room and under the bed.

On Sunday morning, while C.C. and Florence sat in church, Joe left. He printed a short note and put it on the kitchen table.

> 'Dear ma an C.C.,
> Thanks fer everythin. I'm livin
> on me own. Don't worry about
> nothin. Thanks again.
> Joe'

Joe thought bitterly of C.C. standing in line every Friday night at the bank to deposit both their checks. He walked casually down the alley with his suitcase past Mrs. Crispin who was poking her trash fire with a stick.

"Headin out on yer own are ya, boy?" she said, "Well it's about time. You're headed fer ruin, boy! But ain't we all—"

"How old are ya boy?" the landlady asked looking Joe up and down.

"I'm seventeen, ma'am."

"Yer a tall one ain't yese?" she said. "An yer folks where would they be an what do they think of all this?"

"I ain't got no folks."

"No folks? Don't be tellin me lies, boy. No one raised ya I suppose. No mother holdin ya to her breast an right now cryin her eyes red an yer father workin long hours ta put bread in yer ungrateful mouth."

"It ain't like that, ma'am. I pay me own way. I got a job. If ya don't want ta rent ta me just say so."

"I'll rent to ya, boy. It'll be $3.50 a week paid in advance. Ya get yer breakfast an yer supper an clean sheets once a week."

The room at Wickham's Boarding House was large and airy with white wainscotting and figured paper, a washstand in the corner and the bathroom down the hall. Joe lay on the bed studying the ceiling water stain. His light feeling of independence alternated with an anxious sweat. He lay there all day and most of the next.

On Monday evening Joe strolled the cottage back streets until he came to Maple. The big white Plately house set at the top of the lot. The green lawn stretched spaciously to the shrubs and bushes, above which insects danced in the sun's last rays. Joe walked up the steps and rang the bell.

"I'll get it."

Mary had finished the dishes, scrubbed the last pot and wiped the last plate, wearing her red hair in a braid that hung down her back.

"Yes?"

"Is yer dad ta home? I'd like ta talk ta him."

"Won't you come in?"

"Naw. That's all right. I'll just wait here."

"Suit yourself. Dad?" She looked at Joe. "What's your name?"

"Joe. Joe Talldorf."

Mary's eyebrows arched in recognition.

"Ya heard a me then?"

"I'm Mary," she said with a flash of disdain. "Pleased to meet you. Dad? It's Joe Talldorf here to see you." Mary waltzed away and left Joe standing ill at ease.

"Joe," Red said extending his hand. "Come on in."

"How ya doin, Red? I wanna talk to ya alone if that's ok?"

"Sure Joe. Come into the study. Have a seat."

"Red, I'm quittin."

"I see."

"It ain't cause I don't like the work see. Er workin for ya er nothin like that. It's fer personal reasons."

"I. understand Joe. Anyway you've seen what crawling down a chimney does for a man. Just between you and me there's not one of the boys who doesn't drink too much or lose his wages gambling. It's the life of a chimney sweep. You should be looking for a better trade. Carpentry, mechanics, laying bricks."

"Excuse me dear." Elinore stood in the door with her hands on her hips.

"Hello Mrs. Plately."

"Hello Joe. Your mother came to see me today."

"Joe's quitting, Eli."

"Quitting?"

"Yea, Mrs. Plately. I'm gonna find me another trade."

"Stop by the office tomorrow then, and I'll give you your pay. And Joe, please go see your mother. She's worried sick."

Joe sat on a park bench smoking a cigarette. Mary's face stuck in his memory like a photograph.

"Hey kid, ya got a smoke?" Joe pulled out his Bull Durham sack.

"Me name is Slim Hastings," the stranger said and held out his hand. "I was the best winda washer in the 48 states — till I hurt me back. Hey kid, could ya loan me fifty cents?"

"Sure," Joe said, "I just got paid."

Slim Hastings took Joe to the track and taught him how to read a scratch sheet. They rode the streetcar out to the jewelbox setting of Hazel Park and sat in the grandstand. Joe watched the sleek bays prance into the gate, the black horse reared above his trainer. The owl-eyed jockeys crouched in the narrow saddles cradling their whips, the loudspeaker blaring: "They're off! It's Royal Fox in front Jud's Neck second Smart Lady on the inside—" Slim grit his teeth and clenched his fists. "It's Jacob's Run and Smart Lady! It's Smart Lady by a length!" Slim tore his ticket in half and licked his pencil.

"Ya can't win em all, kid," he said. "Pick a horse fer the next race an I'll place yer bet."

Joe gave Slim two dollars to put on Five-O, a ten to one shot that won. Joe picked the last five races with an uncanny bettor's sense, winning them all. "We're rich, kid. I got a hunnert dollars here. I'm gonna give ya the usual ten percent, an I'm takin ya out ta dinner."

"How do ya get ta be a winda washer, Slim?" Joe asked as Slim filled his plate with spaghetti.

"There ain't nothin to it, kid. Ya buy yerself a bucket an a couple squeegees an yer in business."

The next afternoon at Hazel Park Joe picked six races out of ten. "Ya got a inclination fer the horses, kid," Slim said with respect. "Wit this percentage you an me are gonna be millionaires. I keep askin meself, 'Is this kid a genius?' Yer a genius, kid. Just ask Slim Hastings."

Mary Plately had just arrived home from school when Joe Talldorf rang the bell. Joe wore a new snap-brim hat, a dashing plaid suit and duckbill yellow shoes. Mary shook out her red hair and ran downstairs in her blue jumper.

"Yes..." she said, smiling sweetly.

"It's me...Joe Talldorf," he said. "Ya probably don't recognize me in me new duds."

Mary giggled.

"What's so funny?"

"Nothing's funny. You just look so—different. If you wanted to see my dad he's not at home."

"I didn't come ta see yer dad. I come ta see you."

"Me?"

"I brung ya these flowers." Joe handed Mary twelve red roses.

"Oh—They're beautiful, Joe."

"Why'nt ya put on yer coat an come ta the drug store? I'll buy ya a soda."

"I can't go out. I have to fix supper."

"Ain't ya gonna invite me in then?"

"I'm not supposed to."

"I ain't exactly a stranger ya know Mary. I used ta work fer yer father. Me motives is pure."

"Well, since you got all dressed up and brought me flowers —"

Joe became a regular visitor at the Plately house. He always arrived just in time for supper, which always annoyed Elinore.

"He's a drinker and a gambler," Elinore said to Red as he read the paper.

"He's young yet."

"We can't afford it. Why doesn't he eat supper at his own parents' house?"

Red shrugged. "What's one more mouth?"

For the most part Mary's brothers took to Joe at once. Adair and Murray, the oldest, thought he was funny. They laughed at Joe and his jokes. Thomas ignored him. Teddie and Eddie, the twins, took Joe to fish for bullheads in the Rouge River. And sometimes Joe left early with Stanley to shoot pool which made Mary wonder if he was really interested in her.

What Joe liked most was to stay and help Mary in the kitchen after the meal. He cleared the table and stacked the plates while she swept the floor. He took out the garbage while she washed the dishes and scrubbed the pots. The seed of their romance was planted in the pantry among the shelves of canned goods and the flour sacks.

"Right in this house! Behind our backs," Elinore said bitterly.

"We have to accept it, Elinore," Red said. "Joe's promised to take good care of her."

"How? He doesn't have a job. He's always at the track. I can't stand it!"

"All right. All right. Don't get upset. Try to be reasonable for God's sake. He's got some plans. He wants to start his own business."

"He doesn't know the first thing about business."

"Joe isn't dumb. He's good with pulleys and ropes. When he was working for us he learned pretty fast."

"He's ruined Mary's life. She'll never finish high school."

"We've got to give them all the help we can, Eli. I thought we could give them a house for a wedding present. Buy them a nice little cottage, then after the baby comes—"

Elinore covered her face with her hands and began to sob.

Mary's photo had appeared in the *Detroit Free Press*. The wedding invitations had been printed and addressed. The hall was rented and Mrs. Veronski, the seamstress, was working ten hours a day to finish Mary's dress.

"Yer ma don't like me, Mare," Joe said. "She don't like the way I wear me hat."

"That's not true, Joey. She's just nervous because of the wedding."

"Don't give me that. She don't like me an ya know it. If she knew how them guys respect me at the track—"

"What about your business?"

"Slim was tellin me today if it was him he'd pick up one a them new factories. Charge em a nickel a pane on the high ones cause a the risk. Ya know, Mare, some a them buildins got thousands a windas. Slim says it's a good racket. All ya need is a bucket, a squeegee an a couple rags. He says he'd do it himself but he can't. Account a his back."

Joe kicked a tin can along the railroad tracks past another set of grimy machine shop windows. The answer was always the same: "We ain't interested, kid."

He was about to call it quits for the day and return to Wickham's with aching feet again when opportunity gleamed forth from a construction site on the Detroit River. Joe scrambled up the grassy bank. He was still counting the little windows when the sun set. The reflections of the bridge lights twinkled in the glass as Joe's eyes strained," — 4,506, 4,507—" He'd get that job and wash every pane for his sweet Mary.

General Malcom Tire had never gone to West Point. His rank had been bestowed by Teddy Roosevelt in gratitude for Malcom Tire's efficient organization of the trains for moving troops and supplies during the Mexican War, and in recognition of Malcom Tire's father's influence and wealth. Thaddeus G. Tire, the multimillionaire munitions maker, owned mountains of sulphur, fleets of barges and freight cars that stretched into the distance. General Malcom Tire sunk his inheritance in rubber.

General Tire bought plantations in Malaysia and Brazil, bought ships to carry the crude in their holds, built the great factory on the Detroit River with his eye on the future. He envisioned every American family someday owning an automobile, multiplied that number by four and came up with an astronomical figure.

The pigeons had already started nesting in the cornices. The machines were bolted to the floor. Laborers were loading piles of dust and broken brick into wheelbarrows and trundling them off to the docks where draymen were pulled up in horse-drawn wagons and shiny Ford trucks. No one paid any attention to Joe who ran up the steps to the seventh floor.

The offices on the seventh floor were finished and the air smelled of fresh paint. General Malcom Tire sat behind his oval desk with his eyes shut. The General was dreaming of a farmer sitting on a tractor with its cleated rubber tires. He saw two-car garages, freeways, and parking lots.

"Scuse me," Joe said. "Are you General Tire, sir?"

The General's eyes popped open. "Yes, I am. What brings you to this great American enterprise, my boy?"

"Me name is Joseph Talldorf. I come on account a the windas. They're beautiful, sir."

"Why thank you, Joseph. They are beautiful aren't they? I was out on the terrace last night just at sunset and they were indeed a gorgeous sight. I suppose you are a glazier who desires a contract to replace the panes as they get broken."

"No sir. I ain't a glazier. Me idea is ta wash em."

"Ah, window washer by trade," beamed the General on the paternal verge of a panegyric in praise of the integrity of such a high profession and the simple god-like quality of all working men.

"Not by trade, sir," Joe interrupted, "by inclination."

The General's blue eyes twinkled. "What's your price, Joseph?"

"I figure I can wash all the windas once a month. I'm gonna use a bosun's chair, see. I got long arms." Joe stretched his arms to demonstrate. "There's five thousand panes more er less an I charge five cents fer the high ones cause a the risk, an the rest at a penny apiece makes it a hunnert an fifty bucks."

"Done," the General said and stuck out his hand.

Joe Talldorf and Mary Plately were wed by Father Gallaghan in the chapel of St. Boniface's Church on a warm June day. Joe stood in front of the altar in his rented tux as Mary floated down the aisle on Red's arm. Elinore sobbed in the front pew and leaned on Adair's shoulder while the other boys wore varied expressions of solemnity.

At the reception C.C. presented Joe with a check for fifty dollars. He sat bitterly beside Florence, a gob of frosting on his mustache, as Red handed Joe the keys to their new cottage. The bride and groom spent their honeymoon there.

The gray light of dawn crept up from the city's fringes as Joe lugged his coil of rope to the roof. In the distance plumes of factory smoke billowed from smoke stacks. By the time Joe had dressed his pulleys and set the bosun's chair swinging the sun had risen, the river mists had vanished and Joe was sweating.

Joe lit a cigarette and walked down to the seventh floor where he filled his bucket at the sink in the utility closet. Just a pinch of soap powder and the water as hot as he could stand it. He walked back up to the roof, tucked his squeegees into his belt and went over the side.

He lowered himself until he was suspended outside the seventh floor office windows, then jerked the rope and set the dog that held him there.

The panes were covered with a grimy film of dirt. Inside a girl sat at a desk behind a typewriter. Joe scrubbed the glass with his brush until she floated in an underwater blur. He pulled out his long squeegee and peeled off the skin of water revealing her more clearly with each stroke. She scarcely glanced up but concentrated on her work. Her white ruffled blouse was buttoned to her neck. Little gray buttons pinched her sleeves at her wrists; her hair fell to her shoulders in soft waves. She stood up suddenly and twitched away in the warp of her black skirt that fell smoothly to her ankles. Joe shook his head in admiration and suppressed a whistle.

He looked out at the barges and the river boats, at the teamsters on the docks below. He ragged the corners and pecked at the streaks then jerked on the rope and lowered himself to the next row.

When the noon whistle blew Joe went all the way down, ate three ham sandwiches, the apple and the cookies that Mary had packed in his lunch bucket. He smoked a cigarette and walked leisurely up the stairs to the roof.

The sun was hot. Joe lowered himself row by row past the floors of sweating workers who slaved in the din of the machines and the heat from the ovens.

At six o'clock Joe coiled the rope and caught the Oak St. car that let him off a block from their new house.

Mary had stocked the shelves and filled the drawers. She'd put away the linen and the silver spoons; stored the wedding presents they couldn't use, rearranged the furniture and made a set of curtains. Joe was so enthusiastic about his day's work that he failed to notice. "It's gonna take me all month to finish, Mare. That's fer sure," he said as he washed his hands at the kitchen sink and sat down to supper. "Then I gotta start all over again—"

Mary stopped to catch her breath while Joe ran ahead up the embankment. "Wait till ya see er, Mare!"

Mary's back ached with the usual dull ache. Sweat trickled down her face and her ribs. "C'mon, Mare. I ain't got all day."

Mary waddled up the path. Joe stretched out his hand and pulled her up the last few steps.

The windows of the rubber company reflected the city in a shimmering, vitreous mass. The river, the trees, the buildings and smoke stacks trembled in the glass.

"Oh they do shine, Joey! It's really something to see, something you can be proud of."

"There's 250 hours a me sweat in them panes."

Mary gasped.

"What's wrong, Mare? Ya ok?"

Her face was pale. She opened her eyes and took a deep breath.

"I'm all right. Sometimes he kicks me."

"Are ya sure yer ok?"

"I'm all right now."

"Are ya sure, Mare?"

"I feel fine."

"Yer hungry I bet. Ain't ya? What ya need is somethin ta eat, Mare. I'm takin ya out to a real swanky joint, see. We're gonna celebrate."

While Joe hung from the bosun's chair above the Detroit River Mary was busy at home. In the morning her needle flew as she pulled each stitch tight along the neatly basted seams. That afternoon she painted the kitchen and scrubbed the living room walls. She was putting away the ladder when the first pain came. Seventeen hours later the baby lay red and wrinkled on the bloody sheet, his fingers curled into little fists. Dr. Wilks cut the cord and handed him to Mary who put him to her breast where he sucked and gurgled, then fell asleep.

"He's going to be tall like you, Joe," she said as Joe sat staring at his wife and the baby's wizened face in amazement.

Rudolf Victor Talldorf was one year old. Mary suckled him in sweet contentment. Her interest in sex was almost nil. Motherhood was enough for her. Rudy came first. "I'm bustin me balls an what do I get fer it," Joe complained. "Nothin. Me romance is finished."

He usually stopped in the secretary's office and uncorked his thermos but Levanta remained cool. Joe was voluble to hide his guilt. He closed the door, crossed himself and said six Hail Mary's walking to the roof.

The weather was mild. Mary's sexless condition didn't improve. Her joy was obvious. She was attentive and cheerful. She sensed Joe's needs and did what she could to fulfill them but her passion was diluted by her love which was focused on her child.

Joe lay on the couch in his shirtsleeves studying the scratch sheet. "Hey, honey. Where'er me shoes?" No one answered. Joe went to the kitchen window. Rudy slept peacefully in his carriage while Mary hung wet diapers on the line. She never wanted to do much but feed the baby and wash his diapers. She was always too tired now.

"Hey Mare! Where'er me shoes?"

"I don't know, dear. Where did you take them off?"

Joe left the window muttering. He found his shoes next to the bed and pulled them on. He went to the bathroom, put his foot up on the toilet seat and shined the shoes with a towel. He put on his pinstriped shirt with the French cuffs and his yellow silk tie. "Hey, Mare!" he shouted from the back porch. "I'm goin to the track. Don't wait supper ter me."

"Joey?"

"What?"

"I thought we were going to do the budget tonight."

"Not tonight. Some other night."

"Joey?"

"What?"

"Is everything all right?"

"Sure. What's the matter? Do I look funny or something?"

"You look fine. Aren't you going to kiss me goodbye?"

"Jesus." He bent and kissed her forehead. Mary stared up at him with concern.

"Will you be late?"

"How do I know, huh? I might run inta Slim or one a me old track buddies."

"Give me a real kiss, Joey."

"Fer Christ sake." Joe grabbed Mary and pressed his lips to hers. "Is that better?"

Tears grew in the corners of Mary's eyes.

"What are ya cryin fer now?"

"I can't help it, Joey."

"Ya got the kid ain't ya?"

"Joey?"

But he was gone.

Herbert Armbuster sat in the driver's seat as the salesman cranked the new Ford. The Ford was going to be a happy surprise for Estelle, Herbert's wife. The Armbusters would be the first automobile owners on their block. The thought filled Herbert with pride.

The engine sputtered and caught. Herbert waved to the salesman and let out the clutch, just as he'd been taught. The Model A hopped across the lot. Herbert slammed on the brakes and the engine died. The salesman ran up. "Not so fast Mr. Armbuster. You just have to ease it out. Don't worry. You'll get the hang of it."

"Right, right," Herbert said as the salesman cranked it.

Herbert let out the clutch and the salesman leaped aside. The Model A shot into Mitchell St. in front of a team of rearing horses.

Herbert missed second and jammed it into third. The Ford climbed the sidewalk and missed the fire hydrant. Herbert saw the baby carriage just in time. He spun the wheel and the Ford swerved. The baby's mother loomed up before Herbert's horror-stricken eyes. She dropped her sack of groceries and disappeared beneath the hood ornament with a sickening thump. The Ford bumped over the curb, careened to the other side of Mitchell St. and crashed into a lamp pole.

Joe Talldorf stared angrily at the doctor. "I don't believe ya!" he said defiantly. The doctor put his arm around Joe's shoulder but Joe shrugged him off. "Where's me wife?" The doctor turned. "Right this way, son."

Joe followed the doctor through white curtains into a small dark room. A priest stood beside the bed. The priest's lips moved dumbly over the furtive words. Joe pushed back his hair from his forehead. "What am I supposed ta do now?" he said.

He didn't wait for an answer but hurried out of the room, and ambled absently down the corridor. A Sister of Mercy in black habit and hood swept toward him. Joe turned around and pushed through the curtains again. The priest nodded paternally and raised his hand in benediction.

"What am I supposed ta do, Father?"

"My son—"

"Why'nt ya just get outta here huh? Huh? What about you?" Joe said glaring at the doctor. "Why'nt ya just leave me alone!" The doctor shrugged and followed the priest out.

Joe stood next to the bed staring down at the sheet that covered the obvious shape of a human body. He pushed back his hair, raised the sheet an inch and let it drop as quickly. It was Mary's red hair all right. Or was it? There might be a hundred girls in the city with red hair like Mary's. Joe dropped to his knees. "How come ya had to go, Mare? Hey Mare? How come ya left me here like this?"

Joe had the sudden conviction that it wasn't Mary on the bed. It must be, it had to be someone else. He jumped up and pulled back the sheet.

Mary's face, her eyes closed in death, her lips blue and twisted from her last gasp for breath, shone whitely up at him. He touched her forehead, ran his fingers through her hair, his eyes wide with disbelief and fear. He felt a deep pain that opened and swallowed him, then the bubble burst in his chest and he threw himself on her lifeless body.

Joe lay in bed. There was no reason to kid himself. He couldn't sleep. He'd never sleep again. And what about Rudy? Where was Rudy? Joe sat up straight but lay down again. Rudy breathed evenly beside him in the crib.

"It ain't that she wasn't the best cause there wasn't no better girl than Mary. She was the best I'll ever have. She was the best there is. There wasn't any girl prettier er none that ever cared fer me like Mary did. Mare, ya gotta come back. Ya can't leave me. Please Lord, give me another chance. It ain't fair. It shoulda been me. Please send her back. I loved ya, Mare. I loved everthin about ya. The way ya wore yer hair. I loved yer hair, Mare. I loved yer hands an yer teeth. Ya was so beautiful. Ya can't be dead. Ya can't be dead. Yer still alive ta me. Don't let nothin come between us."

The pillow slip was wet when Joe finally fell asleep.

Joe buttered the slice of toast. "I was plannin on payin fer it meself," he said.

"How?" Elinore asked.

"I respect your intentions, Joey," Red said stiffly, taking off his glasses and rubbing his head, "but a funeral is very expensive. Even with a simple casket."

"I'm gonna sell the cottage if it's ok with youse."

"You can't do that!" Elinore said.

"Why not? It's my house ain't it?"

"No, it's not *your* house!"

"Elinore!" Red said sharply.

"It's like this, see," Joe said. "I don't wanna live there. Me an Rudy would be better off someplace else."

"We can decide later if the house will be sold or not," Elinore said decisively. "I think it would be best if you and Rudy lived here so that Rudy can grow up like a normal boy."

"We're all in this together," Red said. "Our lives have been changed, Joey. Nothing is the same."

Joe took out his Bull Durham and rolled a cigarette.

"I'll have to order the flowers," Elinore said. "Will you talk to Father Callaghan?" Red nodded. "I want to get Mary's wedding dress down from the attic and have it pressed."

Joe's eyebrows shot up. "Her weddin dress?"

"These are not pleasant things to think about, Joey," Elinore said, "but they are things that must be done."

"So what am I supposed ta do then?"

"You'll be busy enough with your son."

Mary lay in the parlor of Planchard's Funeral Home. Joe knew that it wasn't her as he stood looking down at the girl in the white satin gown, her hands neatly folded on the bodice among the roses and the gladiolus that heaped the gleaming wood. All day the parlor had been crowded with friends and relatives in the heavy scent of flowers and the smell of candle wax. The men patted Joe's shoulder. The women fluttered around him and pecked at Rudy's clothes.

"Ma..." Rudy said, "Ma..."

Joe took Rudy's hand and led him down the corridor past the sliding oak doors into the garage where Stephen, Mr. Planchard's eldest son, was washing the hearse.

"That ain't yer ma, Rudes," Joe said. "Yer ma's with us."

The black string of automobiles followed the black hearse through the black iron gates of Oakwood Cemetery. The windshield wipers hissed back and forth.

Elinore, in a new black dress and a heavy veil clung to Red's arm. Red held a black umbrella over her. Joe held Rudy who wore a black suit.

"—Wers," Rudy said, "—Wers."

"Flowers," Joe said in a hoarse voice. "Flowers."

The mourners got out of the cars and followed behind as Mary's brothers took hold of the brass rails and raised the casket to their shoulders.

Joe had yielded in every detail and had isolated himself from the ceremony. Elinore had ordered a pink marble monument with two sculpted cupids. Joe couldn't have afforded a headstone, much less the plush casket and the floral wreaths.

He had been revolted by the thought of Mary buried in her wedding dress. He hadn't wanted a wake, and if there had to be a wake Joe wanted the casket shut.

Father Callaghan held his cassock above his shoetops and walked around the mound of wet dirt. He stood at the head of the grave as the boys lowered the casket into the hole.

"Dearly beloved," he said looking out over the clustered umbrellas. "We are gathered here this mornin to pay our respects to one of the Lord's dear children. A dutiful daughter. A kind sister. A faithful wife and a lovin mither, called back to heaven."

Mr. Planchard and Stephen carried the baskets of flowers to the grave as Father Callaghan intoned the last words and crossed himself.

"The Lord giveth and the Lord taketh away. May Mary Talldorf abide with Him forever. Amen."

Each of the boys threw a spade full of dirt into the hole.

"Sovel," Rudy said.

Red handed the spade to Joe who stripped off his coat. The clods of wet dirt thudded on the casket lid. Rudy ran to help. He dug his fingers into the mud and threw in handfuls.

"No!" Elinore said with alarm. "No." Red picked Rudy up and handed him to her. "Naughty boy," she whispered. "Now look at you. Rudy screamed and fought but she held him tightly. "Pa!" he cried, "Pa!"

Sweat trickled down Joe's brow and soaked through the underarms of his shirt. "Here, Joey. I'll take a turn," Red said, but Joe didn't stop shoveling.

Mary's brothers scowled as the hole filled up. The men glanced solemnly at their watches and the women smoothed their skirts. Joe panted and watched the crowd disperse. He wanted to run at them. See them scatter like a flock of startled birds. Hot tears of anger burned his cheeks. He raised the spade above his head, danced a few steps forward and hurled it as far as he could.

Joe took two weeks off from work. When he and Rudy visited the big white house on Maple St. Joe felt like an outcast. Red had started drinking again. The boys were unnaturally loud and there was something in the manner in which Elinore spoke to him that made Joe feel small.

Joe and Rudy spent most of that two weeks at home, indoors. Mary's presence permeated the cottage. Her dresses still hung in the closet. Her shoes were lined up on the floor. Her underwear and stockings were still neatly folded in her drawers.

At night Joe hunched over the kitchen table and worked on his drawings. Rudy woke on schedule at midnight. "Ma!" he wailed, "Ma!"

Joe picked up the scissors and cut into the piece of leather while Rudy played on the floor. Mary's pincushion, buttons, needles and spools of thread lay scattered on the rug.

Joe sat on the couch with Mary's thimble on his finger. It was a tedious and painful job but Joe found satisfaction as his creation began to take shape, stitch by stitch. He forced the thick needle through the leather.

Joe lined the harness with a patchwork quilt that he cut to fit his pattern. The quilt was made from triangles of brightly colored remnants interspersed with triangles of black satin. Mary had made the quilt before Rudy was born.

"It's gonna fit Rudes perfect, Mare," Joe said. "It'll keep him nice an warm."

Red stopped one night to visit. He reeked of alcohol but he wasn't drunk. He pulled a flask out of his hip pocket. Joe got two glasses off the shelf. "C'mon in the livinroom, Red. I wanna show ya somethin."

"What is it?"

"It's a backpack fer carryin Rudy up on me job."

"You aren't going to take Rudy up there."

"Sure I am, Red."

"Elinore is taking care of Rudy. We already decided that, Joe. You can't do it all. A boy needs a woman's love." Red poured himself another drink and drained the glass.

"Rudy's stayin with me, Red. That's the way Mare would want it."

"Mary wouldn't want you taking Rudy up there. It's not safe. She'd want Rudy with her mother. Elinore has already hired a bookkeeper so she can stay home."

"I got me mind made up, Red. Sos ya might as well stop harpin on the subject."

"It will hurt Elinore's feelings. Have you thought about that?"

"Elinore don't care nothin fer me, Red. She never did, an I think she even blames me cause Mary's dead."

"Shut up, Joey."

"I know how it is, Red."

"You don't know anything! You're just a punk kid and you don't even know that." Joe shrugged his shoulders and hung his head. "Listen, Joey. You're going to find out just how tough it is to raise a kid and one fine day you're going to beg for Elinore's help and you're going to have to get down on your knees and apologize for everything you've said."

Joe jerked the rope and let the bosun's chair down to the next row of windows. The bosun's chair swung lightly in the wind, like a cradle, which didn't calm the boy. Rudy cried. He wailed. He screamed. He pulled Joe's hair. "We're almost done," Joe pleaded. "Just let me finish this winda here. All right fer Christ sake! Sit down will ya? Sit down, Rudy."

It was perhaps the conjunction of his mother's death and his father's exasperation as they hung together on that vertiginous job that was responsible for Rudolph Talldorf's later fear of heights. But there were good days too, when puffy white clouds floated above the river like popcorn balls. When the pigeons strutted on the ledges and took graceful flight.

Rudy clung lightly to Joe's back. "Bird..." he said.

"If yer ma could only see us now, huh Rudes?" At such moments Joe was sure that Rudy shared his sense of independence that always came with that distance from the earth and the feeling that Mary hovered protectively near their lofty perch.

Father and son were in a firm partnership though Rudy didn't know it yet. Joe hadn't reckoned on the constant attention that a mother devotes to her child. He carried Rudy every place he went. His shoulders were always stiff, and his back was bent.

Joe carried Rudy to the track. Rudy loved the blue tickets that his father tore in half and the thick yellow pencil that Joe used to mark his scratch sheet.

Joe bet every horse with Mary's name in it. He put two dollars on Mary Come Lately; Miss Mary; Mary D; Lady Mary; Proud Mary; Mary's Choice; Mary's Boy; Mary's Mistake: Mistress Mary; Mary's Lamb; Mary's Hey Dey; and even Merry Prank. But his luck continued bad.

It took him a month and a half to finish the windows. Rudy's limit on the bosun's chair was five hours a day: two hours at a time with a two-hour lunch break and an hour before the sun set.

Joe arrived at the tire plant at dawn and worked while Rudy slept. He ignored the boy's constant demand that they finish. Rudy drank his bottle and wet his pants. He always had diaper rash. He was skinny and sick.

The racing season ended but Joe didn't stop betting. He banked his check with Gus Lipis who could always be found at a back table in the White Way.

"How much will ya give me on this, Gus?" Joe asked.

"I ain't a pawnshop. What is it?"

"It's the deed ta me house."

Gus looked at the deed and studied the fine print. "Ya don't even own it," he said.

"The hell I don't. See me name there?"

"It don't mean nothin."

"It's me house, Gus. Me father-in-law give it to me fer a weddin present."

Joe signed over the house to Gus. He sold the furniture and moved into two housekeeping rooms at the Waverly Arms. He heated Rudy's bottles on the gas stove while Rudy splashed in the claw-footed tub.

The days were getting shorter and the wind was chill. The river moved sluggishly beneath gray clouds. Rudy caught a cold. He hung listlessly in the harness as the rain pattered on the oilcloth that covered his head and shoulders. His fever went up to one hundred and four.

"I need an advance, General." The General came out from behind his oval desk.

"Has the boy been seen by a doctor, Joseph?"

"Yea. I took him meself. The doc says I gotta keep him warm an give him the medicine ever four hours."

"How much money do you need?"

"A hunnert." The General pulled out his wallet.

"Here you are, Joseph. The full amount for the job. Don't worry about finishing the windows until your son has regained his health."

Joe lost half the money on a Hialeah longshot. He pawned the silver at Arky's Pawnshop and moved from the Waverly Arms to the Condor Hotel.

Gus Lipis sat at his usual back table in the White Way Cafeteria. He wore a black topcoat and a new beaver derby from Smithfields. "How ya doin, Gus," Joe said. Gus frowned as Joe sat down and stirred his coffee. "Poon...poon." Joe handed the spoon to Rudy. "Sos how things goin, Gus?"

"Ok by me. How 'bout you?"

"Great. Terrific. It takes me twice as long ta do the job. The kid tears up me winnin tickets. I'm broke. There ain't nothin in the icebox. Things couldn't be better."

"Glad ta hear it."

"Hey Gus, how's me credit?"

"Ya ain't got no credit."

"C'mon Gus. I'm gonna polish off the job end a this week. Saturday I'll pay ya. I promise. I got a longshot fer ya." Joe pulled out his scratch sheet. "Dusty Mary in the sixth at Santa Anita."

"No credit."

"So I owe ya money. What is it? A hunnert. So what. Ya seen me make that in a minute. I been a good customer ain't I, Gus? Ya know how me hunches run. Dusty Mary's a sure thing."

"How many times do I have ta tell ya, Joey?"

"Me luck's been bad, Gus. Ya know what that means? It means me luck is gonna change. I'm tellin ya Gus, just look at these times!"

"I ain't interested."

Joe stared at the ceiling. "Ya ever been married, Gus?" Gus pushed back his new derby with his knuckles. "Ya ever have any kids, Gus? Changin diapers every ten minutes. Washin diapers. Fixin the kid's meals. It's always me, Gus. Ya unnerstan that? It's always ole Joe, ain't it, Rudes? Ole Joe, your poppa."

"Papa—" Joe gulped his coffee and stood up. "I gotta go buy a quart a milk. Hey Gus, lend me a fin will ya?"

Gus glared at Joe and pulled out his wallet. "This is the last time, Joey. I ain't kiddin, the last time!"

Joe handed back the bill. "Go on take it, Gus. It won't bite ya."

"I thought ya said ya needed it fer milk."

"Do me a favor will ya, Gus? Put it on Dusty Mary's nose."

Rudy slept peacefully on the narrow bed while Joe twisted uncomfortably in the broken armchair near the radiator which knocked and hissed beneath the pattern of frost on the window.

"Ya gotta try an unnerstan, Mare. It's too much fer me, see? Rudes ain't got a chance. I'm lookin at the odds. Livin in a dump like this. It ain't right.

Sos I'm leavin him with yer folks. He's gonna be ok, Mare. I'm gonna hop me a freight, bet all them Florida tracks an get rich. I'm gonna put me money in stocks an have Rudy's name typed inta the blanks an keep em in a bank somewheres, sos when he's my age..."

Joe had made his plans carefully. His battered rainbow-colored suitcase was packed. It stood beside the door next to his bucket and squeegees. The wool blanket that he would use for a bedroll was folded neatly on top of the box filled with Rudy's clothes. At one o'clock he and Rudy would sneak down the back stairway to fool Mrs. Bailey. "She'll get her rent, Mare. Cause I'm comin back."

Joe woke reflexively at midnight. When Rudy started to cry Joe gave him the bottle and changed his diaper.

"We was partners, Rudes," Joe said. "We worked pretty good together but I have ta go away, see? I gotta make a lot a money sos you can go ta college. Things is tough, Rudy. I can't make nothin with ya hangin on me neck, but everythin's gonna turn out ok. I'll write ya letters, send ya postcards an stuff—"

Joe slipped two pairs of socks over Rudy's pink little feet. Rudy sucked on the nipple and eyed his father suspiciously. "Gotta dress ya up real warm, Rudes. Don't worry about nothin. Yer ole Joe is gonna take care a everythin."

Rudy didn't protest when Joe sat him in his lap, pulled on his snowsuit and his mittens. "Yer takin this real good, kid," Joe said. "I'd take ya with me but I can't, see. If ya knew how ta talk better I could explain it but I think ya unnerstan anyway. Yer pa's gotta go away but I'm comin back. Yer gonna spend a few weeks with yer grandma an grandpa. I'm tellin ya they're real nice people." Joe pulled the hood over Rudy's head and tied the strings. "Aw, Rudes..." he said. He held the boy close to his chest but Rudy squirmed away.

"Cold," he said, "Cold."

"Yea, that's right. It's cold out there. Maybe it's snowin. C'mon Rudes. You an me is goin out ta see the snowflakes."

The clock in the watchmaker's shop said one thirty but Joe didn't hurry. He stashed his suitcase, bucket, and the box in a vacant lot and walked to Shorty's Diner. Rudy rode on his back, warm and content, the quilt tucked around his neck. "No, No!"

"That's it, Rudes. Them is snowflakes."

The sign behind the steamed windows of Shorty's advertised the turkey dinner with all the trimmings. Joe went inside, lifted Rudy out of the pack and took a seat.

"Hi ya, Joey. What'll it be?"

"I'll have a mug a coffee, Agnes. An the turkey dinner."

"Hi ya, Rudy. Ya want a cracker?"

"An a glass a milk, huh Agnes?"

Joe filled his mouth with mashed potatoes. "This may be me last hot meal fer a coupla weeks, Rudy. Have some pataters. I know ya ain't too hot on the meat. Hey Agnes! Bring a piece a pumpkin pie fer me kid. With plenty a whipped cream."

Joe dipped his napkin into his water glass and washed Rudy's face. He pulled out his Bull Durham sack and his rolling papers.

"Here, Rude. Blow out the match. Now I wanna make sure ya got all this straight. When I drop ya off yer gonna be asleep, see. Yer dad's goin away. Aw, what's the use me tellin ya this? Ya listen ta Red an do what he says. Don't let him pull no wool over yer eyes, but—"

"Say, Joey, you ok?"

"Sure I'm ok. Whata ya mean am I ok? It's colder'n a well digger's ass. Hey, Shorty, how come ya don't plug up the cracks? Me feet is frozen sittin in the draft." Agnes laughed as she cleared the dirty plates. "Where's me check? Eighty five cents. Here, Agnes. Keep the change."

"Thanks, Joey. What'd yer horse come in?"

"Sure. Me an Rudes is rich. We're thinkin a goin South fer the Winter."

"South? No kiddin?"

"Sure. Toledo er Cincinnati."

"Joey, yer a gas."

"Ya ain't so bad yourself Agnes."

Flakes of snow stuck to the fur collar of Joe's leather jacket. His lean shadow with the hump on its back stretched between the gas lamps. He heard a lonesome whistle of a freight somewhere out along the tracks. Rudy was already fast asleep.

"He's a good kid, Mare. Rudy's the best there is. I love him more than anythin. I hope ya know that. I just gotta get outta here, see? This town ain't fer me. I gotta hit a winnin streak. I gotta be right there ta make me picks.

Smell the horseshit an the grass." Joe turned the corner and bumped into Ed O'Grady.

"Joey, me boy."

"Howdy, Ed."

"What would ya be doin out on a cold night like this?"

"Just walkin around, Ed. I couldn't sleep."

"Well, it's good ta see ya. How's the little one? Let's have a peek. Sleepin like an angel, Joey. An lookin more like his mither every day. Ya wouldn't be havin any trouble now would ya, Joe? Somethin Ed O'Grady could help ya with?"

"Naw, Ed. Thanks a lot. Everythin's jake with me."

"Well, glad ta hear it." Ed twirled his stick. "Say, Joey. I seen C.C. the other day and he says ta me, Ed, he says — "

"I don't wanna hear it, Ed."

"Oh, don't ya now? Well I was just goin ta Shorty's ta have me eggs. Come have a bite on me."

"Thanks just the same, Ed. But me an Rudy just had our dinner."

"Ok, Joey. It's too cold ta be jawin sos I'll wish ya good night. An, Joey. Ya might stop by yer dad's place. Yer ma is — "

"Yea, Ed. I'll think about it."

"Goodnight to ya, Joe."

"Goodbye, Ed."

Joe got the box of Rudy's clothes and headed for Maple St. He ducked into the alley and moved quickly through the shadows past the sheds.

Except for the lamp that always burned in the bathroom Red's house was dark. A gust of wind blew off the roof and Joe got a whiff of coal smoke, the clinkers glowing in the grate, a big home for the friendless, warm with heavy drapes on all the windows to keep out the drafts.

Benjy started to bark when Joe opened the gate. "It's me, Benjy," Joe whispered. "It's yer old friend, Joey." Benjy's nose sniffed the air. "It's Joe, Benjy. How ya doin?" Joe scratched the old dog's ears. "I brung ya a present."

Joe slipped out of the harness and laid Rudy gently on the blanket where Benjy slept. Rudy's mittened fists rose convulsively to his face, then relaxed at his sides again. "You keep Rudes warm huh, Benjy?" Joe whispered. He kissed Rudy on the forehead and walked down the steps.

Somebody threw open a sash. "Who is it? Is someone there?"

Joe ran up the alley. His heart pounded in his chest. He felt strangely buoyant, almost weightless without Rudy on his back. He pictured Red bending over Rudy, shining the lantern on his face, and grinned in spite of himself.

"Yer dad's sure gonna be surprised, ain't he, Mare?"

The cold wind made the elm trees dance. The bare limbs moaned as Joe hurried along the pavement. He rubbed his hands together. His knees began to shake and his teeth clattered. The streets were empty. The houses slept. At the vacant lot Joe took a piss. "We gotta get movin if we're gonna catch the southbound freight, Mare." He wrapped himself in the blanket, picked up his bucket and his suitcase.

"Like I promised ya, Mare. We're comin back. It should take a coupla weeks ta earn me stake. I'm gonna pay all me debts, square it with yer folks, the General an everythin. Jesus it's cold, ain't it? I'm tellin ya, Mare. In Florida the grass is green. There's oranges, even palm trees. We deserve a trip, huh Mare? Mare — ?"

He knew she wasn't there. Instead of Mary's presence the air was blank. Joe pulled the blanket closer and walked faster.

Chapter 2

N

Alexander Small grew up in an orphanage. He saw the world created in an instant without batting an eye. Then, like a chick fresh out of the egg, he began to peck around.

There was the woman who approached his crib like a great shadow and he felt better for her visits, though the wetness and burning on his bottom and legs remained.

There was the woman in the room where they played with the toys until she would take them away, and still another who marched the boys down dim halls to eat.

Small was at the disposal of the light, an alternation of darkness and light. It made him feel not quite awake. It seemed he had done something wrong. A luminous grayness filtered through the first years of his life. He recognized the other boys as he recognized daylight in morning and darkness at night.

The boys were marched through the halls where dim light fell from high above, through soiled glass windows.

Rows of boys sat at meals at long wooden tables drinking milk from tin cups. The bigger boys sat at other tables so that forms and faces, as Small looked over his tin cup, arose as they increased in distance like the foothills of mountains. And solemn black men in soiled white shirts moved towering between tables scooping food down onto the tin trays.

Mornings and afternoons they marched in file outside to a cinder playground crammed with boys who looked up at the patch of blue sky framed by high walls around them. The boys were outside just two hours each day.

The monotony of life in dim light and darkness dazed Small. Time spun around and through him until his mind itself was gray. Gray light, indistinguishable from dust, filtered through unreachable windows over everything.

Small was uncertain where he himself left off and dust began. His voice felt tinged with dust when he spoke. The seething mass of them was like a dust pile given life within the high gray walls.

As the boys were marched through the halls from their dormitory to the dining hall, to classes, to the playyard or one morning a week to chapel, Small would reach out to drag his fingers along the walls. His fingers came away smudgy but the touch of the cool hard plaster made him feel real. Then he felt that sometime something might be different.

Small was surprised to discover from the narrow old woman teacher that his life was not like every other life.

It was pleasant to hear the story of Molly's cat, of Molly's lap, and what Mother and Father said to Molly and the cat, and everyone kissing pretty Molly. But it was in the end unpleasant to have his fingers rapped with the sharp ruler when he could not spell Molly.

Small often thought of himself in hell except for the chill worn always like an invisible coat of fur.

So Sundays were a small excitement. The boys plastered down their hair with their little black combs at the wash basins in the lavatory at the end of the dormitory.

Then they would stand at the end of their bunks in silence while Miss Sweatly, who was Mr. Sord's assistant, walked down the center aisle inspecting them critically. She might bend down to pluck an ear and look behind it, or gaze beneath a collar to see if a neck was clean. Face, hands, arms and neck were the special province of Miss Sweatly. Small, however, felt relatively safe because he stood so very still. He felt the safe thing to do was to disappear into himself so that nothing remained for Miss Sweatly to see.

Then Miss Sweatly would cry from the far end of the dormitory, "Two files!" Small would stand beside Peter, whose bed was opposite his, shoulder to shoulder. And then Miss Sweatly would command "March!" and lead the procession out the swinging doors, down the long halls to the very end and into the dark chapel where they slid between the long polished pews to stand in silence.

Mr. Sord in his black suit would stand before the raised pulpit. His red face was somber behind owl glasses. There was no sound but the shuffling of boys into the pews.

"Seats!" Mr. Sord would command, followed by the cushion sound of one hundred boys sitting.

Small would be cheered to see Reverend Westra standing above Sord behind the pulpit. Reverend Westra's face was sunny. He would be smiling. His gold tooth would shine like sunlight.

"Happy Sunday morning boys!" Reverend Westra would say with his golden grin. Only Reverend Westra made him feel happy.

"The Lord is coming boys," Westra would smile, "on clouds of light, light will flood this world boys, light will lift your hearts and joy will shine on every face and love will fill the earth and not a shadow of doubt will remain in any heart." And Small, imagining it all, would grin into Westra's golden smile.

But Reverend Westra did not come every Sunday and the other preachers made the chapel darker.

Reverend Proot was the worst. Reverend Proot's voice echoed like an ocean in a cave. He would always start, "Are you washed in the blood of the lamb—?" gazing down at the boys as if about to douse them with a bucket of blood.

Small was certain Reverend Westra did not wash in lamb's blood. Small would sniff the chill of the stone chapel and feel the hard pew.

"Hell fire and *dam-na-tion!*" swore Reverend Proot, "Do you know what it means?" He hung above them like a walrus on a rock. "I come with a *sword!* says the *Lord*, a SWORD!" and Proot's big lower lip hung above them while his smoky eyes roasted little sinners.

The boys who were awake looked nervously from Proot to Sord, who always appeared to be sleeping.

"A lake of fire to burn forever! Do you know what it *means*?" Small sat bug-eyed wondering.

"We are *against* magic," Proot boomed on, "But—*Ah*—the Catholics have something. With confession. Confession! To confess to God the wickedness that eats out the heart from within like a worm eats the core of the apple.

One rotten apple. Will rot a bushel! Go! Tell God in your prayers of the *cor-rup-tion* that rots in the heart. Or *He* will come like the avenger with his sword. *He* will cut off the *evil* vine. The *evil* vine is *cast* into the firey pit. To burn forever. Oh *God!* We are sinners—!" The noses of boys twitched for the smoke.

The high-walled playyard where the boys played out under the sky had the feeling of the bottom of a pit.

Since their two hourly sessions in the playyard were early in the morning and late in the afternoon the playyard was always in shade. Summer or winter the sun itself was never seen.

The most popular game was bouncing volleyballs against the high walls of the yard. As many as twenty boys scuffled and seethed before either of two walls keeping the balls bouncing. They bounced like the beat of his heart.

Small did not often bat the ball. When he wished to he would slip among the boys like a fish between weeds with an uncanny sense of just where the ball would fall, arrive precisely at that instant, bat the ball up against the wall and slip away.

But when Small played bat ball it made him feel that nothing would ever be different.

Usually he wandered with his hands in his pockets among the other boys who were not playing bat ball. They passed among each other like citizens of a great city too vast to have ever seen each other's faces before. They swirled like chips in a current between quarrels and fist fights and the whirlpools of their own fantasies.

Often Small would squat at the juncture of the two high walls and bounce on his toes to keep warm. It was a spot that only one body could occupy and no one else seemed to have discovered it.

When his age barred him from the playroom and toys, Small's interest turned to books. Books promised bright worlds that contrasted sharply with the grayness of his own. He read poorly and slowly, however, and was considered dull by Miss Brown, the old woman who taught lessons. But it happened that Small remembered nearly everything that he read.

He was most interested in geography which told how varied and unbelievably vast was the world beyond the walls of the orphanage. Small was amazed and delighted, but even in geography he did not receive good marks.

What seemed to be the main concern of geography lessons interested Small not at all. These were facts and figures and graphs of commodities produced and sold by the countries of the world. He did not care if ships were loaded with grain, lumber or steel. But he loved the photographs of the great ships themselves and imagined them sleek and rolling on the high seas and envied the sailors their free and sunny lives.

He imagined his pleasure walking in the fields of golden grain of the photographs, or in the great forests where lumber came from, or even staring into the great pits where the iron ore was dug.

Small loved the maps most of all. By some harmony of instinct he recognized the shape of continents and oceans and the flow of great rivers and saw the blue on the page as water and understood where he was located in the great scheme of it all, on the funny finger of Florida.

He knew, through the pictures he saw in the geography book, of the mountains and great icy glaciers and the snows of the arctic, of wide plains where Indians once had lived and forests and swamps and green farmfields.

And so he liked history which was the closest thing to stories. He sympathized with Napoleon retreating from Moscow. Nobody had welcomed him there. The Cossacks cut down his retreating troops and the rest were freezing. It must have been really cold. Napoleon must have felt very bad. And Small understood that even Alexander Small existed in that long story and that one day he would turn a page to find himself out in that vast and bright world.

One day, from his vantage point where he squatted at the juncture of the walls, Small saw the green drain pipe rising up the gray stucco wall like a vine. He marveled that in all his years in this playyard he had never seen this drainpipe as he saw it now.

Small jumped up and made his way quickly through the bodies. He grasped the green metal. He kicked off his shoes and pulled off his socks. He was jostled by two scuffling boys and had to let go the pipe.

Small grasped it again, and with his bare feet against the cool stucco wall stepped hand over hand up over the heads feeling space expand at his back.

He climbed slowly at first, then more surely with exhilaration as if the freedom of height offered less resistance. The only thing in the world was the green metal drainpipe that his hands clasped and the tension through his body gluing his feet to the rough, cool wall. Sunshine struck his head, his shoulders and his back and Small stepped atop the high stone wall.

He stood in bright sunshine. Wind blew at his hair. The fronds of a palm tree rustled nearby lush and green. A street ran away until it was narrow. It seemed it might end at the ocean. A black automobile chugged past on the street below. An airplane with two wings flew speedily across the wide sky.

Then Small saw the top of the wall stretched out before him like a sidewalk. He stepped along it. And then he noticed the yard full of boys all looking up at him in silence. The silence made Small wobble. He stopped. The playyard had never been silent in his memory.

"Catch, Small!" yelled a voice.

A volleyball came floating up toward Small whose bare feet were firm on the cement beneath them. The ball was rising to his left. Small reached with his left hand and saw that he could not reach the ball. His heart felt as if it floated on air but his center of balance remained unmoved. Small realized, with an airy sensation, that he might have fallen a long way. His body had balanced itself.

Years were to come when Small would consider his balance infallible. And the day would arrive when Small would take a great fall.

"Come *down!* Down! Down! Down! My *God!* Have you lost your mind?" It was Mr. Sord.

"*Alexander Small!*" screeched Sord. Small looked at Mr. Sord far below. "Answer immediately!" he screamed, "Answer me!"

Mr. Sord's face was red. It looked like it might explode.

Small looked away to the wide blue sky and the green palm fronds. He did not know what to answer.

A ladder was brought and propped against the wall. Small climbed down.

Mr. Sord guided him speedily through the dim cool halls by the back of his shirt collar and through the big wooden door with the laurel wreath carved high upon it through which no boy wished to pass. Small nearly tripped on the deep shag of a carpet.

"Stand up boy!" commanded Mr. Sord jerking Small's collar.

"You walk on roof tops and stumble on a carpet? It is boys like you that will be the ruin of me." He let go of Small and led into a room where stood a shiny desk with a sheet of glass on its top. Mr. Sord collapsed into a large leather chair behind the desk and smoothed his black tie under his shiny black vest.

Small stood still in the doorway to this inner room. "Come! Step up here!" said Mr. Sord, "Stand before my desk." Small moved toward the desk as if he walked on eggs. He stopped at its corner.

"You have never been a cause of concern to me," said Mr. Sord, "but then I suppose it is time. Do you know what would have happened if you had fallen off of that tall wall, Small?" Mr. Sord chuckled abruptly. Small wondered what was the matter with him.

Tales had been told of what went on behind Sord's big wooden door with the laurel wreath carved upon it. Small considered the one about death and darkness and a hole in the floor that fell into a lake of fire. He no longer remembered when he had heard this story. He stood as solidly rooted on the carpet as he had on top of the wall. The floor might cave in, thought Small. Mr. Sord's red face would disappear behind the desk as Small fell to his firey end.

"*What* would happen?" glared Mr. Sord and his eyes bulged. "Thousands! Thousands of dollars your foolish little walk on that high wall could cost. It could close this institution! And *you* would be the cause of it. Little matter to me! Save me a stroke. And you could have been killed!"

Boys had been seen passing through the big wooden door never to reappear. Small's eyes darted about the shadowy carpet for the edge of the abyss. A narrow window open to green leaves and sunlight stood on the far wall. He might make a dash for the window. Mr. Sord's eyes followed those of Small.

"Do you know what your punishment shall be, Alexander Small?"

Small was rigid. He made no sound.

"You will not be allowed playyard for one month from this day. You will clean the insides of the windows during playyard and after lessons every day until the buzzer before lights out. You will take your meals in the kitchen alone. I personally will inspect your work. If it is not well-done I will find other tasks to occupy you. Do you understand what I say?"

Small looked at Mr. Sord.

"Speak boy! Do you have a tongue? Do you understand what I have told you? Answer!"

"Yes," said Small.

"You do not do well at lessons. Is it that you are not bright? I cannot give out brains if you do not have them. Apparently you have precious little. Walls are not for standing on. That is very clear to me. You must jiggle your brains a bit and see if there is something inside your head Alexander Small.

"At supper you will go directly to the kitchen and report to Bessie. Tomorrow at playyard period you will report to Edward who will direct your punishment work. Do you understand what I say to you?"

"I understand what you say to me."

"See that you do!"

"I do."

Mr. Sord looked at him sharply.

"If I must bring you to this office just once again you will wish you would have exercised what little brain power you may have. I promise you. You will see my severe side. Now go boy. Go!"

Small did not know what to say about his visit to Mr. Sord's office though the boys asked.

"Were you scared on the wall Small?" asked Peter.

"No," said Small.

He told them about the palm tree he could see and about the airplane. "You couldn't see it down there, but I could see it. It was going real fast across the whole sky."

"I'm going to be an airplane pilot when I grow up," said Eric, who was a blond boy. "I like it cause maybe my father was an airplane pilot."

Small knew that Eric did not know his father at all, but then neither did Small.

"Maybe he was," said Small.

The cook was a large black woman. She had been told by Mr. Sord of Small's crime.

"You call me Bessie, honey. When you come back here to Bessie you has arrived in heaven. Mr. Sord he think he bein mean to you to make you eat alone back here in the kitchen. But, honey, Providence has done you a good turn. You gonna eat better than Mr. Sord does, you can believe your Bessie! Now you sit in that comfortable wood chair there, I gonna fix you up somethin scrumptious."

Small sat down and watched her.

"Here, you start on this peach. It's the best. I saved it for you when I knew you was comin. An you gonna have onions on your meatloaf an real mushrooms in your gravey an if your little stomach is big enough you gets a second helpin of cherry cobbler.

"Yes, sir," said Bessie as she moved between a long table and the big cook stove, "You like a cat landed on his feet when that man send you back here honey. Which one is you?"

Small was eating the delicious peach. "I'm Small," he said.

"Well yes you is honey, I wish I was, but I mean what name has you got?"

"Small is my name," said Small.

"Ohhh," said Bessie. "Well what's your other name?"

"Alexander."

"Alexander! My, that is a mighty fancy name, sounds like you is a prince or a king maybe. Maybe your pappy was a king, you think?"

"I don't know."

"Well maybe you *is* of royal blood?" Bessie grinned a bright big face at him.

"Well someday you goin to fly like a bird right out a this place and you goin have a family all your own an everything will be all right. You standin up on that high wall just tells me you goin to be real high up in this world someday Alexander.

"This whole orphanage seems to me like it's underground," scowled Bessie, "Like all you boys lives in a basement."

Small liked Bessie immediately and he trusted her. He had never eaten so well.

Edward, the old black janitor handed Small a metal bucket.

"Now there some soap in here. See? In this big old sack. You puts in a pinch a that in your bucket there an run it half full of water here at the sink. An here's a step ladder. Don't know you can handle it. It's a pretty big ol thing."

"I'm strong," said Small.

The skinny old man looked down at him. "Well maybe you is, but you don't look it. You younguns look like ghosts ta me. Here." Edward reached into the shadows of the mop closet and handed Small some rags. "You gets the windas all wet with one a these rags then you jus wipes it dry. That's how you washes windas."

Edward stood still, scratching his gray head. "I don't 'member when these windas done last. Ain't got no time 'roun here. I does Mr. Sord's winda an Miss Sweatly an the front door case de mayor come in here to give Mr. Sord a big gold ribbon ta hang 'roun his neck cause he so good ta all you boys."

"What you do boy? How come Sord makin you wash de windas?"

"I climbed up on the wall," said Small, "out in the playyard."

"You up on top a that wall? Why boy you plain crazy, you fall off der you break like a egg. He, he, what old Sord do? He get mad, eh? Old Sord he get all red in de face? He, he. He gonna jus explode some day."

Edward dragged the step ladder out from the mop closet.

"Well if you up on that wall I figure you ain't gonna fall offen dis ladder. An when you done workin for de day you jus stick it back in dis closet. You just take your time cleanin doz windas. Ain't no hurry 'bout it. Don't 'member they ever been clean before."

Small dragged the step ladder along the hall. He was beginning to take an interest in this. He hadn't been told which windows to clean first so he was going to wash the high windows that lit the long hall passages. No boy ever looked through these windows as they were higher than an adult's head.

Small propped open the step ladder beside the cold plaster wall and climbed to the very top. He looked through the grime of a window pane. He could see nothing. He climbed down and lifted up the bucket onto the folding shelf of the ladder. He dipped a rag into the bucket and standing on top of the ladder swabbed at the pane. The grime began to melt away. He squatted and rinsed the rag. He was perfectly at ease on top of the ladder. This time the wet rag swabbed the window clean. Small dried it with another rag. It took a while, but he wanted to see outside. But there was more dirt on the outside of the window. Still he could see the street that he had seen from the top of the wall.

He watched a man in a white suit with a straw hat on his head pass in the sunshine. He saw a woman in a yellow dress who wore a hat of flowers. He watched an automobile and two trucks pass on the street. Where were they going? wondered Small. He waited anxiously for the next new person or vehicle.

Small scrubbed and wiped dry hundreds of the little windows that lined the high walls of the halls, enjoying his position just under the ceilings and looking out upon the unknown world while an increasing light fell onto the heads of the boys marching up and down the halls and their spirits rose and no one knew why. When he was working at the windows Small was happy. He looked forward to his hours of punishment.

One day Small was called from lessons by Miss Sweatly. "You, Alexander Small. Come!" she said from the lesson room door.

"Yes, you. Come out."

Small rose and walked up the narrow aisle and out the door that Miss Sweatly held open into the gloom of the hall.

"Follow me," said Miss Sweatly and she strode ahead. Small followed after the dark flare of her skirts between the high rows of again soiled windows, stretching his legs to keep up.

In the dormitory she led him to his bed where a freshly laundered blue uniform lay folded on the khaki blanket.

All of the boys wore blue uniforms, plain-cut long-sleeve shirts and trousers with no cuffs. These were changed once a week on Fridays.

"You will put on your clean uniform," directed Miss Sweatly. "Immediately. Dust off your shoes so you will not soil the carpet and meet me in the hall as soon as you are finished." She strode away up the aisle between the beds and through the door.

What carpet? wondered Small. He could not remember what day it was, but it was not Friday. Nevertheless he hastily undressed. He kicked off his shoes. The sole of the left was flapping. He unfolded the shirt and pants and climbed into them. When he was buttoned up he pulled the edge of the khaki blanket out and rubbed the surface of his shoes. They did not shine. He folded his old uniform, brushed his hair back out of his eyes and walked quickly into the hall where Miss Sweatly towered in the shadows.

"This way." They were off down the hall.

We are going to the wooden door, Small knew.

He did not trip this time when he followed Miss Sweatly into the gloom of the carpeted room. He remembered the spongy softness under his feet.

"Here he is—" said Miss Sweatly as though she lay down a burden.

"Bring in his file then," sighed Mr. Sord. Miss Sweatly melted through a side door.

"Step up here, Small."

Small moved slowly to the exact spot where he had stood the first time. But now there was the slight difference of his height. He no longer looked up, but straight ahead at Mr. Sord who sat in the big leather chair behind the desk.

"Happy birthday," Mr. Sord said in the voice of an old bird. His bulging eyes darted up at Small's and then away. He leaned forward on his elbows. His finger nails drummed on the fine sheet of glass on the desk top.

Small did not know it was his birthday. He had not known when his birthday was.

"You are thirteen," said Mr. Sord still not looking at Small. "Every boy comes here at thirteen for his identification. Today it is you."

"Here is the file, Mr. Sord," said Miss Sweatly, sweeping in with a chill and handing a yellow folder to Mr. Sord. She took the chill with her out of the room. Small noticed the open window and green things growing beyond it in sunlight.

Mr. Sord was turning over papers.

"All that anyone knows about you is in this folder," announced Mr. Sord. "You are Alexander Small. I myself gave you this name on this document. Alexander for A. It simplifies. No middle name. Unnecessary.

"Your father is unknown. It makes no difference to you if your father is alive or dead." Mr. Sord looked up at Small now as if seeing him for the first time.

"You will never see him of course because he either does not know of you or has forgotten your existence. If in fact your father exists." Mr. Sord sneezed. "Go, Small, close that window."

Small felt a shiver as though again he teetered on the high wall reaching for the ball he could not catch. The stories of the hole in Sord's office where boys were thrown into flames remained in the back of his mind as though carved in a wall.

"Move boy!" said Mr. Sord.

Small stepped like a tightrope walker toward the window across the high colorless nap of the carpet. His eyes filled with the bright green world, the sunshine-yellow flowers, and the street beyond.

"Come, close it Small."

Small pulled the window closed, turned again into the gloom and returned like a soft-footed animal to the place at the corner of the desk.

"Your mother was one Eva Small, deceased in county hospital at your birth. Charity case. No known religion. No known relatives. Buried in paupers' field at Palmcrest number 543."

Mr. Sord looked up at Small. "This means that you too are a charity case. The cost of your support is born by the charitable institutions of your betters, and will be for two more years when you will be turned out to make your own way.

"I see you were disciplined three years ago — ah, yes, climbing up on the playyard wall. Your place is not up high Alexander Small, you will remember that.

"Though you have been little trouble to me or to your superiors you will remember that you owe this institution a debt that you will never satisfactorily repay. Perhaps bringing you up in this home will keep you out of jail. That is all we can hope for, indeed, that is all we expect of you.

"Your lesson grades are atrocious. You are not a bright boy." He snapped the folder closed and laid it on the glass of the desk.

"I hope your stay with us here continues to be an enjoyable one. From now on you will try your best to better meet our standards so that you are not completely helpless when you leave this haven. You have two years to prepare for that day. Then God help you, because we will not. Return now to your classes.

"Miss Sweatly, my tea now, bring me my tea.

"Why do you stand gaping at me boy? Go."

As Small passed out the big wooden door he was no longer afraid of Mr. Sord. And he was determined that he would leave the orphanage.

That very evening after supper in the dormitory Eric, who was now getting tall and had pimples on his face said, "Happy birthday, Small, you're thirteen ain't you? Cause you saw old Sord today. You got any mother or father?"

"Maybe a father," said Small.

"Yeah," said Eric. "Here's a birthday present for you." Eric handed Small a worn comic book. "It tells really how to fly an airplane. Here in the middle." Eric took the comic book and opened it. "See, here is a control panel. It tells you what to do."

Small was so fascinated with the step by step description of how to fly an airplane that he memorized it without intent to do so. He understood how it worked. The simplicity of it amazed him. The only unfamiliarity in the illustrated description was the placement of dials across the instrument panel.

What was familiar was a sense that he would know how to fly an airplane. He thought of the two-winged airplane he had watched cross the sky when he stood on the wall. It seemed now that he knew the pilot too.

How fine to be a pilot, thought Small, flying across all of the sky to any place you wanted to go.

"Alexander!" said Bessie, "What you doin back here, honey? You been wicked again?" Bessie's face was bright with her smile."Come give your Bessie a hug!" She gathered him into her arms like a feather bed. She was laughing.

"You ain't snuck back here to see me in a month but I look out the window there an I see you at meals. How is you, child?"

"I'm *fine*, Bessie," said Small. He looked left and right under the hanging pots. He stepped close to Bessie.

"I'm going to leave here Bessie."

Her big face looked stricken, then a smile flickered at the corners of her mouth.

"You done been adopted Alexander?"

"No Bessie. I'm going to leave tonight to go on my own. I'm big enough."

"You goin to sneak away child?"

"Yes, tonight. I'm going to go up north and work."

"Work? What work you know how to do?"

"I don't know," he said. It didn't seem a problem.

"Why child, you'll starve!" Then Bessie said, "No, no you won't! I know that in my bones. You is gonna go places, Alexander!" She grinned and held him at arm's length to look at him. "An you always know where your Bessie be. You ever need anything or you gets in any trouble — Lord preserve you — you just write me a letter Alexander, now you hear me, an you don't forget? You is one a my children Alexander." She hugged him tightly again and there was in him a feeling that Bessie was what he did not want to leave. It made him feel weak with a sweet dizziness. Small pushed away and looked up into her face.

"I'll always remember you, Bessie. I'll come back and see you, I promise."

Tear streaks shined on her dark cheeks and he turned away.

"Child," she said, supporting herself with one hand upon the long table, "You look under you bed before you go off tonight. I'll have Edward put a lunch there for you in a paper sack. You be sure to take it so you have some food with you."

"Thank you Bessie. Goodbye now." He turned and hurried out of the kitchen.

For an instant he took fright at the shadows of the dining hall wall but he walked through them. Then, alert as a rabbit, he slipped through the swinging doors into the hall.

No one noticed him appear in the playyard. He saw the ball fly up toward the wall. He fished between bodies, arriving beneath the ball and slapped it harder than he ever had up and over the wall.

There was the usual uproar, the boys booed and hooted Small, shoved him and hit at his arm, all in fun, and Small laughed to see their faces. The boys swirled around the playyard. There were yells and laughter. Small was full of the excitement that had accompanied him all day long.

That night before lights out Small sat on his bed watching all of the boys so that he would remember them. Suddenly he lay down and hung his head over the bed and looked. There it was, a brown paper sack. He sat up again watching the boys. With many of them he had slept every night of his life, and mostly in this one long room.

The boys seemed to merge from many into one faceless boy, as if Small's mind's eye was out of focus. This faceless brother was all of his brothers, the brother of his heart. There was nothing to say. He did not have the words. He knew that he was separate from them. Yet he would take the faceless brother with him tonight when he left. So Small sat quietly the last evening with his brothers and his being filled with the life of them.

When the lights went out and the night-keeper had made his rounds through the dormitory and no sound but the even breathing of the boys filled the room Small lay awake with his hands behind his head. He lay quietly for a long time. He was not at all sleepy.

When he was certain that all of the boys slept he slipped back the khaki blanket and sat listening on the edge of his bed. Then he stood and took his blue shirt and pants from the coathanger at the head of his bed and dressed. He pulled on his socks and shoes.

He heard the sharp creak of springs at the end of the dormitory and a boy rose out of his bed. Small melted down lying full-length on his bed as the boy padded barefoot past toward the bathroom. The boy went through the door. Small slipped fully dressed under the cover waiting. After the flushing gurgle of the toilet the boy toddled past to his bed. Small waited again through liquid moments of darkness until again there was no sound but the one breath of sleeping boys. He lay back the blanket and now he removed his shoes, tied the laces together and hung them around his neck. He pulled loose the ends of the blanket and reached under the bed for the paper sack. He set it in the center of the blanket and rolled the blanket into a tube.

"Small—" said a voice. Small froze motionless and did not answer. It was Jake in the bed beside his own. He watched Jake roll over in his sleep. Small sat still listening to the entire dormitory. Quickly he rose and made his way down the center aisle toward the red EXIT sign that glowed above the swinging doors to the hall.

He stopped silently before the doors. He stretched up looking through the small glass window into the dim hall and listened. Slowly he eased the door open. He pushed it further. The night-keeper should be at the big wooden desk around the corner of the hall. Small slipped into the hall in his stocking feet carrying his bed roll and padded silently toward the night-keeper's desk. His blood drummed in his ears. At the corner he squatted, kneeled, and peeked around the corner into the light.

The young black man was leaning back in his chair with his long legs crossed on the top of the desk. The man was facing Small but a newspaper was spread out before his face. Small pulled back his head sitting in the shadows of the wall on his knees. His heart was thumping. He pulled the shoes tight around his neck, tucked the blanket securely under his arm and peeked again. The man turned the page of his newspaper which still covered his face.

Small drew in a long breath and duckwalked out into the open looking straight ahead to the shadows where the hall recommenced. The newspaper rattled and the chair squeaked and Small, looking neither left nor right, moved straight on until he was received into the shadows where he squatted quiet as a mouse. Then he stood and continued quickly down the hall past the dining hall door and under the high windows he once had washed. He turned down the hall toward the playyard and stood at last listening in the shadows before Sord's big wooden door with the carved wreath on it.

He turned the big brass knob slowly, pushed open the door and stepped into darkness, for the third time onto the thick carpet. He stood still listening. He stepped slowly in inky darkness toward the doorway into Sord's office. On the far wall the narrow arched window glowed dimly with light from outside.

Small laid down his bedroll in the doorway and sat down on the carpet. He took his shoes from around his neck, untied the knot in the laces and slipped on his shoes. He was tying them when he noticed the streak of light on the wall above Sord's big desk.

Instantly he was alert. He leaned forward and saw that the light came from that room where Miss Sweatly had gone for his file. No sound came from the room. Small crawled silently across the long nap of the carpet toward the door which was slightly ajar. He stopped and listened. Hearing nothing he pushed the door with a finger. It made no sound, but still he could see nothing. Small did not consider why he wanted to look but gently pushed the door again. It swung further and Small was about to follow with his head.

"What?" said a voice. A chair creaked and Small felt a presence. He scooted and squeezed backward finding himself wedged between a stuffed chair and the wall as Miss Sweatly appeared in the doorway snapping a light switch. She stood motionless, her dark skirt nearly brushing his nose.

"Rats!" said Miss Sweatly stomping at the carpet with quick dull thuds, "Rats! Rats!" stomping in a crazed little dance and her skirts swinging before Small's eyes. He cringed but could move no further. Miss Sweatly danced into the room thudding her feet. Sweat stood on Small's forehead. He remembered his bedroll lying in the doorway across the room but Miss Sweatly turned quickly back still stomping the carpet.

"I'm going rats!" said Miss Sweatly, "I'm going now. Don't you show your faces till I'm gone! I'll step on your heads! I'll crush you to bloody pulps! Bite Sord. Don't you dare bite me or you'll die. Die die die!" she insisted shrilly. She flicked the light switch and slammed the door.

Small knelt trembling in the darkness. What a fury! He didn't move until the crack of light under the door went out and another door slammed.

He scuttled through the dark, found his bedroll and crossed the room to the narrow window. He had unlatched the window and swung it open when he remembered the childhood stories of the bottomless pit in Sord's office. He felt sound and brave. He hadn't even thought of the pit until this moment and he stood unmoving at the window.

Now he set his bedroll on the ledge, turned and stomped back through the darkness over the long nap of the carpet daring the floor to cave away beneath his feet, stomping flat the shaggy nap like a savage partner to Miss Sweatly's own dance and chanting, "Sord! Sweatly! Sord! Sweatly! Rats! Rats! Rats! Bite you in your beds! Bite, bite, bite off your heads!"

Then suddenly quiet he opened the door to the other room. He felt the walls and then switched on the light. He saw a wooden file cabinet. He opened it and pulled out the yellow folders behind 'S' and set them on a wooden desk. He found his. He was going to put the others back but then he turned and carried them to the door of Sord's office. He flung them far into the dark. They bounced from the wall and the crinkle of papers fluttered to the carpet. He took all of the folders and flung them by the handfuls into the dark of Sord's office. He took his own file, turned off the light and scuffed and kicked his way through folders and papers returning to the window.

Small put his file in with the paper bag and rolled the blanket tight. He climbed up onto the window sill, pushed the window wide and, with his bedroll under his arm, jumped out into the night.

Small felt truly small. He crept out of the bushes looking both ways up and down the street. There was no one. He came out onto the sidewalk and walked quickly along under the fronds of the palm he had seen from the playyard wall. He thought it a beautiful tree and then he saw the stars beyond the fronds which made him grin.

He walked quickly past the brick fronts of warehouses, past dark passages and vacant lots passing beneath street lamps and then again into the dark. He was heading toward the sea, he hoped.

In an hour he had come to a broad avenue. The sole of his left shoe was flapping with each step. Already the orphanage seemed very far from him. The city was so big, so many buildings. Were these buildings full of boys too, maybe even girls? What would the streets look like in daylight? There must be *thousands* of people.

As he crossed a street a large truck swept him in its headlights. He hopped up onto the walk and walked quickly on as if he knew exactly where he was going and was in a hurry to arrive. The big truck chugged and rumbled, creeping up the street beside him. Small looked straight ahead.

"Hey kid!" a voice called. Small did not look at the truck, he kept walking.

"Hey you, kid!" Small looked toward the truck. It was shiny in the light of a street lamp and a high tarpaulin covered the back. Small kept walking. The driver was leaning out the cab window.

"Yeah, you! You goin down Chattuck? You want a ride?" Small stopped. The truck stopped too. The tarpaulin sides quivered like the sides of some huge beast, the engine chugged and the powerful headlights beamed far down the street.

"Come on, I'll give ya a ride if you're goin on down Chattuck."

Small stepped into the street and looked up at the driver high above his head.

"I'm going out by the cemetery," said Small.

"Palmcrest? The cemetery? I'm going out to the airport, I go by there. Come around the other side and get in."

Small walked around the front of the cab. The headlights, high as his head, dazzled him like suns. The door swung open above his head and the driver reached down. "Here, throw your bundle up." Small handed the khaki blanket up. Then the man's arm appeared. "Grab hold." Small's hand disappeared into that of the driver and he was lifted up and clutched at the slick seat of the truck.

"Slam it, the door," the man said. Small clutched the door handle and swung it hard. A faint yellow light illuminated the interior of the cab. The light came from dials on the dashboard. His bedroll sat in the wide seat between them.

The driver winked at Small under the brim of a baseball cap. "We're off!" he said, and they lurched forward. Small was delighted to be sitting so high in the cab of a truck.

"I never been in a truck before," said Small.

"This is your lucky night," grinned the man. He had a little pug nose and his eyes crinkled like he was thinking of a joke. Small watched the man's great hand work the gear shift. His wrist was thick as Small's thigh, and hairy.

"I think I'd like to drive a truck," said Small.

"Yeah, and night shift is best, not many folks out to bump into at night," said the man, "ain't a bad job. I just deliver around the city, don't go real far." Small felt like he was flying. This was the best ever.

"What you doin out so late?" the man asked, "You runnin away from home?" Small froze. When he said nothing the man said, "I see ya got your bedroll an all. Get mad at your mom and pop?"

"I got no mom and pop," said Small, "so I ain't running away from home."

"Oh," said the driver. "It's a pretty long walk out by the cemetery though, you wouldn't a got there till morning. Somebody be worried about you by then."

"Nobody's worried about me," said Small. "Everything's ok." He darted a hard little look at the man.

"Oh," said the driver catching the look, "Don't worry yourself, kid, I ain't going to turn you over to the cops or nothing, looks to me you can take care of yourself."

"I can," said Small.

"I ran away from home myself when I was a kid, but not so young as you."

"I'm thirteen!" said Small.

"Yeah, you'll be gettin gray real soon," said the driver and he chuckled. Small didn't understand. "Gray?" he said.

"Yeah, gray, your hair you know, like mine. It's the way we all go kid. Seems like yesterday I headed south. I hitched a freight down here out a Chicago when I was 16. Been here ever since. I didn't like ice and snow, that's why I came to Florida. Ain't sorry I did either." Small looked at the man's face again. Small liked his face.

"I'm going north," said Small. "Maybe I'm going to Chicago. I'm going to get a job and work cause I'm big enough."

The man looked down at him. "You ain't really very big for 13," said the man.

"I know I ain't, but I'm still growing. I can do a lot of things."

"What can you do?"

"Lots of things," said Small. "I can wash windows—I know a lot about geography."

"You know which way north is?" said the driver.

"Yeah," said Small. "I mean I don't right now, but I know where north is." They were rumbling along the cobbled street beside the wharfs.

"I can fly an airplane," said Small.

"Oh, really—" said the man.

"That's right," said Small, "I know all about it."

"Well that's something," said the man. "I never been in an airplane myself and I ain't anxious to get in one."

"I never been in an airplane either," said Small.

"Then how do you know how to fly an airplane?"

"I read about it. There were pictures."

"Well that ain't quite the same thing."

"It *is*," insisted Small. "It told just how and so I know how."

"I see," said the driver. "Still you're too young to get a job doing that."

"I don't know what kind of work I'll do yet. I guess I'll just look around for a while. When I get up north."

"You don't even have a jacket. Don't you know it gets cold up north?"

"Yeah, snow," said Small. "I'd like to see that. I've never seen snow. Only pictures in books."

"Cemetery comin up pretty quick now," said the man. "Where you want me to let you out?"

The street lamps were now infrequent. A great ocean of dark spread out beyond the windshield.

"Anywhere," said Small in a little voice, "Just anywhere—"

The driver had slowed the truck, and now they crept along past an endless iron picket fence.

"Look," said the driver, "I don't think you got anyplace special to go. That's what I think. Since you don't seem to be in any hurry why don't you just ride around with me? I got a delivery to make at the freight terminal at the airport. You might like that since you're an airplane pilot an all—"

"I didn't say I was a pilot, I just said I knew how to fly an airplane," said Small.

"Yeah, right," said the man, "That's just what you said all right. Well you might like lookin close at the airplanes. Then we'll stop and have some breakfast at a diner I know. You hungry?"

"A little," said Small, "I got a lunch in a paper sack in my bed roll."

"Well, you can save that. You got a long way to go to get up north. Ok? You want to ride along a while?"

Small looked into the absolute black of the cemetery. "Sure," he said. "Yeah, I'd like to ride along for a while. Maybe till it gets a little lighter."

"My name's Tom," said the driver. He held out his gigantic hand to Small. Small shook hands with the man.

"My name's Small," said Small.

"Small?" said Tom, "Glad to meet ya Small. Now we'll gas the old crate up an' get on with business." The truck sped up and the iron fence of the cemetery passed in a blur.

"Where do you think the paupers' field is in this cemetery—Tom?" said Small.

Tom looked down at him for a moment then looked ahead at the road. "Well, I think the paupers' field must be on that hill that overlooks the airport. You won't be able to see it now in the dark, but I think that's probably where it is.

"Don't you have another name besides Small?"

"Yeah, Alexander," said Small, "But my mother didn't give me that name before she died. Some other person gave me that name. I don't like it much. And everybody just calls me Small anyway."

"Sure, nothin wrong with Small, that's a good name. Real handy name I'd say. Ain't easy to forget."

Small leaned back now for the first time, relaxing against the big bumping seat. "I never really been to the airport," he said. "I seen it once when we all went fishing one day a couple years ago, the bus went past."

"Catch any fish?" said Tom.

"No. But I liked the boat and the ocean. I went all over the boat. I might become a sailor. I like boats almost as much as I like airplanes."

"You know how to captain a boat too?"

Small laughed and looked up at Tom. Tom was grinning at him. "No, I don't know how to captain a boat. But I bet it wouldn't be hard."

"Well, tonight's an airplane night," said Tom. "See the beacon flash up there, an there's the runway lights."

The truck passed the terminal, and continued along a gravel road passing large hangers.

"Jeeze," said Small. The truck was passing big airplanes with tails higher than the truck, and electric light gleaming in silver flashes along their sides, and men loading great wooden crates into the planes under brilliant lights that turned the night into day.

I would have been sleeping! thought Small. Every night I'm sleeping all of this is happening. "Jeeze," he said again.

"You know how to fly these big ones?" said Tom.

"No, I don't think — not like these," said Small, "Just little airplanes."

"Ah," said Tom. He turned the truck between two great hangers painted with red and white stripes and pulled up beside a concrete loading dock.

"You wait here in the cab, ok? I got to go turn in my bills and then they're going to unload us and I'll pick up some stuff then we'll go get us some grub. You can see the planes good from here."

When Tom was gone Small sat looking at the large cargo liner the men were loading. Soon he saw a plane flash past beyond the hangers with a roar, the green light on its wing and a white light blinking on its tail.

He was pleased to be where he was. He thought of the boys in the dormitory, for many hours asleep. Who could have a dream as exciting as this? Tom had left the motor running and it was warm in the cab.

Small's eyes opened on the black leather of the seat back. Panic gripped him. He didn't understand where he was and jerked up thrashing, tangled in his blanket. Then he remembered.

But this was not the airport. They were parked by a strange building. It looked like a railway car. It was long and the sides were silver but it had no wheels. Across a highway a chill luminous light was pushing the darkness back over the gray waters of the bay.

Other trucks were parked around them.

Small saw his yellow folder sitting on the dashboard with the brown paper sack on top of it. He rubbed sleep out of his eyes and now he was wide awake.

He reached for the sack, opened it and looked inside. There was money lying among an orange, an apple and several packets wrapped in wax paper with rubber bands around them.

He hadn't thought about money. He had never had any. He pulled out three crisp one dollar bills. He studied the green bills. He recognized George Washington. He turned the bill over. ONE it said. And, IN GOD WE TRUST. Small supposed they were real. He folded the three bills and stuck them into his hip pocket.

Then he took the folder from the dash board and opened it. Several papers with printing on them, pink and yellow and white papers.

CERTIFICATE OF BIRTH, said one. EVA SMALL, his mother's name. FATHER: UNKNOWN.

Small leafed through the papers. The last was edged in black: CERTIFICATE OF DEATH. EVA SMALL.

Small closed the folder and looked through the windshield at the blooming light and the ragged pitch of waves in the bay beyond the highway. He put the folder on the dashboard and set the lunch bag upon it. He would have all of his life to understand what was in that folder. It was all his and belonged to no one else. It never had. Those things were his. He was glad he had taken them. He was glad he had scattered the folders of the other boys. Maybe Sord and Sweatly would never figure out who was who now and all the boys could go away.

He watched a large truck bump onto the gravel off the early morning highway, its headlights still on and the tarpaulin covering its back flapping. The truck had three red lights on the roof of its cab.

It sat there staring at Small like a big two-eyed bug; not only a bug, but a creature in itself like the big airplanes had looked. He had never seen anything like them, the airplanes and the trucks. Small patted the dashboard of the truck as if it was the head of a dog. He watched the driver of the new truck climb down from his cab and go into the silver train coach.

Small too climbed down and stood in the gravel. There was a damp morning chill in the air. Gravel crunched under his shoes as he walked toward the warm yellow lights of the train coach. The door was hard to pull open but he squeezed inside. It hissed closed behind him.

He walked up three steps into a rich aroma of food. There was a long counter with men sitting on round wooden stools. It was a cozy place with men's voices and music playing from somewhere and a big propeller fan whirred overhead.

"Hey Small!" It was Tom's voice, and Small saw his raised arm at the far end of the diner. Tom was sitting at a wooden table with several other men. Tom was grinning and motioning to him. Small walked past the tall backs of the men on stools like the bulging bodies of big animals at the zoo.

The men at the big wooden table turned to look at Small.

"Here, I'm goin," said one of the men, "Here's a seat, kid."

Small went around and sat in the vacant seat beside Tom. "What'll ya have Small?" said Tom.

"Jesus, feed that kid, Tom, he's so little can't hardly see him," laughed a man in a corduroy cap.

"Well I ain't so old as you," said Small staring hard at the man. The other men laughed.

"Little dogs grow teeth Tracy," said one of the men, "Be careful he'll eat ya for breakfast."

"Never mind these bums," said Tom, "What'll ya have for breakfast Small?" The men were grinning, smoking cigarettes, raising their cups.

"Betty! Coffee! Where the hell's me refill?" The man was marking a newspaper with a pencil. Small had never seen anyone do that before.

The waitress appeared with a big coffee pot.

"Refills!"

"Right here, gorgeous!" said Joe Talldorf. Without looking up from his paper he pointed at his cup with his thumb.

"Sure, honey, you're always first," said the waitress, "after the handsome ones." She winked at Small. Small looked at her.

"You want coffee, don't ya honey?" she asked setting a heavy white cup before him. Small had never tasted coffee but all the men had their cups.

"Sure," said Small. She poured it to the top.

"Have some eggs?" said Tom. Small hesitated and Tom said, "Give my helper here some eggs over, sausage an grits."

"A man's up all night he's gotta eat," Tom told Small. Small raised the cup like the others and sipped. Coffee was bitter. Small didn't like it. "Cream and sugar in that?" asked Tom.

"Hey, ain't no cream left on this table, Betty!"

"He's a man drinks it black," announced Tracy leaning back in his chair. "Ain't no sissy ya got for a helper Tom."

"Yeah, it's ok black," Small said looking up at Tom. Small saw that coffee was the drink of men. Since he was now in the world of men and drinking coffee, there might be no sugar or cream sometime. Why get upset about that? Small decided in a second, he would get used to coffee black.

"Got a winner! Hot damn!" said Talldorf. "*Boy Baby* in the first. I couldn't figure that one, hot damn! Your little one there give me that winner Tom, Boy Baby!"

"I ain't no boy baby!" said Small. A trickle of coffee was running from the corner of his mouth and down his chin. He wiped it away with the back of his hand. "I'm thirteen!" he said. Small was glaring at Talldorf.

Talldorf raised an eyebrow returning the boy's look.

"What ya want, kid," said Talldorf, "a cut a me winnins?"

"No Boy Baby will win," said Small, and seeing the others looking at him he lowered his head.

"He won't?!" Talldorf was surprised. "Why not?"

"I just know he won't," said Small.

When Small finished his breakfast Tom said, "You really are going north Small? That's what you figure is best for you?"

Small nodded.

"Well, you seem pretty sure. You got any money?"

"I got three dollars," said Small.

"I'm gonna give you five more," said Tom. "That ought to see you through. Hey, Baron," he said across the table, "You know anyone runnin out north today?"

The man called Baron waved his fork before his face while he chewed. "Yeah," he said, "Terry Burns is goin out tonight for Tallahassee."

"Got a passenger for him," said Tom. "Name's Small, right here, needs a ride up that way."

Baron looked at Small. "Sure," he said, "I'll tell Terry at the depot. He be comin in here six tonight, six-thirty."

"See, you be here a little before six tonight," Tom said to Small, "and Burns'll pick ya up. You'll get a good ride. He's a tall skinny guy. He's got a big red nose, can't miss him, an he'll have an eye out for you."

"Ok," said Small.

Tom paid for breakfast and handed a five dollar bill to Small.

"Gee," said Small, "Thanks Tom. I ain't never had so much money as I do now. It'll last forever."

Tom laughed. "You'll see, Small. You'll be able to use it. Up north in the cities you make money but then they take it right away again. So money ain't nothin to take serious. You remember that an you won't get yourself all troubled."

"All right," said Small.

They walked across the gravel to the truck. The sun was up now. A wind was blowing and the morning was bright. The sky seemed immense to Small. He looked up and around at the vastness. Gray- white clouds covered the sky.

"Overcast," said Tom looking up and stretching his arms wide, "But a fine morning, Small."

Small saw the choppy gray waves of the bay as he climbed up into the truck.

"What you going to do today, Small?"

"I got to go to the cemetery," said Small. "I got to see someone."

"Then I'll let you off there."

The truck rolled out onto the wide avenue and they rode along the bay.

"You goin to the pauper field?" said Tom.

"Yeah, the pauper field."

The truck pulled up to a wide gate in the iron picket fence. "I think it's that high hill back there, Small. You walk up an see. You can tell the pauper field cause they don't cut down the grass. They let the grass grow and the flowers."

"Gee, that's nice," said Small. "I'm sure glad I met you last night, Tom. You helped me a lot."

"It was my pleasure, Small. You kept me good company. You got your ride up north for six tonight remember. An you can always find me at the diner mornings if you decide not to go."

"Oh, I'm goin," said Small.

"Then I wish ya the best of luck, Small. I sort of wish I was goin myself. It'll be an excitement, you'll see."

Small dropped down onto the wide sidewalk and Tom handed down the bedroll. Tom stuck his thumb in the air and said, "Up and away, Small!"

At first the path was sand, and Small was surprised to be walking in it. Walking in sand was really walking. He passed only wild weeds and mean little bushes.

Then he scuffed up a sandy bluff and came onto real ground. The vegetation was thicker and a richer green. The path that he followed was very old.

He turned and saw that he had climbed high. He could see across the road far out over the bay. A finger of land reached into the gray waves and beyond was the ocean of the Gulf.

He climbed higher and saw the round tops of grave markers rising from tall grass that moved in wind. The markers were made of wood. There were rows of them. All of the graves of the dead. It was a quiet and open place and Small felt at home here.

Numbers were carved into the gray wood. Who was NO. 1243? He looked suddenly at where his feet stood. He did not want to stand on a person, but he was to the side. When he stepped past the grave marker he felt a largeness added to him and he continued on through the blowing grass and the buzz of insects. The sun did not pierce the clouds but it was bright. The sky was a luminous bowl.

Small stood looking at the number 543 as if they were a face. He sat on his knees and laid down his bedroll. Red wild flowers grew on the grave. His hands petted the grass as though waving an incantation. Grass ran between his fingers. His hands pressed through it and felt the earth. He felt warm and lay down in the grass beside the grave, his fingers touching the wooden marker. The grass smelled warm and insects buzzed. He felt a comforting presence and in a moment Small was dreamlessly asleep.

When he awoke his heart filled to see the wide sky. He felt wonderfully rested.

He looked at the grave marker of his mother. EVA SMALL, said the numbers 543. He was not sad, he felt very good.

Small stood, and beyond the rim of the hill he saw the long concrete runway of the airfield. He rolled his bedroll tightly around the yellow folder and the paper sack. He ran his fingers once over the grooved numbers. Then with his bedroll under his arm and his shoe flapping he walked away down the hill toward the airfield.

Small came along the gray block walls of the small terminal building toward the windy roar of an airplane engine.

It was a pretty, shiny green airplane with a metal skin. The propeller shimmered in an oval of light. Small could see a man inside. Another man stood beside the open door. Small dropped his bedroll and leaned on the wire fence in love with the shiny airplane.

He could stand here and watch the airplane take off. Farther out on the runway a bigger airplane roared into the air.

An idea occurred to Small. He could ask a pilot for a ride. He might get a ride in an airplane all the way to Chicago.

He picked up his bedroll and walked toward the door of the flight office. Just then the two men from the shiny green airplane came walking quickly toward the gate in the fence.

"Why don't you take it back to the line, Mark?"

The men stopped by the gate beside Small and looked back at the airplane.

"No," said the man who must be the pilot, "Ballard said have her ready to go at eleven. She's ready. It's his gas and his time. I'm getting paid. If he drives up while I'm up at weather let him sit."

"Hey, mister!" said Small. The men turned to look down at him. "You're the pilot for Mr. Ballard's airplane?"

"That's me kid, I'm afraid, what's up?"

"Mr. Ballard sent me to tell you he isn't going today and that you should take me instead." The two men looked blankly at Small.

"Say again—" said the pilot.

Small stretched himself tall as possible. "I'm the passenger today. You're supposed to fly me to Memphis, Tennessee."

The men looked at each other, and then looked again at Small. "And who are you?" said the pilot. "I'm Mr. Ballard's nephew, Stephen. I'm ready to go."

"What the hell are you talking about kid?"

"I just told you," said Small. "Mr. Ballard is going to be plenty mad if you don't do like he said. I know lots about airplanes and he wants you to show me more. He can't go today so you're supposed to take me and let me fly a lot of the time."

"I'm going nuts Pete," said the pilot.

"Maybe Ballard's afraid of the weather," said Pete.

"Of course Ballard's afraid of the weather, but this is crazy, a kid comin and tellin me something like this? Memphis? What about Ballard's trip to Atlanta?"

"He can't go," said Small, "I told you. I'm ready. Are you ready?"

"Call his office," said the one named Pete.

"Sure," said the pilot, "Come on, I'll phone and we'll check weather. You stay here kid, I'm going to straighten it all out." The two men went into the flight office. Small watched them heading up a flight of stairs.

He went through the gate and walked toward the shiny green airplane. They would run him off as soon as the pilot made his telephone call.

What an alive thing the airplane looked with its propeller spinning. A yellow cotton rope lay under his feet as he ran his fingers along the shiny green metal. The rope was attached to blocks beneath the two front wheels. Small opened the door and looked inside. There was one wide seat for two people, and two sticks. Either person could fly the airplane.

If there had been a back seat he could have hid inside and gotten a ride to Atlanta.

He dropped his bedroll on the cement and climbed into the airplane. How fine it felt sitting in this soft leather seat. He put his hand on the black rubber grip of the stick. Finger grooves just to fit the pilot's fingers. He felt the vibration of the plane through his body.

There was the throttle in the center of the instrument panel, a round black knob. The airspeed indicator. The dial went to 160 mph. Wow! thought Small, 160 miles per hour! Altimeter. Magnetoes. What was that? Carburetor Ice. Small knew that one. When you cut the throttle you had to first pull out that Carburetor Ice so the engine wouldn't stall.

I could fly this airplane, Small thought. A thrill like a feather passed through him. He waggled the stick. He stuck his head out the door and looked at the tail. Elevators. He pulled the stick back and the elevators raised. That makes you go up, thought Small. He pushed the stick forward and watched the elevators go down. Rudder pedals. He stretched and pushed on the left pedal looking back at the tail. The loose sole of his shoe hooked on the pedal but the rudder moved to the left. That makes you turn left. He pushed the right. You go right.

Small leaned back in the seat watching the bright arc of light the propeller made before the windshield. I could. I could! No one could catch me in an airplane.

He looked toward the flight office. No one. For an instant he brushed his lower lip with his teeth. Then he pushed open the door and dropped to the cement. He snatched up his bedroll and threw it into the plane. He grabbed the yellow rope and jerked hard. The chocks leaped from before the wheels. Small bounded up into the seat and slammed the thin door. He ripped off his shoes and socks. These were no good. He felt the cold steel of the rudder pedals against his bare feet. He yanked the red metal hoop marked BRAKE. There was a whish—like a great spring snapping free, and a small thud. The plane crept forward.

He couldn't see over the dashboard but he could see out the side window. Instinctively he pulled the stick back into his lap. That would keep the tail on the ground and he wouldn't nose over. He stretched and pushed the left rudder pedal with his toes. The plane turned slowly to the left. Small could hardly believe it, he was driving an airplane. He pushed on the right rudder pedal and the plane began turning to the right.

The throttle, thought Small, this is too slow. He pushed gently on the round black knob but it did not budge. He pushed hard, and still it did not move. He pulled. The engine growled loudly and the plane bounded forward and immediately he shoved the throttle back. He saw the tower of the flight office directly in front of him through the high windshield and he jammed hard on the left rudder pedal.

Now the tower swung away from the windshield to his right and through the right window he saw the doors to the flight office burst open. The two men were racing through the gate with their arms in the air.

Small reached for the throttle and pulled it gently and the plane moved briskly across the concrete, turning now slightly left. He corrected by pushing gently the right rudder pedal until the nose headed straight ahead.

A big two-engine airplane came floating down across his path.

The men couldn't run this fast, they couldn't catch him now.

He felt sweat on the palm of the hand that held the stick. This was awkward, because to use the throttle he had to hold the stick with his left hand and he was right-handed. Maybe he was in the wrong seat? By the immediate response to the rudder pedals he understood that the machine was very delicate, that he could not be jerky or make abrupt moves. It would have to be all very smooth. That's what flying was, thought Small, you had to merge all of your movements, graceful, like a bird, or else you would wreck.

Where was the runway? He saw it stretching long to the right and ending at the waters of the bay. Then he saw a flashing red light on a truck racing toward him from the terminal.

He didn't think. He turned the plane toward the bay with the concrete stretching before him and pulled the throttle all the way out. The engine roared and he was pressed into the back of the seat. The truck was gone from his view. The tail banged the concrete once, twice, and Small remembered the comic book. He eased the stick forward. The tail rose — not too far forward — remembering the sweep of the propeller. Now he could see directly ahead through the windshield. He was headed slightly left. He would run off the runway. He stretched touching the right rudder pedal lightly with his toes. The plane skipped on the right tire and lifted from the ground. Small was hurtling at the bay faster than he could have believed.

He eased the stick slightly back to climb. The horizon was cut by the arc of the instrument panel. He darted a glance at the instruments. He was amazed to see the airspeed indicator pointing at 85.

He looked at the ground but the ground was gone. His stomach sloshed. There were waves beneath him. He was flying over the bay. He did not want to be flying over the Gulf because he didn't know how to swim. He eased again on the left rudder pedal to turn back toward land and the plane vibrated ominously.

Instinctively he knew his mistake. He tilted the stick slightly left and together with pressure on the rudder pedal the plane made a banking turn to the left. Small held it so. He saw he was far out beyond the ends of the wharfs. Great ships lay beneath him beside the docks. His eyes did not blink. He passed over the street, full of traffic, that he and Tom must have driven along last night.

Small slowly centered the stick and the airplane leveled out. The engine was roaring very loudly. He eased the throttle knob forward. The engine droned more friendly. But he seemed nearer the ground. Directly ahead on the ground a large oval was approaching. Small watched this oval. He saw horses running in a string and knot upon the track.

Joe Talldorf was bending over the board fence with doubled fists waving, "At a baby, you got it baby you got it *Baby Boy!*" Baby Boy was three lengths ahead and pulling away as he entered the stretch. The cogs in Joe Talldorf's brain were clicking as 30 to one he computed the fantastic winnings. He was kissing the ticket to his lips when a great shadow flashed from the trees accompanied by an exploding roar as an airplane passed up the straightaway directly over his head and Baby Boy passed through the opposite rail as if it was a matchstick, the knot of trailing horses expanding and contracting like a single immense cell gone berserk, whinnies, weavings to and fro, but holding the track, horses riderless, flashing past Talldorf's nose and the airplane climbing now far beyond the track. Talldorf could not believe his eyes. He had never seen anything like it. He pressed his doubled fists to his temples. "Son of a bitch!" he said.

Wow! thought Small. He had never seen a horserace either. There was nothing to this flying. But he mustn't get distracted. He had pulled the throttle all the way out over the race track and he was climbing again, watching the black altimeter needle turn like the big hand of a clock around the dial and the small red indicator move slowly toward the 1 which must mean 1000 feet. At the same time Small maintained a constant airspeed of 85 miles per hour. Balance, thought Small, it's all a balance! Everything is going just right.

He looked at the compass now floating in its bubble. He turned the plane slightly to the right and watched a big black E appear under the hairline of the compass.

Now as he climbed he made a slow banking turn to the left until N appeared crossing the hairline, Small easing the plane back until N stood under the hairline. "I'm going north!" he told himself.

The city was no longer beneath him, only green farm fields and patches of forests. To the left the gray Gulf of Mexico stretched as far as he could see. North, he thought, I'll hold it just to north, I'm going north.

Nothing to it! thought Small. He was elated. Nothing to it! The airplane hadn't blown up or fallen apart. But he was still uncertain. It seemed only an instant since he had left the ground and he had been busy all the time.

He felt a strain in the small of his back. The rudder pedals were too far away. He pulled his bedroll behind his back and propped nearer the instrument panel. That's more comfortable, he thought. Now both feet were firmly on the pedals.

He noticed the seat belt for the first time and buckled it across his lap. Now with the bedroll behind his back he was snug. He dipped the stick forward and felt himself lifted against the seatbelt. "Woo!" said Small. He was learning everything. Flying was all feel, you just had to remember which way was up and down. I'll keep climbing, thought Small, so I can see farther.

Then he saw the other airplane closing in beside him. Small was enthralled to see another airplane floating beside him in the sky. He grinned from ear to ear thinking, That's what *I* look like. There were two men in the other airplane, one in a front seat and one in the rear. They were waving to Small.

The man in the front was the pilot, Mark. Small waved at them. Ooops, too close! The other plane swerved off and away.

He was afraid I was going to hit him, thought Small with glee. He doesn't know how good I am. I wouldn't have hit him.

The other plane closed in beside him again. The men were scowling. They were waving their hands down. They wanted him to go down.

They want me to land, thought Small. He nodded No. He pointed up with his thumb as they pointed down. Now the men shook their heads No and again pointed down. Small nodded No again. The men pointed up, shook their heads No and the man in the rear seat put his hands over his eyes so he couldn't see, pointed up again shaking his head No. Small grinned and pointed up, shaking his head Yes. The men scowled. They looked mad. The man in the rear seat held a blackboard to the window. Written on the blackboard was, 'CLOUDS'. Small looked up. He knew that. The man raised the blackboard again. It read, 'CAN'T SEE ABOVE'. Small smiled and banked nearer the other plane. It immediately shot away to the left, leveled out, and slowly approached again. Small banked toward it more quickly. The plane darted away. He looked at his compass and turned the plane until the N appeared again on the black hairline.

He glanced at the other airplane. The blackboard read, 'NO GAS'. He looked at the gas gauge. It read, F. That meant full. Small was incensed. They were lying to him. But for the first time he noticed a switch beneath the gas gauge reading, LEFT WING TANK, and beside it, RIGHT WING TANK.

He flicked the switch so that it was under RIGHT WING TANK. The needle jumped an instant then held at F. He had *two* tanks and they were *both* full.

Small scowled at the men. He could saw off their tail with his propeller. He stuck out his tongue at the men. They looked shocked.

'BAD WEATHER', read the blackboard. Lies, thought Small. He banked sharply at the other plane. It quickly banked away. The gray waters of the Gulf lay still to his left. He was on course.

Now Small pulled the throttle all the way out and tilted the stick back. The other plane dropped below him, then nosed up, climbing after. He glanced at the airspeed indicator to hold it at a steady 85 mph while watching the altimeter needles creep around the dial passing 2500.

He was not paying attention now to the other plane although he could see it from the edge of his vision.

A shapeless, huge mass loomed before the windshield. Small didn't understand what was happening but a chill passed through his insides. The plane beside him disappeared and so did the ground. It was a fright, and then he understood that he was in a cloud.

All he now saw were the green wingtips hanging above him to either side and the left wheel hanging in nothingness. 85, read the airspeed indicator.

I'll just keep climbing, thought Small, until I pop out the top.

It was weird in the cloud. Small felt strangely uneasy. The comic book had said nothing about clouds. It was like the gloomy halls of the orphanage.

He looked at the instruments. Airspeed, 75. Small tilted the stick forward and the needle moved back to 85. There he held it. They can't follow me in a cloud, he thought. They don't know where I'm at in a cloud. No one could catch him now.

He watched the altimeter needle pass 3500. The engine droned. Small felt lonely. What a big cloud. An overcast. How thick was an overcast? wondered Small. The altimeter needle had climbed past 4050.

Now the airplane trembled slightly and the throb of the engine changed to a whine. Airspeed, 110. Alarmed, Small jerked the stick back and still the airspeed increased. And now he realized there was no reference in a cloud. Where was the ground? How did he know he was not upside down? He held the rubber pedals rigid with his bare feet. The engine was screaming. 130 read airspeed. Small was lifted from his seat and his shoes clunked against the cabin ceiling and sat there above him. Dust from the floor floated past his eyes. He was hanging from the seatbelt and bug-eyed he watched the airspeed: 140. Now he was thrust into the seat: His shoes fell from the ceiling into the seat at his side, 120, 100, 75. He eased the stick forward and airspeed held at 85, the engine droning normally. Small breathed. He had flown upside down. The altimeter read 3600. He had fallen 400 feet. The needle was climbing again.

Small listened to the engine like he had never listened in his life and he did not take his eyes from the airspeed indicator. It held at 85. Now he darted a glance at the altimeter. He was steadily climbing.

The airplane had dived and the engine pitch had been different. Now Small flew by sound, keeping to that drone, not rigid now on the controls but feeling for every tension while his eyes glued to the dials.

A thousand feet of cloud lay beneath him. It was as terrifying to try to go down as to try to go up, so he continued to climb.

It was oppressive, the gloom. Where was he? Was it a dream? He closed his eyes hard, and against his will reopened them.

A flash of blue opened to his right, and was gone.

Small threw the stick to the right pressing the rudder pedal and burst from the clouds.

A hill of white towered before him. He could not avoid it and again was swallowed in gloom. He pulled back on the stick climbing. The gloom lessened, brightened before his eyes, and he burst into the brilliance of sunlight lifting above a dazzling field of white clouds.

He squinted, and his heart seemed to swell and the inside of his ears tingled. He had never seen such brightness: this dazzling blue world and the brilliant fields of fleecy clouds below him.

He squinted up at a firey sun. As far as he could see in any direction he was alone above an endless world of white.

Beneath him the shadow of his airplane, ringed by a rainbow, crossed the clouds.

The compass read, N.

Chapter 3

STRAIGHT ARROW

Rudolf Victor Talldorf passed by the trays of bacon and scrambled eggs, the glazed donuts and stacks of pancakes. Except for *The Superman* by Nietzsche, his tray was empty. He was considering a wedge of cherry pie displayed temptingly behind the glass when the little man hurled up a greeting or an epithet.

Rudolph blinked down quizzically at the top of the little man's corduroy cap. The little man was engaged in reparte with the guardian of the cash register. The little man paid for his coffee and with a final salvo of cheerful banter stepped decisively, briskly, his attache case swinging, his tennis shoes propelling his compact body on the balls of nimble feet toward the table where the little man always sat.

"Move along! Keep the line moving!" The sour-faced woman's mouth twisted in a red smear of lipstick.

Rudolph reached for a cup and turned on the spigot. He fumbled for a dime, grasped his tray in both hands and made his tall- masted rudderless passage through the sea of tables. The want ads lay folded and creased beside his empty water glass. Rudolph sat down, rummaged in the crumpled pack, took a sip of coffee, burned his lip, found his matches and lit a cigarette with awkward unfamiliarity.

Rudolph Victor Talldorf was quick to admit the afflictions of the self-accused. Rudolph suffered the nameless guilt of his generation. The heartache he had caused Elinore and Anne grieved him. He felt sadly irresponsible and anxious and yet he was excited by his opportunity. His love for adventure had sent him careening off to the Windy City. His father, Joe Talldorf, had washed windows in the Windy City.

Rudolph had kept his father's letters in a shoebox on his bookshelf next to the bundle of worthless stocks that Joe Talldorf had mailed from Denver after the market crashed. The battered envelopes each bore the postmark of a different city. Joe Talldorf never left a forwarding address. He'd been up and down the Mississippi and ridden freights across all the rivers of the West.

Joe's last communication had been scrawled in blue ink on the back of a postcard.

'I'm sittin here in the cafe lookin out the winder at the snow-capped peaks thinkin about the day you was born an yer ma. An the only advice I got to give ya, Rudy, is don't never bet the horses don't get married and don't raise no kids.'

Before leaving Detroit Rudolph had read all Joe's letters again. As a boy he had not understood them. As an adolescent he had feigned disinterest, reading them secretly in order not to hurt his grandmother's feelings.

Elinore had raised Rudy as if he was her last chance. Her matronly extravagance, her proud carriage, her pretentions had enveloped him. She had smothered him with hugs and wet kisses. Her face sprang leaks. Her maternal bosom was cleaved with grief. Dr. Sturgis had performed a pelvic sweep. Elinore mopped up the tears that streamed down her cheeks with a lace handkerchief.

The rod in Elinore's closet sagged with the weight of her dresses and suits. Her dressing table was cluttered with a disarray of perfume bottles, powders, jars of cold cream and ointments. Her jewelry box spilled over with brooches, bracelets, earrings and pearls. Her drawers were stuffed with undergarments, girdles, sweaters and scarves. And Elinore kept buying more.

She dragged Rudolph along on her weekly shopping sprees, in and out of downtown stores until his feet hurt. Tea and a creamy pastry at Ulrich's before setting out again. Rudolph trudging in her wake past plate glass windows with the bright bags clutched in his skinny arms.

She was always taking in a stray dog or cat that lasted a week. And she always fed the men who stood, hat in hand, on the steps outside the kitchen door. Rudolph knew her scent: the smell of her love, of an alien correctness that he bore with rueful malignity. Even in the kitchen Elinore was femininely resplendent. Elinore was unctuously ceremonious and devoted to her family. She struggled with her vanity as her beauty ebbed and her sons disappeared into their private lives.

In the tall hallways of the Plately house, with their sliding oak doors, among the potted ferns and stacks of *National Geographics* Rudolph had been king. His dominion had extended from the alley to the front porch swing, included the attic and even went down to the creek that ran through the cement tunnel under Maple St. where he caught crawdads. There had been a pear tree and a peach tree in the backyard then, and Red had planted a kitchen garden every spring.

A gold star on a white satin background hung in the front window for Uncle Stanly. Uncle Eddie, the youngest by six hours of the twins, was killed in an accident at the ingot factory. Uncle Thomas still lived at home as if he was chained to Elinore. It was Uncle Thomas and Uncle Adair who had pitched in to save not the family fortune but Red's proud bearing and the Plately name.

Even when Rudy was a baby his uncles spent more time fishing at the lake or drinking at Slattery's than they did at home. Their photos lined the mantle above the fireplace along with Rudolph's university graduation picture and a tinted photograph of Mary.

The house had grown bigger. The cool rooms were empty. Rudolph stood in front of the tinted photograph taken when his mother was 17. Her pretty face merged with Rudolph's boyish reflection, his sharper masculine features which gave the same impression of an intelligent interest in the rest of humanity, softened by her smoother cheeks and redder lips and capped by curls that spilled over his forehead like a wig.

Even before his freshman year at Henry Ford High Rudolph had started growing precitously. He grew unevenly and he grew too fast. His right leg got longer than his left, then his left leg got longer than his right. His elbows and kneecaps buzzed constantly. Rudolph could barely walk straight. He towered above Elinore and Red, Thomas, and all of his classmates.

Rudolph dropped glasses and plates while drying the dishes. When he tried to help Thomas fix his car, washers, nuts and bolts leaped from his fingers and vanished in the driveway dust. Rudolph's fingers tingled as Thomas crawled out from underneath the chassis, oil smudging his forehead.

Thomas was a perfectionist and preferred to work alone. When Thomas wasn't at work in the Electrical Division of the General Motor's plant, which was every day but Sunday, he was either tuning up the engine or waxing the red fenders of his Chevy. Thomas was taciturn. "Can't you hold onto anything?" he asked.

"I give you a simple job, like mowing the lawn, and it takes you three days to finish it. Is that so hard a job?" Thomas frowned and Elinore toyed with her spoon. "I ask you to weed a flower bed and you moon around as if I'm asking the impossible."

"Rudolph is very intelligent, Thomas," Elinore said. "His I.Q. scores are high. He's cut out for something better than manual labor. He likes to read. Rudy spends a lot of time reading. Don't you dear?"

"It's not his intelligence. I'll tell you what it is," Thomas said menacingly, "You've spoiled him, mother. Rudy lacks gumption. Gumption!" Thomas pounded the table with his fist. "The old stick-to-itiveness!"

When Rudy wasn't at the gym he was shooting at the rim that Red had mounted on the former stable that was now the Plately two-car garage. Rudy shot baskets in the rain; he shot baskets in the winter and dreamed of playing center for the Detroit Bumpers.

He ran up the back steps with his hair dripping and dribbled the basketball into the kitchen.

"Rudy!" Elinore said. Rudolph palmed the basketball in his left hand.

"From now on call me Vic," he said.

"Vic?"

"When I sign with the Bumpers I'm going to sign Victor Talldorf." He dribbled the wet ball vigorously on the linoleum floor.

"Rudy, please don't bounce the ball in the house."

Rudolph palmed the ball in his right hand. "Vic," he said. He cradled the ball under his arm, went to the refrigerator and took out a gallon of milk.

"Rudolph, you'll spoil your supper."

"Vic, Grandmother. Victor Talldorf. How many times do I have to tell you." He got a glass out of the cupboard.

Elinore moved swiftly. She put the glass back and returned the gallon of milk to the refrigerator. "Supper will be ready in twenty minutes, Vic. Now go upstairs and take a shower."

Rudolph ran upstairs, stripped off his wet T-shirt and pulled off his dirty pants.

"When I sign with the Bumpers everybody will call me Vic. I'll sign autographs, Vic Talldorf. I'll have muscles then."

He pulled out the book that Charles Atlas had sent him. Curling the dumbbells each night beside his bed had made little difference. He stood in front of the mirror examining his hairless chest. The glass threw back the reflection of his long legs and knobby knees, the Jockey shorts that clung to his boney hips. He made a muscle. The biceps was flat. His calves were flat. His measurements were the same around ankles, waist, and chest as they were the last time.

"I've enrolled you in the Fortnightly Dancing Class, Rudy," Elinore said. "A gentleman should know how to dance. Dancing will teach you grace and give you a chance to become better acquainted with the opposite sex."

Rudolph was too tall to dance with anyone but Ophelia Nathan and Ophelia Nathan smelled like chalk dust.

Rudolph paid no more attention to the girls who flitted through his periphery than he did to the robins with their heads cocked on the silky Plately lawn or the yellow jackets that clung tenaciously to the mums in the flower beds. His only knowledge of sex came from the movie he'd seen in hygiene class.

Rudolph crept up the backstairs to the attic. The American flag nailed to the rafters muted the light that seeped from the dormer window along the floorboard cracks through used and useless things carried laboriously up the narrow steps and stored forever: mothballed trunks, dusty tables, lamps, a hatrack, gutted armchairs, the dusty Plately Sweeps & Stoker Co. books, an adding machine, two broken typewriters, mess kits and canteens in khaki canvas stenciled US ARMY, the old Zenith radio-phonograph wedged into the corner next to the trunk in which Mary's clothes were packed.

Rudolph dropped to his knees. He opened the trunk and pawed furtively through her dresses, blouses, petticoats and slips for some shred of his own identity.

Rudolph had searched his memory for something more than the sour-smelling shape that dented the mattress, for a more vivid recollection than the stories of a toddler clinging to his father's back. It wasn't Joe's fault that Rudolph was a failure. That his ambition was nonexistent. That his youth had been spent and he looked pessimistically forward to the arid future, seeing his skinny frame bent, his hair coarser and more unkempt as the years crept relentlessly toward old age and death.

Rudolph uncrossed his legs and crossed them again. In spite of the grim premonition he still hoped for something better. One day he had been free and resourceful, independent, his life filled with basketball and his bike, and the next plunged into melancholic gloom.

"I need a car of my own, Grandmother."

"Don't be silly, Rudolph. Name one thing you need a car for."

"To save Julia."

"That's very amusing, Rudolph."

"If I don't have a car Julia is going to fall into the clutches of O'Sheen. They go everywhere together. He drives her home from school. To the dances and beach parties. O'Sheen will ruin Julia, Grandmother. It might be too late already but it's worth a try, don't you think?"

"I think Julia can take care of herself, dear."

"I'll tell you something about a car, Rudy," Red said. "First of all you have to buy gas and oil. You have to maintain the dadblasted thing. There's license plates and insurance. It would be cheaper if you paid Julia's cab fare. And there's always the streetcar. Besides we have two cars already."

The cheerleaders in their orange sweaters with the big blue Fs across their breast kicked their legs and swirled their pleated skirts above their satin panties while Rudolph sat on the bench with a towel around his neck.

"The first thing, the most important thing," Red said, "is your education. I have never had a formal education and I always regret it. Ask your grandmother. She'll say the same thing. If you want to be a lawyer, a doctor, an architect you'll have to get a degree. What do you want to be, Rudy?"

"A professional basketball player."

Red shook his head. "You can't play basketball forever. Don't you have a higher aim?"

Rudy thought a second. His mind was blank. "I just want to be who I am," he said.

"And who is that?"

"Me. I want to be me."

"That's easy."

"It doesn't seem easy."

"Nonsense."

The embezzling bookkeeper, Mr. Riddley, had swept the Plately Sweeps out of business. For ten years the faithful Riddley had burned the midnight oil eating into the books like a termite, nibbling the profits, munching twenties and fifties until nothing was left but the smudged pages that proved Riddley's appetite and guilt.

The books were proof enough to put Riddley away for fifty years but Red had preferred not to press charges and instead had started drinking again. Thomas and Adair sold the lot and buildings, the trucks and equipment, and almost lost the house while Red contemplated runes and ancient writings on tomb walls, not for their meaning but because of his keen interest in design. From a series of Mayan hieroglyphs Red invented a new tread pattern that had revolutionized the tire industry.

Red had rented a small office on the sixth floor of the Pidsulski Building. Behind the drawing board under the gooseneck lamp, among jars filled with pencils and pens, bottles of ink and blueprints, Red sat in his shirtsleeves. Red tinkered with worm gears, pistons, thermocouples and molds until his voluntary retirement at seventy-five. It was Red Plately who invented and patented one of the first hydraulic jacks which alone had made him more money than all his years as the guiding light of the Plately Sweeps.

Elinore kept the budget, paid the bills, balanced the check book and invested Red's money in life insurance. She studied his canceled checks, the shirts he bought at Gimerick's, the earrings at Peacock's, the bar bill at Slick's, monitoring her husband's life from the mahogany desk in the alcove where the telephone sat, adding and subtracting, writing out deposit and withdrawal slips with her glasses on the velvet cord perched on the end of her nose.

"Rudolph! Rudolph! It's seven o'clock, dear." Elinore's voice rises from the bottom of the stairs. The sun streaks the bright green and yellow wallpaper where pennants hang.

Rudolph picks at a grape with his fork, all that is left in the paper cup of his fruit cocktail. "The most popular girl in the Senior class — Miss Julia Peacock!" The scarlet ribbon flames in Julia's golden hair. The sunlight shimmers on her nyloned legs. She tosses her head and rushes to the platform as Rudolph leans back in his chair and cracks his knuckles.

That summer a blue Ford convertible pulled into the Plately driveway. The swing on the front porch creaked with the short jittery contractions of Rudolph's calves. Rudolph recognized the driver of the car immediately — the dark round head and suntanned face of Dirk Mobile the guard and Captain of the University basketball team.

Dirk shook Rudolph's hand. "I'd like you to meet Phil Struthers the President of the Phykes," Dirk said.

"Pleased to meet you, Rudolph. We hear great things about you, boy." Phil looked up at him in pleased appraisement and rubbed his hands together. "Basketball scholarship — four point average. You'd be a tremendous addition to the Phykes."

"I would?"

"Certainly. The Phykes would be proud to have you in their pledge class. We have a great house, Rudolph. I'm not saying the Phykes have the best house on campus but — Not just jocks either but men interested in scholarship. Men who will make their mark in the world."

Rudolph's mild manner compared unfavorably with the avidity of his fellow students. His height and his social advantages were less obvious through the lonely university years. Rudolph quit the fraternity and shrunk a few inches. He pursued his solitary studies in the anonymity of a furnished room. The room was cold. The hallways reeked of the Armenian's boiled cabbage dinners.

Rudolph eagerly read philosophy and Shakespeare, turning the pages long after midnight, wrapped in blankets, wearing gloves and earmuffs.

Dr. Moore opened Rudolph's manila folder and studied the transcripts. "From your test scores, Rudolph, I'd say you could succeed at anything. What interests you?"

"I like to read."

"Excellent. Perhaps you should consider Law or Journalism or Medicine. Have you thought about teaching?"

"Mainly I just want to be myself."

"Of course. That goes without saying. The old Socratic dictum, eh my boy? Being yourself is important, but what do you want to become? That is the big question."

Rudolph dumped the duffelbag filled with dirty laundry in the foyer.

"Anybody home?"

"I'm in the kitchen, Rudolph." Elinore embraced him. "How did the tests go, dear?"

"All right."

"What did Dr. Moore say?"

"He asked me what I was going to become."

"What are you going to become, dear?"

"I don't know."

"Surely there must be something in this world that interests you more than yourself, Rudolph."

Rudolph shrugged his shoulders.

"Well?"

"Maybe medicine ..."

"I knew there was something. A doctor! Oh Rudolph, I'm so proud."

Anne clung to Rudolph's arm. They were a stylish couple. Anne's narrow waist rose smoothly in her gray crepe dress. Her hair was a dark puffy cloud that floated next to Rudolph's bony shoulder. Her pubertal urges had been muted and masked, stifled and appropriated to her studies. She was a straight A student and had been Valedictorian of her high school class. Dr. Bakegart, her father, was a pioneer in orthopedic surgery. Mrs. Bakegart was tall and graceful with the shadow of a mustache on her upper lip. Anne had her mother's long face. Her dark hair was teased and set in two thick auburn waves by Dwight at the Ritz.

"Oh Rudolph, I think I'm pregnant," Anne said.

Once a month they played out the same charade with the fear of a sudden marriage and catastrophic social disgrace. Their plans were made. Rudolph had given Anne a platinum engagement ring with a diamond chip. They had decided to wait until after graduation. It was a weight around his neck. They couldn't wait. Every month brought the same insidious panic that made Rudolph's hair stand on end.

Anne knew the fashions and had excellent taste. She was an only child, which Elinore considered dangerous, but Anne had plenty of common sense, was intelligent, meticulous and intent on sacrificing her own capabilities to help Rudolph carve out a successful surgical career. "Oh Rudolph, it will be so much fun," Anne said.

Dr. Bakegart fixed up a summer orderly's job for Rudy in the operating room at Dearborn Hospital. Rudy washed the bloody instruments and mopped the bloody floors. He pushed the gurney off the elevator, down the polished corridor and through the swinging doors into the operating theater where the scrub nurse stood on a platform arranging her instruments on a sterile tray. Dr. Dare, the anesthesiologist toyed with the dials of his gas machine while Dr. Fellows, Dr. Bakegart's chief assistant, vigorously scrubbed his forearms at the sink.

Dr. Bakegart stood next to the draped operating table with his gloved hands raised while a nurse bent to tie the strings of his gown. The nurse pulled back the sheet on Mrs. Yee's small, emaciated body while the bottle of dextrose continued dripping its increments into Mrs. Yee's skinny arm. "How are you feeling, Mrs. Yee?" Dr. Bakegart asked bending solicitously over the gurney. "Good morning, Talldorf."

Mrs. Yee's leg was yellow and blue. Her toes were black. "I want this leg painted," Dr. Bakegart commanded. "As you can see, Talldorf, the toes are already gangrenous. Take hold of her foot and raise the leg — gently now."

Rudolph held Mrs. Yee's thin discolored leg off the sheet as the nurse painted the bruised flesh with red antiseptic. "We're going to amputate here," Dr. Bakegart said pointing to Mrs. Yee's swollen knee. Rudolph looked from Mrs. Yee's swollen knee to her wrinkled face. Her ancient eyes smiled kindly back at him. "There's a blood clot in the great saphenous vein which could throw an embolus. Talldorf, are you listening? I want you scrubbed for this operation. I think you will find the procedure instructive and interesting. Talldorf — ? Someone grab the leg!" A nurse appeared suddenly. The room spun wildly around the silver eye of the lamp as Rudolph staggered to the wall and was sucked down the tiles into oblivion.

"You'll make such a fine surgeon, Rudy," Anne said proudly.

"I don't want to be a surgeon. I want to be a psychiatrist."

"Well at least you won't be called out all hours of the night like father."

With Dr. Bakegart as his reluctant sponsor Rudolph had been accepted at the medical school. The wedding was to take place on August 25th. The invitations had been sent. Anne was busy doing a thousand errands. She had picked out an expensive ring to go with the diamond chip. A huge pile of gifts had accumulated in the Bakegart's guest room. In a month and a half Rudy would stand before the Methodist minister in a new tuxedo for which he already had been chalked and fingered by Mr. Lubin, the tailor, while standing half-naked in his socks on the cold cement floor.

"This is not the time to get cold feet, Rudolph," Elinore said as she peeled carrots. "Anne is a nice intelligent girl. She will be an asset to your medical career."

"I don't even know if I want to go to medical school."

"You have a better education than anyone in the family. You ought not to question your opportunity or be so indecisive and hesitant. It's not manly. You must learn to live up to your obligations, Rudy. How many times have we talked about this. Medicine is an honorable profession. You and Anne will always have the best. A doctor is a necessary person. He commands the community's respect."

"I've been going to school all my life. I'm tired of it. I don't want to settle down yet."

"How can you say that?"

Rudolph slumped in a kitchen chair. "It's just a thought."

"Thoughts like that are better unsaid. There's no reason to brood about it, Rudolph. You have a wonderful future ahead."

'Dear Grandma and Grandpa,

I have to go away. I have to live on my own to find out what life is. I don't know how to explain all this. I don't want to go to medical school and I don't want to get married. I don't want to be tied down. I have to find out who I am and the longer I stay here the more life becomes a trap. I have to get out and see how I fit in a place where no one knows me. Where I am free to be what —'

Rudolph put the pen down and read what he had written. He crumpled up the page and pulled out a fresh sheet.

'Dear Grandma and Grandpa —'

Rudy trotted up the alley past the ash cans and hollyhocks. He ducked under C.C.'s neglected grape arbor and passed between the garage and the shadowed, overgrown plot that had once been C.C.'s garden. The asparagus had gone to seed. The strawberries had been picked. A single row of leaf lettuce struggled through tall weeds.

Two giant strides put Rudy at the top of the back porch steps. He opened the screen and stepped into the kitchen. "Grandma!"

Florence still lived in the cottage on Acker St. She still scrubbed floors at the Ford Motor Co. offices and she still went to mass. C.C. had died a bitter, jaundiced death, his small angry mouth working beneath his yellow mustache. "Florence!" he had screamed. "Florence!" Florence scurried down the hall with his bedpan.

Florence had taken Rudolph to the movies and the zoo and to the cemetery where she went to cut the grass and leave pickle jars filled with marigolds and daisies on C.C.'s stone. It was Florence to whom Rudolph felt most akin, her hearing box buzzing on the ample bosom of her pink chiffon dress.

Rudy went straight to the refrigerator, took out the quart milk bottle and poured himself a glass. His grandmother's shoes squeaked reassuringly in the hall.

"Joey — ?" she said.

"It's me, Granma. Rudy. The one with the university education. Remember?"

"How are ya, sonny?"

"I'm great, just great." Rudy drained the last drop and refilled the glass.

"From the looks of yer I'd say ya got woman troubles, me boy." She hugged him. "Ya just sit down here while yer granma fixes herself a spot a tea." Florence filled the kettle at the sink and struck a sulfur match.

"Would ya be gettin cold feet, Rudy?"

"They're frozen stiff. I'm going to dump everything."

"Sure'n ya must be foolin, Rudy. What can it mean?"

"It means I'm not going to medical school and I'm leaving Detroit."

"I declare, Sonny—An ya won't be gettin married either I suppose. Headin out fer a shiftless existence same as yer dad. Bumin handouts an ridin the freights—"

Red's bones were thin. He kept his plate in a glass next to the lamp on the bedside table. The freckles on his hands had run together forming liver spots. His short hair was white. He sat with his knife carving little figures from cedar or balsam, or stood at the basement lathe turning out canes, baseball bats, newel posts and table legs.

"What did you say, Rudy? Let me turn off this dadblasted machine."

"I said I'm giving up my place at the medical school."

Red sat down in the rocker and pulled out his pipe. "Say that again."

"I'm not going to medical school. I've been going to school since I can remember. The best part of my life has been spent with books and studies. I don't know anything about life, Grandfather, and if I keep going to school — I don't want to get married either."

Red raised his eyebrows. "You don't say."

"I already feel like Dagwood. I'm always running errands. Anne's wedding plans are like a battle campaign. First she runs me here then she runs me there. I carry the presents. Anne and me. Me and Anne. And it just isn't that great, Grandfather."

Red stuffed his pipe. His blue eyes twinkled. "Tell me, Rudy," he said, "how a man, any man, a man like yourself say—intelligent, educated, good-looking, popular, an athlete—could get himself in such a mess?"

Rudy scowled. "I've got to get out of it, Grandfather. And you've got to help me."

Red sat forward in the chair with interest. "How are we going to do it?" he asked.

"I don't know. I've thought of everything. As far as I can see there's only two ways. I can either skip town like my dad, or tell Anne and Dr. and Mrs. Bakegart face to face."

"Or you could marry Anne and see how it worked out." Red laughed with a loud guffaw.

"I don't see what's funny."

"You don't? Well it isn't funny. Marriage is a serious matter. My advice is to do that." Red lit a match and sucked on the flame.

"Do what?"

"Make up your own mind."

"That's what you always say. Everybody's going to be disappointed in me. They're going to think I cheated them. They're going to think I'm a quitter. Do you think I'm a – quitter – Grandfather?"

"A quitter. No, Rudy, I wouldn't call you a quitter. To be a quitter you have to start something. You don't start marriage until you say your vows and you don't start medical school until the first day of class. I don't know what you are or what you would like to be called, but technically you aren't a quitter. I hope that bit of wisdom will relieve your troubled mind." Red chuckled. "The worst part is going to be telling your grandmother."

"I know. What can I tell her? That I feel obligated to Anne because of a few – hours on a hill? That I'm not interested in pursuing *any* career? All that money wasted on my education. That's what she'll say, and she's right. Grandma's really counting on me making a big hit as a doctor. My great bedside manner! I don't want to be a doctor, Grandfather. I just want to live out there by myself with real people. Get a dumb job or something. Pay the rent. Lie on the grass." Rudy's face twisted in an expression of frustrated enthusiasm for the simple everyday life of the working man. "None of your sons went to college and they're all doing swell. Why do I have to go to medical school? Only Adair is married. Why do I have to get married? I want to go away to another city. Start at the bottom."

Red laughed. "Your grandmother would kill me if she heard me say this but you're a chip off the old block, Rudy. And I'll tell you another thing. Do what you want to do. Don't worry so much about what other people think. Do the things that make you happy."

"I quit," he said.

"You what?"

"I quit. I went to see Dr. Adamson today and told him to cancel my place in the class."

"You're not serious."

"I want to be free, Anne. Please try to understand. I'm tired of being a school boy. I want to get out of Detroit. Go out on my own—" Rudolph winced. "Please don't cry. Just the two of us, Annie. Just you and me. I'll get a job as a carpenter's apprentice or something. Please don't cry, Anne—"

Tears rolled down Anne's cheeks. "Oh Rudolph," she sobbed, "how could you do this to me?"

Rudolph's wing bones stood out sharply against the fabric of his lime-green shirt. The seersucker pants of his tan summer suit fell voluminously to his cordovan shoetops. The long fingers of his left hand curled limply from the french cuff that covered his graduation present.

"Whew—I thought I was gonna boist! So how's the war goin, General?"

The soldier's cap was folded neatly over his belt. "What war?"

"The big war in Europe."

"Yea. I heard about it."

"Youse don't sound too patriotic."

"You fight the war."

"Yer goddamned right I'd fight the war but my draft board turned me down. 'Bonivitch,' the Sarge says, 'yer more valuable at home.' The Huns er tryin ta destroy the world. Yer lucky ta be wearin a uniform, soldier. Ya oughta be proud ta be defendin yer country."

The soldier wadded up the paper towel. "Nuts," he said.

Bonivitch showed his pointed teeth. The band of his porkpie hat wore the exotic pinfeathers of an extinct bird. His baggy black suit was rumpled. His white shirt had the yellow tinge of boiled milk. "How bout you, pops?" he asked. "Ya ever been to a war?" The white-haired man smiled numbly.

"A guy should be happy ta serve his country. Ya know what this war is all about? I'll tell ya what this war is all about."

The white haired man zipped his pants and ignored Bonivitch.

"This war is what all wars is about. We're fightin ta protect the gold in Ft. Knox. I been readin up on it. How bout you, buddy? How come youse ain't at the war?"

Rudolph gulped. "I'm too tall."

"How tall are ya?"

"Six seven and a half."

"No kiddin? When I seen ya get on the bus I says, Bonivitch, if that kid ain't six foot seven he ain't a inch. So what are ya, a perfessional basketball player er somethin?"

I played basketball in high school."

"Couldn't take the pressure, huh? Lots of guys choke up. Six foot seven an not playin pro ball. If I had yer height, buddy, I'd be the best forward in the Association. I'd score fifty points a game an make fifteen grand a year, I'd endorse cereals an I'd make a record. Listen ta this:

"Moon over Miami. . .
Watchin the ships at sea —"

Bonivitch crooned the verse in a frail reedy voice. Rudolph's hair was mussed. The MacArthur sunglasses bit into the bridge of his nose as he peered bleakly down at wadded gum wrappers and soggy butts.

"Not bad, huh?" Bonivitch said. "I used ta be a tenor but my voice cracked. I can't decide now if I'm a baritone or bass. But if I was as tall as you I'd make a record an salt away the cash. I always wanted ta be in show biz. Bonivitch, if them Hollywood creeps knew ya was out here they'd break a leg tryin ta get ya ta sign a contract. So whata ya do fer a livin, buddy? Me, I'm a house painter. I got my own little business. Interiors. Exteriors. Youse name it an Bonivitch does it. Ya ever painted a house?"

"I helped my uncle paint my grandfather's house once."

"Ya oughta try paintin houses. Ya got a long reach. Ya could paint fast. I was visitin my sister in Detroit. That broad'll never change. Ya from Detroit? What a crumby town. I'm a Windy City boy myself. Ya either cut the mustard in the Windy City er ya end up wearin cement shoes on the bottom of the river."

Bonivitch placed his hat carefully on the mirror's ledge and splashed water on his face. "Yer probably wonderin how come one so young as me is almost bald." Rudolph frowned over his shoulder as Bonivitch plastered the long strands of sparse hair to his bumpy scalp. "I had typhoid when I was a kid. I'm gonna lose every one a these bastards. How old do youse think I am, kid?"

"I don't know."

"I'm thirty. Ya'd never guess I was thirty would ya?" Bonivitch scanned his face in the mirror. "So whata youse do fer a livin?"

"I just graduated from the university."

"Congratulations! If I had a college education I'd really go somewheres. I'd have a ritzy house in the suburbs an two Caddies. I'd buy my ma a new refrigerator. I'd eat lunch with da mayor. Sos what er ya gonna be, kid? Doctor, lawyer, Indian chief?"

"I was going to become a doctor but —"

"Wait a minute! Youse coulda been a sawbones an ya didn't?"

"Yes. I was accepted at the medical school but —"

"Ya must be crazy, kid. Them doctors really rake it in."

"I wasn't interested in the money."

"Don't give me that shit. Who ain't interested in money? If ya ain't interested in money ya oughta be thrown outta the United States. Money money money money!" Bonivitch blew on his fist and scattered the imaginary dice across the concrete floor. "Snake eyes!"

He set his hat on his head gingerly and adjusted the brim. "It's yer height, kid. Puts a unnatural strain on the kidneys. You'll be lucky if ya ever piss again."

Rudolph dried his hands and pulled the tie from around his neck. It was the last time he was going to wear a tie. He should have taken it off in Ypsilanti when they stopped for dinner. He hurried along the corridor with his shoulders bent beneath the constant overhanging threat of the ceiling. Past the office with the padded desk chair that held the impression of the agent's back. Through the window the bus waited, exhaust fumes pouring from the metal grating that covered its diesel engine. The driver stood beside the door smoking a cigarette. Rudolph bounded down the wooden steps.

A pretty girl in a green and white dress stood beside an elderly woman in a straw hat. Rudolph got a sweet whiff of violets as he edged past.

"Watch out where you're going, young man. You almost stepped on my foot."

Rudolph fumbled for his ticket.

"Get on," the driver snapped. "I remember you. How could I forget?"

The pretty girl laughed. She mounted the rubber steps and came down the aisle past the seats filled with passengers, her pretty head erect, carrying her suitcase awkwardly in front of her like a battering ram. Rudolph picked up his coat and his book and held them in his lap.

Bonivitch leaped at the pretty girl and snatched her suitcase. "Here sister. Let me help ya with that." Bonivitch struggled to heft the suitcase when Rudolph with his long reach could have easily tossed it into the rack. "Thank you," she said. "Is this seat taken?"

"No it ain't." Bonivitch flashed Rudolph a peremptory wink. As if the pretty girl had purposefully passed Rudolph's seat. As if she had wanted to sit with Bonivitch in the first place.

The driver slammed the door and revved the engine. The wall of buildings and trees threw its shadow across the square, past the courthouse with its four yellow clockfaces and wide stone steps where old men looked up from the benches and the bronze statue of the Union soldier squinted above the cannon and the flower beds.

Past wide front porches where men sat reading the evening paper and ladies in flower print dresses knit beneath the arms of the arching elms. The Armory with its tank and howitzer squatted on the edge of town. Farmhouses set back from the highway on gravel spokes in windbreaks of hemlock, spruce and oak wheeled through the chill sweet-smelling countryside as fleecy summer clouds changed from gold to purple above the misty hayfields and dented hills.

Except for the green glow of the dash and the beam from Rudolph's reading lamp the coach was dark as the bus followed the two-lane highway around the long blue finger on the map.

"What are you reading?" the woman asked.

Rudolph held up his book.

"Friedrich Nietzsche. Mmmmmm."

"Have you read him?"

"No. I heard he was crazy. He actually went insane you know."

"He did?"

"Yes. When they took him from Italy to a mental institution in Switzerland the train entered a long tunnel through the Alps and Nietzsche wailed an ecstatic poem that made everyone's hair stand on end. When they came out of the tunnel Nietzsche never spoke again."

"No kidding?" Rudolph said with enthusiasm. "That's great. Nietzsche was a great man. He was saner than anybody else back then. He was saner than most men today. Don't you think?"

The buses were lined up in the bays like circus elephants waiting to be fed. Rudolph climbed the steps with his suitcase.

The Windy City streets had a surprising carnival atmosphere. Sailors' white caps and black faces of Negroes bobbed among the crowds beneath theater marquees. A skinny man in a blue suit stood behind a card table on which little skinny men in blue suits climbed up and down ladders and turned in circles. A blind woman sat on a folding chair holding a tin cup full of yellow pencils, her fat dog wheezing at her feet. A photographer snapped Rudolph's picture and handed him a brown envelope which Rudolph dropped hesitantly with hundreds of other brown envelopes on the pavement.

The Lindberg Beacon stabbed its cyclopian eye out twenty miles across the waves as Rudolph stared down in amazement at the night bathers and the blankets spread on the crowded beach where whole families slept out of the tenements' heat.

Rudolph saw the policeman approaching and turned from the locker. "Excuse me, officer — "

"Ya got some identification?"

"I've got a driver's license."

"Let's see it."

"Sure. Gladly." Rudolph pulled out his wallet and thumbed through the celluloids. "It's here someplace." He went through his pant's pockets. "I know it's here someplace." His hands were sweating. He went through his pockets again. "It must be in my jacket. My jacket's in this locker. I just put in another dime. Here's the key. Number 39."

"Open it."

"That's the problem, officer. I can't get the darned thing open. The lock must be broken. I was just coming to ask for your help when you walked up."

"Gimme the key." The policeman snatched the key and opened the locker.

"Boy, that's a relief. Thanks a lot, officer. These lockers are only good for thirty six hours, you know. I suppose when the time's up the trap door opens and dumps my suitcase into the river. I'd have lost everything."

"The license."

"Sure."

Rudolph pulled out his coat and went through the pockets. "It isn't here. It has to be in my wallet." He got down on his hands and knees and began to sort the cards, receipts and photographs into neat piles on the floor. "I found it."

"This is a Michigan's driver's license."

"That's right. I'm from Detroit."

"This license ain't no good in the Windy City."

"But I'm not driving."

"That don't make no difference."

"It doesn't?"

"Ya gotta have a Illinois driver's license. See that ya get one at yer first opportunity. In the meantime I don't like nobody hangin around the depot too much. I seen ya before. I been watchin ya fer two nights now. We got strict laws in the Windy City an da Mayor expects me ta enforce em. No loiter'n, see. No perverts. No mashers. No rapists. No queers. No nothin. I see ya around here too often it makes me nervous." The policeman slapped his billy against his palm and frowned.

"I understand, officer. I'm not a loiterer, honest."

Rudolph sat with his back to the green tile wall. His weary brain exaggerated the sordid impressions from the night before — an underworld of drawn and quartered human beings, mercilessly and indefatigably bent on their own scuttling attempts to survive. One moment steeped in sorrow or resignation, the next agitated and full of horrible surprise, leaping onto a chair and haranguing the disinterested crowd who turned listlessly away from any potential excitement in their lives. Their bizarre appearances frightened him. Ranked in a pecking order, separated by the blood in their eyes and the bars of their cages.

Rudolph felt swept from the familiarity of his conventional life into a backwater on the indiscriminate tide that lapped the Windy City's shore. The pools teamed with squirming discordant life while prey and predator alike sought the neutrality of the lights and the stark compromise of coffee.

Midnight Slim had blown through the door, his red neon socks glowing beneath his checkered pant's cuffs. "Ladies and gentlemen!" Slim shouted, bowing to all sides, "Death comes swiftly and rides a white horse." Several freaks applauded. The lady whose hands were covered with warts only raised her veil to sip her tea. The man with the purple birthmark ate his eggs meticulously, staring at nothing. The smiling dog-faced boys sought Rudolph's eye while Rudolph cringed behind his water glass. The epileptics and schizophrenics fluttered in final congregation before the first gray streaks of dawn scattered them across the pavements to their caves and closets.

The normal morning traffic surged through the streets. The normal crush of pedestrians swarmed through the canyons between tall buildings. Horns blared. Tiers of windows soared above the elevated tracks.

Rudolph's eyes were boiled. He stared out through the sunglasses at the travelers moving ceaselessly in line. The floor was waxed to a high polish. The coffee urns gleamed. The day policeman circled on his beat, the big gun mounted on his hip, the visor of his cap pulled down above his seedy black mustache.

Across the room the little man busily stirred sugar into his fourth cup of coffee. His large head gave Rudolph the impression of an uncanny dwarfish intelligence — the small mouth shrewd, the eyes impish and aloof, the heavy eyebrows overgrown above the meaty, resourceful nose.

Rudolph got up suddenly and moved one table toward the little man. He sat for a moment, his hands trembling, then got up and moved again, this time three tables closer. The little man glanced up sharply.

Chapter 4

THE WINDY CITY

"**W**hat a reach, what a reach!" declared Alexander Small. He was holding the spigot open in the Greyhound bus terminal cafeteria two floors under the streets of the Windy City. His coffee cup was running over. Small was staring straight up into the pale face of a giant with flaming red hair who was looking down into his. The giant's eyes were concealed behind sunglasses. The giant's lips puckered as though amazed at the miniature of Small. "Ha, ha. No offense big guy— What a reach—"

"Hey!" shrilled the fat lady at the cash register, "Little man! Watch you're doin you're runnin the coffee over! You buyin two cups?"

"Yeh yeh mama," said Small, "Don't get your bloomers frizzled, keep the change, buy another share of Greyhound." Small wandered from the cafeteria line looking back at the red-headed giant who appeared confused by his gaze.

"What da ya want big fellow?" the fat lady was yelling, "Move it on, people's waitin!"

Small carried his cup away to his favorite table by the window wall where he could look out on the travelers in the terminal waiting room.

What a reach that guy has! thought Small, pouring sugar into his coffee. He makes O'Toole look like a midget. That guy could reach clear across the Wells Street awning!

Small was up against it. For two years he had tried to get the awning cleaning job at the Slippery Tongue ice cream shop on Wells Street, even before the awning was dirty because that awning was such a striking creation, and finally the job was his. The awning was in the shape of a tongue, brilliant red and three stories high. It blossomed out above the sidewalk to shade the Slippery Tongue ice cream shop. It could be seen for three blocks up and down Wells Street. Small could make easier money washing windows, but probably he was the only one who could do this job, and even he could not figure how to place his ladder. He would need a giant extension ladder, 35 feet anyway, maybe 40. He couldn't raise a wooden ladder that big by himself. The only way he could reach all of the awning would be to hook his legs around the rungs, lean way out and do it with a mop. Oh! How that awning would shine when he got his hands on it.

Small lit up a Lucky, stirred his coffee, and pulled his notebook from an attache case. He began to add up projected earnings for the week. Ensardos. Wow, that sign cleaning job was up to a cool hundred and twenty bucks now. It was time to strike! He had outfoxed that sly Mr. Ensardo at last. He had the upper hand. He would slip down there early one morning before Mr. Ensardo could get out of bed and clean the sign before Mr. Ensardo could stop him. Mr. Ensardo would have to pay the hundred and twenty, ha, ha. This week! determined Small. After I conquer the Slippery Tongue. O'Toole would have to help. O'Toole had a long reach — if Small could get him to climb the ladder.

Since Small had left Elvira he had attained landmark peaks in his career as President of Complicated Maintenance. He would out-wit Mr. Ensardo, the Slippery Tongue was in the palm of his hand, and Short had taught him the window washing craft. The Gumm Tower! thought Small, smashing out the butt of the Lucky and burning his finger, sticking the finger into his coffee, plunging it into his ice water, holding it there, gazing about the cafeteria —

That giant was staring at him behind his sunglasses from the far end of the cafeteria. With his free hand Small pulled the brim of his corduroy cap down to his green eyes. He withdrew the burnt finger from his ice water and blew on it. He wrote: 'THE GUMM TOWER,' in the notebook, circled it, put a star beside it and regarded the notation. The Gumm Tower is next! Oh, ho, ho! Wouldn't Elvira turn green? I'll be rolling in bucks! Nobody but me would think of washing the Gumm Tower by hand! Small smiled out at the general cafeteria. He pondered success and sipped his coffee, lit up a new Lucky and gazed out on the busy terminal. All of the homeless people bussing through the Windy City. Small was different. He had come and stayed and conquered.

Alexander Small, who flew away, felt like he had crashed into a basement. There he was, six feet underground beside an alley. He would lean back in his kitchen chair and gaze at the two garbage cans when he pined for a view; or the rear end of Bluey, his beloved old Buick waiting in the alley like a trusty steed.

"Get your head out of the curtains, Small!" It was Elvira, his wife. "You wrinkle them and I'm not ironing them again. And set that chair down on its four legs. That's why a chair has four legs, Small, and we only have two chairs that are safe to sit in."

Small kept his head behind the curtains for spite. He nodded from side to side making the curtains toss over his face, looking first at the garbage cans, then at the rear end of the Buick, a worn and faded blue. "Do you have an audience with me, woman?" inquired Small from the curtains. "That is why you can't see me. It isn't time for you to speak with me."

This basement apartment in the Windy City was his home, afterall, and a man's home was a man's castle. It wasn't the apartment; he paid good money for rent and it was a roof over their heads, and convenient: he didn't have to look for a parking space, he parked right outside the window, they could get in and out real fast. What made it seem like a crash was Elvira. What a shrew she could be. Elvira was still a beauty six years after their marriage. But you never could tell by looks. No, no. Small often mused upon it. Such a gorgeous peach, and such a nag. Small could not decide which was the real Elvira.

She was always trying to tell him what to do. But it wouldn't work; it would never work. Nobody told Small what to do. He tried to keep her happy but he wasn't going to kill himself with the effort. It wasn't her business to know what was good for them. That was his business. He was running this ship. Small was no man's fool, he understood how the world operated. Small made the right moves. Survival was a balancing act and you couldn't trouble your head with other people's advice. Elvira never went hungry, it didn't rain on her head. Discontent was obviously the natural state of women. Nothing was free. The lights didn't go on unless he paid the electric bill. A woman was necessary and

Elvira was his so he had to pay the price. Elvira wasn't the first crash he had survived. And survive he would. Small had the means: he ignored the Elvira he did not like. Elvira had no such talent. Doubtless it was the poor creature's hormones. She had something to say about everything. But Small's head was clear and he wouldn't allow her to confuse him.

"My God, Small!!!" she now howled from the bathroom, "*What* is this!?"

"A little surprise, baby," he called from his chair, the curtains swinging off his head. "You're going to have the classiest bathroom in town." His enthusiasm led him to rise and hurry down the hall to see the expression on her face.

"You cannot draw pictures on the bathroom wall Small! Are you a child that you scribble on the walls of your home? Good Lord, what did you use?" Elvira was rubbing at the black stick figure of a little man with a bow shooting an arrow into the air. Small was appalled.

"Don't rub it Elvira! You'll wreck it!"

"Wreck it? You've wrecked my bathroom! What are these? Little men —"

"There are women too!" said Small, "Look, see the woman, she's picking apples off that tree but I only got the tree, I need red paint for apples, I was going to use your lipstick but the damn stuff is pink —"

Elvira was teetering on her knees on the rim of the bathtub and now she stood up unsteadily holding to the towel rack. She wiped her forehead like she was sweating, "Off, Small, take it all off of my wall, I want it removed, I don't care if you have to paint the bathroom walls all over, I want it *off*!"

"Elvira, you're crazy. You don't understand what I'm doing, I did this for you!" Now Small was on his knees on the rim of the bathtub. "Look, I was just laying here soaking. I saw it all at once in my head —" Elvira was moving toward the door. "No, wait!" said Small, "Look at all of them, I have a dozen of them, I'll do a dozen a day and pretty soon it will be a whole village, a whole civilization! These are ancients, Elvira. I pulled them right out of my own head. I must have seen it first in some book —" Elvira was leaning limply against the door frame looking at the illustrated wall. "What it is, Elvira, is a replica of an Aztec tomb. An ancient royal tomb! They painted all the walls and the ceiling brown and then they drew on these little stick figures just like I'm doing. But I figured it's ok if the background is white, it highlights the figures. I started down here because I was sitting in the bathtub, but at a dozen little people a day I'll be painting them on the ceiling in no time. Little men and women all over, everywhere you look, and they'll be doing all kinds of things! See, this guy is plowing, look, one of those ancient plows an ox pulls, but I don't have the ox. Don't need it — maybe later — but now I'm just figuring out what the people do. They must have had dogs, I'll probably put in some dogs, they just lay around the campfires. People eat them too when things get rough. See, this guy is fishing, it ain't a penus baby, ha, ha, it's his fishing pole!"

"Off, Small, take it off the wall. You will remove them all."

"Elvira, I never knew I had artistic talent, but I can see it all — the walls and the ceilings — You like to burn candles when you take a bath, think how classy it will look, everywhere you look little people living little lives, running around, sitting, holding hands, skipping, dancing, on the ceiling, a million stories in your own bathroom, you won't even have to read a magazine on the toilet, just sit and look! Elvira, there ain't a room in this city — and millions of rooms — there ain't one as classy as this will be. Your friends will want to sit in our bathroom — "

But Elvira was gone. How long Small had teetered on the edge of the tub talking to himself he did not know.

Elvira was sitting at the kitchen table with a cup of coffee. She lit up a Viceroy as Small came into the kitchen but would not look at him. With her regal head high she stared fixedly away saying nothing.

"All right, all right," said Small, "I gotta go out. I'll get paint remover and I'll kill all the little people I made since that's what you want but you'll never know what you missed."

He grabbed his corduroy cap off the nail by the door. Elvira said nothing. She wiped the back of her hand across an eye.

"And I ain't gonna listen to no crying about it, you're getting what you want, I'm going to get the paint remover to kill off a civilization for you, what else do you want?" Small went out and slammed the door. He turned, opened it and stuck his head in. "I'm gonna do that awning job down on the Boulevard, so don't hold dinner — if you make dinner — " He slammed the door a second time and turned into the alley.

Small checked the knots in the clothesline that held the walkboard and two wooden step ladders to the rack on the roof of the old Buick. He checked his pocket to be certain he had the key to the padlock for the bicycle chain that locked the three implements of his trade into a bundle too heavy for a thief to carry away.

Inside the alley gate he turned on the water faucet and uncoiled the hose, opened the rear door of Bluey and thrust the hose into one of two garbage cans sitting in the back seat. Small carried his own water supply for scrubbing awnings. The back floor of the Buick was a litter of floor mops, brushes, soiled rags, half-empty boxes of detergent and bottles of caustic compounds. Small leaned against the car listening to the water swirl into the garbage can, and here came O'Toole up the alley like a shred of cloud in his old overcoat that nearly scraped the cement.

"Hi, O'Toole," said Small, "Come with me, I'm just leaving. Where you going?"

"Nowhere," said O'Toole, "I'm going nowhere." He hung before Small like gloom incarnate.

"Well hop in and we're off," said Small, "I just got to finish filling this one and throw the hose over the gate."

"I know where you keep it," said O'Toole, "I almost broke my neck that night I came over in the dark."

"I leave it like that to catch burglars and peeping toms," said Small.

"Let's have a coffee, Small, before we leave."

"No, no," whispered Small holding his finger over his lips, "She's in a snit, maybe her period comin on, we don't want to go in there. We'll stop someplace."

"Why don't she go visit my wife," said O'Toole, "She's in tears."

"They're all nuts, O'Toole," said Small, "I gave her a gift of my creative art work. She goes into shock and ends up crying." Small jerked the hose from the garbage can squirting the front of O'Toole's old overcoat, threw the hose in a bundle over the gate, had to force the gate open, turned off the faucet, and then they crept away down the alley in the old blue Buick.

"Got a job?" asked O'Toole.

"Yeah, a job—How come you're all wet O'Toole?" Small was turning her out into the avenue.

"It's ok, you soaked me with your hose, but this rag is old, it's waterproof by now—Jesus!" O'Toole leaped forward on the seat nearly knocking his head against the windshield as a great slop of water from the garbage can leaped the seat toward him.

"Sorry," said Small, "I got to go easier around the turns when I got someone with me."

O'Toole reached for a coffee cup on the dashboard and looked into it. He scowled at Small, shook it upside down and dipped a cup of water from the garbage can. O'Toole took a tin of aspirin from an inner pocket of his overcoat and swallowed two, throwing the remains of the cup of water over his shoulder. "Hey, messy!" said Small.

"That's Elvira's influence on you," said O'Toole staring down the street, "Yellow light — Hey, Small, you went through a yellow light."

"You sound just like her," said Small.

"I'm nervous today," said O'Toole. He withdrew a roll of antacids from his pocket. He popped two into his mouth.

"Well I feel great," said Small, "Since I got out of the house."

"Dump her, Small. We're too young to be missing it all cause we're stuck with shrews."

"I don't want to dump Elvira, O'Toole, she's my wife, I love my wife. She drives me nuts."

"I threw away my wedding ring today and Sue got hysterical."

"You threw away your wedding ring?" Small was shocked.

O'Toole laughed, "Yeah, I threw it in a garbage can on the way home from work."

"That's kind of drastic, ain't it?"

"Yeah, I'm gonna dump the broad, Small. I can't stand it, I'm moving out."

"Gee," said Small, "Well. We like you both, you know, O'Toole —"

"Hey, who we," said O'Toole. "You like me but Elvira hates me. And Sue hates you. They hate anything we like. Don't talk for Elvira, Small. We got to talk for ourselves or we're dead men. There won't be no you and there won't be no me, those women will devour us, there'll be four bodies and two voices and the voices won't be yours or mine. They're spiders. They'll eat us up. They're vampires, Small."

"Well, they're different," admitted Small.

"Vicious," insisted O'Toole, "You don't know if they're going to cut their wrists or stab you in your sleep. Small, when a man reaches the age of 24 he should buy a casket and lie down in it because that's his future."

"Not me, O'Toole," said Small, "I'm going nowhere but up."

"Up a ladder, Small, and you're going to break your crazy neck. You won't find me going up no ladder for no woman."

"Not for a woman, O'Toole, I like my work."

"Yeah, that's right," said O'Toole, "Elvira don't like it."

"Elvira don't have to do it."

"She wants you in a tuxedo, Small, smoking a pipe. I don't know why they want all those crazy things. It's like they grew up reading father's day cards."

Small popped a Lucky into his mouth and slammed on the brakes for a red light and a slosh of water lept down O'Toole's back. "Sorry, O'Toole, but you're in the company car. I hate to torment these breaks, try to hit all the lights green."

"Yeah, that's Small, ever the optimist. I'm a stoic, one of those old ruined Roman characters. I know if I don't get run over by a taxi I'll get drowned in Small's Buick and if I don't Sue will make me wish I did."

"You don't look well, O'Toole, your color's bad—"

"You think I'm sunning on the beach? I'm in that mail room on the eleventh floor all day. Sue thinks it's a wonderful opportunity cause it's Tufold, Smart and Glick who got a seat on the stock exchange. I got a seat in the broom closet. 'Hang in there, Roger,' she says when I drag myself home, 'You're learning finance.'"

"You ought to get a job out in the air like me."

"Out in the smog, yeah, soon as I dump Sue. I think I'll sit at the corner of State and Madison with my hat upside down in my lap. I'll make more money and I can look at all the women's legs."

"If I get a big job, O'Toole, I'll give you a piece of the action."

"Just so it ain't high, Small, I'd have to get drunk. Why don't you go international with—what the hell do you call your company?"

"Complicated Maintenance."

"Yeah, well nobody's got any idea what you do with a name like that. A good cover, Small. Yeah, well why don't you open a Cairo office? I'd like to run the Cairo office."

"It's yours, O'Toole. We could wash pyramids. The pyramids must be filthy. They been around thousands of years sittin in the sand. Probably nobody ever thought of it. Or the Sphinx. We could shampoo the Sphinx. Cairo must have thousands of awnings too, you'd be busy all the time."

"Not me," said O'Toole, "I just estimate, you come over and do the job. I don't know how to set up the step ladders."

"You could have lunch in sunny cafes and you'd get some color in your cheeks."

"Right." O'Toole scooped another cup of water from the garbage can and swallowed two more aspirin. "Wait, Small, let me out! It's the zoo. I want to go to the zoo. I got an affinity for the animals, they have it worse than me."

"Sit in the sun," said Small.

"That's what Sue would say if I was managing the Cairo office." O'Toole shook a limp finger at Small when he crawled out of the old Buick. Water dripped from his old overcoat. "Watch out for Elvira," he warned, "Sleep with one eye open."

Small pulled Bluey out into traffic. He wished O'Toole would quit the mailroom job and come work with him.

He fell to musing on Elvira. She had started dressing up in the evenings and going out to the Little Theater. She had drug him around the corner to the second hand store and bought him a tuxedo jacket but they couldn't find pants short enough.

"I look like those master of ceremonies at the circus, Elvira. Do you want to make a laughing stock out of me?"

"You look so *handsome* in it Smally!" Elvira had cooed.

"You want me to get a high silk hat? Who do you think I am?"

"You are the President of your own growing company." It wouldn't work.

"I don't work in a tuxedo, Elvira." They had bought the tuxedo jacket. It hung in the closet collecting dust.

"I wanted you to have it to take me places, I don't want to sit in this basement all my life, Small."

"Don't sit. Get up and sweep the floor once in a while, wash the dishes." She had glared at him, gone into the bathroom and slammed the door. Her hobby was to sit in bubble bath with a candle burning.

She began to go out in the evenings by herself. She had quit asking him to accompany her to the Little Theater. She began bringing one of the actresses home. She was a big blonde with huge tits which Small liked to look at but she made dumb remarks which she considered witty and Elvira would sit there and laugh and jump up to pour her tea.

When the big blonde was in the apartment Small would retire to the bedroom and lie with his hands behind his head staring at the ceiling. Sometimes, feeling driven out, he would jump into Bluey and drive the city streets with a notebook beside him on the seat jotting down the addresses of dirty awnings or soiled signs and an instant price for cleaning them. He would park and go for a coffee reflecting on the signs and awnings and how he would place his ladders. He would walk into shops gazing up at ceilings and walls to see if they were dirty enough to wash, and then approach the manager with an estimate. On a sunny day he would drive into the park and pull up to the lagoon, take the kite and ball of string from the trunk of Bluey and lie on his back watching the kite soar and dive above the yachts tied at the docks.

The big blonde began to eat his food. Once he had walked in the kitchen door as the blonde turned to Elvira and said, "Tell him to get that Jalipino cheese, Ellie, cheddar is so bland, so gauche, utter shit!" Her eyes grew large when she saw Small standing in the door. He walked to where she stood, a head taller than he, picked up the cheese, walked to the refrigerator and put it inside. He returned toward the sink, picked up the wine bottle she had just poured a glass from and, seeing it empty, with one sharp movement smashed it on the sink. He picked up her sandwich, tearing a savage bite from it, and walked from the room without a word. When Elvira attempted to remonstrate with Small that evening he held up a finger, his lips tightly together and gazed at her. The blonde had not reappeared.

Small never faulted Elvira because dinner was not waiting when he came into the basement apartment. He never knew when he would pull Bluey into the alley. But now there wasn't a can of beans to be seen. Only olives and cream cheese and little crackers too tiny to bite. Avocados and colored toothpicks with plastic feathers on them.

Small muttered beneath his breath and shook his head as he drove through the park. Where was the sweet girl he had fallen in love with at first sight?

Elvira had been an orphan like him. She had lived the early years of her life in a country town in Indiana that Small loved to hear her talk about until he imagined that her childhood had been his.

He loved her old father, the grave digger, because he never had to meet him. Small had been grateful to the old man because he had loved Elvira so much and made her childhood happy, until they found him crumpled dead at the bottom of one of his own graves with his spade across his chest and clods of dirt from the walls of the grave tumbled into his white hair.

Then Elvira lived with a maiden aunt in the Windy City who passed brittlely away a week before Elvira graduated high school. Many of her girlfriends went off to college, but the aunt died penniless and Elvira went to work as a maid in a downtown hotel. So far as Small knew she had no friends when he found her walking in the zoo one fall evening when a chill wind blew.

Small had parked his gasping LaSalle sedan illegally and run into the zoo to get a bag of popcorn before the refreshment stand closed. Then he took a stroll past the elephant and wolves on his way to say hello to the polar bear.

And there she came lankily along in her thin gray winter coat. Her honey-brown hair hung down her back and a simple silver beret gleamed dully in her hair. Small marveled at her walk, easy loose strides that waved like trees in the wind. There was something lonesome about her, or was it the fall twilight, or that they were the only two walking in the zoo? Winter was in the air. The girl stopped at the polar bear cage and was watching the huge beast lying beside its cold pool of water like a tourist beside a swimming pool.

"Jeeze, the poor guy is bored to death," said Small leaning on the fence. The girl said nothing. Small looked at her as he ate his popcorn. She had high cheekbones and her lips pouted as she gazed at the lounging bear. Her hair lay in little waves on the gray shoulder of her coat. Chewing a mouthful of popcorn he said to the girl, "No one's around, let's spring him."

She turned her head looking at Small. Her eyes were large and brown. They looked melancholy as a fall evening. Small was touched. He wanted to put an arm around her shoulder and say, "There, there, everything's ok."

So he was totally unprepared for what she said: "Talk is cheap, go get him, I'll wait here." She turned and began to pass when Small put his bag of popcorn in her hand. He vaulted the outer fence, took four steps and jumped up to catch the crossbar of the high iron fence, swung his leg between two pickets and hoisted himself up.

"Get down!" she yelled.

"Give me a chance!" said Small, "You want me to jump in his mouth?"

"No! Get back here, that bear will kill you!" Small perched on the high iron fence like an owl.

"I ain't askin for advice," said Small. The bear rolled onto its back and was contemplating Small hovering above beyond the pool. "Hi," said Small to the bear, "You want to come with me?"

"You're crazy," called the girl, "I'm going to get a guard!" and she turned away.

"And you're a liar," called Small from the top of the fence, "You said you'd wait while I went in to get him. You're stealin my popcorn and you don't care about this bear at all." The girl stopped.

"Please, come down," she said.

"We're going to spring him," said Small, "We're going to give him his freedom. He'll run to the north pole. Nice bear," said Small, "I'm coming to talk to you, we'll sit by the pool and plan it all out." Small dropped lightly onto the concrete floor of the cage. There was an explosion of boiling water as the bear rolled flailing into the pool and the girl screamed.

Small could never remember how he had gotten over the fence. When he recalled the event it seemed he merely touched the crossbar of the fence with his fingers as guide to his flight. He remembered his corduroy cap sliding from his head and the sense of loss, thinking to reach for it and knowing there was time not even for thought, striking the concrete and bouncing like a ball over the outer fence into scattered popcorn at the girl's feet. He looked behind awe-stricken at the mass of erect bear against the iron picket fence with water still streaming from its yellow-white fur and his cap in its mouth. "Jeeze," said Small, "He's fast as me."

Elvira said an angel lifted Small out of the cage.

"You spilled my popcorn," he said as he sat on the concrete, "And I lost my cap."

They left the zoo together just as the gates were being locked. It seemed natural when she climbed right into the old LaSalle. She didn't say a word when he plucked the parking ticket from under the windshield wiper, tore it in half and dropped it over the seat. She seemed to be delighted to be with him, happy and laughing, and they were together every day after that.

How simple it had been before Elvira. When he first came to the city he had done odd jobs for his keep in a barny old rooming house. Soon he had money for all his simple needs. He had gotten a car before he was old enough to drive and then he had gotten the two small rooms above the Chinese laundry where Elvira came.

He had a step ladder which he would throw on top of the old LaSalle and tie with clothesline through the windows, and a bucket and rags and boxes of cleaning supplies. Dirt was everywhere and people were anxious to pay Small to remove it.

He got his clothing in secondhand stores and thrived on potatoes. He had found an abandoned old armchair in the alley and hauled it up onto the tarred roof of the Chinese laundry outside his window. There, among pots of green and flowering plants, Small sat and read in his little garden and looked up from the page to see the treetops blowing beyond a net of telephone wires, and the colors of sunset through the smog.

He read history. He read *The Decline and Fall of the Roman Empire*. It seemed familiar. He read *The Decline of the West*. But Small was far from despair. He read of the French revolution and the rise of Napoleon. He knew all of Napoleon's campaigns to the bitter retreat from Moscow. Military campaigns were fantastic to Small. He would laugh aloud, sitting in the dilapidated old armchair or ejaculate, "No! Oh, no no no..." while some general rushed headlong into disaster.

The newspapers blared of catastrophes in black banner headlines but it appeared no different than it had always been. Tomorrow or in a hundred years sunlight would set in the black pit of death.

Each morning seeing daylight outside his window he was cheerful and light-hearted. He wanted for nothing.·

Into this carefree life came Elvira to add a dimension of passion and complexities. Two weeks after they met, so to speak in the jaws of the beast, they frolicked like lambs in the connubial bed. Small's little apartment had never been so cozy. Elvira went off to work at the hotel early in the mornings. Small would interrupt a basement cleaning job or leave a kitchen wall half washed to meet her before the swank hotel in the old LaSalle. They strolled hand in hand through the winter park and along the lakeshore and often went to visit their friend the polar bear. Small would lean over the outer fence waving the new corduroy cap that Elvira had bought for him and the bear would snap his jaws and Elvira would pull him away saying he was being mean. Small would laugh, "We're even, that bear and me, I don't owe him nothing."

They stayed through spring and summer in Small's little apartment but when winter came on again it seemed too small for the two of them. Elvira found the basement apartment which seemed huge, but there was no view. It cost little more. "It's good enough for now," said Small.

"And if you get that job with the maintenance crew at the hotel, Smally," said Elvira, "we'll have lots of money."

Small took the job and lasted two weeks. "I can't stand it, Elvira, I don't see the sunshine all day. It's like the orphanage."

"I know, Smally," she sympathized, "With all the tall buildings there's no reason why you shouldn't be out of all that dirt and grease and up high in an office." She bought him new white shirts and ties and socks and took him to the bargain basement to buy his first suit. "You can't tell it's cheap, either," said Elvira, "You look so wonderful, Small."

"I don't think I can walk in this, Elvira, it feels like a suit of armor."

"My knight in shining armor," said Elvira nuzzling against him as they walked among the shoppers.

Before the year was out Small found himself working as a skip-tracer trainee in a tall downtown office building. He made more money than he ever had. Elvira was proud. "You work in the Gumm Tower, Small, such an exclusive place!"

"The building's great," said Small as they sat at their table in the basement, "But the job's terrible."

Small hated it. He felt like a rat disguised as a man. He had to lie from morning to night: "No ma'am, I'm not from one of those collection companies. I'm Mr. Marlow's long lost brother. He'll be glad to talk to me if I can find him." The telephone felt like it grew out of his head. He had never had headaches. Now he got a headache every afternoon. He went to the window of the office by the water cooler, threw it open, stuck his head out and gazed over the city, his striped tie dangling.

"You'll have to close it, Mac," said a voice. A window washer stood at the next window belted and leaning out in the breeze.

"Hey," said Small, "What a great job! How much do you guys make?" Small was dazzled by the figure.

"But it's dangerous out here," said the window washer.

"You should see it in here," said Small.

He lasted three weeks. The day he quit the boss was to review his collection files. Small opened the window, pretended to trip and dumped the files out the window. He watched them fall like confetti 33 stories atop roofs, into alleys and before the wheels of taxi cabs.

It was nearly two years before Small escaped the insidious white collar world by landing a job in a bakery where he sweated for a year, and then a job holding the handle of a screaming reamer in the booming gloom of a structural steel plant which he escaped to the freezing flight line of the airport loading cargo. He made good money here but was fired because he was discovered several times in the pilot's seat playing with levers and turning the wheel. Whenever he announced he had been fired or quit Elvira looked at him sadly and began to cry. "We just get enough ahead to start looking for a real house instead of a basement and then this happens," she sniffed.

"I just ain't no good working for anybody but myself, Elvira, it's how I'm made." At last he had refused to look for another job. With their remaining money he bought two wooden step ladders and a walkboard, went after jobs and got them. His time was again his own. Never again, he told himself, never again, a man ain't made for a job.

And finally Elvira had seemed to accept it. "I know you want nice things, Elvira, and I want you to have nice things. I'm going to get you nice things. A yacht. You want a yacht? I'll get you a yacht. You want an airplane? I'll get you an airplane."

"I want a house, and a decent car," she said.

"A house? I'll get a house as soon as I get the money. We got a great car already. I ain't going to be just 'Hey you Small,' I've got a company name, baby, I'm becoming a company now. You want to hear the name? It's Complicated Maintenance. How do you like it? It means I do anything that others can't, especially high things. I charge for it."

"You'll fall and kill yourself."

"I never fall. I'll go up and bring you down feathers from angel's wings," and Elvira laughed at that.

"I just feel you could do great things, Smally. I don't know what. I guess you have to do what you want.

"Daddy was just a grave digger, but he dug a neat grave and I know he was proud of digging neat graves. He didn't ask thanks and sure didn't get any, but I saw the graves he dug. I think they were works of art. And so was our house. It was a little white house with a slanted roof set back on the lot with a long green lawn before it and surrounded with big oak trees. The leaves blew in summer. You could hear the birds singing."

"Yeah," said Small, "I knew a graveyard once."

"Graveyards are neat," said Elvira.

"Lots of grass and bugs and birds and wind and sunshine," said Small, rubbing his palms together. "Your old man had a neat job."

"It was a humble job," said Elvira. She sat on the bed with her full skirt covering her legs, gazing past Small.

"Yeah," said Small, "Well I gotta move. I can't stand in a hole. I wouldn't mind it for a couple of days. But I couldn't do it for thirty years, you know? I seeded four square blocks with those new leaflets, Elvira, every apartment building, so plenty of leaflets at every address and more on the floors for neighbors and friends. I must have dumped a thousand leaflets. If I don't get a wall-washing job I'll kiss my ass."

"Don't be crude, Small."

"Ya get one, ya'll get two. No stopping it. I'll be up to my neck in wall-washing jobs."

"If you'd kept just one of the dozen jobs you've had, good jobs with futures to them, you wouldn't have to be praying for wall-washing jobs."

"I ain't praying," said Small. "I'm a man of action." Small lay down on the bed beside Elvira who lay back in his arms.

"He kept a tidy house, my father did," said Elvira. He loved her when she lay like that and he would watch her chest rise and fall lifting those beautiful tits, her head thrown back, the honey-brown hair lying around her and her eyes wide open talking like a bubbling fountain of clear water.

"My father always kept me neat, clean clothes, not new but always fresh and always there and nice carpets on the floor and oilcloth on the kitchen table. A good table, he built it himself out of oak."

"Did he build coffins?" asked Small.

"Of course not, he wasn't the hunchback of Notre Dame you know."

"Well," said Small, "he could have expanded his business."

"He worked for the cemeteries, he wasn't a businessman."

"I ain't either," said Small, "but I keep the wheels greased."

"He left all his grave problems at work," said Elvira, "When he came home he belonged to me. There wasn't any other place he wanted to be or anything else he wanted to do. I really loved my father."

Small drove on through the park toward Lake Shore Drive. His spirits rose when he drove through the park. He liked the sunlight on the green grass and the blue of the lagoons, and when the yachts came back in the spring his heart rose. When the old blue Buick entered the boulevards of the park Small made believe he was driving through his vast estate and the other traffic was allowed by him because he was an enlightened despot. But he had to watch for the cops. There were more cops in the city than pigeons, and if you drove an old car they shit on you every chance they got.

Just then he saw the squad car in the rearview mirror. The cop had sped up and slowed in behind Small's old blue Buick. The end of the park was coming up.

They ain't got anything on me, thought Small. Not in the daylight, ha, the poor bastards. If it was night they'd see the tail light is out. They were like sharks, always looking for a kill. Small signaled a turn. He turned and the squad car hung on his bumper. Small knew they would get him if they scented a whisp of fear.

He looked determinedly from the rearview mirror and visualized a huge iron box open on the bottom and top and bigger than his car. The great iron box hung above his car by a thread. Small imagined a pair of scissors snipping the thread and the box falling like a shield all around the old blue Buick. With iron walls around his car no one could see his car and so he was perfectly safe. It was a device he had invented and it seemed to work. All he had to do was complete the images before the cop decided to act. And when, in Small's imagination, the box was securely around the car he introduced waves of confusion, like sticking his finger in water and making ripples, and this confusion he imagined in the officer's brain.

When Small came on to Lake Shore Drive he glanced at the rearview mirror. There was no squad car. "Ha, ha," murmured Small, "They're sittin on Astor Street wondering how I disappeared."

Elvira did not believe that Small's defense against the cops worked even though she had witnessed it. She knew that Small could stop his hiccups by mind power because he had taught her how to do it. Small had to admit that this one was still in the experimental stage. And it wouldn't be long before he knew for sure, because Bluey was going to pieces fast. It was missing, on only one cylinder he thought, which didn't seem serious in light of the fact that the engine had seven more. And the electrical system was a disaster. The mechanic told him he wouldn't look at the wiring in a car that old for less than fifty bucks. Small laughed in his face. "I'll do it myself," he lied.

"Go ahead," the mechanic had said.

"The fuel pump or the transmission is probably pinching a wire," Small explained to Elvira, "like a nerve gets pinched in a body. And he wants to rip out all my wires. Wire lasts forever. It's metal for God's sake, wire lasts almost as long as stone. And that guy wants to sell me new wires for fifty bucks, well he ain't suckering Small!"

So even the headlights had begun to blink when the car hit a bump. The first time it happened with Elvira in the car she had grabbed for the steering wheel and Small had to bat her hand away. She complained he had bruised her.

"Don't ever try to grab the steering wheel when I'm driving!" Small had yelled. The lights had blinked on promptly. "We'd both be dead now if you got the steering wheel in your hands, are you crazy?"

"Small, I don't want to ride in this car anymore! Everybody but us has a new car. If you could keep a job more than one week we could have a new car too!"

"Nobody owns those cars they've driving," Small informed her, "Finance companies own those cars, I know! You got me to take that job at the finance company. I know all about those bastards. And I own Bluey. Elvira, we own our car! Those people with new cars don't own them. They pay hundreds of dollars a month to pretend they own them!"

"I don't care, I hate this car! I want a *new* car!"

"Well you ain't going to get one so get used to it!" yelled Small, "And don't talk that way when we're in Bluey," Small patted the dashboard, "She didn't mean it," Small said soothingly to the old blue Buick.

"I *did* mean it! Damn old junk, I *hate* it!" and Elvira kicked the heater with her foot, hurt her toe and began crying.

"Elvira, stop it!" demanded Small, "I'm trying to drive. You can't talk that way, this car is sensitive. It hears things like that." Elvira stopped her sniffling long enough to level a cold look at Small.

"Sometimes I think you are insane," she said. She had hid her face and begun sniffling again.

"Yes, yes, yes," muttered Small, "I got to put some preventive maintenance into you baby." He patted the dashboard, "Hold in there, I'm going to get your oil changed this week—I'll try, baby, I'll really try." The old blue Buick purred. Small had never understood mechanics. His eyes glazed over whenever he raised the hood and looked at the massive V-8 engine. He would lower the hood, turn his back and look at the sky.

The only thing he had going for him was his luck, and Small was aware that he was a lucky man. And now it was daylight. He didn't have to worry about the lights.

Small wheeled Bluey into a drive off the Boulevard between two tall buildings. Too late he saw what looked like a small telephone pole lying at an angle across the drive and didn't have time to pump the breaks. He stomped them but the tire hit the log and knocked it against the wall of the building. "God!" said Small, "A telephone pole in the driveway!" He parked up against the wall of the *Bon C'est Bon* beauty parlor and got out. He had only hit the log with his tire so there was no damage but it had knocked a brick or two from the wall. Small looked around. No one had seen the little mishap so all was well. The log now rested on a brick like a teeter-tauter. Small tapped the end with his toe. It teetered, light as a feather. He nudged it to the side with his toe. The log moved as if on ball bearings and bumped the wall. He teetered it with his toe. The great log bobbed. "Neat!" said Small.

He returned to the car and unlocked the padlock, pulled the bicycle chain from the ladders and walkboard and threw the chain onto the back seat beside the garbage can. He untied the clothesline fore and aft and lifted off the walkboard, carried it to the sidewalk and propped it against the wall of the *Bon C'est Bon* beauty parlor. Out on the manicured parkway grass he looked up at the high, sloped awning. It was white, but dingy. When he left it would be gleaming. Small carried the eight-foot stepladders from the roof of the car and propped them open before the lower lip of the awning. The crowd of homeward-bound office workers was thinning. Pedestrians detoured around his ladders.

Small usually cleaned awnings at night or at sunrise. He explained to the proprietors of the shops that this was to avoid dripping water on their customers, and as an aside — which he considered of little interest to them — to prevent people from knocking him off his ladder. The main reason he did not divulge. This was to prevent the proprietors from witnessing what little time it took to wash an awning in relation to the price demanded by Small for that esoteric operation. And Small didn't like bosses looking over his shoulder. He was finished with all that.

Small had invented the awning-cleaning service. He didn't know of anyone else in the Windy City who did it. It was easier than washing walls and more profitable, and he liked to be outside. The city was full of awnings, especially in fancy sections like this. Down the street he did Baggs for $110 a crack twice a year. Baggs had fancy round white awnings with gold stripes on them. It took Small four hours. When the Baggs job came in he didn't have to do anything else all week. Then there was the Priceless Gallery on the second floor a block farther down the Boulevard. He got $120 for that because it was a second floor job. Small implied a greater danger in the higher work. Actually he went no higher. He stuck the mop onto a long pole, and standing on the walkboard wet down the awnings. No one could see the tops well anyway and their color was black. All he had to be careful about was to bring out the two white stripes at each end of the awnings and these were the only parts he had to scrub.

Not all jobs were so large or lucrative. This *Bon C'est Bon* awning, for instance, required some effort. It was a white awning, and it had to look whiter when Small left. But Small enjoyed doing a good job. He often thought of it as a flaw in his system, but there it was, and he felt good to leave an awning looking like new. The next day he would enter the shop and listen to the praise while they shelled out his fee. "It looks wonderful, Small!" they would say. "Don't it!" Small would answer. At these moments Small felt the benefactor. Here he was collecting money while the owner was still working. Small, sticking the bills into his wallet would tip his cap, say "See ya next time," and whistle out the door leaving the entire staff still working while he was free. That Small had made $15 while the owner made hundreds a day did not enter into Small's reasoning. The proprietor was chained to the business; Small was free and on the move.

Small did not work swiftly, there was never a hurry. He worked steadily and with care.

He made sure the step ladders were soundly placed on the walk before *Bon C'est Bon*. He shouldered the walkboard guiding one end over a step of the ladder, climbed the other ladder extending the walkboard over a matching step of the second ladder. Small climbed down and surveyed his construction. Some passersby looked with curiosity at the construction. Most flowed around the ladders as if they did not see them. Small felt as if he had dropped a rock into a stream and parted the waters. He had changed men's destinies.

He returned to Bluey and filled a five-gallon bucket with water. Into this he dumped a liberal amount of Spic and Span, an equally liberal amount of cleanser, a douse of yet another caustic cleaning fluid and, because the *Bon C'est Bon* awning was white, a huge glug of bleech. It was a wonder the awning was not dissolved before his eyes. Small felt that the owners would balk at the ingredients he used, but they never asked.

That was the marvel of specialization. If you said you were a brain surgeon people would ask the price. If they thought it was a good deal they would beg you to open their skull. Awning-cleaning was virgin territory. By inventing it Small was at once master of the trade. As no one had considered cleaning an awning, no one knew how an awning was cleaned and did not presume to question Small's methods. He made them pay for the scrubbing but mostly for the idea. Small considered himself first of all an idea man.

He lugged the heavy bucket up the ladder and set it on the walkboard. He returned to the car and dipped another five-gallon bucket full of fresh water. This he lugged up the other ladder and set at the opposite end of the walkboard. He brought two new floor mops from the car just as Alfred, the owner of *Bon C'est Bon* stepped out and turned to lock the glass door. Small was disconcerted to see him.

Alfred was dressed in a natty suit that shined and a camel-hair topcoat draped over his arm. He wore a little hat with a brim one inch wide. Turning, he brushed down the lapels of his suitcoat and nearly bumped into Small's ladder. "What — ?" said Alfred, "Small! Yes, how are you Small?"

"Working a little late, aren't you, Alfred?" said Small.

"My yes," said Alfred.

"I had to get out of the house," said Small, "My wife was acting weird you know."

"Oh, don't I *know*!" said Alfred, "I work on their heads all day long."

"Yeah," said Small, "Well I live with one, you can imagine, Alfred."

"I'd rather not. Stop by tomorrow, Small, and I'll have a check for you."

"Right, Alfred, you like my new mops?" Small held the two floor mops in his hands. Alfred looked at the mops.

"They're wonderful!" said Alfred.

"I bought em just for your awning," said Small.

"How nice!"

"The awning will look like snow Alfred."

"Very pleased, very pleased," said Alfred, tipping his hat and stepping off down the walk. Holding the mops by their handles Small tried propelling Alfred away with the power of his eyes.

He climbed up the ladder and stuck a mop in the sudzy bucket. He walked along the walkboard, slightly springy under his steps, and stuck the other mop in the bucket of clear water. The round globes of the street lamps glowed up along the Boulevard though they were not yet needed.

Small took out his pack of Luckies, lit up a smoke and sat on the walkboard dangling his legs as the citizens passed below. He leaned his arm on the top step of the ladder and smoked leisurely watching the flow of traffic like a river of colored metal through the bright green leaves of young trees in the parkways. He watched the pretty girls and young executives pass by. Everyone on the walks was well-dressed except Small reclining above the throng. Small knew why they were here. They liked the gewgaws of fashion and they wanted them.

Elvira wanted them too. Small felt that it would be nice to give them to Elvira but he couldn't. They were all behind the lit shop windows, dresses, shoes, hats, jewelry. He didn't mind taking her to a fancy restaurant once in a while, if you got enough to eat. And a few drinks, and Elvira all prettied up in the candlelight. It was sure to be a nice night in bed.

Small glanced up above the trees at the stone facades of the tall buildings that lined the Boulevard. Small thought the workmanship of the city beautiful, the noble hues of marble ledges adorning the skyscrapers, the narrow fluting of facades that looked like arrows flying skyward. How fine to own a skyscraper one day, 49 stories tall, and you owned it all. Ride the elevator to the top. Walk all the way down running your hand along the smooth iron bannister, spinning at the landings, feet patting the marble, down flight after flight and then across the marble floor of the lobby past the gold-embossed elevator, opening the heavy glass and brass door to stand on the walk in the air meeting the people. It would be like a ship, its course steered through the destinies of its tenants. Thousands of lives, the young, the old, the unborn and the dying living their lives in the offices of a hundred firms who rattled their nets from one end of the globe to another and brought back messages from exotic empires.

The twilight air on Small's cheeks was exotic and from faraway lands. He swung his legs up onto the walkboard, crossed his ankles and leaned back on the ladder.

At night, all the winking lights in the high windows of your skyscraper. What would they all be doing working so late? Was the secretary in the boss's lap? Were they tapping out cables to cartels around the world, moving ships and trains, a thousand tons of wheat here, a thousand tons of rice, bins of spices, five ships to Liverpool with wool, six to the Arabian Gulf for oil, has the shipment of alpacca reached Constantinople by Trans-Afghanistan rail? Thirty tons of rifles leaving San Francisco on the *Angola Lay* of Panamanian registry? I have always despised myself for marrying Jean, Trudy, if you only knew what hell my life has been, let me help you off with that. While Small like a kindly father watching the antics of children stood in the night on the dark roof of his skyscraper with the stars spread out above, the night breeze cool, the roof sailing high above the city. Up so high you would not hear the noise of the squabbling there muted into the harmony of night and wind and the sun and stars passing above. Small would see forever. Even Elvira would shut up. All the gewgaws of fashion would be displayed at her feet.

Small looked above the heads of the passersby up the Boulevard to the Gumm Tower, from which like confetti he had scattered the evidence against a hundred debtors. The Gumm Tower was lit with spotlights from beyond the river. It was a while marble, needle-pointed skyscraper with four clockfaces looking over the city. Small wanted to wash the Gumm Tower. He could make that building glow in the moon and gleam in the sun. He would wash it with terrycloth toweling, suds and rinse it by hand from scaffolds that spanned the towering walls. Half a hundred stories over the alleys his men would polish the Gumm Tower while Small stood on the plaza far below like a great conductor. His men would be paid good wages and so the price for the job would be a bundle. He and Elvira could take a voyage around the world. He would have to work it out in his head, take a closer look at it and the cost of scaffolding. The difficulty would be convincing the building manager of the worth of such a project. Of course they would get more than their money's worth because Small would see to it that every inch of the Gumm Tower was lovingly fondled with the shammies of his scaffold workmen, all dedicated men led by himself. "Feel her, men, in your palms and in your hearts!" Small would shout from his swinging command scaffold, "Let her be your greatest love, massage that marble skin and make it glow! The eyes of the Windy City are upon you! You excel, you reach the heights my men, you have discovered your destinies!" All of the workers would applaud and begin right in with their rubbing of the great blocks of stone and Small would descend in the command car elevator to the street to roll out the vast territories of his mind, to gaze upon them like charts and determine the next stepping stone to empire.

His mind returned to Small from the marble mountain like a bird settling down to a perch. He stretched himself and gazed at the modest hill of awning he must conquer. He took the mop from the sudzy bucket lifting it smoothly full of water and ran it along the awning. Sudzy water cascaded onto the walk below like a downpour. He dipped the mop again spreading the sudzy solution across the awning, dipped and mopped until the entire awning was soaked. He scrubbed the entire surface with the mop and spread a new coat of sudzy water across the awning and dropped the mop into the bucket. Now he would let it sit and soak. Small imagined the solution bubbling into the pores of the canvas dissolving little lumps of grime and dust. Passersby detoured around the wet sidewalk looking up. Small had made it rain.

He climbed down and stood on the wet walk. He might take a stroll while the awning soaked, or stop in the fancy corner coffee shop. Small enjoyed the public life of the coffee shops. It was like a wax museum, but it talked.

Small rounded the corner, hands in his pockets and a rag dangled from his back pocket. He stopped and teetered on his toes rocking by the coffee shop door.

Before him, down the side street, was a long, low, snakey electric sign, an intriguing structure full of glowing, winking light bulbs arching over the broad walk and a canopy beneath the sign. *ENSARDOS,* read the huge snakey sign. A news stand with racks of newspapers blaring black headlines of war stood like a rickety watch tower at the edge of the walk.

Hands in his pocket, Small stepped off toward the sign gazing up at it. There must be a thousand light bulbs. They lit up the dingy superstructure which appeared to be enameled tin, so soiled it was no longer white. Small studied the sign to see where an extension ladder could be set against it. It would be tricky angling a long ladder, but he could guide it in without breaking the bulbs, and maybe *only* he could do it. What was this place? Ensardos? What was Ensardos? There were little lattice windows hung with red velvet drapes. There was no window in the door which was covered with padded leather. Small stepped back to observe the sign once again. It was attached by bars of angle iron and by cables to the second story of the building. There was an electric wire he would have to avoid with the end of the ladder, but he could do it. "Thirty five bucks!" said Small in the twilight air. He backed up further on the sidewalk his arms spreading like wings taking in the whole of the sign one last time, the great snakey *ENSARDOS:* "Thirty five bucks, yup!" He walked toward the leather-padded door with no window in it.

Small opened the door and walked right in onto a fuzzy gray carpet. The walls were papered in intricate patterns of royal red and black. Fancy joint, thought Small. Hands in his pockets he walked across the carpet and looked in at a broad doorway. A fancy restaurant, Ensardos. Candles glowed on tables where people were quietly dining, and along the near wall stretched a darkly polished bar. An elderly man sat at the far end with a drink before him. He motioned to Small with a raised finger. Small walked along the bar and stopped in warm familiarity with the old man who sat on the stool. His rich white hair was combed back from a part that ran down the center of his head. The man was small. He was portly and wore a black suit with a formal black bow tie, his eyes were interested. They smiled inquiringly.

"Hi," said Small, "I'm Small. I do the awnings at Baggs and a few places. I run Complicated Maintenance." Small handed the old man a card which he studied. "We specialize in high work," said Small.

"I see," said the man.

"I suppose you might be Mr. Ensardos," said Small.

"Ensardo," smiled the old man, "What can I do for you, Mr. Small?" Small liked Mr. Ensardo's face.

"Maybe I can do something for you, Mr. Ensardo," said Small leaning on the bar and tipping back his cap. "You have a big sign out there in the front. It isn't what it once was. It's dingy and got dirt all over it. It ought to be attractive like the rest of your place, Mr. Ensardo," and Small indicated the rest of the place with a wave of his hand. "I can clean that sign for you so it shines for thirty five bucks."

"You can clean my sign for thirty five dollars," repeated Mr. Ensardo.

"I can do it," said Small.

"When will you do it?" asked Mr. Ensardo.

"The day after tomorrow, early in the morning," said Small.

"Tomorrow you are playing golf?" asked Mr. Ensardo. His eyes twinkled.

"I'm booked up," said Small.

"Ah yes," said Mr. Ensardo, "Early, Mr. Small?"

"Early, Mr. Ensardo, so none of your customers gets splashed with water."

"Ah yes," said Mr. Ensardo gazing at Small. "Can you screw in a few new bulbs where they are burned out?" Small weighed the proposition.

"Sure, Mr. Ensardo, I'll screw in a few bulbs for you too."

"I will see you the day after tomorrow, sometime in the morning."

"Thanks, Mr. Ensardo, I'll take care of it for you." Small turned and walked up the springy carpet. When he had gone out the door he backed toward the corner looking up at the sign. He could crawl along the top on his knees scrubbing it from the top. There was thirty five more. He was pulling it in this week.

He rounded the corner. It was dark and the yellow lights of the skyscrapers made patterns in the sky.

Small climbed the ladder and flooded the awning with water from the fresh water mop. It cascaded to the walk like a waterfall. In the light of the street lamps the awning gleamed like a pearl. Another masterpiece by Complicated Maintenance, he said in his head as he folded up ladders and walkboard.

The traffic flowed like a yellow river. Small lifted the wooden step ladders onto the metal rack on the roof of the old blue Buick. He swung them above his head enjoying the strength in shoulders, arms and groin. Well-dressed couples strolled along the evening walk through the light of street lamps. Small stood the walkboard on edge beside the two step ladders and climbed onto the hood of Bluey. With one foot on the roof he pulled the rope through walkboard and ladders. He walked across the car roof and stepped down onto the trunk. He tied the rope to the rack and hopped off the car.

Small was proud of the rack he had scavenged from the roof of a junked car. The rack was shiny chromed steel and still sound. Small had taken it down to Piat's to use Piat's electric drill and then bolted it onto the roof of Bluey. Tomorrow he had to clean the furnaces for Piat.

Piat was the building engineer at the Occidental building not far away in the fashionable gallery district. The building was a six-floor red brick structure with ivy growing on its walls and a narrow lawn in front bordered by a low hedge and a black chain fence of iron. It was a modern but homey office building, the corridors bright and roomy. Piat ruled over the Occidental building like a feudal lord over his realm.

Small had explored the entire building following after Piat, screwing in light bulbs or fixing faucets. They had strolled through every office and no corner was concealed from them. Small had been with Piat on the roof and in the elevator shaft. They had turned off the elevator with one of the many keys that Piat carried on a metal ring on his belt. They had laid planks at an angle from one wall to another over the black pit while he and Piat strung a new electrical circuit. Piat had Small propose a written estimate for the installation of the new circuit and had seen to it that Mr. McMillian, the real estate man who administered the Occidental building to the terms of a trust, accepted Small's bid. Small knew nothing of electrical circuits, Piat furnished the expertise and together they got it strung emerging from the elevator shaft, crawling behind flashlights over the rafters of the vast black attic and dropping the wire between walls into an office where it appeared as a socket for a secretary's coffee pot. Small and Piat split the fee.

Small would sit in the basement boiler room watching Piat turn iron wheels, push buttons and monitor the pressure gauges of the great boilers. Small was always welcome. On his arrival he and Piat would dart down the stairs to the boiler room. If it was winter the passages and the huge cave where the boilers sat would be toasty warm from the two oven-like furnaces. In summer it would be cool. Piat had a cot here and a coffee pot, a desk, a clock and an old wooden chair that swiveled and tilted back and a radio playing music. Piat also had a little office with his name on the door just off the lobby. It was the closest thing Small had ever seen to a good job.

Piat took Small up the final flight of stairs to the penthouse elevator control room where a great spool of cable wound, raising and lowering the elevator, and Small marveled at the switching, clicking mechanisms that moved by themselves.

"You get in trouble with your wife you move in here," said Piat, "You live in a penthouse. I'll put a cot in here for you Small and you can shower in the boiler room. We'll hook up a coffee pot and a hotplate. She will never find you and you won't have to pay rent. Come on," Piat led the way out onto the wide roof of the Occidental building. The tarred roof was gravelled with loose white stone. In the heart of the city Piat and Small walked alone amid surrounding buildings that soared into the city sky like two men strolling on a country hilltop.

Piat was ten years older than Small. He was a Pole. He had been in the war and was a bitter man. His hair was thin and blond. His cheeks full, shiny and scarred from the smallpox of childhood. His pale blue eyes were sharp, quick, and ironic. Piat nurtured many hates and instructed Small in the evils of the world.

"Ha!" Piat called from the loading dock where he stood as Bluey drove up, "Pull her right up, Small, give her a rest, how did you get this far, that bucket of bolts should be dead ten years ago. You live on borrowed time Small, your luck is about to run out.

"Ha, ha," and he waved a welcoming hand. "Come on Small, crawl out of that death trap, I have something to show you."

Whenever Small came downtown he would pull off the Boulevard right close to the river, drive a block and a half toward the lake, cut down an alley and pull into the reserved loading dock space. Piat had the cars of executives towed away if they dared park at the loading dock. But Piat knew Bluey and Small could park there anytime.

Small believed that this impressed Elvira. Small would pull Bluey sharply around the red brick corner and nose up to the loading dock. He pretended he was shaking the cops after a daring bank robbery.

Small would lead Elvira up the cement stairs of the dock, past the garbage bins and in the back door of the lobby feeling like a guide to an outlander. He led Elvira down the wide, brightly-lit hall and would swing into Piat's little office trailing the enraptured Elvira, all sparkling now being out of the basement into the daylight and on her way to the fancy shops to see if there was anything she could afford. Elvira was always at her best meeting a new face as if she acquired an energy that lit up her big brown eyes. Small would turn to see all this in Elvira as if presenting the world with a bouquet and wanting to be sure it was perfectly arranged. Then turning to Piat, leaning back in his wooden chair beside the empty-topped desk, his big cheeks gleaming and his blue eyes filled with admiration, and indicating Elvira as if it were nothing for a pauper to be accompanied by such riches: "Me and Elvira are going out to see a little of the town, Piat, how's it going today?"

"It is a pleasure for my eyes to look upon you," Piat would say to Elvira, which would keep her light shining. With Elvira his manner was courtly. Piat was a different man when a woman was around, because he knew them to be so different. Piat would rise from his seat to bow to Elvira, and would accompany them to the front door of the Occidental building as though conducting royal guests, hold the door for Elvira and smile watching her bloom like a morning flower when she stepped onto the fashionable street.

"How did you ever get her, Small?" Piat would ask marveling. "That is a woman with class, Small, do you know what you have? No, you do not know."

"Yeah, Elvira's a peach, ain't she Piat? And I'm finally getting her into line. She's gonna learn to keep the house clean. I don't pay rent to live in a disaster area. I won't tolerate a messy house. I want my decks cleared, I like to be able to see around me."

"I thought you lived in a basement," said Piat with a nasty grin.

"I do live in a basement, it's all I can afford now."

"Do you think a woman cares about what you can afford, Small? Basements are where you hide when the storm troopers come, they are not where a man lives. Don't you know you have a princess, Small? Princesses don't live in basements. You must flow with the woman, you can't expect a natural creature to walk a straight line. Caress the princess, give her ice cream and she will ask what is your wish. That is all there is to it.

"You Americans do not know how to appreciate women, how to guide them, bah! You Americans cannot even grow a potato right. Yet you have beautiful women, it is an absurd universe. Your women run out on you because you are fools. You Americans are clowns, paper tigers, shadows of men. You do now know what women are because you do not know what a man is," and Piat tipped back in his chair and looked down his broad nose at Small as if at an insect.

"You are canned people with trademarks on your foreheads, you are all little peas out of the same can. What do you know of war? Nothing! You do not know that life is war. You know nothing of life, nothing of women. A man knows how to keep a woman. A man knows how to stay alive. If he must kill to live he kills, but your American knees shake to kill a chicken for dinner, you faint at the sight of blood, you faint at the sight of life. You have never grown up. You have hidden from real life which is blood running in rivers, burning cities, corpses heaped in piles and winters squatting in snow starving, dressed in a rag and long rides in cattlecars to the death camps. You think life is a game. Americans are not men and women, they are children and you will burn down your playhouse. What's your game, Mac? you say. Fools! Your minds will change when you feel the bayonets in your bellies. Sheep! The home of the brave, ha! Impertinence — Cowards, shadows, you are not real. You have the arrogance of Huns, the timid cheating soul of the Jew, you are hypnotized by the Pope, you chase the dollar like an ass chases a carrot tied before its nose. You deserve the government of wolves that rules you. Ah! You do not comprehend what I say because you have seen nothing. You do not know what life is. You are *American!*" Piat spat the word like a curse.

"It's good to see you are your usual cheery self," said Small plumping down in the wooden chair beside Piat's desk. Piat regarded him with eyes like shields in a sunset.

"I like you Small," said Piat, "How will you ever survive?"

"Let's get serious," said Small, "I stopped for a coffee break. Is the coffee hot?"

"You will sit and drink coffee while the world burns," said Piat.

"I don't notice you hurrying around," said Small.

"I will get up and get us coffee." Piat did.

"Now, about America," said Small after he had taken a long sip and lit up a Lucky, "It is really not good manners for a foreigner like you to bad-mouth America, Piat. This great land, the land of the free and the home of the brave took you in when they kicked you out of Europe and now you got clean underwear and you look like you eat good. I'm an American, Piat, and I consider myself lucky. I could be a Pole like you, a man without a country, but I'm a born American. I can go to the top here. I could be President."

"Don't believe it for a minute," said Piat.

"You don't know the great country that has welcomed you Piat. Finally you're safe. If any of those foreign powers tries to take over this great land we'd beat em back from these shores, we'd drive em into the sea."

"We?" said Piat, "Why are you not now at the war, little one?"

"Because I ain't crazy," said Small. "I'm an orphan an nobody's got my number. Nobody's got my fingerprints. The President don't even know I'm here, I'm a hidden person, I don't officially exist. I ain't working to give those rich guys taxes."

"Ah, such shrewdness," said Piat impressed, "I didn't expect this of you."

"So I don't mean me, Piat, unless maybe if I could go as a general and straighten everything out right away. I mean America would drive those invaders into the sea. I didn't mean me. I ain't sore at nobody. Here you are a Pole sittin beside me. You could be a Communist, a Jew, or the Pope himself, I ain't got nothing against none of them. I'm a busy man. You got the job, Piat, but I got work, I'm the busy one. You got too much time to think. I keep moving, I mind my business. If there's a war I ain't interested unless I'm running it."

"There will always be war. One day the fires will scorch your heels, little one, and where will you run? You do not even know you should be running."

"Running from what?" asked Small.

"From American ignorance, from the danger of your American life. You are meat for the wolves, Small."

"You live and you die," said Small, "I know that."

"No, I will live and you will die, because I am a man and you are a child. A man has the heart of a lion. Now you listen and I tell you how to grow the heart of a lion. This is so that you may live unafraid and not die that I tell you this."

"I ain't afraid of nothing," said Small."

"That, little sheep, is because you do not know that life is war, that death stalks you like the wolf."

Small got up and refilled their coffee cups and sat down. "Ok, Piat, tell me an animal story."

"Do you know Mr. McMillian who comes in here dressed in tweeds, all civilized and polite and sleek? He looks like a wolf."

Small laughed. "Yeah, now that you mention it, he does, Piat."

"Is Mr. McMillian a man?"

"A man?" asked Small. "Sure, a fine gentleman," said Small, "Yeah, your boss, McMillian, a real likeable guy." Small looked uncertainly at Piat who seemed to be sneering.

"He is a copy," said Piat, "like down the street in these cheap picture galleries. He is not an original. Mr. McMillian came out of a gum machine in the subway. They buy him for a nickel. He was made in a factory on the west side where they make sixty Mr. McMillians an hour. Have you never seen that face before?"

"He's got one of those familiar faces."

"Yes," said Piat, "There is a Mr. McMillian in every office in America. He walks and talks. He looks like a man. He is not a man, he is a copy. A man has heart. Copies have no hearts. Put them in the sun they melt like ice. I say a word and Mr. McMillian steps left. I say a word he turns around. He believes he owns me. Now you listen, no man owns a lion. With one fingernail I cut Mr. McMillian in half. I have cut Mr. McMillians in half. I blow five of them out of a Belgian street with a Mauser automatic. They stand and wait to die because their function is to die. I kill because the function of a man is to live. Do you think I get a free pass from the war, I show it to the Reds, to the Huns, and they smile and drive me to the airport? I live like a lion and that is why I am alive, that is why I remain alive. My parents were of a nobility Americans do not know. I am considered intelligent and they send me early to the university. I am to enter industry. I will have a villa in Italy. I will dine with royalty who will tremble to hear my decision in economic matters because the time has come when money speaks louder than blood. This is to be my future, but while I am at the university the Huns annihilate my city, they kill my family, not a one is left, my sisters and my brothers, my parents. I sneak back to my city, my neighborhood, my house is in ashes. I am in a rage. Before I leave my town I kill seven Huns with their own weapons. I pounce upon them from the fields and drag them into the weeds. I tear them to pieces. I leave a trail of their blood across Europe. I am the scourge to them, I go for their throats. When they meet me they find the war. They die like Jews and each face is the face of Mr. McMillian, the yes man, the copy, the failure. He is meant to die. There is no end to this war, my friend, you live in the war. When you meet a man who will kill you, you have met the survivor. You can trust only yourself. You must rule over everyone you meet. Copies are not men. They are sheep or they are wolves. And then there are men with the hearts of lions. Which are you?"

That day when Small had pulled Bluey up to the loading dock Piat had called, "Come on Small, crawl out of that death trap, I have something to show you."

Small had followed Piat down the basement stairs through the tunnels and the locked metal door into the cave of the boiler room. Piat led Small to the great oven-like furnaces. He threw open a furnace door. They knelt and gazed into the inferno. Gas jets ignited from the long walls of the interior of the furnace shooting jets of fire white blue red and golden toward the center of the furnace where they swirled in a solid ball of fire.

"I want you to crawl in there," said Piat. He closed the heavy iron door and grinned at Small, "When it's turned off, of course, and you must clean furnaces too. Complicated Maintenance does anything, right?"

"Right," said Small.

"Ok, the job is yours, I'll set it up with McMillian. You have to crawl inside. I have a mask you wear. We string a lightbulb and I give you a wire brush and a vacuum cleaner. You brush the ash off the bricks and vacuum it up. Both furnaces. How much you want for the job?"

"How long will it take?" Small asked.

"Three hours," said Piat, "It's a dirty job, you'll look like ash yourself. Bring a change of clothes and you can shower here."

"Twenty bucks," said Small.

"Ok, I'll tell McMillian 35, you get 25. How you like that, little one?"

"Great," said Small, "I never cleaned a furnace before. It's a new specialty for Complicated Maintenance."

"Afterwards," said Piat, "I have a big job for you. I want to get the water tower on the roof painted. You want to do that? After the furnaces."

"I don't like to paint," said Small, "But since it's on the roof I'll take it for the view."

"You have never been in a furnace either," said Piat, "You will get a new view there."

"Some view," said Small.

"Yes, some view," said Piat. "You give the water tower a closer look some day and give me a price. Maybe a couple hundred bucks."

"I sure like to deal with you Piat," said Small.

"Trust me, little one, your future is assured. Come Friday, about five in the morning. Nobody will be around. I will shut down the furnaces. We will get it over with."

Small climbed into Bluey beside *Bon C'est Bon,* started the engine and turned on the headlights. He saw a mouse run along the great log he had bumped with the car when he pulled in. Small watched the mouse run along the log to its end. The log balancing on the brick teetered with the mouse's weight and bumped upon the asphalt drive. Frightened, the mouse turned and scurried to the other end of the log. Its weight teetered the log and again it bumped. The mouse turned scurrying to the other end. Small was fascinated. The mouse ran back and forth, each time tipping the tremendous weight.

"Ah! — " exclaimed Small. He envisioned a huge machine, big as a house, made of heavy beams and tons of concrete and steel and a mouse running it all by the weight of its little body. The mouse was either having a good time or it was too stupid to jump off the log. Small turned off the engine leaving the headlights on, climbed out and leaned on the hood watching the mouse move thousands of times its own weight. Now Small opened the back door of Bluey and tipped the garbage can so that the water ran noiselessly onto the drive. He pulled out the garbage can and tip-toed stealthily toward the teetering log. The mouse was running along the log toward Small, and precisely at the right instant Small lunged, scooping the garbage can over the end of the log. There was a clatter and crash as mouse and log disappeared into the garbage can and the end of the can struck the end of the log.

"Ooooh— " groaned Small, thinking he might have smashed the mouse but he heard it racing around the inside of the garbage can like a marble in a bucket. He jumped over the can straddling the log and looked in. Out of the dark two violet lights approached like tracer bullets and fur brushed his cheek as the mouse rocketed by taking foot-long steps down his back.

"Damn!" yelled Small. He grabbed up the garbage can and turning saw the mouse leap from the other end of the log. Small raced after it holding the garbage can like a butterfly net. The mouse scurried from wall to wall looking for a hole. Small skidded to a stop, whirled, turned and lunged with the garbage can in a flying tackle sprawling onto the asphalt as the can clanged down on top of the mouse.

"Got you! Got you!" yelled Small as the little body rattled around the walls of the can. "Ooooh— " groaned Small feeling pain in his shoulder. He rolled over and sat up. "Ooooh, you damn near killed me Goliath," he said to the mouse. His shirt was torn and his shoulder skinned. "Relax, Goliath, relax, I'm going to treat you like my own son, it's your lucky day."

There was increasing light. A car had pulled up behind his own. Small was holding his shoulder and looking over the garbage can when he saw two cops approach, billyclubs in their hands, and people crowding up along the walls of the driveway.

"Ok, what's going on!" demanded the big cop.

"Everything's ok!" said Small still sitting in the driveway.

"That's for me to decide," said the big cop, "What are you doing sitting on this driveway, who are you, what are you doing sitting on the ground?

What's this?" The cop whacked the end of the garbage can with his billy. There was an instant banging rattle on the inside walls of the can.

"No, no, hey, don't hit my garbage can like that!" said Small, "Goliath's in there."

"I saw it officer," said a little man in a brown suit edging up behind the cop, "I saw it all, he was throwing that garbage can around in here like he was having a fit, like he's crazy!"

Small glared at the man who drew back behind the cop.

"Who's that?" said Small, "He's nuts! My pet mouse got away, Goliath, I got him under the can."

"You got a mouse under that can?" said the big cop.

"Yeah, a mouse, Goliath, a brilliant mouse, he's mine," said Small.

"What are you doing in this driveway?" said the cop.

"I'm Small, of Complicated Maintenance," said Small getting up, holding his shoulder. "I just did an awning job for Alfred here at Bon C'est Bon. The sidewalk's still wet," said Small, "Go look at it. You know Ensardos, around the corner in the fancy restaurant? He's a friend of mine too. I do lots of work here on the Boulevard."

"Hey, I seen him before, Carl," said the other cop, "He's crawling around on ladders at all hours."

"You got a license for this?" said the first cop.

"To catch mice?"

"To work on the sidewalk!" said the big cop and he banged the can with his billy, "Don't get smart with me — "

"*Don't* bang the can!" said Small stretching to his full height, "If you please, officer. My mouse has been through a lot tonight. The mouse under this can is worth twenty five thousand dollars. He's going to be in an act at Ensardos restaurant real soon. This mouse is almost human, you couldn't believe it if you saw it. God! He might be hurt too, I damn near killed myself trying to recapture him. If I lose Goliath Ensardo is going to be real mad!"

"You mean Mr. Ensardo knows about this mouse?" asked the big cop.

"Officer, everybody in the nightclub district knows about this mouse. He's the talk of the town. Goliath. *The* mouse. The mouse under this can you been hammering on. Don't you know any of the acts in the clubs around here, where you guys been living? All the owners around here know this mouse. They'd give a bundle to put him on, but I'm shaping him up exclusive for Mr. Ensardo.

God!" said Small holding his arm across his eyes, "I should have never taken him out. Mr. Ensardo will throw a fit if Goliath gets lost. I just stopped in to see Mr. Ensardo to talk over the deal. I do this ladder work just to keep in shape for Goliath. You see what I have to go through if he gets loose. You got to be real limber to work with a mouse, and good balance gives a sensibility that's necessary for mouse training. A lion tamer, ha!" scoffed Small, "You have no idea. My God, mice are small, you got to be right on it every second."

"Mr. Ensardo is going to put an act on with a mouse in it?" said the big cop.

"Yeah, Mr. Ensardo and me are working up an option for the act. I figure if Mr. Ensardo wants Goliath, Mr. Ensardo gets Goliath."

"You better believe it," said the big cop.

"Stand here just a minute, will you, officer," said Small. "Make sure nobody touches this garbage can. I know how to get Goliath, I need a piece of cardboard, I'll be right back."

"Ok, all you folks move along now," said the cop standing the end of his billyclub on the can and waving them away, "Go on, the show's over!"

Small returned from Bluey with a square piece of cardboard. "Now, officer, I got to slide this under the can real easy so I don't pinch Goliath's toes or break his little legs." Small tilted the can slipping the cardboard slowly beneath it. "Ah, ok," said Small, "He's got to be on the cardboard now." Small looked up at the cop. The other cop was bending next to him, both of them watching.

"Put that club away, officer," said Small, "The mouse can't hurt you, and when I say, lift up real slow on the handles and I'll hold the cardboard."

"Here, Carl," said the other cop, "I'll get a handle."

"No," said Small, "It's best if just Carl lifts it real slow. Two of you might get uncoordinated. Remember, we got 25 Gs we don't want to fall out of this can, Mr. Ensardo wouldn't like it."

"Right," said Carl, "I'll get it." He squatted and took both handles of the can. Small was on his knees holding the cardboard at each side of the can.

"Ok, Carl, when I say lift, lift *real* slow," said Small, "You ready?"

"Ready," groaned the big cop. His teeth were clenched with concentration. Small watched him.

"Now let's not lose Goliath," said Small, "None of us wants to displease Mr. Ensardo, right?"

"Right," said Carl between his teeth.

"Right?" said Small looking up at the other cop.

"You damn betcha," said the other cop.

"Ready Carl?" said Small.

"Yeah, for Chrisake," said Carl glaring from the corners of his eyes, "I'm ready!"

"Ok, *lift* — slowly, real slowly, Carl." The big cop raised the garbage can a few inches from the ground. Small was holding the cardboard snug against its lower rim. "Slowly, Carl," cautioned Small, "Slowly now turn it right side up, I got the cardboard, we don't want to bruise Goliath." The cop raised the can until he held it straight out in front of him. "Slowly," said Small, "Now, start turning it right side up, easy — that's a long way for a mouse to fall."

"Well grab the bottom of the can, Harry, for Chrisake this is awkward," groaned Carl.

"Easy, easy," said Small. "Ok, set him down guys, gentle." The cops set the garbage can down.

"Whew!" blew Carl, "Damn awkward."

"Let's see him," said Harry. Small slid the cardboard aside and the three of them looked in. The little mouse sat on the bottom of the can. Its little sides shivered.

"Looks like a mouse," said Harry.

"It ain't," said Small, "It's twenty five thousand dollars." Harry whistled. "He's trembling," observed Small. "I hope you didn't break his eardrums when you hit the can with your billyclub, Carl," said Small looking at the cop, "That would destroy Goliath's sense of balance. He'd be all washed up. Mr. Ensardo would be sorry to hear that."

The big cop gazed into the can. "Think he's all right?" he said.

"I won't know till I get him home," said Small, "I can't risk putting him through his routine here. I was working him out on his balance beam. I had my headlights on him like spotlights but something scared him and he went berserk." Small lifted the garbage can and carried it back to the car with the two cops following. "Harry," said Small, "get the door." The young cop opened the rear door of Bluey and Small set the garbage can on the rear seat.

"What's that other can?" said Harry, "You got more mice in there?"

"No, that's water I use to clean awnings," said Small.

"You got a fire engine here," said Harry.

"I always wanted to be a fireman when I grew up," said Small.

"I wanted to be a cop," said Harry.

"Let's go," said Carl.

"Oh, I almost forgot," said Small. He climbed up onto the roof and untied the rope from the walkboard and ladders. "I got to get Goliath's balance beam." He hopped off the car. "Carl, Harry, long as you guys are on duty, give me a hand with the balance beam." Small bent and lifted one end of the log. "Ow, damn! Maybe I broke my shoulder." The cops were staring at him. "This is the balance beam," groaned Small, "Help me lift it onto the roof."

"You carry a telephone pole on the roof of this car?" said Carl.

"Come on, guys," said Small, "I can't hold it all night, you just standin there." Harry picked up the other end.

"Carl, help with this end, my shoulder's hurt, boy if I can't work with Goliath Mr. Ensardo will be out of his mind." Carl came and took the other end. "Thanks, Carl," said Small, "Just lift it up guys and set it on the rack. Easy, so you don't smash it. Set it down gentle."

"Jesus," said Carl, "Hold it Harry, don't let it roll off." Small climbed up on the roof and wound the rope around the log.

"If this damn thing falls off it'll crack the cement," said Carl, "That rope ain't going to hold it."

"It's ok," said Small, "I got a chain in the back seat and I drive real slow. Too bad you guys can't see Goliath tilt this beam. I balance it and then Goliath stands on one end and rocks it, it's the funniest thing you ever seen."

"Hey, you be damn careful driving with this on the roof," said Carl, "You need a truck with all this junk."

"What else does Goliath do?" asked Harry.

"You'd be amazed," said Small, "He moves ten thousand times his own weight. He does hand-stands. I'm trying to get him to stand on his tail now and spin but I got to give him more iron pills." Small hopped off the car and reached out his hand to Harry and they shook hands. "Thanks, Harry," said Small and he turned to Carl. "I'll mention to Mr. Ensardo how helpful you guys have been," said Small, and Carl shook hands. "And I hope Goliath's eardrums aren't broken," said Small looking at Carl. "When the show goes on you guys are me and Mr. Ensardo's guests."

"Thanks!" said Harry.

"Come on," said Carl, "Let's get out of here."

"Drive careful!" yelled Small as they got into the squad car. Small fastened the bicycle chain around the log and ladders. I should have had them follow me home, thought Small. How am I going to get it off the roof?

Small backed Bluey into the Boulevard and drove through the side streets toward the docks and bought a bag of fishchips to take home to Elvira. When he got back into the car he dropped one of the chunks of fish into the garbage can. The mouse went crazy, he tore into the fish chip like a lion. "Wow," said Small, "Poor little guy you just been eating garbage. And look at you now! You found a home, Goliath, from now on you eat like the president of Complicated Maintenance."

Bluey crept down the alley and Small eased her in beside the wall and backed up to the garbage cans.

The light was out in the kitchen. Elvira was sitting in bed reading *Glamour Magazine*. She wore an off-the-shoulder nightgown with lace ruffles around the neck. "Hello, Smally," she said, "are you still mad?"

Small sat on the bed, leaned over and kissed her bare shoulder. "Mad? About what?" he said, "Hey, I got a surprise for you baby!"

"I mean about the bathroom wall. I'm sorry I got so upset, Small, but I'd worked so hard painting that bathroom and I'd got it so nice an—"

"Oh, I forgot the paint remover, but it's ok, baby," Small kissed her shoulder and she snuggled up to him, "I'll get some tomorrow. I got to go down to Piat's and clean the furnaces for him then I'll be up for the water tower job."

"Small, you aren't going to climb around on a water tower? Don't do a water tower."

"I tell you I never fall, don't you listen to me?"

"What about the first time?"

"The first time is the last time," said Small, "So there can't be a first time. Tomorrow morning I'll be in a basement furnace. I won't fall out."

Elvira leaned back on her pillow propped against the wall and her look was moody.

"Now don't be telling me about safe secure jobs with a future, ok Elvira? Hey, I brought you something. Close your eyes and open your mouth."

"No, Small."

"Trust me, baby, you'll love it."

"No. What have you got?"

"I won't tell," said Small.

"Tell!" Elvira hit him in the arm with her fist.

"Ow!" yelled Small toppling off the bed onto the floor, "My arm, you've broken it—torn my shirt—oooh!" He lay still with his eyes closed.

"Small! Blood!"

"You don't know your own strength, oooh—" groaned Small. He looked from one eye. She was pale and staring. "Smally, did I hurt you?"

"You've killed me," said Small. He jumped up and grabbed her by the front of her nightgown, "Ok, Tits, out on the floor an we'll go a few rounds, I can still whip you." Elvira boxed his ear. "Ow!" Small went into a clinch fondling her breasts.

"Oooo—I give up," said Elvira, "Smally, how did you get hurt?"

"I tangled with a beast but I whipped him. He's my prisoner, it ain't nothin, just skinned. Look," said Small. He pulled the waxed bag out of his pocket.

"Oh, Small, that was nice of you."

"Someday it will be diamonds, baby."

"Sure," said Elvira spreading the sauce on the fishchips, "Some—day—" she sang, popping a fishchip into her mouth. They sat and ate the fishchips. "I cooked some dinner for you, Smally," said Elvira.

"You're kidding," said Small actually surprised.

"But it got cold. I don't know when you get off work you know, like other wives. Ah, the last one and I get it!" but Small snatched it from her hand.

"I got to save this one, Elvira. It isn't for me, I got another surprise for you. Oooh, you'll love this, you never seen anything like this."

"What—?" Elvira was suspicious.

"You'll see," said Small, "Put your shoes on, you got to help me bring it in."

"What is it?"

"A surprise, you'll have to see it. It's on the car."

"Small, I have my nightgown on, I just took a bath, I don't want to go out in the alley."

"Then you can't see it."

"All right." She swung her feet off the bed and pulled on her fluffy slippers.

"Get your housecoat, so you don't get your nightgown dirty," said Small.

"What is it? I don't want to get my housecoat dirty either." But Small had gone out the kitchen door. When she arrived he was propping open the gate with the garden hose. "Small! I want you to get one of those wheels that fasten to the wall and rap this damn hose up on it or I'm going to stuff it in a garbage can."

"Right," said Small, "Come out here and see it." She saw the log immediately. She didn't know what to say. Small was on the roof untying the rope.

"Bet you don't know what it is," said Small as he hopped down into the alley.

"Sure," said Elvira, "It's a telephone pole. It's crushing the roof of the car. Why don't you just drive this car into a wall, Small? It's a wonderful surprise. I'm going inside."

"No, wait. There's something else. Now just step aside, I got to roll it off the roof."

"Wait!" Elvira hid behind the car. Small rolled the log off. It sounded like thunder when it hit the concrete.

"That cop was right," said Small, "It cracked the concrete. Grab an end, Elvira, I got to get it in the house."

"Oh no, no no, you aren't bringing that tree in *my* house."

"Elvira, grab an end, we can't leave it in the middle of the alley. I told you it was dirty. Help me get it into the gangway. I'll wash it with the hose."

"No, Small, that is not coming into the house!" Small had spun it around and was rolling it toward the gangway gate.

"Ok, now all we got to do is drag it into the gangway." Small lifted an end. "Now push on the other end if you can't pick it up. The least you can do is push."

"I'm not touching it!" said Elvira.

"Helpmeet!" groaned Small.

"All right, pull it farther," said Elvira, "I won't have that thing blocking the door." Small dropped it beside the wall.

"Ok, I'll wash it up good tomorrow."

"Burn it tomorrow."

"Elvira, come here now, I want you to meet Goliath." Small took her by the arm, "Goliath's in the car. This will knock you out, oh, have I got plans!"

"Goliath? Is that the something else?"

Small opened the rear door of Bluey. He lifted out the garbage can. "We better go in the kitchen, you can't see here." Small carried the garbage can before him, "Come on."

"*What* is in there, Small? Is it alive?"

Small set the can on the floor. Looking inside he grinned, "Goliath! You're home with Papa and Mama." Elvira approached cautiously drawing her housecoat around her, her swan-like neck bending from a reserved height. "Goliath, meet Mama," said Small. Elvira peered into the garbage can.

It seemed to Small that her scream dimmed the kitchen light bulb. Goliath slept in his roomy garbage can in the back seat of Bluey and Small slept tangled in a skimpy blanket on the lumpy old couch.

"You don't look good, Small," said Piat, "You look like you're ready for the furnace."

Small told Piat about the mouse and Elvira as they sat in the boiler room drinking coffee. "You are hopeless," said Piat.

"Piat, you got lots of experience, I thought you'd understand."

"You're trying to get rid of that woman. You don't even know it."

"I love her Piat, she's my wife, I ain't trying to get rid of Elvira. I'm just interested in many things. I can see this machine in my mind and Goliath can run it. People will marvel at it when I get it built."

"What good will it be if you build it?"

"None," said Small, "That's the beauty of it. It'll be a gigantic, elaborate, complex machine like nobody ever dreamed of, except me. It'll make a watch repairman dizzy it's going to be so intricate and little Goliath will run it and it won't do nothin. Nothin at all." Small chuckled.

"You're going to build it in your apartment?"

"Yeah, where else? The newspapers will want pictures of it, my mouse will be famous."

"The newspapers have pictures of famous madmen every day, why not you and your mouse? Into the furnace with you, Small."

Piat gave him the mask. "It looks like a gas mask, doesn't it?" asked Piat. He snapped the black rubber bands around Small's head. "There, now you look like you're in the war." Small's voice came muffled and indistinguishable. "Don't talk, little one, it's too late. I don't understand you." Piat put a light bulb in Small's hand. It had a wire mesh around it and was attached to a long black cord. "To light your way to hell," laughed Piat. "When you get in I'll hand you the vacuum cleaner. Hook the light to one of the gas pipes and brush the soot off the bricks all around and vacuum it off the floor. Are you ready for your new adventure?"

Piat opened the iron door of the furnace. Small put a leg into the blackness, ducked his head, turned his shoulders and squeezed into the furnace. His hand on the porous bricks felt the warmth still radiating from the walls and ashes crumbled at his touch. He was in an abbreviated tunnel eight feet long, the walls and arched ceiling of which were lined with pipes with tiny gas perforations all along them. Small could stand but he had to bow his head. He turned and looked back. The doorway of the furnace was a small square hatch bright with the light of the boiler room. Crouching, he turned and went to the far end and began brushing the bricks of the ceiling with the wire brush and black ash fell like a veil. The oven was still warm and Small began to sweat. Ash clung to his clothes and blackened his hands. Sweat ran into his eyes and burned. This ain't going to be a regular feature of Complicated Maintenance, vowed Small.

When he emerged from the furnace Piat was sitting with his feet up on his desk cleaning his nails with a penknife. "Don't come near me!" said Piat, "Stand right there, I'll bring you a chair and a cup of coffee."

"Muffummm —" said Small.

"Take the mask off, you're back in the world," said Piat, "How did you like hell?" Small stripped off the mask.

"What a wonderful job," said Small, "You got another one like that?"

"Right behind you," said Piat, "Sit down and drink this. How come you're sweating?"

"Give me a cigarette, Piat."

"Sure, I'll light it for you, I don't want you touching my lighter. Just one more to go, Small, you're making ten dollars an hour."

"Money ain't everything," said Small.

"Right," agreed Piat, "Breath is, isn't it, little one?"

When Small completed the second furnace he had handed the vacuum cleaner and light out to Piat and turned to retrieve the brush when Piat called his name. Crouching, his feet warm with the heat radiating from the bricks of the floor he turned toward the square hole of the door. Piat's broad face looked in at him.

"Small," Piat said, "Do you want to know how the Jews felt?" An evil grin transformed the shiny white face. I don't know him, thought Small. The face was replaced by the furnace door slamming shut, the sound reverberating through the emptiness of his mind into the bones and blood. Vision retreated from the iron door of the furnace into unknown realms of himself where was no up or down only infinite space with no identity whatsoever, and from this mystery realm a world appeared filled with the grinning face of Piat, his pale blue eyes warm and laughing. "Come out now and tell me about your new view. Coffee break, Mr. Small."

Small came from the furnace like green toothpaste out of a tube. He sat limply on a chair, Piat bending over him, extending a cup of coffee and a lit cigarette. Small's mask dangled in his hand.

Piat looked like the first human being he had ever seen. Small looked at the sunlight streaming golden through the high basement windows and found it good. The soft music from the radio was beautiful. "I know how they felt," said Small, "If you had turned on the furnace I wouldn't have felt a thing, there is somewhere else you go."

"But you are happy to be here, aren't you Small? A little lump of dust and ashes, tired and filthy. Maybe you would have gone into one of the many mansions. I have seen that other world in the barrel of a burp-gun but like you I am pleased to be here. Now you see how sheep die, right in the Windy City any time your back is turned. War is near as your neighbor, the sheep you follow to your doom, the wolf that leaps when your head is turned. What will you trust, Small? The Jews? The ring of the Pope? The lies of the thieves who govern the land of the free and the home of the brave? Will you trust your life to the whims of a woman? Trust anyone but Small and you are a victim. And now you know where that leads." Small was shaking his head.

"I'm sure glad I got a friend like you," said Small.

"Ach!" said Piat bitterly, "You are hopeless."

On the way home Small stopped and bought a can of paint remover. "Here's the paint remover," he said to Elvira when he came into the kitchen. "I'm going to rub out that whole race of industrious happy people I created."

Elvira said nothing. She had not spoken a word to him since the castigation that had driven him to the couch the night before. She was reading the entertainment page of the newspaper. Small went into the bedroom. He grabbed the chest of drawers and began pulling it across the concrete floor. Elvira arrived holding the newspaper as he came out of the bedroom sliding the chest into the hall. "What are you doing?" she said.

"You'll see, I'm going to be busy today, I got lots to do in here. I don't suppose you'll appreciate it, but it's going to be done whether you appreciate it or not." He picked up the throw rugs and dropped them in a heap in the hall.

"Are you going to repaint the floor Small?"

"No!" A troubled look crossed her face.

"Well, just so you keep that mouse out of my house!" She headed for the kitchen.

"A *mouse!*" scoffed Small, "There's a war on and you worry about a mouse!"

"What does war have to do with it?" asked Elvira stopping in the hall and looking at Small.

"Everything," said Small, hurrying back into the bedroom. He came out dragging the rocking chair that Elvira had bought in the second-hand store and he set it against the wall in the hall. "I know what I'm doing!" he said, "All you got to know is you don't have to worry about Goliath. Got it? Goliath will never touch you. He's terrified of you. I'm in charge here! I'll make the decisions here! You got that, woman? Don't ask me questions, I'm busy."

Elvira watched him disappear into the bedroom. Small had never spoken to Elvira like that in the seven years of their marriage. Elvira was secretly gratified, yet troubled.

'A Titillating Spoof,' read the advertisement for a play at the Little Theatre. Elvira wanted to go. Small came through the kitchen and went out the door. She heard water squirt from the hose. Small appeared in the door. "Where's the scrub brush? I don't suppose you know, the scrub brush like housewives use to scrub floors!"

"The shelf beside the refrigerator," she said. Small grabbed it up and disappeared out the door. Elvira looked out. Small was hosing down that telephone pole, scrubbing it with the brush. Elvira looked at the sink heaped with dirty dishes. She almost felt like washing them. She stood at the door in indecision. She would dress and go out. By the time she returned Small's spring might have run down.

Elvira's return was by no means joyful. Small had cleared the bedroom of everything but the bed which sat on building blocks on the floor. One end of the telephone pole sat propped on the bed, the other end stuck into the hall.

"What have you done?" screamed Elvira.

"I'm building the Goliath machine," said Small, "I can't fit the log in yet, I'm going to have to move the bed to the other end of the room."

"Not in my bedroom!" wailed Elvira.

"There isn't any place else I can build it. Should I use the kitchen? The living room is too small."

"Out! out of my house with that telephone pole! Put every stick of furniture back into the bedroom! Oh—oh, Small, I can't stand it!" Elvira whirled and Small heard the door slam.

"Can't be helped," Small muttered, "Can't be helped—no imagination. She'll love it when she sees it working." He got a chair from the kitchen and with much effort lifted the end of the pole off the bed and set it on the chair. The chair leaned slowly and then the legs seemed to explode. Small got his bare feet out of the way just in time. Soon he had the pole propped again on the debris. He pulled the bed to the other end of the room.

Small spent the evening scouring the alley for odd items. He brought an old wooden sawhorse into the bedroom, about twenty house bricks, a bicycle frame, the rim of an automobile wheel, five curtain rods, the tubular attachments to an abandoned vacuum sweeper, a perfectly good bowling ball and several long boards.

By ten o'clock Elvira had not yet returned. Small sat crosslegged in the doorway of the bedroom eating two boiled hotdogs wrapped in a piece of bread and drank his coffee and smoked a cigarette. The telephone pole now lay balanced over the sawhorse which was propped for safety's sake by the building blocks that had supported the bed. The bed lay flat on the concrete floor against the far wall. The items he had scavenged from the alley lay strewn about. It was no longer a bedroom, but a workshop where something unidentifiable was taking shape. Small had screwed six heavy iron hooks at irregular intervals across the ceiling. Steel cable hung from one supporting the end of a long two-by-four the other end of which propped six feet away on the floor. "It'll come to me," he murmured. "All the way, the bowling ball's got to roll all the way from the ceiling at one end to the floor at the other end. Maximum power, ha, ha, what a crash, but I'll mute out the effect some way...distribute it through the machine, vibrate like a spiderweb, tremble like the leaves of a tree, a thousand pounds of action and little Goliath will work it all!" He got up and went to the garbage can that sat at the far end of the room from the bed. "Hi, little fella," grinned Small, "I'm going to get you a nice little box you can see out of just as soon as I can, I know you got no view in the bottom of that can. Here, grow strong." Small dropped the end bite of his hotdog to the mouse. "And be quiet tonight, if Elvira hears you we got problems."

When Small awoke he did not know where he was because the room looked so different. Elvira was not in the bed. He felt a little trepidation creep in his guts. He padded barefoot out of the bedroom. Elvira was sleeping half covered on the lumpy couch. It was later than he thought.

Small hurried out and got the building manager's extension ladder from the storage room, tied it to the roof of Bluey and headed for Ensardos. In the morning light the Ensardos sign appeared larger. He hoisted the end of the heavy ladder raising it against the front of the building. Then deftly maneuvered it under the electric wire bringing it to rest against the sign without touching a single bulb. He climbed the ladder, sat on top of the sign and considered his plan of attack.

A window raised at the end of the sign and the cheerful face of Mr. Ensardo appeared from the lace curtains.

"Don't you ever sleep?" asked Small rather abruptly.

"Good morning, Mr. Small," sang Mr. Ensardo. His white hair was combed neatly, his cheeks were rosy and his eyes bright. He even had his dinner jacket on.

"I am the early bird that gets the worm," said Mr. Ensardo. His gray eyes narrowed upon Small. "I have so much to oversee," continued Mr. Ensardo, "I have little interest in sleep, it will come to us all too soon. More frequently now I journey up to the woods where I keep an estate—when Ricardo is available to tend the business. Ricardo is my son." Mr. Ensardo smiled paternally. "Then I rest and enjoy the calming influence of nature. The city is not for sleeping. Here my eyes are always open, believe me."

"Yeah," said Small, "Well I got a late start myself this morning, Mr. Ensardo. Just now I'm trying to put my thinking on this job here—"

"May I add to it?" asked Mr. Ensardo. "As you clean my sign, Mr. Small, dirty water is likely to drip on my awning, is it not? And so I suppose you are prepared to clean my awning?"

"Well, no, Mr. Ensardo," said Small, "I didn't have that in mind."

"An oversight, Mr. Small?" Small looked down on the metal awning that stretched beneath the sign. Metal was easy enough to wash.

"First off, I'm an awning cleaner, Mr. Ensardo."

Mr. Ensardo leaned forward on the window sill, his eyes brightening. "I see. Then you will also clean the awning?"

"For a price, Mr. Ensardo."

"Ah — And what price?"

"Ten bucks." said Small.

"Thirty five for the sign, ten for the awning. Forty-five dollars for both?"

"Right," said Small.

"Now this is a larger commission than we had first considered, Mr. Small. You might wish to do the complete job on another day when you can start earlier?"

Small was delighted. He would get here earlier when Mr. Ensardo would be snuggled warm in bed, not peering down on his every move.

"Fine, Mr. Ensardo, the day after tomorrow, real early."

"Excellent," agreed Mr. Ensardo, "Now you can have a round of golf yet this morning. Did you enjoy your game yesterday?"

"Golf?" said Small, "No, Mr. Ensardo, I don't play golf. Yesterday I was cleaning furnaces."

"The day after tomorrow then, Mr. Small. Forty five dollars. Is the arrangement suitable?"

"Perfectly, Mr. Ensardo." Small climbed back down the ladder feeling rich.

"Mr. Small?" Small looked up to the window.

"Yes sir?"

"The fee includes the inside of my awning as well as the outside." Mr. Ensardo smiled.

"Ok, ok!" said Small, "The inside too."

Small sped away in Bluey to a coffee shop, parked in the alley, carried his coffee and chocolate donut to a window table and enjoyed the morning rising over another free day.

That day Small put Elvira straight: "You are my wife!" he yelled. "You sleep in my bed! If my bed is in the alley, woman, that's where you sleep! If you don't, you're no wife of mine. Go find yourself a millionaire. Be in our bed tonight or I won't be tomorrow!"

With the exception of a single night, Elvira never again referred to the incomprehensible machine that grew like a mushroom in what had been a bedroom. She maintained a lofty silence. She was chillingly aware also of the presence of Goliath in the bedroom because the mouse now resided in plain view on a shelf that Small had constructed for him; nor did she refer to the mouse. Nor did she complain that the bed now rested on the floor deprived even of its brick supports. With a stony stare she noted the spread of the mechanical cancer toward and above the very bed.

Elvira was out nearly every evening while Small worked on the Goliath machine. She kept the rest of the house presentable and when she cleaned Small knew that she might bring a few of her growing circle of friends home after a play at the Little Theatre. Elvira introduced them to Small who came out of the bedroom to see what was going on.

Small sat with them several times and had a glass of wine. There was laughter and loud talk in his living room. It was like walking into an Armenian restaurant. He had no idea what they were talking about. It was theatre talk, as the women and men were actors and actresses. Small did not know why they laughed, and Elvira's laughter was prominent among that of the others. Small would glance at her, and catching his eye she would lick her lips, assume a straight face and look away. It appeared to Small that each vied with their fellows for attention, that burdened by the sharper wit of another they guffawed and shrieked with laughter not from amusement but from envy. They slandered their absent friends and the next night praised them to their faces. All the while Elvira ran back and forth offering what she called canapes, microscopic sandwiches and olives speared on those feathered toothpicks. The first time she offered the platter to Small he said, "God, Elvira, I could eat the whole tray, are you feeding mice?" Elvira's face crimsoned in the silence. A ripple of laughter arose and then Borozsky, the oldest of the actors, who had graying temples and wavy hair said in his voice like an organ, "Small is indeed a man of perception. What muscle save that for nighttime use alone doth canapes serve?" and this followed by bursts and shrieks of laughter. Borozsky patted Elvira's arm and took two of the morsels, "Nevertheless tis fuel for my inclinations." He directed a dazzling smile at Elvira. Though this was Borozsky's joke everyone looked at Small and laughed. Small grinned into the laughter as he chewed and shortly excused himself. In the kitchen he made a peanut butter sandwich, put slices of raw potato on it and returned to the challenge of the Goliath machine.

Small hoisted a five-gallon bucket of water up the ladder and set it on the *Ensardos* sign. The sky was light but the sun had not yet risen. Surely Mr. Ensardo was dreaming in his bed. The sign would be clean before the old man could stick his white head out the window. Oh boy, thought Small, forty five bucks! He climbed onto the top of the sign and knelt like a raccoon on a limb. The window flew up before his face. Small could not believe his eyes. At the end of a black-coated arm a pistol pointed at his nose. Small threw his arms into the morning sky: "I give up! I'm Small! I surrender!" He was stone-still on his knees. "Don't shoot! I ain't a burglar! I'm Small! I got a card—" Small reached for his breast pocket.

"Touch that pocket I blow you into the lake!" said a steel voice.

"Right!" said Small, his arms again skyward.

"Who sent you, cracker? Cheap punk on a second-story trick! Stand up! Come to the window!"

"Stand up!" said Small, "Right!" and he stood as though on the sidewalk. "I'm coming, don't shoot, there's a misunderstanding."

"Shut up! Move!" The arm withdrew behind the billowing curtains.

"Right, shut up," said Small, "I'm coming, don't get nervous with your gun."

"In the window—slow," instructed the steel voice.

"Yes sir," said Small, "Real slow, I'll be glad to come in and straighten out this misunderstanding, Mr. Ensardo wants—"

"Shut up!"

"Right!" said Small. He climbed onto the ledge poking his head through the curtains. An opulent carpeted room spread before him, little lamps glowing on endtables, a polar bear rug before a flickering fireplace, the bear's great head attached and its teeth gleaming in the firelight, oil paintings adorned the walls, and across the room stood a slim man in a tuxedo, the gun in his hand. He looked like an ad for cognac, like a young banker. His eyes looked like the heads of nails.

"Sir?" said Small from the window sill.

"Get in or I blow you out the window."

"Right! I'm in, I'm coming in," said Small, "Don't shoot, blood on the rug." His arms were above his corduroy cap.

The man approached smoothly like a snake on its tail. Small could not look away from the eyes, black as the suit. "Everything's ok!" said Small, "Mr. Ensardo likes me, I'm the sign cleaner. Small. Everything's ok!"

"Who sent you, punk?"

"Right! Mr. Ensardo sent me," said Small, "Mr. Ensardo won't like it if you kill me."

"I'm Ensardo, you fool!"

"Right, I'm your sign cleaner, bucket on the sign, ready to go, forty five bucks, cheap, good deal—" The man hovered before Small. His face was like stone under the wavy black hair.

"Turn around!" The lips barely moved.

"No," said Small, "I don't want you to shoot me in the back."

"I'm frisking you, punk, I ain't shooting you here."

"Frisk me frontwards," said Small, "so I can watch you."

"Ricardo, Ricardo!" Mr. Ensardo came into the room, "What is this?"

"Mr. Ensardo—Call 'im off!" said Small.

"Put that away, Ricardo." Mr. Ensardo's pale hand moved the gun aside and Small felt the blood begin to move. "Ricardo, this is Mr. Small, he's doing a job for me."

"Clear it with me!" snapped Ricardo, his hard eyes pointing at his father, "Am I running the business or ain't I? Punks creeping on our window sills!"

"Ricardo! Mr. Small, please, lower your hands. I apologize for this inconvenience. Mr. Small, my son, Ricardo. Shake hands with Mr. Small, Ricardo."

The gun disappeared inside Ricardo's coat. He extended a naked hand. A punk! thought Small. Ricardo looked vulnerable as a child without his gun.

"Please, Mr. Small, no hard feelings, Ricardo is over zealous with his responsibilities, he means you no harm." Small discovered his hand above his head, lowered it taking the icy palm of Ricardo who then turned without a word and left the room.

"Do you people sleep in tuxedos?" asked Small. He sank into an over-stuffed chair.

"You will join me for coffee?" said Mr. Ensardo looking at Small with concern. He turned striking a gong with a wooden stick and called toward the door, "Coffee!"

It was good coffee. "You must understand," said Mr. Ensardo, "My son is my pride, Mr. Small. His nature is so extremely delicate. I have had to raise him under the strictest of rules. His social graces are somewhat wanting, but his instincts are sure. He is now a finely honed executive yet bridles under the leash like a doberman. But enough of a father's concerns, you have come to do my sign and awning?"

Small reclined in the chair like a convalescent. "Yeah," he said, "I came to do the job."

"Forty five, was it?"

"Right."

Mr. Ensardo sat forward now, his eyes brightening. "Mr. Small, would you accept an added commission? I want all of the bulbs in the sign replaced."

"How many bulbs?" Small's head rested on the back of the chair.

"Seven hundred twelve."

Small's eyes closed and slowly reopened. Without interest he said, "Fifty bucks."

"Sign, awning, bulbs, total fifty dollars," said Mr. Ensardo.

"Sign, awning inside and outside, bulbs replaced, total ninety five dollars," replied Small.

"Ah—" said Mr. Ensardo with a little smile, "Total ninety five." He glanced at his gold wristwatch, "How time flies, perhaps—"

"Right," said Small, "I'll come day after tomorrow, early. Ninety five. Do you think you could make Ricardo stay in his room, Mr. Ensardo, or tie him up or something?" Mr. Ensardo chuckled showing Small to the door.

"Ricardo finds golf very relaxing. How is your game by the way, Mr. Small? It is early enough for you to get in a game this morning."

"I'll never play golf," said Small, "I might get in front of Ricardo."

As Small passed down the stairs Mr. Ensardo called after him, "Mr. Small, the bulbs must be replaced alternate red and white, I trust it won't be an inconvenience?"

"Ok, ok," said Small, "Red and white. Ninety five!"

The evening visits of Elvira's new friends became habitual. Small observed that when he came into the room to sit for a few moments with them that conversation flagged; that when he left from sheer boredom the talk rose and laughter resumed. At last he ceased to acknowledge their presence. He worked with the Goliath machine.

He stayed up too late. In the morning he phoned Mr. Ensardo: "Mr. Ensardo, I got this job I just can't get away from at the moment – "

"Any time, any time, Mr. Small, at your convenience. The total is fifty dollars?"

"The total is ninety five dollars, Mr. Ensardo."

"Ah yes, of course. Inside of the awning and you'll alternate red and white bulbs?"

"Ninety five," repeated Small. "Is Ricardo relaxed?"

"Ah, my boy, yes, keen as a razor, Mr. Small."

"I'll get at it just as soon as possible, Mr. Ensardo."

Small returned to the Goliath machine. For nearly two months it had been his sole occupation outside of his jobs. Now the Goliath machine stood so near completion that no other work could interest him. His eyes glowed when he looked at it.

The boards, ropes, cables, free-swinging levers horizontal and perpendicular, sheet-metal troughs, rails as if for little locomotives, pulleys, a two hundred pound block of concrete suspended inscrutably at waist height, a ten-foot clear plastic tube, the tire rim suspended just beneath the ceiling on a pole, a bicycle wheel connected by its axle to the intricacies of the machine in a manner the human eye was scarcely capable of following and resting on a bed of marbles contained in a metal dishpan, curtainrods connected to boards and pipes, the bowling ball sitting at the top of a slanting troth near the ceiling, the entire construction filled the bedroom from wall to wall, from floor to ceiling, yet through this maze Small wove his way nimbly as Einstein through an equation, tightening a screw, testing a lever, pulling a rope, stretching a cable and then standing in the midst of it like a heretic held by the Inquisition to an unheard of torture. Goliath would jump upon his shoulder and Small would absently stroke the mouse with a finger as the two of them, brows furrowed, surveyed and pondered the glory of their enterprise.

"Small, I might be late tonight," said Elvira, "I'm going to the Elegante Restaurante with the cast. It's a new French restaurant. You're welcome to come. I don't suppose you want to?" She was painting her lips before the hall mirror. Small had just returned from a rush job washing the walls of a stairwell so that a new bride would not soil her gown.

"Oh no," said Elvira, "Don't touch me, you're filthy."

"Yeah, I been working," said Small, "Dirt is my business."

"I try not to consider it," said Elvira as she brushed out her hair.

"I was hoping you'd be home tonight, Elvira, I just got a few adjustments to make. Then I'm going to run the machine. I want you to see it work. Tonight's the night."

"It is," said Elvira, "They're discussing a new play and I am in line for a part. They like me tremendously, Small, and they think I have talent."

"I like you tremendously too, Tits, and I know you got talent." Small nuzzled under her hair to bite her ear.

"Off! Back off, Small, you're mussing me, and I do not appreciate being called Tits. That is crude. I've told you a thousand times."

"Well you better be home early or you'll miss it," said Small.

"Miss what?"

"The Goliath machine! I just told you it's finished. Tonight I turn it on. I've created a miracle in the bedroom. You could bring those friends of yours by even, if you want, and they could watch too."

"I think not," said Elvira.

"Is there anything to eat?" said Small.

"I'm not sure," said Elvira, "You'll have to look."

"Yeah. Maybe you could bring home a chicken neck or something in a doggie bag. Elvira— Never mind! I ain't hungry anyway, I got work to do. But hurry back tonight. The Goliath machine will be waiting for you."

"When isn't it?"

"You'll see tonight, Elvira, you'll be amazed."

"I have to go, Small, you'd better not wait up."

"Elvira! I want you home early. I want you to see the Goliath machine work. Who the hell are you married to?"

"Small," she said with compressed lips, "I may get a part in a play. Someone has recognized that I am of value. I will not miss this opportunity. As to who I am married to I have lately wondered, is it a man, a machine, or a mouse? I will be back as early as possible. Goodbye."

"Early!" called Small as she headed for the door, " — woman!" The door banged and Elvira was gone.

The mouse was asleep and so was Small when Elvira climbed into bed and muzzled up. "Huh — ? Who?" said Small.

"Hi — ummm," said Elvira, "It's me, Smally, the great actress — " The bare bulb was shining in his eyes.

"Elvira! You're drunk," accused Small.

"Just a little tipsy..." murmured Elvira, squirming and nuzzling.

"Elvira, what time is it? I told you to be home early."

"I'm going to be female lead — " She nuzzled her nose into his chest, "Knew I was a better actress...Smally be Mr. Tits in lights — "

"Elvira! You're soused!"

"Oh — I don't feel good, Smally — ?"

Small got a wet washcloth and washed her face and brought her a cup of black coffee. "Here," he said propping her up on the pillow against the wall. "Drink this, Elvira. If you go to sleep like this you'll think you're dead in the morning. Why did you drink so much? You got no business with people like that Elvira."

"I'm female lead, Smally, will you come see me?"

"You're the female lead right here," said Small. "This is where I want to see you. I don't want you hanging out with those people no more, Elvira, they're a bad influence. I don't want my wife going out with strangers and coming home drunk."

"I have to be in the play, Small, I want to be. I'm not drunk." She tried to sit erect and focus her eyes on him. "I was very proper, Smally, I am not drunk."

"Drink the coffee," said Small. "I told you I wanted you to watch the Goliath machine, I finished it tonight."

"I want to see the machine work," said Elvira, "I want to see the machine work."

"You're drunk for sure."

"I'm not drunk, Small, I promise. I'm sorry I'm late for the great machine. I want to see the great machine work." She tried to sit erect. "Please, Small, work the machine for me."

"You really want to see it Elvira? I ain't run it yet but I know it'll work. Ok, now's the time. I got to get a piece of cheese." Small returned from the kitchen. He crawled into bed beside Elvira. "See this?" he said.

"Cheese," said Elvira, "I don't want it, I'm drinking coffee like you said."

"It's not for you, it's for Goliath to make him run the machine. Now just sit here and watch, Elvira. You ready?"

"I'm ready to see the machine run, I want the machine to run." Small set the piece of cheese on what looked like a little silver tray and snatched away his hand.

"Watch, Elvira, it's off!"

The little silver tray moved. It gathered speed, it slid on a little rail toward the center of the room bouncing into a taut string. A bell rang. "What's that!" said Elvira, "The doorbell—"

"We don't have a doorbell," said Small, "Watch, that bell's to alert Goliath. It's right above his cage."

The taut string had rung the bell when struck by the little tray carrying the cheese and caught on a hook allowing the little tray to pass on the rebound, gathering momentum and colliding at the far wall tripping a switch connected to an automobile battery that lit green Christmas tree lights throughout the room—"Ooooh—" said Elvira—activated a phonograph at high volume beginning at the cannonade of the 1812 Overture as the tray tipped upside down depositing the cheese onto a ferris wheel mechanism the rotating axle of which simultaneously released two paddles, one swinging horizontally, the other swinging down, both of which pulled strings one of which dropped the ten-foot plastic tube across a fulcrum raising it instantly from near Elvira's head, the other opening a door in Goliath's cage onto the tunnel expanse of the tube while the chunk of cheese tipped from the ferris wheel onto a platform elevator in slow rise due to the threading of twine around three sprockets of varying size, switches clicking in the passage of various items as they moved turning off green lights, turning on red lights, the music blaring, Elvira sitting round-eyed against the wall as though assailed, knowing not where to look, the chunk of cheese in its elevator having reached the ceiling beside the round black bowling ball on its perch was tripped onto yet another conveyance that carried it past Goliath's cage who now was seen hurtling himself up into view with piercing squeaks.

"Small! Don't let it out! That mouse!"

"He won't get out, watch!"

The chunk of cheese passed on through the midst of vibrating members of the machine, was scooped off by a tablespoon with a screw through its handle into a funnel, tumbled into a trough above their heads and landed in the open end of the plastic tube as the music marched marshally on.

"He's getting the scent!" cried Small in a crazy shriek.

"Who? What scent?" cried Elvira in alarm, "Small, that music, turn it off, those lights, everything's moving, I'm getting sick!"

"I can't turn it off. The mouse! Goliath, he'll smell the cheese, then things really start happening. Watch the plastic tube!"

"Small, that tire rim by the ceiling is spinning. Is it spinning Small? The bicycle wheel—"

"Perfect!" yelled Small, "Watch!" Elvira didn't want to watch. A vertigo beginning in her head was corkscrewing into her bowels but her eyes unblinking hung on Goliath's cage where his body was visible hurtling up against the wire mesh and shrill squeaks pierced like needle-sharp teeth through woodwinds, horns and booming percussion of the New York Philharmonic Orchestra.

"The mouse is mad!" wailed Elvira clawing at Small's arm.

"Ow!" yelled Small, "Everything's all right!"

"I want out of here Small, turn it off!" The lights had gone into a new phase of blinking, red, then green, red, green—

"Go! Go Goliath!" yelled Small, "We're losing momentum!" A white light bulb lit above Goliath's cage and the plastic tube above their heads shivered as the mouse shot through it like a projectile and the tube fell toward their heads like the barrel of a rifle.

"The mouse!" screamed Elvira trying to crawl behind Small's back.

"He ain't in the tube no more!" shouted Small, "It works! It works! Look!" From a two-pound coffee can slowly upended Goliath fell, the little body stretching like that of a human leaping from the upper story of a burning building, the golden chunk of cheese in his jaws, landed on a foam rubber pad one end of which was lifted by a tightening string that ejected the mouse into a metal bucket immediately struck by the hollow ringing blow of a swinging vacuum sweeper tube and Goliath leaped into a metal pipe drummed down its successive length by wooden-ball mallets like a xylophone and Goliath came from the other end racing like a greyhound around a spiraling ramp the first circuit of which passed near their heads and Elvira howled.

"He ain't loose, he ain't loose!" said Small holding her down, "Don't get up, don't touch a thing!"

"Let me go!" she yelled, "I'll kill it if it touches me!"

"Faster than a racehorse!" yelled Small, "Look at him go!" and as Goliath neared the ceiling all of him that was visible, like a spiraling sun leaving the universe, was the golden chunk of cheese clutched in his jaws. "Watch out now!" yelled Small, "Stay on the bed! Keep your feet up! Mr. Goliath, put a shot across her bow!" and Goliath raced across a strip of tin near the ceiling, from before the loosened bowling ball the draft of which passing surely chilled his tail, Elvira watching it hurtle toward her like a cannon ball down a chute crashing deafeningly into a metal bucket beside the bed instantaneously stretching three steel springs rotating the bucket with a mighty force smashing a metal plate driving a gigantic piston to the mid-section of the telephone pole with a withering thunk that sent it rumbling from its perch down three two-by-fours like a redwood down a hillside toward the opposite wall triggering in its momentous passage innumerable reactions that blazed in light, tinkled, rang, chimed, gonged and clashed, metal on metal, sticks on bottles, clanging old pots, three waterfalls of marbles cascading like rainbows from separate altitudes into troughs of tin swirling there in spiral like lightning out of the storm of the heaving, vibrating, whirling, spinning members of the machine with ripping finality into mason jars, every piece of the machine in astounding maniacal motion reflecting light as if in the last calamitous expiration of a universe pinwheeling surely into hell and even Small's brain was numbed on the lurching bed as the telephone pole collided with unbelievable force against the foundation blocks of the wall streaking them with a crack like a geological fault severing cables, wires, cords, strings, dropping objects like heavenly bodies felled by the stroke of a cosmic sickle from the realms of the ceiling clashing, bouncing, bounding technology transformed to junk above which towered one solitary pole atop which like a last survivor cheese-less, bereft, yet undeniably victorious rose the mouse Goliath in a graceful leap into a purple silk scarf descending with his weight into a throne-like cage atop the mysteriously suspended 200 pound cement block where his cheddar award awaited and Elvira rising dumbly, stumbling blindly through the junk littering the floor knee-deep —

"No! Elvira!" yelled Small, but she had grabbed at the remaining pole to steady herself, "Look out!" the pole crashing to the floor, Goliath leaping straight into the air with the golden chunk in his jaws and disappearing into the rubble, Elvira falling backward as the great block of stone flipped in a crescendo concussion above which dust of flattened debris rose in spirals like smoke and Elvira crawling out through the hall door with whimpering sounds and Small clawing through the debris calling "Goliath! Goliath! Answer me —" standing as though in the midst of the city dump in a reigning silence from which not a squeak arose.

She wasn't hurt a bit and she didn't have a tear for poor Goliath. Small told her she could use the cement block for a table but that he would not remove it from the bedroom and since her father had been a grave digger she shouldn't mind if it was Goliath's tombstone, that that mouse was dear to his memory and he must have been reduced to powder because there was no smell at all but Elvira wouldn't listen.

Elvira was always at the Elegante Restaurante now with her crazy friends. She said she would not remain stunted in a basement day after day with a dead mouse and a madman who refused to better himself. She said that she did not want him to come with her to the Elegante Restaurante because he would not fit in: "I would be embarrassed to be seen with you there. You do not know how to conduct yourself in public, you would blow your nose on the tablecloth."

"I ain't footin your bill at the Elegante Restaurante, Elvira, and I won't have none of those crazies in my house. If those are your friends keep em out of here. I don't have time in my short life for play actors. You don't need rehearsals, you're an actress already. You pretend to be a wife. It's a lousy job of acting too."

Elvira said she met cultured people in the Elegante Restaurante, and women with their own careers. An unbreachable distance grew between them. Small said she had regressed into a high school mentality, she was out for fun, for fluff, that she had never grown up. And Elvira accused Small of that very defect: "You're Peter Pan," she accused, "You think life is play, you refuse to work."

"I *am* working, are you blind?" shouted Small.

"You appear to be sitting in the kitchen chair drinking coffee with no shirt on, unshaved, and your pants unbuttoned," said Elvira.

"Yeah, thinking," said Small, "Thinking how to survive, thinking how to buy the groceries, how to pay the rent for this mole hole, that's all I'm doin, Elvira, considerin how to pay for your welfare as well as my own, Elvira, that's all I'm doin, nothin at all."

"Get a job."

"I don't work jobs, I work work."

"What language are you speaking, Small?"

"When you grow up you'll recognize it," said Small.

"You certainly claimed the bakery was work. It was the perfect opportunity for a man of your talents when you worked on the garbage truck. That was *work*, you said. A government job with the best security."

"Your father the grave digger!" said Small, "And still you believe in security. I slaved at the loading dock too, and at the crazy toaster factory, and at that loan agency, that was the worst job I ever had."

"Clean clothes and a necktie and you sat down all day," said Elvira, "You called that work!"

"More than a man can stand," said Small, "Jobs are nonsense."

"Then nonsense could buy a house for us."

"You're never at home. Do you want to rent it out? Believe in my ability to keep us alive. Stop sticking pins in my balloon when I try to get off the ground."

"I'm not going up in balloons with you."

That was women for you. They thought their feet were on the ground but their feet were stuck in mud. They could dance all night but they couldn't rise one inch off the ground. They only kept a man down. They stuck his nose into the ground and claimed they had saved him a terrible fall. Men were meant to fly but women were baggage. They could never be moved.

Small marveled: How had he been so bamboozled? He had thought he had been in Eden and seen an angel. She wore no makeup, she had been seventeen. She looked like an orchard, cheeks like apples and wind in her hair, breasts like peaches, her like a sapling in the breeze, eyes like dew, teeth like pearls. How his heart had danced. He was going to show her the grand sights of the world. He would get her whatever her heart desired. She stuck to him like glue.

"Where should we go?" she asked, "I've got half an hour for lunch."

"We could go to my place and jump in bed," said Small. She stopped on the spot, wrenched him around by the hand, "Let's go, Small." He had been under her spell for years, and now she turned off the faucet. The day after was the same as the day before but Elvira had decided it was winter. Ice glared over the dew in her eyes. She started to wear that pink lipstick that made her look like a dress shop dummy. She plucked her eyebrows out, she was destroying the orchard.

"I liked you the way you were!" protested Small.

"Well I don't!" snapped Elvira. "I have a brain and I'm going to use it."

"You're making a mistake, Elvira," said Small, "You're the one with the looks, I'm the one with the brains, keep it straight."

"Small, you are suffering from a delusion."

"It's that crowd you're hanging around with, the Little Theatre, the Elegante Restaurante, I should have thrown them out the first time they stepped into my house!"

"You will not intimidate my friends, Small! You will not lay a hand on my friends! I will not tolerate it! They are terrified of you, I tremble when I bring them home."

"You better because the first one that steps into my house I'm going to throw into the alley!"

"My house!" contradicted Elvira.

"I thought I lived here," said Small, "I thought a man's house is his castle! I thought a man's wife was in his house, not traipsing around the streets at midnight with guys that ain't her husband. That's what I thought."

"You are hopelessly antiquated, this is not the dark ages."

"The hell it ain't!" shouted Small, "You don't even see what you're doing. You're crazy out of control, Elvira."

"Out of your control. I'm thinking for myself."

"Oh — bad mistake, Elvira. You promised to honor and obey. Did you lie to the judge? Did you lie to me? Have you suddenly got a college education? What do you want, to be president of my company?"

"*What* company?"

"My Complicated Maintenance company, what do you think I do every day?"

"I can't imagine. You hurry out of here with your garbage cans, load them with water, drive away in that hopeless Buick and come back with a few dollars crowing like you've won the Irish Sweepstakes. Well those few crumpled dollars won't get one far these days Small, let alone two. Company!" she scoffed.

"I warn you," said Small, holding up a finger, "Don't defame my Buick, I love Bluey like I loved my mouse!"

"I believe you are insane, Small. You got that piece of junk because it had gone 100,000 miles so it had to be a wonderful car —"

"It *is*!" insisted Small, "Just because it's rusted out a little and it only shines when it rains — you can't understand that doesn't affect an engine at all. That engine will last another hundred thousand. There ain't nothing wrong with it that kicking the left rear fender don't fix, and you seen me do it a hundred times." Elvira offered a withering look.

"A tank," she said.

"Better than a tank!" insisted Small, "The military would pay me two grand for it if they knew what I had."

"Never again speak of the war," cautioned Elvira, "That is just one more thing I cannot take pride in. You are a draft dodger, Small!"

"You think that is *wrong*?"

"I don't wish to discuss it."

"You want me to be dead so you can be proud of me," marveled Small. "You rather have a star in your window than me!"

"They wouldn't even have you," said Elvira, "You're much too little!"

Small took his corduroy cap from the nail beside the door and left the basement forever.

Small rode the bus downtown. He was familiar with the city landmarks raised by the 138 Broadway in its course to the city center, landmarks of love and lust and fear and greed and loathing. Small pulled the visor of his corduroy cap over his eyes and his sandy hair stuck out at the sides.

He had awakened to a grim day. He was going downtown to apply for a job. There was no escape. If he was to survive in this jungle he had to get a grubsteak. Bluey's battery was dead, they had turned out his lights, disconnected his telephone and cut off his gas. And soon winter would come. It got so cold in the Windy City that Small grieved for the pigeons. How could they survive? But they had pigeon secrets. They did survive. It was a pigeon wisdom that eluded Small. People had lost their instincts for survival. If he had no money he would be dead.

The fear of death drove him to the rash act of seeking a job. Wouldn't Elvira be proud!

He had crawled out of bed earlier than he wanted, which boded ill for any day. He couldn't heat even a pot of water for coffee. They hit you where it hurt. Small had shaved in cold water, an abomination. What did they care if you cut your throat? He brushed back his hair so it pretended to lie down, plopped the corduroy cap onto his head, tromped down the wooden steps and passed through the gangway into the morning street. As he headed for the bus stop the words of a forgotten general recurred to his mind: 'We are surrounded. Excellent. Attack!'

He would go to the window washers union. He would tell them that he was a window washer and ready to work. A chill crisped the morning air. Maybe he would survive until he got to the first cup of coffee.

Small slouched in the bus seat and watched the poor bastards step aboard hanging to their lunchbags. Wouldn't Elvira be proud! To hell with Elvira. He was the luckiest man in the world to be rid of her. And there were the young executives, the well-paid slaves in their tailored topcoats. They were crazy. Well, he wouldn't be keeping his job long. Just a few weeks at some window washing company. Then he would have another trade to add to Complicated Maintenance. He would make the rent money. True, his rent was so cheap it was a miracle. The star of his luck was not dead. Miss Deerly, his landlady, would give him her ragged coat for a blanket her old heart was so big. She had offered to loan him money. No greater love had anyone in the city. He was safe on the rent till he could scrape it together, but he had to get the gas turned on so he could eat and wouldn't freeze to death, and the phone hooked up again so he could get awning, sign and wall jobs.

Small craned his neck to find a clock through the passing windows of shops. He knew where to look: barber shops, currency exchanges, cafes, a tailor's shop was perfect. Good! It was already too late this morning to be sent on a job. He would go straight for coffee and make sure it was too late. To apply for a job was trauma enough for one day.

The bus pulled up to a stoplight. Small found himself gazing through the window of the Elegante Restaurante at Elvira smiling toothily at that old actor

Borozsky, that old fool, a man who would laugh stumbling into his own grave. What was Elvira doing out of bed so early? Her hair piled up on top of her head like Small had never seen it. And dangly earrings big as coffee cups. They were toasting each other — with bloody marys? At 8:30 in the morning? The bus rushed ahead replacing Elvira with brick walls, plate glass windows with the latest ladies' fashions blaring out at Small's smitten eyeballs. What a terrible omen for the day! She must have spent the night with that old fraud. Small rapped his fingers on the seat before him. Amazing! In a city of millions he looks out of a bus window and sees his wife with another man. My ex-wife, considered Small. "My, my," he muttered, "My, my." He pulled the visor of his cap completely over his eyes.

The 138 Broadway snaked hissing through the streets like a devouring serpent swallowing up bodies, packing them into the aisle. Small scrunched in his seat, knees against the seat-back before him, his feet dangling off the floor. He gazed with foreboding out under the visor of his cap:

The gray bastion walls of the Bible Institute. He couldn't see the top; black iron pickets like ancient spears, shadowed arched entries into hidden courtyards. He'd always wanted to go through one of those arches to see if there was a coffee shop. You probably couldn't smoke. He imagined the clean white shirts of the serious young students. What had them? He'd like to know.

John's Violin Shop. Small craned his neck to see the varnished depths of old violins hanging from cords like victims wandered here from the Middle Ages. And then it was gone: Dog food, soap flakes, a pile of apples screaming red through a dingy grocery window.

People piled on at Chicago Avenue; the huge YMCA up the street: a neat cafe on the ground floor, low-ceilinged and wide with ten thousand ghosts in the dim air, men from nowhere, like him, drinking coffee from white cups, imagining King Kong in the streets, you can see it in their eyes. Lucky he was scared of nothing, thought Small: "Nothing!" he said aloud. "What!" shouted the ancient man in a black suit like a talking sack of potatoes in the seat beside him, "What you say?" When Small came out of that he was staring wide eyed and innocent at the great white blocks of stone that rose up into the spires of the Catholic Cathedral of the Windy City. 'Black magic!' hissed the pendulous lip of Reverend Proot. To Small it was no more than a caution. His mind tip-toed on behind the great blocks of stone, up a stone-cold aisle to a dim-lit recess, to a chair old as a Strativarius where the skirts of the Cardinal were noted, and out of the wary corners of his mind's eye, the caskets of mob members sprinkled with holy water; he rode in his bus seat through the ghosts of limousines lining the curb — the Cardinal has license plate number one, not the governor: ghosts that fascinated Small.

The nightclub district where Goliath might have performed and only he the sole living memorial to the greatness of a mouse.

What is that, Tudor? The heavy block brick, gray, of three-floor walkups, can't tell if the rent is high or cheap, depends who the owner is, they come in all shapes, Miss Deerly and the king-pin realtor downtown, a faceless unreachable guy out on some yacht in Belmont Harbor getting soused. You could rent a corner in one of them and hide out. Inside, those places were like castles where Bluebeard lived, like that princess with the long hair who laid it out the window for her lover to climb up, or someone very old was dying in the shadows down the hall, stealing away with a lifetime of living — Hey wait! yelled Small in his mind, What do you know? as lives slipped away into ghosts and rooms and buildings slipped behind, and the skyscrapers of the city center now towering, fire escapes in black webs above alleys, ack! — O'Brien's Fish House flashing by, elite little place disguised, by an alley, dark, delicious sea food and a cold beaded bottle of imported beer and Elvira warm as french fries nuzzled beside him in the dark booth and outside snow blowing white in the night street — Small tore his mind away, he didn't want to hear again what she had told him then.

The serious iron bridge across the river: suicide, yachts, fire boats, white chunks of ice floating in green water, the moat around the temples of commerce, everyone piling off like the bus had sprung a leak, people blowing away like dry leaves to the four winds. Small wouldn't get off.

He rode past two cross-streets where pedestrians swarmed, got off finally and darted into the Greyhound bus station. Small descended the escalator toward the lower level cafeteria. All the way through the line, cup of coffee, grab a spoon, sat at a table by the window wall looking out onto the terminal. Ah — the first cup of coffee.

They couldn't keep a good man down, you just had to be mobile. Light up a Lucky and see which way the wind blows. Regroup. Get the lay of the land.

After a refill Small went to the telephone booths and stepped into the most anonymous, closed the door, stood like a spy under the yellow light looking out at his fellow travelers, imagined himself hiding from the cops after knocking over the First National down the street, turned to his fate, hoisted up the gigantic telephone book, flopped it open like a dead fish hitting the deck. Who was that German baron turned hobo who tore it in half with his bare hands? a grinning, bearded old man with a fierce, mysterious light in his eyes — Small looked in the yellow pages under 'Window' — ok, he knew where it was, flopped and dropped the phone book like a rock dislodged in a cave, lit up a Lucky, pulled down the visor of his corduroy cap and stepped into the world.

No mistake, Small had found a job. Or rather, the job had found Small in the form of Short, the master window washer.

Short had snatched Small from the clutches of the window washers' union, from the threshold of the very office just as Small was to put his signature to the union agreement that would wring fifty dollars from his first month's wages. Short was an independent, the bane of the Windy City window washers' union, dedicated to the overthrow of all bureaucracy, bandoliered with his window washer's belt and bucket of protruding brass-handled squeegees like arrows in a quiver, like bolts of lightning, a teetering, tipsy, wobbly, dancing ancient little man in gray coveralls and a wilted old train engineer's cap held up by big hairy ears. Small was Short's prize of war on that memorable day which changed the course of his life.

The door to the window washers' union stood open. Small closed his eyes, swallowed, walked in to apply for a job. A fat man with a bald head chewing on a cigar, dressed in a dingy white shirt and colorless tie, was reading a newspaper: "Whatda ya want, kid?"

"I'm a window washer, I want a job."

"Who ya worked for?"

"Myself," said Small, "I taught myself all about it."

"In other words ya don't know nothin about washing windows."

"First job I ever had," said Small, "I was a window washer in Florida."

"You was in the union there?"

"Naw, I was a slave there. Now I want to be a slave for you guys. How much of my check do I have to give to the union? Make it easy, I got to eat once or twice a week."

"I see you're a smart kid," said the union agent. "For a hunert off the first month's checks I get you scaffold work on the new buildings."

"No," said Small, "I don't want on a scaffold someone else is runnin, I want belt work."

"Seventy five bucks I put you with one of the best companies. You work every day, no fly-by-night outfit."

"Come on," said Small, "You guys are the champions of the poor. Look at this." He held his shoe up not long enough for the fat man to see the sole, "Holes in my shoes, I'm back in my rent, no food on the shelves, I can't afford lunch downtown, I can't pay no more than 25 bucks, I ain't no rich man, what do you think I'm doing here?"

"You got yourself Ace Window Cleaners," said the union agent, "Fifty bucks off the first month's checks, that's rock bottom. Fill out these forms. And take scotch tape with you, their belts are old. Have the fifty in here ta me personal by the tenth of next month or ya'll never wash a window in this town again."

Small took the forms and bent to sign them. "I'm certainly proud to have you guys protecting me from greedy employers," said Small.

"This is a union town, kid. You work, you pay."

"*YOU*!" blared a voice that made the hairs prickle on Small's spine. The union agent was on his feet banging his fist on his desk:

"Out a here you wino bum, you crazy old goat!"

Small had turned to see the crazy old goat in the doorway, formless, boneless-appearing in old gray coveralls. He was staring at Small.

"You! Don't sign the papers! No graft to the oppressors! Follow me!" He spun away out the door. Small felt himself drawn out the door and into the hall. He was still carrying the papers and the union agent's pen.

"Sign those papers!" yelled the union agent. The little old man stood by the stairs crooking a finger at Small. Small walked toward him. The union agent in the doorway was stomping his feet like Miss Sweatly had stomped at the rats: "You gotta go through the union, kid! Short, you'll find yourself face down in the river!"

"Ha, ha, ha," cackled the little old man, "Who's afraid of the big bald wolf? Follow me, kid!" He bounced down the stairs like a rubber ball. Small followed him out onto the walk where the little old man addressed him nose to nose, and so standing they might have been mirror images at opposite ends of a time warp:

"You do high work!"

"Yeah!" said Small, "I go high as I want!"

"Wrong!" said the little man, the stubble on his cheeks bristling like white-hot wire, "You go high as you can, *I* go as high as I want! It's your lucky day! You're talkin to the best window washer in the Windy City. I need an apprentice. That's you. I ain't union cause I ain't no fool. You ain't union neither. You got me to thank for that. I ain't offerin no job, I'm givin you work. Welcome aboard, my name's Short!"

"No fooling!" said Small shaking the old man's hand, "I'm Small!"

"Ain't that marvelous!" said the little old man whistling and rolling his eyes, "You're Small. It's me that's Short. Don't forget it."

"Right, Short," said Small.

"Down ta business. You're late for work your first day, what ya been doin? Drinkin coffee. I know your kind. Well here you are an this is how it lays: You're new, wet ears, snotty nose, a tiny talent. I'm old an I know it all. Do as I do an you'll be a master window washer an the fortune of your life is made. I show, you watch. I do, you do like I do, got it?"

"Sure Short," said Small, carried away with the little man's magnetism, "But money? Short? I mean you got a company? I mean—What do we do?"

"Ha, money!" Short spat in the street, "Trivia! Didn't I tell ya your fortune is made? Listen, don't ask, watch, don't look, unnerstan, don't wonder, unnerstan?"

"Maybe, I guess. I'm workin for you washing windows?"

"Brilliant," said Short, "Follow me!"

Short took Small up to a second-story room in a flophouse beyond the river. "This is where I stay," he said, "I'm a transient. My real home is heaven. While I'm here I work in the clarity trade." Short did a little dance step. Small watched with fascination. Short looked like he could barely stand up yet he was unbelievably nimble. He must be seventy years old. His eyes flashed. "Belts!" he announced and leaped onto the narrow bed springing under his weight. He snatched two window washing belts from hooks on the wall and bounced to the floor. He handed one to Small, swung the other over his shoulder dropping to his knees and dragging two metal buckets from beneath the bed. "Your bucket," said Short handing one to Small. Three rags appeared in his hand, "Stuff these in your pockets. You got three squeegees an a brush in your bucket. Never lay your squeegees down on the rubber, these precious little strips of rubber serve us to the degree we respect them. Never drag your squeegee across a cracked pane of glass. That will cut the rubber and successive panes will acquire the scar of a streak. Is that clear? Is it credible? Do you think you might remember that?"

"Sure, Short," said Small.

"Follow me," said Short and stopped directly in front of Small who nearly ran him down.

"On your toes always on your toes!" cried Short, "Never follow me off a ledge, you don't unnerstan what I unnerstand, unnerstan? You represent the youth of a decadent age. We ancients throw you the torch. Any moment the trumpet of destiny may sound for you. Be ready. Follow me!" Short tottered off toward the stairs, Small following more cautiously after, admiring how Short wore the webbed and gleaming leather belt with its ropes and iron hooks draped over his shoulder. Rags hung from his pockets; his metal bucket with the brass window squeegees rising from it hung on the crook of his arm. "Hands off the railing," said Short over his shoulder, "You'll smash the roaches." Small threw his window belt over his shoulder and carried his bucket like Short. They emerged from the stairwell gloom onto the littered walk of a windy corner. Short spun like a top.

"In here!" and Short blew in the side door of a saloon. Small followed across the sawdust through a rubble of black wooden chairs and tables up to the bar.

"I thought we were going to wash windows," said Small.

"I'm Short, I'm Short!" declared Short, "You're Small. Short is boss. Later for Small, now for Short. Ain't it morning? You think you're done for the day?" Short whistled rolling his eyes. "We stop for coffee before we go on the job. It's a workman's right! Coffee before work is a divine right! Don't forget it. Die for it if need be. Or live a slave. We take coffee breaks when we want coffee breaks. A divine right. Give me white wine, Hank, the kid wants coffee."

They sat at a round black table and the postmen from the main office by the river came in to cash their checks after the night shift.

"Workin stiffs!" said Short nodding his forehead at the postmen. "Birds in a cage. Think they got it made. Hidin behind pillars in the basement a the post office, hidin from the foreman in the mop closet, gettin a raise this year, two weeks off next year, gettin a new car, gettin a TV, gettin drunk ta forget it, gettin fucked an takin it. A window washer is a free man. Don't forget it."

"Do I get a refill?" asked Small.

"You bet," said Short, "Get me one too, sauterne, for the higher altitudes."

Small returned to the table. "Don't you worry about getting out on a window ledge when you drink?"

"I float a lot," said Short. "My feet are fly feet. I have suction cups on my soles. I got holes in my shoes. Best way to travel. I was born that way. My mother used to hang me from the ceiling when she swept the floor. I carry a belt so other folks don't get nervous."

"Right," said Small, "I'll carry it so I won't get killed."

Short rolled his eyes and tapped his forehead, "What you don't unnerstan! My work is cut out. Busy busy! And I'm gettin old." He raised his glass toasting the air and drank half of it off. "You ain't met the Angel. You have to have a pure heart. Then you meet the Angel. Then you never fall. Even if you fall. Don't believe me, do you?" Short's eyes crept from under his feathery brows to regard Small sharply.

"I don't know," said Small.

"When you know the Angel it's all you need to know." Short tossed off the wine and picked up his bucket. "Follow me!" They marched out of the tavern.

Short was even shorter than Small, but Small had to hurry just to keep up, especially at intersections where Short never hesitated, where the light was always green, where Short's old brogans did a curious shuffle that sent him sailing into the street and up again onto the walk.

They crossed the rumbling iron bridge over the river beside the opera house. Short spun in the door of the old building beside the river so abruptly that Small, finding himself alone, retraced his steps hurrying into a cavernous lobby. "On your toes!" yelled Short already mounting the marble stairs.

They entered an office on the second floor. Short kissed the pretty receptionist on the cheek as he passed but she eyed Small warily. The office looked like a doctor's office in 1880 Abilene, wooden chairs with round backs ageless under their varnish, old wooden desks with green blotters on them and shadows from high plaster walls. Short went to a closet door which hid a sink. "You will notice a peanut butter jar in your bucket," said Short as steaming water poured into his bucket. "This contains detergent. Use a pinch in half a bucket of hot water." Small filled his bucket as Short had done. Short pushed a wooden chair near the window sill and climbed onto it. He swung wide the window and stepped out. Small climbed onto the sill looking out. Short stood at ease on a ledge rolling a cigarette and looking over the river, the traffic below and crowds of commuters flowing across the bridge and along the wide walk. Small held to the window frame. Short popped the cigarette into his mouth, raised his old brogan standing like a heron on one leg and struck a wooden match on his sole.

"You must trust your belt," said Short turning to Small. "We are independents, which means freedom. But you might be more interested to know it also means we ain't covered by insurance. We don't throw coin in the wishing well of the leisure class. If we fall and kill ourselves we don't get paid for it. So my apprentices get belts that don't bust."

Short strolled away up the narrow ledge smoking his cigarette. Small stuck his head out the window watching Short who turned and strolled back, a hand in the pocket of his gray coveralls. "Never mind how I know what I know," said Short, "You won't unnerstan till you unnerstan. You got a talent for faith, a gift you are unaware of. To survive, nurture that gift. You fretted about takin a job. Wasted energy, cause here you are workin with me. You'll make the money you need. You'll enjoy your work. You'll find out you're a window washer. Worries are straw, let 'em go with the wind. If you panic no ledge made of stone will hold you. Fear can kill you, and you are the one that creates fear. You can't help being alarmed, but you can refuse to be afraid. Don't hang out here in your belt and drift with your thoughts. Always be attentive. Always on your toes. You never know when fear will look you in the face an you better be ready to look right through that ghost. Pride tells you Small can't fall. It's a lie designed to destroy you. Pride always falls. Respect the natural laws with immediate emphasis on the one about gravity. Then learn from the pigeons, they fly by faith."

Short handed his own belt to Small, took Small's and buckled it around his own waist. "Watch," said Short. He hooked the belt to the window bolts. He bent slowly backward out over the walk until his silver hair hung from the railroad cap. Short waved his arms once, his feet rose into the air and he flipped over backwards landing on the edge of the ledge. Small's eyes were big. Short loosened one side of the belt and cast himself from the ledge returning in an arc to stand before Small. "You see," said Short, "You can trust the belt."

He stripped off the belt, handed it to Small and put on his own. "Put on your belt and come out here." Small emerged, holding to the window frame. "Close the window and hook onto the bolts." Small hooked onto the bolts and leaned back resting in the belt, turning his head and gazing down on the passersby. Short stood on the ledge watching.

"You trust your belt," said Short, "So you think you're safe?" Small glanced quickly up at him. "What about those window bolts you just attached that belt to?" Small clawed his way rigidly up and stood on the ledge. He inspected the bolts. He looked at Short. "Why do you trust the ledge?" asked Short. Small gripped the window frame. "The frame of the window?" said Short. Small looked at Short standing beltless on the ledge smoking his cigarette. He leaned back in the belt saying nothing. "You trust the bolts and you trust your belt," said Short. "Made by fallible hands. With better reason you trust your next breath. Balance is like breath, none of your doing, it's a gift. Trust that balance that you can't see, trust it always before belts or bolts or ledges. Now pay attention, we're going to wash windows." He slid Small's bucket toward him with a foot and hooked his belt to the bolts of the next window. "Do as I do," said Short.

Small brushed his window wet like Short did to his. "Get the corners," said Short, "Scrub it. We get windows clean. Run the end of your squeegee across the top of the glass just under the frame, it gives you a dry strip. Now set the blade of the squeegee a fraction of an inch below the sash. When you pull the squeegee down from the sash suction dries the space between squeegee and sash and you don't drag mud to streak the glass. Draw the squeegee down, not hard, the less pressure the better." Small watched Short and then made his first stroke with a squeegee. "Wipe the blade." Small wiped the blade with a rag. "On this next stroke tilt the end of the blade down into the dry part so water runs out the wet side and not on the dry pane." Small watched and did it. "The next stroke is exactly like the last," said Short. Small brought his squeegee down and the window looked clean.

"Looks great!" said Small leaning back in his belt.

"You ain't done," said Short. "Rag those edges." Short wiped a rag down one side of the pane against the sash, then wiped the other side. Small did the same.

"With infinite variations," said Short, "this is how you wash a window. The variations can fill up a lifetime. This of course is unbelievable to you, but remember you don't know nothin. Long as you wash windows, if you're a hunnert an eight, you will find it to be true."

"You want to come check this window, Short?" asked Small.

"No," said Short. "That window you get on grace. The rest I'll be on your ass about. After that it's credits or blotches on your conscience." Short stood straight on the ledge. "This one is wide enough to walk on. You seen me do it. But until I tell you different you move buckled to the bolts. This is how ya do it." Short unhooked the left side of his belt and stepping to the right refastened it to the left bolts of the next window and stepped before that window. Reaching back to the window he had left he unhooked the right side of his belt refastening it to the right hand bolts of the window before him. "That's how you walk windows. Let's see you do it."

Small noticed the wet ledge beneath his tennis shoes. "Right," said Short, "always attentive."

Small felt the ledge through the soles of his shoes and picked up his bucket without being told. Short said nothing. With his left hand Small unbuckled the left side of his belt and moving toward Short hooked it to the left side of the next window stepping before it. He reached back unhooking the right side of the belt and correctly hooked himself before the window where he stood. Unbuckled now Short stepped behind Small passing to his left. "Keep going," said Short, "Right around the corner and down that wall far as you can go."

Small again unbuckled his left side, hooked it to the next window bolts and stepping easily stumbled over Shorts bucket, grabbed for the right window bolts, would have glued his knees to the very concrete of the ledge but the belt not allowing such latitude swung Small sickeningly out and backwards where he pivoted from foot to foot his bucket clutched to his chest. He looked at Short standing with his own bucket in his arms, looking at him pleasantly. "What's your left hand doin?" asked Short. "Pull yourself up here." Small gripped the belt and pulled himself up straight on the ledge where he set down the bucket breathing deep.

"There is a place for the window washer's bucket," said Short, "That place ain't under people's feet. Pedestrians will be anxious to sue you if they trip over your bucket. You can kill yourself or someone who's workin with you. Now would you move your bucket safely back toward the window so that I don't fall over it?"

Small slid his bucket against the window with his foot and Short passed again around him. "You'll never again find my bucket in your way," said Short. "I don't want to find yours in my way. You been out here fifteen minutes and already you quit watchin where you're stepin. Watch where you walk. Now walk the windows around the corner and down that wall. If you get there alive start washin em back this way. I'll work toward you. No streaks. We get windows clean."

Small stood for a moment more until his fright was gone then unhooked and hooked himself to the corner of the building. He stuck his head around the corner into a sweep of wind. The wide green river lay not one floor below like the sidewalk in front, but five. Small looked down upon it holding to the corner. He could not reach the bolts of the next window, but here, as in the front, the ledge was ornamental and wide. There was no reason why he could not walk so wide a ledge. He unbuckled his belt and with the bucket on his arm moved carefully around the corner, the sweep of river wind in his face. His eyes watched the ledge where his feet fell, the brick wall caressed his shoulder. He stopped in the whistle of wind and without moving his head, so that balance was still the focus of attention, he allowed his eyes to rest on the green water far below. To stand so was elation to Small which he dared not celebrate with movement. He shifted his eyes again to the ledge and moved slowly on until he reached the window and buckled his belt to the bolts. Such a view! Never while awning or sign-cleaning did he get so high. His chest swelled — like a pigeon, he thought. He gazed up and down river, far down skid row and over the neighborhoods beyond the river. The pale blue sky hung above. In the midst of the city he was alone and glad. He looked down the ledge. He could walk it all without being hooked to the bolts. But Short was boss. Small walked the windows hooking his belt to the bolts as he made his way along. At the last window he hooked both sides of his belt and leaned back. Between his legs ran the green waters of the river. In dreams Small had dived such heights. Wind blew the sandy hair that stuck from the sides of his corduroy cap. Small turned to the window and dipped out his window brush with the black bristles and wooden handle and bathed the dusky panes. When he had squeegeed them dry and wiped the edges with his rag he had brought out his own reflection in the glass. Small stared at himself belted and soaring upon the dark hues of the room beyond the window, the hues of 1880 Abilene, beneath the clearer image of the Windy City spread below the soaring Small. High above the flowing river he leaned back in his window washer's belt and grinned up at the sky.

Small walked jauntily in the company of Short week after week through the streets of the Windy City. Small had out-witted the world. He worked with Short only three days a week and made enough to live on. The other days he leisurely pursued the affairs of Complicated Maintenance or flew his kite above the lake-front lagoons. Every day with Short he was somewhere new and Short paid after each day's work. They were out in the open and washed windows high up out of it all, and the view was splendid.

Short and Small appeared a pair of strange birds high on the walls of the Windy City skyscrapers, the old man above with his gray hair blowing from the faded railroad cap, the younger following below. The old man seemed to float on wind, he danced on his toes and turned in his belt wielding brush and squeegee, gazing about above and below, talking to the younger man as though guiding his flight. Small below waved along jerky, like the tail of a kite, as if he stubbed his toes on realities marring his dance from window to window.

Small hugged a great stone pillar as he stood on the window ledge and talked to Short as though pleading his case. "I was me, see. I went high as I wanted to go. I ain't never forgot how bright the sun looked on top of those clouds. And I land in a basement. It was lust overcame me," he asserted, "and possession and power." Small shivered. He buttoned the collar of his jacket.

"Pay attention," said Short from the floor above.

"Right, Short," said Small. He buckled onto the next window and swung around the pillar.

"You wasn't in no danger on top of those clouds, but you crashed in the basement."

"Right, Short."

Short was sticking his hip flask back into his pocket after a nip. "There's salvation in this dark jungle," he said. "You could fall all the way from here an land on your head but your heart get's lifted up." Small had grown fond of

Short though the old man was obviously senile, he had such strange ideas. But he was always done with a set of windows before Small. Short must have been doing windows for half a century.

"How long you been washin windows?" Small said up to Short. Short's look was condescending. He always looked like that after a nip.

"For all eternity," said Short, "Time doesn't matter. You heard of the Wandering Jew? I'm the Floating Gentile."

Small tried at times to be morose about Elvira, but really he couldn't bring her up here with him. He enjoyed the high ledges, looking over the city or many floors below seeing the street between his legs, the crowd swirling along the sidewalks, the bug-like roofs of tiny cars, taxicabs and buses. And Short was always there for instruction and entertainment. Short knew everything about window washing. Small hoped Short didn't kill himself before he could pick up all the little tricks of the trade. Window washing was the best work he had come across, yet still there were conquests to achieve in the awning and sign trade.

"I see ya in the windows, Small, I see ya an you don't even know it. You think ya see me too but ya don't. You do a passable job just ta see your homely reflection. There's two sides to the window."

"I look through the windows all the time, Short, not a secretary escapes my sharp eye. I think you're so old you don't see the dolls no more. Ain't it coffee break time?" Small was holding to the pillar as he stood on the ledge looking up, "You're always nippin and I'm dyin of thirst."

"Ok," called Short, "Then I'll burp you."

"If I ain't in the hall," called Small, "It's cause I'll be enjoyin my youth in the broom closet with the secretary, Short, and you shouldn't open the door."

"My coffee's black," said Short, "It's your turn to buy still."

"Still?" echoed Small as he climbed through the window onto the desk of a thin man who did not answer when Small greeted him. The thin man held anxiously to the papers on his desk threatened by the wind through the open window and squinted up his nose at Small.

"I threw bigger piles than that out a window," Small told the man. "I got fired," he said. He set his bucket on the desk blotter and leaned on the desk. "Then my marriage fell apart."

"If you please," said the man tightly, "Close that window and remove that bucket from my desk." Small closed the window raising an eyebrow at the thin man's stare and walked through the office looking at the nylon legs of the girls in the typing pool who drew back at the raw appearance as he passed whistling under his breath and went to join Short over coffee.

"Follow me!" Short commanded day after day. The formless figure in gray coveralls led off the bus. It looked like the end of the world to Small: a wide intersection, and beyond rising fantastic out of the straight streets and city blocks, Funland, the Windy City amusement park.

"Follow me!" Short stepped over an iron chain into the park and walked onto the green grass straight into a sprinkler, getting doused. He bent like a drinking bird into the spray, picked up the sprinkler and turned the water into his bucket. Small came up. Short handed him the sprinkler and walked away. When his bucket was half full Small stood directing the sprinkler at the grass. He saw Short watching him from the sidewalk. He looked again at Short and then set the sprinkler down easily on the grass looking into the spray washing his face and drenching his clothes and walked out of it jauntily up to Short.

"What did ya do that for?" said Short, "You're all wet. Follow me!"

The walk before them widened into an apron of gray cement.

"Guess what?" said Short, water dripping from his bristly old cheeks.

"What?" said Small, shaking himself like a dog to throw off the water drops.

"The world is going to end."

"When?" asked Small.

"Soon," said Short.

"Ha, Ha," said Small, and then looked hard at Short, "Today?"

Short didn't answer. The green grass was gone and concession booths opened on the left and the high wooden cross-hatchings of a roller coaster rising into the sky that was disappearing over a world warping to a concentration of hawkers, shooting galleries, cupie dolls, and colored lights.

"You mean the whole world?" pursued Small, very interested.

"The world as we know it," said Short. "Everything you know and love will die, and you too. The beast of greed is loose on the earth. Iron clashes with iron and smoke and fire and destruction are loosed on the peoples of the earth. Blood runs in rivers from the mouth of the beast. It revolts the very earth. She is going to shake and rid herself of the corruption so she will be able to rest in peace. First was the flood. Soon is the time for fire."

"Do you know a guy named Piat?" asked Small.

But the noise as they entered the midway rose with ceaseless flashes of colored lights through which ran children with cotton candy and cries. Ticket booths painted like clowns with barred windows stood beside ramps up which crowds moved into infernal machines of fun. A tinny female voice sang:

'Don't it make your brown eyes,
Don't it make your brown eyes,
Don't it make your brown eyes
Blue — ?'

"Follow me," said Short and started up one of the wooden ramps. *SILVER BULLET* said the sign.

It was a roller coaster. Not the fastest, perhaps second fastest to the Bobs around the park on the far side, and by the time the adventurer reached there he was ready to grit his teeth, fasten his belt in suicidal acceptance of the world as fantasy and step even onto the Bobs. His girlfriend was afraid to go. Let alive off the Bobs he was a hero as they wheeled away, and tales of heroism his to tell on the way to Aladdin's Palace, the fun house, to face each other in warping mirrors, to discover themselves absurd. After such dreams they walked from Funland to stand at bus stops aimed four directions through the Windy City where life was real, tomorrow the same as yesterday, nothing fun, and nothing new but age where death at last came creeping to gobble them alive.

"Hey! It's Wet Man!" cried the Puerto Rican boy who kept the turnstyle through which passengers boarded the Silver Bullet.

"Ah — Gonzales!" said Short, "Will you never go?"

"Hey!" cried Gonzales with laughing liquid eyes passing Small through the turnstyle, "Two wet men!" A group of boys in white coveralls who ran the cars of the roller coaster gathered around Short. A Negro boy, taller than the others, who leaned back when he talked as though exhorting from a podium said, "What you have to know to get wet like you Mr. Short when you come here? I know you ain't ride the boats at the Chutes yet. You ain't been in the tunnel of love or there somethin I don't know, and I know you ain't been in the kiddy pond cause you ain't come that way. Youse the cleanest person I ever see!"

The cars of the roller coaster rumbled into the platform, the first car lurching to a stop before Short. As passengers piled dazed and wobbling out onto the platform and girls squealing hysterically and bending with laughter,

Short bathed the windows of the cars with water from his window brush and squeegeed his way back while new passengers boarded the cars and was standing again beside Small, so distracted by the commotion that he had not moved, and the cars rumbled and clanked away toward the first high hill over which the train would plunge and by the bottom of its dive the windows would all be dried and the train careen on through its curves like a wayward silver bullet.

Short easily hopped over the tracks and boys in white coveralls followed as Small stepped across the rails.

"They ain't payin us no good money, man," a fat big Mexican boy was saying and tapping his fist in his hand.

"There ain't no good money," said Short, "What do you need? A new car I suppose. A diamond for your girlfriend? You want to own your own roller coaster? You think a car tastes better than tortillas and beans? Can you eat a diamond? How will a silver bullet taste? Go to the villages of your ancestors and listen to them. Listen when you're young, talk when you're old. Greed led your fathers here, greed holds you here. There is nothing you need here, none of it is worth having. Take your girlfriends to where the sky is and the sun shines. All of you, you Puerto Ricans, you are slaves in the white man's world. You leave paradise to live like rats in city basements. Go home while you can. The longer you stay the more you pay."

Short put his hand on Small's shoulder and led him to the end of the platform. "When she comes in wet-brush the windows to the middle of the train where I meet you, then squeegee back." Short walked away to the head of the platform where the boys surrounded and hid him in a circle of white coveralls. The train came rolling in, the passengers looking like wilted and windripped flowers. As soon as it stopped Small flooded the windows with his brush moving toward Short who approached easily doing the same. Small set down his bucket beside Short's and they squeegeed away from each other while a new mob filled the cars. Small worked fast and did not finish his squeegee strokes as the Silver Bullet jerked out from under his hand with a new cargo of fun lovers.

"Cheap thrills," Short was saying as Small arrived and picked up his bucket. "That's what you buy with your pay." He leaped the tracks while the boys bobbed down across and up onto the platform after him crowding around. Small could not make out what the excitement was. Small stuck his face among the shoulders of the white coveralls trying to see Short's face. "You heard of Babylon?" Short was saying, "Open your eyes. Where do you think you are? You are captives in a strange land. The slaves of the city are not the sons of the city. Pity the young white faces that come dazed off these trains in their party clothes, they are worse off than you. Pity the children of the master made in his image, a fate you have all escaped. You will never get more than crumbs from the master's table. I know this ship inside out, up and down, I was born in it. Rust holds it together. You live below decks. That's where the slaves are kept, and this ship is going down. Tell your brothers not to come. Nothing that is for sale nurtures you. You are sons of nature, corruption is not of your blood. Find your homes, build lives with dignity and restraint. Never allow your children to know such insanity as this. If your faces are here when I return you'll be far wetter than me. Follow me!" he said turning to Small and they went back down the wooden ramp like a gangplank past the barred window of the ticket booth painted like a clown and into the midway.

"What was all that about?" said Small.

"I'm just a steward," said Short, "I keep everyone informed about the passage."

"What do you mean, the world's going to end?" said Small.

"I mean the ship is sinking," said Short.

Over their heads red white and blue pennants whipped in the wind as they washed the windows of ticket booths down the midway. Short ragged the lens of the camera that snapped funny pictures of people who stuck their heads through the holes in comic cardboard sets. They washed the windows of the red popcorn wagon and cleaned the little windshields of the little boats that the children sat in to ride around the Kiddy Pond. Short had the little children laughing as he polished windshields before their faces and Small was laughing with the children while he worked. Short spun on his toes like an iceskater. He put a rag on his head and polished windshields with his old cap. Children who wore glasses lined up for Short to polish them. Short invited the adults but none would dare. Small was laughing when they left and Short was in good humor. He said, "The world's going to end."

"Let's get a coffee break first," said Small.

They entered the beer garden. Short had a glass of beer and Small had coffee.

"What a view," said Small sipping the coffee, his elbow on the round metal table, lighting up his Lucky, "I could sit here forever." But Short's chair was empty. Small looked out on the midway. For a moment he imagined himself another fun lover come to Funland and thought he might walk out into the flow of people and pick up a doll and take her on the rides for lots of fun. Where had Short gone? To his amazement Small saw Short come strolling down the midway with the crowd. Their eyes met as Short passed Small's table and went strolling on. Small gulped his coffee, grabbed up his bucket and hurried out of the beer garden. He made his way through the crowd and caught up beside Short. "Where you going, Short?" said Small.

"To work," said Short, "The night is coming when man shall work no more. It's a devine right. Don't forget it!"

"I looked up and you weren't there. I thought you went to the can, where were you?" said Small.

"Where were you?" Short echoed.

"At the table drinkin my coffee."

"That's Funland," said Short stopping to stare into the dark canal of the Tunnel of Love.

"We got somethin to do in here?" asked Small.

"If a Chinaman falls in a canal and you pick him out, he's your responsibility for the rest of your life," said Short.

"I'll never do that!" said Small.

"What makes you different from anybody else?" said Short. "Follow me."

ALADDIN'S PALACE, said the big wooden sign. Short knocked on the window of the ticket booth. The lady waved them on.

"What's in here?" said Small hurrying after Short and a blast of air from the floor made Small jump. "How come it didn't do that to you?" said Small hurrying after Short through narrow twisting and darkening passages.

"I float over things you step on," said Short.

"Aw, Short—" said Small,

"AAAWWWRRG!" howled a green beast looming out at Small from a recess lit with eerie light.

"Holy smoke!" said Small, "What do we have to wash in this madhouse?"

"The green beasts will get ya if you don't believe me," said Short.

"If you float how come I don't float?" said Small.

"If I'm old how come you ain't old?" said Short.

"Hey, wait, Short, not so fast, it's dark, I ain't never been in this place."

"Ha!" croaked Short with a whistle.

"Whew!" said Small crowding up to Short's back as they stepped into a cubicle of mirrored walls, "Look at all of us!" Endless reproductions of Small and Short holding their buckets surrounded them.

"Pay attention," demanded Short, "You don't want to step off the end of the world. Follow me," and Small saw Short disappear in four directions at once and stood alone staring at replicas of his own consternation.

"Short? Where are you?"

"I'm right here," said Short appearing innumerably beside Small. "I said follow me," and infinite Smalls were again alone with themselves. Small pushed at a mirror with his hand. It was a wall and did not move. "Keep your hands off the mirrors," said Short, "If ya followed me like I told ya you wouldn't be laggin behind. Do I have to do everything?"

Small was pushing at mirrors with his elbow, "I'm coming," said Small, "Just as soon as I find my way out of here."

"About time," said Short appearing before his face as the last mirror opened into a doorway, "I already got these, follow me," and infinite Shorts disappeared replaced by infinite Smalls. "I told ya I got those," came the disembodied voice. Small reached for the glass he thought was a door. "Hands off!" said Short though those present were only Smalls who said nothing. Small pushed a mirror with his elbow. It was a wall. "Small! I got these half done," called Short, "I want ya to stay ahead of me, not draggin behind admirin my work. Get up here ahead of me and earn your keep."

"Well how am I supposed to—" began Small who caught Short in infinite reflections squeegeeing the last mirror of a new cubicle.

"Don't touch it, it's all done," said all the Shorts putting all their squeegees away in their rear pockets. Short took Small by the shoulders and many Shorts and Smalls guided and were guided through a mirror door, turned and passed into another cubicle of mirrors, were turned and guided into a third. "Set down those buckets," said the Shorts to the Smalls who set their buckets down. "Now see if ya can have 'em done by the time I do the other two. How long you been workin with us?" demanded all the Shorts.

"Ha, ha," said all the Smalls, "Which of us?" But the Shorts disappeared leaving Smalls dipping for their wet rags in their buckets.

Small washed the first mirror and was about to squeegee it when he decided to wash the mirror behind him too. When it was wet he looked in a clear mirror and saw his numberless replicas standing between endless water-falls. Then he washed the third mirror until it was a swirling mass of spiraled water, turned to the one left and saw his one mirror image alone with him in a watery box. "How come you and not the others?" said Small to his reflection.

"You done? I'm comin up on ya," said the voice of Short from somewhere in the watery depths.

"I'm in here with another Small," said Small, "Just one Small beside me, the one I know."

"Get the others," said Short, "Don't dilly dally with a job half done."

"Right, Short," said Small. He watered out the remaining Small. "I'm all alone," said Small.

"Now you're up to zero, start producin."

"Right, Short." Small squeegeed one mirror where his replica emerged stroke for stroke. They smiled at each other. "Now let's liberate the others," said Small to Small. "Right, Small," said Small. They turned and worked side by side bringing out another Small each. "Hi, Small," said Small to Small. Every Small turned to his right and told that Small that he had uncovered another Small. "Are we all here?" said the Smalls to other Smalls. "No!" they answered one and all, "There's more of us!"

"Oh no!" yelled Short from somewhere beyond a universe of Smalls.

"Oh yes!" yelled all the Smalls to the feeble voice of one Short, "There are more of us yet unseen! Let's find them fellows! We're coming!" they yelled to the yet invisible Smalls, and all Smalls stretched busily to bring yet more Smalls into the company, and more appeared, an endless row of Smalls squeegeeing out of oblivion like miners digging out of a cavein until they all stood with smiles of happy greeting before and behind as far as the eye could see. "You see what can be done by a little industry," said all the Smalls turning to the single Small beside him in the watery box, and now they turned their backs and found another endless row of squeegeeing Smalls and at last stood there smiling at each other like brothers, Smalls before and behind, to left and right, a world of Smalls who in their pleasure leaned their palms against the neighboring mirrors and at once were all aghast at their mistake and all the Smalls that even Small could care to see were busily dusting handprints off the glass and standing humbled, even impatient before themselves.

"Hey Short!" yelled Small, his eyes tightly shut, "Show your face, I'm tired of looking at this guy."

A mirror opened slightly and Short's voice said, "I'm here."

Small opened the door wider with his elbow and found himself infinitely in the company of infinite Shorts sitting in the air while he stood foot to foot with himself in space and deep beneath through a crystal world bucket-bearing Smalls stood foot to foot like rumpled stars amid which grinning Shorts sat like cherubs, and looking wonderingly above, his balance effortless as there was nowhere to fall, the same constellation of Smalls and Shorts. "This is how it feels to meet the Angel," said all the floating Shorts, "You walk on air."

Small reached up to touch the nearest Short floating above him. "It's you, Short," said Small.

"Who did you expect?" echoed all of the Shorts.

"Is the Angel lettin you do that, Short?" said all the Smalls.

"You bet," said all the Shorts, "An look at you balancin on your own feet."

"It's mirrors," said all the Smalls.

"Sure," said the floating Shorts, "Nobody's goin to fool a sharp guy like Small," and all the Shorts dropped down and up landing foot to foot before foot to foot right-side-up and up-side-down Smalls. "It's a crystal ball I was sittin on," said a real Short before a real Small, "Hop up on it, you can float like I did." Small set his bucket down on the mirrored floor while infinite Smalls likewise set buckets bottom to bottom through mirrored space.

"Whew!" said all the Smalls balancing erect then reaching up and down for a nearly invisible silver cord boosting themselves with abandon up and down through infinity to sit swaying on crystal balls in a bottomless, topless, sideless world where an army of Shorts waved foot to foot looking on. "Whew!" echoed all the Smalls, "I don't know which is more secure, standin on my own feet or sittin in nothing."

"Six of me, a peck of you," said all the Shorts, "If the Angel's with you you can float on your head."

"Is the Angel around, Short?" asked Small.

"Without a doubt!" affirmed all the Shorts.

"Where? I don't see no Angel," said the Smalls dangling infinitely.

"Ain't time for you to see her," said all the Shorts, "First you feel her in your balance. If you're balanced she's with you, when you're afraid she ain't. Put away the fear she's with ya again."

"I ain't afraid dangling here," vowed Small and all the Smalls with him.

"Pay attention!" commanded all the Shorts and dark doors opened throughout the spacey world of dangling Smalls through which hopped all of the Shorts, the doors closing on a world of Smalls floating alone amid bottom to bottom buckets.

"Whew!" claimed the Smalls clutching their silver cords and upside-down Smalls appearing even more forlorn. "Hey, Short," said all the Smalls, "I'm alone with all these Smalls, I don't know if they can handle it."

"You ain't alone," said the voice of Short, "Don't you hear me?"

"I don't see you," said all the Smalls attempting to look behind themselves.

"Well, obviously I'm here," said the voice of Short. His whistle was heard.

"Where's the Angel?" said the Smalls.

"I told ya!" said the voice of Short, "Am I a parrot, a parrot?"

Small sat erect now on the crystal ball and swung a bit. All of the Smalls swung with him rocking through the infinite world among buckets set bottom to bottom. "I like it better when I can see you too," said Small and all the Smalls with him who now looked at each other and smiled encouragement.

"Mother light a light for me," crooned the old voice of Short.

"But I'm doin all right," said all the Smalls together, "I'm just swingin along."

"Then the Angel's with us," said the voice.

"I hope she stays," said Small looking at the faces of other swinging Smalls. Smalls swung on among swinging Smalls. "Short?" asked all the Smalls. No answer. The Smalls looked at each other, looked away swinging on in nothingness. "It's just that all these Smalls bore me a little," said all the Smalls pretending not to look at one another. Still there was no answer from the voice of Short. "I know you're there even if you ain't talkin. Maybe I ought to help you. You washin mirrors?" No answer. Small reached for the presence of an angel within while he hovered on his crystal ball. "I don't know where balance comes from," said all the Smalls to each other, "But it's there. Why don't you speak, Short, you're there too, you ain't foolin me. But this crystal ball is what's holdin me up, I don't know about no Angel."

"Did you fall down?" came the voice of Short. The faces of all the Smalls lit with pleasure. Doors opened through the universe of swinging Smalls and through them hopped the Shorts.

"Right, Small," said all the Shorts, "Can't fool a smart guy like Small. Come down off that thing." Small and all the Smalls dropping down and leaping up before the Shorts who spun on a toe. "Get your buckets, follow us!" mirrored doors opening, Shorts waving at Shorts and Smalls, and Shorts waving back echoing, "See you later, fellas!"

"Wait!" wailed Smalls in tiny lamentation, clutching up their buckets, watching the Shorts float out the doors of their world, clambering heavy-footed after.

Immensely relieved, Small found himself up behind the gray coveralls of a single Short walking briskly down a ramp to the midway.

"Now we'll prop you up with a cup of coffee," said Short, "The Angel is somethin else."

Small was free to walk the windows of the skyscrapers without hooking his belt to the bolts. He walked the high ledges like a captain on his bridge imagining the tugs on the river moved at his behest and ships from the docks sped on personal errands. He cut the water with the squeegee blade and fanned the larger windows. Small wondered if he had learned all the old man had to teach him.

In the midst of such days when Small felt his power, he had a dream.

Green needles dripping rain, trees and rocks were his habitat. The immensity of Asia filled bones and blood. He was neither young nor old. Fogs of morning moved upon the canal that ran before the Manchurian Palace and he came down to the canal and pushed out in the small red boat to drift at the pleasure of his fate. He gazed into the water where the orange heads of carp rose to its surface as clear through the water as the bow of his boat in the air, puckering their lips to see him, floating placidly on in their wisdom. There was a commotion in the waters or heavens. A creature was flailing the waters not knowing to sink or soar. A man in the water. Naturally he reached out, pulling the long body aboard. It rocked his boat, there was no end to him, surely a royal Chinese courier come to grief who spoke in high Mandarin with the water running off his face, "May you live in an interesting age," said the survivor.

Short announced that he was going to Florida for the winter. "I might find the fountain of youth," he said, "I'm feeling the chill in my old bones. It's time you went on your own, Small. Pay attention. I fear you have plans?"

"Now that you mention it," said Small, "I do. I'm thinkin of this advertisin campaign with matchbooks to overwhelm the moguls of the city for their window washing contracts—I could undercut the prices of any union window company—Their greed will put em in the palm of my hand. From there it's only a step to the aldermen, to city contracts, to city hall."

Short yawned.

Small was not motivated to move until the defenses of time were cut to ribbons around him. When there was no gas to heat his morning coffee water he put on his corduroy cap and sportscoat and took his green attache case in hand. The lights were out, the telephone was disconnected, and he was behind in the rent.

But they couldn't keep a good man down. He enjoyed dueling with them. He enjoyed going downtown to the gas company, swinging through the revolving doors, skating across the marble floors of the cathedral of commerce, poking the elevator button and stepping into that spaceship of piped music and the lights in rows popping off and on: Alexander Small in disguise: in appearance a normal taxpaying citizen; under his corduroy cap tipped over one eye, under the rigid grooves of enduring corduroy disguising him in the perpendicular lines of buildings, halls, elevator shafts, streets, alleys, telephone lines, and the minds of his fellow citizens so that none could tell here was a madman who did not want a job, a subversive impostor.

"Mr. Spotneat," intoned Small somberly, his cap against his chest, his hair brushed hastily back before entering the august presence, seated in the soft leather chair that faced the huge desk with the shiny glass on its surface— Small enjoying the lush nap of carpet underfoot, the luxury of the leather armchair in which he sensed he belonged, suffering little remorse that his highness Spotneat paid for it with bags beneath desperate eyes, while he, the delinquent Small, enjoyed himself so thoroughly—"Mr. Spotneat, I am Alexander Small." Small hesitated, allowing this mystery to impress itself upon Mr. Spotneat.

"I am pleased to meet you, Mr. Small—" appearing yet more harried with Small his curse or salvation. Small crossed his foot upon his knee.

"May I smoke, Mr. Spotneat?"

"Please do, Mr. Small!" with a shaking hand sliding an ashtray that looked like a priceless Egyptian antique across the glass desktop. Small lit a Lucky. With a glass of ruby port he could sit here all day observing the mayhem.

"Uhhh — Mr...?"

"Small," allowed Small.

"Yes, ah — Mr. Small? Of what service might I be to you today?"

"A beautiful day!" said Small, "Not so cold as it's been. Could it be the Indian summer we didn't get? I suppose not, we'll be buried up to our necks tomorrow — "

"But sir, it is summer," advised Mr. Spotneat.

"Summer!" exclaimed Small, "By God, so it is! Where does time go? I've been working myself blind! Yet pity the poor with no gas heat frozen dead in their beds. Well, this morning I strolled down the Boulevard, all the pretty girls with roses in their cheeks, had my morning coffee at the Bug an Germ. You ever stop in there Mr...?"

"Spotneat, sir..."

"Yes, Mr. Spotneat. Well, I enjoy not rushing in the morning. I'm convinced it's bad for a man. I *know* it is, your bones wailing Lay me down, lay me down, damn the clock! Don't you agree? And God knows we have problems enough just surviving in a declining age like this. May you live in an interesting age. Do you know what that means? That, Mr. Spotneat, is a Chinese curse. Ha! Well some Chinaman must have been cursing us, huh? Did you ever read *The Decline of the West?*"

"No — Yes, it is not easy these days," said Mr. Spotneat with a grieved look. "Sir — Mr. Small — may I be of some assistance? Time — " he wavered, "Time marches on — "

"Ah — " chuckled Small, "You said it! Right over our skulls. I see you are a student of history besides being a man of business, Mr. Spotneat. Troublesome business — Mr. Spotneat, sir, I have a troublesome little overdue bill here for the gas in my little apartment which is also my office."

"Ah! May I see that sir?"

"Yes, please look at it Mr. Spotneat, sir." Looking at the bill through his bifocals Mr. Spotneat appeared to regain life.

"Yes — you see — Mr. Small, you are in arrears — "

"That's exactly where it hurts, Mr. Spotneat, ha, ha—" He leaned forward through Spotneat's vacant stare and assumed a serious face, "Yes, arrears, sir. And I propose to you that I put down ten dollars on that bill immediately! This very morning. Cash! I would be extremely grateful to you personally, Mr. Spotneat, if we might put the remainder off until the next billing period. Mr. Spotneat, sir, I rarely see the light of day, I am working so hard at present, job after job, and you understand that the better establishments that I do my services for withhold checks until the following pay periods — nipping an extra month's dividends on their assets before paying up—ha, ha, sly devils—and I cannot hurry such esteemed customers, you understand, I am sure, being a man of business, sir." Small's cap now rested in his lap as he sat erect in the good leather chair beaming sincerity upon Mr. Spotneat. "I am trying as hard as I can, you know sir, and it is not easy these days getting a business off the ground—I am president of Complicated Maintenance of course—Perhaps our reputation for quality work has reached your attentive ears?—No?— though you give the best service and right from the heart. Because I know, sir, that is the way to survive. To treat your customers like the loving human beings they are!" Mr. Spotneat looked at Small as at a Chinese puzzle. "And I want you to know personally that my intention is to pay this bill first thing on the next billing period."

"Of course, of course—" said Mr. Spotneat, scribbling his initials onto the bill. "Just take this to Miss Bibbs at the second window. She will defer payment."

"A pleasure to do business with a man of your stature, sir." Small rose and bent across the desk to shake Mr. Spotneat's hand. "I hope we can meet again soon to have another pleasant chat." Mr. Spotneat showed his teeth.

In the subterranean Grayhound bus terminal Small returned to the cafeteria line for a refill. The fat lady at the cash register smiled because he had told her to keep the change. Small returned to his strategic window table beyond which the travelers milled, dumped sugar into his coffee and pondered success dead ahead.

That redheaded giant appeared to be swimming closer, table by table.

Small blinked. Where had he seen this before?

Small lit up a Lucky, rested his elbows on the table and studied the strange creature from a wary, self-contained repose.

The giant's hands were trembling. Suddenly he jerked himself to his feet, tucked his book under his arm and reentered the food line. He passed between the shiny rails and reemerged out among the tables without anything. He spun in a complete circle, flapped his arms and headed straight at Small who looked up in alarm. "Pardon me —!" he croaked.

"What's your problem!" demanded Small, "I'm self-employed. I got my own business. Whatever you're sellin I don't need it. No insurance, pens, cardboard flowers!" Small dragged furiously on his cigarette. "If you're one of them religious nuts I don't wanna hear it. Here's a quarter, get yourself a cup of coffee!"

"I've got my own money, sir."

"What do you want then?"

"Sir, I am looking for honest work. My name is Talldorf — Rudolf Victor Talldorf." He extended his hand.

"No foolin — Small's the name."

Talldorf's limp fingers were in a hairy iron fist.

Part Two

THE CHINAMAN

178 TALLWORLD AND SMALL

Chapter 5

THE LADDER

Rudolph Victor Talldorf followed Small up the escalator rising above the throng of strange travelers.

Rudolph felt light-headed, useful and relieved of all responsibility. He carried Small's green attache case happily and his suitcase knocked against his knees. Small had handed the attache case to Talldorf, "You work for me, Talldorf. I wanta make sure you got it straight." He followed Small through an arcade of shops and out the tall glass doors into the noisy glare of morning traffic hurrying to keep up with Small's quick pace. Rudolph was grateful, an idiotic grin flickered beneath his sunglasses and flaming red hair as Small bore back the tide.

Small paused in a backwater in front of a hotel with carpeted steps and ornate lobby and flipped out a Lucky.

"This ain't where I live, Talldorf. This is the Emerald Isle Hotel. The bars and restaurants of the Emerald Isle is where big city politicians hang out. A smart business man can buy the right guy lunch and sign a big contract." Talldorf watched the doorman hold the door of a cab for a pretty woman who handed him a bill. Chauffeurs in black hats and sunglasses loafed behind the wheels of black limousines and the cab line went around the block. Small plunged into the human flood which spilled them out beneath sheer dark walls, tall brass doors and black iron bars of the financial district.

"That's my bank, Talldorf. We got assets over a billion dollars. That's my car." Small pointed to a battered blue Buick with ladders tied to the roof parked in front of a fire hydrant. "Get in, Talldorf." The door didn't work. Small kicked it open from inside. Rudolph squeezed in with his suitcase, his knees against the cluttered dashboard. Small balled up the yellow paper and tossed it into one of the galvanized garbage cans in the back seat. Small frowned, "I hope you ain't gonna bring me bad luck, Talldorf." The engine coughed alive and died. "I'm immune to tickets." Small jerked his thumb at the roof. "Ladders are proof. The cops lay off. I never get a ticket. C'mon, Bluey, start up!" The Buick roared to life and Small wheeled her into traffic.

"I'll take you right down the Boulevard. We Windy Citiers call it the Monstrous Mile. I got big plans for me and the Windy City. Dust and filth, there's a fortune in dirt. You gotta start at the bottom. That's where I been. Lately I been sticking to eye-level dirt. See that skyscraper? Gumm Tower. Very dingly. I'll change all that." Rudolph stared up at the soaring white column against the summer sky. Small appraised the white spire leaning out his window oblivious to flashing fenders and honking horns. "I'm gonna wash every inch of Gumm Tower, Talldorf. I'll cover it with a spider web of ropes. A. Small is going to the top in this town!" Rudolph felt an impulse to cheer but Small swerved into the center lane and floored it through a yellow light leaving the pack behind. "Those awnings with the red and white stripes. My awnings. I clean em. I do quality work, Talldorf, and I demand the same from my employees."

"I'll do my very best, Small. I can learn, can't I?"

"You askin me?"

"Yes."

Small glanced misgivings at the pale face behind the sunglasses. They arrived in an alley faced with the backs of unpainted coachhouses. Small parked beside a board fence. "Get out on my side, Talldorf. Follow me." Rudolph followed through a gate and up a flight of wooden stairs into the kitchen: heaped ashtrays, coffee cups, a red telephone and a black telephone, a litter of papers, pencils and books. The sink was filled with dirty dishes and cobwebs hung from the ceiling. Between two filthy windows stood a dingy refrigerator. The windows were open and the room was cool.

"Small himself here, baby," said Small into the red telephone. "Any calls for Complicated Maintenance? Nothing, eh? I'll keep in touch." He hung up.

"You bunk in the Executioner's room, Talldorf. I ain't got time to clean it out. I'm a busy man. Maybe you wanta wash up."

"Thank you, Small. I brought my own towel so I won't have to dirty one of yours. I can't wait to take a hot shower."

"No shower. Bathtub. And I only got one towel. I only need one towel. Ya hungry, there's bread and peanut butter. I'll be back. Rest up. We work at two a.m. sharp."

Rudolph took from his suitcase a Turkish towel, his robe and slippers, a plastic soapdish and a toothbrush. He undressed in the gloom of dust-laden Louis Quinze curtains which hid the living room windows. The bathroom was small. The apex of the slanted bathroom ceiling over the sink was the only place where he could stand up straight. The sink was clogged with iron filings scraped from Small's jaws. A bedraggled toothbrush lay in a rusty puddle behind a faucet. While the tub filled Rudolph inspected Small's small house. Small's bedroom was the size of a big closet. Small's bed was small and beside it lay a large pile of dirty clothes. Rudolph returned to the kitchen and examined Small's papers covered with small, unintelligible figures. The refrigerator's small freezer unit was a block of solid ice; a solitary tomato moldered on a shelf. Through the keyhole of the locked yellow door Rudolph spied an odd collection of junk: cables, coils of electrical wire, boxes and automobile batteries.

Rudolph soaked in the small tub. "I'm your friend," he said to the cockroaches that regarded him from the walls. He felt fortunate to have found an employer. Invigorated by his bath and enthusiastic he dressed in clean clothes and went out for a brisk walk around the neighborhood.

Women gossiping on the stoops and ragged children playing in the dirt stopped to watch Rudolph stride along the cracked walks. This was the Windy City, and Rudolph Victor Talldorf was now a part of it all. *FUCK YOU,* said the painted message on the brick wall: *IMPERIAL SAINTS; GOLDEN COONS; COPS SUCK.* In the laundromat Negro women leaned against the washers. Rudolph's nose led him around a corner to a butcher shop where three white-smocked butchers swung cleavers above big chopping blocks. He bought T-bone steaks, bacon, eggs, a gallon of milk, a bottle of red table wine, a jar of pickles and five pounds of hamburger.

"Talldorf!"

"How do you like it, Small?"

"My desk —! Where are my important papers?!"

"I was very careful with your papers. I put your papers in a neat pile."

"Where, Talldorf!"

"Look here, Small." Rudolph held open the refrigerator door. "I bought enough food to last us days." The inside of the refrigerator sparkled. "Dandy," scowled Small. Even Elvira had never defrosted the refrigerator.

"And look at the bathroom, Small." Sink and tub were spic and span. Two toothbrushes hung side by side beside a clean glass. "You're good at housework, Talldorf. I hope you're good at work work. But don't be gettin ideas about livin in my house. My house is just big enough for Small. What's on fire?"

Talldorf leaped to the oven door. "Just in time. Dinner is served, Small. I hope you like steak and baked potatoes and French green beans. You don't like your steak rare, Small. I'm a pretty good judge of character. You, Small, are the kind of man a person can rely on. From that fact I drew the conclusion that you like your meat welldone."

"You burn good steak an ya talk like a professor in a psychology class. Ya think too much but ya never think that this is Small's kitchen, that this is Small's desk and this is Small's small house. I want my important papers. That plate you're about ta eat off of is from my marriage." Talldorf was already eating.

"The wine — I almost forgot." Talldorf jumped up and poured the wine.

"Them wine glasses are from my marriage, Talldorf. And the fact is, I like my meat rare. I like the blood oozing. But I'm gonna eat the steak anyway."

Talldorf teetered sleepily at the sink washing the dishes while Small busily littered the table anew with his important papers. The yellow door of the Executioner's room was open. Talldorf would sleep on the Executioner's work bench. "It's a great bed, Small. I won't have to curl my legs hardly at all." Rudolph was anxious to lay down on that grotesque sheet of plywood nailed to the walls. "I'm so pleased to be here, Small." Rudolph stretched his arms feeling at home. Talldorf's wing span rendered Small's formerly roomy kitchen small. Talldorf's red hair was too bright. Talldorf's pale face glowed like the moon. And worst of all the giant had collapsed into Small's chair.

"Up, Talldorf! That's my chair. Other side of the desk." Small pointed and Talldorf sank into the low armchair. Small however did not take his seat, but locked his hands behind his back and paced the linoleum.

"The Slippery Tongue awning!" announced Small. "That is our objective. I will clean the Slippery Tongue. You will assist me, Talldorf. To you it's just a job. To me it is a stepping stone." Rudolph was impressed.

"To what?" he asked.

Small chuckled and his eyes rolled as though he pondered mysteries. "It is now four hours to zero, Talldorf."

Small awoke with the startling memory of Talldorf's occupancy at the opposite end of his small quarters. He padded barefoot into the dark. Talldorf must have turned out the bathroom light. Small cracked his shin against the armchair.

"Get up!" he yelled. "It's time for work!" Small pounded on the yellow door. "Get up!" He opened the door and switched on the bare bulb. Talldorf stumbled out of the Executioner's room in red striped pajamas like a barber pole. "When you get out of the costume there's coffee. How many eggs, one or two?"

"Two'" managed Rudolph. Small peeled off two strips of bacon. He could eat them both himself. In a gesture of largess he threw two more into the skillet. Talldorf was a big guy, he'd need energy, and God knew where the homeless giant would wander after the job. It's a traveler's world, Small mused. Talldorf slumped into the armchair with his shoes in his hands. His cheeks were rosy but he didn't look like he could talk. "Have a rough night in the wars of the dark?" asked Small and chuckled as he turned the bacon in the skillet.

"It's dark outside," Talldorf observed.

"My business is conducted at odd hours," said Small. "It's an odd business. Here's your eggs. Eat fast. Leave two of the bacons for me. You got to pack your junk and don't forget your toothbrush." They came down the steep flight of wooden steps and out the door into the small courtyard. It was pitch black. "Follow me," commanded Small.

"Where?" inquired Rudolph. An iron claw grasped his jacket and pulled him through the dark. "Bend over," whispered Small, "feel the ladder. It's leaning against the wall. I'm going to the other end of the ladder and we're going to carry it to the car. This baby stretches to the stars, Talldorf. It cost me eight bucks at Jake's Rental. And be quiet. We don't want to wake Miss Deerly's dogs." The 45-foot wooden ladder felt like a redwood tree. "Why are you holding it so high, Talldorf?" hissed Small.

"I'm just holding it, Small," hissed Talldorf.

Small rested the ladder on his shoulder. Talldorf was obliged to walk sideways dragging his suitcase behind while the ladder pulled him on. "It's slipping, Small—"

A jarring crash hammered Small's teeth together and drove him to his knees. "Dammit, Talldorf!" The gangway filled with the screech and yowl of Miss Deerly's dogs and yellow light flooded a window above Small's head. The window rattled: "I'll get it high enough to get the barrel out—!"

"Now, Al!" cried the voice of old Miss Deerly.

"Al! don't shoot! It's me, Small!"

"Smally?" called Miss Deerly. "You out workin so late, deary?"

"Get a daytime job before you get yourself killed!" yelled Al.

"Shutup!" Miss Deerly yelled at the mad dogs.

"Pick up this ladder, Talldorf!" They labored onto the sidewalk into the dim light of a street lamp. "Slow it down, Talldorf. You're gonna ram me into the side of a car." Small would not let Talldorf help tie the ladder to the roof of Bluey. "It takes talent to tie these babies so they stay." Small drove into the alley and parked beside the gate. "Stand here, Talldorf. Don't move. I'll throw out the hose. Fill up the garbage cans in the back seat." Small went up the stairs, uncoiled the green hose connected to the hot water heater and dropped it out the window. A cry rose from the darkness.

"You ok, Talldorf?"

"I think so."

"Excellent. When one can is three fourths full fill the other one." Small turned on the hot water, poured himself a fresh cup of coffee, sat in the armchair and lit a Lucky. If I could get this dummy trained, thought Small, I'd have more time for brain work. Rudolph awoke with a start. The hot water was running onto the back seat. He stuck the hose into the other can and began bailing with a coffee cup. "Ain't they full?" yelled Small.

"Yes, they're full, Small." The hose leaped from Rudolph's hands and snaked up the wall through the window.

"I spilled a little water on the back seat," said Rudolph when Small was behind the wheel.

"No problem. I always spill a little. Probably rusting out the floor. Hang in there, baby." Small patted the dashboard. As they swung out of the alley a great slop of water leaped the seat onto Talldorf. "Holy Toledo!"

"A little water never hurt nobody, Talldorf. Normally I'd stop for coffee at one of the many interesting Windy City coffee shops but you been stumbling around so much we gotta get to the job."

Bluey sped down empty Clark Street past the park and swerved onto empty Wells Street where globes of street lamps filed away to a point. "There she is, Talldorf, the Slippery Tongue." The three-story red awning glowed dully above the saplings. Rudolph was astonished to see that the awning was actually shaped like a tongue splayed out above the sidewalk.

"Talldorf! You flooded my car. Can't you hit a garbage can with a hose?" Small dumped great doses from bottles and boxes into the steaming buckets he dipped from the garbage cans. Small walked the perimeter of the huge tongue surveying its rise like a rocket on a launching pad. Rudolph craned his neck up at the awning then looked at Small wondering what the master craftsman might be contemplating.

"Grab the end of the ladder!" It might have been the captain's voice cracking from the helm. "I got the foot. Swing your end around." Talldorf crossed the street, stumbled over the curb and backed the ladder into a doorway. "Follow me, and don't ram me into the wall."

"I never carried a big ladder before," shouted Talldorf.

"Imagine that!" shouted Small. "Back it up, I gotta put this end against the tree. Ok! Walk it to me rung by rung so it's standin straight up." The ladder rose slowly, even majestically above the walk.

"It's heavy," groaned Talldorf.

"Damn right," Small grunted pulling on the rungs from the opposite side. "Straight, Talldorf! Don't let it fall!" Small strained to balance the ladder upright amazed at its height towering above them. "Don't manhandle it, Talldorf! I'm balancing it! If it falls it'll wipe out this end of town. Everything's ok!" Rudolph peered questioningly through the rungs. "Don't laugh, Talldorf. Ya get a hernia if ya laugh when you're workin. We got to walk it to the wall. Don't move it— I'll move it. Just keep it straight up. Here we go. Walk, baby, walk... Don't push against me, Talldorf! Hold it. Ease it down—" The ladder crashed against the wall beside the red canvas.

"Good work, Talldorf. How we get it down is another problem. I'll take care of it. Set up the step ladders and walkboard under the lip of the awning."

Small climbed onto the walkboard. "Climb up, Talldorf." Rudolph climbed awkwardly. "You never climbed a ladder either? Were you raised in a glass bowl, Talldorf?"

"Yes, kind of, I was." Rudolph crouched and held to the awning.

"Stand up, Talldorf! You're a grown man." Rudolph balanced precariously on the springy walkboard while Small flooded the bottom of the awning with a mop. "Ok, Talldorf, do what I been doin." Sudzy water from the mop flooded Talldorf's shoes. "On the awning, Talldorf." Rudolph mopped jerkily, nervously glancing at the sidewalk.

Small hooked a bucket over his arm and climbed a third of the way up the big ladder. "Watch, Talldorf, this is what you do next." Small tied the bucket to a rung, leaned out and began mopping. "You'll be able to reach all the way across." Small bounced down to the sidewalk and lit up a Lucky. His work was done. The rest belonged to Talldorf. They could knock it out in two hours. "Up you go, Talldorf."

Rudolph peered up the narrowing ladder. "Up, up, Talldorf. I ain't payin you to stand and stare." Rudolph tested the steadyness of the ladder, stepped briskly up four rungs and stopped. "Up," yapped Small. Talldorf climbed slowly three more rungs.

"Small, I can't move."

"How the hell can you clean the awning if you can't move?"

"My hands don't work." A pathetic whimpering sound reached Small's ears. "Relax!" Small demanded. "You're tight, that's all that's wrong with you. Relax just like you was standin on a sidewalk."

I'm not on a sidewalk —"

"Come down here immediately, Talldorf!" Rudolph descended in a manner painful for Small to witness.

"Small, I'm terribly sorry. Everything is different up there. I thought I'd had a stroke."

"Nothing is different up there! That's your mistake. Your ineptitude is wasting half the night. Now watch me and watch good because you're goin back there or you get nothin for this job!" Small sped up the ladder and untied the bucket. "I tied the simplest knot known to man. What more can I do for you?" Small grew smaller up the ladder. "I tie the bucket! I hook my leg through the rungs. I mop!" A great slosh of water cascaded down the awning showering Talldorf who watched Small lean sickening out above him. Small mopped high and low. A story of red awning rose yet above his head. Small tripped down the rungs.

"Now we heist it Talldorf. We run this beauty up all 45 feet." Small jerked at the ladder with great force and raised it two rungs before the ladder fell back to the wall. Rudolph grasped eagerly and pulled. "Talldorf, please. Pull when I pull." Small raised the ladder climbing ever higher. "What a view!" yelled Small. "Now you got a better shot at the awning cause the angle puts you way out over it. You can reach the whole thing here." Small returned to the sidewalk. "Ok, hit the boards."

Rudolph began a deathlike tread up the rungs. He went on so steadily that Small felt a thrill he might inspire such devotion to duty. Rudolph climbed in hopeless reckless daring, the inheritance of weightless mornings when a world swung below, looking up at the swinging bucket, advancing rung by rung. "Untie the bucket. Take it up!"

"Untie the bucket," echoed Rudolph. He jerked on the rope and the bucket plummeted so alarmingly he grasped the ladder in a bear hug sliding down with a sickening sense of loss. Small stepped back instinctively but at the last moment reached out to break Talldorf's slide and could not escape as Talldorf fell back on him and they rolled across the sidewalk.

"You're fired!" Small shouted from the gutter. "If you're hurt we ain't got insurance. I might sue you myself." Arising, Small shook the ladder which stood firm. "What a ladder," he said with admiration. "Heavy as lead, springy as rubber and it goes to the stars!" Small retrieved the empty bucket. "He almost broke the bottom out of you, old bucket." Small dipped it into a garbage can.

"I could mop the awning up a little way —" Rudolph suggested. He fretted in the silence that followed. The night was a blank unfriendly wall. He had been fired. Should he take his suitcase and start walking? Perhaps Small was so outraged he wouldn't tell him how to get back to the bus depot. Small climbed a few rungs and paused. "Move the stepladders and the walkboard to the other side. Work from the walkboard."

"I will! I will!"

Small looked at him curiously and continued up the ladder. Vigorously Rudolph scrubbed the soiled red canvas. Grime peeled off like onion skin to reveal the bright mucosa of the Slippery Tongue. "Ok, Talldorf, don't wear a hole in it. Fill the buckets with clean water." Small paced the sidewalk. Rudolph thought he noted a mollified light in Small's eyes.

"Now we rinse the awning." Water and suds sluiced off the awning and they finished as the sun rose. "A beauty!" exclaimed Small. The Slippery Tongue pulsed in the light.

Small climbed the ladder and lowered the extension. "Get under the ladder, Talldorf, and take hold. I'll ease the bottom out and we'll slide her down the wall." The weight bore down on him but Rudolph hung on in a desperate effort to prove his loyalty, until his arms buckled and were pasted to his sides as the rungs passed before and behind him and the great ladder slammed the concrete. "I never seen that before, Talldorf. Why weren't you killed?" Small walked the length of the ladder shaking his head and nudging the ladder with his toe. "Fortunately the ladder is all right so you won't have to buy a new one."

Small tied his nimble mysterious knots on top of the car. "Oh- oh—" said Talldorf.

"What's wrong now?"

"The front tire is going flat, Small."

"I knew it! The ladder's too heavy for these baldy sours. An no spare."

"Oh — oh —"

"Stop the oh-ohs, Taldorf!"

"All the tires are going flat, Small."

"Damn!" Small leaped to the pavement and kicked the rear fender.

"Use my pay to fix the tires, Small. If I have any pay coming. I haven't been much help. I could have hurt you. I'll probably kill myself in a week or so. God, if I'd become a doctor do you know how many people I would have killed before they stopped me? I should crawl away into a manhole so I can't hurt anybody." Talldorf's head drooped mournfully.

"I can't pay ya till the owner gets in, Talldorf. Let's go have coffee."

Small stared thoughtfully out the plate glass window smoking his Lucky. "I'll buy your breakfast, Small,"

"I had breakfast."

"I'll buy your lunch."

"It ain't lunch time."

"A slice of pie —"

"Nothin, Talldorf." Talldorf went through the line while Small mumbled: "Hire an employee, work twice as hard."

Rudolph neatly transferred large quantities of food from plate to mouth while Small juggled figures in his notebook. If Small would only give him a chance to learn. Rudolph wiped up the last bite of egg with his whole wheat toast.

"I just figured it out," said Small. "I gotta buy four used tires, I'm supposed to pay you ten bucks, rent is due, I'm thirty-five in the hole. I spent my last dime on this cup of coffee. I'm not worried. In fact I got an idea. I been kinda hard-nosed with ya, Talldorf, but what would you say to a little loan?"

"Red always said never loan money to a friend. Red said it will ruin the friendship. Shakespeare said so too. A friend won't pay you back. A friend will take all you have and ask for more." Small scowled.

"We ain't friends, Talldorf. I'm your boss."

"I'd like to consider you my friend, Small. You pulled me out of the doldrums. You gave me work. I feel indebted to you for life itself."

"In that case I got another idea. You wanta learn the business, right? You're unskilled. You pay me and I train you. As my apprentice you live in my house and eat my food and work with me on my jobs. I'll teach ya how to climb ladders, do handstands on window sills and ride the clouds."

"How much?"

"How much you got?"

Rudolph opened his wallet and counted the bills. "Seventy-six dollars, Small."

"That'll cover the first month, Talldorf." Small scooped the money off the table. "You know as an apprentice you don't make no salary."

"I suppose not."

"And it still sounds good to you?"

"When do we start?"

"After I get a refill. Here's a ten-spot for your personal expenses for the month." Small folded the bills into a wad and stuffed them into his shirt pocket. "Welcome aboard, Talldorf. You're workin for me permanent."

CHAPTER 6

THE BOSS

"**I** n here," said Small. Talldorf followed out of the chill night into a bright bakery toward glass cases filled with donuts and sweetrolls in the pungent odor of coffee. The bakery aroma made Talldorf ravenous. He hung over Small's shoulder gazing at the pastries. "I think I'll have coffee instead of milk, Small, and — "

"Great," agreed Small. "It's cheaper. Give me one chocolate donut," he said to the counterlady, "and a cup of coffee. Give this guy what he wants." Small walked toward the steamy windows and sat at a smooth-topped table.

Talldorf had ordered not one sweetroll but two. They were immense and bristled with chopped nuts and raisins. Small scowled and took a transfusion of coffee. "You said I could get what I wanted," shrugged Rudolph.

"In the future get what you need. A growing company has to watch expenditures. Maybe it's good you got two sweetrolls cause I want some work out of you this morning. Ensardo is mafia and we're going to be working right under his nose and be done and rid of him before he knows we're there. Then I pay the phone bill, sweep up odds and ends and go for Gumm Tower. When I got Gumm Tower I got any job in the Windy City. I don't split with politicians because Small calls the shots. You begin to see, perhaps Talldorf, how a job is not simply a job in my business but a stepping stone to higher things."

Talldorf had devoured his first sweetroll with a delirious look and was brushing crumbs off his fingers. He tore off a large section of his second and chewed. In Small's steady gaze Talldorf appeared in the advance stages of a nervous disease. "How come you left home?"

"My mind was being destroyed."

"Did you say you was in the hospital?"

"I worked in a hospital. I was studying to be a doctor."

"You should have studied how to relax. You know what a tightrope walker is? A tightrope walker is any old common person who is afraid of nothing. So he's relaxed. He could stand on the head of a pin. You can't even sit still in your chair." Talldorf felt calmed by Small's words. He was wide awake from the coffee. "Those are the kinds of things I'm anxious to know," he said looking at Small's chocolate donut. "I'm sure I'll be of use on the ladders real soon, Small. I'm getting my bearings inside my head."

When Small peered out the steamy window to make sure no thief was stealing his ladders Talldorf took Small's chocolate donut and put it into his mouth.

"When we get to Ensardo's don't speak a word. Don't do anything unless I tell you to do it. Two things: relax, and stay awake." Small tapped his saucer, glanced down at the tiles of the floor and lit another Lucky. "I ain't sayin I'm perfect," said Small exploring his poor teeth with his tongue for donut crumbs. "Sometimes I ain't aware of what I do myself. But in our work it pays to be awake."

Small wheeled Bluey off the deserted Boulevard and drove slowly past Ensardo's surveying the darkened front of the two-story brick building, made a U-turn and pulled up before the long snaky sign. Small held his finger to his lips. "Radio silence. Set the ladders and walkboard under the sign. Quietly."

"Right, boss."

"Shhhhhh."

Small was having no difficulty with the extension when Rudolph hurried over thrusting the ladder up with such force the top banged loudly on the wall. A window flew up and the cheerful face of Mr. Ensardo appeared. "Good morning, Mr. Small." His white hair was neatly combed, his cheeks rosy, he wore his dinner jacket.

"Don't you ever sleep?" asked Small.

"I wasn't going to disturb you, Mr. Ensardo, but I got a nincompoop for a helper. Talldorf, meet Mr. Ensardo."

"I'm pleased to meet you young man."

"Go shake Mr. Ensardo's hand, I'll sit in the car while everybody gets acquainted."

"Delighted!" called Mr. Ensardo.

"Up!" commanded Small. Rudolph mounted the ladder. "Come, young man," Mr. Ensardo called. Rudolph began to climb. He tried to relax but as he passed above the awning his body stiffened, his heart pounded, his steps flagged. "Up!" shouted Small. Mr. Ensardo was smiling not far away like a kindly encouraging father. I'm doing it! thought Rudolph. He reached out for the old man's extended hand and saw the cement far below. "Hold me!" yelled Rudolph grasping the hand. "Release me!" cried Mr. Ensardo bulging at the window.

"Talldorf! Let go of Mr. Ensardo!" Small struggled to keep the ladder from falling. "Get down here, Talldorf!" Rudolf inched down the ladder. "Go stand by the wall and don't touch anything!" Talldorf walked to the wall and stood staring at Small.

"Quite a nervous young man, Mr. Small," said Mr. Ensardo smoothing his lapels. "I'm pleased to meet your entire crew."

The Ensardo job was jinxed from the start. Each time Small arrived before dawn. Each time Mr. Ensardo appeared at the window as if waiting for him. Each time he requested additional services and Small postponed the job. Now Mr. Ensardo wanted the metal legs of the awning polished.

"Twenty dollars," said Small. "That makes the total job $145. Let's call it $150 so we don't forget. I can't possibly do it tonight. I'm upset. I can't consider working tonight."

"When shall we do it?"

"I will do the entire job one week from tonight."

"Excellent," agreed Mr. Ensardo. "Now you can have a round of golf yet this morning."

"I told you I don't play golf, Mr. Ensardo."

"Two weeks from tomorrow, Mr. Small. One hundred and fifty dollars. I admire your decisiveness. Good morning to you and to your lieutenant."

"You lost the job," said Small in the car. "I got nothin else lined up. I don't know what you do puttering around my place all day but I know what I do, Talldorf. I hit the streets, I poke my head into every store and office, I run up and down flights of stairs and drive all over town, I yes-no on the telephone, I work, Talldorf!"

Talldorf was snug as a mouse in Small's small house. He had constructed a clothes line from piano wire in the Executioner's room. The cluttered apartment became clean and Spartan, an improvement Small noted with approval and pride. Talldorf shopped for groceries and took Small's large pile of dirty laundry to the laundromat. In the evenings when Small arrived dog-tired Rudolph filled Small's cup and set supper dishes under his nose and the odors of hot food rekindled the light in Small's eyes.

"Have you ever read the novels of Lewellyn Fairchild?" asked Rudolph after supper as Small sat at his desk plotting with important papers. "Fairchild died young. He committed suicide."

"I know you think a man ain't civilized till he's read every dead author, Talldorf, but I ain't got time. You got time. I'm trying to build a business. I'm tired. My eyes don't even shut when I'm asleep. When the alarm clock rings I start workin again."

The honeyed sun carved gold bars on the scarred linoleum as Talldorf dried the breakfast dishes. Small's forehead ridged with mentation, his head was bowed and hands folded as he focused energy on the red telephone. Neither ever rang. Not a salesman, bill collector, enemy or friend. Not even a wrong number. The black telephone rang.

"Good morning! Complicated Maintenance."

"Is this A. Small?"

"In person!"

"This is the Downtown Library to ask if you will recommend Rudolph Victor Talldorf as a card holder, Mr. Small?"

"Yes I will."

"Thank you, Mr. Small."

"You're welcome." Small hung up. "It was the library. I okayed your card."

"Thanks, Small."

"Think nothin of it."

Small bumped the bumper of the car in front and banged the bumper of the car behind across from the Start The Day Rite Restaurant. He side-stepped the *Please Wait To Be Seated* sign and sat down in a booth with his back to the wall. Talldorf scanned the entrees.

"Just coffee, sweetheart." Small opened his attache case on the table. "Let me give you a little advice, Talldorf. Don't eat so much. Not only is it bad for your health, it's bad for the company." Small sipped his coffee and watched Talldorf wash six donuts down with a glass of milk. "I gotta go." Small blew his nose on the napkin and snapped shut his attache case. "Wish me luck." Talldorf picked up his books and headed for a day at the library, admiring secretaries in their twitching skirts as he walked down the Boulevard.

"Hi, Mr. Perkins, ha-ha," said Small. "I tracked you down through the web of your many stores. I'm Small of Complicated Maintenance." Mr. Perkins sat in a swivel chair in a littered office in the rear of a men's clothing store. Studs with fists full of bills from steelmill paychecks patronized this particular store of the Dick King clothing chain. Mr. Perkins' rumpled gray suit didn't make him look shabby. He was not old but might have desired age so comfortably did he wear the air of benevolence to all who came to him. "I'm happy to meet you, Mr. Small. What can I do for you?"

COMPLICATED MAINTENANCE
Walls Floors Ceilings Awnings Stairwells
Your Filth Is Our Profit
999-9999   A. Small

read Mr. Perkins.

"I was in the Greek Town store, Mr. Perkins. The walls and ceilings of that store are filthy. I stopped in Lincoln Park: dirty walls, dirty ceilings." Mr. Perkins received these reports with visible concern. "I have dealt in dirt for several years, Mr. Perkins. I'd like to wash the walls and ceilings of all the Dick King stores."

"Monumental," said Mr. Perkins.

"It's nothing for me, sir. I'll use a scaffold on wheels and roll it down the aisles. I got dropcloths. Your manager can lock me in at night and the job will be done by morning."

"I want a price on this store, Mr. Small. I don't doubt this is the dirtiest of all."

"Seventy dollars, sir."

"Do it, Mr. Small. If this works out we will do the others."

Small left the Dick King store feeling a proprietary interest in the welfare of the clothing chain which now was mysteriously welded to his fate as he rose toward a position of power in the Windy City.

Miss Deerly stopped Small as he started through the gangway. She came out on the high cement stoop, her pillar-like legs wrapped in flesh-colored elastic to keep the swelling down and a swirl of dogs barked and wiggled around her. "Smally, I wonder if ya might have time to do a little thing for me. Al is ailing, you know." Miss Deerly leaned forward over the iron rail and whispered loudly, "I don't think he's got much longer, poor fella, he can't let the bottle alone. He's in there in bed now and I'm tryin to get some good potato soup down him. It's awful for a person to let himself go like Al does but it's his family, you know. His ex-wife just wants to bleed the poor man till he drops. Well Al can't help me the state he's in, Smally, and I need a side porch tore down."

Miss Deerly would probably want to pay him too much. "Sure, I got tomorrow afternoon free. Me and Talldorf will take care of it for you."

A strange enticing aroma greeted Small as he ascended the old board steps in the dark. Talldorf loomed over the gas range. "What's that smell?" said Small slapping his cap on the nail. "Mushrooms," Talldorf beamed.

"I don't like mushrooms. You could get a toadstool and be dead."

"I never heard of anyone who didn't like mushrooms."

"I just told you *I* don't like mushrooms. The party's over, Talldorf. Tomorrow we tear down a porch. You oughta be good at that. And I got us a big job for Friday night. Boy, look forward to a workout. This is an integral in my plans, a very useful step. If we do this job well, we got the whole chain. I'll shift my office to a highrise with a lake view."

The next afternoon there were loud bangs on the door downstairs and Miss Deerly's voice: "Small! Smally dear! Come on down, dear. It's time to wreck the porch!"

"All right. I'm coming! Be right out!" yelled Small. "I ain't ready. I just poured a cup of coffee. I don't have my socks on. Are you ready?"

"Rearing to go, Small," Talldorf towered up out of the easy chair, "Except I don't have my shoes on."

"Can't you be ready for work even in the middle of the day, Talldorf? Go tell her I'll be right down."

Miss Deerly's old van pulled up under shady trees in a side street. An old frame house stood near the walk with a shaggy lawn. "Where's the porch?" demanded Small.

"It's around on the other side of the house, Smally. There's crowbars on the steps. And don't trust those steps, you boys." Talldorf hadn't seen the Windy City like this, the old houses and lawns with little fences around them and the big elm trees. "Come on, Talldorf. We're going to eat this porch. I'm a busy man, I got things to do today." It was a big porch and high. "I hate to charge her a big fee but this ain't a little job. Ok, Talldorf, we wreck it from the top down. We got to start up by the door."

"Miss Deerly said the stairs aren't safe."

"Who's the boss? Is Miss Deerly the boss? Follow me up the stairs." Small broke through the second step. "She's right, the steps aren't safe. Come on, we're going up anyway." They reached the porch where Small stomped heavily and Rudolph hugged the door. "It's solid," judged Small. Rudolph looked out over the concrete alley and the garage roofs. Small was already standing on the railing, a stubby leg around an upright prying with his crowbar. "A good old porch. Old as Miss Deerly. They didn't use bolts in those days. They just spiked this porch into the wall and it lasted this long."

"Sound," Rudolph said hopefully.

"Not for long. Pry that stud loose. Do something Talldorf!" Splinters fell into Rudolph's red curls as he squinted up. "When you get your side loose let me know," said Small.

"It's loose. I see the sky through it."

"Good. Stand in the doorway. When my side is loose you pry the center hard and I'll shove when she starts to go. Now!" Rudolph heaved with the crowbar. The roof tore loose, swung down smashing away the uprights and carrying away the railings as Small leaped to the doorsill, the floor and staircase collapsed into ruin like a child's construction of blocks. A pillar of dust arose. "Everything's ok, Talldorf. Keep calm. Hold onto the door knob."

"I'm holding the door knob!" They stood like two men passing in a closed doorway that no man would use placed as it was high on the wall. "Smally!" called Miss Deerly from below. "Be careful up there, boys. This is an excellent job. You got it down so fast. You didn't drop any of it on the garage?"

"The garage is ok," said Small.

"Smally, you boys will have to take all these boards apart and we'll stack 'em long and short. Why are you boys standing there when the porch is gone? Why don't you go in the door and come down the other stairs?"

"Turn the doorknob, Talldorf." The door swung open and they toppled into a vacant apartment. "Good," said Small getting up from the floor. "You fell the right way. Come on, the job isn't over."

When it was, night had come. Small was exhausted and Talldorf was bumping into things. "She said to sweep the sidewalk, Small." Small snatched the broom away and tossed it into the darkness. "We're done. This job has to be worth an arm and a leg," said Small drooping along the walk toward the van where Miss Deerly dozed with her head on the wheel. For the first time Small had seen Talldorf work. He kept going like a machine, hammering out nails, crowbaring boards, stacking lumber. Tell him what to do and he'd do it so long as it wasn't off the ground. Small would get enough to pay Talldorf something for his efforts.

Though Small wanted to go home Miss Deerly insisted on taking them for a delayed lunch at the Bright Castle. The hamburgers were exquisite to Rudolph because they were bought with his honest labor. "I always come here," said Miss Deerly spooning her chile. "My husband, bless him, was a big man and he ate a lot and did a lot of work."

And now he's dead, considered Small. Miss Deerly didn't mention the pay. It was saving him money since Talldorf was feeding at her expense. As they drove home down the lamp lit avenues and penetrated into the sidestreets of the indigenous poor Small found no opportunity to mention their pay to Miss Deerly so grievous were her groans and sighs as she turned the van around the corners and into the alley. They held the brokendown garage doors as she inched the van in. "I thank ya, Smally. An I thank you, Talldorf, you boys have done me a great service. Just close up those garage doors Smally dear, and you boys have a good rest, the Lord knows you deserve it."

In the kitchen Small said, "Do you ask a doctor for a free operation? This apartment ain't free. I pay her for it. She never thought of paying me! It never entered her mind. I oughta wear a sign on my forehead, FOR SALE."

"Boy, I'm tired," said Talldorf.

"Another sunset and you ain't made a dime."

"I had a delicious supper. The bathtub is going to feel good. Do you want me to run your bath, Small?"

"What for? We have to work tomorrow. You think this afternoon was hard, Talldorf— Ha! Wait till tomorrow."

They pulled up to Jake's Rental off a wide boulevard in Uptown where winos and Indians fought it out each night in cut-throat bars, a section of the city distinguished by prowling police cars and blowing newspapers, the torn families of the poor and the stumbles of the old. Small had phoned to reserve the scaffold. It was painted orange and was made of iron. Small noted the roof and tires flatten as they hoisted it onto Bluey. He had to buy rope to secure the load.

They arrived at the milltown Dick King clothing store just before closing time. Small parked in front of the bright windows. They sagged into the store under the iron scaffold and planks and stood them in a side aisle. "By morning, Talldorf, we've made sixty bucks clear, almost," said Small as soon as the manager had locked them in for the night. They had to get the scaffold erected and planks on the top level. It was another hour before they were ready to start, dropcloths spread over tables and racks. Crouching now on the planks and gazing the length of the ceiling Small was appalled. "This ceiling's got no end and the dirt hangs like moss. It looks like a coal mine. I got to look closer at ceilings before I estimate. Boy, I think you got yourself a deal, Mr. Perkins."

By three o'clock Small knew they would not finish the job by morning. Rudolph sat on the floor of the hat department leaning limply against the wall. He looked done up for a minstrel show and Small, blackened from head to foot, walked the aisles looking up at the ceiling. A third of it glowed milky white. The rest appeared to be painted black. "Oh, what a job," blew Small like a dolphin wearied by the sea, seeing through the plate glass doors a cop writing a ticket for Bluey. Small yelled, ran and banged on the door with his fist but the officer did not hear. He just went maddeningly on writing out the ticket and put it under the windshield wiper. "Damn!" yelled Small. "That would cost me five more bucks! If I paid it, which I won't!"

Rudolph had risen to see Small standing with his fists doubled at his sides and his stubby legs wide as though he would invite the night in for a final brawl. But when Small turned back toward the job his face was already brightening. "Wait till Gumm Tower!" said Small coming up the aisle like a vagabond in the king's wardrobe, "When I get Gumm Tower I got the Windy City in my hand. Then I'll wise up some of these cockeyed officials. Your honor, Mr. Mayor, and you in the blue uniform. I got a few things to tell you guys. Like who the hell do you think you are?"

Small jumped up the scaffold and began rubbing a rag across the ceiling raining down a shower of dirt that was profit in the accounts of Yankee Steel even now sending more of the same from chimneys not many blocks distant over the cottage and tenement roofs of its sleeping servants. Rudolph followed Small up the scaffold and with no other thought worked on against the dirt.

CHAPTER 7

LOW GROUND

The *Sunday Tribunal* lay scattered around Small's chair on the linoleum floor. "Those crooks in Washington think war is a sport. If the President gets a day off, we get a day off. We're going to the zoo, Talldorf, I hope you like wild animals."

"I love all animals, Small."

"Then the company is going to spend some hard-earned capital. I'm proud of the way you been working for the company and to show you the company rewards loyal service I got a surprise for you." Small scurried to his bedroom and came back with a dusty shoebox which he handed to Talldorf.

"Thanks, Small. You shouldn't have. What is it?"

"Open the box. Open the box."

Talldorf was coughing up Dick King dirt and would continue until he was coughing up a different brand. Talldorf was proud of the dirt he coughed up, proud of his blisters, proud of himself. Modestly he lifted the lid of the box.

"If they don't fit we'll cut out the toes," said Small. Talldorf squeezed his sixteens into the new tennis shoes. "You'll walk up walls," Small boasted. Those tennis shoes would give Talldorf his new bouncy working-class roll.

"Slow down, Talldorf!" Small shouted as they strolled the walks past displays of mums transferred from the hot-house to the flowerbeds by the park gardeners. The air was crisp. The sky was blue all the way to St. Louis.

"I always liked this zoo cause they don't charge nothin," Small said. "The birds of the air and the beasts of the field should be free for all Americans. Look at those furry little animals pacing in their cage. Those are fennic foxes, Talldorf, brought all the way from the Sahara Desert with great difficulty and cost just so we can enjoy the world's wildlife on our day off." Talldorf was pale. "It seems a crime to cage any creature, Small."

"Wait till you see the hunks of sirloin they toss to the big cats for free, Talldorf. I want to keep a sharp eye on your chronometer. They feed the lions at four o'clock. Which reminds me, the company is buying whatever you want. Today is your day, Talldorf. A one day all expenses paid vacation is one of the fringe benefits I didn't tell you about. Today management and labor walk arm in arm, cooperating, putting a smile on the face of our great American economy."

To Talldorf it was a small miracle that Small's long experience in the school of hard knocks had not destroyed his sense of humor nor stunted his generosity. "I could eat a hippopotamus, Small." Talldorf was wolfing down his fourth hotdog.

"I ain't complaining. Eat as many of those sawdust weanies as you want, Talldorf."

Rudolph stared at the hotdog and dropped it discreetly into the trashcan. Talldorf's temperament inclined him toward ascetic vegetarianism. Conversely, as a working man, he craved meat as he craved sex. As one second he was freezing and the next sweating, so his blood ran hot one minute and cold the next. "You got a few brains, Talldorf. Stick with me and I'll teach you how to stay alive."

"Tomorrow is Monday, Small. You have to go downtown as usual. I've been giving the company's finances some thought. You could save the company a lot of money if instead of driving you walked." This was followed by a silence so prolonged that Talldorf wondered if Small had heard him.

"I don't have to walk, Talldorf."

"Red told me once that it's cheaper to ride in cabs than it is to own an automobile. You could take the bus or the elevated."

"I'll put up a suggestion box when I need advice from employees, Talldorf. I brought you to the zoo to leave behind the pressures of big business. We'll rent a rowboat. You can row me around the lagoon."

"I'm really good with oars, Small. Red and Elinore used to take Stanly and I to the cabin on Lake Refuge every summer. We spent all our time in canoes and rowboats."

Small sat in the bow holding to the gunnels while Talldorf flailed the water with the green oars. "Talldorf! You said you knew how to row."

"I think I've forgotten, Small."

"I want my money back," Small told the man at the boathouse, "We wasn't out an hour. You might say we wasn't out at all." The man said nothing. He stuffed his pipe, struck a match and turned his back on Small who fumed. "C'mon, Talldorf. I wanta see the polar bear. I been so busy I never told him me and Elvira got a divorce."

"Look, Small, bicycles! Small, it's fun to speed along free as a bird on a bicycle."

"Do you know how to ride a bicycle, Talldorf?"

"Everybody knows how to ride a bicycle, Small."

"I never learned to ride a bicycle."

"I'll teach you. I ride a bicycle with real skill. All summer long it was me and my bike, my bike and me. I took my bike to college. I rode my bike in rain and sleet and snow. I probably would have ridden it to the Windy City if Dr. Steelpin hadn't backed over it with his Chrysler. A bicycle built for two! I've always wanted to ride one of those."

Small peeled two more dollars off his roll of ones and the man in the checkered hat unlocked the lock and snaked the chain out from the spokes. Small grabbed the front handle bars. "The back of the bike, Talldorf. You're strong and willing but you ain't got my sense of direction."

"My legs are too long to sit back here, Small. I'd better ride in front."

"Small's the boss," said Small. "Small is first. We saw what happened when you tried to row the boat. I can't reach the pedals, Talldorf."

"Trust me, Small. I know how to drive a bike with my eyes closed."

"I don't like it Talldorf."

"Relax, Small. Are you ready? Here we go."

Talldorf flung his weight into the pedals and the bicycle built for two weaved down the ramp, picked up speed, wobbled among pedestrians, swung in a wide arc watched by a little girl in a pink dress and smashed into an oak. Small was gingerly raising a pant leg to examine his skinned shin. "It proves one thing, Talldorf. Some are born to follow and some are born to lead. You're lucky you didn't kill us. I'll take the two bucks out of your wages if it'll make you feel better. We can find a safe bench and twiddle our thumbs or discuss literature. There's O'Toole and his old lady! Hey, O'Toole!" Small yelled.

O'Toole was wearing his Sunday best and Sue was dressed in her finery. They had come to the park on Sunday as usual to thrash out the week's domestic difficulties. Sue had shed tears as they strolled around the lagoon and watched the monkeys. Now she dried her eyes to look like a happy, obedient wife in front of the preposterous struttings of Elvira's ex-husband who Sue considered a ruffian and buffoon. "You're lookin good, Small," O'Toole said. "Plenty of broads, huh Small?"

"No time for trivia, O'Toole. I work every minute. This is the first day off in six months. I just caught the Dick King Clothing chain. That's for openers. I got big ones on the line."

"Glad to hear it, Small. I ain't doin shabby myself, am I, baby?" O'Toole winked conspiratorily at Sue. "I made a few investments, bought a few stocks, traded a little gold, play the pools. All my longshots run in the money, Small. Feel the threads. Look at Suzie's outfit. Turn around, baby. Fifty smackers for the shoes alone. Can you believe it? Who are you, tall guy? Introduce us, Small."

"This is Talldorf, my apprentice, O'Toole. Talldorf, shake hands with a guy who'd give you his shirt off his back." Talldorf pumped O'Toole's hand and offered his friendliest smile. This was the famous O'Toole who Small often talked about. "I'm very happy to meet you, Mr. O'Toole."

"Easy, Talldorf. You'll wrinkle the fabric. My pleasure. Don't call me mister. Don't let the bags under the eyes fool you, I'm not much older than you. If you want to know the truth I'm still in the sweet bloom of youth, right baby?"

Sue O'Toole smiled grimly. She was attracted to Talldorf's boyish awkwardness, his pale complexion, his aristocratic nose. She held his long fingers in her small hand squeezing them warmly, tentatively, watching the blush spread from the roots of his red curls.

"Talldorf's from Detroit, O'Toole. He's a college graduate."

"How come he's working for you? Small, I gotta talk to you. Baby,me and Small got important business to discuss. I'll meet your back at the apartment at five o'clock. We'll go out for a pizza. Show Talldorf around the zoo. I can tell the way his eyelids flutter he wouldn't mind a guided tour." O'Toole draped his arm over Small's shoulders and off they went. Sue was furious. Talldorf dangled like a participle.

Rudolph preferred short girls. He had always been paired with the tallest girls at school. Sue O'Toole was five foot two, eyes of blue and lips like cherry wine. That he should be turned loose with this succulent married woman was woefully absurd and beyond Talldorf's most extravagant hopes. Is this the one? Talldorf looked briefly up at heaven. Talldorf faced the sparks which might ignite the whole works.

Sue and Rudolph walked the cinder bridle path beneath the umbrella trees. "You're the first woman I've had a chance to talk to since I left Detroit, except for old Miss Deerly," said Rudolph, then brightly, "I like talking to women. I always talked to my grandmothers. I didn't realize how much I liked talking to a woman before I left home."

"Most men I know don't think a woman is even human," Sue said, "much less intelligent."

"I think women are very intelligent. My ex-fiance had an IQ of 185." Talldorf winced.

"I don't put any stock in IQ scores," Sue said.

"That's an intelligent view. I have a high IQ myself but it hasn't done me any good. I could make a long list of all the things I can't do. I think IQ isn't the whole story, especially when —"

"What is your first name?"

"Rudolph Victor Talldorf. You can call me Talldorf."

"I'll call you Rudolph if you don't mind. There is something elegant about you Rudolph. I'll bet you come from a blueblood family. Why do you talk so negatively about yourself?"

"I try not to but I can't help it, Sue. Small is teaching me the fundamentals of scratching for a living. I still don't know very much. I make a lot of mistakes. I'm still nothing much but a headache to Small."

"I think you and I are two of a kind, Rudolph."

"You do? I do feel like myself right now. Usually when I'm with another person I feel like somebody else."

Over the next few weeks Rudolph and Sue's friendship began to bud. They worked out a code of rings to make sure neither O'Toole nor Small was at home and spent hours talking on the telephone. They arranged clandestine meetings, held platonic discussions while strolling around the lagoon and sipped wine at covert cafes.

Meantime, scurrying like a rat, Small's nose was to the pavement. He sighed for gratitude to gaze from the height of a third-floor window down onto the elevated tracks where the trains sped through the canyons of commerce and pigeons strutted on window ledges and Small remembered the high and magic days with Short. Small walked down the dingy hallway to a door of opaque glass on which was lettered DICK KING INC.

"Hi, honey," Small said to the plain girl who sat at a desk amid a pile of papers, "A. Small to see Mr. Perkins about a little check." He winked as he handed her his card. She watched A. Small warily as she slid around the desk and through a door. "You can go in," she said returning.

"Hi, Mr. Perkins. Did you get a look at the ceiling and walls at milltown?"

"I did, Mr. Small. Please take a seat. I was not only pleased but impressed."

"Yeah, and now I would like to discuss the other stores with you, Mr. Perkins."

"They are yours, Mr. Small," said Mr. Perkins leaning back in his old swivel chair. "All of our stores."

Unaccountably a small cloud crossed the countenance of Small. He could not immediately compute the vast sum this might amount to. Ooooh, all that work!

"Ahhh — Mr. Perkins, I can do the jobs for you but I will have to charge more because the quality way we work in Complicated Maintenance requires more time than other fly-by-nights. Our work is a craft, like masonry. We take great care. So whatever price I gave you is raised by one-third and that's still a good deal, Mr. Perkins, because it brightens a class line of clothing."

"It does indeed," agreed Mr. Perkins. "Let's do the store on North Lincoln, say Friday night? And we will do one store a week thereafter."

"Fine, sir. Next Friday night it's Greektown. I'll make it glow like the Acropolis."

"I hope our association will be long and profitable to us both, Mr. Small."

On the way out Small stopped at the receptionist's desk. "Say, honey, how about you and me — " The girl's eyes widened with fright, her face grew deathly pale, her mouth hung open and not a word came forth. "Maybe later." Small retreated out the door.

The Dick King check was drawn on the First National Bank. Small often passed through it cutting across town. He swung his attache case and anticipated a decorous cup of coffee at a square table in the bank cafeteria while he computed his new wealth. He sped past the security guard into the center of the great marble lobby. He gazed up at pillars supporting the vaulted roof and noted high narrow windows dusty with city life through which dim yellow beams fell. "A thousand bucks!" announced Small turning completely around. The old head atop the blue uniform interrupted Small's view. "May I be of assistance, sir?"

"Yeah," decided Small. "You can direct me to the office of the purchasing agent. I'm going to clean up this joint."

"I'm afraid we have a cleaning staff."

"I don't blame you. Look at that ceiling, Captain!" The guard looked upward. "Dingy!" said Small, "floor shines like moonlight and the ceiling is a black cloud. Do bankers wash behind their ears? This is not a good image for finance. The whole con breaks down if a customer looks up. Who's in charge? He's looking for A. Small of Complicated Maintenance." Small handed a card to the guard.

"Yes — thank you, sir. You might wish to speak with Mr. Weatherby, he is a vice-president of the First National."

"Better than vice-president of the Last National, ha ha," said Small. "Yes, Weatherby." Jotting the name on a business card. "And your name, Captain? I won't fail to mention to Weatherby how helpful you've been."

"Really sir, it isn't necessary."

"Carson," Small read the plastic name tag on the guard's lapel and wrote it down. "Never be ashamed of service, Captain," advised Small, "One's work may be humble in the chain of command but such is the foundation of empire."

"Sir?"

Small wheeled on a tennis shoe and sped toward the wall of cashier cages. The giraffe, the wolf, the fox or the marmot. Small walked from the marmot's cage snapping crisp new bills into his wallet, tapping down marble steps to the basement cafeteria. Small did not value the red leather upholstery and white drapes of the First National cafeteria over the less ornate decor of other downtown coffee spots, but imagined he absorbed some arcanum of finance while here. He propped open his attache case on the tabletop like a shrapnel shield at field headquarters, pushed back the china cup and opened his notebook. He wrote *LOW GROUND* dropped his pen, took a quick gulp of coffee, rose and sped out of the cafeteria to return with the yellow page listing of the Dick King clothing chain ripped from the telephone directory. The addresses appeared landmarks in his brain, pierblocks on which to build higher achievements. Sixteen store locations spanned the city. It would amount to approximately sixteen hundred dollars. Small preferred the figure 2000. He wrote that down and considered it working capital. Just a little labor once a week, thought Small, won't be long now. On the next page he wrote

SKY HIGH
Gumm Tower

and circled it to isolate its importance. That would be a powderblue suit day. Dirt and grime, thought Small, dirt and grime, and was scarcely comforted by the bulky wad of bills in his wallet. Small was grateful to the star of his luck that Talldorf was available as his lieutenant in his projected campaigns and experienced a poignant sense of omission that Talldorf this moment might be carrying out an order to further the success of his plans but as usual Small had left Talldorf with nothing to do. He's probably exercising his annoying reading habit, drinking milk and eating food, worried Small. He sped out of the cafeteria, dropped a dime into the telephone and dialed his own number. The line was busy. Small scratched his head and dialed the Glibb Answering Service.

"Complicated Maintenance," said the faceless female voice. Small brooded. *"Hello!* Complicated Maintenance! Can I *help* you?"

"Yeah baby, a lot better than you're doin. I pay good money to get service and you ain't providin it for me. Am I throwing money away I wonder? I have instructed Speers, who I assume is still your boss, that this number is to be answered cheerily, *'Hello* Complicated Maintenance, A. Small President.' You left out the most important part. And you wasn't cheery."

"Oh, I *am* sorry, sir, you are Mr. Small the president, in person?"

"I am he, dear."

"I'm Joanie, Mr. Small. I hope you won't report me to Mr. Speers, I just started today. I couldn't stand to lose this wonderful job."

"Don't worry, dear. Maybe one of these days I'll have the pleasure of making your acquaintance."

"Ooooo," said Joanie.

"But please, dear, be cheery. It's what I pay you for. And add, 'A. Small, President.' Advertise or be forgotten, as the brain washers say, and A. Small don't plan to be forgotten. Very fine, dear, any message for me?" Joanie had no message. "Then I got a message for Talldorf, my lieutenant, in case he contacts you. Are you ready?"

"Ready, sir."

"Talldorf: I want you to get to work while I'm out here pounding the pavements and knocking my head up against brick walls — "

"Do I write all this down?"

"That's why I'm bothering to communicate it to you, dear."

"Yes, sir."

"Continue: Talldorf, I want a sign constructed of two pieces of plywood attached at the top by two hinges. You will find these in the Executioner's room."

"Executioner — ?"

"Actually it's Talldorf's room. Continue: you will find paint and brushes. Print on both boards the name of our company in capital letters. Underneath print, 'Cleans Up Again.' Got that, honey?"

"Yes sir."

"Now Talldorf may not call in, he's probably out playing in the sunshine while I rack my brains but that's the burden of us in command. If he don't call in I'll pass the message on personally. My business is moving, honey. You'll probably be getting a lot more calls and if you handle them the way I like there might be a Christmas bonus."

"Oh, thank you so much, Mr. Small."

"It's nothing," said Small. "I'm happy to welcome you to the Complicated Maintenance Team."

Small did not expect Talldorf to call the answering service. Indeed, Small had not extended him that authority, but Small considered the sign idea brilliant. They would prop it on the sidewalk before the Dick King clothing stores while they washed the walls and ceilings and it would attract business. Small would have Talldorf build a little shelf on the sign on which to set a pile of business cards so that everyone could have one of his own. Small sped back to his square table thinking, more, more, more — So intense was his obsession that he was seated and reaching for the coffee cup before he realized the old man with the sorrowful gaze sitting across from him.

"I seen you a mile off!" the old man cackled. His eyes glimmered like black rocks. His nose hung over his chin. He wore a gray homberg, an expensive black overcoat and a gold stickpin secured a striped silk tie. Was the man in mourning? Gray gloves lay across the top of the cane on which his hands folded and his flat old chin rested, "Stop. Right now!" he demanded.

"Stop ,what?" inquired Small.

"Stop scurrying around, scoundrel."

"You're mistaking me for someone else!" The old man rapped his cane smartly across the tabletop. "Whippersnapper! I opened a million car doors. You're the one who stepped out. I owe it all to you!"

"I was here first," Small said patiently, "this is my table. I am conducting important business. I never got out of a car in front of you in my life."

The old man poked Small's toe with the end of his cane. "Tennis shoes! Never saw that one before."

"I move fast, I can't afford to slip."

"Don't I know! But you'll slip like the rest of us and take a great fall. I did you all one better. I stood there in my uniform. They loved me and called me General. And the nincompoops imagined I wasn't. General Timmy O'Malley, doorman at the Windy City Athletic Club fifty years. Stayed on my feet, you bet your boots, but it was a great slip up. Wore my footprints into concrete under that flapping awning rain, wind, snow and cold. Sweat myself to a bone two hundred campaigns, got hard as rock, two hundred seasons I served your likes. Everybody loved the general and saluted and tossed me market tips. I scooped them off the cement bowing low when they stepped out of the limousines. 'Hello, Timmy, buy Booger King, good evening, General', winking at their trollops, 'buy Exlax'. I did and retired worth a million dollars. And when I applied for membership in this outfit I'm wearin like a new-minted dollar you scoundrels black-balled me."

"I didn't!" denied Small.

"Did!" cried Timmy O'Malley slapping the table with his cane. The coffee cup jumped in the china saucer. "Did! And you wouldn't speak to me. Couldn't see me. I was invisible. I'm invisible now! Do you believe it? Why I know half the people in this cafeteria by their first names, scoundrel! They wouldn't see me if I yelled in their faces. That's reality, sonny boy. There's ice in the hearts of men. Under this spiffy topcoat I'm chilled to the bone. Got a natty little suit hidden away in the rubble of your devious life, don't you? Well, don't you!"

"I dress for proper occasions." admitted Small.

"Proper!" cackled Timmy O'Malley revealing toothless old gums. "That's a good one!"

"I got business, Grandpa." Small slid his attache case between them. Glaring around the barrier Timmy O'Malley said, "We're in the same line, you and me. It gets worse and never gets better. All we get is ashes."

"A million bucks. Some ashes, Grandpa."

"Wrapped in a black overcoat," sniffed the old man in a crushed tone of grief.

"I'll buy you a cup of coffee," Small hazarded.

"Buy, buy, ashes, ashes," stuttered Timmy O'Malley, "It's three million now. It grows like cancer once you got it. The General's dead and I'm invisible."

"I see you!" Small peered around the attache case and the old man's head swiveled on his cane like a weathervane.

"Then listen well, scoundrel. You'll be just like me unless you drop your low-down no-good sneak-thief ways. You and your speedy tennis — for shame — generals are crazy and you are no exception."

"Small's the name, Grandpa. You're confusing yourself with me."

"All generals are small, nincompoop! Scheming under ground drinking crafty brain juice when your future is ashes. Look at me!" The voice grew shrill. "I'm you! A bag of ashes!" Snapping shut his attache case Small beat a hasty retreat up the marble steps. "Ashes!" screeched the old voice. Was everybody in the Windy City crazy? wondered Small. Old Alphonse, the bum in the alley, was crazy. O'Malley was crazy. The poor were crazy and the rich were crazier.

Small shivered in the chilling wind that poured through the concrete canyons. Well, Small wouldn't freeze this winter with the Dick King clothing chain in his pocket. But he needed more. A job a day, a firm foundation and then he would capture the big ones. He stopped on a busy corner amid the swirl of shoppers and caressed the bulge of his wallet with a buttock, a technique he had invented to determine if his pocket had been picked, knelt on the sidewalk up against the wall of a skyscraper, set his attache case on his knees and opened his notebook to *SKYHIGH*. He wrote, 'Goldbogen awnings, $180 — blue suit,' and closed his office. Small was like a cat in the jungle of the busy street ready to spring any direction on the instant without doubt that he would survive and instantly optimistic he charged on into the day.

"Hello, Mr. Ensardo? This is Small, the man who has worked for you longest for least, ha ha. How you doin? Me and my lieutenant are coming to do the job Wednesday for a mere $150."

"Mr. Small, I cannot talk now. A rare occurrence is taking place here at this very instant. I shall be indisposed for a time, Mr. Small. We must arrange a date for the work you are to do for me."

"That's why I'm talking to you on the telephone, Mr. Ensardo."

"Until then, Mr. Small." Click.

By chance Small was looking at the beauty parlor listings in the yellow pages. There must be a thousand, thought Small. They got to keep their walls clean. He had five dimes, dialed five beauty parlors and got five estimates. I'll make a fortune on beauty parlors! I'll have to hire more men! It took a day to estimate the five beauty parlors which lay scattered to the furthest fringes of the Windy City. The proprietors invariably addressed Talldorf, whom Small had brought along for the purpose of instructing him on the waste of company time. Talldorf's curls hovered near the lowered ceilings and he hung back in the face of devastated beauty. Small was forced to speak up sharply. "It's *me,* A. Small, President of Complicated Maintenance. He's just my lieutenant, R. Talldorf. You got some filth for our profit?" Small got one depressing job beyond the mills for $25 and scheduled it for the following week. He had wasted a day to get one job that would not pay expenses for going to it. Besides Small couldn't stand washing the walls of beauty parlors. They couldn't rid their rags of human hair. It clung to pantlegs and socks. It smelled like a shipload of drowned rats.

Small was in a black mood the evening they arrived at the Dick King job in Greektown with the iron scaffolding crushing the roof of Bluey. The young manager was not expecting them. "You haven't heard," he said to Small who stood before the cash register with two buckets in his hands. "Mr. Perkins died. No new expenditures are to be made until they straighten out his papers."

"The job is off?" blinked Small.

"Right."

"Mr. Perkins set it up."

"Mr. Perkins is dead."

"Well I ain't," said Small. "I got to keep eating!"

"I'm sorry, sir, you'll have to contact the main office."

Small was pale when Talldorf met him coming out of the clothing store. "Job's off, Talldorf. Perkins skipped on us." A cop was climbing off his cycle and heading toward Bluey with his ticket pad. "Off, off!" yelled Small waving his bucket in the air, "I'm unloading, I'm loading up, I'm a commercial vehicle!"

"You're a sedan," countered the officer, "with a dangerous load on your roof."

"I'm getting out of here! You going to throw me in jail for driving away? Don't distress me, a close friend has just died!" So intense was Small's objection that the cop backed away. "Five minutes," he said and walked away slapping his ticket book against his thigh. "The whole chain could be down the drain, Talldorf. I don't understand it. I get a big pile of jobs, break my back on the first to prove myself and before I get to gravy the boss dies. Poor Perkins, he was a nice guy, a fine man who understood quality because he hired us. He'd want me to finish the jobs. Maybe he left a note."

Mr. Perkins left no note. Mr. Perkins stood in the doorway to his office that particular morning with an immense sense of weariness, an acute sense of the overwhelming weight of his duties, a paralyzing sense of irrelevancy, and slumped to the floor with his hat in his hand and his overcoat on. The doctor surmised he had caught a chill. Mr. Terwilliger, a younger man, was to take up Mr. Perkins' abandoned duties. Terwilliger was overjoyed at this unexpected boon. It would mean more money for Christmas. Terwilliger determined to slash expenses to the bone and introduce a more flashy line. Terwilliger was tired of old-man ideas. Small's telephone call gave him the idea of walling the stores with mirrors, the better to play on the vanity of the customer, an omission he speculated had cost the chain untold thousands. "No," said Terwilliger into the telephone. "We will definitely not continue washing walls and ceilings. Out with the old and in with the new!"

"It's cheaper than painting!" said Small, "Mr. Perkins wanted me to brighten the places up."

"Perkins doesn't care now," said Mr. Terwilliger.

"Oh yes he does!" and Small slammed the receiver.

Small sent a bill for the rental of the scaffolding he hadn't used to Terwilliger who directed the girl with frightened eyes to throw it in the wastebasket.

Small ran before the bills hungrily snapping up any little job, a silly round awning over the door of a Chinese restaurant. "I feel like a callgirl, Talldorf. Any guy who'd open his eyes could climb up here on a stepladder and clean this himself and save five bucks." When Small returned next day for his pay the manager started speaking Chinese. The only American word was no. "No! No!" and he slapped Small's bill on the cashier's desk. The Chinaman disappeared in his white dentist's jacket behind a bead curtain leaving Small like a Banzai tree wide-legged on an Oriental carpet cautious amid gongs and reeds. Small wondered what he awaited. A stern-faced Chinaman with black hair parted in the middle wearing a black coat came toward him with sabre eyes, nailed the bill to the desk with those eyes, rang open the cash drawer and laid a five dollar bill before Small. "No more," said the Chinaman, "It is too much."

Small cringed through the icy gangway swinging his attache case, climbed into Bluey and ground the battery to zero. He held his head in his hands. By the time he had the battery disconnected his fingers were numb. He boosted it onto his shoulder and it ground him into the concrete. Small bore it three city blocks, the attache case banging against his knees. "Treachery," said Small. The battery had deserted him like Perkins had deserted him. "Keep warm, Perkins, pant, pant." Small left the battery on the cold concrete floor to be charged and escaped the garage. Garages reminded him of factories. He didn't like the dim light, the metal, the grease, or the bone-chilling cold. He hurried to a cafe by the bus stop to thaw his hands on a coffee cup prior to diving again into the byways of downtown looking for his piece of cheese.

Downtown was so cold there wasn't a single pigeon under the elevated tracks. Awnings were so brittle they didn't look like they could roll up. He would not consider outside jobs. He wandered into nighttime lingerie stores, his eyeballs warming on sexy nightgowns and lacy brassieres. Small appreciated this facet of his business which allowed him into forbidden precincts where his eyes fell upon the astonishments of modern civilization. To warm his feet he wandered through giant department stores and wandered out the revolving doors into a new street where the cold forced him into another cafe where he warmed his hands again on the cup and stared dazedly out plate glass windows. Something was wrong. He didn't want to solicit jobs. He didn't want to do jobs. It seemed his blood was congealing. It was like carrying the dead battery. "Scratching!" said Small to himself. "For crumbs! I suppose the brakes go next. I can't get off the ground carrying this load around."

Burlesque houses strung a faded necklace down the dingy street in the barren afternoon light. Optimism lit the walls of his skull like a marquee lightbulb. The burlesque houses were dingy, the signs ornate and showy and rusted and filthy and the awnings like scabs. They were supposed to sparkle and Small imagined them so. "Summer's coming!" he announced bounding across the icy intersection.

Bluey's brakes went out as Small was approaching a stoplight on the Boulevard. He went through the light, over the curb, knocked over a wire wastepaper container and swerved around a corner into a small and expensive garage. No cops had witnessed his little mishap and he had hit no one. He thanked his star. The new parts cost $100. Small couldn't get Bluey out of hock for a month. The icy hand of winter slowed his steps. Rudolph gazed at him with concern. Small looked like a tire that was losing air. He did not speak of his great plans. The clang and clamor of the Windy City was a wire-tense din in his brain relieved only at night in his small house where Talldorf waited like faithful Penelope stirring the stew while winter bore down.

Chapter 8

WINTER QUARTERS

Wet gray flakes drifted past the windows. Talldorf, wrapped in a blanket, shivered with his latest book beside the water heater while Small sat at his desk in a T-shirt sweating over important papers. "Sue O'Toole is an attractive intelligent woman, don't you think, Small?"

"I told you to stay away from that broad."

"Sue doesn't have anyone else to talk to. O'Toole ignores her. She tells *me* her problems. We have wonderful discussions. I'm certainly not guilty of any misconduct, Small, but I hate sneaking around. Wherever I go lately I see O'Toole. Maybe he's following me."

Small threw up his hands. "I don't have many friends, Talldorf, but O'Toole is one of them. For my sake, your sake, his sake and her sake stop playing around."

"I'm not playing around, Small."

"Sex is what you're talkin about, Talldorf. I bust my balls while my lieutenant is wastin company time on a foolish affair with a married woman. I don't want O'Toole or anybody else accusin Complicated Maintenance of adultery."

In spite of Small's sound advise Talldorf continued to meet Sue O'Toole secretly. Sue took him to the symphony and to the latest foreign films. They spent entire afternoons roaming the corridors of the Art Institute in animated conversations about the value of art. "Do you ever think about anything but the big questions in life, Rudolph?" Sue asked.

"There's not much else to think about if you think about it," Talldorf replied nervously.

"Rudolf, I love your intellect. I love your white teeth, Rudolph, and your nice straight nose. Kiss me, Rudolph —"

An icy wind tore at the skirts of secretaries on the Boulevard. Talldorf held Sue's hot little hand and stared wretchedly at the snow blowing over his tennis shoes. "We could go to a hotel, Rudolph."

"I think Small would fire me if he knew I was seeing you. Besides I have a conscience, don't I Sue?"

"Oh Rudolph, how can we pass up such a wonderful opportunity? I know I can make a red-hot lover out of you. I'll turn your inhibitions into a peeled banana."

They kept up the brisk pace along deserted beaches where the ice crunched, past empty benches and abandoned life guard stations as the purple snowclouds puffed themselves up above the choppy whitecaps.

> "Let me be a sharer in the fierce
> and far delight
> a portion of the tempest
> and of thee..."

said Rudolph.

"Rudolph, that's beautiful!"

"Byron," said Rudolph miserably.

"Such an interesting mind, Rudolph. I love your brooding eyes. We can't go on like this."

"I've been doing a lot of reading about our moral dilemma, Sue, but I haven't reached a conclusion. All the heroic thinkers say to live life to the hilt. Fling away tradition, inhibition, morals. They say that to disregard our impulses is the worst sin of all. Worse than murder! Worse than incest! Worse than fornication! I've jotted down a few paragraphs." Talldorf pulled out his notebook.

"Kiss me!"

"I feel like a traitor, Sue. I think about you day and night."

"Oh, darling, your arms are so strong."

Where does she go? O'Toole wondered. He considered hiring a private detective to follow her. Instead he took a hot shower, fixed himself a scotch and soda and lay down on the couch to watch television.

It didn't take long for O'Toole to go from winning to losing. O'Toole lost his last fifty on a filly that trampled his money in the mud in front of an empty grandstand at Pimlico while O'Toole sat in a rear booth at Ensardo's watching his ice cubes melt.

And then Mr. Ensardo had shown O'Toole the generosity that made him the man he was. Mr. Ensardo had talked with O'Toole in his private suite as a father talks to a prodigal son. Mr. Ensardo had counseled O'Toole, admonished him and let it be known that O'Toole's talents had been noticed. But like all men O'Toole must start at the bottom. Mr. Ensardo offered O'Toole a job driving a Mother's Bread truck.

"I quit drinking and I quit gambling and I've got a steady job," O'Toole told Sue. "What else do you want?"

Patches of dirty snow glittered under street lights, sullen bedraggled clouds scudded above shadowy wet walks in Lincoln Park where Talldorf and Sue huddled on a bench under the bronze statue of William Shakespeare.

"Marriage is horrible, Rudolph," Sue sniffed, wiping her eyes. "O'Toole is sick. He agreed to give up drinking and gambling. I got him to quit smoking for his own good. I convinced him to take a steady job, but nothing helps. Last night we had a terrible argument and he beat me. Oh, Rudolph, I feel so lonely and confused."

Talldorf held Sue limply in his skinny arms, his blue eyes mournful as he stared up at Shakespeare's words carved in stone:

'WHAT A PIECE OF WORK IS MAN! HOW NOBLE IN REASON! HOW INFINITE IN FACULTY! IN FORM AND MOVING HOW EXPRESS AND ADMIRABLE!'

"Hold me, Rudolph. Kiss me, Rudolph. Be gentle with me, Rudolph."

Rudolph walked Sue to within two blocks of her apartment refusing to come closer though she assured him that O'Toole wouldn't arrive home till ten o'clock from his first meeting at Alcoholics Anonymous. He felt better having endured the agony of his strict moral principles under fire. A spontaneous brotherly affection sprung up for O'Toole the moment Sue was safely around the corner and Rudolph was striding home across the Windy City. Talldorf was troubled by pains shooting through his balls.

"It must come from walking so much, Small," said Rudolph.

"Lover's nuts!" Small said with disgust. "You've been out with Sue O'Toole again. Don't lie to me, Talldorf."

"I had to see her. I can't throw an old friend to the dogs, can I, Small? O'Toole struck her. It ought to be stopped."

"Obedience is a virtue in an employee, a soldier and a woman, Talldorf. Having had little experience with women, you tend to sympathize with Sue. Don't take her side. Take it from a guy who knows the heartache a woman can cause. Stay away from that broad. That's an order!"

One evening when Talldorf had set up his chess board to solve the *Daily Tribunal* chess problem O'Toole came out of the wind and cold. Talldorf grasped O'Toole's hand and shook it with fervor. "You are looking good, O'Toole. Really exceptional. It's so good to see you, O'Toole, you look extremely well. Doesn't O'Toole look well, Small?"

"Why don't you let go of my hand, Talldorf? Am I missing something, Small?"

"You gotta forgive Talldorf," Small said. "It ain't entirely his fault. Talldorf ain't had much experience with nothin. I couldn't tell you all the things he don't know nothing about. He was eatin silver spoons when you and me was eating baloney."

Talldorf withered under O'Toole's sharp appraising eye. "It's true," mumbled Rudolph, "I went to school instead of earning my living. But I too have suffered like every human being. I'm trying to be worthy of the great American labor movement."

"You're cuckoo, Talldorf," said O'Toole with a sidelong glance over his toothpick. "So who plays chess?" Talldorf leaped forward. "I play chess. Do you play chess, O'Toole?"

Small shouted into the red telephone, wadded a sheet of paper into a ball and threw it across the kitchen.

"I haven't played for a few years, Talldorf, but chess is like swimming. This is the knight?" O'Toole held up the bishop. "I was champ of the Park District three years running. I got time for a game. How much you want to bet? It's all right if I bet just so it ain't more than a buck. I promised Sue."

"I don't have any money," said Rudolph.

"Give your partner a buck, Small."

"I'm broke," said Small.

"Here, I'll loan you a buck, Talldorf."

"I don't believe in borrowing—"

"C'mon, you might beat me. Then you'll have a buck of your own." They sat down at the chess board. O'Toole wet his finger and tested the air. "Not much of a wind chill factor here, Small." He got up and put his overcoat back on.

"They shut off the gas, O'Toole," Small explained. "I'm gonna burn the furniture if we don't get a job."

"Light a candle, Small, it'll take the chill off. Small, I feel like a new man. I gave up smokes and even java. I don't miss em. You oughta try it. Everybody tells me how good I look. And I feel good. But something ain't right. It's Sue. I can't put my finger on it." Talldorf could not raise his eyes to O'Toole's. "Something's fishy." Rudolph gulped. "It's just little things, Small. Sex, for example. She wears curlers to bed and long underwear. She burns my dinners. Your move, Talldorf. I can't sit here all night waiting for you to move."

Small paid scant attention as he pleaded and cajoled, harangued and swore into the red telephone, jotted figures and tore his hair as snow fell beyond the rattling windows, over weathered board fences, garage doors and ashcans.

Talldorf moved his queen, trembling with excitement and dread at the trap he had laid for O'Toole.

"What are you shaking for, Talldorf? Small, you should stuff newspapers under the door. Checkmate, Talldorf! I got time to play again. Don't take it so hard, Talldorf, it's just a game. How about a little refreshment before we begin?"

"Fix O'Toole a catsup sandwich, Talldorf, and get him a glass of water. This poverty is unbecoming to the dignity of my citizenship, O'Toole."

"How'd things get so bad, Small? How much do you need? Ten? Twenty?" O'Toole pulled out a roll of bills. "When O'Toole's got money Small's got money. If I'm hungry you guys must be starving to death. Get your coats, guys. I'm taking you both out for dinner."

"But won't Sue expect you home for dinner?" asked Talldorf.

"Friendship is eternal, Talldorf," announced O'Toole, "but a woman is a sometime thing."

While Small and O'Toole ate the bread of brotherhood Talldorf twitched through the meal with pangs of betrayal.

O'Toole was not the only visitor to emerge from the winter snows. Like a blaze of lightning the Executioner appeared. Small knew he was coming because the toaster popped and the door buzzer which Talldorf had never heard slashed the silence.

"He's in the gangway!" exclaimed Small.

"Who?" Rudolph was amazed at Small's anxiety.

"Don't call him the Executioner, Talldorf! His name is Bill. He's a crazy electronic wizard. I took this apartment off his hands so he thinks I'm his friend."

The door burst open, the doorway filled with a powerful man in a black leather jacket closing his switchblade, his eyes glittering black fire. Rudolph's spine tingled.

"Hi, Bill," said Small. "Don't have to tell Bill to come in, Talldorf. He rings the buzzer by remote control. If we had a mixmaster it'd be throwing batter on the walls. He slips the latch with his blade. They couldn't keep Bill out of Fort Knox. Talldorf, shake hands with Bill."

Bill crushed Rudolph's hand. Bill's teeth flashed like guillotines. "Ouch!" said Talldorf, "I'm happy to meet you Mr. Ex — Mr. Bill."

"Death to all aristocrats!" snarled Bill. Rudolph moved backward toward the living room.

"My cathode ray is designed to disintegrate leather! Wallets will burst into puffs of smoke!" The powerful man let out a sheet of screaming laughter. Small chuckled. "Ha, ha," he said.

Bill strode into Small's small bedroom. Small and Talldorf peered around the corner. Bill was on his knees with his head and arms under Small's bed.

"Lose something, Bill?" inquired Small.

"Just adjusting the springs so you will sleep more soundly," explained Bill. He pulled a metal pan filled with flashlight batteries from under the bed. "See how these batteries are all connected, Alexander?" Bill's teeth and eyes flashed. Rudolph thought of wolves in snowy wastelands.

"Don't use electricity! Hook your radio to these batteries. Never pay the running dogs of capitalism one penny! I'm going to blow up the telephone exchange as soon as I get my blitzer perfected. They'll burn with their money, with their headsets on their exploding heads, the rotten sons-of-bitches!"

"Wonderful," said Small rolling his eyes at Talldorf who was appalled at such insanity.

"You are a poor man, Alexander, so you are my friend," said Bill filling Small's small bedroom with his glittering blackness.

"Right!" agreed Small, "I'm your friend, Bill. So is Talldorf here. Any friend of Small is a friend of Bill. What did you want to see me about, Bill? I was just going to bed."

"Yes, yes, go to bed just as soon as I leave, Alexander. I'm hurrying home too. I have work to do in the laboratory."

"Well such a short visit, Bill. Bye bye."

"Not yet. I have to show you something in the basement. Come!"

"Come to the basement Talldorf," said Small. "You never seen the basement."

Talldorf followed cautiously down the wooden stairs. The Executioner popped the latch with his switchblade and flipped on the light. The room was filled with Miss Deerly's clutter accumulated over half a century. Bill showed Small a hidden breaker switch. "I installed this and forgot to tell you about it. It bypasses the meter. Your electric bill will go to zero. They can't trace it."

Small was delighted. "Wonderful, Bill! Talldorf, no electric bill from here on out!"

"That's illegal," said Talldorf. Bill cast him a glance that knocked him backward.

"Bill don't like that word, Talldorf."

"What I mean is—it's illegal the rates they charge—" fumbled Rudolph.

Mad laughter shrieked from the Executioner. "Yes, yes, *they* are IL-LEGAL! But they'll have to deal with me! I'll fry them all, the rotten bastards!" and the Executioner slammed his great fist into a piece of plywood that shattered before their eyes.

Small was rocked onto his heels and he patted Bill's leather arm. "Bill, it's ok. Everything's ok, Bill. Let's not destroy Miss Deerly's things, she's a poor old lady like us."

"Woe to you, Alexander! Woe to you if you ever succeed. If you become one of them you will no longer by my friend."

"I'll never succeed, I'm hopeless. Elvira always told you that, Don't waste your wallet-burner on my wallet, ha, ha. I don't have a dollar to my name. You know me, Bill. Hopeless Small hopes you blow up the telephone exchange tomorrow."

"We're terribly poor," agreed Rudolph. "I've been hungry ever since I got here. Small hardly eats at all."

"Damn them! Damn, damn, *damn* them!" howled the Executioner. He smashed the plywood and splinters flew.

"I ain't hungry, Bill! Everything's ok!"

Small led the Executioner to the door. "Hurry home now, Bill, and get a good night's rest. Don't worry about me. They won't put nothin over on me. Well, nighty night — "

"Are you going to bed now, Alexander?" asked Bill.

"Yes, we got to go to bed right now, Bill."

"Then I'll hurry home to my laboratory."

Small rushed upstairs. Talldorf found him in his small bedroom with his head under the bed. The springs were webbed with a network of electric wires and a mysterious cylindrical object hung from them. Small slapped it with a slipper. It buzzed. "The crazy bastard was going to electrocute me in my bed by remote control! That's why he had to hurry back to his laboratory."

"I thought he was your friend," said Rudolph.

"This is a good omen, Talldorf. The Executioner doesn't believe I'm hopeless. He thinks I'll get rich. He must be right. He's very smart."

"He's insane!" said Rudolph. "He's the craziest person I ever met."

"Open your eyes, Talldorf. Everybody in the Windy City is crazy or they wouldn't be here. I'm beginning to wonder about myself." Small cut the wires from the springs wearing rubber gloves.

"I don't feel safe here," said Talldorf.

"It's all in a day's work," said Small. "But the sooner we're safe in the penthouse the better."

"Hello, Rudolph." It was Sue. "I had to call. I have to see you. I must talk to you Rudolph."

Talldorf met Sue like old times at one of their secluded cafe rendezvous.

"Oh, Rudolph, I'm so happy to see you again. It makes me feel better just being with you. I've missed you, Rudolph." She squeezed his sweaty hand under the table. "I know you're starved, Rudolph. O'Toole told me all about it. Order whatever you want. I can loan you money if it will help. Small, that tyrant! If his company doesn't make any money he'll send you to the blood bank like he did Elvira. Promise me you won't go, Rudolph."

Talldorf's stomach growled as he studied the menu, "I can't take O'Toole's money, Sue."

"It's my money now," said Sue.

"I'll have a cup of coffee," he told the waitress.

"Bring him the roast beef dinner and cherry pie ala mode," Sue said.

The roast beef tried to choke Talldorf.

"Sue, I don't think it's wise for us to see each other."

"Rudolph, I feel terrible. I need your advice. I have to tell somebody. I can't keep it a secret any longer. Rudolph, I had an abortion."

Talldorf felt sick to his stomach. His face twisted as he sought an appropriate response.

"How's the baby, Sue?"

"Rudolph! How can you say such a terrible thing?"

The storm sent out advance scouts which drove across the lowering sky above choppy white caps and the purple clouds ripped out their bellies on the skyscrapers.

"Don't tell me any more, Talldorf!" Small shouted pacing the kitchen. "I don't want to hear nothin about it. Treason! Mutiny! Insubordination! You disobeyed my orders. If this was war I'd have you shot."

"Women are such pitiful helpless creatures," mourned Rudolph.

"Pitiful? Helpless?" scoffed Small flinging the coffee grounds from his cup. "That's how much you know. Fangs and claws, Talldorf. Is a woman who twists you around her little finger helpless? A broad will tear you open and eat out your heart. I was married, don't I know? You can't be screwing around behind my back, Talldorf. We can't have secrets from the company. Secrets eat into the mouldings."

"Do you mean I can't have a private life, Small? You have a private life. Surely there are things you don't tell me."

"I have no secrets, Talldorf. Yeah, I got a secret. I paid Miss Deerly the rent yesterday. I tell you everything. I told you all winter to lay off O'Toole's wife but you wouldn't listen."

"I never intended to do it, Small. I didn't plan to let it go this far."

"How far has it gone, Talldorf?"

"There's been no penetration, Small. I wouldn't allow that. I'm innocent in the eyes of the law."

"The law knows nothin, Talldorf. It's the heart that knows."

Talldorf promised Small to obey all further orders. He concentrated on his books and took long forlorn walks. He felt sad but exonerated, rehabilitated, proud. From atop the bridge he looked at the condoms floating in the turgid green water. Thousands of the little creatures, schools of rubbers, swam enmasse on the tide of modern love from motels, apartments, offices, schools or wherever a toilet flushed. It appeared to Talldorf that he was the only person in the Windy City not engaged in such activity.

"There ain't nothing wrong with sex, Talldorf," Small explained, "If you got time and a woman. Which you don't. Someday your woman will come along. But now you will put nonsense behind you and turn full attention to our new campaign. The spring offensive is at hand! There will be no woman in your future or mine. Complicated Maintenance is opening a full scale invasion of the suburbs."

Chapter 9

THE SUBURBS

Spring came with the trees along the streets greening and a blue breeze wafting earth odors through the open kitchen window. Small was sketching the final details of the spring offensive. Suburban telephone directories lay open on the kitchen table and piled beside his feet.

Small tapped his temple. "It's knowing little things like capitalism, Talldorf, that makes me boss. To get ahead you exploit society's weak points. Spring cleaning is a weak point. Women are crazy for it."

They moved out at dawn with their coffee cups on the dashboard driving up the ramp onto the expressway.

"Look at em." Small leered at the early rush hour traffic. "Packed like sardines. Tied to mama's apron strings, the poor bastards. At least we ain't trapped like them guys." Small puffed his Lucky and sipped his coffee as the industrial smokestacks of the electric plant slipped past, through the outskirts of the city, past rows of brick flats, blocks of cottages behind the cyclone fence and then out into the open expanse of tract houses, trees, billboards, motels and gas stations.

PEA RIDGE, read the green exit sign.

"The people in Pea Ridge ain't slaves like them guys, and they ain't peons like us. The people of Pea Ridge drive Mercedes and don't go to their offices till ten o'clock. They have bloody marys for breakfast and martinis for lunch and they're in love with golf. What they hate to do is work, Talldorf. I got wire brushes, bristle brushes, rags, steel wool, a shovel, a rake, buckets, squeegees, mops, a broom and a saw. We wash the windows, scrub the floors, and clean their dentures. We tell it to em quick and we sell the whole package. And we emphasize quality. We give em the slogan: 'Pea Ridge ain't the place for filth.' The success of this operation depends on speed. You're gonna have to work faster, three or four houses a day. And you're gonna have to display more discipline than ever before. The company can't afford to spend nothin on lunch. So we don't eat lunch. Got that, Talldorf? There's no such thing as lunch."

Small had lined up a job at a big stone house with brown shutters which backed up to the 19th hole of the Pea Ridge Country Club.

"She wants tree trimmin done," Small said as he turned off Bluey's motor. "Follow me, Talldorf. On this one I'll demonstrate my salesmanship. So keep your mouth shut and pay close attention to my technique." They marched up to the kitchen door.

"I'm so glad you've come," said Mrs. Proot. "We should have had the limb trimmed off months ago." She pointed to a gigantic elm. A thick dying limb, like an iron arm, threatened a corner of the house.

"Don't worry about a thing, Mrs. Proot," Small said as Talldorf stared up at the tree in horror.

"My husband, Amos, gave me strict orders that such a difficult job should only be attempted by professional workmen. Do you have some proof of your experience? Do you have insurance? I rather expected you to be wearing uniforms."

Small whipped out his wallet. "My driver's license," Small said with assurance handing it to her, "And notice my calluses. I am as you have seen for yourself, A. Small, in person, President of Complicated Maintenance, an honest and talented working man who has journeyed way out here from the city to deal with that terrible limb personally for you Mrs. Proot."

"Well, I suppose Amos would approve. Amos is famous you know. Amos idolizes the common working man. Here is your driver's license."

"Yes, that's my driver's license," said Small returning it to his wallet. "And to ease your mind I'd like you to meet my lieutenant, Rudolph Victor Talldorf, of the Detroit Talldorfs. Talldorf cut up the bodies of the poor in medical school. Him and me will saw that limb off with no damage to the house. The garage might cause a problem but we'll drop it in the side yard like a feather."

"Your helper doesn't look well. Why, you're positively pale young man. Would you like a glass of water?"

"He don't drink water. Go to the car, Talldorf."

"How much will it cost, Mr. Small?"

"Two thousand dollars."

"Amos said not more than five hundred dollars."

"For five hundred dollars Complicated Maintenance will have that limb down before noon."

"Small!" whispered Talldorf as Small laid out his ropes, "This is Amos Proot's house, the famous liberal lawyer I read about in Mine Magazine. If we scratch his house we'll be in a liberal prison in a minute. Small, we shouldn't do this job!"

"We're rich again, Talldorf. But you almost blew it there. Liberals don't scare me. You gotta keep up a good front. No matter how impossible the job never admit you can't do it."

Mrs. Proot drove off to the women's luncheon in her maroon Mercedes with the promise she would pay them on her return.

Small looped a noose around the limb and ran the ropes through an ingenious network of pulleys and soon the limb was cut three-quarters through. "Hold onto this rope and don't worry about nothin, the limb is secure." Small scurried up the tree like a squirrel. As the teeth of the saw bit into the wood there was a ripping sound.

"Pull!" Small yelled. A strip peeled down the trunk as the limb tore loose, pivoted away from the house and disappeared in a splintering crash through the garage roof. Talldorf and Small gathered up their equipment and retreated hastily from Pea Ridge.

"He's a lawyer, Small! A big-time political lawyer!"

"Calm yourself, Talldorf, he idolizes the common working man. That's you and me. Besides, she'll never remember the company name, it's too complicated."

Small pointed Bluey's nose toward a different suburb. It was noon before Small got the ladder up against the front of a two-story brick house to wash the windows.

Talldorf's stockinged feet sunk into the carpet. Hunger gnawed at his stomach. He grabbed a piece of toast off the top of the coffee grounds and gobbled it. He went outside where Small was filling his bucket. "It's no use, Small. I have to eat or I'll pass out."

"Do you think I ain't hungry. Do you think because I'm Small my hunger is small? We're gonna be lucky to finish this castle by sunset." Small started grimly up the ladder with his bucket over his arm. "Discipline, Talldorf!"

Talldorf went into the kitchen. "I wonder if you might have any leftovers—" he asked the nonplussed housewife. He devoured five toasted cheese sandwiches, three pickles, and drank a quart of milk.

"I hope you're satisfied, Talldorf," Small fumed as they flew along the expressway toward the city lights, "Because of your noon meal we had to finish washing the windows in the dark. They'll be streaked. They're gonna judge us by our work, and we can't afford to get bad-mouthed. When we get the word-of-mouth goin our phone will be ringing off the hook."

Each new house presented new difficulties. Small tracked mud from a flower bed across a white shag carpet. Talldorf in his enthusiasm with the squeegee swept a priceless vase off a table top. There were amoniac drops which stained a teak floor and broken screens that housewives noted and complained about and a hundred little accidents they would have complained about had they noticed. Sums were subtracted and word-of-mouth was rife. It spread their peculiarities and strange working habits from suburb to suburb, from house to house. Dining rooms and breakfast nooks buzzed with rumors of mishap and warning.

"I'm telling you, Carl," the stockbroker said pulling on his golf shoes in front of his locker, "the tall guy was going through Edith's drawers. I would have caught him red-handed but he heard me coming. I think those two nitwits are professional robbers."

The phone was not ringing off the hook. The suburban campaign appeared to be foundering.

Talldorf and Small parked on a sidestreet. Small was depressed and irritable. "I told you what to say. It's not like we're cheating people. We're offering them a service. Somebody has to do the dirty work. That's us. Now walk up to that door and knock!"

"I sense that these people don't trust us, Small."

"I'm going to count to three and you're going to get out of the car and start knocking on doors like I been doing all morning. One, two—"

A little girl in a yellow dress and yellow kneesocks came down the walk from the house. "Hello, little girl," Talldorf said getting out of Bluey. "We're your friends. You don't have to be afraid of us." Little Trudy Peck, the petulant spoiled beauty, kicked Talldorf in the kneecap. He bit his tongue and hopped on one foot.

"Child molester!" a woman shrieked from across the street. They sped away in Bluey.

The woman who shrieked happened to be Felicia Breed-Mork who had recently married Mosiah Mort Mork the insurance executive and son to the famous General Merriwether Mort Mork who commanded on the Western Front. Felicia also was the beloved sister of the distinguished and dashing air ace on the Eastern Front, Colonel Wilifred Breed III. It was she who informed the police of Talldorf and Small's presence in the neighborhood. Feeling her good deed for the day had been done Felicia hopped into her Jaguar and sped off to meet her lover.

Chief Nugget sat behind the blond oak desk at police headquarters. "All right, boys, nobody's accused you of anything." "I know my rights!" Small yelled. "I'm an American businessman conducting free enterprise. This is a free country."

"Calm your friend down, son," Chief Nugget frowned. "I'm only doing my job. It's best for everybody concerned that you stay away from our nice little town."

Talldorf leaned responsibly and awkwardly toward the law, proud to be taken into the confidence of high authority. "I understand perfectly, Chief."

"This is what I think of your nice little town, Chief!" Small put his thumb to his nose.

"Get him out of here," the Chief said. Talldorf hauled Small out of the office and down the corridor. "Take your hands off me. Turncoat! Traitor!" Small brushed off his lapels. "Don't you recognize the enemy? Do you want to be shoved around all your life? I'm going to have to make a million dollars quick to hire a smart lawyer to protect my Constitutional rights."

"We better not hire Amos Proot, Small."

Though the most memorable suburban moments lay yet before them, the spring offensive ground to an ignominious halt.

It was the middle of summer and Small was still broke. Tar bubbled in the streets; beaches were littered with scorched faces and peeling backs; musclemen strutted and girls paraded in bathing suits. Talldorf tiptoed along beside Small who stared out across the lake from beneath a cork helmet and a pair of bubble sunglasses. They made their way through the throng of bathers and settled by themselves on the breakwater.

"Shazam!" cried Small stripping to his gold swimming trunks. "Talldorf, ain't ya goin for a dip? At least take off your shirt and get a suntan."

"I don't know how to swim, Small, and the sun would burn me to a crisp." He watched Small poise on the balls of his nimble feet and throw himself recklessly off the rocks into the waves.

"Next we do the hospital," Small said rubbing his wet head with a towel. We wash the windows inside and out. I'm gonna get you your own set of brass Eagle squeegees for the job."

"That job will take us a month," Talldorf observed professionally.

"A week, Talldorf. I do the high work. That leaves you with hardly nothin to do but keep from breaking some expensive piece of equipment or tripping over crutches. Hand me the suntan lotion.

"We're finally hot on the trail of the great Short." Small said as they arrived at the hospital. "Short laid on me my greatest talent. In very reality I am a window washer. And you will be a window washer too. In recognition and appreciation of your diligence Complicated Maintenance rewards you with your own set of professional squeegees. Brand new, Tallie, and crafted by the Brass Eagle Squeegee Corporation of America. I picked them out at the janitor's supply house myself."

There were two squeegees in the box, a long and a short one. They gleamed like weapons. "With these," Small said, "the company confers on you an equality hitherto reserved for myself."

"I accept these squeegees with humility, Small, and I promise to do all in my power to live up to the company's trust in me."

They sat on the grass eating the sandwiches that Talldorf had packed. Nurses in trim uniforms, radiating youthful exuberance, passed briskly to and from the hospital and the nurse's home. Talldorf's prediction was coming true. It was their fourth day on the job and Small was still washing the great oval window that rose above the lobby to the seventh floor. His scaffolds had risen with unforeseen expense. Small fought rusted pins in the rented iron and spent much time teaching Talldorf expertise with the squeegee.

"No no no! Never, never start squeegeeing a window from the bottom, Talldorf," Small said in disbelief. "I thought ya had a college education. I love America, Talldorf, but when I see the results of our educational system I fear for our great republic. People think washin a window is easy. People are generally nuts. Don't bear down. A light touch, like leadin a symphony orchestra. No steaks. Don't leave sparrow tails. Clear and clean. Pay close attention to my technique and stop eyeing the nurses. Now, try it."

Talldorf was eager to please and worked meticulously. "You gotta work faster. Don't think about nothin. Especially women." The long awkward reach of the fledgling was marvelous to contemplate. Everything about Talldorf was from the off side, Small observed. He was left handed, left footed and left out. The only thing right about Talldorf was the part Elinore had plowed through his red hair in her ceaseless efforts to flatten his turkey tail while eradicating any vestige of the vagabond nature of his irresponsible father. The Abraham Lincoln Grammar School had twisted Rudolph from a lefty to a righty which had left him cross-eyed for a time and was responsible still for his stumbles. Rudolph's long white fingers which Elinore had imagined dancing on a concert keyboard and Anne had envisioned enshrined in the Hall of Surgeons, those pale cold fingers so apt at fumbling, were becoming nimble under Small's stern tutelage. Now those esteemed fingers brushed lightly as feathers at irridescent streaks until window panes trembled with clarity.

"Keep your attention on your work, Tallie, and you can't get hurt. We're only five floors up. See down there, a nice soft row of bushes. There's nothin to it. Pick up your bucket. Follow me."

"Perhaps the company should buy some insurance, Small."

"Don't think and you won't fall. There ain't no insurance against falling no matter how much the policy costs. And if you fall you're right here at the hospital."

The job lingered into the third week. Every sickroom Talldorf entered brought a stronger whiff of floorcleaner, ether and the smell of death. Rudolph tiptoed past catheters and bottles of blood and oxygen tents. Wasted faces acknowledged his presence with the flutter of an eyelid or the twitch of a lip while he clung to his squeegees.

"I feel sick," Rudolph told Small on one of the numerous coffee breaks. "Hospitals reek of my past." But Small was enjoying himself. From the formica table in the hospital cafeteria Small ogled the nurses. "Talldorf, I can't believe you gave up all these fringe benefits."

Talldorf stood rooted on the ledge, his window brush dripping, staring through the window. Small bounced toward him. "What's going on?"

"A man's dying," said Talldorf. "Look, Small. He's dying."

Small pushed his nose against the glass. A rugged black man with curly white hair was kneeling beside a bed where an old man lay. "What do ya expect in a hospital, Talldorf? Look in the baby window, you'll see em gettin born. They come an they go."

"That black man is giving the white man last rights," said Talldorf.

"That black man is a janitor. He's wearin overalls. Come on, it ain't nothin to us."

The old man's body lay like a child's under the white sheet. He was squeezing a rubber ball in his hand. "What do you think, Snowball?" asked Short, "the Angel is coming?"

Snowball's black hand took the ball and spun it on a finger and Short grinned. His silver hair shining with life stood out in whisps against the pillow.

"I think the Angel is here," said Snowball.

"Is that how you do the whirl, Snowball? On a finger?"

"That's how I do the whirl. I got the squeegee handles bored smooth and my finger inside spins the world, Short. My fingers is bird feathers on the wind."

"And your feet too," said Short. "See out the window there. That's Small, my last apprentice. He's washing the windows right here at the hospital. Ain't that strange. Small's got his apprentice, the tall guy. They haven't discovered Luigi yet, there's no healing in those squeegee strokes. Look at those clowns. Small don't even recognize me. Follow me, boys..."

Death did not concern the commander who was busy living, but it obsessed the mind of his lieutenant. Small hurried Talldorf onto the sixth floor ledge where it ended abruptly high above the hospital entrance.

"Pay attention to what I'm tellin ya, Talldorf. I'm gonna bridge this gap in the ledges with the ladder so I can walk across and we won't have to rent no more scaffolding. I'm gonna stand over there on the end of the ledge and lower the end of the ladder to you over here. You got to grab it so it don't fall six floors. I'm gonna put it right in your mitts, all ya gotta do is catch it. Talldorf! Are you listening?"

Talldorf held to the window frame but stood firm with death in mind gazing fatefully across the abyss where Small appeared on the ledge opposite pulling the extension ladder out of the window. What drove Small? Look at him heisting the ladder up rung by rung while holding to the ledge with nothing but his tennis shoes until the ladder towered straight above him. Small set the foot of the ladder where the ledge ended and Talldorf came awake.

"No! No, Small. Don't lower that ladder to me. I'll miss it! It will fall and kill a dozen people and I'll be responsible."

"Shutup! Catch the ladder. Here she comes right on the money! Grab it!"

The top of the ladder came down on Talldorf like judgement. He caught it perfectly and was driven to his knees.

"Great work, Tallie!" Small yelled. "Set it down. Get out from under it. Watch out!"

Talldorf was kneeling on the ledge with the end of the ladder in his lap and the next moment he was dangling from it by his knees gazing through a window into the blue inverted eyes of a nurse he took for an angel. Small bounded across the rungs.

"Don't move, Talldorf, that's an order!" A thin wail like an air raid siren rose from Rudolph piercing even the consciousness of the dying Short who knowing it all so well was seized with gales of laughter that raised him from his bed and carried him away through the ceiling in the arms of the Angel.

"I got your leg, Talldorf!" Small had locked Talldorf's leg in his arms. "Don't thrash!" Small bit through Talldorf's pantleg to get his attention. "All you got to do is reach up and grab the ladder rungs, Talldorf. Do that!" And Talldorf did.

In the urology laboratory where they climbed through the window Small berated Talldorf for wasting time and refused to listen to his jabber about angels. "You don't see the Angel unless you fall at least twelve floors. Short told me that and you didn't even fall. If the company forbids you to think about women you think about angels!"

"I apologize for my ineptitude, Small. Now you see what kind of a doctor I would have been. I don't know that I am ready for the responsibility of the squeegees. I will return to my post and hold my attention to my humble task."

"You must be Rudolph, Alexander's apprentice," she said standing over Talldorf who was on his knees scrubbing a row of low windows in the lab. "My name is Cynthia. I've been admiring your work. If there's one thing I appreciate I think it is clean windows."

Cynthia moved closer and held out her hand while Talldorf inched backward. "You have beautiful hands, the hands of a surgeon or a pianist. Probably a lot of women have told you that."

"Not a whole lot of women. A few women. Two women to be exact." Cynthia turned over Rudolph's hand and studied his palm. "Such an interesting lifeline," she said. "Would you like me to read your future?"

"Do you think it will help?" Rudolph asked. "How can a lovely girl like yourself work in a hospital day in and day out in the midst of death and despair?"

"Oh!" exclaimed Cynthia, "What a bright future I see for you, Rudolph. But I mustn't tell you more now." She bent and kissed his cheek. "Thank you for cleaning my windows, Rudolph."

"I think she likes me, Small!" Talldorf said excitedly.

"Of course Cynthia likes you, Talldorf. You're a likeable guy. And Cynthia is a likeable girl." Small sliced the top off the water on the glass with his six-inch squeegee. "Cynthia and me already had a provocative interchange, Talldorf." Small winked. "She's got a townhouse out here in the suburbs. She wants me to estimate her windows."

"She just asked me to ask you if we would come to dinner, Small." Small started to whistle.

"Of course we'll come for dinner. Take over here, Talldorf. I'll answer the fair damsel in person."

Talldorf scrubbed the windows and saw himself reflected in the finished panes, handsome, intelligent and debonaire. Hastily he obliterated the pulcritudinous image of Cynthia that rose unbidden in his brain.

Not so Small whose eyes glowed like charcoal briquets as he plotted conquest with bold acumen. She's mine, Small thought. And she knows it. How she stroked my brow and kissed my lips! And when I held her in my arms how eager her tongue. Good God! How long since a woman pressed my head to her breasts. I despise a man who chases a skirt but when the woman comes to me, is blinded by my spell—Poor Talldorf. He'll be jealous. He'll accuse me of being a hypocrite. I'll admit it. I'll explain the ancient Chinese practice of self indulgence. I'll tell him about the variety of religious experiences that crisscross man's life..."

Small donned his red plaid shirt and knotted his forest-green tie. He whistled as he tied his polished shoes and clicked his heels together. Talldorf had never seen his mentor so assiduous in his toilet.

Small had staunched his shaving nicks with Carnal Cologne, splashed scent of cloves behind his ears and on his neck, soaked the tip of his green handkerchief with the monogrammed 'S' which he explained matched his eyes, and stuffed it into the breast pocket of his powderblue coat.

"I think the company should present Cynthia with a bottle of wine, Small," Talldorf said following Small down the steps.

"I'll take care of strategy, Tallie." Small whistled all the way to the supermarket.

"I'd suggest a fine wine, Small." Talldorf held out an expensive bottle of rare vintage for Small to inspect.

"No wine, Tallie. The company's gettin hard liquor. I know what women like."

"Cynthia would appreciate a bottle of wine, Small. Cynthia is a refined girl, Small, she lives in the suburbs."

"Ok, Talldorf. Get the wine. We'll drink a bottle with dinner."

"What's for dinner, Small?"

"Probably chicken."

"Then this bottle of white wine will be fine."

"Four bucks? Outrageous, Talldorf. Here's a bottle of spaghetti wine for a buck."

"It probably tastes like nail polish, Small."

"Who cares what it tastes like so long as it gets Cynthia drunk. You're gonna need your sleep tomorrow, Talldorf. I'm gonna give ya the keys to Bluey and let you pick me up at Cynthia's house in the morning." Talldorf was indignant. "Let's get one thing straight right now, Talldorf. I can tell a hot broad when I see one and Cynthia ain't interested in you. She likes ya but she don't want you horning in. I hope you enjoy dinner. Eat as much as you want. Eat till you're stuffed. Stuff yourself, Talldorf."

Small shaved the fender of the car before and backed into the car behind, gunned Bluey and sped toward the suburbs.

"I'll carry the sack, Small," Talldorf said as they approached Cynthia's townhouse at a double trot.

"I told you I'm handling it." Small cradled the sack of bottles beneath his powderblue coat next to his heart, ran through the gate, leaped up the steps and pounded on the door. "Open up, baby," he shouted. "It's Small!"

The table was set, the candles lit.

"Pretty classy joint you got here, Cynthia," said Small. "I'd estimate the windows at thirty bucks but for you the company will do em for twenty five." Small took off his coat, loosened his cravat and tucked his napkin into his shirt collar.

"Would you please carve the fowl, Alexander?" Cynthia asked.

"Talldorf," Small said, "Cut the chicken."

"Red taught me how to carve," Talldorf explained as he tried to saw through the leg bone. "Ive disected frogs, pigs, sharks, cats."

"Please, Talldorf, a lady is present."

"I don't mind, Alexander," Cynthia said, "I'm not offended by science."

"That ain't science, my dear. That's Talldorf's childhood. Talldorf had a very unusual childhood." The candles' flicker wove an intricate pattern of Small's desire over Cynthia's face and breasts. "But I didn't come here to talk about Talldorf." Small splashed more wine into Cynthia's glass and smacked his lips over the fowl. "You can cook up some hot stuff, Cynthia. If we was Romans we'd puke and start all over. Allow me to pour us a touch of scotch, baby, and you and me can get better acquainted while Talldorf washes the dishes."

"Don't bother about the dishes," Cynthia said. She filled three glasses with ice and whiskey. "Excuse me for a moment. I'm so anxious to hear how you two met. I'll be right back."

"Here's Bluey's keys, Talldorf. Scram. Don't drive too fast and don't drive too slow. Take the keys. Talldorf!" Talldorf was pretending to study the books on Cynthia's book shelf.

"Oh Rudolph," called Cynthia.

Small leaped to his feet. "She's callin ya, Talldorf."

Cynthia had changed into a sleek dressing gown. "It seems my zipper is stuck," Cynthia said. Talldorf's fingers lay like icicles on her hot flesh. She breathed deeply and looked into Rudolph's eyes as he zipped her up.

Small, standing splay-footed in the middle of the mustard colored carpet crushed out his Lucky in the rubber plant. His nostrils flared. The flame of lust raged beneath his cheeks and his lips twisted in a wolfish snarl. His eyes were burning coals as he looked from Cynthia to Talldorf. "Two's company, three's a crowd," he barked.

"Arithmetic is so silly," observed Cynthia. "It's all right Alexander, I like Rudolph too." Cynthia led Talldorf by the hand. "You don't want to leave do you Rudolph?"

"No," admitted Talldorf looking hesitantly at Small.

"What we all need is another nice drink," said Cynthia.

"Right, baby, I'll fix them," said Small. He would make them doubles. Cynthia would be putty in his hands and Talldorf would pass out. But to Small's surprise he found Cynthia cuddled under Talldorf's arm on the couch.

"Drink up, Talldorf," ordered Small.

"A toast!" said Cynthia raising her glass, "Here, Alexander, sit on this side of me. What more could any woman ask than to be between such men as you?" Small slid down beside her feeling the warm fullness of her thigh.

"To woman!" growled Small.

"To Cynthia," said Talldorf.

"To togetherness—" purred Cynthia and their glasses clinked. Cynthia sipped and said, "Won't you put your arm around me, Alexander?" Small snaked his arm under Talldorf's and Cynthia took their wrists and pulled their arms tight around her, sighed contentedly and her slippers fell from her ivory toes while the eyes of Talldorf and Small met in amazement across Cynthia's boobs.

"Please, oh please don't let me go," breathed Cynthia sipping from her glass. "This way you both have a hand for your glasses." Small took a hasty slosh. "And each of you have a free hand for me—" Talldorf gulped his drink.

"I mean—I see the philosophy of it, Cynthia—" said Talldorf.

"Hold me, Rudolph." She drew his hand down where his wooden fingers lay against the rise of her breasts beneath the silk gown while moulding herself to Small's hard torso with a heat he felt in his teeth.

"I see the whole of it," claimed Small as Talldorf watched the breast nearest him suffer the hairy paw of Small. It drove Rudolph mad with passion. He felt dizzy, lightheaded, and pressed kisses to Cynthia's cheek.

"I know, dear," whispered Cynthia turning her lips to his. Small's chuckle seemed that of a satyr behind a shrub and Cynthia's laughter the trickle of waters. Whose glass was whose Talldorf scarcely knew, whose hand was whose he was never certain and the darkness of Cynthia's bedroom to which she led them gamboling and tumbling obliterated Talldorf's very sense of civilization. The last thing he remembered was Small's cry, "Bombs away!" Cynthia's "Yes yes yes—" and Talldorf's own "Whoooooeeee!" climaxing the suburban offensive.

Chapter 10

THE BRASS EMPIRE

T he Exclusive Men's Wear Store accessible to any fool with a few bucks on the world's busiest corner wore an amazing amount of dingy brass.

Small stood on the curb as shoppers scurried and traffic howled. He balanced on his toes studying the brass fluting around the show windows and the solid brass revolving doors, the dreary hue of a dusty arid land like Mongolia.

I can turn it into gold, thought Small. I'll corner the brass market. This city will gleam. They'll call me the Brass King. I'll be on the cover of *Mine Magazine*. I'll have a brass empire that will shine like gold.

"Mr. Hope will see you, sir," said the matronly receptionist. Small entered, hat in hand. He had chosen to appear a worker rather than in his powderblue suit for the shock value of a workman with a brain.

Small noted in the instant the friendly and honest face of a man who enjoys his work, and was comfortable with Mr. Hope immediately.

"Complicated Maintenance, sir, is a small company which prides itself on quality work. Among our satisfied customers are Baggs Fifth Avenue, the Look-Up Gallery, Ensardos Restaurant and numerous downtown stores, a diversity of work, Mr. Hope, with quality foremost and price a secondary consideration. I know of no other company in the dirt business who can make that statement. Considering your location on the world's busiest corner I would think the brass trim on your store would gleam like gold."

"It doesn't," said Mr. Hope, "but it should."

"I can make it gleam like gold," said Small, "All of the brass on the facade and the revolving doors, for three hundred dollars."

"That's a good price, Mr. Small. What do you use on the brass?" Small had not considered it.

"I prefer not to say, sir. Trade secret, you know. We try to improve on existing methods. What lends quality to our work is the dedication of my staff."

"You speak like a competent man, Mr. Small. I will take up the matter with the board this afternoon. Ah—! Those pigeons at the windows, that is a real problem, Mr. Small. They roost on these ledges and drop on window shoppers and make an infernal racket."

"I can get rid of those pigeons," said Small.

"My god, man, how?"

"Rubber snakes," said Small. Mr. Hope chuckled.

"Rubber snakes," repeated Small. "Lay them on the window sills and the pigeons will leave."

"Really? Will you get rid of those pigeons for me?"

"I will," said Small.

"I know the rubber snakes will work," Small told Talldorf, "But I ain't taking no chances. There's rain puddles on the ledges. I'm going to electrocute them. If I get rid of those pigeons the brass contract is in my pocket. We'll be doing every piece of brass in the Windy City. We'll be millionaires."

Bluey swerved into the alley behind the world's busiest corner. Small raised the hood. "If the cops don't believe I'm a work vehicle they'll think Bluey is stalled."

They darted across the street into a dimestore and went to the basement toy department and found piles of green rubber snakes with black eyes and red tongues. "Give me two dozen snakes," Small told the counterlady, "and a discount."

They crossed the street in the rain with two paper bags full of snakes. Talldorf got his box and they went to the second floor. "Give me the bags,

Talldorf." Small climbed out the window and walked along the ledge distributing green snakes at intervals while pigeons fluttered up squawking.

"Ok, Tallie, hit it downstairs and be ready. Birds are gonna rain from heaven and they're all ours."

Small drew ten feet of electric cord from his pocket, plugged one end into a socket and approached the window with the stripped wires. Small plunged the live wire into a puddle on the ledge. A universal squawk like the plucked harp of heaven reverberated above the man-made noise of the world's busiest corner. Small peered along the ledge where no pigeon sat as feathers floated away from his view.

From Talldorf's view it was a pigeon waterfall. He didn't know which way to dart first. Where he stood a pigeon fell into his box with such force it fell from his hands. Either way on the walk men and women were on their knees, parcels scattered or stumbling among the bodies of pigeons. "My god, I'm killed," declared a lady with her hat askew. People declared it had been an earthquake and stood dazed against the walls as Talldorf stuffed pigeons into his box and hurried away to dump the bodies in the back seat of Bluey. The cop who had been directing traffic questioned witnesses, and traffic began to snarl.

Having replaced the electric wire in his pocket Small directed Mr. Hope's gaze along the ledge outside his office windows. There lay the green rubber snakes and not a pigeon.

"Masterful, Small!" said Mr. Hope. "I heard the pigeons squawk when they saw the snakes. Say, quite a traffic snarl down there."

"I'm glad you're satisfied, Mr. Hope, I'll submit my modest bill, sir. Just now I must dart off to other pressing business."

"I'll tell you now, Small," said Mr. Hope, "I like your style. Obviously you know what you're doing. The brass job is yours."

Small collected an armful of warm pigeons from the gutters and sidewalks that Talldorf had not yet gathered. The cop had returned to the blaring intersection but pedestrians still milled about scowling at Small's activities.

"A lunatic!" a fat man said to his skinny companion as Small passed. "A long redhead dumped boxes of those damn pigeons into that blue car in the alley."

"Da mayor really runs this town snappy, P.J.," said the skinny man, "Those guys are department of sanitation workers."

Small was appalled at the heap of steaming bodies that occupied the back of his car. They overflowed both garbage cans and the box and were knee-deep on the back floor. Talldorf sat in the front seat panting from exertion and looking distressed. Small slammed down Bluey's hood and leaped into the driver's seat.

"We got the brass job, Tallie, and I'm charging Hope fifty bucks for our brief activity here. Now it's off to some low-life grocery store where the natives eat squab. Ho, ho, Tallie, this is the kind of operation I like. By a stroke of authentic genius I hold the brass heart of the Windy City in my palm."

Small sped out of the alley. Bluey darted out of downtown traffic, past the dour stone face of St. Francis Cathedral, past the loading docks of the railroad yards onto the long ribbon of Lake Shore Drive where the park flew past on the way to the ghetto. "We gotta hurry, Tallie, before the corpses begin to stink."

"Oh god, Small, it's terrible, terrible," said Talldorf hunched like a grasshopper and wringing his hands. "We must have killed two hundred pigeons, and just for money."

"What do you think we're working for, Talldorf? The humane society? This is valid business. Like hauling dead cows to the butcher shop. People got to eat and I know those people eat em. In all foreign countries people eat pigeons. I seen pictures. They lay em out on boards all in rows. We got a car full of gold!"

"Small, you're overexcited, you're driving too fast."

"Two hundred pigeons are rotting behind me." Small patted Bluey's dashboard. "When you get on the open road you can't hold her down."

"Too fast, Small!"

"Our turnoff's the next one." Small swerved into the curb lane. A squad car curved in behind with its red light flashing. "Damn, the sharks are on me again! I ain't stopping for them bandits!"

"Stop, Small, he's a cop. He's got a gun."

"I got a car full of dead bodies! How do I explain that? I ain't makin explanations, Talldorf, we ain't stopping. I know this neighborhood. What the hell!" yelled Small momentarily alarmed. He flipped a spare rubber snake over his shoulder.

Talldorf and Small barely escaped with their sanity. The pigeons had been merely stunned by their recent unfortunate experience and with the snake now in their midst revived careening within the car as if a shell of beating wings and feathers had penetrated Bluey's armor exploding in bird shrieks, stabbing bills, and ripping toenails. By the grace of God the windows were open. Pigeons billowed forth like a living smoke screen so alarming the officer who was trained to expect anything that he ran his squad car over the curb into a briar of lilacs, an event not witnessed by Small who was riding the steering wheel with shoulders hunched nor Talldorf whose head was buried in his arms like a spare tire. "I hope you're satisfied!" Small yelled at Talldorf as Bluey raced down an alley past a blur of garbage cans. Feathers floated about the car as Small swerved around corners but the cop was gone.

"That's what insanity must be like," said Talldorf.

"That cost us! We could have got two bits a bird. I never understood electricity, electricity's got no heart. Never say we don't give service, Tallie. Not only did we get rid of Hope's pigeons, we taxied em to the other side of town."

Bluey nosed through the financial district at midnight. They were looking for maintenance men cleaning brass, but none were to be found. "They're like cops, Talldorf. When you need one where the hell are they?"

Small went downtown in broad daylight and brazenly penetrated the bowels of the Board of Trade. "Who are you?" said the maintenance man guiltily dropping his feet from the desktop. "Nobody's suppose to be down here."

"Relax," Small said, "I'm a friend."

"They got vaults down here with stocks and bonds in em, buddy, probably gold bullion too. The public ain't allowed down here."

"You don't have to cover up for me," said Small. "I ain't your boss. I got a maintenance company of my own. I only want info. I want to know what you guys use to clean the fancy brass on this pile of rock." It was the wrong tack. The maintenance man returned his feet to the two grooves on top of the desk. His eyes narrowed.

"I don't know," he said.

"You know."

"You said you got your own company. You're a boss. You ought to know all that stuff. How come you ask a plain old worker like me?"

"I'm a plain old worker like you."

"You union?" asked the maintenance man, his eyes more narrow than ever.

"I ain't nobody's slave," said Small. "So I ain't union."

"You're a boss," accused the maintenance man.

"I got one guy working for me, he's my friend."

"You ain't union and you're a boss, so when you need knowhow you come to a poor worker like me and you think I'll just toss it out to you so you can make big bucks while I eat beans and you eat steak!"

"I eat donuts and peanutbutter." This nearly broke the resistance of the maintenance man but he recovered himself. "I don't know what they use to clean brass. I work the day shift."

"Let's look in the lockers," suggested Small. "They must have a can of some kind of compound."

"You better just get out of here the way you came. I ain't at all sure you're who you say you are. All I got to do is pick up this telephone and call the guards."

"Guards? You think guards are your friends? You been in this dungeon so long you're blind as a bat. You don't know who your friends are. You're a puppet of the executives at the top of this rock pile. They pull the strings and you dance in your hole. They throw you a bone and you gobble it and hoard the crumbs. You're so blind you think the union is your friend. You don't know a worker when he stands in front of you. I'll see you in the street sometime with your tin cup. Then you remember me and hold your breath. You think work is sittin on your ass. You ain't a worker, you're a lackey!"

Well, it couldn't be hard to clean brass anyway. He drove to the Windy City's biggest hardware store and bought a can of Kopper Kleen, the picture of a happy housewife holding a shiny pot on its label. "Give me the biggest size," said Small. "Just rub it on and wipe it off, huh?"

"Yes, sir, easy as pie," said the counterman.

"I'm giving us more time than we'll need, Tallie," Small said as they drove downtown at midnight. "Hope himself will be down at six a.m. to open the revolving doors so we can get the other sides before the store opens."

"That can will be enough, Small?"

"Sure, there's a gallon. It ain't like washing a wall, Talldorf, it's only strips and curlicues. We'll finish in a couple hours and be sitting in Pixie's the rest of the night drinking coffee and making three hundred bucks. This will be my record, Tallie. I never made more than a hundred in one night and that was awnings and that takes muscle. Hope's gonna broadcast the name of Complicated Maintenance all over town and we'll be polishing brass fireplugs on banks and I'll make em pay."

At midnight the world's busiest corner was deserted. Small pulled Bluey right up to the curb. "It's the best time to work, Tallie, nobody crowding us or getting jealous at how easy we pick off three hundred smackers. Set up the ladders and walkboard. I'll start dabbing with the Kopper Kleen and tell you how to do it."

When Talldorf had the walkboard set on the ladders so they could reach the brass strip above the show windows he knelt beside Small who was rubbing furiously at the brass strip beneath the windows. Rudolph saw no gleaming brass. A dank gloomy compound coated the first two feet of the brass strip. Small rubbed with all his might.

"Is it hard, Small?"

"I think you got to let it set," said Small.

"It looks like mud," said Talldorf. They stared away at the long strip bearing off toward the intersection. Small dabbed the mud away. It was no brighter. He polished it briskly with a flannel rag. No gleam of gold rose out of the metal. Small tried steel wool. They left the mud on the brass and walked around the block. Small puffed on a Lucky and scrutinized gleaming brass fireplugs as if they held a mystery.

"When we get back and wipe it off it will probably shine like gold." Talldorf's voice was optimistic. He felt relaxed walking in the warm city night. Since he rarely saw any of the money they made he was not greatly concerned, but Small was gloomy.

"Maybe it's got to set for hours," Small said. "And Hope expects it to be done by six a.m. Why don't guys help each other, Talldorf? Did they explain that to you at college? I burn when I think of that maintenance mole in his hole. We're all in this together, but one guy gets his crumb and he'll beat you over the head if you look at it. We ain't no better than cavemen. Don't I share, Talldorf? Ain't I always thinking about your welfare? I'm the boss and I think of others, and that guy calls himself a worker and don't think of nobody but himself. So here's two guys goin hungry because he don't recognize a brother when he sees one."

"Brother, I'm hungry!" said Talldorf, "Let's get a couple donuts and let it set longer, Small."

"It ain't dinnertime, it's work time. Give you guys an inch and ya take a mile. We got a mile of brass to clean in five hours, and the rate we're going it'll take five years. That's ten cents a day, a nickel apiece."

"Ok, Small, I'm ready to go back there and rub her till she shines!"

Small removed the mud that had set for half an hour and polished it lightly. It was the color of Mongolia. He rubbed hard. There was no change. Small stood up and walked in little circles on the sidewalk gazing up at the skyscrapers.

"I'll rub hard with steel wool, Small." Talldorf stooped and rubbed with all his might. "I think it's helping, Small."

"It's scratching the hell out of it, Talldorf. Stop it. They'll sue us."

Talldorf was infected with Small's gloom. "Let's rub the Kopper Kleen all over everything and let it set two hours, Small. I bet it will shine when we rub it off."

Small continued pacing. He imagined how disconcerted Hope would be to arrive in the morning, so confident of Small's ability, and see the same dingy brass which had always been there. "Shameful," announced Small as he paced. Rudolph stared absently in the show windows remembering the clothes he had worn in Detroit. The displays now seemed fantastic to him. They were the uniforms of an alien army.

"Fold up the ladders and walkboard, Talldorf. We're getting out of here."

"We're quitting?"

"We're retreating. The only way to clean this brass is to rub every inch like a Turk. I ain't a Turk. This is a three thousand dollar job, not a three hundred dollar job. No wonder Hope snapped up my bid. I don't have to do it and I ain't."

And Small felt a sense of relief, his dream of a brass empire fading into the debris of his past.

"I had an inside connection with Hope, Talldorf. Hope would have said, 'I was the first man the Brass King ever worked for.' Now he'll want to forget my name. It wasn't even dirt, it was corrosion and I ain't a miner." Small pulled Bluey up before the lights of Pixie's all-night cafe.

"C'mon, Tallie, we still got coffee and donuts."

Chapter 11

THE BLOOD OF TALLDORF

Small sat for coffee in the Greyhound cafeteria at the same subterranean table where he had met Talldorf. His eyes itched under the fluorescent light. Small had lived long among the concrete caves of the Windy City with his sights on the heights looking to scale skyscrapers and what had he found but illusion: his youth, Elvira, his great plans. He was broke again and not an inch higher.

Under such a burden Small crossed the concourse among the travelers to the information counter and inquired for the Purchaser of Services.

"I don't want the walls washed," said the Purchaser, a lean man who looked like a greyhound, "I want someone to clean the upholstery in all of our buses."

"All those seats in all those buses?"

"Precisely." The Purchaser beamed and rubbed his thin hands.

"The buses park underground, don't they?" asked Small.

"Yes."

"No."

"I beg your pardon?"

"I don't work underground. I ain't a mole. I don't crawl around in sewer pipes."

"Sewer pipes?" The Purchaser stepped back from Small's dark little figure.

"I came to you in good faith to brighten up your waiting room walls and you want me underground picking up hairs."

"Good heavens, man, I'm offering you a big job. Are you a maintenance company or not?"

"I'm Complicated Maintenance, the best for quality work. But I don't work in holes no matter what you pay. Good day!" Small bounced up the escalator like a swimmer rising to the light.

Small sagged along an unlikely sidestreet next to the railroad station and wandered into the Western-Eastern Building. He thought he might get the walls and ceilings in the outlying telegraph offices. Instead the Purchaser had him estimate the walls and ceiling in the enormous employees cafeteria. It would take Talldorf and him two months to clean that cavern. "No, no..." said Small pushing the vision of that ceiling from before his eyes. He stumbled out onto the sidewalk. "I can't wash every wall and ceiling in town for peanuts," Small told the shoppers who scurried by.

"You don't happen to have a bridge in your mouth with gold in it, do ya, Talldorf?" Small asked that night.

"No, Small. I have perfect teeth."

Talldorf's graduation present got them $12 for gas and groceries at the pawn shop.

Small reasoned he could make a killing in the ghetto, that blacks would leap at the opportunity of having a white man do their dirty work. He went from door to door with his hat in his hand. "A. Small, my card, sir." The man invited A. Small inside and set him like a trophy in the midst of the family enjoying exotic, aromatic dishes which A. Small had never before tasted. He shared the repast and sipped the glasses handed him and furnished an oral history and projection of the meteoric rise he anticipated for himself in the high affairs of the Windy City. "Crazy, man," murmured the black men nodding and bobbing their heads. Small enjoyed their company, he was stuffed with food and slightly tipsy and yet unaccountably he could not get the first kitchen wall to wash.

"That sky is gray, Talldorf, but beyond those clouds my star is shining."

He got a job washing all the windows in a twelve story building for two hundred dollars. "First you gotta crack some windows," the building manager said. "I think some of them are painted shut."

It took Talldorf and Small two weeks to crack the windows open. "He knew damn well they were *all* painted shut!" stormed Small. He told the building manager there had to be an adjustment on the price. The building manager wrote a check for $100 and fired them. The wind blew colder. The only difference between Small and the captains of industry was that they were dealing in millions while he was dealing in peanuts.

"Good evening, Mr. Small," the butcher said. "What can I get for you? The lamb chops are especially nice. How is business, Mr. Small?"

"Up and down, up and down, Joe. I got a check here I want to cash."

"Certainly, Mr. Small. Only too happy to serve our good customers. The hamburger is fresh. I ground it myself. And how is your apprentice, Mr. Talldorf? Such a pleasant young man. How many times have I looked out the window in the middle of the night and said to Edith, there they go, Edith, off into the night while the rest of us are cozy in our beds. Here you are, Mr. Small, eighty, ninety, one hundred dollars. I have some nice smoked bratwurst."

"Six hotdogs, Joe. And put em on my account."

"Certainly, certainly, Mr. Small."

Alphonse materialized out of the darkness, exuded from between the bricks of the wall, his rheumy blue eyes, his broken nose jutting from his white whiskers and his ripped salt and pepper overcoat. Old Alphonse, born in the bosom of the Confederacy blown North to his doom where ice and snow had numbed his childhood memories and his toes. Small felt an ungovernable rush of generosity that caused him to pull out his wallet and hand a dollar to Alphonse.

"Things ain't so bad, Alphonse," Small said as the old man shuffled off. "Buy yourself a good meal and cheer up!"

It had been a mistake to give the old man anything, Small admonished himself. Alphonse now watched for Small like a hawk. Alphonse anticipated uncannily the spot where Small would park and sat complacently in the doorway. He rose laboriously and approached Small with his hand out. Small was forced to park ever farther from the house.

"Don't give him nothin," Small cautioned Talldorf. "Alphonse is a drain-pipe, the more you pour down him the faster it pours out." But Talldorf disregarded Small's advice. "False pity," Small ranted as Rudolph emptied his pockets into Alphonse's outstretched claw. "You're encouraging a public nuisance! There's institutions for em. I was raised in one. This country wasn't built by beggars askin for handouts."

Talldorf could not refuse to give and Alphonse continued to hound Small, accosted him at every corner, bearded him in public. When Small saw Alphonse coming he crossed the street or went around the block. He ducked down the alley with Talldorf. Alphonse caught Small bent behind a garbage can while Talldorf did his best to hide behind a telephone pole.

"Grubbin in my garbage cans, eh?" Alphonse mumbled, "Invadin an old man's territory. I know your kind. Wait till the young derelicts find out. Your life won't be worth a wooden nickel, he he he." Alphonse bent his neck and looked up at Talldorf. "Sonny, can ya spare an old man a dollar?" As usual, and to Small's disgust, Talldorf emptied his pockets into Alphonse's talon.

As the days grew shorter Alphonse began to appear at their door in the morning when Talldorf and Small went out, and in the evening when they returned home. Small lost his temper.

"You miserable scrounge!" Small yelled and doubled his fist to club down the dottering old man but gained control of himself with a supreme effort. He shook his finger under Alphonse's dripping nose. "I hit you and you fall down and sue me and I pay the bill while you warm your ass at County Hospital. I'm not your ordinary sucker, Alphonse. Winter's coming, but you ain't staying in my house. The answer is no. The house is big enough for Small and too small for Talldorf and Small so there ain't room for Alphonse an if there was I wouldn't want ya around so go flop in a snowdrift!"

"Goodnight, Alphonse," said Talldorf. Small gave his lieutenant a black look.

Small put a big silver padlock on the gangway gate and warned Miss Deerly to send out her pack of ferocious little dogs if Alphonse tried to come in the front way.

"Small," Talldorf pleaded, "I could make Alphonse a warm little bed on the sofa — "

"You pity winos, whores and orphans!" shouted Small. "Well I'm an orphan and I tell ya that orphans don't need your pity. Do you want to be pitied, Talldorf? You give away the company's hard-earned funds to worthless bums and suggest they sleep on my sofa. You oughta be ashamed."

Small eased out the window of the fifteenth floor and hooked his belt to the bolts. Rudolph washed the insides in his shirt sleeves while Small shivered and slipped on the icy ledges. Small dumped three shots of Four Roses into his bucket and two into himself according to Short's formula but it didn't help. "A guy could freeze to death out there, Tallie," Small said through chattering teeth. "Let's get a cup of coffee. We'll hit it again when my eyeballs thaw."

December darkened the sky over the lake. The wind howled. The snow drifted over the fenders of automobiles and closed the alleys. Wooden houses and naked trees shivered and creaked in the cold. "I wonder where the pigeons go?" Small said looking out the frozen pane. Talldorf waded through the snow and looked up cautiously at the thick icicle that hung from the gutter as he stuffed orange peels and coffee grounds into the garbage can. Talldorf looked down at a human hand blue as stone sticking out from a furry cuff. Talldorf's trembling fingers brushed away the snow. The red earmuffs and the crooked nose and the blue face with eyelids frozen in repose belonged to Alphonse.

Small was strutting around the apartment in his T-shirt when he heard Talldorf's call. While they waited for the cops a small crowd of housewives and unemployed husbands gathered to discuss Alphonse's strong points.

"Poor old fella," Miss Deerly said as she stomped around Alphonse's stiff body in the bearskin coat her dead husband Henry had purchased from a Russian fur merchant before the Depression. Talldorf's head was bowed. Small frowned wondering how cold it had to be to crystallize a man's blood. "He must have been drunk," Small speculated. There was a discussion about brandy and St. Bernards, car radiators, and how much alcohol a man would have to imbibe to survive such a night and if Alphonse could have had that much when the police arrived and slid Alphonse like an icicle into the paddy wagon.

Since that first simple act of generosity which had precipitated all his uncomfortable encounters with Alphonse jobs had sprung up like mushrooms, and with Alphonse's death the jobs ceased. The coincidence did not escape Small who pondered it in silence.

Talldorf studied the empty egg carton.

"No breakfast, Talldorf," Small said coming into the kitchen in his long underwear.

"Just give me a minute, Small, I'll whip up something."

"No breakfast. We're going to the blood bank. If you eat anything they won't buy your blood. Have a glass of water and jump into your pants. I want to get you to the blood bank before you start to think."

Talldorf and Small sat at wooden desks filling out medical forms in the naked gloom of fluorescent tubes with two solemn-faced Indians and a blue heroin addict covered with tattoos.

"I feel like I'm volunteering for my funeral, Small."

"Think of the ten bucks."

"I'm starved. All I can think of is food."

"As soon as they get your blood they'll sell you a bottle of orange juice. Cheer up, we're almost in the money again."

The nurse pricked Talldorf's finger and squeezed a drop of his blood into a test tube.

"I demand to see a doctor!" Small said. "Thank God you're here, doc, this nurse don't want my apprentice's blood."

"I'm sorry," the doctor said, "But as you see for yourself Mr. Talldorf's blood floats. He needs iron. You should be eating more meat, Mr. Talldorf."

"I'll tell you who eats meat, Doc," Small said, "Doctors and lawyers. Me and Talldorf are honest workmen. Of course I own my own company. Here's my card. You got any filth just give us a call. Times are tough, Doc. We need money. I'll take full responsibility. Talldorf's in perfect health. His folks grew him up like a prize orchid. Do some push-ups for the Doc, Talldorf."

"I'm sorry, Mr. Small."

Small lay on the table with his sleeve rolled up and his eyes tightly shut seeing Alphonse lying in the dark frozen ground.

"I hate needles," Small confided to the nurse who slipped the hollow steel shaft deftly into the vein that bulged in Small's hairy arm.

The Commander leaned on his lieutenant like a wounded soldier as they slipped up the block to the coffee shop. Talldorf was alarmed, Small looked so spiritless and wan, but his color and vitality returned with the third cup of coffee.

"What will you have for breakfast, Talldorf?"

"Coffee is quite substantial, Small, thank you."

"I thought you was hungry."

"I didn't contribute, Small."

"Suit yourself, Talldorf. I'll have ham and eggs, honey, fried potatoes, a chocolate milk shake and keep the coffee coming."

Chapter 12

THE CONSERVATORS

S mall stood before the mirror in his powderblue suit. "You are really something to behold, Small," said Rudolph. There was an unwholesome perfection in Small's appearance. He looked packaged to be sold.

"Yeah, pretty spiffy," agreed Small, "but what we know and they don't, Tallie, is that it's me in here. I'm like the Shadow in my powderblue suit. I cloud men's minds so they can't see me. I dance a neat little step—" Small skipped around the refrigerator like a boxer. "I'm going for the Goldbogen awnings, a block-long row of awnings we can clean in a night for a hundred eighty bucks. I never tried the big department stores but when I get this job I'll beat out the union for the Goldbogen window washing contract too. No telling where we'll end up when Small gets into his powderblue suit."

Small stood in the executive offices of Goldbogen's, his green attache case in his hand.

"Miss Marman will see you now, sir," said the receptionist.

"Now dear, I don't care about no Miss Marman. I want to see the Purchaser of Services like I told you. I'm A. Small, President of Complicated Maintenance. I don't talk to secretaries."

"Miss Marman *is* the Purchaser, sir."

"A *woman*?"

"More than half of us are, sir."

"Certainly, dear, and I love all you poor things."

Small strode into Miss Marman's paneled office. There was no carpet on Miss Marman's office floor but rather bare wood stained long ago. Miss Marman's desk was huge, of heavy hewn oak. The chairs about the office walls were upholstered in severe black leather. Miss Marman herself was barely visible, a trim muscular torso in a black dress bent in her chair over the waste basket and as she turned, her lips red and straight, her bosom wonderful, her eyes sized up A. Small.

"Well hello, Mr. Small. I'm Bridget Marman, my friends call me Bitty. Just pick up one of those chairs and bring it over here by my desk and we can chat."

Small set his attache case in the center of the floor with a grin, such pleasure did those wicked eyes afford, turned with the grace of the high ladder man lifting the chair as Bitty's eyes watched with equal pleasure the ripple of muscles under his powderblue coat.

"My friends call me Small," said Small his face now close to that of Bitty Marman's.

"What's in a name?" asked the husky voice.

Before he left she loosened the knot in his tie, her nyloned athlete knees brushing his powderblue ones like hot winds of passion sear leaves of flesh and she purred, "That's the well-dressed man, Smally, with the hair on your chest showing. Now give me a break, hon, and don't let me see you till tonight."

"And you'll see plenty, baby," Small promised Bitty as he left her office rolling his shoulders. The last thing Small considered was the Goldbogen awnings, which were certainly in his pocket.

God, what a woman! thought Small, an earth mover. No wonder she's an executive. But the little dear has found her match in A. Small. He did not consider calling on another customer but walked the park paths anxious for six o'clock.

Small met Bitty Marman at Diamond Jim's and suggested a drink at the bar and forget supper.

"No, look, hon, *I'm* the purchaser. Bitty knows where the deals are. Goldbogen pays tonight. I sign my little name, hon. You don't worry about a thing."

"That's a privilege I'm happy to grant you," said Small slipping his hand about her waist as they walked to a secluded booth.

After the Roman banquet they moved on to a nightspot Bitty knew, a cave where the music was loud, her hand caressing Small's powderblue thigh under the table, her breast soft against his arm as they toasted each other with champagne.

"To bed," Small said as their glasses touched.

"My maintenance man," said Bitty.

And soon Small was dancing and Bitty was tossing out her black hair, her shoulders firm, breasts trembling like jello while her hips in that same black office dress flowed like the river Styx.

She provoked and enticed him over their drinks. She bit his earlobes and honed Small to a fine flame.

"Not yet, not yet, hon, let it flow—" Her dark eyes flashed and Small's green ones smoked. "And when the fire bursts out we'll both go up like moths!" Bitty pulled him again to the dance floor and the night went on like a crescendo.

Small found himself talking to a politician from City Hall who appeared at their table dark as Satan, slick as a shark while Bitty took ten on Small's powderblue lapel, flashing open her black eyes with increasing fire and purrs approaching a growl.

"Well I'm saying what the hell do you do?" demanded the shark.

"I'm an alchemist," Small said. "I turn dirt into money. I clean up the Windy City wherever I touch it."

"You clean up and I clean up," grinned the shark. "How much you want to clean the glass at the Conservatory?"

Small burst into laughter thinking of how Elvira had loved to stroll in the steamy heat of the Conservatory amid the exotic vegetation because it made her passionate. He drew Bitty closer beneath his arm.

"That's an acre of glass," Small told the shark.

"What's your price?"

"A thousand bucks," said Small, "Aaaah—" Bitty's fingers were rippling through the hair on his chest.

"Fourteen hundred," said the shark, "Four hundred's mine and the job is yours. Call me at City Hall tomorrow at ten."

"If you're there and I get an advance for supplies, total eight hundred, you get four hundred," said Small.

"It's a deal," said the shark.

"It's a bribe," said Small, "But if that's how you guys do business I'll be a Roman like the best of em."

"Boy," said Small when the shark slid away from their table, "What this powderblue suit brings into my life, baby."

"It's what's under the powderblue suit that brings me into your life, hon," breathed Bitty.

"Let's go to your place, baby," growled Small into her dark hair. "I'm about to bust out of this disguise."

"When *I* say," replied Bitty and she led Small into a jungle dance on the black dance floor.

Small's shirt was soaked with sweat. "I ain't waiting no more," he said guiding her toward the exit. "It's your place or right here."

"Why of course, hon," said Bitty.

"I bribed a city official in there," remarked Small rising from a hot kiss in the back of the taxi.

"Congratulations," said Bitty, her fingers doing unmentionable things to Small's person.

They were in Bitty's luxurious apartment high over the dark waters of the lake no more than a minute when it was a standoff between two wildcats. She ripped Small's brilliant tie from his neck and with the next move all the buttons off his only dress shirt bearing his hairy chest and she danced away.

"Don't touch me!" she said, her fingers teasingly unbuttoning her dress a little black button at a time. "But first I think I'll just look at the new issue of Mine, I haven't had a chance yet. I'm a busy woman as you know—"

Small's eyes gleamed beyond smoke. He stood crouched on the carpet slowly removing his shirt, dropping it to the floor and kicking off the shoes Elvira had bought for him. "I think you better think again," he said moving toward her.

"I'll buy that." She backed in a small circle that became a ring of trampled clothing and leaped onto a stuffed Ottoman and from there to the back of the big wing chair.

God, who would believe it? Black lace panties one inch wide, those tits point-blank cannon, a feline worthy of the passion of Small. Red lips that would talk until he pressed them shut commanding from her height, "Kneel! You may kiss my foot!"

But Small was beyond words and quicker even than Bitty Marman and his hairy arm caught a thigh and her flesh riding his shoulders like a hot-blooded python, biting at his ribs while she rode, her nails like thorns digging at his thighs. Small threw her into the shadows of the bed. It was pink ruffles, he knew, though there was no light to see. Small ripped the panties from her thighs as she flowed upon the bed.

"I'll buy it, I'll buy it— " she moaned pulling Small toward her but he thrust her back and held her there until he saw her flashing eyes.

"I ain't selling," said Small.

She reached again for him and still he held her away.

"Please— " whispered Bitty Marman. Small threw himself upon her like Icarus into the rolling sea.

She was gone when Small awoke but there was a note:

'You do quality work. Call me—'

Small called three times. Miss Marman was always out. When he understood he laughed. "The only ace she's got is to deny me the awning job, Talldorf. She got what she wanted. A broad like that only knows the whip. I got her marks on me too but they were worth it. If I ever see her again she'd be putty in my hands. She cries herself to sleep at night thinkin about me. But back to serious business. Monday we start the Conservatory."

Small had not told Talldorf how he got the Conservatory job. Rudolph considered Small's silence on this point the mark of a nature more noble even than he had supposed.

"You are a great salesman, Small," said Rudolph.

"It ain't talent, Tallie," replied Small gloomily. "It's fate. I always wanted city contracts and I always knew I'd get em but I figured they'd see I was the only one who could handle em with quality."

Business is business, Small told himself over and over, but his conscience flailed him. Quality had always been the one recommendation of his company and in a mad moment he had stooped to buy a job. That shameful moment flew in the face of Small's cherished if obscure ideals. It tarnished the once spotless name of Complicated Maintenance. He had degraded himself and compromised Talldorf who believed in him.

"Dirty, dirty, dirty," muttered Small as he paced.

"We'll make it shine, Small," said Talldorf enthusiastically. "Sit down now and eat your steak, Small, before it gets cold."

They stood before the Conservatory, a gigantic dome of glass covering acres of tropical and exotic vegetation. Under its vaulted glass grew banyans, rubber trees and palm trees seventy feet tall.

"We're going to do this careful and systematic, Talldorf. We start at the peak and we wash the glass section by section all the way down to the ground. We use mops and hose and then we squeegee. You're gonna have to glue your brains to your feet cause if you step off one of those catwalks you'll go through the glass and kill yourself. Jesus, I wish I'd never got the damn job."

Talldorf shifted springily from foot to foot as he watched Small mount the glass dome dragging the long line of hose.

"Come on, Tallie!"

With his mop in his belt like a sword, rags dangling from his pockets, squeegees, steelwool, razorblade scraper, Talldorf mounted up the dingy glass world. The hose steadied and helped to reassure him. He could not avoid looking down but focused his gaze on the iron steps and not the misty green world blossoming beneath.

Small climbed yet higher until at last he stood at the very top of the dome with the Windy City spread out before him. "Halt, Talldorf! You work that ring of panels. I'll work down from up here. We want those plants to see light, Talldorf. Give it our Complicated Maintenance quality touch. You're doin fine. I'll give you plenty of water."

Small turned on the hose and sprayed the glass like a man watering the tomatoes. The water came rolling down in transparent waves. Where an instant before there had been the linear geometry of latticed rectangles Talldorf now saw undulating liquid curves. Obscure greenish tones of vegetation far below came swirling up vividly. Rudolph clamped his teeth on his vertigo. He mopped the glass and grime flowed away beneath his feet. He looked up to see Small wielding his mop like a dancer and Talldorf's brain reminded him that a dance was a two-step and so he moved though his eyes plainly told him he must not step where he did.

Small had turned to glance at Talldorf and saw that fatal step, saw Talldorf's leg sink as if through ice, the mop that rose like a standard last flourished by the avant guard and carried to his doom as Talldorf disappeared in the exploding crash carrying away in glittering shards the entire panel far down into the green jungle below. Frozen in horror, Small stood alone atop his glass world.

And smote numb by the reality of his disaster, his blood given up in utter surrender, aglow with the release of his will happily beyond hope at last Talldorf plunged beatifically toward the green welcoming arms of life.

Ever alert, the gracious Woomblybah tree, from somewhere east of Tasmania, received Talldorf into its resilient foliage severely spiking and securing him by a buttock on one of the seven thorns appearing on that rare species. It took six firemen and the cherry picker from Hook & Ladder Company No. 9 to get him safely down on a stretcher which they slid into the ambulance that sped Talldorf to County Hospital.

"I'm finished!" resolved Small holding up his hand contritely. "I don't mean to upset you, Tallie. I'm trying to talk in a low voice but it was my fault you almost got killed. I made a clean business dirty. I should have never taken that job. It was dirty from the start. And I led you right into it. It was me deserved what you got."

"No, no," said Talldorf lying delicately on his stomach, "I did exactly what you told me not to do, Small. I forgot my feet." Talldorf munched a chocolate from the box Small had brought him.

"Have a chocolate, Small, and forget it. I'm doomed to live. I pity the world. I'll probably become President."

"I'm glad you're alive, Tallie," said Small uncomfortably sitting on the edge of the bed. "I miss ya at the house but everything's ok there. I'm gonna clean the stove for you while you're in here. And I put the pillow from my own bed in your chair. This has changed my life, Tallie. I hope to lead a clean life in the future and not get us into such messes."

"Me too, Smally," said Talldorf. "I'll be back at your right hand, Commander, and I'll follow you anywhere."

Chapter 13

THE GUMM TOWER

I t took a mere month of five and ten dollar jobs for Small again to climb into his powderblue suit and the dress shoes Elvira had bought for him. He slicked back his sandy hair.

"I ain't waitin no more, Talldorf, it's straight to the top and I ain't takin no for an answer."

Small strode across the marble lobby of the Gumm Tower. So smart did he appear rocking on his heels before the black building directory that the security guard did not give him a second glance. He rocketed to the 42nd floor and his heels clicked along the marble hall with resolution. He pushed open an opaque glass door and stood on a springy carpet.

"Mr. Buble!" announced Small to the big blue eyes, "A. Small is here to see Mr. Buble. I don't have an appointment but Buble may fire you, dear, if you don't announce me immediately."

Small seated himself near a decorative lamp and snatched up an issue of *The Fall Street Journal*. Scarcely had his eyes time to rove the chicken tracks of stockmarket quotations when the very picture of the Gumm executive appeared before him with pink cheeks and silver hair.

"I'm Mr. Buble, Mr. Small. Would you care to step into my office?"

Rising, Small cast down *The Fall Street Journal*. "Ah!" he declared, "Construction costs are going through the roof! I for one refuse to go along,

Mr. Buble! A. Small vows to keep the rates of Complicated Maintenance at a sane level!"

"Capital!" beamed Mr. Buble, "This is rare talk, Mr. Small, the kind of talk I like to hear." He laid a friendly hand on Small's powderblue shoulder and guided him to an inner office. "A curious card you have, Mr. Small, I see that our filth is your profit. Will you have a seat?"

"No," said Small continuing across Mr. Buble's office. "Allow me to show you something, sir." He went to the window, opened it and reached out. He turned and displayed a dirty finger before Mr. Buble's nose. "Isn't that disgusting? I bet you, Mr. Buble, that the profits of Gumm Gum plunged last year."

"Yes, indeed they did, Mr. Small. You keep your eye on the market — "

"I don't waste change on The Fall Street Journal, Mr. Buble. I just got good vision. Gumm Gum profits fell because of this!" Again Small raised the disgusting finger. "The image of Gumm Gum is soiled, sir. The Gumm Tower, a famous national monument, stands dingy and soiled in plain view of the public. Step over here, sir." Mr. Buble approached the open window with some reluctance. Small took Mr. Buble's hand, stuck it out the window and rubbed a finger on the white marble of Gumm Tower.

"My Lord", said Mr. Buble visibly contaminated. He hid the soiled finger in a Kleenex.

"Would you put a piece of Gumm Gum that looked like that in your mouth, Mr. Buble?" Though Mr. Buble had never before conceived of such an operation he agreed to an estimate for washing the Gumm Tower.

Small sped to a third-floor cafe across the bridge in the Tribunal Building which faced the Gumm Tower across the river. Small sat at a window table over coffee and cracked a new pack of Luckys. He opened his attache case on the table, and glancing at the sheer peak of the clock-faced white spire began jotting figures into his notebook as though sketching for his master-piece. He returned to Mr. Buble with an estimate of ten thousand dollars.

"The Gumm Tower will be so bright when I finish with it, Mr. Buble, they'll see it in New York."

Mr. Buble appeared to be in a state of profound contemplation. Small willed optimism into the air of the office, he willed light into the executive brain, he willed affirmation, he willed joyous assent. His green eyes were like traffic lights when Mr. Buble looked at him blurting, "Your idea brings light to my mind, Mr. Small! I'm riding with you, sir!"

Small was in a festive mood. Over the 69-cent bottle of wine he brought home from the drugstore he made account to Talldorf: "It was the magic of the powderblue suit and beyond that my keen vision informed with my infallible sense of when to strike and how to aim my artillery. Ho ho! Buble didn't have a chance. I always knew I should start at the top. We're finished with landlevel dirt and second-floor jobs, Tallie, we're out of the latrines of the Windy City. In one beat of the wings of vision and brilliance we are at the top. You are now my field marshal. You, Talldorf, will direct our huge staff of workers from the scaffolds!"

"Scaffolds?"

"We'll swing around Gumm Tower like busy spiders. Up and down. Busy scaffolds of happy workmen on every wall. The view of the lake will take your breath away. From Gumm Tower we leap the river to that baby Matterhorn, the Stone Container Building, and then to the Rookery. We'll do the Board of Trade and stand on Ceres hat and shammy her bronze tits. None of them new tincan buildings for us, Talldorf. I'm aiming at the landmarks designed by architects like Shadly Left, Farlow Highpoint and Elmer View. And we start with Gumm Tower, Left's masterpiece. Imagine, Talldorf. We'll be rich! Oh ho ho! But it requires strategies and tactics you've never dreamed of."

Talldorf was astounded; and he wavered.

"I might better serve the company at a desk, Small. I can man the phones, write press releases, sign checks..."

"Nothing doing, you are my right hand in the field where the action is hottest. I handle tactics, strategy and finances while you drink milkshakes and keep your eyes peeled. That's the way it's gonna be forever."

Two thousand dollars was to be drawn against expenses. "Captain Carson," said Small staring up at the slim old guard in the security uniform, "Good to see you still on the job, my good man. I got this little check for two grand I got to cash, can you direct me to a window?"

"Oh most certainly, sir." Small bounced beside him.

"Weren't you going to take over the cleaning contract here at the bank, sir?"

"No time, Captain," said Small, "Maybe I can get to it later in the year. Here's a card. Give it to the vice-president. Have him give me a call."

"Scoundrel!" shrilled a cracked old voice. It was Timmy O'Malley waving his cane not far distant.

"Throw him out!" demanded Small, "Do your duty, Captain, I'm a withdrawing customer!"

"Oh, never mind him sir," whispered the old guard, "He's crazy."

"I know he's crazy!" said Small. "Does the First National allow its customers to be insulted by madmen off the street?"

"Well you see, sir," advised the old guard, "we must bear it because Mr. O'Malley owns half of the bank."

Small glared at the old doorman.

"Which half? I'm cashing this check in the other half!" Small placed an ad in the *Tribunal*:

Scaffold Men: $50 a Week
For the best view of
Your Lives
COMPLICATED MAINTENANCE
A. Small Pres.
(etc.)

A wretched line of the poor, dispossessed and degenerate appeared at his door.

"None of these guys can hardly stand up, Talldorf," complained Small. Nevertheless he hired ten he hoped would not fall off the scaffolds.

"You'll have to keep these guys moving, Talldorf. And stop worrying, they all know how to run scaffolds."

Jake's Rental was delivering four scaffolds to Gumm Tower by truck. Small had paid cash in advance. The corps of brigands Small had hired were to gather on the plaza at eight o'clock sharp. Talldorf and Small rode downtown in a taxi. Small was dressed in his powderblue suit, his attache case in his lap. Talldorf wore his baggy work pants and a white shirt and, so that crew would not forget who the foreman was, a black plastic bow tie which Small had insisted on, and a red baseball cap.

They stepped out of the cab onto the wide plaza before Gumm Tower rising like Mount Blanc into the blue sky. Small could not refrain from a little dance step, swinging his attache case in an exuberant circle. "It's all ours,

Talldorf! I told you I'd get us the Gumm Tower. And today is the day. From here I'll look down on City Hall. With ten G's I'll rock the boat. They'll all be looking up saying, 'Who is this Small?' Well I'll let em know. Oh ho ho ho, Elvira, you blew it, baby."

But Talldorf was nervous. He had never commanded men before; he didn't want to command men.

"I don't think I can do it, Small."

"You can do it, Talldorf. You *will* do it! Repeat over and over, 'I can do it, I can do it.' Your dad, Joe Talldorf, was a high climber. It's in your blood. You got the build and the talent for high work only you don't know it. Up there is where the glory and the money is. We're reachin for the sky. What do you say, Tallie? Duty is calling. I'm puttin you in the clouds like I promised you. All you got to do is keep those rummies rubbin marble, assholes and elbows. Excelsior, Talldorf! Find the men! Bring them to me. I'll give them the word. I'll be sitting here on the fountain."

Presently Talldorf returned across the plaza trailing a gray straggle of men through the early morning shoppers.

"The men are here, sir," reported Talldorf.

Small stood up on the rim of the fountain, a powderblue nob taller now than any save Talldorf.

"Men!" announced Small. "This glorious morning we are gathered together here to scale— Hey, you! With the bald dome! Is that a bottle you got in that bag?"

The bald man wavered forward, "Breakfast, Chief. Have a slug—"

"You're fired!" yelled Small. "Give this man bus fare, Talldorf. Get him out of my sight. Any other man with liquor on his breath is canned! Talldorf, I got nothin more to say to these bums till they prove themselves to the company." But at such a moment how could Small remain silent? "Loyalty, men! I have given you a place over all workers in the Windy City!" Small held up a powderblue arm with a finger pointed to the sky. "No men hang higher than you this day! Take em away, Talldorf. Get the scaffolds hung on the river wall. If any of these stiffs fall I don't want em messing up the plaza. I'll be in the Executive Inn in the lobby. And I warn you, men, I'll be up to check on progress. A heavy hand, Talldorf! The Windy City is watching."

Inspired despite himself Rudolph saluted. "Men!" he cried.

There was grumbling in the ranks:

"Sheit —"

"What the hell —"

"Men! Men!" demanded Talldorf, his head now set like a fiery eagle's. "Follow me, men! To the freight elevator."

Talldorf led away across the plaza with his ragged band following, and Small found a white-clothed table over the green waters of the river. With his coffee he ordered a magnificent breakfast. And, indeed, success was all that Small had imagined.

Talldorf pulled his red cap down tighter, his men trudging sullenly behind: Charlie Spotted Chicken and Leonard Hands In His Pockets, two silent, bronze-faced Indians; old man Swenson with his constant chant like the beat of a Viking drum, "I climb Empire State Building, I climb Empire State Building," nodding and bobbing his head. Bartholomew and Dominic, the twin Italian sign painters with heads like Michaelangelo, who inspite of Small's warning and Talldorf's disdain passed a bottomless pint of dago red; Gus, whose pitted cheeks, walrus mustache and craggy face made Talldorf trust him, Gus who spoke no English, only Greek; Danny in a black watchcap and black turtleneck sweater who chainsmoked cigarettes and moved like a cat; and two stumbling gray shadows who Talldorf's anxious eyes never quite focused on.

"As Commander Small told us, " Talldorf said stooping over his crew in the freight elevator, "there will be no drinking on the job, men, it's too dangerous. Does anybody know how to start this thing?"

"What floor, Commander?"

Talldorf winced. "I'm not the Commander. That's Small, who just spoke to you men. I'm only your foreman, Talldorf. You can call me Rudy." Talldorf grinned. No face returned the favor.

"What floor?"

"Yes, the very top," Talldorf said.

Talldorf had been up on the Gumm Tower parapets before with Small who had explained the job's mechanics while the wind whipped their jackets and Small leaned sickeningly out over the railing. Talldorf had bolted back down the steps to the elevator.

"Come back, Talldorf. You're the foreman on this job. You don't have to do anything but hang on. The men will run the scaffolds. Everyone of those guys has plenty of experience. Leave it all to Danny. The guy knows his stuff.

None of those guys are afraid of heights. Just show them where the scaffolds are. They'll do the rest."

"I climb Empire State Building, I climb —" The doors of the freight elevator opened on the 50th floor.

"The scaffolds, men. I want them carried one at a time up the steps to the parapet. Who wants to volunteer?"

Dominic passed the bottle to Bartholomew. Gus blew his nose in a red bandanna. The Indians sat down cross-legged and Danny lit another cigarette. No hands were raised, no voices chorused, no one stepped forward but Swenson.

"I work for Rigbsy Hitch, you bet," Swenson's blue eyes sputtered behind his glasses, "Swenson knows business. I carry scaffold up steps on my back." Old Swenson danced in a circle.

"Do you see that, men?" Talldorf exclaimed and bent to help the old man. The others reluctantly began to lend a hand. They walked the first scaffold to the top of the steps and pushed the doors open to the blue sky. The wind snatched away Talldorf's red cap and flattened his hair.

"Holy Mother in Heaven," Dominic said and passed the bottle to Bartholomew.

"A guy could get blown off of here," Bartholomew observed and took a swig. Talldorf looked askance deliberately ignoring the sign painters. "Who knows how to work these ropes?" he asked.

The river sparkled like a ribbon far below. Gus inspected the cables and the pulley drums and mumbled in Greek while Danny ran his fingers over the motors.

"What time is lunch?" Dominic asked.

Talldorf glanced at his graduation present. "Twelve o'clock."

"When's our first break?"

"If you need a break you have only to call that fact to my attention and

"Sir," Dominic said, "I need a break."

"Me too," Bartholomew added.

"All right, men. At ease. You are the first men in history to put a scrub brush to this stone. We're going to make her shine, men. The Commander will smile. The Commander may consider a bonus —"

"Fat chance."

"Cheap bastard — "

"Men! I am on my way to report to the Commander now and I shall return with the equipment. Each man will be issued one new bucket, one new mop, and one new scrub brush, and a bunch of rags. The company expects you to treat this equipment as if it were your own. While I'm below I expect you men to be hard at work. I don't want you to feel rushed or to hurry. Remember, safety first. The Commander and the company and myself would appreciate it if you could hang that scaffold while I'm gone. I won't be gone long. Thank you."

Talldorf found Small sipping coffee in the elegant river-front dining room.

"What's wrong, Talldorf?" Small asked anxiously.

"Everything is fine, Small," Rudolph said excitedly, "The men are hanging the first scaffold now."

"Wonderful, Talldorf, wonderful. *Garcon*! A cup of coffee for my lieutenant."

"This job is going to take a long time, Small."

"Nonsense, Talldorf. If it takes us longer we charge Buble more. Don't worry. That marble's gonna shine like an ivory tooth. Everybody in the Windy City will be talkin about it. Gumm will probably promote Buble to president of Gumm Gum."

"The men don't like the idea of scrubbing stone. No one has said anything but I can feel an undercurrent. From the way Mr. Swenson is acting I'll be lucky to get him out on the scaffold."

"Fire Swenson, Talldorf."

"He's old and he's scared, Small, but he knows his business. I think."

"I'll have a talk with Swenson, Talldorf."

"He only understands Swedish, Small."

"He'll understand me, Talldorf. What else?"

"The two Italian sign painters are obnoxious and won't follow orders. They're drinking, Small. I wouldn't be surprised if they were drunk by now."

"Fire the sign painters, Talldorf."

"I think they're going to quit, Small."

"Good riddance. How about the other guys?"

"You were right about Danny, Small. Danny knows his business."

"All right, Talldorf. You"d better get back up there. I'll join ya as soon as I finish my work. An iron hand, Talldorf! And Talldorf... I'm proud of ya."

When Talldorf was gone the waiter brought his coffee. Small poured it into his own cup and moved his breakfast dishes aside, lit a Lucky, and gazed with satisfaction over the river at the spires of the Windy City rising on the opposite shore. By one inspired act Small had brought himself from eye-level dirt to this white linen table while his own staff labored at the great and lofty project conceived by his brain. Small twitched the cheek of his ass feeling the comforting bulge of his wallet. He, A. Small, had set the wheels in motion and now they flew at his bidding. His trusted lieutenant, Talldorf, gentleman and friend and the Commander's right arm stood at this moment on the bridge executing the orders of his chief. At this instant the scaffolds must be swinging high above on the river wall. Small now prepared to roll out from his limitless imagination the great charts of immediate and future campaigns to determine the next step toward conquest. Should he take on the great architects or shall it be the First National? His men might sandblast City Cathedral while he personally would replate the cross atop the dizzying steeple with gold. Or would it be the Gross Steel Building which was rusting, all 55 floors of it. His men might lovingly rub it with steelwool until it shined like a silver dollar. Or City Hall itself? His name this instant must be on the lips of great tycoons in dark board room: 'Who did you say got the Gumm contract, Jasper, a newcomer? Why that is a twenty thousand dollar job, Jasper. How can the man do the Gumm Tower for half our price? Mark my words, Jasper, this Small is not a man to have at your back! God, that we had such vision, brains and drive in this organization!'

'I fear we must step aside, Mr. Millionworth, sir, there is no competing with such a man as A. Small.'

As so on.

So fantastic were Small's reveries that he scarcely believed when he saw a gigantic scaffold pinwheeling down from the sky.

Mr. Buble reached Mr. Gumm at Gumm's summer headquarters on Gumm Slough. Gumm stuck to his wheel chair, his jaws working furiously a piece of Gumm gum as he shouted into the phone.

"Complicated Maintenance??? What the hell is that, Buble, another one of your fly-by-nights? Get those nincompoops off the job. Get Slash and Rasp and have them file a suit of criminal negligence against Little or Tiny or whoever he is. I want his name smeared across the front page of the Tribunal. Give each of the workers a thousand dollars. I will see to it that fool does no more business in this town or any town where Gumm gum is chewed. And, Buble, you nitwit, I warn you, no more slipups. You'll find yourself cleaning spittoons in the halls!"

Small was arrested and released on bail. He was charged with everything but bribery. A photo of Small and Gumm Tower appeared on the front page of the *Windy City Tribunal*. Small was being booked with his tie askew and his mouth wide open. A black arrow pointed to where the scaffold hung and a dotted line marked its plunge to the river. A scurrilous article beside the war news defaming Small and Complicated Maintenance and hinting at blacker deeds yet uncovered resulted in an overloaded switchboard at the Glibb Answering Service and more messages in a single day than Small had ever received in his life. All without exception were to cancel jobs, some of which he did not even know he had.

Small held his head in his hands. "I'm ruined," Small said.

"No one was killed, Small," Talldorf said. "I know you think it was all my fault, but if you'd let me explain —"

"Ruined," echoed Small.

But the case was dismissed. The scandal in Washington and reverses on the Northern, Southern, Eastern, and Western fronts captured again the front pages, and no witnesses could be found to testify against Small. The workers on the Gumm Tower job, every man with his thousand dollars in hand, displaying no civic responsibility, had melted from view.

Chapter 14

THE HIGHEST SIGN

A spectre haunted the soul of every citizen who passed through the heart of the Windy City on the expressway. This was the prominent and somehow sinister sign of *Smart Shafter and Engels* which in the flat country of mid-America, with a good telescope, might be clearly seen for fifty miles in any direction so high it stood atop the rock bastions of the clothing manufacturing buildings now interfaced by the expressway which the sign, lit at night, spanned on steel girders six hundred feet above the whistling concrete lanes.

Small, who had nothing left to lose, recognized the sign while walking haggard in disgrace down a sidestreet with his hands in his empty pockets.

In Bluey and in cars forgotten he had steered the expressways by the highest sign as though guided by a star many nights returning from forays to the foreign ends of the city. What Small had never realized until this moment was that the figure represented on the sign was young Doctor Talldorf, a man who did not exist. It was a dead ringer if Talldorf's unruly curls were covered by the gray homberg, if Talldorf wore the paisley scarf and silk tie and stood with a hand in the pocket of the cashmere topcoat casually open to reveal a Smart Shafter and Engels suit while squinting with confidence into painted snowflakes. It was the highest sign in the Windy City, smitten and bitten by the foul pollutants of the age.

Small set out with quickened step homing on his last vision of the sign before it was blotted out by tall gray buildings, and arrived before a wide flight of concrete steps in time to be forced aside as a bedraggled mass of humanity burst like smoke from the building. *Smart Shafter and Engels* was changing shifts. It was as if all the nations of the world were represented as the workers poured past Small and though their eyes were hopeful one and all were tattered and all were women. The *Smart Shafter and Engels* clothing industry was manned by women who ran the infernal interminable sewing machines in a screaming din day and night wielding pinking shears and needles with flying fingers in the harsh glare of electric light behind glass block windows. This scene was repeated many factory floors into the sky, above which were the executive offices where men in *Smart Shafter and Engels* suits riffled papers and talked into telephones.

The uniformed guard moved to intercept Small the moment he entered the door, but so determined was his approach the guard stepped back. "Purchaser of Services!" Small announced.

"Elevators to the right, sir!"

The bell captain, disguised as an admiral, scanned the winking lights of the elevator control board. His shaggy brows furled down a twitching nose at Small.

"Well, do they work or not? Open one up, Captain! Take me to the Purchaser of Services. A. Small here. You know of me if you read the newspapers." The bell captain personally took the controls and they shot toward the 48th floor. The eagle come alive in the eye of the bell captain indicated the heart of the matter: Small strode across a red carpet to the great desk of the receptionist unaccustomed to men not dressed in *Smart Shafter and Engels* suits.

"A. Small who struck fear into the Windy City is here to speak with the Purchaser of Services! What's his name?"

"Tite — ? Mr. Tite — ?"

"Tell Tite A. Small consents to speak to him." Small locked his hands behind his back and walked in small circles.

"Mr. Small — ?" Hyram Tite licked his thin lips and eyed Small with suspicion.

"Even so, Tite. It is I, in person."

"Will you come into my office? What is it that I can do for you?" Small flipped out a Lucky and took a chair.

" I don't care what you think about my recent infamy, Tite. No man is my judge."

"Who is to judge, sir?" said Tite dryly.

"My company, Complicated Maintenance, is a noble and misunderstood company."

"I see," said Tite, straining his senses.

"It is my vision that conceives of the work to be done before the one who needs my services knows he needs it. I battle with light against the enemy dirt. Only men of quality recognize the need for my services and I am here to point it out to you, Tite. You are personally responsible for the maintenance of the highest sign in the Windy City and that sign is soiled. You should have had it cleaned years ago. This might come to the attention of your superiors. You are in a tight spot, Tite. You are in need of my services."

The narrow *Smart Shafter and Engels* suit set off Tite's complexion well, and also his thought: he is a madman and a ruffian, thought Tite.

"I ain't askin for nothin, Tite. I'm here to make you money." Hyram Tite's eyes sharpened and his ears pricked up. "I advise you to put all your money into stock. When Complicated Maintenance has cleaned your sign, Smart Shafter and Engels will sell twice as many suits. You'll have to rent a train to get enough wetbacks north to run your sewing machines."

"It might be true—" whispered Tite.

"It's simple: Get the highest sign cleaned by me and make money, or get fired. Business is merciless, Tite, but my price is right: $999.95. I'll start Monday night."

Hyram Tite leaned back in his chair rubbing his thin palms together while a sly smile creased his face. "It is an obscure investment you proffer, Mr. Small, but a compelling one." The deal was struck and Tite got on the phone to his broker.

"It's a thousand bucks," Small told Talldorf. "But it ain't the money, Tallie, it's a command performance. With one night's work we touch a million lives!" This was the first job Small had gotten since the defeat at Gumm Tower and Talldorf was delighted with Small's enthusiasm. "We'll need O'Toole on this one, Tallie, or we won't finish in a night. We only go up there once."

Rudolph brooded. There had been no news of Sue O'Toole in months, which Talldorf attributed to his virtue. But what was ominous was that O'Toole himself had not been seen in weeks. Talldorf explored the dread possibility of O'Toole's knowledge and so entered into the depression which Small at long last had vacated. Rudolph determined to follow his fate: he deserved whatever O'Toole considered just.

Small found O'Toole in a near comatose state in his cheap apartment. Sue had left him.

"There's some guy," O'Toole said, "I'm going to break his legs." But O'Toole would not get up from his chair. "It's all right, Small, I sit here every evening. I'm waiting for my life to end. I don't drive a bread truck anymore. I got promoted, I'm dispatcher of all Mother's Bread bread trucks, I got a raise. Ensardo promises me the moon. I have to play golf with him. I like golf but I gotta listen to all his black tales about fathers and sons."

"Maybe Sue don't need you, O'Toole, but I need you. And I got a cure for your blues. Listen to this—" O'Toole would meet them in O'Flynn's Hideaway under the elevated tracks at sunset.

Small spent the following day scurrying through the chill gray town buying telescopic aluminum poles, wide brushes and bottles of cleaning supplies. It was like the hours immediately before a voyage, or those times in the future when technicians would run busily about the base of the rocket tightening screws and checking fittings, a joyous work because its pettiness would soon be obliterated in the vision of a new world.

For Talldorf the day crept by in torment and raced blindly toward sunset when he would face O'Toole under the elevated tracks. The more Talldorf thought the more conscience convicted him and the more certain he was that he went to his doom. I won't raise a hand! vowed Rudolph. He wrote a note and put it in his pocket. It absolved O'Toole for murdering him and declared that Talldorf had brought, as he put it, 'the righteous hand of vengeance,' onto his own head. He may shoot me in the tavern, considered Rudolph. It would be quick. At last Elinore would know who he really was: the wretched son of a gambler who fittingly met his death by violence in a saloon. The rank odor of spilled beer and sawdust in the nostrils once expected to hover above the concert keyboard or behind the surgeon's mask, as he lay where he belonged with the holes in his chest. Or would O'Toole wait and push him off the highest sign? By the time Small returned home Talldorf was in a catatonic state.

"I got a couple of zombies to help me on the highest job of my life!" said Small. "You look like you died last week, Talldorf."

"I will be with you till the end, Small."

O'Toole was in worse shape. They found him drunk in a back booth at O'Flynn's. Talldorf was appalled at the condition of the man and held himself responsible. Small slapped O'Toole awake and sent Talldorf for coffee.

"I'm perfectly aware of everything around me," O'Toole protested.

"You are?" asked Talldorf.

"You damn right and I fear nothing and no man!" They poured coffee down O'Toole. "You don't understand, Small, my courage is at a peak. If I was sober I couldn't do what I'm going to do."

"What are you going to do?" inquired Rudolph.

"I'm going to be right behind you, Talldorf."

"How many fingers am I holding up?" asked Small.

"Two," lied O'Toole.

"Close enough," said Small, "The cold and wind will do the rest."

"Let me help you up, O'Toole," offered Rudolph.

"Hands off, Talldorf." Talldorf's compassion returned to him ignominy which he wore out into the chill dark feeling it fitting raiment to his last misunderstood hours on earth.

O'Toole sat in the back seat between the garbage cans. "I need a drink. My wife left me, Talldorf."

"I'm sorry all this has caused you such grief, O'Toole," said Talldorf. "I consider you justified in any action you might take."

"He deserves to die, doesn't he, Small?"

"I — I — " said Talldorf.

Small wheeled Bluey between the elevated abutments. "I need workmen with wings!" he shouted, "And I got two gravediggers."

The frigid night spit flakes of snow as three men in a box like a tomb rose up the spine of the brutal tower with poles, mops, buckets of steaming water, and one hundred feet of rope. O'Toole's bloodshot eyes enlarged at the lit numbers of floors winking above the door as they rocketed up through the night. There was gray concrete lit by bare bulbs where they stepped out and black iron stairs up which they hauled equipment to the sheet-steel door kicked open by Small to a howl of wind and unearthly light inviting them into the night. Wind smote them, but more shocking still was Small's mad laugh which awakened Talldorf to the supreme moment and sobered O'Toole.

"Oh no, Small—" said O'Toole.

As Talldorf stared upward he felt in the presence of an immense enigma, as though he stood before the Sphinx. Its awesome presence swallowed even the fear of death. The highest sign, so far above, appeared unattainable even where they stood. Talldorf felt nostalgia for the unaccountable feats of man, for slide rules, logarithms, and Homer. He wondered at engineering that dared thrust such a monstrosity at the heavens. Bare girders shot above, latticed with steel crossbeams merging in filigree at the end of the great sign lit like a window in the black heavens and soaring across nothingness. Beneath the sign hung a narrow iron catwalk.

"What's that noise?" asked Small. O'Toole's teeth were chattering.

"It's freezing. It's snowing. We'll blow off that thing," said O'Toole.

"Not your average humdrum day on the job, eh O'Toole?"

"We'll slip Small—"

"We won't slip, O'Toole, cause we'll kill ourselves if we slip."

"Talldorf, you ain't going up there are you?" O'Toole was confounded by Talldorf's calm voice: "We have a job to do, O'Toole."

"You've made him as crazy as you, Small. I ain't goin up there with two madmen!"

Small was unwinding the coil of rope and tying it under the arms of Talldorf. He dropped loops onto the roof where snow blew and tied the rope under O'Toole's arms heedless of his protests, dropped more and tied the end under his own arms. Like a prisoner, O'Toole moved only when the rope tugged at him. Small led the little party like mountain climbers toward the foot of the sign. O'Toole felt momentarily better because this was the center of the windswept roof.

Small grasped a rung of the black iron ladder and started up with two steaming buckets over his arms, two mops through his belt and brushes sticking from his pockets. The rope tugged at O'Toole's armpits and Talldorf saw O'Toole's eyes close as he grasped the rungs and began to climb. O'Toole stared straight ahead as the rungs passed. The weight of the bucket on his arm gave him little time for thoughts such as, 'I won't let go; why would I let go?' The icy wind buffeted O'Toole and whipped his pantcuffs and snow bit his face. Talldorf, with a bucket over each arm and poles in his belt, could look down with barely a qualm to where the roof lay a small black square on the embers of the city and expressways swirled red and white arms into the night, because his hope and his pride were in O'Toole moving steadily above. O'Toole saw Small crouching before him, pulling him onto the sidewalk of black steel mesh where O'Toole crouched holding with his fingers. Talldorf and Small were on either hand.

"On your feet, O'Toole," said Small, "We're almost there. Get your bucket." Talldorf held O'Toole's arm and bending near said, "I'm right behind you, O'Toole." When the rope jerked O'Toole followed. Linked by a thread three tiny figures treked across the sky.

Driving in from the suburbs to meet her lover at the Tip Top Tap, Felicia Breed-Mork, who like her brother the air ace had excellent vision, wiped a gloved finger across the windshield of her Jaguar but the specks were indelible.

And a thousand women sewed beneath them through the night on the layered factory floors. The brilliance of the sign before them was dazzling. It pulsed in the blows of the snow as if it wore an aureole. O'Toole was enchanted despite himself as they approached out of the night like pilgrims toward a shrine.

"Halt!" cried Small. He took the bucket from O'Toole's hand. "You've arrived, old trooper." O'Toole saw the expressway between his legs like a river of light flowing through a black canyon. He sat down and clung to the grating of the catwalk. "You're doing fine, O'Toole," said Small. "You'll get used to it in a minute."

Talldorf laid a comforting hand on O'Toole's shoulder. He was inspired by the view and he felt no fear. It was as if they stood atop clouds where falling was unthinkable. Rudolph looked up at the best-dressed prince in the sky and was disconcerted at his own likeness. Small yelled through the howling wind: "A mile down the expressway he looks like a man!" It was merely the caricature of a man. Talldorf yelled into the wind: "Let's clean him up," and snow shot like silver bullets through the light.

O'Toole would remember this night like a dream in which he fought with a javelin shoulder to shoulder with his brothers in the face of impossible odds and won a great victory which he could never explain.

Water from their brushes fell as hail onto the Windy City. They scrubbed young Doctor Talldorf's face in snow and laundered his clothes and with slush on their brushes bathed even the painted snowflakes of his winter fantasy. No one slipped and no one fell as they wielded their poles through the storm of that other-worldly place and when the sun arose on a white world, not the least of which was the highest sign, they were gone.

Hyram Tite was upbraided by the executive vice president, Cyrus Scythe, for throwing a thousand dollars down the drain, and though Tite quivered with hate for Cyrus Scythe yet he fawned before him begging pardon while taking great pleasure in the knowledge that not even Cyrus Scythe had made more than he on the unaccountable rise in Smart Shafter and Engels stock.

O'Toole's feet were on the ground; Talldorf was ready for anything; Small was buying an airplane.

Part Three

INITIATION

Chapter 15

THE STEERMAN

T hey stood beside the biplane in powdery snow blowing about their ankles. Wind sang in the wires that braced the wings. Talldorf and Small turned toward O'Toole. They both wore leather flight helmets and their goggles were in place.

"Our air force," said O'Toole. "I'm proud of you guys, but I still don't believe it. This is the last time I'll see you two alive, you're going to kill yourselves. It was nice knowing you, Talldorf."

Rudolph peered at O'Toole from behind his goggles and shook his hand. "We'll be all right, O'Toole," said Rudolph. "It's me who gets us in trouble and Small is doing the flying."

"In that case he should leave you here," said O'Toole. "And since you don't know how to fly, Small, why don't you stay too?"

"Man the plane, Talldorf, the back cockpit," said Small jerking his thumb upward. Rudolph stepped up on the tread of the lower wing and angled his leg into the cockpit.

"I've got three hours in this baby," Small told O'Toole, patting the gray canvas skin of the Steerman.

"Small, you don't have a license," objected O'Toole.

"Neither do pigeons, O'Toole." Small climbed onto the wing and was looking into Rudolph's cockpit.

"This is the throttle, Tallie, just crack it like that. When I yell contact she's gonna roar and you pull the throttle back. Keep your feet on the brakes or you'll grind me into hamburger."

"I have my heels on the brakes right now, Small."

"Seat belt buckled?" asked Small.

"Seat belt buckled, Commander." Small jumped into the snow beside O'Toole whose wool scarf whipped at his neck. The two friends shook hands.

"You've come a long way from Elvira and the basement, Small, and this is the end."

"This is the beginning, O'Toole."

"You should have traded this ladder for those parachutes that guy offered you. You'll need parachutes if you try to fly with this ladder."

"I don't buy insurance, O'Toole." Small squatted in the snow and yanked at the aluminum extension ladder tied with rope to the belly of the airplane. "It'll never come loose. I'm giving you Bluey, O'Toole, because you're the only guy I would trust her with, but I need my ladder."

O'Toole followed Small around the wing. "I heard it on the news and we're standing in it right now. It's the worst blizzard in 75 years!"

"What do you expect from the Windy City, O'Toole? The town with the heart of ice." Small climbed up the step ladder and grasped the cold steel propeller. O'Toole held a leg of the ladder at arm's length ready to flee the instant Small was sliced in half. "Switch off!" yelled Small over the howl of wind.

"Switch off!" yelled Talldorf. Small pulled the great propeller around twice.

"Switch on!" he yelled.

"Switch on!"

"Contact!"

"Contact!" Small gave a high kick with one leg, swung the propeller and leaped off the ladder as the engine roared. O'Toole was running through the snow dragging the step ladder. He turned to see Small mount the wing and sink into the front cockpit. A black gloved hand waved above Small's helmet and the Steerman crept forward onto snowswept concrete, turned blowing winter into O'Toole's face, and disappeared into a squall of snow.

O'Toole folded the step ladder and slid it onto the garbage cans in the back seat of Bluey. "Now I'm your rightful owner," O'Toole reminded Bluey as he turned the ignition key, "Small gave you to me. Work for me like you did for him." Bluey wouldn't start.

"Talldorf," said Small through the rubber hose intercom, "Can you hear me?" The airplane was bouncing along the snowswept apron.

"I hear you, Small."

"All you got to do is keep your hands off the controls back there and your feet off the pedals. Everything's going to be ok."

"I can't see a thing, Small. Is it safe to take off in a blizzard?"

"This communication system isn't for you to question my judgment, Talldorf. It's for me to give instructions to you. If you want to fly this airplane say so now or leave it to me."

"I leave it to you, Small. My eyes are closed, my fate is in your hands."

Small braked the Steerman at the end of the runway and ran up the engine. "Magnetoes ok," said Small, "Damn, I can't see a thing." Small turned her into the blowing snow and shoved the throttle full forward. They were pressed into their seats. The tail rose. Small could barely make out the runway through the beveled glass. They broke from one squall of snow to be swallowed by another. Small felt her lift and saw the roofs of the hangers pass beneath and Bluey creeping toward the exit before all was obliterated in ripping gray clouds. Small felt a sense of deja vu as he continued a climbing turn seeking S on the black compass face.

"Small?"

"Yeah?"

"What's that singing sound?" Small stuck a finger under his flight helmet lifting an earflap. A shrill whine alarmed him before he understood. "It's our ladder, Talldorf. It's singing in the wind."

"Small?"

"Yeah."

"When will we get out of the snow? How can you see? I can't see anything."

"That's cause you're looking outside. I'm watching the instruments. They tell us where we are, and I know where we're goin. By the time we cross the Ohio River the blizzards will be behind us. It don't snow in the sunny south."

"Small, how do you know the blizzard will be gone by the time we get to the Ohio River?"

"Talldorf! I'm tryin to fly an airplane. I know the blizzard will be gone because we'll be out of gas and we got to land. And I don't want to see no blizzard there." Rudolph remained silent for a moment.

"I'm cold, Small. I think I'm freezing to death."

"Talldorf, please don't think unless I call you on the intercom for advice." They burst into sunshine soaring above white fields of clouds.

"How will we get down?" came Talldorf s voice.

"Stop worrying out loud or I'm going to unplug you Talldorf. Our past is way back there under the clouds. I feel like a million bucks."

"I'm cold, Small." Small pulled back the stick and eased it quickly forward. "Oooooo —" wailed Rudolph.

"Did that take your mind off your worries? I'll bring her down lower as we get south and the storm dies away. In a few hours we'll be in warmer air." Small had no doubts.

And the air did warm. To the song of the ladder Small banked and turned out of high spirits as the clouds below began to break and they glimpsed farm fields in sunlight. "We should pick up the river real soon," Small said into the intercom.

Rudolph was rigid with cold and stiff with sitting. "Is that where the clouds end?"

Ahead the clouds dropped away and sunlight flooded over green rolling hills and there, amid them, lay the broad river. Small pointed the nose of the Steerman at the river and down they went as the hills grew around them. Rudolph watched the river rise between the wings to meet them, wide waters flashing below, the green hills beyond and again blue sky. They flew over the hills and brown dirt roads of Kentucky. Small began circling over blue mountain woods.

"Where is Nashville?" said Small's voice. Rudolph's confidence in Small did not flag, he did not even know Nashville was supposed to be near. "It's half an hour late." Rudolph stuck his helmeted head over the side and peered through his goggles. "There's powerlines running into Nashville and we haven't passed any. There —!" Ahead a long march of powerlines moved across the hills. Small followed them into Nashville and brought her down over the hills onto the runway smooth as pie and they taxied to the pumps. It was a lovely late afternoon.

They sat over coffee in the airport cafe. "I really hardly believed you knew how to fly, Small! I didn't think it was possible to leave the Windy City in a blizzard. Small, I shook hands with O'Toole because I didn't want to go to my grave with bad feelings, and here we are in a summer world. It's like heaven. It's beautiful. Let's live here! I'll bet there are oleander bushes and honeysuckle and Georgia peaches. I could be happy here, Small."

"If you think this is something, Tallie, wait till you see Florida. We got to go all the way, that's why we started. If a guy's as easy satisfied as you he ain't going to get nowhere. We're going to the glitter and bright lights of Miami Beach, to the Fountainblew Hotel where women wear diamonds and rubies and pearls and bathing beauties lie out on the beach just waiting for wonderful guys like ourselves."

"I'm with you all the way if it's better than this, Small. I'll never doubt you again."

They slept in a little wooden motel near the airport. In the morning a lanky lineman propped the Steerman, they taxied to the end of the runway, and got a red light. A C-47 cargo plane was in the pattern from Atlanta. And a CAA inspector had noted with horror the ladder tied beneath the Steerman.

"What does that red light mean, Small?"

"I don't like red lights, Talldorf. Let's get out of here." The canvas rudder shined in the morning light as the Steerman turned its gleaming propeller into the wind and roared down the runway into the air."I didn't buy my own airplane to stop for red lights, Talldorf. So long, Nashville."

Eric, who grew up in the orphanage and slept in the bed next to Small and once gave him a comic book which told how to fly an airplane, was at the controls of the C-47 arriving from Atlanta and could not believe his eyes. In any case it was too late. The cargo plane crossed Small's vision like a silver dinosaur. Small felt its belly with his hair. It seemed to Rudolph they flew through an airplane factory. And then it was gone. The Steerman with its two wings shining rose up through the morning sunlight above the green mountains.

"That pilot was blind, Talldorf," Small commented into the rubber tube.

"I'm really impressed with your skill, Small. I'm glad you missed him."

"I'm glad you missed him too."

Small headed straight north, edged toward the mountains and when out of sight of the airfield swung abruptly south; he was leaving no tracks. They soared among the green mountains following the ribbon of Hwy 41. It would be the only place to land in case of an emergency. Nevertheless Small had strayed, climbing high over the mountains when the airplane seemed to halt in midair, soar wildly left and then wildly right, like a blowing leaf.

"What's happened, Small!" Talldorf yelled into his ears. "Will we crash?"

"Talldorf, the ladder's loose! Did you mess with my knots? Talldorf, what did you do?"

"I didn't, Small. Save us!"

"Calm down, everything's ok. But we can't land with our ladder hanging down. You'll have to get out and fix it. And tie a good knot."

"No," said Rudolph, "I can't get out of an airplane when it's in the air, Small."

"Then you got to fly the airplane, Talldorf."

"I can't fly an airplane."

"Grab the stick. Put your feet on the pedals, that's an order!" A jolt set them swinging wildly across the sky. "Talldorf, you fool, let go of the stick, feet off the pedals!"

"I told you I can't fly!"

"Don't rip the controls out of the airplane, Talldorf, a soft touch, keep her nose on the horizon, feel it out, don't tense up— see how easy it is—"

Small disconnected his rubber audio tubes and was rising from the front cockpit when Talldorf allowed the nose to fall away and having neglected to fasten his seat belt, felt himself lifted perilously from his seat. His bony knees held him in the cockpit. Not so Small. To Rudolph's horror Small rose in front of him helmet shoulders trousers and tennis shoes as though ascending to heaven, his arms at his sides as he passed the upper wing over Rudolph's head and Small was gone. Rubber-necking in paralytic panic to follow the flight of Small, Talldorf executed an Immelman turn the Red Baron himself might have admired. This was a half loop with a barrel roll at the top where Talldorf himself was emptied from the cockpit out over the green mountains of Tennessee while the extension ladder cut a singing arc through the morning sky.

Barley Poakes, a twelve year old entrepreneur of the hills had just lighted a marijuana butt after watering his promising hilltop patch of excellent Columbian and did not believe his eyes as he witnessed the aerobatics of the biplane high above. Barley could not make out what the ladder was as it whipped around the airplane, or the two specks which emerged from it. Barley scratched his pantleg with his bare toes, looked admiringly at his homegrown cigarette and lifted his gray eyes again to the sky.

As with every event of his life, Small accepted this with acute interest. He stood in space with the best view of the world ever presented him. His goggles were in place so the rush of wind did not impede vision. He watched the biplane plummet away before him. He had a clear view of the silver ladder trailing behind. He watched the Steerman rise in the tightest of loops with the ladder standing directly above it. He glimpsed Talldorf emerge from beneath the airplane. He watched it roll over and the ladder swing below. He saw the Steerman float toward him like a vengeful eagle, the silver swath of its propeller gleaming in sunlight. Small drew up his toes but it would not be his fate to be ground up by the propeller of his own airplane in the morning sky of Tennessee. He levitated above the canvas wing and was offered the leather-padded safety of the cockpit he had so abruptly quitted only an eternity before. It was necessary merely to turn and Small was again at the controls as another jolt nearly lifted him out of the cockpit a second time but Small held on as anguish at the loss of Talldorf overwhelmed him. There was but one hope and Small nosed the Steerman into a screaming dive seeking his friend.

We know there was a brief period when no mortal hand held the controls. The question arises: who steered the Steerman? Small would surely avoid the question by claiming that his star guided the entire incident; Talldorf would have no opinion. The face of death which alone could not surprise him and which ceaselessly failed to make its appearance was masked at this moment in the brilliant light of a never more vivid world, a world of events and objects into and by which, since his meeting with Small, he was thrust and confronted without the grace of even time to use his brain to save himself. Such was the case when Rudolph found himself a mile high without an airplane.

The limits of anguish had been strained when Small had disappeared into the sky so that none remained for his own miserable fate, and indeed a buoyancy filled Rudolph's heart in the realization that all choice was removed and that he shared the fate of Small. Talldorf soared on his belly against the rush of wind like an airmattress, without remorse, without fear since the initial instant when his stomach was left behind and he peered through his goggles at the slowly rising green hills of Tennessee from which the face of death would surely emerge to view if he were quick enough to glimpse it. A single last mortal wish occurred to him, that he might meet Small on the way down and take his arm to travel this last mile, and Talldorf's blue eyes scanned the brilliant void when the ladder sliced through his vision like a pendulum he took for a neurothrombosis impairing his vision. When it passed again before him he recognized it as the ladder, but it was gone before surprise renewed the cruel pang of loss. And then the ladder stood before him as though extended by an angel and Talldorf actually hesitated to take hold of it. Tentatively his long fingers reached, and as imperceptibly it began to withdraw. Rudolph read the label before his eyes:

> 'DO NOT STAND HERE YOU
> MAY LOSE YOUR BALANCE'

A breathless lunge and the grace of his long reach saved him as the ladder jerked away with Talldorf on its end like a banner.

This was the jolt Small felt as he took the controls upon reentering the cockpit after his eternal seconds in space.

Barley Poakes experienced the first paranoia of his young life: Revenuers were diving on his marijuana patch from out of the sky. He clearly saw the bomb trailing behind the diving airplane. He dropped his smoke and snatched up the 12-gauge shotgun to defend his crop to the death. Through his goggles Small saw Barley Poakes. He saw a contorted dusty country road wending through the green mountains and three rushing creeks, several garden plots, a broken wagon, a sway-backed mule, two cows, five horses, twelve crows, six squirrels, one hundred thousand trees and no Talldorf.

Talldorf had jabbed his leg through the third rung. The airplane was going to crash, he was going to hit the mountainside like an artillery shell but it was better than being alone. The roar of the engine was deafening. The green mountainside loomed, and Rudolph stared as it came for the black face of annihilation.

The airspeed indicator to which Small paid no heed registered 200 miles per hour as Small pulled out of the dive at the depth of grief knowing Talldorf was lost forever, the knot in his throat threatening his breath and tears splattering his goggles and the singing roar laid back the ears of little Barley Poakes who closed his eyes and pulled both triggers. And to his credit Talldorf never batted his eyes at the orange explosions flaring like peacocks from the green trees that passed in a blinding blur out of which emerged not the face of death but the immortal glance in the depthless eye of the unknown bluebird passing like a bullet and the vertigo of empty space again as Steerman and ladder and Talldorf and Small cleared the ridge.

Rudolph began a weary climb up the ladder. It was something to do. He climbed without fear and without hope. *Poor Small, Poor Small, Poor Small.* Talldorf sorrowfully hoisted himself onto the tread of the wing and looked into the goggles of Small. Their arms were around each other. Small sat, pulling Talldorf near by the collar of his jacket.

"Smally! Smally!"

"Did you fix the ladder, Talldorf?"

"No, No, I didn't, Small—"

"As long as you're out there—" Small handed Talldorf a long rope. "I'll keep her nice and level."

They landed at Murfreesboro at a small airfield that was like a barnyard. They stepped through the summer streets in high spirits wearing their flight helmets, past old red brick buildings to a coffee shop where they ate donuts, and the old men in bib-overalls slouched in their chairs and slapped their knees to see the two animated Yankees who must be from a sideshow come to town. Small declared that Talldorf had tied the perfect knot, and Talldorf maintained that Small was a pilot second not even to the great air ace Colonel Wilifred Breed III. And when they tired of telling their stories to each other they moved into the lounge of the old hotel and told it to the drinkers who didn't believe it, and late at night Small climbed onto a barstool to hit the biggest unbeliever, but Talldorf hauled him away like a sack of potatoes up the stairs to their room.

It was noon by the time they left Murfreesboro because Small had a terrible hangover and said he wished he was dead. "Buckle your seat belt," he grumbled. Small said they would reach Macon before the sun set. As soon as the Steerman was in the air Small felt wonderful. "Tomorrow, Tallie, you'll get your first view of paradise, good old Florida where I spent my boyhood."

The sky clouded over. It appeared to Rudolph that they were flying into the center of a storm that lay dead ahead. Small decided to climb over it. The clouds closed beneath and behind and still lay below when Small estimated them over Atlanta. "We'll go on to Macon," Small said into the intercom.

"Isn't it going to get dark soon, Small?"

"Everything's ok, Tallie. We'll see the glow of Macon even if it's cloudy. I got the maps. They light up the airport in a big place like Macon. I'll bring her in."

"You'll bring her in, Small. You'll bring her in." Talldorf fell into silence.

Light died slowly in the west out of the great bowl of the sky and stars grew down from the heavens. Rudolph was enchanted. Never had he seen the stars so large and bright. Small turned the Steerman and found the big dipper lying above. His eye followed the arrow of the cup seven times its own depth and found the North Star. The compass read N. Small turned south.

"Don't get upset, Talldorf, but Macon ain't here."

Rudolph peered over the side into darkness. "I'm sure you'll bring her in," answered Rudolph.

"Yeah, we're bound to hit the ground. The storm is hiding Macon, but maybe we can beat it to Augusta. I think we got the gas. They'll have lights at Augusta."

"What if the storm is there too, Small?"

"With your luck, Talldorf, I'm surprised you would ask a question like that."

The stars burned noncomitally as Small strained his hawk eyes for lights on the ground to assure him they had outrun the storm. No lights were seen. "We got an hour's gas left, Tallie," sounded Small's voice. "Look for the glow of Augusta."

Night encompassed them round: "A half hour, Tallie."

"I'm sure you'll bring her in," recited Rudolph.

"Don't go into one of your fits!" Small yelled into the tube. "Talldorf?"

"Right, Small. I'm peaceful, Small. I don't care what happens."

"Well *I* do. I got a ladder under this airplane that I don't want to dent and it's your responsibility. If that ladder is damaged when we get out of this airplane I'm holding you responsible! You want to drive a taxi in Georgia to buy us a new ladder? Peel your eyes for lights, we got to set this baby down gentle. If you don't see Augusta in the next fifteen minutes it don't look good for the ladder."

When the engine sputtered, not a light from below was visible, never the glow of an illusive, storm-lashed Augusta. Small played the throttle. The engine caught, thrust them onward, coughed, and stopped.

The steel propeller glinted in starlight. Wind rushed in the wires like fingers upon a harp. Rudolph was silent, in awe of the great bowl of night with its brilliant crown and the angelic song of the wind. He heard Small's calm voice.

"I'm sorry, Tallie, I miscalculated. I believed in the star of my luck. I gambled and I lost."

The sun was rising like a bucket of blood over Afram-Dar on the Eastern Front where Colonel Wilifred Breed III, dashing young air ace and darling of the base reached for his ivory cigarette lighter as his Mock III soared into the sky. With his ninety-ninth kill the Colonel's first star was not far away. In the boardrooms and salons of Boston, old Wilifred Breed II, the Colonel's father, wore his sacrifice to the war effort like the falconer wears the wings of his bird and business was booming. Felicia Breed-Mork, the Colonel's winsome sister, thought fondly of him as she raced beneath the highest sign in her Jaguar on her way to an assignation with her lover. The Colonel thought of his sister with fondness, tilted his dashing overseas cap and his plane at a rakish angle and opened his eyes to the face of death in a barren mountainside.

"We gambled and we lost," echoed Rudolph. The wind sang on. The altimeter told Small they had 3000 feet between them and the reckoning.

"We'll probably find a storm down there, Tallie, but whatever it is I'll have my hand on the controls till the end."

"I'm right behind you, Small." It was all Rudolph could think to say. The stars disappeared. Small's eyes strained. Then, like a mariner long at sea, he read the looming form of the earth close at hand, eased up the nose of the Steerman noting dark umbras flash beneath which he took for trees.

"Everything's ok, Tallie—" as if talking to himself, "I've done this before—"

Small knew it was a farmhouse past which they flashed and now, revealing itself to his peering eyes in the instant before impact, what he accepted as a miracle and believed to be a haystack.

Chapter 16

MIAMI BEACH EXPRESS

All four wings of the Steerman lay strewn behind the fuselage where Small stood talking to the farmer with the straw hat tipped back and a sprig between his teeth.

"All you gotta do is rake up the hay," said Small. "That motorcycle can't compare with an airplane. Maybe you don't understand I ain't a sucker to be had. I had a big company in the Windy City." Small thrust his card into the farmer's hand.

"Your filth is our profit," read the farmer. He looked down at Small with his cool gray eyes, and up at Talldorf who looked dumbly back at him through cracked goggles. "What the hell does that mean?"

"Never mind," said Small. "I'm tellin you ya gotta throw some cash in with the motorcycle or it's no deal."

"Ya got ten minutes ta get off my land," advised the farmer. "Sheriff'll throw ya in jail if ya find a way ta drag it out on the road." The farmer in his bib-overalls sauntered easily away through the dewy grass.

"Where are you going?" yelled Small.

"Get my shotgun."

"All right. All right! If you can get this antique to run."

Talldorf sat jack-knifed into the sidecar to which the miraculously unscathed ladder was tied with wire and rope. The ladder jutted fore and aft.

Small had gained control of the angry machine and they roared along dirt roads between broad expanses of fallow cotton fields.

Talldorf rejoiced: I'm alive! He had been out cold but didn't seem to have a concussion. His shins were barked, he was covered with dust, and his throat was parched but no bones were broken. He saw the tropical vegetation etched on the horizon and rose enthusiastically in the sidecar.

"A palm tree, Small!"

Through bug-spattered goggles and heat puddles Small saw the limp brown fronds of that singular palm tree which stood sentinel above the low roofs of the distant town.

"You seen one palm tree you seen em all!"

MOLASSES, GA., said the sign full of bullet holes, *ELE 100 POP 59*. Motorcycle backfires reverberated between vacant storefronts. A few old men craned their necks from the front porch of the Mercantile Exchange. Small pulled up to the pump and shut off the motor.

"Gas her up, Tallie," Small pulled off his gloves. Talldorf fell out of the sidecar.

"We're only a hundred miles from the ocean," said Small reading the map. Rudolph was guzzling his third bottle of Croak. "Soon we'll be on surfaced roads."

Small kicked the starter and they were off through the stares of old men. Talldorf's legs had come back to life. His resignation to danger and discomfort in their new life exalted him. They rocketed down Main Street toward the royal palm tree which had been planted before the Civil War by Colonel I.O.U. Riddley who built Molasses' first sorghum mill, and at the age of 70 donned the butternut in a vain attempt to halt Sherman's march to the sea; the Colonel was wiped out. The palm tree marked the Emmitsville-Moffitsburg fork.

Small knew that a left turn to Moffitsburg would bring them to Hwy 15 and a straight run to the Florida Coast but the road signs had gotten turned around. He swerved left by inclination, right against his better judgment, left again— There was a blur of scenery as the ladder fetched the palm tree.

"Jump!"

Small lifted himself out of the dust as the motorcycle snarled around the trunk, the ladder whirling like the blade of a windmill.

"Shut off the ignition!"

Talldorf gave no indication that he heard. His knuckles were a white ring where he gripped the sidecar. A geyser of dust like battle smoke poured upward through the withered fronds. Three black children arrived with wide eyes. The old men hobbled up from the Mercantile. The Sheriff pulled up in a battered Ford.

"Defacin a historical marker...disturbin the peace...drivin on the wrong side of the road."

Small held his card under the Sheriff's nose. "A. Small wasn't born yesterday, Sheriff. If ya wanna give me a ticket you'll have to talk to my lawyer. I got big city connections."

The Sheriff tore up the card.

"Infernal racket. Cost yall twenty dollars."

"That's outrageous!" Small yelled.

"Twenty-five! Resistin compliance."

"I'm a free-born American citizen!"

"Thirty! Offendin the Confederacy." The Sheriff held up a big finger until Small closed his big mouth, stomped his tennis shoes in the dust, peeled off the bills and slapped them in the open palm.

"A man is trapped alive in that unfinished accident! All you think about is graft!"

"Ah figger ta rescue that individual in accordance with my duty," said the Sheriff. "County don't charge a penny ta rescue a human life, son."

Small glared through his goggles while the Sheriff cleared the ring of spectators to the side. He drew a six-shooter from his holster and emptied all chambers at the roaring dust cloud.

"You've killed Talldorf! Get an ambulance! I'll have your head!" Small raced into the silence where the motorcycle sat on flat tires like a slain beast and Talldorf's head lay against his breast.

"Just got himself some motion sickness," advised the Sheriff. Talldorf's eyes opened in a hollow stare. "Gork," he said.

Talldorf looked like a zombie, walked like a zombie, and said gork. The doctor in Moffitsburg suggested a rest home. Small stuffed Talldorf into the sidecar and sped out of town. He set his shoulders against the wind and peered stonily out his goggles at a lifetime of pulling Talldorf around in a wagon. To drive that image from his mind Small talked:

"Then there was the time I took Elvira down to meet Ma and Pa Sphincter, Talldorf. That was the family I belonged to in Indiana after I escaped from the orphanage. Elvira didn't like Ma and Pa Sphincter right off. I warned her before we got there: Don't act snooty, Elvira, Ma and Pa Sphincter are good folk but they're made hard from toiling on the land and they have to be thrifty. We unloaded the groceries we'd brought and Ma Sphincter put em away in the cupboard and said, 'We done et, Small Sphincter.' Her and Pa Sphincter called me Small Sphincter since the day I walked barefoot up their lane. Gave me their name right away. 'He come barefoot to us,' Ma Sphincter always used to say to explain where they got me. But neither Ma nor Pa would speak to Elvira. They said they wasn't invited to the wedding and didn't believe there was one. You can imagine how that lit Elvira's fuse, but I wouldn't let her get a word in edgewise which was some feat, Tallie. Elvira wasn't one to keep her mouth shut, so I got her off to bed in my old room.

"'You sleep in your old room, Small Sphincter,' Ma said, 'And I spose you'll take her with ya. Thank god it ain't under my roof, I'm blameless before the eyes of heaven,' Ma said. Ya see my room was in the old pump shed that was a separate little house by itself beside the windmill. Elvira said, 'This is a shack! My poor old father didn't slave his hands to the bone digging graves so that I would wind up in a shack without supper!' She was yelling, Tallie, so I had to tell her she'd have to respect my family if I had to lay her out with one in the chops. She quieted down then. She just stood there lookin at my old room saying, 'Impossible! Impossible!' I told her it was just like I left it. She said it was a pig sty, a chicken coop. I said it wasn't, it was a pumphouse. She went right on complaining she was hungry when I was pointing out my blanket that had covered me some cold Indiana winters that she should have took an interest in if she really loved me, but she said it was a rag and Ma and Pa Sphincter were criminals and yelling she's hungry, she's cold, and you know how a woman can go on— or maybe you don't— until she finally fell asleep.

"Pa banged on the pumphouse door at sunrise and said it was time for chores. It was just like old times. Pa Sphincter didn't have to tell me what to do, I still remembered. But some years had gone by and Pa was even weaker. I couldn't see how he could manage it when I wasn't around. I carried the slop for the pigs and shoveled out the barn and harrowed five acres. Ma had come and got Elvira to help with some canning and the wash and by the time I got back she was sitting in Bluey with the windows rolled up and the doors locked and she was in a fury. It was like an explosion when she opened the door. I told her to come on out because Ma Sphincter said she'd miss supper if she didn't. She got out the other door and marched right off down the lane and wouldn't stop. She went to the old cabin across the road where old Edgar Smith lived with his three little granddaughters. They weren't much more than babies, Ella was the oldest and sort of mothered the other two who were Trudy and Scarlet, the youngest. They were just little flowers, those little skirts, Tallie, and old Edgar and the little girls mellowed Elvira right out. They never got any visitors way out in the boonies like they were and they treated Elvira like she was ice cream. Well, old Edgar Smith was my favorite person there. I mean Pa Sphincter never had much to say, or Ma either except tellin me what time it was and what to do next. Old Edgar just worked out a couple of farms as hired man and I worked with him some when Pa Sphincter would send me. Old Edgar would always give me a dollar for my own, that's the money I came to the Windy City with.

"So old Edgar Smith and the girls welcomed Elvira, Tallie, and that much again when they seen she was with me. Old Edgar kept a tidy place since he got the three new girls to bring up and they made a happy man happier. He took in his only son's daughters when their ma and pa got ground up when the train hit their car."

"Gork!"

"Yeah, terrible tragedy. But the little girls landed on their feet like kittens. So Elvira and I stayed with them the rest of our visit to the country and I'd go across the road to help with the chores. Elvira purtied up old Edgar's cabin like an angel touched it with a wand. She put up curtains and pictures on the walls and cooked dinners and played mother to Ella and Trudy and Scarlet. They called Elvira Mama and called me Papa Small, and I figured it would be like that when Elvira and I had our own kids. But we never did."

"Gork!" A sense of belonging rose in Rudolph's consciousness with a drowsy feeling of light and heat. Small saw Talldorf's head tip forward and nod loosely, so he pulled the cycle up under a roadside palm and sat smoking a Lucky gazing at the white breakers and the golden sand. While Talldorf slept in the shade Small continued:

"Old Edgar wanted to pay me for the things I helped with at his place but he was needin all his money for Ella and Trudy and Scarlet. He hoped he could live long enough to see the girls proper married and I told him he could send them up to me and Elvira anytime. Elvira was all for that too, but old Edgar said he hoped he'd never have to part with his girls. Well, old Edgar and the girls made Elvira's stay, and she even went across the road and said goodbye to Ma and Pa Sphincter when we left to please me. Elvira sent Christmas cards to old Edgar and his little brood for several years. Then I heard he died. I never found out what happened to the girls. Ma Sphincter wrote in a letter it was all for the best wherever they'd gone."

"Gork!" From the whirling edge of a centrifugal roar Talldorf answered to some brass ring of hope ungraspable behind the goggles Small placed over his eyes every morning and removed every evening as from a casualty of the omnipresent war.

Small took a nuts and bolts approach: "I know you hear me, Talldorf!" he yelled over the roar of the motorcycle. "Two things: first, I ain't gonna drop you off at a nuthouse. Second, don't give up."

Gork, gork, every time he saw an orange tree, and there were groves of orange trees, and the balmy air was laden with the sweet scent of frangipani.

"You gotta learn to take the good with the bad. You gotta snap outta this, Tallie."

Small ordered deep breaths as they stood watch on the sea wall. "Smell it, Tallie," Small said expanding his lungs. Nature was straightening Talldorf's shoulders and firming his resolve. The salt air was doing him wonders. Whistling combers boomed under tropical stars, and spread milky aprons onto sunny beaches. "We never have to look at another snowflake, Tallie!" Small shouted as they sped toward Miami.

"Half a dozen donuts and two coffees, honey," said Small.

"D-d-d-donut!" said Talldorf.

Purple reflections of the Gulf Stream and the green fronds of palms sparkled in the windows of beach hotels. The vertical rows of glass assured Small he would have little trouble earning an extravagant living. Small veered into backstreets zooming past houses pushed together on small lots among spiky foliage. Florid blurs of exotic blooms flashed from every yard.

Small set up headquarters in an empty motel. The stucco cottages, once white-washed with pink trim, were as faded as the sign that squeaked in the sea breeze announcing a worn welcome to the *Pink Pelican*. Small paid a month in advance to the bony-faced woman in the baggy housedress who struck a kitchen match against her fingernail and lit the pilot light in number

12. "Toaster works, skillet, pots, pans, there's silver in the drawer. You can smoke if you got to but no drinkin, no pets, no gamblin, no girls."

A dilapidated wooden stairway led down to the beach where Talldorf sat recuperating in a torn deck chair. Talldorf's voice and mental faculties had returned like gray dawn though he had the tendency to fall asleep suddenly and unexpectedly. He took to salt water like a flamingo.

The first day he braved the surf Mimi Winda picked him from the foam where the wave dumped him. Mimi Winda had seen the wave crash down from her blanket where she sat with her boys, her fashion magazines, and her lotions while the sun burnished her deepening bronze. Mimi Winda diagnosed Talldorf's case of boils as sun poisoning and smeared on a soothing ointment which she brought from her trailer in the trailer park.

Could she be the one?

While Talldorf was combing the beach, Small was reconnoitering the town. "We got a window washer," they all said smugly, their teeth sunk into the butts of creamy green cigars. They laughed out loud when Small gave them a figure for the sheer walls of glass. They spoke of Archie Winda and his non-profit window washing company, The Brothers of Light. "Archie does it for half your price."

"This town is infested with window washers, Talldorf," Small said dragging himself through the screen door and mopping his brow. He was exhausted and disgruntled by a week of failure. "We're runnin out of money. No more lobster, no more prawns. I brought home some beans and hamhocks. We're goin on field rations. No more jai-alai. And I ain't takin you to the dog races tonight like I promised. I better invest in a fishin pole so you can be useful while you're out sunning yourself."

The next day Mimi asked if Rudolph would mind watching the boys while she ran to the beauty parlor. "I'm sorry I'm so late," she said when she returned five hours later, "I decided to do a little shopping. I can't resist a bargain."

Rudolph didn't mind. He liked building sand castles with Charlie, Aaron and Benjamin. It took him three trips to carry Mimi's packages into the trailer. He didn't mind that either. Mimi looked so pretty in her new hairdo. There was the atmosphere of wholesome family life, children, a woman. Rudolph played with Charlie and Benjamin on the rug while Mimi busied herself at the stove.

"I'm home," Archie said dropping his bucket and picking up his boys.

"Rudolph is a window washer, Archie," Mimi said, dumping Aaron into his highchair, stuffing a spoonful of mashed potatoes into Benjamin's mouth, turning the pork chops and handing Archie a bottle of beer.

"Put'er there!" said Archie, "Always glad to meet another member of the fraternity. The Brothers of Light are dedicated to the proposition that mankind needs all the light it can get. If you need a job you came to the right place. Two dollars an hour. Work for me and I get you a cheap spot in the trailer park. I want you to read this book Rudy. Keep it, I got a closet full. It represents my non-profit company's high ideals. Right now I'm trying to throw a little light into those crummy Miami Beach joints. I got plenty of work. I'm always willin to take on an inexperienced guy."

"I work with Small," Talldorf said. "Small studied with Short."

"Small studied with Short—" echoed Archie. "Ha-ha, you're puttin me on. I never heard of em. How much does he pay?"

"Small doesn't pay. We're partners."

"He ain't gonna find any work. If he wants work bring him to me. Charlie!" Archie yelled. "Get in here if you want your supper."

Mimi hadn't exactly invited Rudolph to eat supper. Besides, there didn't seem to be enough chairs.

"Where you been, Talldorf?" Small asked. "What's to eat?"

"I think I got us a job, Small. Archie Winda says the Brothers of Light are ded—"

"The Brothers of Light! They're blind! They don't do quality work. The glass is speckled with paint bumps that ain't scraped, it's littered with streaks," Small ranted. "If you worked like that I'd fire ya. I met some of those dodos. Harry was a good belt man and now he works with a pole like the rest of em. No pole works like a man's arm. Them guys think they're independents cause they ain't union. What they are is slaves of Archie Winda. The brotherhood of free window washers! Routine gives em a dead sense of security. Complacency, Talldorf, the certainty that ain't certainty. That's where Small is gonna nail em. I never need a union and I don't need Winda. I can smell jobs Archie Winda don't even see. Quality, not quantity! No drips! No smudges! No streaks! Magnetism, not mediocrity! We take our coffee breaks and smoke our cigarettes when we please. We're independents in the true line of Short, my master. They think A. Small can't make a living? I got my personal star of destiny. Freedom forever! Let me see that book..."

Instead of looking for work Small sat in the armchair reading *The Doctrine of Light*:

'...Monarchs and emperors yet contended for power with Popes. The Dark Ages of Europe had fermented its medieval fruit on hidden shelves and the Renaissance sent seeds on the wind from Italy to Continental cultures where tendrils had taken root in the Gothic stonework when Luigi Medici Squeegee (1740-1850) was born into the aristocratic Venician glass-making family.

'After his marriage and signal success in the family business, Squeegee carried his glass-making secrets to Paris, the City of Light. It was his formula, used to cast superlative replacements in the Hall of Mirrors, that raised Squeegee to renown in the vain and venal court of Louis XVI. Squeegee's vitreous absorption magnified his image in the eyes of his peers. He was intimate with such luminaries as J.C. Bach, Goethe, and the great lens maker Von Leeuwenhoek. After a marathon metaphysical dialogue of seven days and nights with the German atheist, Von Blott, Squeegee invented the ouija board.

'To clean the mirrors at Versailles, Squeegee invented the instrument which today bears his name. The invention of the squeegee seems to have been a catharsis for that nobleman whose fame reversed to infamy when he abandoned wife and children in the pursuit of light. He espoused freedom. He forsook the privileges of the court to prowl the streets of Paris on the lookout for dirty windows. Those were bright days for the *Parisenes* as Squeegee squeegeed his message across the windows of shops and cafes. Squeegee accepted whatever his customers paid: a sou, a glass of wine, a crust. What he could not put into his stomach he gave to the poor.

'Luigi Squeegee was a taker of chances. He was squeegeeing the French doors of the Directory on 19 *Brumaire*, Year VIII, when disgusted with what he viewed within, he flung them wide inviting the hesitant dragoons on their restless steeds who at a nod from Napoleon swept through to scatter the Directors. It was rumored Bonaparte spent millions in a futile effort to locate the man with the gleaming weapon in his hand and reward him with the title of Count.

'Squeegee sought America by traveling east...'

"There's a chapter on medical techniques, Talldorf," said Small. "Squeegee discusses squeegeeing techniques for curing a lot of ailments like kidney stones, heart disease and depression. If I'd known how to make light patterns when we did the hospital job we'd a been able to help them sick people back to health. If a woman wants to have a baby and is havin trouble conceiving Squeegee tells ya the strokes to use to get her pregnant." Talldorf blinked skeptically as Small read on to himself:

'In disguise, with rags dangling from his pockets and a laughable rubber weapon in his belt, Luigi Squeegee entered Mecca. He cleaned the windows of the sacred city as an offering and applied his implement with impunity to the panes of the harem. He swung in his bosun's chair from the Potala Palace of the Dalai Lama in Lhasa. Saint Squeegee, as he came to be known throughout the Orient, traveled on foot spreading his doctrine of light. He crossed the Himalayas with Tibetan salt caravans. Squeegee taught the peasants in hovels in the hamlets how to blow out globes of glass from which he cut panes for their windows. He taught them to mix antimony into the silicates and soda ash to get clear glass without the green tint. Whole villages were animated by Squeegee's presence as apprentices clustered around the Master who sat cross-legged on a holy prayer mat.'

Squeegee's geometrical figures and progressions decorated whole pages of manuscript, illuminated hexagrams, stars of David, innumerable illustrations of interior and exterior reflections.

The Doctrine of Light in Archie's hands was a pearl before swine, considered Small, as he read under the only lamp, jumped up from the only armchair, and leaped to the kitchen table to add another detail to his own diagram.

'...Seeking Buddhahood Luigi Squeegee crossed the Gobi desert. Leaving his streakless mark of light on Asia he left the Orient forever. By the time he piloted his sampan to the Pacific coast of North America, Squeegee was 100 years old and spoke twenty-four languages. What he did there is unknown. He died among the savages in the Seven Rivers wilderness at the age of 110 near the present town of Paradise, California.'

"We were there, Talldorf," said Archie. "Nothing but hicks. Tell him, Mimi. I couldn't find Squeegee's grave. Nobody in Paradise ever heard of him. Squeegee was like a Zen master. He wasn't in it for the money and neither am I."

"You can say that again," Mimi said as she shuffled around the sink in her bathrobe and bedroom slippers, Aaron on her hip sucking on one of her naked breasts.

"Filthy lucre, Talldorf," Archie said, "I'm doin my best to clean up the Establishment."

Archie practiced his *asanas* on the livingroom rug.

"Whose junk is this!" Archie screamed. "Charlie, pick up these toys before I bust your little ass. This one's called the Grasshopper, Talldorf. Try it. It'll make ya feel better."

Rudolph managed to get his legs in the right position, twisted behind his neck. Pains shot through his calves and down his arms, his breath came in gasps.

"Pull his leg this way, Archie," Mimi shrilled, "No, not that way!"

When Archie and Mimi got Rudolph unpretzeled he was more skeptical than ever of Archie's promulgation of Count Squeegee's doctrine which suggested the exercises as part of his easy method to Nirvana. He was skeptical of Squeegee himself and skeptical of Small who, though spiteful and envious of Archie's success, spoke on Squeegee's behalf.

" 'Glass conceals itself while revealing the world,' read Small. 'A wavy stroke is better than a straight stroke. Light resonates at higher frequencies as the squeegee approximates a circular motion. The Whirl is the most difficult stroke of all and should only be performed by one, who after long years of experience, has mastered the trade.'"

Across Biscayne Bay fancy Miami Beach shop windows glittered. Harry stood in front of Hookum & Sakim's Pharmacy with three squeegees tucked into the loops of his belt and the fourth at the end of his pole.

"I like watchin a good window washer work, Harry," said Small. "You're too snazzy for a policman."

Harry ushered Talldorf and Small into a soda fountain booth.

"Just so I make enough to buy my booze and pay the rent, that's my independence, Small. I been around. Don't make no difference to me what

Archie says. I give a damn. I keep my feet on the ground. I make enough to bet the nags. I don't eat much. Stella calls me an alkie. I ain't a alkie. I'm happy as a kid and free as a bird. I worked on the Empire State Building for Rigsby and Hitch once. Worked for Smear & Smudge on the Chrysler Building when they first put it up. I paid my dues; I gave my blood. It didn't hurt me but it didn't do me any particular good neither. I read Squeegee's book sitting in a union hall twenty years ago. Some fellas say they got something out of it, but damned if I ever did. Squeegee must have been a smart fella though. Ahead of his time. There was a time after Stella and me broke up I couldn't get along with people. I'm all right now. Stella always wanted to be respectable. Pettyness, greed, bickerin all the time. 'Harry, if only you worked a steady job we could have a mink coat.' I began thinkin I was on the wrong track. Now I think I got it straight." Harry pulled out his pint. "Hair of the dog. Go ahead, Talldorf, it ain't poison. So how's it goin, Small? You line up a job?"

"I'm thinkin, Harry," Small said tapping his skull, "It'll come to me."

"Pour a slug in your coffee," Harry said, "It might help. America took over the glass industry, and it was America developed the squeegee to it's industrial potential, improved it, unionized it, and created a fraternity. The clarity trade suffered by the victory of elite unionism. Fear of losing a job put the working man in a hole. The big window cleaning companies have the cities sewn up with long-term contracts. A fly-by-night like yourself, Small, can forget about car agencies and banks and hotels. Pound the pavements, solicit them all, and you come up with nothing. Yet the true window washer is a will-o-the-wisp like you guys. Get too steady and you die. Have another slug.

"There were some great belt men, but most of them are dead now, or too old to climb. I'm not old. But then I was never great though I got to watch a few. Funk and Pell used to wash Grand Central Station lying on their backs. Now the skylights are covered with so much soot seeds have taken root. Aluminum siding cut a lot of business. That's corporate crooks who want no light on corporate books. Society's windows are going generally unwashed. The Ink brothers have been washing the White House windows for a hundred years. Leo Ink started as a boy workin for his father, Ivan Ink, and his Uncle Slivermore Ink, before Lincoln was president. The Inks have left a blot on history. The White House windows look terrible. It's cause of the soap they use. The Inks still use the formula that Joshua Ink cooked up in 1852. That soap is made from tallow and its tinted the windows with a permanent gray film. The Inks are greedy, rich and stingy. What do you think of that? They ain't window washers at all. I've taken my falls. Last time I went up I fell eleven floors. Landed on a Cadillac roof and got sued..."

Small burned his old business cards.

"We gotta have a new motto, Talldorf. 'The light we save might be yours...' A catchy slogan, use the old bean, Tallie. 'The alpha, betas, and gammas and all the forces of the stars, the influence of eternity which defines our code of quality craftsmanship brought to you at a cheap price...' Too long! Something subtle, 'A small price for a better view? A brighter life at a cheaper price?' "

Small's enthusiasm was contagious. Talldorf began to read Squeegee's book too, and though he harbored doubts, his skepticism was beginning to dissolve.

"We could donate our profits to charity, Small," he said in the spirit of Squeegee's vow of poverty.

"We gotta eat, Talldorf, it ain't a free world. We'll fight greed, hate, and adultery by doin our work cheerfully and always aiming for the highest quality. We'll dedicate our efforts to the common good and make lots of money."

"Poor Mimi," Talldorf sighed.

"What's wrong with Mimi?"

"She's married to Archie."

"That rat is probably a wife beater. But it's none of your business, Talldorf. Forget it! You can't be in love again. I know you can't help it, but stay away from Mimi. Focus is the word, Tallie. Squeegee explains it all right here." Small tapped the book. "If you wasn't obsessed with your personal life you'd see somethin more interesting is goin on. Focus on molecules and photons and rods and cones. Learn to use your X-ray vision."

"Surely you don't believe in X-ray vision, Small?"

"X-ray vision!" insisted Small. "Squeegee points out how there's other worlds goin on right under our noses. Listen to this:

" 'We can perceive the inner workings of our perceptions as well as the workings of the ethereal immaterial worlds. As outside so inside.'

"To me, Talldorf, that's vision. It gives a person a greater sense of purpose.

" 'Count Squeegee's work with light has been recognized by the modern scientific community. His indefatigable research predicated the Morley-Michelson experiment and presaged Hisenberg's Uncertainty Principle, Plank's Constant, and the Theory of Relativity.'

"Window washers are messengers of light, Talldorf! We got serious business on Earth. We were sent to dispel darkness and cast rays of hope into the dungeons of people's lives. And all you think about is sex with another man's wife."

'...It is to the aspirant's advantage to judge his position in life through the depth of reflection. There are two sides to each pane. Expect the unexpected. Relax. Never worry. Face the world with a light heart and the world will fill with light...'

Archie Winda leaned on his pole in front of the savings and loan.

"One of the differences between you and me, Winda," said Small, "is you limit yourself to windows. Light is my business. Another difference between you and me is height."

"So you're short. It doesn't make any difference to me."

"I ain't short I'm Small. And you're a poleman. To be a window washer you got to like high places. You like low stuff, Winda. And the low stuff will make you an old man fast."

"Height don't mean nothin, Small. I ain't afraid of heights if that's what you think. You know them third floor windows at the movie tower? Five hundred dollars twice a year. So don't think the Brothers of Light don't take risks. I pay em good. If you want to do high work I pay extra five floors and up. You and Talldorf want to work I just might have room. Harry's gettin old. I'll get you your spot in the trailer park and pay ya two twenty-five an hour."

"And next you open a company store. I don't work by the hour, Winda."

"Don't take such an attitude, Small. There ain't a decent job left in this burg. I've been everywhere they got a pane of glass and give em an estimate. You ain't a scab. You ain't gonna underbid me. What the cleaning services and the union ain't got, I got. I'd even get the Fountainblew Hotel if the union didn't have it. You and me are brothers cause all window washers are brothers. I wish ya luck, Small, but when you get hungry come see me. And remember, it's quantity. The more windows we wash the more light we let into people's lives."

Small walked away. "Polemen!" He held his nose. "The chickens of the earth. Afraid of ladders, guardin their selfish little lives — I wouldn't work for a gyppo like Winda if he paid me twice what I'm worth which is ten times more than he makes himself."

"I think we should go to work for Archie," Talldorf said. "He'd get us our own trailer in the trailer park. We could live in this wonderful tropical setting for the rest of our lives."

"If you itch to be a whore, Talldorf, I ain't gonna stop you. You'll end up with a pole in your hand like Archie and your feet on the ground. You'll end up with window boxes and a wife to run your life. Not me. Small is and remains free. If you think I ain't gonna find us work, abandon ship like a rat. See what I care."

"It was just a suggestion, Small."

'...The window washer's work affects the mood of all people in places where he practices his art. The mistress and master of the house are subject to his influence. The occupation requires selfless application, patience and diligence. He brings light to inn and church, state-house and hovel, dissipating the dregs of the past and lifting the curtain on what is springing new. Do not interfere, is the wise window washer's code. The window washer, humble but not subservient, obedient to the light, places himself as inconspicuously as possible where he can do least harm and most good.'

"Eureka!" Small shouted leaping from the armchair. "I got it! I see it! Every little crystal shining, refracting the light, scattering sparks on all them rich bald domes. Some guy is gonna feel the effects of our work so piercingly that in appreciation for such selfless ingenuity he'll hand us a million bucks!"

Small rushed to the kitchen table and put the finishing touches on a geometry he now recognizes as *ropes*.

"Sometimes I think I must be a genius, Talldorf. Grab your sunbonnet. We're ready for Miami Beach."

Chapter 17

THE CHANDELIER AT THE FOUNTAINBLEW

T alldorf and Small strolled beneath the elaborate awning of the Fountainblew Hotel.

"A four hundred dollar awning job," Small said from the side of his mouth. "Peanuts," he added. Small wore one of Rudolph's short sleeve shirts from college. The short sleeves covered his elbows. His cap was low over his eyes which, like Talldorf's, were hidden behind shades.

"Act natural. We'll case the joint. They'll think we're tourists."

The domed lobby spread before them ornate as Versailles. The royal red carpet was crowned by a chandelier. Rudolph blinked at this conflagration of the aristocracy.

"That's it, Talldorf. That little gem is why we came to Florida. It's got more glass than Niagara's got water. Let's stroll around it so they don't get the idea we're gonna heist it."

"It would take a crane to heist that, Small. My grandmother, Elinore, must have stayed here. She sent me a postcard of this chandelier. I've seen it before."

"Every aristocrat is born with this chandelier in his brain, Talldorf. You'll never forget it either. You're gonna slip through that crystal forest like

Tinkerbell. We're gonna wash that chandelier for two thousand bucks. A smashing victory! Money, money, money!"

"That's no way to talk," counseled a gentle voice. An Indian princess sat nearby sewing tiny colored beads onto a strip of leather. Her eyes were dark, her lips and cheeks were radiant. She wore a beaded dress and feathers flew in her raven locks.

"Pardon me, my dear," said Small tipping his cap, "Did you address me?"

"Sit down," she said, "You guys look real weirded out."

"I'll be happy to." Small dropped instantly onto the soft divan beside her.

"I discern you are of the Indian nation," said Small. "A Seminole, I expect. I'm a native of Florida myself. Have you aborigines struck oil in the swamps? It couldn't happen to a more charming representative of your race. Maybe you'd like to take a motorcycle ride?"

"Motorcycles are violent," she informed Small, "Why would I put my body on a roaring machine and race through traffic?"

Small did not have the answer. Rudolph was splashing helplessly in the dark beauty of her eyes.

"You guys are the real yin and yang of America," she judged. "Come with me right now. I'm going to give you something that will help you."

She swung off across the royal carpet on bare feet. She took them to her suite of rooms on the twelfth floor and poured them each a glass of orange juice which she squeezed herself. Her name was Leewing, she said. Her name meant Grace in the Yahwese language, she explained, a tribe inhabiting the exact geographical center of the American continents in the paradisiacal swamps of Nicaragua. She had chosen the name herself. Her parents owned a large portion of the great hotel.

"I wondered why they didn't kick you out," said Small.

"Wasn't your mother hurt when you chose a different name than the one she gave you?" asked Rudolph.

"Golden is your *real* name," Small informed her, "Since that's what your parents named you. This Lee-wing is just a little game you're playing with your parents — your bare feet and your Indian costume and all here at the Fountainblew, the center of ritzy America. When you grow up, dear — in your mind I mean—" and Small chuckled allowing Leewing a wink, "you'll see that you ain't no Indian but just little Golden. It's immaturity, dear, you're rebelling."

"Leewing has always been my name," she said, "because I discovered it in my heart. This has been my home since I was a child. It's an awful place. I don't want to rely on my parents anymore, or on any of this," gesturing from the balcony at the private beach with its cabanas, tennis courts, gardens, patio bars and restaurants below where the stylish guests strutted and flounced.

"You must be nuts," said Small. "What more could you want?"

"I wish I was a true Indian," said Leewing. "I wish I had a big family with brothers and sisters and babies and children and old people and that all of us loved each other and that we lived outdoors under the sky and sang songs."

She lit a cigarette which she puffed in an absurd manner and handed to Small.

"Thanks, dear, but I'm an old Lucky man."

"Smoke it," Leewing directed. "Don't waste it."

"An Indian custom," Small said across the coffee table to Talldorf, "We're smokin the peace pipe." Small took a long drag.

"Hold the smoke in," Leewing said. She took the cigarette from Small's fingers and gave it to Talldorf.

"I smoke a cigar on occasion, Miss Leewing," he said, "but if it's the peace pipe I'll take a puff."

Small's eyes appeared strange to Talldorf. Small was attending the unique sensation of his blood flowing through his brain and down his back to his toes and up through his nose into his brain again. Small had discovered a current inside himself. This enlarged his eyes like headlights.

"What's the matter with your eyes, Talldorf?" asked Small.

Rudolph found the cigarette again before him. "Oh? It's a mysterious custom. I would like to hear from you, Miss Leewing, how, precisely, did the peace pipe custom originate, in the beginning?"

Leewing only looked at him. Rudolph turned to Small.

"Well, Small, anyway, you know— No, you don't know this about me, Small, but I have some interest in archaeology. Even to the little daily customs of other races, little daily doings of all mankind. In fact, I know a few things that people have never suspected that I know—"

"Smoke," directed Leewing.

Small carried a small bag of marijuana back to the Pink Pelican and he and Talldorf smoked one after breakfast and one after supper. Small's plan lost all importance. Small was always misplacing his shoes. "Where are my shoes, Talldorf?" I must be losing my marbles, thought Small. Small would stand barefoot in the warm sand and gaze at the tall beachfront hotels as if he could not comprehend what they were, turn and walk aimlessly on where water met land.

Talldorf walked shaded sidestreets of North Miami talking to vegetation. He hung over fences examining flowers and smiling at housewives who looked at him suspiciously. Rudolph mumbled apologies and wandered on.

Leewing was the sister Rudolph never had. He went to sit for hours with her in her suite or under the chandelier at the Fountainblew while she made necklaces of beads and feathers of flamingos and parrots. A gouty tourist insulted Leewing in the lobby. "Riffraff redskin!" he complained, "Get a job and buy yourself some shoes!"

Rudolph was incensed. He stood up.

"You are an insensitive barbarian, sir! She is not an Indian. Her ancestor was Moses himself, the chosen one of God."

"Religious fanatics and savages," muttered the tourist stomping away. "This place is going to the dogs."

"Why are people mad at me because I like to go barefoot? Everyone is so bitter. Maybe it's the war. Everyone is so unhappy."

"Everyone should love you, Leewing," said Rudolph, " because you never tell a lie."

Leewing told Rudolph that he was not at all like he thought he was. She said he was like a Greek god and that he should be a leader of men because his heart was pure.

"Me?" said Rudolph. His kneecaps touched and he felt awkward.

"How can you doubt?" asked Leewing.

Small too had become very fond of the little rich girl who wanted to be an Indian. As they sat together on her balcony Small stumbled over the business drawer in his mind and sat up. "I got to get us a job, Talldorf. The chandelier, two thousand bucks."

"We could buy a lot of marijuana for two thousand, Small."

"You can have all you want from me for free," said Leewing. "You guys should have something better to do than work for money."

"I need a lot of cash," said Small. "For motel bills and paying off the cops."

"You are really caught up in the American craziness, Small," Leewing said. "Police can't bother you if you don't let them into your mind. All police can do is kill the body. I am ready to die and go to the happy hunting ground. This is a vale of tears. My people are all poor and oppressed—"

"Leewing," Small interrupted, "your people own the Fountainblew Hotel!"

Leewing went on as if she had not heard.

"I want to be with them. I could be a nurse, I suppose, in the war— No, there is misery enough here. I should live in my native land and care for my own people."

"If Senator Quiggley becomes President things will be different," said Talldorf.

"If he does they will kill him because he is a good man," said Leewing.

"He ain't old enough," said Small. "And besides he's a rich kid and they don't know nothing."

"Not all rich people are stupid, Small," Leewing said. "I'm not stupid."

"Yes you are," Small said. "You want to give all this up to go live with poor Indians."

"You better smoke some more, Small," said Leewing. "They really have your brain washed."

"A job. The chandelier," said Small.

"If you really want to clean the chandelier then you must do it," said Leewing. She led them into Butram's office. The hotel executive listened politely to Small's proposal, merely nodded and said, "Um—hum—" when Small said $2000.

"Will you take it up with the board right away?" said Leewing. "Daddy would want the chandelier to be still more beautiful, you know how he prizes it. When you get an answer, Mr. Butram, just let me know."

"With two Gs in our pockets life won't be any harder," Small advised Talldorf.

"Let's smoke," suggested Rudolph.

"Not now. We can't afford for me to forget what I'm doin. I'm gonna hit the street and get us a job today."

Small stood before the Southern Confederate Bank which commanded a beach view. It looked like Mt. Vernon, and it elbowed back the parvenu highrises. The squat structure had little stature but that was where the money was. There were hundreds of dingy little lattice windows—cutups, in the trade—through which Small imagined the light streaming. He and Talldorf could make a jewel box of the Southern Confederate Bank, and Small had always wanted to do a bank job.

"*Small*?" roared from behind the president's paneled door. "By God, send the man in!"

"Alphonse!" cried the robust old man who rose from behind an ornate desk as Small entered the office, "You're not Alphonse — "

The old man's white hair grew in a ring around his bronzed dome, a white walrus mustache trembled beneath the hawk nose. "Alphonse Small of the Windy City— You favor him, boy. Do I have the pleasure of looking on the son of Alphonse Small?"

"Alexander Small, sir," said Small shaking the old man's hand. "That's what the A. stands for. Can I have my card back? The rest caught fire. I don't know any Alphonse but I bring good news. My business has expanded to Miami and I'm at your service."

"Sit down, young man, you've given my old heart a shiver. You are the spitting image of Alphonse Small who was close to my heart in the old real estate days on the coast. Oh, it's all gone, back these many years. Alphonse was a great friend. What was Alphonse's was mine and what was mine was Alphonse's. And, by God I'll say it, he was sharp as me, but he sold short and the last I heard he was in the Windy City. I expected for years Alphonse must be dead. Well, he could have stayed. I fought their narrow- mindedness and the family accepted Alphonse. With the connections of the family he could be where I am today, but he said it was nepotism. By God, nepotism!" thundered the old man. His mustache quivered and a red tint suffused his tan.

"So Alphonse went north. Betrayal, I called it. You said we were brothers! I reminded him. Well go on you damn Yankee. I loved Alphonse, young man, but I came to see my family had been right all along. You must be born an Oglethorpe. Alphonse didn't have Oglethorpe blood in his veins, never could have ruled in the Confederacy. Alphonse had brains, I'll give him that, by God, he was the delight of my heart. But there was no Oglethorpe blood, he was not legitimate."

Mr. Oglethorpe noted Small's raised eyebrow across the desk.

"No, no, I don't mean Alphonse was a crook, Mr. Small. Absolutely no shady dealings with Alphonse, he was a stickler for ethics. Balderdash! Into the garbage heap of frivolity with Alphonse and his ideals. There's Oglethorpes and there are commoners. My family, sir, the Oglethorpes whom I have the honor to represent have been on this soil for thirteen generations, the Oglethorpes *are* the South."

"Yes, well this is very interesting, Mr. Oglethorpe, but I ain't who—"

"The Oglethorpe hand is on the rein, boy, we have been here longest, we deserve to rule."

"What about the Seminoles?"

"In the swamp where they belong! You are a damned Yankee like Alphonse! What's your business?"

"As a matter of fact, Mr. Oglethorpe, I'm a native-born Floridian. I went north in my youth and now I've come back home."

"You didn't look all bad, boy."

"I'm a window washer. Our motto is, 'Let light smite blight'."

"Poppycock," said Oglethorpe.

"I want to wash your windows," continued Small.

"Because of your name, boy, I am giving you the job."

The Southern Confederate bank job was worth $300. And in the midst of the job Butram told Leewing that the board would have the chandelier cleaned.

Old Oglethorpe stood for some moments each day below the windows where Small worked gazing up at him, or if he caught Small on the ground would stand talking interminably of heredity, honor, lineage, duty, brotherhood, blood, slavery, and Oglethorpes in a tangled monologue. Small shuddered wondering why old men were mad. And with what volubility he came at Small so Oglethorpe passed by Talldorf in icy silence.

Talldorf and Small stood on the walk opposite under the palms. Rudolph was enthusiastic, "Look at it shimmer, Small!"

"Our usual quality touch, Tallie. And where are your no-quality friends now who don't even come around to give it the once over? They're blind with envy. I got the Southern Confederate Bank and I could keep it and there'd be more bucks than those pole pushers ever saw."

That afternoon as Talldorf was about to mount his ladder on one of the last tiers of windows a slender young woman in a white dress approached. She wore a white gardenia in her blonde hair, and white gloves. Her blue eyes appraised Rudolph with delight.

"Mr. Small," she said. "I'm Priscilla Oglethorpe? Daddy said you were a new member of our great big family here at Southern Confederate and I feel it my honored duty to welcome you. Why, I declare, Mr. Small, you're not at all like Daddy described you. I'm tickled to death to have you with us. Why if I was to conjure up a window washer I think you might just be my ideal—"

"Priscilla!" It was old Oglethorpe himself stomping across the marble floor, his cane raised in his hand. "Get into my office, Priscilla! Wait for me there!"

"Daddy, I was welcoming Mr. Small—"

"That isn't Small, you ninny! Don't know who he is, don't care!"

Priscilla's blue eyes lingered on Rudolph's with a sense of loss. Oglethorpe rapped the ladder with his cane, "Up, up there! On with your work, whoever you are. Mind your business. Don't let me catch you making eyes at my daughter again or I'll have your hide on my wall!"

The girl scurried toward her father's office.

"Sir!" objected Rudolph, "I—"

"I don't care about you! I won't hear you, by God, man, you'll learn your place!"

"Mr. Oglethorpe," said Small, "What's the problem?"

"Get your man to work, Small! His indiscretions are an outrage. We do not behave that way in the South. Makes my blood boil! Common lust! Disgust! Animals—"

Small shot Talldorf a glance with raised brows. Rudolph went up the ladder, relieved to remove himself from the bilious old man who laid his hand on Small's shoulder and led him aside.

"It's endemic, Small, boy," began Oglethorpe. "You must beat it down the moment it rears its serpent head. The filth of all the world is in the minds of creatures like that."

"Talldorf is innocent as a child. He comes from a rich family too. Talldorf don't have to work like this. Talldorf could have been a doctor."

"I have a place for you, Small, boy. Southern Confederate has twenty more offices. All of this can be yours, Small, boy, but I won't have that stringbean villain with his filthy mind. Get rid of him. You may be from the working class, but I favor your name. I'm willing to overlook your origin, I'm willing to forget what is no fault of your own. I take a personal interest in you. Under my hand you can amount to something."

"To what?" asked Small.

"Money, Small, boy. You'll be on salary at first but I'll see that you want for nothing. Alphonse wouldn't want you to miss this opportunity. I have hounds, did you know? You never thought you would ride to the hounds, now did you, Small, boy?"

"Talldorf is my friend."

"No, no. You work for me, Small, boy. Your standards will be mine."

"You ain't George Washington, Oglethorpe, and I ain't the house nigger."

For an instant a look appeared on the old man's face not unlike that in Priscilla's eyes when she learned that Rudolph was not the esteemed Small. And as quickly was it gone in the purple storm gathering on Oglethorpe's brow as Small's voice rose:

"This was my first and last bank job! I ain't a thief and there ain't no other reason to be in a bank. Kiss my ass, Oglethorpe."

Oglethorpe sputtered, he turned away with raised shoulders and stomped toward his office as tellers quailed with signal alarm at his awful approach. Small yelled across the lobby: "Wrap it up, Talldorf, while the old skinflint gets our money out of his sock."

Oglethorpe did not get the money. He got the cops. Talldorf and Small were ejected from the Southern Confederate Bank, Small yelling at the top of his lungs: "I've been robbed!"

Leewing welcomed them back. She cut and stitched broad leather straps lining them with wool for ankles and wrists to which they attached gleaming steel rings to snap to the thousand feet of white cotton rope she retrieved from a trunk forgotten by a circus that once played the terrace of the Fountainblew.

Talldorf and Small stretched the white rope from gleaming brass rails past the chandelier, arching above, around, through and beneath, a spiderweb gleaming in dizzying geometric precision that entranced Leewing and made her laugh. They worked nights, Small playing a rotary switch dimming and brightening the various tiers of the chandelier to highlight or offset areas they worked, and the light illumined Leewing strolling the mezzanine around or perched on throne-like benches, her beadwork lying still in her hands.

Hooked by their gleaming rings within that web Talldorf and Small rode and floated wearing gloves of white flannel. They dove into the depths of gleaming tiers of glass like fish dipping into luminous grass, swam up from beneath, disappearing within or splayed like butterflies, lay on the air plying their trade.

Mr. Butram arrived to look on with dread: "Good Lord, if they fall the Fountainblew loses a chandelier that never can be replaced. That web! It's dizzying." Mr. Butram fled to the solace of his bed.

The fingers of Talldorf and Small removed shadows which loomed as the cleaning progressed. They worked within a silent intent that late night voices of merrymakers below did not penetrate and light blossomed out and stars were seen in the midst of the chandelier which Leewing had dreamed were there. The movements of Talldorf had become graceful, precise, and assured as he glided among falls and tiers touching flannel fingers to tear drops and rays of glass so that every facet gleamed, Small like an elf and Talldorf a gull rising, dropping, gliding away and back to touch again.

And the night Small told Leewing they would finish she wore hibiscus blossoms in her hair, her eyes sparkled and the beads of her Indian dress shimmered. The chandelier was resplendent with a magic unknown since her childhood.

"I am going to find my people," said Leewing. "I'm going to see the Seminoles. I *am* an Indian, I am not a poor little rich girl."

With $2000 in his pocket and wanderlust in his heart it did not take Small long to decide to leave Miami.

"You don't have to worry about gettin wrapped around a palm tree in the sidecar no more, Tallie."

They were flying along the Ta-Miami Trail in an old rust and scarlet Studebaker with the ladder tied to the roof.

"She's way out there, Tallie, beyond the shadows and mist hanging over the grasses. That ain't land, them's the Everglades where Leewing went. But I personally ain't no primitive. I think I'll like New Orleans. Maybe I'll get a pipe and smoke it on a veranda.

Talldorf had become fond of cigars. "Miami has good ones, Smally, but I heard Tampa has the best. We could start up the business there. It could be our home."

"You can buy yourself a case of the finest Tampas, Tallie, but Small ain't stopping where he started."

"I'm with you, Smally, the worker's life is a good life like I always thought it would be." Talldorf tilted his long cigar in his white teeth and watched the world roll by.

In Tampa Small stopped at the cemetery gate through which he had passed many years before with his bedroll in his arms. He led Talldorf up the same old path through the sand to the height of pauper's field and the wooden marker.

"My mother, Talldorf. Eva Small. She died in county hospital the day I was born."

"I'm honored," said Talldorf.

Small pointed out the airport, now much enlarged. "That's where I took off, Tallie, when I swiped the airplane. I went right out over the docks there and swung her back around, didn't know what I'd got myself into, almost killed a bunch of racehorses. That's the track, it's still there."

Small looked up the orphanage in the phone book. It wasn't there. He drove through neighborhoods recognizing nothing but suddenly slammed on the brakes. Talldorf followed him out of the car. Small looked at the crumbling brick wall of the playyard and, where the orphanage once stood, clinkers, weeds and foundation pourings under a lone palm tree.

"There's plenty of light now," said Small.

Chapter 18

WIND

"This is the hurricane season, Small," said Talldorf, "The lady where I got the coffee said a hurricane is coming."

"Good," said Small, "I always wanted to see something like that." Small sipped from his cardboard cup of coffee and set it on the dashboard as the white sand beaches of the Gulf ran beside the open window. Gentle waves broke sparkling in the sun.

"She's nuts, Talldorf, there ain't a cloud in the sky."

"It looks good to me, Smally," said Rudolph upwrapping one of his Tampas, "but maybe she heard it on a weather report."

"Ain't no wind can hold Small back, Talldorf. I'm from the Windy City. I've done up Miami and New Orleans is my objective. We're goin to New Orleans come hell or high water!"

"On to New Orleans, Commander!" Talldorf puffed his cigar grinning at the passing vegetation.

As they passed through little towns people bustled busily about. "Very active people," observed Small, "Must be the sea air."

In the next town they were boarding up windows.

"They're preparing for the hurricane, Small," said Rudolph. "They think it will blow out their windows."

"They're nuts to board up windows, Talldorf. It's obscene. They can't see what's comin. Where's their respect for light?"

"Hurricanes really wreck buildings, Small. I've seen pictures."

"Hurricanes is their only claim to fame, Talldorf. They got to make a big thing over it. I seen the best pictures in Mine Magazine."

"They have a touch for disasters, Small."

"They're right on top of it, Tallie. I figured someday they'd cover Complicated Maintenance. I'd be the cover story, 'Man at the Top.' All across this great country in corporate offices from coast to coast they ask, 'Who is this man at the top?' And flip open Mine and see that the face is mine."

"Yours!" rejoiced Talldorf brandishing his cigar.

In the next town there were no people.

"We'll just help ourselves, Tallie. I'll leave plenty of cash to cover it." They got crackers and bread, a jar of peanut butter, a head of lettuce, a quart of milk for Rudolph, and six oranges. "There's a coffee pot here and it's still hot!" yelled Small, "Bring in the cups. They won't begrudge wayfaring strangers a spot of java for the road."

"That's the first car I've seen, Small," said Talldorf coming in the door of the old store. "It was a squad car."

It was the highway patrol out of Mobile clearing the coast highway.

"Well don't call em back, Tallie. Those are the last people I'm looking for."

They carried out the groceries and their two cups of coffee and set out on the deserted highway. They stopped for a picnic on the beach in the breathless air.

"Paradise," said Small.

The sky was turning green.

"It looks eerie, Small."

"Green," said Small. "A beautiful green day."

The wind came. It was not there and the next moment it came. At first imperceptibly high in palm fronds then in Rudolph's hair then wind touched their faces and played with their clothing as waves rose booming and foaming onto the beach.

"I think it's time to be moving on," said Small.

Talldorf already was standing clutching his cigars to his bosom. They made sure the ropes that held the ladder to the roof were secure, jumped into the scarlet Studie and made off.

Wind tossed the palm tops and surf boiled on the beach and sand blew across the roadway.

"Pretty exciting, huh, Talldorf?" said Small squinting in the wind that blew in the open window. "Looks like they're going to get a little storm. What we need is a couple coffees."

Rudolph guzzled from the milk bottle and peered worriedly out the windshield.

"I love it, Tallie, listen to the sea boom! I always wanted to be a sea captain!"

"Not me, Small. You could be killed out there!"

Small laughed and stuck a Lucky in his mouth. "Not when you know what you're doing, Tallie." He had to grip the wheel with both hands. The wind was pressing on the car. "Wind is a paper dragon, Talldorf, and I'm a man! I'm Small! Muscle and bone and brain and balance, let it do its worst! Small's ready, ho ho ho!"

The sky glowered down. "What time is it, Talldorf? It ain't time for dark."

"This is the hurricane coming, Small. It isn't daytime. It's storm time!"

"Don't get overexcited, Talldorf. Everything's ok. Small is at the helm."

"Let's find a place and stop, Small."

"Stop? You're crazy, Talldorf. You stop you're dead!" Small laughed crazily above the wind.

Miss Bibbs, late of the Windy City Electric Company, thought that she had found a better position, but now was having second thoughts. Her hands covered her ears and her eyes were closed because she was sick of the childish violence that was Ricardo Ensardo. "If you don't like the wind why don't you shoot it!" she screamed. Four shots rang out in the night and were lost like spray on the wind of Baroque Key and terror filled the brain of Miss Bibbs as, largo, her nipples rose against the black silk Mr. Ensardo's son had dressed her in.

"It's pouring!" Rudolph was staring bug-eyed out the windshield and his Tampa was cold in his fingers.

"My keen vision will see us through!" yelled Small as he wrestled the wheel. It seemed they were racing but he was doing only fifteen miles an hour. "By God, we're moving, Talldorf! We're safe in this scarlet baby. She's sound as a dollar."

Daniel Proot, renegade son of a line of Southern Baptist clergymen, now himself but skin and bone dressed in a rag and his mat of gray hair blowing like a banner came out of the rising waters of the bayou like ripped fog to glare ecstatic at the blast of the storm and bang his staff on the concrete of the coast highway and the sound was sucked up and gone as if it had never been.

"Water!" announced Small, a bare mile away, slowing to five miles per hour and glaring down headlight beams shot with silver rain.

Rudolph yelled: "Small! A wave! You're driving into the ocean!" But Small, watching the water recede jammed the scarlet Studie into second and raced the next wave at forty miles an hour.

"It ain't the ocean, it's the highway, Talldorf!" And Small saw from the corner of his eye foaming white rise into their racing headlights and pass behind as if they left a wake and, sheltering palms and vegetation to windward, slowed her to ten miles per hour.

"Small, we could have been washed into the sea! Waves are washing over the highway. We should have stopped. We're trapped, Small!"

"You're trapped in your head!" yelled Small. "Everything's ok. The wind would have blown us toward land."

"That isn't land!" insisted Talldorf, "That's a swamp! We drown either way!"

Another highway patrol car bore toward them, its headlights about to pick out crazy Proot when a wave snatched it from the highway into the nighttime sea not a bubble different or a word heard in the sighing roar that combed the hair of man and beast for a hundred miles, who instead greeted the lights of the scarlet Studie with brandished staff and saucer eyes.

Rudolph yelled. Small braked the Studie. "It's a man!" The halted car trembled in wind, and rain slammed. "Let him in, Talldorf. The lucky bastard is rescued by Complicated Maintenance."

The bent figure crouched through the headlights and clawed at the fender waving its stick as if conducting. Rudolph threw open the back door but the face stood in a swirling stare outside his window.

"Get out and shove him inside before we get run over by a Greyhound bus, Talldorf!"

Rudolph lept beyond the call of duty. He hung to the car door, the water a whipping sheet in his face and corraled the bony sopping figure into the back door, slammed it and climbed in drenched and gasping.

"Hey, what the hell's the pole for?" said Small ducking, "Throw that log out, grandpa, you're safe with — " Small's words froze on his lips when he saw the firey eyes. Rudolph, who saw at the same instant, moved to the edge of his seat. Never, never, never, pick up hitchhikers! Elinore always told his uncles. Old Proot howled into their faces:

"They sow the wind and reap the whirlwind!"

Talldorf and Small turned their backs and the Studie crept on, a madman behind and a hurricane before.

"The pole, Talldorf!" Small yelled from the side of his mouth, "Do something with that pole before he brains me. I'm lookin for a safe harbor for us to pull into!"

Talldorf had grasped the staff, at least to steady it above Small's head and read in the eerie light from the dash panel the manic will of the old man of the swamps.

"At Babylon fall the slain of the earth!" yelled the man with the voice of the sea. It flattened Small to the wheel and they rushed headlong into the hurricane.

At Weather Headquarters of the Pensacola Naval Air Station the hurricane was a calculated constant of increasing intensity the greater length of the Gulf coast and the calculation was absolutely wrong for singular blows of the storm shot with unerring accuracy, with a perfection that annihilated a bulwarked mansion that had stood one hundred years reaping in a moment the accumulated debts of the scions of five noble families and the pregnant maid in the scullery was left untouched; the Doberman kennels with their occupants vanished without trace while the stray skulking beneath the shrubbery under the library windows licking his chops and wondering had not a whisker ruffled as the house removed itself from his presence. The yacht and the playboy, from whose father Small had once stolen an airplane, went in his brocade robe and silk underwear to the bottom while Carlos, the Cuban boy who had been surly denied a berth as galley help, ate an unexpected lobster dinner on shore.

And Small in his wickedness drove on with Talldorf who could not believe his eyes or ears and who rode without hope.

"The Lord God of recompenses shall requite!" boomed the voice.

Small watched ghosts of waves break across the highway before them and drove on, the old Studie rocking and sliding like a sled through the nightmare of an Eskimo from which was no escape, for the voice of doom drove him on.

"Behold! I am against thee, Gog! Rain upon him overflowing rain! Great hailstones! Fire and brimstone!" Talldorf and Small stared into the terrible storm. "Fish and fowl and beast and creeping things and all men upon the face of earth shake at my presence! Mountains shall be thrown down and steep places fall, sayeth the Lord!"

"Right —" agreed Small. Talldorf chanced a glance and turned back to the storm seared by those eyes. Trees with ancient roots lifted from earth before and behind as the scarlet Studie with the ladder on the roof crept on.

Small never tired of telling how the sea rose into the headlights and did not pass them by. Not a wave, but the sea itself unleashed in greenish tint before the lights went out.

"Behold!"

Small beholding the star of his luck in his mind, the pile-driving thrust of the sea the blackened swirl and dazing crunch. Stunning unabated wrath of wind and, drowning in his mind, Rudolph awaited the lovely face of his mother.

Neither Talldorf nor Small wet their feet. By morning light the eyes of the son of Reverend Proot, who had mercilessly belabored the orphans of Tampa, glowed like the eyes of an owl over the seat. The aluminum ladder was wrapped around a palm tree like a fender. The scarlet Studie was wedged among mangrove roots not far from the silt covered highway where they stood gazing on a world whose hair was trimmed.

Talldorf and Small were already setting off down the salt-crusted highway even before the man of rags with his staff raised cried:

"Ye that escape the sword! Go! Remember the Lord afar off! Let Jerusalem come to mind! Go ye out of the midst of her! Deliver ye every man his soul from the fierce anger of God!"

"Amen!" murmured Rudolph striding beside Small.

"Amen," seconded Small and looking back to see the old man no more reached thankfully for a Lucky.

Chapter 19

MR. CHARLIE GETS THE BLACKS

S mall's star rode high over the hood of the scarlet Studebaker with the bent extension ladder on its roof as they entered New Orleans.

Talldorf gripped a cigar in his teeth. His face was green. "Let's live, Small, before it's too late. We'll have fun, Small! What is life without fun?"

They took a large room where an overhead fan with mahogany blades still stirred the air in the Calhoun Hotel. Small bought a bottle of mint julep mix at the drug store which they drank sitting in their shorts and socks on the balcony overlooking chimney pots and the swiveling eyes behind lace curtains of the *Vieux Carre*. They passed out and woke up feeling fine. They walked out into the afternoon sunlight and exchanged their sand-filled sneakers for wingtips, and T. Raggs fitted them in white Panama suits and straw hats. Small bought a bamboo cane which he swung dangerously as they strutted along Canal Street.

Two black men dressed in livery leaning on a lamppost, grinned and rolled their eyes at the pigeons.

In their bright Panama suits they dined on oysters Rockefeller and breast of squab. Sex strummed the lamps of the French Quarter and reverberated in the street cobbles. Sweating backs of black dancers flushed with firelight in Congo Square echoed days of slaves and pirates. Talldorf and Small drifted from one Crescent city bar to the next. Rudolph was anxious to throw himself into the dark arms of passion.

Small banged on the big wooden door in the dark. "Are you sure this is a whorehouse, Talldorf?"

Talldorf had watched the place, a big Victorian house on the Rue St. du Shade. He had seen lawyers, politicians, and flashy young executives welcomed through the front door. The blonde woman with a fur boa around her throat had come out through the back door. Talldorf had followed her to Canal Street where she nonchalantly boarded a trolley.

The peephole opened on a square blue jaw:

"Beat it, you guys."

They sat on high stools in a waterfront dive. Drummers pounded bold jungle rhythms. Talldorf, head and shoulders above the heaving crowd, was pale with excitement.

"Bachelors, Small! Maybe you and I are always going to be good old bachelors." They put their arms around each other. "Small, I've never seen such beautiful women in all my life!"

"Why don't you dance, Tallie? You're the best-dressed man here except for me."

"What girl belongs to who? We might get in a fight with some greaser with a knife. Pardon me, sir, I didn't mean you. Can I buy you a beer — a glass of tequila then? I never learned to tango, Small. Dance on! Go on and dance! By jeezes, Small, I think I'll have another drink and dance myself!"

Talldorf threw himself around the dance floor at the edge of the heaving mass without a partner. The music in his blood expanded with joy so exquisite that he passed out. Small grabbed him from the bouncer.

"You can let go of his collar. Talldorf ain't no common drunk—he's uncommon."

Talldorf was always trying to steer Small into a black restaurant. "I need to go in there, Small."

"We just ate for crisake. Are you still hungry?"

"I'm not very hungry. It's ethnics, Small. I studied ethnics in college. But I never got a chance to see it in person." Small relented, smoked his Lucky and drank the bitter coffee.

Talldorf was taking an unprecedented interest in his life. Small followed him up another sidestreet toward the bridge lights set like rubies in a crown where the river moved and freighters rode in twinkling gleams of adventure. Talldorf led into colored bars where they sat like maggots on an eggplant and Small backed toward the doors while Talldorf continued naive conversations with his black brothers.

"No more white women for me, Small. There's something about a white woman that makes me panic."

"You're riskin your life, Talldorf," Small said, "I hope you know that. You don't realize that somethin is goin on in the world that's got nothin to do with desire or the dark. Have you forgotten Count Squeegee? Man is destined for greater things than sporting with whores. I ain't standin under no more street lamps till four a.m. I'm gettin a library card and tonight I'm going to the opera. I plan to discover the meaning of the universe."

Talldorf continued his nocturnal prowls alone. He appraised the ebony tints of the black women and their lips, curled to a fine edge of sensuality and grew heady with their dusky scents. He sat on a stool in the raucous din at the Camel Club sipping tomato juice as black musicians on the small stage snapped sweat from their faces.

Iris was coal-black with sausage breasts like pictures of Cameroon girls in the *National Geographic*. "I ain't beautiful, Skinny," Iris corrected. "I'm ooggly."

Her sensuality was protuberant like African statuary, her dark eyes bitter, happy or shockingly devoid of everything. Iris allowed herself to be kissed, wriggling back suddenly, barely brushing his lips with her own.

"Sammy," growled the black man, "Give Mr. Charlie a shot a Johnnie Red."

"Rudolph Victor Talldorf, sir," extending his skinny hand.

"You looks like a educated white boy. I been askin myself. Morris, I says, how come Mr. Charlie —"

"Talldorf."

"How come Mr. Charlie come pokin roun black folks? Mr. Charlie, I think youse a money-fucker."

"You must have me confused with someone else," suggested Talldorf looking down disconcertedly at the two-fisted black man.

Iris snatched him away. "Don't pay no mind to what he say." Iris cradled Rudolph's head against her breast, her velvet skin like lampblack, and ran her fingers through his red curls.

Talldorf howled his primal scream over his jungle sister and bent the bedposts.

The hair on his arms grew in thicker, and long-dormant follicles on his chest shot out sprouts. "This one must be an inch long, Small!" Talldorf was standing proudly before the mirror. Small looked up from the fat volume he was reading.

"It's all the pig tails and greens you been eatin, Talldorf."

Talldorf, who had been keeping his liaison with Iris a secret, was compelled to spill the beans. "I have crossed the racial barrier, Small. Black people are my people." The only evidence he could muster was his fair skin, red hair and freckles.

"I'm an albino, Small."

"You are not an albino, Talldorf. You're a white man. While you're traveling with me in the south don't forget it."

In his spotless suit, his straw in hand and wingtips Talldorf was quick to dance off the sidewalk to let Negroes pass. By God, thought Talldorf, if anyone has to bow and scrape let it be me. He sat at the back of trolleys. He used only bathrooms reserved for the colored who backed against the walls when he entered as though witnessing a vision. He drank copiously from *their* fountains.

"I love you, Iris. I want you to marry me," said Talldorf.

"Fool," answered Iris.

"People in love get married where I come from, Iris. We will soar over racial barriers together. We'll have children. We'll pattern our lives on the brotherhood of man. We are all one people, aren't we Iris?"

"What a skinny educated white boy want with a nigger wife?" Iris wanted to know. She wrapped her ebony legs playfully around Rudolph's white chest. "You sure crazy, Skinny."

At the track Small clattered his cane over the backs of folding chairs and announced it was Scion in the first. "It's Fleet Beat," contradicted Talldorf. They bet Scion and Fleet Beat won. In the second Small said it was Mousey Girl. Talldorf held out for True Price. They bet True Price. Mousey Girl won by eight lengths. Talldorf picked four winners. Small picked four winners. They bet the losers and lost three hundred dollars.

Amos, who cadged drinks at the Camel Club and was into Talldorf for a hundred and fifty bucks skipped town.

"Small, Iris doesn't have a refrigerator."

"Don't think we're gonna buy your intended a refrigerator with my half, Talldorf. You spent your half. The answer is no. Vacation draws to a close. We got to find some windows to wash."

But Small was busy pursuing the meaning of the universe through the rubble of culture, and Talldorf was busy keeping Iris company.

Morris bent toward Talldorf at the bar. "Us niggers got a old test we gots to pass befo we men, Rudolph. Ain't no fine lady like Iris goin ta respect no pansy white boy don't pass dat test."

"What is the test?" Talldorf asked.

"Mos of us swims de ribber in flood time," Morris said, "Or wade de bayou when de baby moccasin hatchin."

"Yikes!" said Talldorf.

"But no one got courage 'nough ta pick up de serum cause de man be watchin. It a dangerous mission. We's gettin dat serum from nice Yankee white folk fo our po sick chillen likely ta die. But de wicked govment say it illegal cause dey cain't make no tax money on dat serum sos we got to smuggle it. Some mans got to pick up dat serum. We all done already passed our mans test. Dat leave you. You picks up dat serum at midnight on de ribber an saves our po chillens' lives Iris see youse a real man, white boy."

Iris was hanging on the shoulder of the banjo player after leaving the sway-hipped pool player at the back of the bar.

"Morris, I will submit myself to the test."

"Give Mr. Charlie a shot a Johnnie red."

"Iris," said Talldorf proudly, "Morris and I have an understanding."

"Don't you have nofin to do wif Morris, Skinny. He a bad stepper."

"I don't fear Morris, Iris. I fear a government that keeps serum from dying black children."

"Huh?" said Iris.

Meanwhile, his cane over the arm of his white suit and his nose in the air, Small was slapping a guide book in his palm appraising the stained glass of St. Ignatius Cathedral when the old lady came upon him. Her ancient face appeared in the drawn light of votive candles. She clutched his sleeve and led him past niches of saints until they were threatened by the blast of sunlight at the open door. She drew him to a halt against the cold stone and pressed her bony nose to his.

"I am Mrs. Pontchartrain Cock. My name and culture are synonymous. I will give you the key to the door of culture. Get rid of that dreary guidebook. Come!"

Her black skirts braved the sunlight's blast and before two liveried black men who materialized behind him Small was hurried into the shadowy back seat of a limousine. Mrs. Pontchartrain Cock draped herself in a far corner like a dusty doily. The car shot up the narrow street.

Small followed as though charmed by a witch up stone stairs into a sprawling mansion, into the cave of high culture. The rich, the defenders of tradition were afterall perhaps privy to a knowledge which might have escaped Small in his plebian origins, he considered judiciously.

Mrs. Pontchartrain Cock did not speak of stained glass. She told a tale of evil times, of the loss of plantations and how the cotton mills were swindled away by modern corporados. Through the flickering candelabra of the dining table the shadowy caverns of the crone's face merged before Small's eyes. He seemed to see the belle Louisa du Bois lift her glass and toss her golden curls and her blue eyes flashed while slaves, to be sure, did a soft-shoe down cotton rows off the veranda. Louisa du Bois of the peanut du Bois, beauty of beauties, heiress to an autocracy suffered the blight of a marriage to the dashing scoundrel Pontchartrain Cock who burrowed into her patrimony like a boll weevil, and dissolute and unregenerate to the end was at last carried off by apoplexy, his dying words: 'Frankly, my dear, I don't give a damn,' leaving her on the lip of ruin where she must turn her hand to her own devices.

"My eyes have been opened since I was a silly girl. I am still belle of the ball and none will defy me!"

"As you have perceived, Mrs. Cock, I am on a quest through the halls of culture," Small said. "I am curious to know if people like yourself might know the secret of the universe."

"Who would if we don't?"

"What is it?" Small asked.

"Money."

"Are you sure?"

"Certainly."

"How much money?"

"So much money that one never considers money. As a child I spent an entire day throwing my dolls down the incinerator. I never came to the end.

What fathomless joy! Where my eye fell, that belonged to me, things and men." Her eyes flashed like dark lightning.

"What is it that I can do for you, Mrs. Cock?"

They adjourned to the drawing room where even oil paintings adorned the walls. Mrs. Cock spoke from her wingtip chair in the shadows. "Your dress and manner, Mr. Small, inform me that you are a gentleman above reproach. I am engaged in a business where discretion is paramount. I push dope."

Small's surprise had little time to invest itself in indignation. "I will pay you thirteen thousand dollars for one night's service as my supercargo. Of course I have servants, but I will trust my reputation only to a white man."

Mrs. Pontchartrain Cock told Small that she had observed him for some days and that he had impressed her favorably. She especially admired the manner in which he swung his cane. Small's fingers touched the fat knot of his white tie. Mrs. Cock said that she had observed him at the opera, at the ballet, and had watched him dance down the library steps.

"I require the services of a discreet gentleman, Mr. Small, one capable of handling himself and my concerns with decisiveness and valor. To insure your anonymity you will dress as a nigra, a top hat and tuxedo will do, preferably with moth holes and you will wear blackface."

In the shadows of the room the liveried black men smirked, teeth and eyes gleaming. How peculiar that neither Mrs. Pontchartrain Cock nor the sharp-eyed Small appeared to notice their antics.

"You are to receive a barrel of pure cocaine from a launch at mid-river tomorrow at midnight. You shall make payment and return the barrel to me. Prove yourself capable and I will make you a rich man. I shall open to you the priceless doors of culture."

She handed him a white envelope which contained a retainer she considered sufficient. As Small tucked it into the pocket of his white coat, at one and the same moment, a black fire inhabited Mrs. Pontchartrain Cock's ancient eyes and they sparkled winsome, blue and young.

"The evening after your little service, Mr. Small, I would be enchanted to have you escort me to the opera which you shall enjoy from my box." She offered her hand to be kissed. It came like an alighting dove but to Small's lips it was cold as stone.

In the back of the limousine on the way to the Calhoun Small counted ten crisp one hundred dollar bills. He took no note of the liveried black man who opened the car door but twirled his cane smartly across the walk and strode into the hotel, his heart warmed by the thousand dollars.

Talldorf was leaving the Camel Club because Iris had failed to show up and he had no more money to buy drinks for his black brothers. He stepped quickly aside at the door to permit the entrance of the two liveried black men who had just left Small. They danced by on the toes of their shiny boots like a pair of gay Nazis, doffing caps with shiny black brims. Talldorf marveled at the native politeness of his black brothers as he strode into the cut-throat dark. Iris might treat him flippantly now, he considered, but she would sit up and take notice when he delivered the serum for the sick black children. Then he would loom large in her eyes. He would stand as tall as a black man. Iris would quit hanging on the shoulder of that banjo player.

"We better get some windows to wash, Small," Talldorf told him on entering their room at the Calhoun. "I've run out of money."

Small pulled a twenty from his wallet. "Enjoy yourself, Tallie. I can't be bothered with windows. Maybe I'll never bother with dirt again. My new suit might get soiled. I've met a fancy lady who is taken with me. I'll be gone all night tomorrow."

Talldorf was delighted. "We can double date, Small."

"This dame don't hang out in dives, Talldorf. She's about a hundred years old, but she's bewitching. My association with her can be very profitable. I'm takin her to her box at the opera. Diamonds and singing."

"My grandmother Elinore had season tickets. I was always uncomfortable, it was boring and profitless. Those people knew nothing about real life."

"Those people know where the next meal is coming from, Talldorf, which you wouldn't if I hadn't handed ya that twenty."

"I hope you have a good time, Small. I too will be out tomorrow night. I must be with my black brothers."

"I warned you about the riff-raff, Talldorf. You're headed for trouble."

"Thank you, Small, I consider myself capable of directing my life. In fact tomorrow night I expect to be a new man." Talldorf was adjusting his straw before the mirror and experimenting with grave expressions, narrowing his eyes, raising an eyebrow. "I can get you into Morris' late night poker game, Small. They respect me there." Small was laying on the bed in his shorts.

"Watch out they don't use you for alligator bait, Talldorf."

When Talldorf was gone Small switched out the light and lay brooding on the pillow. Apparently she recognized him as a resourceful man. He imagined the bundle 130 one hundred dollar bills would make in his pocket. And more where that came from. He would float that barrel through fire for thirteen Gs. Small was her man. Feeling rich he fell asleep.

And beyond the rim of the watery globe on Baroque Key, Ricardo Ensardo with his foul retinue, Miro, Maxie, Tony, and Blister, was stepping into his private launch, the *Faerie Queen*. Having had his way with Miss Bibbs, late of the Windy City Electric Company, Ricardo had locked Miss Bibbs away in the slave quarters and thrown away the key; more exciting prospects were at hand. Having forged a link with the South American drug empire Ricardo was delivering a barrel of raw cocaine to the New Orleans market. It was Ricardo's boldest stride beyond the prohibitions of his father, Mr. Anthony Ensardo, who preferred distilleries. Bullets would fly from east and west and Ricardo Ensardo would rise to the top of the heap. He took a snort, slapped the hands of his henchmen when they reached for the bag, climbed to the flying bridge and shot holes in the waves as they sped through the throbbing night toward New Orleans.

Small awoke with a hangover; the champagne at Mrs. Pontchartrain Cock's packed a punch. Talldorf was chipper and rosy-cheeked with only a few hours sleep. The day was torrid. Everyone was sweating including Small standing in the morning shade having his wingtips shined, and under the fan at Jacques over a sumptuous breakfast.

Talldorf met Iris early in the afternoon. They ate fish and chips on her rumpled bed behind the plastic curtains blowing in the breeze off the river and Talldorf's joy was ecstatic while Iris lolled like fudge.

Despite the heat and the crimping knot in his tie Small went to the Museum of Art with his cane. He sat on the handle reconnoitering the masters. He found them to be a passionate bunch. They drank a lot and never had any money.

He went for a mint julep in the courtyard cafe, drank it as he smoked a Lucky and looked at the wilted rich at other tables. He kept seeing the matrons naked. He wiped his brow with his handkerchief, had another julep and took a long stroll through the heat along the levee swinging his cane and sweating. "Eez too hot to fuck," a Latin girl counseled the glistening boy beside her on the park grass. The muddy river glinted and female lightning bloomed in the western sky. Money could buy women and men, Small reflected, but it couldn't keep it from raining. Mrs. Pontchartrain Cock was living in a dream. He should know better than to ask a woman the meaning of the universe. Mrs. Cock had connections and cash. He was the one with vision. With his direction her business might prosper. Small dined on oysters and returned to the Calhoun to await the arrival of Mrs. Cock's car.

Talldorf was on his way out when Small arrived.

"I'm glad I got to see you before I left, Small. Wish me luck."

"Good luck, Tallie. You're goin to meet Iris, eh?"

"No, Small, I won't see Iris until tomorrow when I face her with the pride of a man. I must be with my black brothers tonight."

"Don't knock over a liquor store, Talldorf."

"My association with the Negro race is of interest humanistically and anthropologically, Small. I might say that tonight I am to be initiated into that culture as a new and equal member. I can't say more at this time."

"That's plenty," Small said, "If I was you I wouldn't let any of em get behind me."

"Tonight I expect to pass beyond fear, Small."

"Try to stay out of the morgue, Talldorf."

Talldorf stepped blithely out into the twilight of the sultry evening. Small awaited his call from the desk.

The car had just left the Camel Club, an unauthorized stop, piloted by the two in livery. Their faces in the passing lamp-lights were expressionless masks. One called for Small at the desk and, stern and severe, awaited the opening of the elevator doors. Small strode briskly out tapping his cane past the liveried one without a glance and entered the car without acknowledging the one who held the door. The car sped into the darkness. In the front seat the grins returned to the faces of the two in livery like cats with the canary near.

When Talldorf entered the Camel Club Morris hustled him into the back room almost roughly. "Youse almost miss yo manhood test, boy."

"I'm sorry, Morris, but I was just chased around the block by a man with a knife. However I'm ready whenever —"

Two cut-throat types emerged from the shadows. One wore a red cap and the other a scar across his forehead. Red Cap draped a soiled towel around Rudolph's shoulders. Talldorf surrendered his will to his dark guides. The man with the scar held a coffee can.

"Put some color on dat boy," Morris said, drinking from a pint produced from his hip pocket. Scar's broken teeth shown gleefully and Talldorf's nose quivered at the bourbon breath. Scar wiped greasy blackface from the can across Talldorf's face, his blunt fingers probing even Rudolph's red curls.

"He look a lot better already," judged Scar.

"Hold still you puss," Morris instructed. He painted huge red lips on Talldorf.

They took the towel from his shoulders and turned him to view from every angle. Morris scowled with his hooded eyes. Their faces were sour. "His hands is wrong," Morris said. Scar rubbed them with blacking. Talldorf watched with anxiety as the cuffs of his white suit were soiled.

Red Cap popped open his switchblade. "We gots to cut off dat red hair." Talldorf felt anguish: Iris loved his red hair.

"Don't want dat mop on dis floor," said Morris, "He jes be a wimpy albino."

"That's just what I've often thought, Morris," Talldorf ventured.

Morris spat on the floor.

"He need dis," said Red Cap putting a cane in Talldorf's hand not unlike the one Small carried. "Do us a soft shoe, white boy," instructed Red Cap.

"If you wants to pass yo manhood test, mother, you bes dance," suggested Morris. Talldorf began a self-conscious shuffle on the bare old boards of the back room while his guides passed the pint.

"Swing de cane," said Red Cap.

"We wants a shit-eatin grin," instructed Scar.

"Dance, mother," said Morris.

Talldorf followed the instructions with vigorous pursuit and turned quite a step especially when the banjo player hit hot licks in the doorway.

"He ain't much," they all agreed, "but he all we gots."

Talldorf was sweating and winded, more from excitement than exertion. Morris handed him the pint.

"Take a slug," he said. "It loosen you up an put some spine in you. Don't wants nobody recognizin you. You got ID on yo person?"

Exhilarated by the whiskey, Talldorf's head felt quite large and emptied of all concern. "I have a wallet, Morris." Talldorf handed it over.

"Ain't got nothin in it," Morris said.

"There's my library card and my Michigan driver's license," said Talldorf.

Morris grumbled but slipped it into his pocket. "Fo safe keepin," he said. "Gimme dat watch, boy. It goin to glint in de searchlight an give way yo position to de man an we don get de serum an all de po chillen die an you done flunked yo manhood test."

"Certainly, Morris," Talldorf said feeling stripped naked. His graduation present followed his wallet into Morris' pocket. The banjo player in the doorway did a nice accompaniment.

"Check yo pieces," Morris commanded. All three flashed huge black revolvers, spun the cylinders, spit bullets into their palms, reloaded and replaced the guns in their pockets. Red Cap tested a flashing straight razor on the hairs of his wrist. Scar snapped open his blade and twirled it in his fingers. Talldorf appreciated their dexterity.

"Are we expecting trouble, Morris?" Talldorf asked.

"I ain't," said Morris. "Into de car, white boy." Talldorf accompanied his dark guides into the night.

Meanwhile, in her mansion, Mrs. Pontchartrain Cock confronted Small with a ragged tuxedo and a silk top hat. "They dress so foolishly," she said. "We will see that you look like them." She clapped her old hands and the two in livery appeared. "Go with my nigras, Mr. Small. They have their instructions."

Small accompanied them with the clothing to an adjoining room where what had been done to Talldorf was now done to Small down to the big red lips painted over his own. Small bristled.

"You guys got no idea what a nigger is," he told the two as he looked into the mirror. He looked like a dressed up ape. It made Small furious. The two in livery held their white gloves over their gleaming teeth and rolled their eyes.

"My cane," Small said. It was handed to him. Leaning upon it did little to improve his appearance. "I'm only doing this for the money," Small told the two in livery. "See that my suit and straw are well cared for. There'll be a little something for you later."

"Perfect! You look like Mr. Bones," said Mrs. Cock. "If the police launch picks you up in its light they may run you down but they will not bother to rescue a drunk nigra. If you should fall into their hands I will disavow any knowledge of you. You must be at mid-river precisely at midnight. You are expected by the Faerie Queen. You will exchange this sealed packet for a barrel of raw cocaine. You will return the barrel to the dock from which you will embark." She withdrew a shiny automatic pistol from the Afghan on her lap and handed it to Small. "You know how to use one of these, of course. You will guard the packet and the barrel with your life. You might kiss my hand but I will not be soiled. My nigras will drive you to the dock and await your return."

Small put the pistol in his pocket and the packet into his waistband, doffed his top hat and bowed to Mrs. Pontchartrain Cock who curtsied, and Small withdrew.

The low limousine knifed easily through the night toward the docks while not many streets away in a hiccoughing old clunker Talldorf and his black brothers paralleled Small's approach to the river.

Scarcely two miles downstream the *Faerie Queen* slid languidly upriver through the torpid night showing no running lights. Ricardo was at the wheel, his red eyes burning holes in the darkness ahead. Maxie, Blister, Tony and Miro who had been into the prohibited barrel twitched and jerked on the aftdeck and threatened the dark with their tommy guns. They paid scant attention. They were embroiled in argument. With hisses and whispered threats, so as not to disturb the boss who muttered over charts and steered with one hand, each declared that Ricardo had promised him personally the pleasure of blowing away the nigger after they received payment for the barrel.

Ricardo consulted his chronometer and screwed up his red eyes to blink at buoy lights. He might have hired a competent pilot and afterward shot and dumped him overboard, but Ricardo must do everything himself. He should have met half a dozen Coast Guard launches during his trip from Baroque Key but had seen none and been seen by none. He would indeed reach the rendezvous precisely at midnight blundering through a mine field of them. Ricardo mistook balls and brains for the charm of a dark purpose which preserved his course, so he steered toward the fire next time in his perennial agitated state of ravenous excitement, maddened at the slow pace the *Faerie Queen* must pursue. If Ricardo Ensardo knew what awaited him he would have done well to turn and run hard for Baroque Key.

The limousine was parked behind a warehouse at the end of a pier whose oily boards extended into muggy darkness and fog which had risen from the river. Small, in his ridiculous outfit, cane tapping, followed the shiny black boots of one in livery followed again by bootsteps of the other as he peered ahead for a view of the boat. It was a slender gray dory lying below on the luminous green water.

"Synchronize your watches," Small commanded. The two in livery looked at their watches. "I'll need one of those." Small slipped a watch off the nearest wrist onto his own and the faces of the two registered sorrow. Small consulted the watch. "Time to move out." He patted the packet, and the pistol in his pocket, adjusted his top hat, hung the cane over his arm and tripped down the ladder into the boat. He sat down beside the outboard motor and took in the eerie world, green and gray, dank and silent save for the distant ominous moan of foghorns and water slipping against the piles. Small yanked at the cord and the motor roared. He peered over the river, strangely luminous with artificial fires of the city night and saw no light, he saw nothing at all, and opening the throttle sped into that darkness.

Not far up river in the glow of a butane lantern Talldorf tripped over his cane and sprawled in the bottom of the dinghy. He recovered himself and settled precariously with the knees of his Panama suit sticking up like wings. Morris' hooded eyes peered over the boards of the pier at Talldorf.

"Youse watch de lantern here and you drives straight to de middle of de ribber a good piece an you see de Faerie Queen. Dey hails you an say, who goes der. You says, Ahoy Faerie Queen, I come fo de coke. Dats de password fo de serum. Dey tells you come on long side. You does dat. Dey give you lot a funny talk like, where de money, fool? You jes talk along any ol thing come in yo simple white boy head an if dey pokes you roun you know it part of de nitiation to yo manhood an soon dey sees you a real nigger an give you de serum. You got dem structions?"

"I believe so, Morris. I will do my best. But it's terribly foggy. I can't see anything."

"Groovy. Shove off, white boy."

Talldorf managed to hold on when he gunned the little boat and roared between the pilings of the pier, emerged at the end and shot with terror into the darkness.

He was well out from the end of the pier riding the dinghy like a race horse into the bowl of fog before he was able to throttle down so abruptly that the bow sank and wallowed in the swift current. He was drifting. He looked back to see a lonely pinpoint of light from the lantern. He proceeded slowly, straining his eyes for his benefactors somewhere ahead with the precious serum. He thought of Iris. It was possible he might fail, he might never return. The 'man' might spot him. It was unthinkable he would surrender. He would escape them. Somehow he would elude them in the fog. He would return the serum to the dock and his black brothers. Would they hug him at the successful completion of his test? Would they open their veins with a switchblade and mingle their blood with his? Iris would behold him with awe and love, the saviour of black children. He would have her for his own. Talldorf realized he was not paying attention. He cut the throttle so abruptly the bow again foundered. No light. There was no light before or behind.

Small roared past what he considered mid-river, but there was no *Faerie Queen*. His dory was slicing a large figure eight through the fog when a tiny dinghy bearing a ridiculous gangly Negro appeared and swept past his bow. Small saw the whites of his eyes roll and he was gone.

Talldorf had scarcely recovered from the apparition of the flying madman in the top hat when a white launch arose before him. He cut the throttle. The dinghy wallowed.

"Who goes der!" It was loud-mouthed Maxie.

"Ahoy Faerie Queen," Talldorf cried, "I come for the coke!" Instantly he was blinded by the floodlight Ricardo turned on him.

"It's the nigger, Boss," said Maxie. When Talldorf neared out of the direct beam of the floodlight he was astonished at the gun barrels protruding like spikes from the side of the launch. Behind each barrel was a Windy City fedora and the glow of a cigarette butt.

"Throw us your line," he was commanded. Talldorf threw the rope as the dinghy bumped the hull of the *Faerie Queen*.

"Get aboard, nigger," said Ricardo.

"Get aboard, nigger," echoed Tony.

"Shut up," Ricardo told Tony.

Talldorf angled his leg aboard and climbed in towering over the crew.

"How's the weather up there, nigger?" snickered Blister.

"Shut up," Ricardo growled.

"What a stupid lookin nigger," judged Miro.

"Shut up," Ricardo told Miro.

"I wish to thank you in behalf of humanity and the black race for bringing the serum, Faerie Queen," Talldorf said to Ricardo who slapped him smartly across the face knocking Talldorf's straw into the river.

"I ain't the Faerie Queen you insolent spade. That's the boat! His black came off on my hand!"

Maxie curled his lip looking at his master's blackened hand.

"That's cause he's an albino, Boss. Albinos are the sickly ones," Miro said.

"Disgusting!" Ricardo wiped his hand on Talldorf's white coat. "I despise doing business with you people. Let's see the color of your money, nigger."

"Certainly you are aware, sir, that I have no money," Talldorf said.

"If you got no money you're a dead nigger," Ricardo said.

"Yes, sir," Talldorf agreed. "But I am aware the serum — excuse me, sir — the *coke* is free, and that you have come on a mission of mercy. I have volunteered to risk life and imprisonment to come to you and I must be on my way quickly."

"Maxie! Frisk the lunatic. If he's got no money kill him." Talldorf was not alarmed. They couldn't be serious.

"I don't want his black comin off on me," Maxie pleaded.

"I'm countin to one," Ricardo told Maxie.

"Ok, ok, Boss."

Miro, Blister, and Tony shoved the muzzles of their tommy guns into Talldorf's ribs as Maxie frisked him.

"This nigger ain't got a gun, Boss. He ain't got money. He ain't got nothin."

"Kill him," said Ricardo.

"Surely you jest," Talldorf hastened to say.

"You promised I could kill the nigger, Boss," Tony said.

"You promised I could kill the nigger, Boss," Blister said.

"Shut up, shut up," Ricardo howled.

As they crowded near jabbing him with their gun muzzles Talldorf saw Red Cap rise over the side behind them with his big black gun in his hand, his straight razor in his teeth and step silently onto the deck. Then Scar with his big black gun in his hand and his switchblade in his teeth, and at last Morris stepped onto the deck leveling a sawed off shotgun.

"Look behind you, gentlemen," said Talldorf immensely relieved.

"You think we'd fall for an old one like that?" they said in unison.

"Don't turn round, white boys, or we blow off yo heads," said Morris. Ricardo and his foul retinue froze like statues. "Drop yo pieces on de deck an raise up yo hands fo we cut youse up in pieces." Guns clattered to the deck.

"Niggers, Boss," said Maxie.

"I gonna cut out yo tongue, honkey," said Scar.

"Shuddup you mof," Morris told Scar.

I gonna cut out der gizzards," said Red Cap.

"Shuddup yo mof," Morris told Red Cap.

"Morris! My friends!" said Talldorf, "Thank heaven you've arrived!"

"Shuddup yo mof, Mr. Charlie."

Talldorf gathered his initiation was not yet concluded. Morris sipped from his pint while Red Cap and Scar collected the tommy guns and relieved Ricardo and the foul retinue of their concealed pieces.

"We done come to relieve you a dat little barrel a coke, Mr. Charlie," Morris was good enough to explain to Ricardo.

"My Papa is gonna get you dumb spades," Ricardo threatened.

"Shuddup yo mof, Fairey Queen," Morris told Ricardo.

"That's the name of the boat. I'm Ricardo Ensardo! My Papa is Anthony Ensardo and he runs the mob in the whole country and he's gonna get you!"

"My ol man make sour mash outta you ol man," Morris told Ricardo.

"My Papa is the biggest man in the whole country!" insisted Ricardo. "My Papa is bigger than the President!"

"President a piss ant," Morris decided and popped the lid on the infamous barrel.

"My Papa—"

"Shuddup yo mof, white fairy."

"I'm not! I'm not!"

"Easy, Boss," counseled Miro.

Morris dipped a finger into the barrel, sniffed, licked it, and took a shot from his bottle. "Dat's de real stuff," he said. "You boys gets a good sniff." Red Cap and Scar stuck their faces into the barrel and arose with exclamations of delight. "Put de lids back on," instructed Morris, "an gets dat barrel into dat boat Mr. Charlie come in. We goes back first class."

"May I help put the serum in the boat, Morris?" inquired Talldorf.

"You knows what we does to white boys mess wif our womens, Mr. Charlie?" Morris asked approaching Talldorf and looking up from his hooded eyes. Talldorf looked inquiringly at the sawed off shotgun which Morris poked into his navel. Morris was undoubtedly testing him, but the strain was beginning to tell on Talldorf. In Morris' other hand a switch blade clicked and shimmered in the eerie light. Morris answered his own question: "We cuts off dey balls."

"*Freeze, you white trash!*"

The voice seemed to come from the sky. And yet no man made a move save Morris who with bug eyes turned slowly bearing his shotgun at the darkness.

"Lay it down, barfly, or kiss your ass goodbye," came the voice.

"Who do dat talkin?" Morris said, carefully laying down the shotgun.

"SUPERNIGGER!"

A startling black figure like a bat or giant spider dropped with a thud onto the deck from the flying bridge. A shiny automatic was in his hand. He crouched, spun, waved a cane wildly, kicked the shotgun into the pile of tommy guns against the rail and lunged like a swordsman at Red Cap and Scar who retreated warily from the barrel to the comfort of the crowd boxed under the roof of the launch. A top hat sat erect over the mad face, the tails of a tuxedo swept the deck.

Talldorf, whose nerves were beginning to jingle, saw it was the small mad black man who had nearly run him down in the speeding boat.

"Who the hell is *that*?" Tony inquired from the crowd.

"Shut up," Ricardo answered, "It's Supernigger."

"Shut up," Small told Ricardo.

"Hey you, dwarf," ventured Morris, "Ain't no way you goin to take dat coke fom all of usuns."

"You bet your life I'm doin just that. Supernigger does the talkin and the takin here. Next man to open his mouth without bein spoke to gets hot lead in his tonsils. Captain Faerie Queen! Step forward!"

Jammed shoulder to shoulder as if in the elevator to hell Ricardo grinned and waved his hand. "Here I am. My boat, my coke. Out of my way!" he snarled elbowing Maxie in the ear to get out of the crowd. "Pleased to meet you Supernigger. Let's make a deal."

Small recognized Ricardo Ensardo, his old nemesis, and was appalled at his wretched luck. Holding the automatic on Ricardo, Small thrust his cane at him. "Far enough, junior! Supernigger is mad and bad. I'd as soon blow you away as look at you. I see you planned to do me in with this mob of riff-raff, take the money and keep the coke and dump me overboard to the catfish."

"Certainly not. With Ricardo Ensardo a deal is a deal. I bare the proud honor of the mafioso. I could use a classy nigger like you in my class organization, Supernigger."

"Shut up," Small told Ricardo. He backed to the barrel and stuck a finger into the white powder and sniffed. "Is this coke?" he asked.

"Yeah, Supernigger," said everybody but Talldorf.

"But you ain't gonna get away with stealing it," threatened Ricardo.

"I'm buying it," said Small pulling the packet from his waistband and tossing it to Ricardo.

"Why thanks, Supernigger. You're the nigger I've been looking for. It's grade A pharmaceutical," Ricardo said pulling a handful of shredded newspaper from the packet.This was perhaps even more unsettling for Small than for Ricardo.

"Ha, ha, Boss. He was foolin you," said Maxie.

"Ha, ha, Supernigger, I guess you're playing a little joke on me."

And then Talldorf, who had finally recognized the mad little black man as his partner, friend and mentor, A. Small, yelled:

"Behind you!"

Small whirled. The two in livery with delighted grins were strutting across the deck toward him. He understood why they kept coming even though he held his gun on them. He didn't pull the trigger. He knew it was empty. He handed the automatic to the nearest white-gloved hand. Another relieved him of his cane and deftly broke it over Small's top hat. As he sprawled groggy on the deck they slipped the watch off his wrist. Small crawled over to join the crowd while one in livery covered them and the other began wrestling the barrel over the side.

"Small, what are you doing here?" Talldorf asked.

"Greed led me astray, Talldorf. You want to be black so bad you painted your face, huh? Look where you wind up. Maybe you'll listen to me when I warn you about the company you keep."

"Morris," said Talldorf, "you intentionally deceived me. I feel that you have failed me terribly. I can barely restrain my bitterness. I—"

"Shuddup yo mof, money-fucker," Morris told Talldorf.

"Shut up, nigger," Ricardo told Morris and then predicted his future: "You ain't never gonna get out of the trouble you're in."

The sudden light was blinding. The fog had covered the police launch until it was well within pistol range.

"Everybody freeze in the name of the law!" The crackle of the bullhorn was loud in their ears: "Stand by for boarding!"

"Talldorf," said Small, "Take my word for it. This is the time to leave."

Small took two quick steps, the crushed top hat still on his head when he dove over the rail and Talldorf too was in the air when he saw Small's wingtips disappear under the swift gray surface. The top hat was gone. They had struggled out of their shoes and coats. When the light swept them and the shots rang out they ducked and swam, surfaced, ducked and swam again until the light no longer came. "How do you know you're swimming toward shore?" worried Talldorf.

"I feel lucky," Small sputtered, "C'mon."

Who would be surprised that the pilings of the city wharfs arose from the fog before Talldorf and Small, and a wooden ladder from the river's current. When they had regained their breath and stood dripping and barefoot in what remained of their finery they made their way up the rail tracks. When they turned the corner of Terpischore St. they were met by Iris on the arm of the banjo player. Iris and the banjo player shrieked with laughter at the sight and slapped their thighs.

"You white boys take de cake," sang the banjo player.

"I'm still a better nigger than you!" Small challenged the banjo player.

Rubbing at the blackface and lipstick with the wet tails of his white shirt Talldorf succeeded only in smearing it.

"Iris," he said indignantly, "how we loved just this afternoon! How can you step out on me as soon as my back is turned? You can't imagine what I've gone through to prove my love to you."

"Baby, check you out later," the banjo player told Iris, "Dees white boys a downer," and he slipped easily from Iris' grasp. "When you comes bring a pint." He strutted off into the shadows snapping his fingers.

Iris wouldn't stand still and Small wandered after them, Talldorf talking, Iris walking and refusing to listen.

"It's never been like this before Iris," vowed Talldorf. "I'm seeing stars and planets. I'm in love with you, Iris."

"You all wet, Skinny. I ain't marryin no white man. I got enough troubles, thank you kindly."

They had entered a late-night commercial area, Iris was heading for the liquor store. She stopped. "Skinny, I gots to get a bottle. Borrow me some scratch."

Talldorf slapped his empty pockets like a seal. "Morris stole my wallet — and my graduation present — I'll borrow it from Small — Small, loan me five dollars."

Small refused to even acknowledge Talldorf's request. He stood a few steps away leaning on a lamp post with a sorrowful countenance. Perhaps he was remembering ten one hundred dollar bills and his wallet in the pocket of the fine Panama suit at the mansion of Mrs. Pontchartrain Cock, who had betrayed him.

"*Please*, Small" Talldorf pleaded.

"I have recently discovered I am a man of light, Talldorf, after the example of Count Luigi Squeegee. Who are you?"

It was the moment fate had chosen to reveal itself to yet another pair of star-crossed lovers: The late-night revelers in town for the Legion convention arrived exuberantly at the liquor store and stayed to stare. Talldorf gallantly took Iris' hand and smiled into the indignant faces of his countrymen. Iris shook loose her hand:

"Gwine, we both gonna get in trouble."

"They're in blackface," someone said.

"Commie pinko bastards," judged another. "Tryin to pass for niggers on Saturday night just sos they'll have more fun."

"Let's give it to em —"

"Lynch the nigger lovers!"

Iris was the first to leave kicking off her high heels and running like a gazelle, Talldorf behind her and the sprinting Small was gaining.

With curses, cries, and pounding footsteps behind, in the light of a passing lamp as she darted forever into a shadowed passage her beautiful eyes kissing his goodbye, Talldorf swerved from the passage, turned and yelled at the charging mob, "Yah yah yah! I love niggers! I love niggers!" pausing to lure them past and in a few steps was abreast of Small as they rounded a corner and raced into the dark.

None that night were so fleet of foot as Talldorf and Small.

That terrible night bowed out and the glorious light of a new day shown on the nose of the scarlet Studebaker pointing north through the mangrove swamps.

Talldorf had the blues.

"We're takin these back roads for our health," Small explained. "We're gonna see plenty of indignities, Tallie. Who knows what great hand pulls the strings of this show. It's a mystery."

Part Four

UP THE RIVER

Chapter 20

THE INSANE ASYLUM

Thousands of dollars gone with the wind.

Not only that, they had lost the highway and the river taking Small's short-cut. Hours ago the last car had passed, the last gas station, the last shack, the last barefoot inhabitant. The gnarled oak limbs dripped with moss. The road had gotten narrower until it was nothing but this strip of macadam raised above watery corridors.

"We're lost, Small."

"Nonsense! The only time I'm gonna be lost is when I'm dead. Give me the map and try to steer straight this time. Here we are, at the end of my index finger, the Sink Hole Wildlife Refuge, interesting and educational, Talldorf, so don't start sniveling. We might get to see an alligator."

The clearing appeared suddenly, the watchman's shack resting comfortably on pierblocks under the oaks. Small drove up the shell driveway and stopped next to an armchair in which sat an old man in a blue uniform smoking a corncob pipe. Uncle Floyd Farks poured two cups of coffee in his small kitchen and refilled his own.

"Farks been runnin the asylum since before the Civil War," he said. "A Farks son inherits his pappy's job. Had some lean years. Depends on who gets elected."

"We're looking for work, Farks," said Small tipping up the pot for a refill and getting a cup full of coffee grounds.

"We're window washers, Mr. Farks," said Talldorf.

"Ain't never known no Farks to wash a winder," Floyd said.

"What about it, Farks," said Small. "A watchman needs clean windows."

"The less I see the better. Dr. Mudd at the asylum might be interested."

"An asylum, Talldorf, ha! My star has led us to a gold mine hidden in the middle of a swamp. Much obliged, Farks." Small backed the Studie out of the driveway, his eyes glittering.

The asylum was completely fenced by wrought iron pickets which stood in sinister defiance against the world outside. Small drove through the iron gates under the ironwork arch, up the overgrown drive and parked in front of the ancient administration building. That moss-covered brick structure which had once housed the asylum's entire population was slowly sinking into the swamp. The tower leaned at a rakish angle. The iron rings to which madmen had once been chained rusted now in dungeon cells below the waterline.

"This is the perfect place to practice Count Squeegee's doctrine, Tallie," said Small as he got out of the Studebaker. But Small felt uneasy, and the sallow-faced clerks picking their teeth over pecuniary details in their cubicles didn't help, nor did Dr. Mudd who seemed a little crazy himself.

"Of all people, Doc," said Small, "you oughta be the first to realize the importance of clean windows to a nuthouse. My name is A. Small. This is my partner, R. Talldorf. Talldorf is my medical advisor. Tell the doc, Talldorf."

"We are dedicated to spreading the message of light to all mankind, Dr. Mudd. We don't wash windows for money. We wash windows for humanity."

"I knew you'd come," sang the delighted Dr. Mudd, "you're going to wash the windows of this institution for nothing?"

"No, no, Doc," Small jumped up. "That's not what Talldorf meant. You take the gray of the windows right here in your office and multiply that by the number of windows in the whole joint and you'll have a partial understanding of how much dirt burdens the average loony's life." Small gave Dr. Mudd a brief summary of *The Doctrine of Light*. "About $600 worth," said Small, "as a rough estimate."

"What did you say your name was?" Dr. Mudd asked.

"I'm Small, Doc. He's Talldorf."

"I like your idea, Mr. Small. Light therapy. I might agree to it. I could do a before and after study, deliver my long awaited paper to the Society—but can I squeeze the money out of Brother Buddy? Have you men ever heard of Brother Buddy Farks? Brother Buddy is a thorn in the side of civilization. I send in requisitions to try to help ease the horrible suffering of these poor insane people and Brother Buddy ignores them. I try to change inhumane practices perpetuated at this institution and Brother Buddy cuts my budget. I'm responsible for these simple honest souls. I need a competent dedicated staff. Can I do it alone?"

Dr. Mudd suppressed a sob. He blew his nose. "I like your theory about light, Mr. Small," he said soberly. "I'll find a way to wring the money out of Farks. I'll charge it off to housekeeping. The job is yours, men."

"It's a nice cozy room, Small," said Talldorf packing their socks and underwear in a dusty bureau drawer on the second floor of the Administration Building. "Nice gauzy curtains and a sink, pretty wall paper."

Small was suspicious. He looked under the big brass bed, examined the empty drawers of the secretary and tapped on walls.

"Something funny's going on here, Talldorf."

The lights went out. The asylum grounds spread for a hundred acres beyond the sill: a dark undulance splotched with clumps of live oak. Crickets shrilled, frogs croaked, warped floor boards and ghosts moaned as the swamp sucked at the foundation.

"Are you asleep, Talldorf?"

"No."

"Well go to sleep. We need a lot of rest. Tomorrow we gotta be on our toes. Don't worry about nothing. Small has it under control."

They ate breakfast in the asylum cafeteria. There were Farks swilling at every table: uncles, cousins, aunts: burly red-faced, wedge-shaped women who stirred kitchen pots, supervised linens and changed bedpans. Every Farks wore a white uniform which made it easy to distinguish them from the patients.

"By thirty a Farks gone ta seed," said Junior Farks to Talldorf between mouthfulls of oatmeal. "The old folks ain't had no kids since me." Junior, the youngest living Farks, was twenty-three.

Babies born from sexual unions between inmates were sped to the Buddy Farks Foundling Home, a New Orleans supply house for a lucrative non-profit adoption agency called Children, Inc.

Each day the modern new steep-roofed Admissions Building did a brisk business in new patients. Talldorf eyed them warily on his knees in front of thermal panes as they crawled out of black marias and filed up the walk between deputies. All able-bodied men and women were recruited to serve under the Farks. The Farks found a place for them in the laundry or the dairy barns or the fields of the asylum farm. There were plenty of jobs for healthy inmates. The brick yard, for example, or the salt mine. The workers were housed in segregated barracks and when not working had free run of the grounds, while the bed-ridden, the uncommunicative, and the less coopera- tive were crowded into four two-story red brick buildings where cots filled the aisles of wards and corridors.

Talldorf crouched beside his bucket in horror watching long rows of old women tied into their rockers for another day of watching television. The fixed schizophrenics droned in and out, their shaved heads wrapped in white bandages, platinum electrodes sticking out of their skulls like antenae.

Craig Bitterroot sat rigidly in a straight wooden chair on the second floor of one of the red brick buildings which had been named after former governor Alonzo Alphonso Farks' palomino stallion, Sunshine. Governor Double A. Farks had dedicated the Sunshine Building on a bright spring morning, but the brightness had faded and the Sunshine Building had become a euphemism housing a gray community of incurably insane men.

The soup had thinned: tatters of yellow fog still drifted in Bitterroot's brain, but for the first time since he'd been a cub reporter, since his notebook which had contained enough evidence to sentence Brother Buddy Farks to life at Angola had been confiscated by Colonel Claude Snoopier of the New Orleans Police Department, since the morning he had been shoved out of the black maria in front of the Administration Building in his straight jacket, Bitterroot was again beginning to see the light of day. He sat rigidly in the wooden chair reaching for the ceiling as Talldorf scrubbed the pane.

"Sure does make a difference, feller," said Clyde Farks, who moseyed over. "Ya want me to move that feller. I'll just stand that feller over there in the corner."

"I'll work around him, Mr. Farks," said Talldorf.

Bitterroot glanced up at where his eyes had been. Rays of light entered his pupils and slanted down through yellow fog where he huddled like a prisoner on a pallet. A big brown rat watched with concern as Bitterroot rose and began to pace the floor. The brown rat had arrived in Bitterroot's cell with the yellow fog.

"I'm going up," said Bitterroot.

"It's no use, Craig," the rat grumbled. "I've been around humans longer than you. They'll never change. Sit down. Let's have another piece of cheese and forget some more."

Bitterroot glanced skeptically at his friend the rat, dug his fingers into the bricks and began to climb the wall. He pulled himself up to his cob-webbed dusty sockets and gazed out on the ward's brilliant din and squalor just as Clyde Farks turned from the medication counter and headed straight through men and wheelchairs toward him with a paper cup full of yellow pills. Dr. Mudd had issued a general order to suspend all medications but Clyde Farks had more than one reason to disregard young Dr. Mudd's orders.

"Durndest thing I ever seen," said Clyde to Talldorf. "I seen him hold his arms up like that three months. Once we run a lottery but he held em up so long we got tired and asked Cousin Finny Farks for our money back."

Clyde pried open Bitterroot's mouth and began tossing in pills, then held Bitterroot's jaws closed.

Bitterroot jumped lightly back down to the floor of his cell and listened, powerless to stop the machinery of his throat as it raised his adam's apple like an elevator and gulped down the pills. He counted the pills as they splashed into his stomach.

"What's up, Craig?"

"They've gone back to the old dosage, Ratty. I've got to get out of here. It's now or never." Anxiously, affectionately, he clutched the rat's front paws. "So long old pal."

"Goodbye, Craig."

Bitterroot leaped for the wall. By the time he had pulled himself up to the windows in his skull the yellow fog had obliterated the cell below and was rising. Clyde was moseying off to stop the 19 year old motorcycle wreck from beating the old man with lead pipe arteries over the head with a urinal and the tall redhaired guy was moving on to the next window.

"Get me out of here!"

At first Talldorf thought it was his own voice. He looked at Bitterroot who sat rigid, his face gray as stone and decided that he hadn't heard a voice at all.

"Get me out of here!" rasped Bitterroot.

"Pardon me," said Talldorf.

Bitterroot's blue eyes blazed. Not a facial muscle twitched or a finger moved. He tried again and felt his voice slip over the threshold of stone. *"I'm a reporter. Get hold of Murphy at the city desk. Tell him..."* The acrid stench enveloped him, choked him. He lost his hold and fell backward into the yellow arms of fog.

"We're you speaking to me, sir?" asked Talldorf bending closer. "Can I be of help?"

Bitterroot's blue irises paled. Talldorf caught a glimpse of drifting yellow smoke as he stared into the burnt ends of Bitterroot's hopes.

"I told ya I'd be glad to move that feller, feller," said Clyde hurrying over.

"He spoke to me," said Talldorf.

"That feller ain't spoke in 12 years. You best let that feller alone."

"It must have been my imagination," shrugged Talldorf as he moved on to the next window.

"They got nuts stacked up like cordwood," scowled Small as they strolled across campus toward the barracks, their buckets over their arms, their white rags dangling. Inmates and Farks alike smiled in recognition which made Small fearful that they were being absorbed slowly into the asylum's population.

"Nice shady lawns, plenty to eat, friendly people," Talldorf said optimistically.

There was commotion in the aisle of the first barracks they entered. One of the black women had tried to burn her mattress. Now two muscular Farks women pinned the frightened creature to the table while Uncle Dudley Farks, the electrotherapy technician, smeared conducting grease on her temples.

"It ain't gonna hurt, Emma," Uncle Dudley said. "You won't feel a thing."

"Stop!" yelled Small. "You can't do that!"

"Get those nuts out of here," shrilled Dudley.

While frightened black women clustered around poor Emma Dudley's two female assistants bore down on Small.

"What's going on here?"

It was Dr. Mudd.

Fresh from the university, Phi Betta Kappa, after a meritorious internship, Dr. Phillip Mudd with his new little family had arrived at the asylum eager to begin his residency. Young Dr. Mudd had not been discouraged by his tour through the backwards. He had ordered the Farks file clerk to excavate the archives. Dr. Mudd tirelessly burned the candle at both ends studying exhumed medical records. Mudd had transferred neglected patients, one by one, to the infirmary, pressing on with his heroic efforts. The infirmary was soon overcrowded. Emaciated human beings babbled incoherently from every nook and cranny but Dr. Mudd had not been deterred. "This woman must be turned and her sheets changed at least twice a day," Mudd had cried to the Farks nurse in charge of the ward as he examined the ulcerated wing bones of an old woman who tried to sink her two remaining teeth into his leg. "Maggots, Margaret," Mudd wailed as he sat at the dinner table. "The Farks just let them rot. But I'm not a Farks. The Farks are ignorant people, Margaret. It's not their fault that they are such stupid ignorant people."

"Am I glad to see you, Doc," said Small. "This maniac is trying to electrocute this poor woman."

"And who are you, sir?"

"I'm Small. That's Talldorf. The window washers. Remember?"

"Of course. Good-morning, men. Get on with your therapeutics. Dudley, I told you, NO MORE SHOCK TREATMENTS!

"Poor, poor Emma. Let me get these horrible electrodes off your head. Wash this paste out of her hair. Dudley, if I ever catch you giving another shock treatment, I'll...I'll... Get this awful machine out of here. Take it to my office. No one is going to use it on another human being ever again!"

The gutters were rotten and slate shingles slippery on the roof of the ancient Administration Building. Small tiptoed across the peak and climbed the iron rungs to the top of the tower.

Talldorf followed Junior up the narrow spiral staircase inside the tower through a maze of chicken coops where single Farks men slept. Single Farks men had scrawny necks, sharp beaks, and hard blue eyes that regarded the world from a cold distance. Their nests honeycombed the tower which rose to the windows in the cupola and the cell in which Capps had been a fixture for thirty years.

"Used to tear out patches of his hair and throw turds when they brought visitors. Played chess with my Uncle Brewster. When I first seen Capps he had a regular old ball and chain on his leg," Junior said. Mercifully, Capps was now dead.

The ranch houses where the young doctors lived stood in sharp contrast to the asylum buildings. The young doctors left the asylum grounds every evening and went home to their families where they drank martinis and played with their children on neatly clipped grass. The young doctors depended on the Farks to run everything and concerned themselves with new admissions sent from the capital and New Orleans for ninety day observation.

As permanent inmates depended on Farks for their well being so the Farks depended on the permanent inmates for their income. While Brother Buddy, the fat bayou politician, grew fatter his kinfolk clung to the pork barrel that was Farks Parish. Nickels and dimes and dollars, term insurance and welfare checks, bribes from provisioners of every kind as well as a per capita royalty the state paid the asylum for each crazy citizen, poured into Buddy's coffers.

The monumental window washing job was performed at a new high level of conception. The mechanics had been simple. Small had quickly thrown together the necessary equipment and outlined the logistics.

"Almost got it whipped eh, men?" Dr. Mudd said. "The light means so much to me. Since you did my office I feel less depressed. My head is clear. My mind is keen. You're Mr. Small, right? You see I have it right this time and you, sir, are Mr...Mr..."

"Talldorf."

"Of course. Mr. Talldorf. I think I'm losing my marbles, men. I need your help. The entire Farks clan is ranged against me. And the patients suffer. Nobody cares about the patients. Do you know that, Mr. Small? Nobody! I can't be everywhere at once, Mr. Talldorf, can I? Can't you do something?"

"We're doing our best, Dr. Mudd," said Small.

"You're doing a wonderful job, Mr. Small. Both of you are. I see smiles on faces where I've never seen smiles before. Wonderful work! But it's not enough! These people can be cured. You men are fortunate. When you're finished you'll pack up your ladder and your buckets and drive off. Won't you? Don't deny it! I tell you they can be cured, Mr. Talldorf. What time is it? I have to hurry home. My wife Margaret is a very intelligent woman, Mr. Small. I envy you, sir, and yet it must be a lonely life. No children. No one to fix your meals. And you, Mr. Talldorf, what must it be like for you, traveling the country without a home. Some men are not disposed to domestic life. I happen not to be one of them."

"It's seven o'clock, Dr. Mudd," Talldorf said.

"Of course it is," said Dr. Mudd looking at his wrist watch. "Perhaps you men would like to come to our humble abode for supper, eat a home cooked meal, have an interesting dinner table discussion. Margaret would be delighted."

Dr. Mudd's modern ranch house was the last house on the row.

"This is Mr. Small, and this is Mr. Talldorf, have I got it right? Welcome to our happy little home. Mr. Talldorf and Mr. Small are our friends, Margaret. Mr. Small and Mr. Talldorf are apostles of *Light*. Look at them. They look like ordinary people don't they? But they're not. They are window washers."

"I'm so glad to meet you," Margaret said. "As you can see, Phillip, I didn't have time today to pick up after your son."

"Perfectly all right, Margaret. I'm sure our guests won't mind. If they don't mind I don't. Shall we all pitch in and clean it up? I'll get the vacuum cleaner. I like a tidy house. Forget it. Let's sit down to supper.

"They built these houses for the doctors and I'm a doctor," explained Dr. Mudd. "I don't regret it. Don't think I regret it. I don't regret it, do I, Margaret? I still have my ideals and a truer sense of purpose than ever. Healing, Mr. Small, is the answer to all of humanities problems. All of us are sick, Mr. Small. Physician heal thyself, ha ha ha. And I'm well qualified, trained in the finest schools, the best hospitals. I'll break Brother Buddy with my will! Those poor insane people. They're our people, Mr. Talldorf."

"I'm sure Mr. Talldorf cares in his own way, Phillip."

"Of course he does. Of course you care, Mr. Talldorf. Let me tell you your efforts with the windows have been appreciated. Nobody at this God-forsaken hole respects me, Mr. Talldorf, but I respect you. And you, Mr. Small, I know are a man of high principles. We don't have many friends here.

Doctors Marx, Cox and Thompson are competent men but prefer to parlay their Hypocratic oaths with big shots. Marx, Cox and Thompson are under the thumb of Farks. They are, in short, cowards, men, as I know the two of you are not. Margaret used to go to their wives bridge parties. Now they are without a fourth. They liked you, didn't they, Margaret? Then I started making my discoveries. It is indecent, Mr. Talldorf. Torture and punishment inflicted on innocent minds by that bovine clan of swineherds. But my hands aren't tied. I have two arms. If you could witness the despair of men and women cast away by their loved ones, despised, victimized, huddled in the miserable rags that Farks provides, see the spark of affection kindle suddenly in the ruined eyes of a fellow human creature — " Dr. Mudd started to cry.

"Mr. Talldorf, Mr. Small, forgive the tears of a man torn apart by life's harsh injustices, the cruel practices of Buddy Farks. I will not stand for it, men! But I need help. Should I see a psychiatrist, Mr. Small, ha ha ha. I am a psychiatrist. I can't stand it. I hate life. Margaret knows how much I hate life. I hate it, don't I, Margaret. Margaret wants a divorce. Don't be alarmed. It's the truth for Christ sake, Margaret. Excuse me for a moment, men."

Small rolled his eyes at Talldorf who picked at his burnt chicken with his salad fork.

"Margaret will be all right, men. I hope my little fit didn't spoil your appetites. Margaret is an excellent cook. Wonderful woman."

Dr. Mudd filled his mouth with mashed potatoes. He ate absently and silently.

"There's ice cream for desert!" he suddenly shouted. "We always have ice cream for desert. Margaret has instituted that custom. Our son will remember his parents for the ice cream and will in turn serve his children ice cream. I come from a strong family background, Mr. Small, as you no doubt don't. You look like a man with no deep roots. I envy a rootless man, Mr. Small. Mr. Talldorf, you sir, strike me as a rooted man. An intelligent man, an anxious man. Let me give you some professional advice, Mr. Talldorf. Don't be anxious. The future lies before you. You and Mr. Small carry the torch to an ungrateful public and I too — " Dr. Mudd slumped. "I too strive to lift the veil of ignorance." He sat bolt upright, " — to reach out and touch a human heart. Men, we are tired. But we must not give up. Margaret, where's my coat? Margaret — ? She won't come. I can't blame the poor woman. We must all strive to maintain our integrity. The effects of life can be devastating,

Mr. Small, as I'm sure you know. But I am the only man who has any idea of the degradation my people, our people, suffer. The Farks wring the blood out of the poor bastards. They are decent ordinary people, aren't they, Mr. Small? Their faces haunt me. Then I see the fat face of Farks." Mudd closed his eyes and stamped his feet on the rug.

"Impotent rage, Mr. Talldorf. Is God in heaven, sir? Am I having a nightmare? When will I wake up? Where are the happy days of childhood? I was a straight A student, Mr. Talldorf. My opinions were respected at the university. I had confidence in myself and my profession. Now I shrink in horror from the vanity of it all, I lay awake beside Margaret. Margaret doesn't know, Mr. Small. I tried to tell her. Heaven knows I have tried to demonstrate to Margaret the extremity of my concern but my outbursts only provoke her contempt. What is the next step, men? I need your protection. You'll take me with you won't you, Mr. Small? Please say you will. Together we will cross life's great desert. We will scale the highest mountains and journey to Paradise."

Dr. Mudd did not leave the asylum with Talldorf and Small. Neither did he get the check for the monumental window job past the sharp eyes of the pecuniary Farks in their cubicles in the subbasement of the Administration Building.

The next morning, the job completed, Talldorf followed Small down the corridor past the ash stands and spittoons through the door on which Small didn't pause to knock into Dr. Mudd's office. Dr. Mudd lay on the leather couch. He didn't have his shoes on, and his toes twitched in his monogrammed socks. Dudley Farks had pulled the plug on his shock machine. Dudley was busy winding up the cord. He had already removed the electrodes from Dr. Mudd's temples.

"What have you done to the good doctor?" Talldorf was alarmed and knelt to take Dr. Mudd's pulse. Dr. Mudd was as white as the picket fence around his house. Big drops of perspiration stood out on his upper lip and his forehead. His pulse was faint but his eyelids fluttered. Hilda and Gretchen swaggered forward. They looked like warrior women in tales of the Norsemen.

"We've come for our money, Dudley," Small said.

"Shake the money out of Dr. Mudd's pockets, girls," Dudley ordered, and the two strong women picked Dr. Mudd up from the couch and turned him upside down. Dr. Mudd's wallet, two dimes, three pennies, a gold pen, and a rubber fell onto the threadbare carpet. Dudley picked up the wallet, extracted the few bills that were in it and threw them on the carpet: twelve dollars in all.

"Pick it up, boys," Dudley drawled, "and get on out if ya'all know what's good for you."

"This is criminal, Mr. Farks," said Talldorf. "You've electrocuted Dr. Mudd."

"Nonsense, son," Dudley said.

Small picked up the money and steered Talldorf down the hall and out to the car. "Get in, Talldorf," Small said and jumped behind the wheel of the Studebaker.

"We'll have to report Dudley to the authorities, Small," Talldorf said as Small headed the old car back toward the river and Hwy 61.

"The Farks *are* the authorities, Talldorf," Small said.

"We have to do something, don't we, Small?"

"Look at it this way, Tallie," Small told his friend. "We did a little service for humanity. We're probably the first window washers in history to wash the windows of a nut farm. After what we did to those windows maybe some of those nuts are going to want out."

Chapter 21

THE GREAT WRITER

A thens was a most unlikely spot to find a man with the talents of Jagger Fitzroy. Athens, Missouri had a home for unwed mothers, a general hospital and an arts council to which the enclave of doctors' and lawyers' wives and the president of the coupling works wife and his executives' wives contributed their spare time. The big cake-work houses boasted the feminine pride in people chosen to do God's work. The ladies in those houses had raised their children and were growing older. The men in those houses had passed on their businesses to their sons. Their gray heads were replaced by a younger sleeker look on the city council.

Athens' sense of culture was still supported by an opera which stopped on its winter tour. The girl violinists still rosined their bows, the fat conductor still flourished his baton, Athens' matrons still sat in the front rows beside their snoring husbands. There wasn't a radical thinker amongst the men, Jagger knew. He had been toasted by the Kiwanis, gored by the Elks, torn to shreds by the Eagles, lionized by the Lions, made to feel odder than he was by the Odd Fellows, taking precious time from his arduous task of writing his novel to speak at their luncheons. It was part of a significant publicity tour that would put his contract over a million dollars. There was no one to talk to in Athens. Not Fuddley Dart, the banker, who didn't know a pork chop from a homburg.

The house with its sloping roofs, latticed windows and hardwood floors was lonely by himself. Everything had changed. Jagger hardly remembered it, or his childhood. *Mine Magazine* as well as *Death* and *Wink* had sent out photographers who shot pictures of Jagger, his hair tousled, in a fresh white shirt, his eyes hardboiled, smiling on the front porch. Jagger Fitzroy had returned with fanfare to Athens, to refresh his memory, to perform living research.

> 'Prize-winning novelist returns home to research his *tour de force...*'

The Times said.

Stories had been spread across the nation in Sunday supplements and the imagination of the American public had been stirred. Now the fanfare had died to a dull roar that Jagger heard every time he put his lips to a whiskey bottle. Jagger felt restless, forgotten, unsung. How many times a day did he have to call Sol just to keep up his courage.

"Hello, Solly, I feel like a prisoner. Solly, you've got to find a way to get me out of this burg."

Bernice was off in St. Louis doing valuable research. What would he do without Bernice? The facts that Bernice brought back would shed new light on his work.

Jagger stood on the porch, rings of sweat expanding under the arms of his white shirt. He watched the scarlet Studebaker with one raised eyebrow as it bounced over the curb and came to a stop a foot in front of the fire hydrant. Small popped out of the car and bounced jauntily up the walk ahead of Talldorf, who appeared to be reluctant.

"It certainly is a beautiful house you got here, Mac, and the windows are filthy. Crown glass, just like I told ya, Tallie. This is the original glass, Mac. You got a palace in fine glass- blowing right under your nose. My name's A. Small and this is R. Talldorf, my partner."

"Jagger Fitzroy," Fitzroy said. "I own the place. It's the family manse. What do you want? I haven't got all day. I'm a busy man."

"Jagger Fitzroy, the great writer?" asked Talldorf.

"The same, lad."

Talldorf who had read several of Fitzroy's novels in college was impressed. "Will you autograph the road map?" Talldorf asked.

"I want to tell you about our expert window cleaning service, Fitzroy," said Small. It didn't take Small long to convince Fitzroy that clean windows would benefit his creative efforts.

"It can't hurt," Fitzroy said. "I can use all the help I can get. Besides, I need expenditures. I can't imagine anymore how much money I am worth. Hundreds of millions. People hound me for money, boys. Yesterday Sol purchased an African diamond mine. I've got steel and gold and oil. I own railroads, forests, ships."

"I'll give you an estimate," said Small.

"I'll drink to that," Fitzroy said.

Fitzroy followed Talldorf and Small as they walked around the house counting windows. "I see you boys know your work. In a world of corporations it gives me inspiration to see somebody dedicated to little details of a small enterprise. Brighten my life, Small! Flood my life with light! Lift the veil from the Muse, bring her back in all her freshness. She awaits me now. Go to it, boys!"

Jagger Fitzroy had left New York forever. He had shaken hands with his friends and thumbed his nose at his critics for the last time. He had stood dolefully with a tumbler full of whiskey in his Manhattan study as two men from the Move It or Lose It Moving Co. picked up his desk, dollied out sofas, endtables, crates of books and paintings, carpets, Bernice's collection of cacti, plaques and other memorabilia of Jagger Fitzroy's career. He had fled that great whore New York where friends stabbed him in the back. His friends, ha! Academicians, critics had torn his corpus literario to shreds, established their reputations picking at his scabs, giving the great writer migrains and ulcers. His last book, *The Main Vein,* a story of a blood lust set during the gold rush in the high Sierra had been mercilessly panned. How they envied him, and his next book, *Branches,* would have to be even better.

Small raised the long extension ladder to the doghouse where Jagger sat behind his desk amid piles of manuscript and files of information stacked and heaped and scattered around him like an avalanche. Chills were running down Jagger's spine. He lit another cigarette and washed down another Tums with half an inch of cold coffee. The big house was quiet except for the banging of the aluminum ladder as Small scurried up the rungs. The thought of Small climbing the ladder made Fitzroy sick to his stomach. He mumbled an excuse to his typewriter and hurried from his study only to run into Rudolph Victor

Talldorf, gawky and self- consciously struggling to preserve the veneer of his education, his red hair the only indication of a fiery spirit.

"Do you believe in death, Talldorf?" Fitzroy asked.

"Death, Mr. Fitzroy?"

"D-E-A-T-H, Talldorf."

Fitzroy felt his stomach contract and rushed to the bathroom. The nausea occurred more regularly now. Perhaps the wart had invaded his blood stream. Sol would have to make another appointment for him at the Mayo Clinic. Bernice was to return tomorrow and he'd better have something finished. The wastebasket was already spilling over with paper balls: one hundred starts on the first page. She'd know he'd lost his courage. He'd been drunk since Bernice's departure. If she knew she'd kill him, horrid woman, yet Fitzroy knew he'd be even more miserable without her. There had been plenty of blandishing beauties who had thrown themselves his way only to encounter Bernice, his mainspring and watchdog. It was true that Bernice had all the right connections to get him published.

"Enterprising, Talldorf," Jagger said, "Free travel, supporting yourselves on the idle rich. Not that I'm idle. Too many ideas in the old noggin. Every breath I take is worth money. The royalties keep rolling in."

"Your work must offer you great satisfaction, Mr. Fitzroy."

"Not satisfaction, Talldorf, M-O-N-E-Y! I get to travel. I like the publicity tour. I like walking into Club 21 and knowing everybody knows this mug belongs to Jagger Fitzroy. I have shingles and insomia. Don't tell anybody! Shingles, Talldorf! I'm getting a wart on my middle finger. Look at this! A stinking corrupting virus! If it gets any bigger I'm not going to be able to type. If I can't type I'm finished. Bernice can type but I can't stand Bernice touching my manuscript. That woman knows all my secrets. Do you know what it's like to live with a woman who knows all your secrets, Talldorf?"

Talldorf listened with his unpracticed ear. He watched Jagger's brow ridge in despair and felt sympathy. "I don't think I ever want to marry, Mr. Fitzroy."

"Smart boy, Talldorf."

Twenty-three years married to Bernice and no children. Jagger himself had foolishly slipped the gold band onto Bernice's third finger. Bernice was a mighty woman with that bun in her hair. Bernice had squashed his Celtic spirit like it was a bug. And what of the bardic singer Jagger had hoped to be, had all his songs run out? His well dried up? Jagger had been ecstatic when CockWalk Books had decided to publish his first novel. After the first one Jagger had been sure the rest would come easy. His second novel was more difficult and worse. Jagger kept writing, following the same moth-eaten plot diligently to its unsurprising and disappointing end. It was hard work. He wrote his novels with pick and shovel, hacking his way through jungles of statistics, laying out the chapters, digging the ditches of his narrative, typing until his eyesight flagged.

At noon Fitzroy served lunch.

"Poke salad, boys. One of Athen's few homegrown delicacies. A gourmet experience. It's all I eat." He fixed them each a plate of poke salad and buttered toast, filled their water glasses with whiskey and sat down himself to munch the coarse greens.

"I agree with the critic, Clyde Snide, Mr. Fitzroy," said Talldorf. "Your books do make good movies."

"Clyde Snide is a liar and a coward, Talldorf. Snide's remark was that the movies are better than my books. Snide has tried to relegate me to the shelf of pulp writers. He once compared my prose to instructions for putting together a Jap bicycle. I've made Snide famous. An evil business, boys." Fitzroy was bent double by a spasm from his ulcer.

"Milk, boys! Milk!"

After draining the glass he appeared to be all right.

"I'm all right, boys. I will counter the accusations and innuendo with real creative work. I will bind the wounds, boys!"

Fitzroy hurried to his study while Talldorf put the finishing touches on the alcove windows and Small sat down in a shady spot on the roof to smoke a Lucky and admire the view.

Keys clicked merrily, insects buzzed, bougainvillea climbed the lattice work. The prairie sun bore down like a bronze hammer on the plenitude of cornfields while Jagger sweated over his magnum opus.

If the rest of them were junk, *Branches,* was going to be literature. The book had everything: irony, suspense, realism, set in a town not much different from Athens called Mothball, Missouri, in a house not much different from the house in which Jagger was typing like a freight train and to which the hero, alcoholic writer Roy Bannon, had nominally returned. Like Athens, Mothball had changed. Factories had replaced cornfields; parking meters had been installed, the trailer park spilled over with unemployed veterans and their households.

Small was on the ladder squeegeeing the conservatory windows when Fitzroy ran into the room waving a sheaf of manuscript. Fitzroy looked rumpled and worn out. His hair hung over his brow, the whites of his eyes were more red-veined than ever.

"Have a shot of the old sode, Small. Warms the blood and clears the eyesight." Fitzroy handed a cup of Irish coffee to Small through the open window. "You and your partner have brightened my view. The Muse whispers in my ear. The plot thickens. Fifteen pages, Small, and the words ring true! Listen to this. No! On second thought it doesn't seem just right. When will I get it right? Take what you get, Small. Don't ask for more. You have worked your magic here. I owe you money. You earned it. Where's my checkbook?"

"We're not finished, Fitzroy," said Small.

"Strike while the iron is hot, Small. I too should work. A nap would help. The Muse avoids me. I am rejected by Morpheus."

"I wonder what the Muse looks like," Talldorf asked Small as the two partners turned the corner of the house.

"A goddess, Talldorf," said Fitzroy from the shrubbery. "She floats to my desk on a zephyr with ruby lips and creamy breasts. She is in my study this moment and I am sprawled helplessly under this bush. Coffee, boys. A cup of coffee for the great writer who has been wounded, an officer in the front lines of literature shot from behind, toppled, as it were, from his horse."

They helped Fitzroy into the house. The telephone rang.

"I feel good, Sol. Strong as an ox. I got two guys doing the windows. The window panes, Sol. I'm coming to New York, Solly. Wire me a ticket. If you're trying to swindle me, Solly, I'll break every bone in your money-hungry body. Let me worry about Bernice. I make the decisions. I'll leave her a note. Sol? Solly?"

Fitzroy slammed down the dead receiver. Fitzroy hunched over his typewriter. He was typing the one hundred and fifty-first draft of the first page of *Branches*, the Roy Bannon saga for which he had been advanced two hundred and fifty thousand dollars. I'm a professional. I work best under pressure, Fitzroy told himself as he opened the bottom desk drawer and took out the revolver. He spun the cylinder. There was a bullet in every chamber. Fitzroy visualized the alcoholic writer Roy Bannon stumbling down the hall toward the bathroom, six-gun in hand, to end it all. Fitzroy stumbled down the hall and stared at himself in the bathroom mirror, the cold steel of the barrel pressed to his temple.

Small stared incredulously in through the window.

"Don't do it, Fitzroy!" Small yelled.

Fitzroy was startled. "Don't do what, Small," he said with annoyance.

"Don't pull the trigger."

"I'm rehearsing a scene, Small. Roy Bannon feels lost in his old hometown of Mothball, Mo., the little river town where he's come to dry out, to try to recover his dignity, where there's no one to talk to: He gets loaded and contemplates suicide. Who hasn't? To be or not to be is one of the themes that run through all my novels. Can the hero find a nest in the family tree? Can he return to the enthusiasm of his youth, walk streets where he dreamed in greener days? Is the answer no, Small? What did Roy Bannon live for? To be *free*! You and Talldorf are on the right track. Stay away from women and booze. Don't desire fame or money. Become hermits. Humility, Small!"

BANG

The bullet shattered the pane and whined past Small's left ear. Fitzroy slumped against the sink. He stared at his bloody horrified face in the glass. What would Bernice say? A lilly- livered act. Her nostrils would quiver with contempt. Maybe Sol would take him more seriously. This was certain to make *Mine Magazine*. Good publicity for *Branches*. Had it been accidental? Or had he actually had the courage to pull the trigger? Maybe he was dying now. He could feel the warm blood trickle down his neck, see it dripping into the sink. His white shirt was turning red with a spreading crimson stain. The sink was cold and reassuring. The drops of blood exploded against the porcelain and ran down the drain, down the drain, down the drain. Fitzroy toppled sideways. Small scurried down the ladder yelling for Talldorf to call an ambulance.

"I hovered near the doors of death," Fitzroy said, propped up in the hospital bed, his head swathed in bandages. "Pour the great writer a drink will you, Small. And hand me my checkbook. Mum's the word, boys. Jagger Fitzroy was almost killed while sitting on the toilet cleaning his gun. Rumors will run like wildfire through the literary establishment. If I ever finish it, *Branches* will sell like hot cakes. How much do I owe you, Small?"

"Thirty-five bucks."

"Nonsense. That covers your work perhaps but you deserve a bonus." Fitzroy signed the check with a flourish that made him wince with pain. "One hundred dollars, Small. My compliments on a job well done. No tongues must wag."

"I can't take it, Fitzroy," said Small. "Talldorf and Small are honest craftsmen who want no part of chicanery or mendacity. You can't buy our silence, Fitzroy."

"Well spoken, Small. You saved my life and I'm deeply indebted. I'll just change this check to five hundred dollars."

"You don't understand, Fitzroy," said Small. "We didn't save your life. We only helped carry you to the ambulance."

"I thought I was dead."

"You almost took me with you," said Small.

"Take this check, Talldorf. Let it be known that Jagger Fitzroy is a generous man. Above all nothing you say must lead Bernice to suspect that I would wantonly destroy our marriage neither must she suspect that I had a drop to drink. Think of me as the worm I am, boys, but take the money."

A nurse entered. "Your wife is here, Mr. Fitzroy."

"Bernice! Oh no. Hide the bottle. Send her in. Hi, Bernice, my love. How was your trip? I'd like you to meet Talldorf and Small, window washers by trade, who have journied to our village in pursuit of their mythical occupations, light dealers who have eschewed the conventional life to shed the blessings of the outdoors on poor unfortunate shut-ins like myself. These boys, Bernice, are responsible for my being here today. It was an accident, I swear it, Bernice. My two friends will attest to that, won't you boys?"

Bernice sat down on the bed and pinched Jagger's ear.

"Ouch, let go, let go!"

"You've been drinking. I smell it. You were practicing the suicide scene again."

"Yes, dear. This time in the bathroom just in case. Small was outside washing the window, lucky for me but almost unlucky for him. He and Talldorf carried me to the ambulance."

"Such a silly dear," Bernice said. "I hope you're satisfied. You've interrupted my trip but I was able to bring you a new carload of facts. Sol is flying in tonight to personally handle the publicity. What's this?"

"What's what, dear? Oh that. That is a check for five hundred dollars to Talldorf and Small who won't take it. These men have integrity, Bernice. They are itinerants who are on their way to becoming free men. They do not wish to involve themselves in mendacity or chicanery. Free men Bernice! Oh, my head."

Bernice snatched the check and tore it to bits over the wastebasket.

"How much do we owe you for the windows, Mr. Small?" Bernice asked.

"Thirty-five bucks."

Bernice opened her purse and counted out the cash into Small's hand.

"Now if you gentlemen will be good enough to leave us alone, Mr. Fitzroy no longer has need for your services."

Chapter 22

THE BELLY BUTTON OF AMERICA

T he scarlet Studebaker sped north along Hwy 61 in the shadow of the levee. Small kept the gas pedal to the floor. They burned up the road at 35 miles per hour. The megawatts of St. Louis' great iron heart throbbed on the horizon. The fly-weights of industry were going to get some big league action.

They drank their tenth cup of coffee and smoked their last Lucky in a diner near the waterfront. "If ya get another donut I ain't got enough to tip the waitress. Ya don't wanta be takin bread out of her kids' mouths do ya, Talldorf?"

They strolled the quay inspecting the cobblestones for butts as the river rolled along. The fretwork of the bridge soared above and muggy air wriggled in heat waves. The sun promised that by noon any fool could fry an egg on the sidewalk.

"We could try panhandling, Small."

But Small's eyes had wandered shoreward. He grasped Talldorf's sleeve. "That's it, Tallie!" Above them, as if sheltered by the bridge, rose seven stories of stone with tall windows rounded at the tops. Alternate windows were bricked up.

"Anyone who bricks up a window is nuts. My eagle vision tells me those beautiful unbricked windows are filthy, Talldorf. I bet there ain't a window washer in St. Louis daring enough to handle that job."

Small nosed the Studie up the bluff and turned the corner. The street was busy with rumbling trucks raising clouds of dust. The Belly Button's elegant lines outclassed squat utilitarian bulwarks of neighboring warehouses. A garbage truck was parked at the service entrance. A steel door was open and two black men were carrying out garbage cans while a white man in a T-shirt sat in the cab smoking a cigar.

"At ease, boys," Small saluted, bounced up three cement steps, passed under the overhang and went through the door onto a rubber runner that led down a hall.

"Motha fuckhin, motha fuckah..."

"Quit complainin, Justus," said his partner.

"Good morning, men," said Talldorf who was hurrying to catch up with Small.

"Goin to de motha-fuckhin ho-house whilst we carries out de ga-bage," said Justus Fustus who had got out on the wrong side of bed. "I sweats in de hot sun whilst dey traipses to de motha fuckhin ho-house. Ain't right! Ain't fair! Ain't just!" cried Justus Fustus raising his fist to heaven to proclaim injustice.

"What kind of a warehouse did he say this was, Small?"

"A mother-fucking warehouse, Talldorf. Now shut up! Let me do the talkin."

Rosie, the black cook, was busy in the kitchen forking steak and eggs onto platters which Rosalinda, her brown-skinned daughter, carried out through the swinging doors.

"Good morning, Madam. Permit me to introduce myself—"

"Get outta my kitchen! We ain't open fo' business."

"I'm distressed you're in such a foul humor, Madam. I have arrived to brighten every dreary corner of this warehouse and bring the sun back into your life."

"You ain't heh fo' business?"

"Of course I'm here for business. I'm a serious man. I follow an itinerant trade. My lieutenant and me might not look like your average businessman but neither did Jesus."

"Doan nobody here wanta buy no Bibles, mistah!"

"I'm not selling Bibles, woman. I'm selling light. I told you I'm here to brighten up the place."

"Rosalinda, will you get that food out to them peoples, an tell Miss Wanda I got businessmens who ain't come fo' business wants to see her."

"Yes, can I help you...My, my, dear boy," said Wanda Wistunka sailing in through the swinging doors. Wanda's cheeks were thick with rouge, her lips red as blood, her teeth studded with real diamonds. She took Rudolph's arm enveloping him in pink perfume that rose like a cloud from her bosom.

"Do you like them?" asked Madame Wistunka flashing her sparklers.

"They're very...unusual," stammered Rudolph.

"Yes, that's exactly what my dentist thought. He has the most wonderful machine, don't you know, dear. I didn't feel a thing. I even enjoyed myself. My, such exquisite long fingers, dear boy. I shall read your fortune. I shall tell you all. And you shall tell me what I can do for you."

"Well, ah, that is to say...Small?"

"Nonsense. I thoroughly doubt it. Spit it out!"

"I'm the one who does the talkin, Madam. You'll have to excuse my lieutenant who is easily flustered. I happen to be A. Small, a messenger of light."

"Tut, tut, Mr. Small. Do come to the point."

"Lieutenant R. Talldorf and myself—"

"R. Talldorf. My, my, my! And what is your first name, dear boy? No, don't tell me. Let me guess. Rodney? Roger? Reginald? No, I won't give up. Rudolph? Yes, it fits you. Rudolph, the Red, such a fine figure of a man! So long, so tall. My name is Madam Wistunka. Call me Wanda. You may kiss my hand, Rudolph."

Rudolph the Red dutifully pressed his lips to the blue veins above the glittering rings and purple nails which curved over the ends of Wanda Wistunka's pale fingers.

"Talldorf and me are window washers."

"What a perfectly fascinating occupation."

"We'll light up every room in your place for a cheap price. At a glance I'd estimate it at 500 bucks."

"By all means, *wash my windows*, Rudolph," said Madam Wistunka squeezing Talldorf and rolling her eyes as if his nearness made her giddy.

"We'll get started right away. Talldorf, get the equipment while I eyeball the joint."

Talldorf got the buckets, rags and squeegees, and climbed back over the iron gate which the garbage men had locked.

"Coulda used de front doh," said Rosie. "Lucky you dint rip you trousers comin ovah de fence like dat."

Most of the girls had finished breakfast. Madam Wistunka was seated at the head of the table where the remaining girls lolled in their wilted finery. "Girls, girls," sang Madam Wistunka rapping on her water glass. "I want you to make Mr. Talldorf feel at home. Ah, so long, so firm, just like Bert. Isn't he fine looking and he's mine, tee hee. Give Rudolph plenty of room, girls."

Madam Wistunka flashed her dazzling smile at Rudolph who bowed and moved past highboys filled with china and peacock feathers out through a fire door into a hall.

The inside of the Belly Button had been gutted, remodeled, and decorated in the rococo style of Armand Fabulous the fabulous interior designer. Alternate windows had been bricked up according to instructions from Armand himself who had done all in his power to recreate the atmosphere of a Turkish seraglio. Talldorf found Small talking with a bullet-headed man on the second floor.

"Wanda okayed the job," Small was saying as the bullet-headed man thumped his gold-headed cane on the carpet.

"Who sent you?"

"Nobody sent me. I was lookin up from the river when I seen—"

"Come!"

They followed the man through a dark paneled foyer into a dark paneled office. The big desk under the bricked-up window was cluttered with account books. The man picked up the phone.

"I tell you no more. How many times I have to tell you, Wanda! No, no, no. What? Room and board?" He wiped beads of perspiration off his glistening dome.

"I just came through the dining room, Small," whispered Talldorf. "What kind of a place is this?"

"Snazzy dames, huh, Tallie?" whispered Small. "It's some kind of hotel for workin girls."

"Why aren't they out working?"

"They probably don't have to be at their offices till ten o'clock. Shhhhhhh!"

"Ok, Wanda. I leave it to you." The man hung up. "Do good job, boys."

When they left Uncle began to pace his office. Embezzlement had been uncovered in the Belly Button of America. Mr. Ensardo's sister's husband, the man called Uncle, was behind the eight-ball. Neither was Wanda Wistunka free from blame. Mr. Ensardo had dispatched his son, Ricardo, and was coming himself to act as arbiter in a complete audit of Uncle's riddled books. Uncle had had a sizeable corner of St. Louis to himself but now, with the rabid Ricardo poking his nose into every nook, Uncle crept from pillar to post dreading another encounter with the dripping jaws of his nephew-in-law. Understandably Uncle was nervous, though blameless of skimming one penny off the profits of Madam Wistunka's skillful team of girls.

Talldorf and Small filled their buckets in a utility closet and took the elevator up to the roof. The broad river rolled along under the frying sun.

"Quite a drop, Small."

"You won't have no trouble balancing on those ledges. They're a foot wide and you're tall enough to reach the tops."

Talldorf peered over the dizzy edge. "Too dangerous, Small. We can rent bosun's chairs."

"We ain't rentin nothin. If you won't do it, I'll do it. Small is always glad to get the exciting work. I try to give you opportunities—"

"What's that, Small?"

"A helicopter."

The helicopter beat its way straight toward them through the shimmering expanse above the broad muddy river. They watched as it hovered overhead and shrank back as it fanned down churning a whirlwind of dust. The pilot shut off the motor; the blades stopped convulsively; the bubble-door opened and Mr. Ensardo got out followed by his bodyguard, Al Salami.

"I tell you, Mr. Small, a man should take care of his health," said Mr. Ensardo as Talldorf and Small rode down with them in the elevator. It was indeed Small's ex-unaccountable client, the impeccable Windy City restauranteur, known in underworld parlance as The Flounder. Mr. Ensardo's trim diplomatic stature glowed salubriously, his eyes twinkled as he returned his small elegant hands to his pockets.

"Honor, Mr. Small, is my most precious possession. I protect it with my life. My word has been law. I have not made too many mistakes but my son has already made many. Poor Ricardo. I assure you he will not bother you in my presence. If I didn't have pressing business I would join you in a round of golf, Mr. Small. Perhaps we will find time to play when you come to wash the windows of my summer home."

The kitchen was closed, so was the Heartbreak Lounge.

"Go get the pass key from Wanda, Talldorf!"

"Please, please go with me, Small."

Small hammered on the dutch-door of Madam Wistunka's parlor.

"Rudolph, dear boy, you've finally come to do my windows."

"All in good time, Wanda," said Small.

"Oh, do please keep your nose out of this. It's such a lovely idea washing the windows, Rudolph. I have talked it over with Uncle and we have decided to provided you and your man with board and room and any other services either of you might desire. You are of course reserved for me, dear boy," cooed Madam Wistunka pinching Rudolph's arm to the bone.

"Ask her for a cup of coffee, Talldorf."

"Would you like coffee, Rudolph?"

"Coffee would be swell."

"Come then." She clapped her hands and Rosalinda came running. They sat on a velvet covered love seat in Madam Wistunka's parlor.

"Cream, Rudolph? Rosalinda, please give this small gentleman his coffee in the kitchen," said Madam Wistunka turning her icy profile.

"Wait a minute," said Small.

"Small is my partner, Madam Wistunka. Rather, I am Small's partner. Where I go Small goes. That is to say, where Small goes I go, if you follow me."

"Very well. But if I were you I shouldn't stoop so low. For Rudolph's sake I will bear your presence, Mr. Small. Now then, I will keep track of your expenditures, Rudolph, but it isn't important. It's only money. It is love that counts."

"Wait a minute," said Small. "I said 500 bucks."

"Of course, Mr. Small. We will deduct your expenses from your bill. That is fair enough, don't you think, Rudolph dear?"

"It sounds fair, Small."

"Good. Then it is settled. Do you smoke, Rudolph?"

Talldorf took a cigarette from the elegant enameled box Madam Wistunka offered. Small looked at Talldorf who handed the cigarette to Small who handed it back to Talldorf.

"For heaven's sake," said Madam Wistunka extending the box to Small who grabbed a handful.

"Put em on my account. We need a pass key, Wanda."

"You'll have to get Mr. Kribble's pass key. Mr. Kribble lives in the sub-basement."

"Come on, Talldorf!"

"Visit me soon, Rudolph," Madam Wistunka called waving her lace handkerchief as Talldorf waved over his shoulder and gratefully followed Small onto the elevator.

They descended past the underground garage into the bowels of the Belly Button of America.

Kribble was squatting before the open furnace door in a sweat suit. Sweat beaded Kribble's forehead and trickled through his pencil-thin mustache. The inferno lit his perspiring countenance with an orange glow. He checked his steam gauge, eyed his thermometer and slammed the furnace door.

"If it ain't the shortstop and left fielder. You guys in wrong place if you come for action."

"I know where the action is, Kribble. The name's A. Small. I come for the pass key."

"Says who?"

"Wanda."

"I'll just give Wanda a tinkle," said Kribble picking up the phone. "Wanda hates Kribble's guts but Kribble is indispensible. No one gets hot water up to girls like Kribble. What you guys do?"

"We're window washers."

"Ha ha ha. Hello, Wanda. I got coupla window washers down here. Yeah? How come you don't give em yours? Yeah, sure Wanda." Kribble hung up. His hands took a ring of keys. "Kribble opens doors. Kribble knows prickles in his blood."

Small rolled his eyes at Talldorf. "Relax, Kribble. We all got prickles."

"You guys sit down. I fix you Atomic Cocktail."

"We don't drink during working hours."

"Not alcohol, shortstop. Carrot juice, cabbage juice, ginseng root."

"The name is Small, Kribble. And no thanks. I ain't keen on vegetables. Besides, it's too hot down here. Get up Talldorf."

"Here," said Kribble slipping a key off the ring and handing it to Talldorf. "Treat with reverence. Don't forget who it belongs to. And if you think you're gonna get some on side forget it."

"What did Kribble mean, Small?"

"The guy is whacko, Talldorf."

A handful of girls lived in the Belly Button, the headliners had private suites on the 7th floor. If the girls weren't sleeping or washing out stockings and underwear they had gone downtown to shop, to the beauty parlor, or to a matinee at one of the movie houses.

Al Salami, who was waiting for Mr. Ensardo who was closeted with Uncle in his office, didn't look up from *Death Magazine* as Talldorf and Small struggled to get their ladder onto the elevator. They got off at the 7th floor and Small knocked on the first door.

"Window washers, my dear. Put the ladder here to get the skylight, Talldorf. Set it down. Help me move this coffee table. Talldorf, set it down! Miss, would you mind putting on some clothes."

The girl, whose professional name was Dolly Madison, slithered up to Small in her nightgown.

"Would you boys like to make a little whoopie?"

"We never get laid during workin hours," said Small. "Talldorf, go see if you can borrow a step-stool from Kribble while I get started on the job." When Talldorf was gone Small began stripping off his clothes.

In the sub-basement Kribble was busy cutting up vegetables for his third Atomic Cocktail. "Fresh garlic, cayenne pepper, tamari sauce," said Kribble cracking two eggs into the blender. "I'm telling you, Long, it goes straight to balls."

"My name is Talldorf, Mr. Kribble. I wonder if you might have a step-stool we can borrow?"

"Sure!" Kribble stuffed the blender with vegetables. "I'm gonna be in Ripley's, Dorf. I been keeping track. I figure, averaging three a day last six years, is seven thousand times on green with putter."

"I never understood why men chase around a little white ball, Mr. Kribble."

"It ain't the ball, Dorf. It's the hole. I been workin up slow. Stayin in training. I got fifteen punches left on ticket and today's payday. This is best job Kribble ever had. I couldn't have picked better place to keep sharp in plumbing arts. A joint leaks, pipe bursts, Kribble is right there with his wrench. I do little sweeping up just so Wanda don't get nervous. Boiler's blazing. Plenty hot water. Feels good, don't it? Sweats out poisons."

"Rrrrrrr Rrrrrrr Rrrrrrr," said the blender drowning out Kribble who started doing deep knee bends and continued talking. "Two hundred Marine push-ups, hundred-fifty chins, hundred sit-ups..." Kribble shut the blender off. "Have to keep up strength." Kribble prodded Talldorf's stomach. "You're young. Don't have to worry about flab around gut. Eat like horse. How many fluffs you stuffed in last forty-eight hours?"

"Fluffs?"

"Hens, females!"

"Oh," said Talldorf. "None."

"None? Pitiful answer, Dorf. Are you a walking dead chicken? Don't let your meatloaf, Dorf. The trouble with most guys is diet." Kribble filled two glasses and handed one to Talldorf. "Down hatch, Dorf." Kribble drained his off and nodded at Rudolph who gulped down the frothy concoction. A jolt of raw power shot through him as soon as the liquid hit his stomach. "Yikes!" he yelped.

"Powerful stuff, huh, Dorf? Cockle-doodle-doooo!"

Kribble leaped to the insulated pipe and twisted his body into a knot. Talldorf's eyes watered. He clutched his throat. "I'd like Small to try a glass of your atom juice," he croaked.

"Never mind! I don't give out cocktail to every bantam would be cock-of-walk who visits hen house." Kribble was back on the floor doing jumping-jacks. "Nine more hours Kribble be ready. I like to wait till sunset. Top shape. A piece of steak." Kribble was running in place. "Hundred twenty-five pops a month, Dorf. That's four and a third pops a day. Here's a step-stool."

"I'll bring it back as soon as we finish the hotel, Mr. Kribble."

"Are you on level, Dorf?"

"I finished the insides, Talldorf. Give me the step-stool. And be quiet. The lady is asleep in the bedroom."

"She seems to like you, Small."

Small flashed Talldorf a wicked grin and crawled out the 7th floor window. He leaned the closed step-stool against the stone wall and stood on tip-toes on the top step hanging from the pane by the friction of his nose while Talldorf, sick with guilt and vertigo, tip-toed into the hall.

Talldorf knocked on the next door. When no one answered he inserted the pass key, turned the knob, took the key out, got down on his knees and was about to insert the key into the lock upside down when the door opened. Nefertiti had taken off her working clothes and slipped into a frilly dressing gown.

"I have come to let in the light, miss."

"Come in window washer."

Nefertiti read the future in the faces of her sisters who passed down the line. She had worked the bordellos of Memphis and the bagnios of Cairo, had learned the ropes getting out of airplanes with her suitcase on the macadam at the edge of town to work the cribs of her youth before rising to the status of a call girl and was still working a hot spot like the Belly Button in the midst of the bacon futures and sorghum politics of St. Louis. When the moon was full it was Uncle who pressed his crushed physiognomy against her finely moulded brow, rooted over her like a hog and left a stack of bills chilling in the refrigerator beside the buttermilk.

While Talldorf diligently applied brush and squeegee Nefertiti reclined on her heart-shaped waterbed. The bed turned beneath the mirrors as she gazed out the grimy windows at the river. Talldorf kept his eyes on his work in accordance with Count Squeegee's instructions for dealing with an attractive woman.

"I suppose you think Nefertiti wants out of this racket? I get whatever I want. Can't you talk? Stop looking at me like that! What rock did you crawl out from under? I'll shut up. Don't listen to me. I get like this this time of the month. Uncle won't let me work. He's a Jew you know, and a bastard! He says you can't mix milk and blood. Forget it, Slim. I like window washers. You guys are all right. I've screwed some real nice window washers. Come here. Sit down. Don't be shy."

Nefertiti unbuttomed Talldorf's shirt. "What did you say your name was?"

"Rudolph Victor Talldorf. My mother named me after Rudolph Valentino. I've never told anyone that before."

Nefertiti unbuckled Talldorf's belt, undid his pants' buttons and pulled his pants down.

"Wait a minute," said Talldorf. "I hardly know you."

"Nefertiti doesn't have to sleep with every two-bit jerk who comes along, you know. Take off your shoes! Men, you're all alike. Crawling into cracks like scorpions. I used to be shocked when they didn't take off their shoes. Nothing shocks me anymore."

"I don't want to take my shoes off."

Nefertiti lay back on the waterbed. "Don't take them off then."

"I'll take them off."

Just as Rudolph dropped his second shoe Uncle walked through the door. Uncle stood pulling on a pair of leather gloves.

"Mr. Talldorf, is it not —" hissed Uncle.

"I was just putting on my clothes, sir."

"That won't be necessary."

Talldorf, carrying his pants and shoes, hurried down the hall. When Small found him Talldorf had his clothes on.

"Where you been, Talldorf?"

"I just met Nefertiti, Small. I think she likes me."

"The girls are pretty friendly around here, Talldorf. But we got work to do."

Talldorf, who couldn't stand to watch Small risk his life on the ledge of Marty Washington's suite worked across the hall in Paula Revere's bedroom. He passed through her bathroom with its fancy fixtures and sunken Roman tub. Her bathroom was well stocked with phallic rubber goods. He was examining two hinged cups studded with rubber prongs when the front door flew open.

"Where did you come from?"

"I'm the window washer," stammered Rudolph.

"Good. I'm in a hurry." She headed for the bedroom leaving behind a trail of riding clothes. "The first thing is pick up the duds!"

Talldorf gamely followed Paula's instructions.

"Next!" she howled over the sound of water pouring into the tub. "Go down to the desk and bring up my packages."

Talldorf did as he was told.

"Where the hell are you going?" shouted Small coming out of Marty Washington's door.

"I'll be right back."

"Give me the pass key!"

Talldorf gave Small the pass key and was swallowed by the elevator.

Al was sweating in the lobby, his coat off, his shoulder holster in plain view. Uncle passed Rudolph like a robot, his massive head set on his shoulders like a bowling ball.

"Put them over there," said Paula. "Why are you waiting around with your tongue hanging out? I suppose you want a tip. A window washer, *geezuz*! I learned early. For a girl it's simple. You know who taught me? The family doctor. Open your trousers!"

"Madam!"

"Unzip your pants! I'll clamp on the ball-squeezer and you can have a free squirm while I put on my make-up."

"Thanks, but I'd prefer just to wash the windows."

"Well get on with it. I got an early customer."

When Talldorf finished he stood helplessly in the hall wondering where Small was. Small came out of Pat Henry's door.

"Where have you been, Talldorf? I got this one finished. Down to the sixth floor."

Blister had already picked up Ricardo's monogrammed silk pajamas and hung them in the closet. Breakfast was over and Ricardo was standing in front of the mirror while Miro brushed off his $400 Smart Shafter and Engels suit with a whisk broom.

"What's the schedule?"

"Elmo the barber, then lunch with that jerk Costello."

"Scratch it," Ricardo snapped on his sunglasses. "We're goin out to Sportsman's ta watch the Cards."

"Are we goin to the *ball game*, boss?"

"Shut up! Tell Costello, dinner at the Mirage at nine o'clock. Tell him he better be there! Now let's get outta here. I'm sick of the smell of broads."

Ricardo led his retinue down the hall past potted palms, across Persian moons of Armand Fabulous' magic carpets. He spotted Uncle sneaking between columns and cornered him in a broom closet.

"If the investigation shows you was skimmin, Unc," snarled Ricardo, "I'm gonna tear out your throat and when I catch Shapiro I'm gonna cut off his balls."

"You're own son, Anthony," groaned Uncle, wiping his sweating dome with his handkerchief. "I can take no more."

"Calm yourself, my dear Uncle. I will speak to him again. I am only sorry that Ricardo's beautiful mother died so young and my son forgot her love."

"Yooo-hooo, Rudolph," called Madam Wistunka. "When are you coming to do my windows, dear boy?" She deftly pinched his cheek. "Do come now.

"It's not that I don't believe your small friend doesn't have sterling qualities, dear boy, but you would be better off without him. If you would like to become a St. Louis window washer, for example, I might be able to make arrangements. Just a tiny bit of money seems to have disappeared but there is always enough money to set an enterprising young man up in business. Oh my, you do so resemble my dear Bert. Of course if *he* wished he could work for you until he made enough to clear out. Tut, tut, don't make up your mind yet. Come give your Wanda a kiss. I have to see the Police Commissioner this afternoon. Such a greedy little man. Well, it's only money," and Madam Wistunka clutched Talldorf to her bosom. "You are so sweet, Rudolph." She dug her fingernails into the back of his neck and kissed him again. "Lock the door when you have finished, dear boy. And do come see me tonight. Until then, ta- ta—"

Talldorf followed Small who picked his way along the buffet table selecting choice morsels. Music blared from the bandstand as couples squeezed together on the postage stamp dance floor of the Heartbreak Lounge. The spangled band jackets the two partners had been asked to don were the same size, cutting off circulation at Talldorf's elbows and bagging Small in the mummery of a simian trumpet player.

"Feast your eyes on the broads, Tallie. Hi baby," Small winked at a six-foot platinum blonde who passed without noticing him.

"There's Nefertiti, Small. Nefertiti! Nefertiti! Nefertiti, this is Small, my friend and mentor."

"Pleased to meetcha," said Small. "So you're the Egyptian Talldorf's been tellin me about. Talldorf graduated from the university. I bet he didn't tell ya that. He ain't rich but he's loaded with integrity. You could have a good time with Talldorf," said Small tossing down his scotch.

"Men, what are they? Drips to shut off. Leaky faucets. I love men," said Nefertiti. "Let them live I say. I have read The Doctrine of Light so I do have some conception of your mission. Forget I said anything. Are you window washers comfortable? Excuse me for just a moment."

Nefertiti returned with a long haired blonde named Abagail Adams. "Now we're getting some place," said Small. "Drinks for the girls, Talldorf!"

Drinks went on the cuff of Madam Wistunka's blouse as did time spent with her girls. Wanda added a quarter every time Talldorf's or Small's head swiveled from a pane for a look at the curves in the Belly Button of America.

"How about a dance, Abbie baby," said Small.

"Sure, honey, why not."

Small gripped Abbie in a bearhug and waltzed her around the floor. "What do you say I get a bottle and we rent a room for the night?" asked Small.

"Sure, honey. I'll sleep with anybody."

"You ain't sleeping with anybody tonight, baby. You're sleeping with A. Small. Don't forget it! You won't forget it!"

While Small escorted Abbie to the elevator Nefertiti escorted Talldorf to the dance floor. She led firmly, conveying the music's rhythm with her pulses as they glided over the polished boards. By the time they returned to their table Talldorf was hearing wedding bells. "You'd love sleeping under the stars, Nefertiti."

Nefertiti shot Talldorf an oblique glance and inserted an Egyptian cigarette into her ivory holder.

"I know Small wouldn't mind. Maybe you could fix him up with one of your friends. We'll sell the Studebaker and buy a houseboat. Doesn't that sound like fun?"

"Spare me the maudlin details, Rudolph."

Rosalinda stopped at their table. "Ain't you Mistah Rudolph Talldorf?"

"Yes."

"Miss Wanda wants to see ya."

"Pardon me, Nefertiti. Don't go away. I'll be right back.

"Why does Madam Wistunka wish to see me?" asked Rudolph following Rosalinda out of the smoky din into the corridor.

"She say she gonna make a new man outta you."

Madam Wistunka's parlor was abustle. "Oh there you are, Rudolph. It was so good of you to come." She kissed Rudolph on the cheek with her blood red lips. "Answer the phone, Denise, dear— It goes on like this all night, Rudolph, my pet. The sound of the telephone is music to my ears."

"It's Senator Buzzard."

"Hello, dear Senator Buzzard. Nefertiti? Yes, of course she would be delighted to go to the opera. Will you send a car around? Spendid, Senator, ta-ta."

Rudolph winced. Battle casualties appeared from the wars of love: "They oughta put guys like that in prison," shrilled Carmine. "I hope Uncle breaks his fingers. Look, he ripped my dress. My best favorite dress."

"There, there, dear. Let Wanda wipe away your tears. I'll put this exquisite orchid Judge Thorn brought in your hair. I'm sure the Judge won't mind a bit. There now, aren't you pretty. Rosalinda will mend your dress, won't you, Rosalinda? Go to the sewing machine. That's a good girl. We must return to our battle stations. We have so many wonderful guests. Did you run the tub, Rosalinda?"

"Yes'm, Miss Wanda."

"Come with me, dear boy."

Madam Wistunka led Rudolph into her boudoir.

"So we are finally alone. After you've bathed, dear, I want you to try on some of Bert's old clothes, though they're not really old. Oh, I miss Bert so, Rudolph. Bert was a tall man. Bert was even taller than you, ooo-la-la."

"Nefertiti is waiting for me Madam Wistunka. I—"

"Tut, tut. I will take no foolishness, dear boy. And for heaven's sake do call me Wanda. Off you go now."

Reluctantly Rudolph went into the bathroom and took off his clothes. As he eased himself into the steaming tub Wanda burst through the door. "My dear Rudolph. Your Wanda is going to make you feel better than you've ever felt before."

She submerged Rudolph in the hot water and anointed his head with warm fragrant oils. She dried him with a rough towel, wrapped him in a silk dressing gown and laid him out on the satin sheets of her four poster. Her fingers probed his skinny muscles. "Are you familiar with the female's anatomy, dear boy? I have so much to show you. There are no tricks to love, but Wanda will teach you all.

"I don't understand it," she sighed. "I'm afraid I'm losing my touch." She broke a vial of a pungent substance under Rudolph's nose which almost blew his head off.

"It's been so long since I've had the pleasure of knowing a man so tall, Rudolph. The spit and image of Bert, but of course you're not Bert. I work so hard to keep everyone happy. I try to meet Uncle's quotas. Have you had this problem long, Rudolph? I know just the thing for it!"

Wanda sat at her dressing table smearing on a flagrant red lipstick which distorted her mouth into a crimson scar. She roughed her cheeks brusquely. "When all else fails—" said Wanda brightly, opening a jar of vaseline. "It will begin deep in your inner darkness, dear boy. It will grow and whisk you off like a mote of dust lost in the cosmos." Wanda loosened her garments.

"Don't touch me!" said Rudolph.

"But Rudolph..."

"Don't Wanda! I'm going to put on my clothes."

"I won't hurt you, dear. Do stop acting silly and come right back here and lie down."

"I'm getting out of here and no one can stop me," said Rudolph jamming his feet into his shoes.

"But it's on the house, dear boy."

"Good night," said Talldorf.

"But what about Bert's suits? Oh dear, what have I done?" A tear cracked Wanda's eyeliner and trickled through her rouge. "Rudolph, come back! Oh Rudolph, please don't leave me now."

Mr. Ensardo was known as a fair judge and was swift to render justice. The fist in the till had not belonged to Uncle, but to the notorious arch-criminal Emil Shapiro. Anthony Ensardo chuckled to himself. Shapiro had ingeniously penetrated Uncle's Belly Button. Uncle had learned his lesson and the Belly Button was now in the organization's hip pocket.

"Mr. Shapiro did us a favor, Ricky," Mr. Ensardo counseled as he sat and sipped a snifter of brandy.

"Shapiro is my pigeon, Papa. When I catch Shapiro I'm gonna pump the whole magazine into him."

"Ah Ricky—" Mr. Ensardo wiped an eye. "I see it is not time for me to step down. I forbid you to hunt Shapiro, and if you continue to harass Uncle I will suspend your soldier's privileges and confine you to headquarters."

"Grrrrrrrrr," Ricardo growled.

In the morning the party was over leaving dregs in glasses which the maids cleaned up and stains in sheets which they washed out downstairs in the laundry.

"Oh, my head," groaned Small waking next to Abbie's voluptuous body.

"That's the first good night's rest I had in seven years," said Abagail. "I feel like a million bucks."

Small found Talldorf asleep on a couch in the lobby.

"Wake up! We're goin to breakfast."

"We have to get out of here, Small. Madam Wistunka tried to rape me last night."

"The ladies are really oversexed in this joint, Tallie. Don't worry. Small's got everything under control."

Breakfast was the only meal the girls took together. After a hard day's night they ate like lumberjacks.

"Fortunately I'm not in it for money," quipped Dolly.

"Like my momma told me," said Angela, "there ain't nothin lower than a man except snake shit."

"Angela!" exclaimed Madam Wistunka. "I will not tolerate obscenities at table. Please answer the phone. Oh there you are, Rudolph, dear. Do sit down." Madam Wistunka's smile was dazzling. "I do hope you have forgotten last night's little episode. Did we keep you and your little assistant up too late, dear? Christina! We do not pick up our steak with our fingers. How do you expect to marry respectably if you don't practice proper etiquette?"

"What's the bone for?" Christina wanted to know. Nefertiti was conspicuous by her absence.

"This is real sweet of you, Wanda," said Small as he tucked his napkin into his shirt collar. "Talldorf always has a big appetite. Pass the meat, Talldorf, and some of that French toast and pour me a cup of that excellent coffee."

Talldorf was on his knees scrubbing the bottom panes of an ornate door while Small stood on a step-ladder squeegeeing above his head.

"Do either of you gringoes play Hearts?" asked the Virgin of Guadalupe.

"Anyone in his right mind can see that me and Talldorf are tryin to clean windows."

"I'll play," said Talldorf who had passed many a Dirty Dora to his grandmother Elinore. Sacajawea, whose mirrored T-shirt reflected the spangled words across her breasts,

A BUCK WELL SPENT

dealt the cards. It was a dime a point and Talldorf lost ten dollars.

Al was perched on a stool in the Heartbreak Lounge reading *The Sporting News* and sipping tomato juice. Talldorf worked meticulously behind the bar.

"I heard you was playin around with Uncle's girl, Red," said Al shifting his toothpick under his nose.

"No, sir," said Talldorf glumly. He spread the soapy solution on the mirror, and as he studiously peeled off the suds the Heartbreak Lounge brightened. The limpid glass brightened Al's countenance.

"Not that I give a rat's ass about Uncle, Red. Just a little friendly advice. Avoid Wistunka. She'll charge ya for breathin the air in the Belly Button. And stay away from Ricardo. Ricardo's homicidal. Don't say Al didn't tell ya."

"Thanks, Al," said Talldorf, admiring his work.

"Looks good, Red. I can see I need a drink. Dump three fingers of that gin into my tomato juice." Al's beeper began beeping. "The Flounder! I wouldn't work for nobody else. Here's to ya, Red. Keep it clean." Al scuttled off.

The mirrors gleamed, the small panes in the kitchen were clear as crystal, the glass blocks in the regal bathrooms sparkled like ice cubes. The dark glass held the riverfront in its fast reflections as Ricardo Ensardo sat tilted back in the naugahyde recliner and squinted out the window. The helicopter was just a speck now and there had been enough dynamite in that bomb to blow up St. Louis. Ricardo uncovered his ears and grabbed the phone.

"A ham sandwich and a glass of milk pronto!" Ricardo growled his first order since his father and Al had departed from the roof. Before Rosie got his order Ricardo was striding down the hall. "Heads are gonna roll!" he snapped to Miro and Blister who scurried after him. Ricardo turned the corner and ran headlong into Small and Talldorf.

"The cockroach and the grasshopper," he snarled.

"Watch where you're goin," said Small.

Ricardo struggled with his gun, got it out of his shoulder holster and aimed point-blank at Small's forehead. "Now see here—" said Talldorf. Ricardo wheeled and fired twice.

Talldorf looked over his shoulder at two smoking holes in the velour wallpaper. Madam Wistunka ran out of her parlor.

"Ricardo behave yourself! Act like a gentleman! Think of your father!"

Ricardo's lips foamed. "I'll show you what I think of my father. Dance, cockroach!"

Dum-dums ploughed the carpet as Small hopped from one foot to the other. Nefertiti appeared from nowhere and hit Ricardo over the head with a vase of long-stemmed plastic roses.

"How come that maniac ain't in the war?" demanded Small.

"The boss is 4-F!" said Miro defensively.

"Put him down here," said Madam Wistunka gesturing to her canopied bed as Miro and Blister carried the limp Ricardo into her boudoir.

Fortunately, Dr. Diddle was in the Belly Button making his weekly examinations and issuing weekly health certificates. Thanks to modern medicine, and Diddle, the girls were no longer prey to syphilis though a host of unsung organisms rioted through their birth canals. It was due to Diddle's diligence that the Belly Button was known as a clean house.

Dr. Diddle examined Ricardo's laceration, opened his black bag and applied a mustard plaster to Ricardo's scalp.

"Keep him in bed twenty four hours," ordered Diddle.

"Who hit me?" said Ricardo. "It was that skinny broad with the little tits, wasn't it, Blister? Don't try to cover for her. Let me outta here!"

"Doc Diddle says to stay in bed, boss."

"That blood-thirsty nitwit. My head is burning up. Pull this tape off my head. Ouch! Ouch! Get away from me you numb skull!" Ricardo leaped to his feet, his bright eyes glazed over and he crumpled onto the carpet.

Kribble was busy with his hammer plugging the holes Ricardo had blown in the floor while Talldorf and Small put the finishing touches to the windows. They dumped the crud from their buckets into the gutter as the sun set.

"Thank you so much, Rudolph dear. The glass does look marvelous," said Wanda Wistunka taking Rudolph's arm and flashing her forty thousand dollar smile.

"Wait a minute, Wanda," said Small. "I'm the one who handles finances."

"Your bill, Mr. Small."

They sped out of St. Louis over the mighty Mississippi on the green steel bridge. Small puffed his Lucky looking puzzled while Talldorf stared dumbly out at the stars.

The girls in the Belly Button of America were already busy entertaining customers.

Chapter 23

THE GIRLS' REFORMATORY

The Girls' Reformatory was set back in the gloomy woods off the old highway like Count Dracula's castle, ragged with towers against the full moon. Small felt a chill as he wheeled the Studie past thick old oaks up the long gravel drive and stopped at the spiked gate. A hunchback appeared with a lantern and a shotgun. Small stuck Mr. Ensardo's card out the window. The head that looked like a balloon said, "Five dollars gate fee." The claw changed the bill by magic into a clinking ring of keys. The iron gate swung open.

"Anytime you want to come through, day or night, you take out girls I keep my trap shut cheap, heh heh heh." His mouth hung open like a dog's.

"He's got worse teeth than me," said Small. "Be sure to get the guard house windows, Tallie. That guy's in desperate need of our services."

The barking of dogs arose in sheets and they discerned four racing black-as-night Dobermans seeking the jugular of the Studebaker. Small pulled up to a beamed portico lit by a hanging lantern. The door opened on a tall woman in a long black dress.

"Whistler's mother!" said Talldorf.

Her face was thin. Cold severity looked from the eyes and her gray hair was rolled into a tight knot behind a ruffled white collar. A knife-sharp command silenced the dogs which sat at her feet with dripping jaws. Miss

Kleen had been expecting them. They were quickly quartered down a ghostly hall in a hospital-like room.

"We'll have to squeegee through bars, Talldorf. What a shameful thing to do to a window."

"We don't want to get locked in the wrong place here, Small."

"It might not be all bad," said Small scratching the hair on his chest. "We ain't nobody's prisoners, Tallie. We're Mr. Ensardo's personal representatives. This joint is only a school where they teach wayward girls the right way."

The wayward girls this late at night were not snuggled in their beds, even as Small had been during his years at the orphanage because times had changed. Indifference had bloomed into exploitation. In a distant wing of the castle the most homely of the waifs neared the end of their twelve-hour shift in the dogtag works. They padded like disembodied spirits in their pressed paper slippers over a stone floor. A matron standing at the barred door drew them to her in a line like metal filings. The girls answered rollcall in weary voices like notes struck from a broken xylophone and were led out to lockup cells where they fell onto their pallets without desire or strength to splash their faces at the buckets in the shadows which provided water for all their needs. The room which housed Talldorf and Small was separated from the brutish sleep of these lambs by a courtyard of hard pack earth.

In the second story resided girls who had escaped the fate of the gray drudges below. The second level housed girls considered intelligent and presentable enough to carry on secretarial functions of the Ensardo enterprises who, when their time was served, would be offered clerical jobs in the underworld empire. They were destined to become the wives of bookies or liquor dealers or nightclub managers or to run operations themselves at the blessing of the organization with a cut due for education and insurance to protect their reputations. Such girls were thus brought into the organization from shanty lives in the environs of smaller cities for such crimes as having an uncle who would sign a paper releasing the girl's guardianship to the Ensardo Benevolent Association; for having a mother who would take a similar check to be relieved of a tramp's guidance; for being apprehended wayward on back roads of the Great Emancipator's state with no papers to show to a local deputy who knew where the money was. The second floor was full of American girls who didn't run fast enough. The girls had no appeal, nor was access to them allowed during their stay at the Reformatory. When the gates closed their identity was lost to any on the outside who might have cared. The local constabulary maintained a special patrol of roads near the institution and for their vigilance received Christmas bonuses from a long black limousine which pulled up to their humble abodes. Second floor windows were meshed with heavy steel wire resembling money cages like those to which the girls would graduate upon parole.

On the third floor resided the most comely of the girls, who were allowed access to the grounds by a pair of private elevators. These were girls chosen by Miss Kleen to receive training for future escort work. The girls were told that they were being groomed to riches beyond their wildest hopes. They received elocution lessons and read *Mine Magazine* and were tested on it so they might respond in an enlightened manner when senators caressed their young flesh and spoke of high achievements. They were to wear jewels, the names of which they learned in this finishing school. They played volleyball and did calisthenics and were allowed, in fine weather, picnic luncheons on the greensward where manners and refinement were emphasized while keen black Dobermans patrolled. From time to time a debonaire representative of the organization paced before the girls who stood against a wall in identical sheer chemises. His cold eyes snapped, his finger pointed and Miss Kleen made notes while the chosen trembled, uncertain if this was for good or ill yet excited, knowing they would soon leave the Reformatory. They never returned. No letters were ever received from the departed ones. Yet often they were to meet again in the Belly Button of America or in other elite bordellos across the country.

At the time of the visit of Talldorf and Small it happened that three sisters were incarcerated in the Girls' Reformatory, Ella, Trudy, and Scarlet Smith, granddaughters of kindly Edgar Smith who once had called Elvira, Mama, and Small, Papa, in the Indiana countryside across the road from Ma and Pa Sphincter's farm.

This is how the innocent children came to be lodged in the Reformatory: Ella, Trudy, and Scarlet were bouncing happily home from school singing together a rhyme that had occurred to Ella,

> "Two cats and three little mice,
> Oh you can truly bet your life
> They'll get et in just a trice—"

At that very moment Pa Sphincter brooded that no new idea for turning over a dollar had occurred to him all day and with melancholy wondered if senility was invading him. Ma Sphincter stirred the watery porridge and counted again in her mind the money she had hidden from Pa in a sock under the floorboards. Edgar Smith, across the road, rested for an unaccustomed moment in the old cane chair on the cabin porch wondering what he must do before the girls got home when, no end to his amazement, he was called to his blessed reward.

What a sight the terror-stricken, tear-stained faces of the girls presented with Edgar's corpse behind them and the two hard faces of the Sphincters before. Was it Pa, or Ma Sphincter — but if one how could it not be both — who spoke the word that brought the cat that swallowed the mice?

Miss Kleen brooded, gazing through the smudged window of her office on the long and short one pulling buckets and rags from that ridiculous car. It would not be too shrewd of old Ensardo to send spies. They had Ensardo's card with his own scribbled signature. Ensardo himself had telephoned to instruct her to render all assistance to the window washers and to deny them nothing. Well, they would report to Ensardo nothing amiss in her operation in human lives; the wheels she kept in motion were swift and ground her sinister product fine.

The gray matrons who stood like posts at the locked doors had been instructed to pass the little and the long one but Small nevertheless flashed Mr. Ensardo's card: "In the name of Mr. Ensardo, open up!"

The blue haze of surrounding woods hung in the morning light as the summer sun bathed the grounds. At the gabled windows of the third floor girls leaped back from the panes at specters of men, then crouched nearer in quivers of joy to see if it might be true. Brushes scrubbed at dirt and girls' eyes brightened as squeegees allowed sunshine in and girls threw windows up.

"Hello," said Talldorf, "I'm your window washer."

Small would have been alarmed to see Talldorf's figure at that moment half in and half out of the window if his eyes had not been filled with amazement of their own.

"Papa Small!" repeated Scarlet Smith over and over as though her fingers turned precious stones to learn their value. "You have come to save us!"

Small clambered into the room and stood alone with Scarlet Smith. "What could you have done, Scarlet?" Small implored.

"It's Trudy and Ella too, Papa Small. We have done nothing." Scarlet burst into tears and threw herself into the safety of Papa Small's arms.

"There, there, my child," said Papa Small.

After Scarlet had dried her eyes Small sat on the pink ruffled counterpane at her side. "We are prisoners, Papa Small. If we do not progress as they wish they send us to the second floor cages, or worse, to the dogtag factory cells where girls live on cockroach soup and sleep on straw and are beaten with whips and fucked by the hunchback. We do exercises and read that horrible Mine Magazine until we cry and never drip a drop of tea and we learn coy looks—" her lovely cheek fell to the left, her lids sunk over her blue eyes, "for not to obey they promise will be our ruin!"

"I promise you," said Small appalled, "I'll get you out, and Trudy and Ella too, and I'll never again go to a whore—horrible, it's horrible—"

Meanwhile Talldorf had fallen in love.

"I would go with you," said Nancy Shanks to Talldorf, who sat on her ruffled bed, his hands locked in hers as once he had sat with his fiancee.

"Will you take me away, Rudolph?"

"I will go to the legislature. Small will go to the Governor. I'll do your time myself."

"Do you love me?" murmured Nancy Shanks.

"I do," said Rudolph, for all his compassion for the world of his lost father and beloved and lost mother was drawn out by those yearning eyes. Before the day was over Talldorf had pledged more than any man possessed to seventeen girls on the third floor of the Girls' Reformatory, though Nancy Shanks was the first.

When the two partners came along the third floor hall late in the day the girls were lined up in rows before Miss Kleen. The girls' faces turned with longing toward the intrepid window washers.

"Ach! Small and Talldorf!" said Miss Kleen in her grating voice. "You see the personal attention I give to every detail. My dears will learn their places. Watch! You see they do not flinch when I slap their faces."

"Small! I won't stand by and watch!" claimed Talldorf.

"Stop the slappin," said Small.

Miss Kleen blanched.

"Surely you approve of discipline," she squeeked.

"Take me to your office," said Small. "I got to make a telephone call."

"You can have nothing ill to report about my operation, Mr. Small."

"I want to see the second-floor girls on our way down."

"Certainly, Mr. Small— Mr. Talldorf. My pride is the reformation of my children. Four! Three! "she barked to the gray matrons with the rings of keys, "Go! Mr. Ensardo especially prizes my efforts with the girls of the second floor. It is our largest group. Not all girls have correct bust and hip measurements and can not meet the customers' expectations, though we exercise them like thoroughbreds. I fabricate American beauty from most common material, you understand, but here on the second floor, Mr. Small, he he he, I manufacture the very backbone of Mr. Ensardo's empire. Look! Is it not a progressive sight?"

It was a huge business office full of girls with their heads bent and eyes straining at an ocean of papers where electric lights burned all day for the windows were filthy. The faces of poor waifs wore dazed and lifeless looks with the absence of the least enthusiasm in their sallow forms. Though none were so striking as girls on the third floor not one lacked the gentle appeal of girls their age. Denied the sunlit grounds the girls had fallen to lives of sums and figures documenting the mob's activities throughout the nation, nor like their older sisters of the industrial revolution were they permitted the diversion of a Saturday night stroll with a beau, or a family or home to which to return however humble before the next week's work would again demand their blood and youth, for Miss Kleen was indeed efficient and the girls rarely raised their eyes from the work they accepted as their fate.

"Infamy!" exclaimed Small. "You allow dogs to run free and lock poor girls in this cage!"

"Oh no, Mr. Small, they would forget themselves, they would chase butterflies and roll in the grass. I make adults of children!" The two gray matrons, Four and Three, stared dumbly at the unaccustomed consternation of their mistress.

"They will be allowed the grounds," snapped Small. "Mr. Ensardo would have light flood into these lives. It shall be done!"

'Papa Small—' formed the pale lips in a face just risen from tallying baccarat totals by percentage. Small's green eyes drank Trudy Smith's rekindled faith in her freedom and such was its intensity that it was transposed to brows of other young girls now looking up from their accounts, and their eyes glowed at the honest and handsome face of Talldorf afire with indignation at the reformation of precious girls into pitiful, drab and careworn creatures.

"There will be change!" vowed Talldorf. Miss Kleen gazed with trepidation at this marshal image so recently that of a bumbling lackey.

"The wind of change will touch these cheeks!" confirmed Small. "To the first floor, Miss Kleen. I would see your reform of the waifs who remain."

Miss Kleen preceded them down iron steps to the musty chill of ground-level corridors of stone, as though she grew more frail and old as they descended the floors of her domain of ruin. "Twelve-hour shifts," she squawked over her black shoulder. "We make every dogtag in America. I get work from the beasts if they drop like oxen at their machines!"

"People are not oxen!" exclaimed Talldorf. "Girls are not beasts!" A tremble rippled through the loins of Four and Three and Miss Kleen's back ached as if weary of her rectitude.

"This is where I started in the old times and soon I saw the right way and I rose up out of these cells because I was crafty. Mr. Ensardo noticed me in the secretarial pool and set me over all of these, even the trollops on the third floor and there will be no mercy for shiftless ninnies who cannot do as I did. Four! Three! Open the cell!"

A matron raised a lantern that shown on a huddled figure on the pallet. "Ella!" Miss Kleen grasped the figure by a thin wrist and jerked her upright but Small moved Miss Kleen aside with a hairy arm and knelt before the dumb figure with its stringy hair and vacant eyes.

"Little Ella, my favorite, don't you know me?" He scooped a dipper of water from the bucket and brought it to her lips and as it wet them they moved: "Papa Small...You've come at last—"

Small spoke into the telephone. "Right Mr. Ensardo, it's me, Small, at this sinkhole you wanted us to clean up. It needs more cleaning than we anticipated. No sir, money is no object. I've discovered a special interest in three of the girls who are getting reformed—" Small was interrupted by Talldorf: "*All*, Small, not just three. All!"

"A step at a time, Tallie—Mr. Ensardo, this is what I want in the way of support down here—"

"Fools!" cried Miss Kleen from the shadows.

By evening the three granddaughters of Edgar Smith were lodged in the room next to Talldorf and Small. Scarlet cradled Ella's head in her lap and Trudy fed Ella spoonfuls of soup. Ella's consciousness returned slowly from a madness of claking machinery as she received the fond caresses of her two sisters.

Next day Talldorf and Small cleaned the windows of the second floor unlocking iron screens and swinging them wide, nor locking them again when they passed on. Papers blew from desks and girls looked up from their duties where gray matrons could not hold their attention. Girls fluttered to windows like moths to light and laughter was heard where it had not been before.

"It won't be long, darling," Rudolph spoke the good news to the girls as he washed the panes. "Small and I are going to Mr. Ensardo himself. Be brave. Your freedom will come to you!"

The clerical errors girls made on this memorable day cost the Ensardo empire upwards of an insignificant hundred thousand dollars and by extension the life of Mr. Ensardo's Director of Procurement who saw the embezzlement he had perpetrated on the organization for the past year clearly revealed on a mistyped debit statement and leaped head-first from the window of his Nero, Nevada office. The girls beheld the green of the outside world, blue sky and sunlight which they had been trained to imagine mere illusions, and the web of the corrupt empire shook.

The thin lips of Ricardo Ensardo hardened in the Belly Button of America as he noted with increasing rage consistent irregularities in the courier pouch from the Girls' Reformatory.

"Maxie!" he barked and the brute stooped before his master's desk. "Get the car around front. Get Tony, Miro, and Blister. I'll have the hag's head on a picket. I'll feed that old bitch to the dogs!"

Small worked inside on the ground floor while Talldorf easily reached the outsides from the ground. Light fell into cells and factory where machines creaked and clanked seeming to resist it, and the gray matrons narrowed their eyes, and those of prisoners raised to behold it with the deathless hope that makes of women fit vessels for the divine.

Ricardo Ensardo spit on the shoe of the dwarf at the gate and drew his .38 as the black limousine shot up the drive. When the first Doberman streaked from the trees Ricardo's .38 blazed and the second dog rolled over the first and gained its feet to run face-first into the next slug and Ricardo cursed the two that howled and fled for the woods.

"You senile old whore!" yelled Ricardo, "What the hell do you mean it ain't your fault!"

Miss Kleen cowered behind her desk. "It's those spies your father sent!" she squealed. "Your father has lost faith in me, Ricardo. He has sent two spies in the guise of window washers!"

"Those punk screwballs!" snarled Ricardo clutching his gun, "I'll shoot their fingers off. You're right, you old witch, they are my father's spies!"

"Get your things together, girls," said Small.

"Papa Small," said Trudy, "Is it time to go? Can it be true?"

"We're all packed," said Scarlet. "I'm the only one who has a toothbrush."

"Wretched injustice!" said Talldorf stomping his foot.

"At last, to freedom, dear sisters," sighed Ella.

It was in the hall our little group met Ricardo Ensardo, Maxie, Tony, Miro and Blister like a solid black wall with scarcely a glimpse of Miss Kleen bringing up the rear.

"Stop dead or I stop you dead," snarled Ricardo needlessly. "So it's you and your noodle friend been turning the heads of my girls, eh?"

"I'm getting the feeling you're following me, Ricardo," said Small.

"You cheap punk. I shoulda blowed you away first time I seen you creepin on the restaurant sign. I'd fill you full of holes right now but I want you to get a straight report to my old man. I want you should tell my old man that his light is about to be shut off. That I control the organization. That his days of kid gloves are over. That it's time for the iron fist of Ricardo. You give him that message and if I ever see either one of you again, it's curtains."

"Let's go, girls," said Small.

"The girls stay," barked Ricardo. "You two get out before I send you to Papa in boxes."

"Go to your room and wait for me there," said Small to Edgar Smith's girls who trailed fearfully back down the hall.

"We'd better leave, Small," advised Talldorf. "We'll see this gentleman's father and —"

"We don't leave without our supplies, Talldorf. Let's get the garbage cans." Small elbowed between the retinue of thugs.

"Big business!" mocked Ricardo. "What a big business, ha ha!"

They carried three shiny garbage cans past the toughs sitting in the lobby passing a bottle while their leader made a tour of the third floor. They carried the garbage cans back past the drinkers one at a time depositing them in the back seat of the Studie. Ella huddled in the last garbage can refusing to leave before her younger sisters were safe.

"Stay low in the cans, dears," said Small as the trusty Studie sprang to life. "We got to get past old claw fingers at the gate. You got your bucket, Talldorf?"

"My bucket! Yes, Small. It's here between my feet."

"A good omen," observed Small.

They pulled away from the portico and wound down the drive among the oaks, and the gatekeeper's house came into view.

"Who you smuggling out in the garbage cans?" said the wizened little voice.

"Those are the bodies of Ricardo and two of his friends," said Small which sent the hunchback into peals of hysterical laughter.

"Then you get out no charge!" he squealed and swung wide the gate. But Small jammed her into park and leaped out of the Studie.

"Talldorf, you never washed this guy's windows. Don't shut the car door, I'll be right back. Stand aside, little man."

Small moved in a blur around the gate house, his arms whirling like a windmill, wet rag, black blades and gleaming brass of the squeegees before the windows which bloomed before the eyes of the dwarf whose mouth hung open in wonder. Small appeared to be in all places at once and again in the driver's seat as the Studie shot through the gate and the hand of the hunchback waved farewell.

Chapter 24

PEACE

"A prosperous college town, girls," said Small puffing on his Lucky while Scarlet flounced beside him. "It won't be nothin for professional window washers like me and Talldorf to set you up with a nice little grubstake."

Here indeed appeared a wonderful community in which to situate the Smith sisters, a clean and righteous capital of learning where the carillon chimed in the evenings and church bells rang on Sunday. Bucolic dairy farms on rolling green hills circled the town. The lawns were neatly clipped in the cemetery. There were only a few winos and just one Negro, Roland Snowball, the window washer, known to adepts of the trade as Saint Snowball.

Already Trudy had wrapped Talldorf around her little finger. She sat on his lap oooing and aaahing the gewgaws and frocks in the smart college shops. Ella raised her head from the pillow in back.

"Where are we?" she asked.

"Poor Ella. How do you feel, dear sister?"

"Don't worry about me," Ella said. "I'm all right." She slumped back unconscious.

"Crack open the ammonia again, Talldorf," said Small.

Small was exuberant. The town held great prospects. The university buildings stared down from the hill, their windows glinting with the golden light of sunset. Small turned off the highway onto a dirt road and parked in a wide place between two cornfields.

"I'm starved," said Scarlet.

"Potatoes and peanut butter," said Small.

Trudy and Scarlet groaned.

"Trudy, help Talldorf gather firewood while me and Scarlet set up camp."

Talldorf stumbled over clods while Trudy grudgingly followed between the rows. "There's no firewood in a cornfield, Mr. city- bumpkin." To Trudy's amazement Talldorf collected an arm-load. Soon coffee was boiling, and potatoes were steaming in the saucepan. Ella whispered weakly that she wasn't hungry. Scarlet and Trudy refused to eat. Talldorf and Small spread peanut butter on the potatoes and ate with gusto.

Ella was toasty in the back seat wrapped in blankets and rags. Small crawled into his sleeping bag. Trudy and Scarlet crawled into Talldorf's sleeping bag. Talldorf paced the road, pausing in his star gazing to add another stick to the dwindling fire. Everyone awoke unrested and ill-humored at the crack of dawn.

"I wish we were back at the reformatory," Trudy said.

"Where's the coffee," grumbled Small.

Ella had a fever and chills. She clutched at Small's sleeve. "Please don't let them take me back to prison, Papa Small," she pleaded.

"She's hysterical," said Small drawing back. "Talldorf, you're my medical officer. What's wrong with Ella?"

"I've captured several mosquitoes. They are anopheles mosquitoes, Small, which means Ella may have contracted malaria."

Small turned his back on his medical officer.

"Everything's ok, Ella."

After a cup of hot water and a piece of burnt toast Ella felt much better.

Roland Snowball, who had sat at the deathbed of Short, stood barefoot in the dewy grass reaching for a peach when he saw the scarlet Studie bump across the Mainline Trainline track on the way into town.

"This is a job for *Snowball*," said Snowball.

Roland and his wife Martha lived across the tracks in a shack with hounds under the porch, chickens pecking in the yard, peach, pear, plum and apple trees which never failed to bare, a large garden, seven cats, a nanny goat, and a well that never went dry. Martha was under the impression that she must drive her husband from the house each morning, and Snowball was happy to go. Snowball cleaned virtually all of the windows in town. Martha berated Snowball for charging too little for his work; she was mercifully unaware that he charged nothing at all. The only money he received was what people were moved to give him out of the generosity of their hearts.

Snowball glanced about him and, seeing the coast was clear, he ducked into the bushes. The sparrows, drying their feathers in the first light, didn't take fright. The birds chirped happily on when Snowball dematerialized. Snowball reappeared on the physical plane inconspicuously across the street as the Studie pulled up to the *White Owl Grill*. Snowball was cautious where he re-materialized since the time he had chosen the phone booth beside the ice cream parlor which happened to be occupied by a blonde coed.

While in New York City Roland Snowball had learned the secret of unclouding his mind so that people could not see him; people could not see him because their minds were clouded. The only ones who shared his secret were his beautiful companions, that high-flying flock of blackbirds, Carter, Williams, and Stevenson who materialized one, two, three, in his cell at the Gotham Reformatory to instruct him out of *The Ladder Testaments*, by Henry Lindquist Shine. It was only right that they should do this for Snowball since they were responsible for his incarceration.

Carter, Williams, and Stevenson had taken on Snowball to teach him the window washing trade when they were working the Grave Stone Tower job behind Rockefeller Plaza. They started at six in the morning and dropped thirty stories on their swing scaffolds before the noon whistle blew at the shirt factory: sixty-nine floors of white secretaries screaming in ecstasy at the way those black men swung. Many fainted. The bosses called in squad cars and fire engines and mounted cops to quell the riot. The district attorney pointed the tell-tale finger and the judge sent Carter, Williams, and Stevenson up the river, and Snowball to the reformatory. The baffling and simultaneous jailbreak from Sing Sing by the three black fly-boys never made the papers because the warden refused to believe his eyes.

Few had believed *The Ladder Testaments* either, with the exception of Carter, Williams, and Stevenson.

'NEW BOOK NULLIFIES EINSTEIN'S THEORY', *The Daily Mirror's* caption had proclaimed.

The book was written on the basis of Shine's meeting with an envoy from the planet Nearfaria. The Nearfarian envoy had picked Henry Shine out of the subway line one morning when he was on his way to work at the Johnson Screw Machine Co., where he had been going for fifteen years to punch out brass donuts, took him by the arm, bought him a cup of coffee at the automat and explained the importance of keeping skyscraper windows clean. Henry had to quit his job to work on the Nearfarian project. His wife left him. His oldest son tried to plant him in a vegetable farm. Shine barely had time to scrounge the money to have a vanity publisher print *The Ladder Testaments* before he died.

The Ladder Testaments explained the Nearfarian ability to exceed the speed of light. Shine explained that Nearfarians, a transmuted race, rode light beamed from the clean glass of Earthling windows at instantaneous velocity. When the Nearfarian applied the breakers of thought he became visible, only to disappear the instant he chose to explore beyond the space-time warp galaxies beyond any star chart. Henry Shine's book was subtitled: *A Handbook For Window Washers*.

The brevity of his stay in the Gotham Reformatory surprised even Snowball. In the twinkling of an eye he had accompanied Carter, Williams, and Stevenson to China where he first met Short in Peking floating over the cobblestones with *The Ladder Testaments* under his arm on his way back from Manchuria where he had landed by accident.

Short was hot about labor relations and had been talking to a lot of coollies. Snowball was fascinated with the delicacies of bamboo scaffolding. Snowball thought the Chinese were busy and happy as ants. Short visualized man with freedom to wash the glass he chose. Snowball perceived freedom and his own transparency in the frozen element of glass itself; all was light to Snowball. Even the soiled cotton boot of the Chinese cop who kicked his face and the familiar iron bars of the cell, and he had to calm the volatile Short before Short remembered how he had gotten there in the first place and who he was so that they both could materialize back in the Windy City and get to work.

It was clear to Snowball that Nearfarians were talking to themselves, that Nearfarians were merely people who understood that they existed at the speed of light, that freedom allows such perception, that speed is not miles per second but rather the immediacy of perception. Time and space, like dirty glass, need not exist.

'Be ye wise as serpents and innocent as doves,' Henry Lindquist Shine admonished his readers, and Roland Snowball was both. The only nigger in town had entered a peace beyond understanding. He washed windows for the Nearfarian within, locked inside space and time, never had a bad word for anyone, calmed people with his presence, and with his squeegees showed them many things. There was even a group of lunatic fringe students who read obscure poets and called Snowball Superman because of the tale of the blonde coed in the phone booth. Such young people sought him out as though he were a teacher.

Snowball watched the scarlet Studie pull up in front of the *White Owl Grill* and then he melted from view.

"We're all goin inside," said Small. "Talldorf, carry Ella."

Talldorf lifted the sharp-nosed bundle and carried it into the restaurant with Small striding ahead guiding Scarlet by her elbow while Trudy reluctantly held the door. The White Owl was nearly deserted at this pristine hour. Menopolis, with his pot belly under a soiled apron, brought coffee himself. The man looked like he had been up all night.

"The name's A. Small, first class window washer. Ten bucks to wash all your windows."

"I get a cheap price from the nigger," said Menopolis. "Free, ha ha!"

"I beg your pardon," challenged Talldorf, his nose twitching at the scent of injustice.

"You see that sign?" Menopolis pointed to the sign which said *Waitress Wanted* backwards. "I got a cute little uniform would fit nice on the blonde."

"None of that stuff, pal," bristled Papa Small.

"Nice college boys," Menopolis assured Small, "Nice and rich, big tips."

"You know any nice cheap apartments for three nice girls?" asked Small.

"Nice yes, cheap no," Menopolis said. "I don't care what professors say, money makes the world go round."

"That's what professors say," affirmed Talldorf.

"What you have to eat?"

"We ate," said Small. "Water all around."

"Cheap, cheap!" muttered Menopolis. He disappeared through the kitchen doors.

Small outlined the day's strategy. "Here's a couple bucks. Get Ella some hot chicken soup." Small handed his last two dollars to Trudy. "Talldorf, you and me hit the streets. We sweep through the shops and up the hill. We make a hundred bucks and give seventy-five to the girls. You girls can buy new clothes and we'll send you post cards." Papa Small offered himself a Lucky.

"Who wants to spend the day in this crumby grill!" complained Trudy.

"Can't we go with you, Papa Small?" Scarlet pleaded.

"The Greek ain't gonna mind if we prop Ella in the booth all day," Small said. "As soon as me and Talldorf hit the golden vein of light in this town we'll be back with the loot."

Ella roused herself from her stupor: "Papa Small is right, sisters." Ella was the most mature and sensible of the girls. "We must follow Papa Small's instructions. We owe our freedom to Papa Small." She slumped back. Talldorf and Small gained their freedom in the scarlet Studie.

"Wonderfully clean windows, Small," exclaimed Talldorf as they inspected the shops. "This town receives the attentions of some master squeegeeman."

"It ain't the work of an amateur," Small admitted.

They crept in the Studie past the columned porches of fraternity row, past the library and the humanities buildings where pretty girls swung their long hair and laughed in the sunshine. The windows hummed with the blackness which is the hallmark of a first-class job. Windows were so clean it seemed foolish to solicit. Small solicited. Talldorf stood by loyally on the sidewalk, trudged behind Small down alleys and around blocks of sparkling windows. The only windows that weren't clean belonged to people who didn't want clean windows. Small wouldn't give up.

"Is it the nigger?" yelled a man's voice from inside the house. "Tell him to kiss my ass."

"Up yours !" yelled Small.

"Are you all right, Small?" said Talldorf helping his friend up after he leaped the fence just ahead of the German shepherd's dripping jaws. Small limped ahead.

"I'll try this house," said Talldorf in an impulsive attempt to relieve his guilt and share Small's load. He sailed up the walk of a small neglected house whose windows looked like they had never been washed. A dingy brass nameplate beside the bell proclaimed:

OSGOOD VILE, PhD. HUMANITIES.

The faces of two old people hung above the oilcloth where they sat drinking coffee and smoking cigarettes, oblivious of Talldorf's presence. The bell didn't work. When neither answered his knock Talldorf opened the door.

"Excuse me, Professor Vile. I couldn't help seeing you enjoying your coffee. I'm a window washer and I would be proud to be clean your windows for a low price."

"Are you Jewish?"

"No," said Talldorf, surprised.

"Wonderful. If there's anything Ethyl can't stand it's a Jew."

"Won't you come over here under the light where we can see you, young man?"

"You're not a Mexican are you? I can't stomach a Mexican."

"No sir, Doctor, I'm not a Mexican, my name is Rudolph Victor Talldorf."

"Sounds German. Good hard-working people, the Germans."

"I'm not German, sir."

"You aren't a nigger are you, boy? Ethyl can't tolerate niggers. If you're the nigger we are not interested in having our windows washed."

"I don't think the young man is that Negro, Osgood. Look at his pretty red curls. Are you Irish perhaps, dear?"

"My mother was Irish."

"You're not Catholic are you?"

"I don't belong to any church, ma'am."

"Good! How Osgood hates the Catholics. Let's not get him started on a tirade against the Catholics."

"I loath the cloying smell of them!" Doctor Vile ground his yellow teeth. "I hate their stench! Their plastic Christs! Their bleeting-sheep Latin mumbo-jumbo! I abhore—"

"Do be quiet, Osgood. Poor Osgood. How he loves to lecture the students on evils of the Roman Empire. How much would you charge to wash our windows, young man?"

"Small and I would be happy to do them for ten dollars."

"Small?"

"My partner."

"I hope he's not a midget."

"No ma'am."

"How tall is he?"

"About five feet."

Ethyl curled her upper lip. "I do dislike little people. Midgets, dwarfs, children— They make my skin prickle, and how I hate cripples, Osgood knows. Cripples have been the bane of my life, young man. Father and mother were wheelchair cases. Everyone knows that. Horrible people. Can you assure me that your partner has no deformities or visible handicaps?"

"Yes ma'am."

"It's going to rain," Dr. Vile said. "I feel it raining in my big toe."

"It wouldn't be intelligent to have the windows washed when it's going to rain, young man. Perhaps you could come again another day. By the way, you don't happen to have any Chinese ancestry, do you?"

"I don't think so," said Talldorf.

"Good! Osgood and I reserve a vast hatred for the yellow race. I don't think there's anyone Osgood detests more than the Chinese."

"The Manchurians!" shouted Dr. Vile. "Rotten, deformed, mal-nourished, vile little devils, yellow cockroaches—!"

Talldorf hurried down the walk.

"Small, the window washer who does this whole town must be one of our black brothers. They call him the Nigger."

"I'll call him a few things when I find him," Small promised. "He don't leave a dirty window for the poor."

The poke Small had promised the Smith sisters was turning into an albatross. He was expected to provide a dowry when Destiny called him elsewhere.

The faster they delivered Ricardo's fearful message to Mr. Ensardo the better Small would feel, and the quicker they would get the two thousand smackers.

"Talldorf, I got it!" exclaimed Small. "We got to put those girls to work. Let's go pump a free cup of coffee out of the Greek and I'll spring my plan."

The Smith sisters sat like an island of wilted flowers in the middle of a boisterous college crowd of carefree students resolving with ease the issues of a war-ravaged world. Ella smiled wanly.

"Some greedy window washer has got this town sewed up," Small told the girls. "How would you all like jobs in a restaurant? While me and Talldorf are out pounding pavements you girls could be serving meals to customers."

"I was trained in mathematics, Papa Small," said Trudy.

"You gotta go to work sooner or later."

"I'm not interested in slinging hash to a mob of college joes," said Trudy. "How about you, Scarlet?"

"I think they're cute," said Scarlet.

"I ain't gonna be around to rescue you all your life, Trudy," said Small. "You have to start thinking for yourself."

"I always think for myself, Papa Small."

"I used to go to a wonderful university just like this one," said Talldorf. "You and your sisters can profit from working in such a stimulating atmosphere."

"You have to be joking."

"You could get an education," insisted Talldorf.

"I have an education, Mr. red-headed woodpecker."

There seemed to be no hope. Ella raised herself from a crumpled heap in the booth. "Oh dear, oh dear! Mr. Menopolis is coming at last to throw us into the street."

They all looked around and indeed Menopolis was bearing down like a maddened bull.

"You think this is the soup line?" yelled Menopolis. "This is the flop house? — "

But at this very moment the restaurant fell into a hush. Small saw Menopolis' face change from beet-red to an expression of wistful peace as the light softened and every head turned for the source of a dim celestial choir. Menopolis leaned a hand on the table. Menopolis was not the same man. His teeth glittered in a winsome grin, his eyes sparkled. He had sucked in his gut. He stood erect. Small had not noticed the pointy little mustaches before this moment.

"Gentlemen," he said to Talldorf and Small, "it is such a pleasure having the company of these delightful young ladies. It has made my day. I will run and bring the French menus. You must order lunch on the house."

Small's eyebrows raised. Talldorf looked as blissful as Menopolis. The girls were smiling and Ella was sitting up straight. All eyes were turned to the plate glass window where the window brush of Snowball, like the baton of a great conductor, had painted the Last Supper. It was impossible; it was unmistakable; it was so. With a squeegee in each hand the black man with the Santa Claus beard twirled aureoles around the sudzy heads of the Apostles whose gazes peered upward to the expanding light. It's the suds running, thought Small. The light expanded until the whirling squeegees blazed above the head of Him and sunlight reclaimed the glass as if no window was there. Instantly Snowball stood between Talldorf and Small, a hand on either of their shoulders.

"Gentlemen," he grinned, "I have just demonstrated Principle One of The Ladder Testaments by Henry Lindquist Shine: 'Permit the light.'"

Immediately Snowball was outside laying his brush to a new window. Small felt a sense of vertigo. Where had he seen such legerdemain except in his mentor Short? The buoyant black man, limber as a ballet dancer, spread a soapy tapestry on the glass. Civilizations flourished with his brush and perished with his squeegee blade which never left the surface of the pane. Snowball dangled from the waterline and Small imagined he was floating. Small's eyes were narrow and Talldorf's mouth dropped open as Snowball depicted his favorite subject, the First American Civil War: cannon roared shattering infantry and horse, spewing blood and smoke through the Wilderness and across the swamps of Cold Harbor.

"He's terrific, Small!" cried Talldorf.

"Too much soap," mumbled Small.

Snowball went to work on a lacy pageantry of King Louis' court. They watched sudzy columns topple and heads roll, saw lawns catch fire and Versailles explode and burn until nothing was left but four soapy corners which Snowball extinguished with two vertical strokes.

"Bravo!" shouted Talldorf to the wonderment of the customers in the *White Owl Grill.*

"Pardon us, girls," said Small. "I gotta give that window washer a piece of my mind."

"Hey you!" Small yelled as he went out of the door with Talldorf right behind. "So you're the nigger who cleans all the glass in this burg!"

"Yehsuh, boss, Roland Snowball's the name, window washin is my game." Snowball did a little softshoe and doffed his cap, "Iz de only nigger in town."

"Oh please, sir," objected Talldorf, "be assured we do not think of you in those terms. We have noted your consummate skill with the squeegee...Small is just upset — "

I ain't upset I'm outraged! I'm A. Small, big-city itinerant will-o-the-wisp fly-by-night specialist in the art of light. This is R. Talldorf, my lieutenant, we're on a world tour. You gotta be rakin in hundreds of bucks a week and I demand my fair cut."

"So it's work you're lookin for. Would you boys like to help me do the Old Folks Home?"

"That's more like it," said Small. "What's the cut?"

"One hundred percent of nothing. I do it for nothing."

"Nobody cleans windows for nothin. You ain't serious — "

"You understand that not everyone will pay to have windows cleaned, and since it is necessary to clean windows I clean windows for nothing."

"You're serious! How can a sane man compete with that?"

At this moment Menopolis appeared on the scene. But was it Menopolis? The pointy black mustaches had grown. Small was certain of it. The man was slender and wore a chef's hat and his sour nature was replaced by a tangy French accent:

"*Bonjour! Bonjour! Monsieur* Snowball! You come as usual een zee neek of time. Zee beeznees has drive me mad. I nearly trow zees fine gentlemen into zee street and now I feel so wonderful. I am again zee great chef zat I am in my heart. Herc! Today I pay you weez your favorite!"

It was a slice of watermelon.

Menopolis, if indeed this was Menopolis, rubbed his palms together in anticipation of Snowball's joy.

"I know you people like zee melon best!" chuckled the chef waggling his finger at Snowball and dancing off into the restaurant.

"Who was that frog?" said Small.

"That's Pierre Menopolis. He feels his best when I clean his windows." Snowball cracked the slice of watermelon on the curb into three equal pieces. "Join a nigger for lunch," he said.

Small was stunned. "You wash his windows for a slice of watermelon?"

"Remember the birds of the air, Small," said Snowball. "They don't sow or reap or gather into barns, but they eat."

Talldorf flapped his arms. He sensed he was in the presence of a man who belongs to life as the bird belongs to its song and there was not a problem in the world. Small sank in dejection to the curb with melon juice dripping through his fingers.

"This reminds me of a story," said Snowball. "I bought a parrot when I was a young man. I thought I had the smartest parrot in the world. He wore glasses and he read books all day. But he wouldn't talk to me. I said, 'Polly want a cracker? Polly want a cracker?' a million times but that parrot just kept on readin and turnin pages. One evening he took off his glasses, laid down his book, looked me in the eye and spoke."

"What did he say?" asked Talldorf expectantly.

"Nigger want a watermelon?"

"I ain't in no mood for witticisms, Roland," said Small. "I'd like ya to know that you've rendered destitute three waifs who depend on me, and Talldorf there, who ain't got no sense."

To prove it Talldorf said, "Small, it's a wonderful idea to wash windows for free. That way we can wash any windows we want to wash."

"*Never fear,*" said Snowball in such a way that Small could almost believe it. "True window washers serve the bedazzlement."

"You don't understand the situation. We got no money."

"Mr. Snowball," said Talldorf, "both Small and I have sensed a secret wisdom in the trade. Both of us are seeking that wisdom. We have read *The Doctrine of Light* by Count Squeegee and we wish to discover the true path."

"Brother Talldorf, the Sidereal Society of Window Washers welcomes you into the fold. I, myself, have been honored with a seat on the board of the S.S.W.W. It will be my pleasure to take your first dues payment of fifty dollars and issue your official membership card."

"Wait just a minute!" said Small glaring at Talldorf who reached for the wallet he no longer had. "We ain't joining nothing. Me and Talldorf are independents."

"Besides your official membership card, Brother Talldorf, you get your own personal copy of *The Ladder Testaments* by Henry Lindquist Shine which take up where Count Squeegee left off. That book will introduce you to the Nearfarians who travel faster than the speed of light without gas."

Small held his head while Talldorf and Snowball babbled about spaceships. But strangely, as Snowball talked his crazy talk, Small began to feel better. What was the use of brooding? He had done all he could do. The girls would have to go to work whether they liked it or not.

"Where is Nearfaria, Mr. Snowball?" Talldorf was asking.

"Right here. Everything is right here. The difference between you gentlemen and Nearfarians is that you think you're just sitting here on a curb."

"Where are we really, Mr. Snowball?"

"Everywhere," said Snowball.

A fat black lady came barreling up the walk. "Roland Snowball!" she shrieked.

"Uh-oh," said Snowball, "my dear wife, Martha. Martha, dear, I'd like you to meet Talldorf and Small. Small learned the trade from my late great friend Short—"

"Say, how did you know that? Did you know Short? Hello, madam, I'm pleased ta—"

"Why ain't you home eatin your supper stead of jabberin trash to a lota white trash. I won't stand for it!"

Bam, bam, bam! She hit Snowball over the head with her umbrella.

"Like Short always said—" called Snowball as Martha drove him away down the walk, "Follow me!"

"No wonder he's crazy with a wife like that," said Small.

"I think he's a genius."

"If you didn't have me, Talldorf, you'd end up as nuts as Snowball. He's just the poor town nigger, he said so himself. Forget everything he told you. It ain't done him no good and he ain't done us no good. C'mon, let's squeeze a coffee out of Menopolis, or whoever he is."

Inside the restaurant the girls were not to be seen.

"When they get back from the powder room I'm gonna tell em they got to go to work, Talldorf."

"May I take your orders, monsieurs?" It was Scarlet in a tight-fitting little waitress uniform with a lacy coronet on her head.

"Chef Pierre has hired us all," said Scarlet. "Isn't it wonderful? I met the nicest boy, Joseph. He's the cute one in the last booth. He's going to be a nuclear physicist to aid the war effort and make lots of money. He has a sports car. He's going to take me for a ride. Trudy is going to be Chef Pierre's bookkeeper and Ella is chopping vegetables. I think Pierre likes her, tee hee. Papa Small, you and Rudolph get dinner on the house, Chef Pierre said so.

Our choice this evening is pati-de-fa-grass, or hamburger steak with onions. I'll bring your coffee right away."

"I don't like it, Talldorf," said Small. "This is the spookiest day I ever lived through. Everything's out of control."

After a free supper Small sat at the table scowling at the war news in the paper while Talldorf helped the girls clean up the restaurant.

"With your permission, Monsieur Small, zee girls will sleep peaceful as chickadees in zee leetle cottage beside Chef Pierre's house. We have already make zee arrangements."

"Who are you really, Chef?" asked Papa Small. "This morning you were a Greek running a greasy spoon and tonight you're a French chef."

"*Oui*, Pierre Menopolis," said the chef. "My mother was French, I loved her dearly, she ezz zee best part of me. Zee leetle Ella reminds me of her. Someday perhaps zee wedding bells may ring for me and zee marvelous Ella, *sacre blue!*"

Ella tried to touch her ear to her shoulder in a shy, self-deprecating gesture meant to hide her embarrassment, and Scarlet giggled.

"Menopolis is zee 'orrible mathematician so zee smart Trudy weel do zee books, an Scarlet eez zee best waitrez I ever have. Zee restaurante was full tonight!"

Pierre Menopolis appeared boundlessly happy and it was a great relief for Small to know that Pierre was taking the Smith sisters off his hands; triplet albatrosses are too much for any man.

"I need zee dishwasher too," said Chef Pierre beaming at Talldorf and waving his eyebrows.

"Talldorf stays with me, Chef," said Small.

Beside the day's wages Pierre had paid them, Scarlet made sixteen dollars in tips. Compared to Talldorf and Small the Smith sisters were rich. Trudy sat on Talldorf's lap counting their earnings and Scarlet sat on Small's lap and gave him a kiss on his cheek and Ella brought a bag lunch she had packed for them.

"Give the money to Papa Small, Trudy," instructed Ella. "Papa Small has rescued us. May the Lord bless you Papa Small and guide you and Rudolph on your important mission to Mr. Ensardo's mansion."

"We appreciate your heart-felt generosity, girls," said Small stuffing the bills into his pocket. "Take charge of the change, Talldorf. There's one thing you girls can count on: Papa Small always pays his debts."

Chapter 25

WAR

Ricardo Ensardo, power-maddened son of the Flounder, and his retinue of violent death streaked blindly past the cornfields. The enemy was advancing on Little Versailles, Mr. Ensardo's vast estate in the Wisconsin woods. They roared through the mid-western night in four high-powered black cars bearing license plates that no cop in seven states would stop. They moved out of Springfield on 125, swerved onto 67 at Virginia, sped through sleeping Macomb and aimed for the river at Moline where Ricardo would take care of business. In the rear seat of the first limo, in the dim light of wall lamps, to the slap of the finest nylon on the tar cracks of the highway, Ricardo cheated Miro at poker and blew cigar smoke into Blister's eyes.

Talldorf and Small had followed precisely the same route in the scarlet Studebaker which had served them so well in their trip up the river, and had been welcomed by Mr. Ensardo at Little Versailles the day before.

Little Versailles was a fortress surrounded by high brick walls and electrified fences which permitted the forest within the grounds though not a living creature larger than a mouse could move outside the infra-red, closed-circuit surveillance of those in attendance upon Mr Ensardo. But the fortress aspired to loftier heights. In a strange mixture of contemporary American architecture the main chateau resembled a hybrid of a bank and a temple; there was even a hall of mirrors modeled on the original.

"See how fine your lieutenant, Mr. Talldorf, looks in the glass. You are a courier out of mythology, Mr. Talldorf, and a worthy figure in this mansion. For it is a mansion, is it not, Mr. Small?" and Mr. Ensardo's tuxedoed elbow touched Small in the ribs. "And the golf links lie behind the whole layout. There is no estate on Corsica itself so fine as Little Versailles. Come, gentlemen."

He led them off the grand and glimmering hall into a leather room where a wood fire burned in the grate and billiard tables crouched like fairyland meadows in pools of yellow light, and seated them in great chairs. Mr. Ensardo rang for cognac and offered fine cigars.

"Now, if we might talk business for a minute, Mr. Ensardo," said Small.

"If you wish to speak of business you have come to the right man, Mr. Small. How I have enjoyed our dealings. My sign and awning in the Windy City look worse than ever. Will you ever clean them up for me, Mr. Small? You should see the rust! But I tell you, still they come to Ensardo's, the rich and powerful. Not a mayor of the Windy City has not sat beside me at the bar of Ensardo's. If my sign and awning is ever cleaned they would not know the difference. But do you propose a deal, Mr. Small?"

"First, I am proposing you pay me $2000 as to our agreement for washing the windows at the Girl's Reformatory—and I got to discuss that sink-hole with you, Mr. Ensardo—and ten bucks extra because the dwarf at the gate charges to get in."

"Boys will be boys," chuckled Mr. Ensardo. He rang, and spoke with a servant who returned with an envelope from which Mr. Ensardo counted out $2010 to Small who folded the pile into his hip pocket. Small raised his glass.

"To your virtue, Mr. Ensardo, prosperity you got."

"Ah, virtue, Mr. Small, what can it be? I live for the great dice game with Virtue. I believe I have done well, just look around you. And here am I, the ruler in my house. And yet I have no peace because my son, Ricardo, is my constant concern. Mr. Small, if Ricardo were more like yourself, of an even temper, not given so recklessly to his passions—If I had such a son, Mr. Small, I could rest easily giving over to him his father's inheritance. The weight of my duties rest heavily on these shoulders for my businesses are great."

"I can't call your business at the Girls' Reformatory exactly great, Mr. Ensardo," said Small. "If that's good business, it stinks."

"How refreshing, Mr. Small, after the stale air of the boardroom."

"Innocent girls are held prisoner in the Girls' Reformatory, Mr. Ensardo. I have no doubt that you are unaware of this, sir, but not one of the girls either Talldorf or I talked to have been convicted of a crime. They were captured by law enforcement officials whose law is money."

"Disgraceful!" exclaimed Mr. Ensardo. "I will send an order out immediately to admit no new inmates until I myself make a personal inspection. If my business has outrun my integrity I will not sleep until my debt is repaid, I promise you."

"Mr. Ensardo," said Small. "There's something else. I have a message for you from your son."

"Ah, you have seen Ricky more recently than I. What words does he have for his father?"

Talldorf shoved his cigar into his mouth.

"Ricardo said to tell you that he was going to turn your light off. He said that he controls the organization. He said that your days of kid gloves are over."

Mr. Ensardo rose to his feet. "Please, Mr. Small and Mr. Talldorf, you will clean all the windows and especially the mirrors of Little Versailles. Be at home here, as if you are the sons of Mr. Ensardo. Your presence comforts me."

Three more limos were added to the caravan at Moline where, in the wake of Ricardo's advance, a number of new widows grieved as the cars roared across the span at Dubuque.

"The goddamned Mississippi again!" glared Ricardo from the back seat.

"Easy, boss," said Miro, "it's only a river."

"I hate it!" screamed Ricardo.

The tiny town of Willow Springs had been unknown, except to the few local inhabitants, before Mr. Ensardo had chosen the site for Little Versailles. One local inhabitant was Harry Slim Krankoffer, the ner-do-well son of old Hans Krankoffer who kept all the years of his life a modest dairy farm near Willow Springs.

"Boy, you ain't gonna turn out worth a cow's tit," predicted old Hans when Slim began to dabble in real estate to support his drinking habit. It was to Harry Krankoffer's weather-beaten little office that Mr. Ensardo's representatives had come to negotiate the purchase of the site for Little Versailles.

Krankoffer sold the acreage for one hundred thousand dollars transferring to the estate of the blind widow who owned the property and who now resided in the Plixen County Old Folks Home twenty-five dollars after his deduction for expenses and services.

Krankoffer had gone to his drinking buddy, Mabley Pot, and together they had organized a construction company that built Little Versailles by subcontracts and kickbacks for Mr. Ensardo who was pleased to employ local help. 'My people,' mused Mr. Ensardo in moments of whimsy. And from the well-intentioned generosity of Mr. Ensardo, Krankoffer and Pot were raised to figures of prominence in Willow Springs as the unaccustomed odor of money made heady the virtuous and simple folk.

Krankoffer and Pot were elected to governing positions in the town on the crest of their new affluence with the slogan, 'Progress and Prosperity, Open Willow Springs to the 20th Century'. In the seven fat years since the appearance of Mr. Ensardo's representatives, Krankoffer, now Mayor of Greater Willow Springs, and Mabley Pot in control of the city council, had enticed a tractor factory, a rubber works, a new spur of the Mainline Trainline from its crooked course along the great river itself, a plastic cigarette lighter factory, nine new trailer courts and two shopping plazas into the once peaceful community.

Krankoffer had so changed that his old schoolmates could hardly believe this obese man who looked as old as his own father was really Slim Krankoffer who used to hang over the pool table downtown. And Pot, who had always been sneaky, now sent shivers down the spines of his fellow townsmen and it was rumored that he carried a gun to enforce his business deals.

The noxious gloom of industrial waste hung over the pleasant site of Willow Springs and fruit trees were dying. The germ of credit buying had infected the blood of the townsmen: men were driven to drink, happy homes were fraught with dissension and despair, and children presented with bad examples had gone wrong. The townsfolk, whose arrival Little Versailles had awakened to the ways of the world, now fed off the monetary body of Mr. Ensardo, cheating him on every dealing his attendants had with the new town of Greater Willow Springs from the inflated price they charged his chef for beef to the gouging the plumber made replacing a leaky water pipe in the tulip garden. Mr. Ensardo smiled with forbearance and thought, 'My people.'

The rise of Harry Slim Krankoffer into a bilious and dottering old man decades before his time would not be unaccompanied by his fall. Whiskey, if anything, preserved him and was not responsible for his physical ruin; that was due to his increasing horror of what his rash greed had unleashed upon him. Harry had wanted only a good wad to gamble at Lacrosse and wine and dine some slick dame once in a while, but it had gotten out of hand. It was so easy he couldn't believe it. It was like a bad dream. No more easy days hanging over the pool table or drinking with the boys in the backroom. The boys hated him now. They smiled and called him Slim but they didn't mean any of it. The first one who got the chance would stab him in the back; he never stood on a carpet for fear someone would pull it out from under him. He had eaten himself sick and diabetic, and worst of all something had gone wrong downstairs, he couldn't get it up, he suffered headaches and he hated to wake up in the morning. And now Ricardo had laid the fifty Gs on his desk and informed him that he owned him, a proposition old Ensardo had never even imagined. He was as good as dead if he dared cross the rabid young mafioso. All Harry wanted was out, and he could not get out. Ricardo had growled into the telephone that tonight at the city council meeting he expected Krankoffer's and that skinny weasel Pot's unconditional support. Ricardo's meaning escaped Krankoffer, but he knew it would be a black day.

Talldorf and Small moved easily among the associates of Mr. Ensardo who nodded as they passed with their buckets, squeegees, and the rags dangling from their pockets. Small and Talldorf knew these businessmen as Mr. Ensardo's inner guard and that each was armed in a ring of steel. They knew because of the thin film of ice that clung to their persons. The guards sat at lawn tables conversing like socialites on holiday, but their dark gaze continually swept the grounds and they spoke into two-way radios in terse commands. Small marveled at the firepower that ringed Mr. Ensardo's mansion. He had seen the chainlink fence topped by barbed wire and the great stone wall, none of which would keep out Mr. Ensardo's greatest enemy, his son.

"Ricardo's on his way, I figure," said Small as they walked the second floor windows where the new ivy grew. "I ain't anxious to be here when he arrives."

Mr. Ensardo himself stepped out on the lawn below.

"Mr. Small, they look wonderful, your work brings light to us all. Tonight I am inviting you to a little diversion after supper. You will come to the boardroom in the north wing. Our little town of Greater Willow Springs is conducting a Council meeting. You must meet these good people whose protector I am. I say, Mr. Talldorf, you do fine these days don't you? With scarcely a thing to hold to! Look at him, Mr. Small! Good work, my boys," and Mr. Ensardo disappeared from their view.

That evening Small ate the grandest meal in his experience. The table was lavish and long, white-draped and sparkling with candelabra beneath the glowing chandelier in the grand dining hall. Representatives of major corporations in the Middle West, tailored in their traveling tuxedoes, dined this evening with Mr. Ensardo. As this was a gathering of the essence of Mr. Ensardo's enterprises business was the topic and heart's blood of the evening, and no women were present.

In their work clothes Small and Talldorf sat to the right hand of Mr. Ensardo and were introduced to the table.

"Two of my people," said Mr. Ensardo, "Mr. Small and Mr. Talldorf. It is too rare a privilege to have such men at my table, for their talents are dedicated to a rarer product than those we deal in. Let us rise, if not of our own understanding then in deference to the memories of our humble mothers, and the precious feelings hidden in our hearts. Join me in a toast to my window washers, Mr. Small and Mr. Talldorf!" Glasses glimmered aloft in the white hands of corporados.

"You will all profit by cleaning your windows," suggested Mr. Ensardo, and various lieutenants, who stood in attendance behind the diners, hastened to gather behind the chairs of Talldorf and Small to deliver business cards with requests that their masters be contacted at the earliest convenience.

Small could not contain himself. "What did I tell ya?" he said *soto voce* to Talldorf. "We're in like Flinn. We'll be doin the Chrysler Building, we'll chisel gunk off the windows of General Motors and be rich! Deal with em, Talldorf, make sure we got the names of the big shots, ho ho ho. We'll remember this night as the great clean-up."

Talldorf and Small puffed Mr. Ensardo's cigars and sipped brut from tall-stemmed glasses while deals wheeled around the table and a check for a million dollars to replace the last extant factory manufacturing rubber baby-buggy bumpers with the manufacture of plastic bumpers dropped into Small's wine glass.

"Let it be a good omen," laughed Mr. Ensardo lifting the dripping check, "It has tasted the wine of an American craftsman. See that the children of America have the smoothest ride business can provide."

"I think I'm poisoned," said Small and others laughed.

Rudolph was absorbed in the conversations around him. Two debonaire men across the table outlined the finances of American auto makers, who by showing an operating loss, were reaping their greatest harvests. A Mr. Smith, who had begun with a popcorn machine not far beyond the river in an Iowa movie house and had built his ten-cent bags into a worldwide empire of Hello Motels welcoming American tourists to Dubuque in such exotic settings as Zanzibar, wheedled to no avail for Mr. Ensardo's intercession on Corsica to locate a Hello Motel at Ajaccio.

"Who will deny I am a generous man, Mr. Smith? But my native soil is sacred to me and if I am honored to see it again before I leave this vale of tears I do not wish to be greeted by a Hello Motel. Leave these great advances of American know-how to the capitals of the world. I will not trouble my native soil."

"Certainly, Mr. Ensardo," agreed Mr. Smith affably, "Not all locals are suited to Hello Motels. I shall respect your wishes."

As Mr. Smith returned to his seat beside the board chairman of Consolidated Steinmetz, the power conglomerate that lit the eastern half of the American continent through the lower- productivity hours of night, the genial cosmopolitan thought, 'Ricardo will set a Hello Motel on your grave, you senile peasant.'

"Come my good friends," said Mr. Ensardo taking the arms of Talldorf and Small. "We will see democracy in action at the Council meeting of our little town whose good people will be directed and enriched under my roof this night."

And Ricardo's black caravan was roaring along the county highways shattering the twilight. Meadowlarks died of heart attacks, and gravel flew.

Slim Krankoffer, the crooked mayor, waddled from his Mercedes toward Ensardo's door with Mabley Pot's anxious nose bouncing over his shoulder and his words like a dentist's drill shrieking in Harry's brain.

"Off, Mabley, off," groaned Krankoffer, "Don't you see these worries are killing me? You'll be sucking up bucks like an anteater when I'm dead, how do you do it, Mabley? You aren't human. Crazy Ricardo's going to be here, don't give me new troubles to burden me, I beg of you."

"Just this, Slim!" insisted Pot, his narrowing eyes making him look even more like a rat.

Mabley told Harry that he would back him on any vote that favored Mr. Ensardo over the violent faction of Ricardo.

"We know where our interests lie," drilled Pot's voice, "Old Ensardo is our benefactor, Slim, only in old Ensardo lies our safety."

"Right, right," mumbled Krankoffer.

Pot's lids blinked over his sharp eyes with the gaze of the predator as Krankoffer preceded him up the steps to the portico. Pot's health was due to his singlemindedness: he never worried about it. He thought only of money. He thought of the money Ricardo had passed him to betray his old friend Krankoffer.

The electronic gates of Little Versailles were now thrown open for the general amnesty of the monthly Council meeting, one of Mr. Ensardo's favorite hobbies after golf. Cars bearing prominent citizens of Greater Willow Springs trailed up the drive like so many vassals called to the lord's castle.

"It's a privilege, a real privilege, really a privilege —" repeated an occupant of one of the cars to the sanitation engineer of Greater Willow Springs.

"Well shut up about it, will you, Kevin? I didn't say Mr. Ensardo would give you a deal. You talk to him. Don't mention my name. I don't want my neck sticking out. I got my bed made in this town and I ain't getting kicked out of it."

"Yes, certainly, I understand," said Kevin. "But it's such a privilege."

Now that Kevin was at last drawing near to the powerful Mr. Ensardo he could taste and feel the fortune that might be his. Kevin hoped to capture for his new law office legal representation for Mr. Ensardo's organizations across the river in the state of Minnesota through the intercession of his father's old friend, the sanitation engineer of Greater Willow Springs.

"A powerful, a hidden man, a man of many secrets," said Kevin taking a new tack with the sanitation engineer. "A great man in our society. I have followed his activities in the press. It would mean so much to my father if I could represent such a significant client." When Kevin had enthusiastically outlined his plan his father had actually said, "You'd best keep your nose in your own yard, boy, but I 'spect it ain't no use advisin an educated man like yourself."

And innumerable others, for Council meeting nights in summer were a social affair for the citizens of Greater Willow Springs, not one of whom sought the environs of the mysterious Mr. Ensardo without consideration of profit. The ancient Mongol aphorism has it: 'The best guest stays home.'

The auditorium that Mr. Ensardo had constructed for policy meetings with his staff served as the City Council chamber. It was the shape of a piece of pie; the felt-cushioned folding seats were cherry red. And a double-level basement beneath housed the largest arsenal in the state.

Into such a room crowded the eager social world of Greater Willow Springs and, for what they imagined a humorous aside to the day's business, the proud and elite of corporate America. And, in honorarium, seated in the front row before the red carpeted dais and the polished oak table where Mr. Ensardo sat nodding sagely down on them, Talldorf and Small.

"How many cards did you get?" Small asked Talldorf.

"Maybe thirteen," said Rudolph.

"Why don't you say a dozen if it's a guess?" inquired Small.

At this moment a rear door opened and Ricardo Ensardo strode through with eyes gleaming and a thin smile on his lips. More than a ripple of applause welcomed his entrance.

Ricardo was holding his arm aloft, his fingers forming a V-for- victory sign. Murmurs ran through the audience. Mr. Ensardo rose with a smile and embraced his son and they turned to acknowledge the applause with arms raised like political candidates.

Rudolph slid down in his seat at the sight of Ricardo but his legs stuck out so inordinantly that he was sighted immediately. As their eyes met Small watched Ricardo's smile freeze.

"My friends!" said Mr. Ensardo. "And my townspeople, and honored members of American business. To you who may not be so familiar with him I introduce to you my son, Ricardo. Welcome my son and extend to him the honor which you give to me." There was abrupt and strong applause. Ricardo's eyes narrowed scanning the faces, none of whom dreamed that at this moment Ricardo's forces were overwhelming the guard stations around

Little Versailles. Mr. Ensardo made room at the great table for Ricardo between himself and Mayor Krankoffer, who looked sick, and beside him Mabley Pot gazing with undisguised glee at Krankoffer.

With his son, his great failure which denied peace to his days, his cross, his burden and his sorrow beside him at the director's table, Mr. Ensardo opened his heart to the assembly:

"Are you not all my children? Am I not he who made something of nothing, who gave to the people what they wanted? — "

Ricardo interrupted, extending his tuxedoed arm before Mr. Ensardo, "Papa, you are boring!"

Mr. Ensardo's face betrayed his amazement, but with great self-control he continued, his palm raised as if in benediction.

"My children, the abundance of my business has enriched you all. I bare the slander of some who prefer chaos to order — "

"Enough, Papa!" sneered Ricardo, making of his sneer a grin for the assembly. The eyes of Mabley Pot gleamed as though he could see his reward. But Mr. Ensardo continued with great patience, stilling the murmur and nod of executive faces with that raised hand.

"I saw to it that you had what you desired. I have created business where no business existed. I have put many of you in charge of my affairs and you have prospered. Even to you humble representatives of Greater Willow Springs who grew up in drafty farmhouses and now enjoy central heating in your homes. Have I wronged you with these benefits? Speak and tell me if it is so."

A dottering old man who sat beside Small began a feeble clapping of his paper-thin hands which was picked up by others in the assemblage. Small turned to see who applauded: the elder executives. The younger executives appeared stern, even dour.

"Yes, there are those who understand my mind," continued Mr. Ensardo, "who grasp the intention behind it to elevate our children beyond what we have achieved."

"Crap!" exclaimed Ricardo.

A sharp tearing sound of applause cut the stillness, and Ricardo's sneer was on his face. "You got the ball rolling, Papa, but you lost control. All you can do is look back, you and your old fogeys. Now are new days and new ways.

You carry a dull old blade, Papa. I carry a razor. If heads are in the way, they come off."

"Justice, my boy! My principle is justice to all of my children."

"Justice is mine," said Ricardo, "I want ice cream and cake! I want it every day and I'll have it! I want more than you ever knew existed!"

"You see, there is no temperance in you," said Mr. Ensardo.

"I want it all and I want it now!" yelled Ricardo. "I want it all right now!"

"My son, you must calm yourself. We will put it to a vote. Let the proposition be this: That temperance and justice shall guide our affairs, and not undisciplined and ruinous greed. Do I hear a second?"

What was heard was the murmur of the assembly. Ricardo's hard narrowed eyes searched for the face that would dare. Those executives of corporate business whom Mr. Ensardo had made by his genius, who yet belched the abundance of his princely table, glanced from one to the other. The younger executives looked daggers at the elder who meeting such sharp stares bethought themselves and remained dumb in doubt.

"Second it, second it —!" Mabley Pot hissed into the ear of the blanching Krankoffer: "It will make you Ensardo's right hand!" But Harry could not make his lips work or his head raise.

"I'm going to second it!" said Kevin, seated beside the sanitation engineer.

"No you ain't!" hissed the engineer, his hairy hand holding the young lawyer to his seat.

Small expected the feeble old man seated beside him to second Mr. Ensardo's motion and was astounded when Talldorf leaped to his feet and yelled, "I second that!" Small's eyes bulged and the hair prickled on his neck.

"How was that!" said Talldorf to Small. "It was an impulse, Small." Small rolled his eyes at the ceiling and shrunk in his seat.

"Ah yes," smiled Mr. Ensardo. "My honored guest whose business is light."

Ricardo's eyes burned into Small's and Small moaned.

Mabley Pot gazed down at Talldorf like a bird observing a worm. "He did it! He did it, Slim!" hissed Pot. "Who is he? He stole your thunder. You got to back old Ensardo *now,* Slim, or we're lost!"

"Gentlemen, I must protest!" rose the cultivated tenor of Mr. Smith, the creator of Hello Motels World Wide. "Is a mere window washer to have a voice in this august assembly equal with our own?" He laughed shortly, "Be reasonable, gentlemen."

"I third it, I third your motion, Mr. Ensardo," said Krankoffer and wilted into silence under the crazed stare that now shifted from Talldorf to the mayor, and Mabley Pot drew back to show Ricardo the distance between himself and Krankoffer who had said such a damn-fool thing.

"You got a second and even a third," sneered Ricardo. "Now, Papa, put it to a vote." Ricardo turned to the assembly. "I'm giving everybody a vote who sits here. Vote your votes." He chuckled coldly. "And hope you're on the winning side. You who are tired of looking to Papa to throw you a scrap and who are ready to follow me and get it all, vote Nay! And the rest of you—I warn you—there will be no place for you in the new order. You have smelled the change in the wind, and now it is here. I am the new blood, the new voice, the new brains, and the new muscle. I await your votes. Vote. Just for the fun of it." Ricardo sat beside his father, his face impassive, cold and hard as flint.

"So you would take such an inflexible stand, Ricardo," said his father looking at him like a papa who has reached the limits of patience. "You, my own flesh and blood, would stand to oppose me in open revolt."

"Put it to a vote, Papa. I ain't afraid of the democratic process."

The Chief of Surveillance, who had received his payoff from Ricardo, sat calmly in a room not far distant watching what might have been mistaken for a late-night movie as shadows grew into men who dispatched Mr. Ensardo's guards before his eyes. The man turned from the surveillance screen so as not to witness the demise of those who had eaten with him that day at the same table. The assassins relieved the corpses of their weapons and advanced toward the main structure of Little Versailles. Their objective was the arsenal housed in the lower levels of the auditorium, the doors of which were thrown open to their arrival by one who had received Ricardo's money after he had dragged away the body of his fellow guard and dumped him into the shrubbery. The alarm blinking insistent red lights annoyed the Chief of Surveillance who turned away in his swivel chair, removed his automatic from beneath his coat, released, inspected the clip, slapped it again into the butt of the gun and remained at his post as to the orders of his new master.

"Say, my children, what shall it be, aye or nay to our proposition: That temperance and justice shall guide our affairs and not undisciplined and ruinous greed. Who says Aye?"

"Aye!" yelled Talldorf, the man of the people, at once on his feet. Talldorf had sealed their fate. Small stood raising his arm, "Aye!"

"Aye—" sounded the feeble voice of the old man who had risen beside Small. "Aye!" cried Kevin breaking loose from the restraining grip of the sanitation engineer, "Aye, aye, aye—" a chorus rising until it seemed to Small that a clear majority had carried Mr. Ensardo's proposal of reason.

Ricardo's face showed no concern. He pulled Krankoffer back into his chair and told him to shut up and turned to the assembly a face so confident, cold and deadly that hardened executives blanched at its sight. Mr. Ensardo raised his hand bringing silence to the chambers.

"And who says nay?" he asked.

"Nay!" bellowed Ricardo, and nays erupted like gunfire, united and became the voice of the night, Ricardo conducting its desperate insistence with the gun drawn from his coat.

"No, No! My son! This is not the will of the people!"

"This is democracy, Papa!" He turned toward his father and blew Mr. Ensardo out of his chair as the voices of women who had accompanied their prominent husbands from their comfortable homes in Greater Willow Springs rose in a single horrified scream at the spectacle on the dais and the doors to the chamber burst open revealing Miro, Blister, Tony, Maxie and other shades surging from behind as the toughs moved into the chambers slapping the hysterical ones and no man raised a hand to stop it.

Ricardo bent behind Krankoffer's chair and pinched the flabby cheek. "Do I off then, Mr. Mayor, I want to off those two spies of my poor departed father, those dim-witted window washers, I want to blow them away, Mr. Mayor, may I have your permission?"

"Off, off, I say blow blow, yes, Ricardo, you know best, Sir—!"

Small's eyes met those of Ricardo. Talldorf saw in the instant and they dove from their seats as slugs ripped through the backrests. Pandemonium. Pledges of allegiance howled by Ensardo's proponents were denied by the Ricardo faction as guns flashed in the hand of every businessman out of suit coats and tuxedoes and it was Chinese New Year. The rattle of tommy-guns, the reverberations of battle ballooning the walls of the auditorium, ricocheting slugs cracking the cement of the floor where scurried Small in the lead on all fours like a greyhound, stopping only to wave on Talldorf whose red head rammed Small, their collapsing tableau framed at that instant by two bursts of tommy-gun fire sawing up the carpet before and behind.

"THE DOOR!" Small shouted against the din and they scurried as before as bodies toppled left and right.

Krankoffer had lost his mind and pulled his automatic with the intention of assassinating Ricardo but Mabley Pot, his old schoolmate, was an instant quicker blowing Krankoffer out of his chair as a burst of gunfire blew open the doors just as Small flew at them with his head, the very sound of battle casting then outwards into darkness where they rolled on the dew-drenched lawn, regained their feet on the instant in the glow of the open doors of the arsenal from which moved a phalanx of shadows fanning across the lawn, and a tongue of flame leaped out of the night toward them as in timeless dreams from the dragon's jaws, their clothing scorching and the new ivy vines of the auditorium glowing up like sparklers, steaming and hissing and evaporating in a cloud of white smoke as Talldorf and Small, deprived of their shoes by four slugs from an army of Mr. Ensardo's men from the Windy City throwing open car doors, blazing away at the flame-thrower troops with a sound that drowned even the inferno in the auditorium dove, tumbled and rolled through stereophonic crossfire loosing like a ball of yarn untwined bullet-severed threads of pantlegs and shirtsleeves, Small's $2010 sailing up into the consuming tongue of flame which burned city men in their suits like torches before they fell onto the smoking lawn and then the most brilliant light of all turning the woods before their faces to daylight as the long and the little one flew—

"RUN TALLIE!"

and the explosion of the arsenal lifted the roof of Little Versailles from its walls like the lid of a sardine can, the pie wedge of the auditorium rising into the sky, doric pillars tumbling like ten-pins and clean glass sparkling like diamonds before it went out in the dewy lawn, and the force of the blast casting the two far into the woods and the open arms of blackberry vines as bricks, bent spoons, belt buckles and shards of torn squeegee brass, still aglow, fell around them. Small felt the hand of an angel lift him from briary snares as he bounded barefoot through them and Talldorf too felt lifted honing on the course of the bounding Small; together they flew through the darkest wood of their lives, bare skin of hindquarters prickling in the night air for the death that stalked them and the singed hair of their legs like arrow feathers guiding their flight. They came upon the barbed wire and rolled over it, and the high brick wall was nothing, Small leaping onto Talldorf's shoulders, bending, heisting up Rudolph and they dove into the waiting dark, raced across a road into a copse wearing on their bodies only the living velvet cloak of night, Small flying on, scarcely stumbling through the brush amid the trees, down to a stream, slipping on rocks, rolling in the balming waters, stings and scratches and aches barely beginning as they raced up the opposite bank into a wheat-field broad in starlight, and Rudolph amazed to see Small naked as a savage treading on before him, and Talldorf feeling his own ribs and flanks under-standing he too wore not a rag and felt the soft wheat bend beneath bare feet and sucked into his lungs the delicious air of life.

So they traveled all the night wordlessly past dairy cattle, raising their heads from sleep to low at the apparitions, until just before dawn streaked the sky with her bloody finger they crested a rise to look upon the Father of Waters. And here they crouched under the morning star, bare-ass on the bank, gazing on the river endlessly flowing like new-born babes at the begin-ning of time.

Chapter 26

I DON'T KNOW WHAT TIME IT IS

A ndrew Drew stood among the pale tombs with his arms spread and his empty palms skyward. "I don't know what time it is," he said. His gray hair made only dingy by the few remaining dark strands stood out as if electrified. He wore a shiny old plaid sportscoat and his white shirt was open at the throat and his trousers had been slept in.

Small was crouching before Andrew Drew and Talldorf behind him so that it appeared to Andy a two-headed naked man stood before him. He was not surprised. "You don't know what time it is, do you?" Andy asked. The two heads shook. "Are you real or are you spirits?"

"We need pants," said Small. "Two pairs of pants. Can you help us out?"

"Sure," said Andy Drew, "Welcome aboard. You want shirts too?" I'll give you shoes. I'll buy you shoes. I don't care. Were you in a shipwreck? An honest-to-god shipwreck? My god, I've had a shipwreck I could tell you. You guys look like you've been in a war. A war, have I been in a war? Poor Agnes they say. That's all they can say but poor Andy, I say, I mean that poor old bastard Andy Drew, that's me, I'm pleased to meet you, sir," extending his hand to Small who grasped it, still hunched, his eyes burning up into Drew's bloodshot ones. "My name is Small."

"Ta-ta-Talldorf," said Rudolph crouching around Small to touch the hand of Andy Drew.

"Small and Tall?" said Andy Drew. "Come, I'll take you to the shop. We'll have lots of time to get acquainted. We can sit there forever. All the clocks have stopped. I'm ruined. I'm probably dead and don't know it. It's all right with me but I come to bring flowers for Agnes. I think I'm alive and she's dead but who knows. I got no way of telling. I don't know what time it is. Everybody depended on me and now nobody knows and I can't make anything work. They bring them in and in two days they stop. The old Benbow I've had for thirty years and hung over the door of the shop, it stopped. That's what brought on Agnes' heart attack. She said, 'I thought I was dead, Andy!' She thought she was dead when she came in the morning the old Benbow had stopped. Everybody in town was late to work. Problems, ha! They got problems? I know what problems are, I could tell you about problems!"

Talldorf and Small limped behind, from tomb to tombstone like cats following their master on a Sunday walk.

Andy Drew, kindly old soul that he was, took them to his clock shop in the near-by town of Ripple Forks, Wisconsin. Beyond the rippling river, on the other shore, ran Highway 61.

"It's new," said Andy Drew of his shop. "It don't look new but it's new. It's Main Street, isn't it? For thirty years I was on Back Street, fed my family, raised up thirteen kids, fed em all from clock and watch repair on Back Street. Then one of em, Harry, I call him Hank, but he's an important man now — was before his brother, my youngest son Cliff, the D.A., indicted him. Only professional jealousy I told em both but now Hank's waiting trial — God, what day is it? I gotta be there, God knows why. Hank sent me a thousand dollars — wasn't near enough — and told me to take the place in the Tibbs Block on Main Street — this is it, the Tibbs Block — and get the business cranked up so I'd be sure to have something to take care of Mama, that's Agnes, when I'm gone. Now she's gone — funny, huh? Said it was a man's duty to take care of his own, my own son telling me when who was it worked his fingernails off putting him through State U? Me, Andy Drew, that's who, his papa. So we put the down payment on the Tibbs Block and moved in while the remodeling was going on and I lost four grandfather clocks, one of them Grabem's, the banker, and one Sheen's who owns the department store and two of em mine on consignment, dropped a big oak beam on em. Tock himself couldn't have put em back together, missed my last premium on the insurance cause of the shift from Back to Main Street so they weren't insured. Agnes took it hard, ha, you can imagine! So they charged us $2500 more for the redecorating than they said. Two guys looked something like you two, names Little and Long, blew into town calling themselves the American Traveling Fixit Company. Said they done this interior stuff in all the big cities. Long, the little one, was the fast talker — "

"I ain't surprised," said Small through chattering teeth in the back seat of the car.

" — and the long one was named Little, a quiet fellow. They spent most of the day hazin at each other trying to get the other one to do the work but they wasn't lazy about getting their money, half down to start and only worked two days when they dropped the beam on my best clocks and I ain't seen em since. I owe so much money I had to cash in the grave plot next to Agnes and if it wasn't I didn't have a place to lie down in eternal like I provided Agnes through the Mainlawn Perpetual Rest Company, that's a Mainline Trainline company, I'd cut my throat. What time is it? You see? You see it, the Benbow clock? Hangin up there in front of the shop? Four faces on her, might look like black iron and that's what it is, but Imperial design. Says midnight. Or high noon? Shocked Mama to death. It always ran, never had a problem, but I'm so poorly now I can't get up there on a ladder to work on it and I ain't got the money to get it brought down. I suppose it's dead. That's what I say of em when they're not going to run anymore. You can put new springs in em you can get from London, platinum gears, rebuild em all but if you leave one part in from the old clock it won't work I don't care if you take it to Tock himself, that clock's just turned up its toes, its spirit has gone out of it and the hand of man won't make it run no more after its dead. So's Tock, he's dead, God rest him in eternity, Bernard Tock, that's who taught me watch-repair as just a tyke in St. Louis. Tock came from generations of Tocks who got to the dock in time to catch the Mayflower and Tocks took care of the clocks for the Pilgrims and anybody else who was anybody up to the time I apprenticed at Bernard's shop. Many's the Tock clocks the wagon trains took west on the Oregon Trail. Tock clocks ticking across this great nation and me taught by a Tock himself, the last great Tock. There's Tocks left but they don't know what time it is. I don't know what time it is. I didn't sniff it in the wind till Hank got prosperous and all this came down on our heads but the kids are gone to the dogs, and don't I know with thirteen of my own. There's something gone wrong right here in Ripple Forks and it don't make a difference I'm off Back

Street and on Main Street cause my world's gone to hell and everybody in it and I tell you I ain't the only one don't know what time it is."

Old Andy Drew looked into the back seat where Talldorf and Small huddled asleep in opposite corners of the old Ford and, forgetting momentarily, thought them dead bodies, red with scratches and cuts, blue with bruises and cold as they were.

As the morning business had begun on Main Street and he could not wake the naked figures he had met in the graveyard he pulled the Ford into the alley and dragged them in the back door on the dolly he used for grandfather clocks. Since his ancestral home on Washington Street, where he had resided the past thirty years of his marriage, had been repossessed by Grabem's bank Andy slept on the floor in the back room of the clock shop where he laid Talldorf and Small, covered them with a blanket, wandered into the front of the shop, unlocked the door and fancied with a thrill that this could be the day when the Grim Reaper might strike him happily dead like the tickless clocks that stared at him from every shelf, dumb and useless and absurd.

Talldorf and Small slept through the troubled day untroubled by the troubles Andy Drew drew to himself with the surety of one destined to utter destruction. Like wounded soldiers in the comparative safety of the field hospital, so slept Talldorf and Small making undecipherable sounds like those of demons or animals amid the dumb clocks.

Andy Drew at the front door lifted his gaze above the statue of the Union soldier across Main Street where the victory lamp burned to the morning sky above the wide river to see if it was evening when he would shut up his useless shop on Main Street and go again to the cemetery to talk to Agnes. But it was morning and Andy Drew looked down into the freckles and blue eyes of Penny Pool on her rollerskates who was the child of Mike and Sue Pool who had come to Ripple Forks from the Windy City opening a new branch office of Pinchin & Penny Collection Agencies Inc. Sue had married Mike when O'Toole divorced her and Penny, named in honor of Sterling Penny's wife, Penny Penny, at ambitious Mike's insistence, was the first fruit of their prosperous union. She stood chewing bubble-gum with her yellow sausage curls flopping as she held to the door of Andy Drew's clock shop and thrust an envelope at him.

"Penny," said old Andy, hoping against hope, "I don't know what time it is. You've brought me news," and he took the envelope. The little girl was blowing bubbles and clattering to keep her balance. "Penny, what time is it?" Penny shook her head making her curls swing, blowing a pink, sugared bubble.

"God protect you, child," said Andy. "Go away now before I read the bad news." It was a dun from Grabem's bank threatening foreclosure proceedings to be introduced against him by the District Attorney's office of Clifford Drew, Andy's son, all notes to be made payable to Pinchin & Penny Collection Agency Inc., signed by Mike and typed by Sue.

So he wouldn't have to wait long, thought Andy. He'd be thrown into the alley any minute. He put the bad news in his pocket and headed to the alley to move his Ford where already the town constable had hung a parking ticket, loth to stop in to deliver it personally because all old Drew said was, 'I don't know what time it is.'

Andy didn't get to the alley in time to collect the ticket. A semi delivering hot TVs to Sheen's Department Store destroyed his old Ford where it sat. The driver threw her into lower reverse and ground the Ford through the wall of Flem's Bakery.

Sheen and Flem would sit at their separate desks before noon talking to John Sly, the worthless lawyer son of old Guy Sly, Andy Drew's best friend before he died, and institute new suits against Andrew Drew. John's first words were, "What, another one? I don't know what'll be left for you guys but it looks like I'm going to own me a clock shop."

Small wallowed in a nightmare. Small fought an endless war. He was Supreme Commander of Allied Forces and consequently was allowed no peace. His white dress uniform with gold buttons, epaulettes on his shoulders, shiny black boots and golden sword never suffered spot or speck though carnage reigned about. Roaring cannon pained his head, a thousand hoofs of cavalry smashed the earth before his eyes and waves of armies disappeared into waves of armies. He thrashed about for the right chart always a battle behind. If he had just a moment he would know the correct course but a moment would leave him defenseless and he would lose the world and he had not the moment nor ever would.

Andy Drew did not distinguish the demolition of his Ford from any other factor of his morning. He was interested in the structure, laid bare, of the brick wall of Flem's Bakery, how sturdy before, how flimsy and ragged now, crumbled to dust. Before wandering back to his tickless and tockless shop he asked Flem, fat and furious in his white apron covered with brick dust, what time it was. "Time you wake up!" screamed Flem. "You want to ruin us all?"

"I don't know what time it is," Andy informed the truck driver. "It's late as hell," said the truck driver.

"It's time to get up!" said Elinore to Rudolph, "Time to eat! Time for school! It's time for dancing class! It's time for church! You're late, Rudolph! Rudolph, can't you ever be on time?" "Young man," said Red, "It's time you thought about your future." "What time shall the wedding be, Rudolph?" insisted Anne. "Wait! Wait! I'm late," yelled Rudolph running for the bus.

"What time is it?" Andy asked the mailman who appeared at his door.

"Time for the mail," said the mailman. "When you going to get the big Benbow fixed, Andy? Everybody's asking me."

"It's dead," said Andy. "We all have to go sometime. There's a ringing in my ears."

"Are you all right?" asked the mailman.

"I don't know," said Andy. "What time is it?"

He got a letter from his son Peter who was in prison for stealing cars. Peter wanted spending money and twelve character references for the parole hearing. Andy got his income tax forms early because he was among a select number to be honored by audit of the Internal Revenue Service. He got thirteen bills and an overdrawn statement from Grabem's bank. He tore open an official notice from the Department of the Navy which informed him that his triplet sons, Max, Morie and Martin, all seaman last class, were missing in action and presumed dead. He knew the announcement was in error but his mind refused to grapple the issue. Actually Max, Morie and Martin had been isolated in the brig at Okinawa and fed radio-active breadfruit by a crack team of government-funded scientists to test human tolerance for projected limited nuclear warfare in tropical zones and had succumbed. "What time is it?" barked the head scientist as each expired.

Andy unwrapped the monthly book selection that Agnes had ordered and he had no time to reject. It was an explosive best-seller by a Justice of the Supreme Court which proved England was responsible for all problems that America had suffered. It was entitled, *Fuck You Jack*. Wondering about English platinum gears Andy Drew looked in the index for clock. There was no index.

Only curiosity seekers came to the clock shop now, for news travels fast in a small town, and Agnes scarce cold in her grave, dust on the cash register, and Andrew knew the Lord had withdrawn skill from his hands, the magic gone from his fingers and no clock would respond to his cursed touch. People stayed only long enough to add their two cents.

"Your dog, Spot, has been soiling my yard, Mr. Drew," said Miss Miss, the old maid who had lived next door to the Drews for twenty years. "When people move out they should not leave their pets to be another's burden!"

Andy Drew's bloodshot eyes brimmed with tears. "Spot?" he asked. "My old friend, Spot, Miss Miss? I'll come get him. How could I have forgotten? I don't know what time it is. I don't know how to thank you. Have you fed Spot? How is he?"

"He's dead," said Miss Miss. "The vet put Spot to sleep this morning." Andy Drew showed no surprise and Miss Miss stomped away offended.

Mr. Hitt, principal of the Ripple Forks High School came through the door. "Drew!" he said.

"Yes sir, Mr. Hitt. How good of you to stop by. What time is it?"

"Get a grip on yourself, man," said Mr. Hitt coldly. "I wouldn't have stopped in to interrupt your self-pity but I cannot pass by degeneration. I am taking the liberty of revoking your honorary member status in the PTA. I observed you asking little Penny Pool, tender young thing, what time it was. That question from a man of your age to a sweet little girl can be nothing but perverse. Watch yourself, Drew. When one link in the chain weakens it endangers us all. Remember, I am watching you."

"Thank you," said Andy who had no idea what Hitt was talking about but knew it wasn't good. Andrew Drew now accepted what came, looking hopefully for the last face, the last word, blessed oblivion.

Mine had a picture of the moon on the cover. *Death,* a picture of Earth taken from the rocket. *Wink* had a photograph of the President, JFQ, standing handsomely beside that big rocket they shot into the sky and his pretty wife beside him and their little girl in her pink dress. With these Andrew Drew spent the lingering afternoon in the tickless and tockless shop interrupted by nothing more important than an official notice from his draft board that he had been drafted, and locking up the front door at last when twilight came down on the river and rosy red clouds lined the east he put his old plaid hat on his head and remembered that he had no car to visit the cemetery. Then he remembered the two in the back room, Tall and Small, and went to sit beside them in case he might be of some service.

Small's eyes opened on those of Andrew Drew, then Talldorf opened his eyes. "Welcome back, friends," said Andrew Drew. "It is night. That's all I can tell you. I don't know what time it is. There are pants and shirts on the chair for you both. If you're going to get up you're supposed to wear clothes. I don't know why."

Andrew Drew brought them each a glass of water. When they were dressed, long and short versions of Andrew Drew himself, and shod in the cast off shoes of the sons of Andrew Drew they walked out into the Wisconsin night. Drew took them for donuts and coffee in a sidestreet grill.

"This coffee is so good, Andrew," said Small. "If I had a Lucky I couldn't ask for anything more."

"Oh, ask for whatever you wish," insisted Andrew Drew. "Anything I have left is yours, my friends. Could you use a clock?"

Andrew Drew had never been a smoker, but he was willing, and hopeful that the company of his new friends might lead him to the end. He bought a pack of Luckies and the three men sat smoking. The bristles on Small's chin stood out. Out of the ravages of what he had seen glowed a youthful appearance that unnerved Rudolph. Small seemed barely older than himself. "We can go anywhere, Tallie, anytime," said Small apropos nothing. "We're alive."

"That's right," agreed Andrew Drew. "We can go back to the clock shop. But we don't have to go back to the clock shop."

"I could go home," said Rudolph.

"Home..." Small repeated as if a word he had never heard.

Andrew Drew looked at Talldorf and shook his head in disbelief.

"We don't even have a car, Small," said Rudolph. Andrew Drew shook his head again. He puffed smoke looking from one to the other.

"We don't even have underwear," said Small.

"Forgive me," said Andrew Drew. "You can have mine."

"Elinore would still be at home," said Rudolph.

"Where is home?" asked Andy. When Talldorf said Detroit the old man appeared no better informed.

"Should I Small? I could start over."

"Do what you want to do, Talldorf. You're free as a bird," Small answered. "Just don't ask me no more. I can't give no advice because I don't know nothin."

"It's best you stay just like you are, Tall," advised Andrew Drew. "Nobody's got anything except me. I got a lot of dead clocks. It's best to have nothing. No one can take anything away from you. Isn't that nice?"

"Clear sailing," said Small.

"In Detroit—" said Rudolph.

"It don't matter, Talldorf," said Small. "Let's go back to the clock shop."

A dark figure rose up as they neared the clock shop. "Message for Andrew Drew," said the telegraph boy, not knowing which to hand the message to. "Oh, there you are, Mr. Drew. Are these your brothers? You all look alike."

"My brothers—" said Andrew Drew.

They went into the shop and sat on the old mattress in the back room.

"Aren't you going to open your telegram, Andrew?" asked Small.

"Why not," said Andrew. He read it aloud:

> "IT HAS BEEN DETERMINED THAT YOUR PROPERTY ON MAIN STREET IN THE TIBBS BLOCK IS SITUATED ON A VEIN OF HIGH CONCENTRATE URANIUM ORE STOP WE PROPOSE TO PURCHASE YOUR MAIN STREET SITE FOR CONSIDERATION OF $500,000 INCLUDING ROYALTY TO YOU OF 15% AGAINST GROSS YIELD PER ANNUM STOP"

Andrew Drew balled the telegram and cast it from him as if it burned.

"You're rich, Andrew," said Small.

But Andrew Drew had found out the time and turned up his eyes for a greater reward, the happy man he had once been and his well-ordered life merely a dream in the reality of his plunge to destruction. He had done his duty by family and country as had been expected of him, had paid his bills, had kept Ripple Forks on time for thirty years, and time had come to an end.

Talldorf and Small bent near and saw that Andrew Drew was dead. Andrew's face showed no surprise. He looked like he hadn't a care in the world. They straightened him on the mattress and covered him with the blanket. "It's time to go," said Talldorf and Small at the same time.

"There's the bridge, Tallie," said Small. "I'm going on over the river. I guess you'll be goin back to Detroit. It's a nice night. Stars burnin up there and the grass smells good. I guess you'll be snug between the sheets in the mansion in a few days. You won't get hungry there, Tallie."

"I'm not hungry, Small," said Rudolph gloomily. "Where will you be, Small?"

"Where I haven't been before, Tallie."

"Will you send me a postcard once in a while, Small?"

"I'll think about you, Tallie. You've been more than just my partner. You been my friend and I don't hold it against you that you got to go home now that it's hard times. I'm headin west. See that star over the river? That's my star. You go home where you belong and have a good life. Good-bye, old Tallie."

Small turned and headed up the concrete approach to the bridge. His figure with the rolled up sleeves and cuffs receded as the knot grew tight in Rudolph's throat, then Small was gone.

Talldorf broke into a run and ran until at last he saw Small's bouncing form.

"Small!" yelled Talldorf, "Small!"

Small turned and waved him on.

Part Five

MAKE WESTING

Chapter 27

LET'S CLEAN IT UP
MR. PRESIDENT

A|t this time there reigned in the White House the star of the Western World. His ascent had been noted from his birth. He was raised in great capitals of the world in tutelage of his father, prince of commerce and ambassador-at-large, Matthew Quiggley. Sons of royalty, prime ministers and cabinet members were companions of his youth. He was graduated from Oxford and the London School of Economics. At 25 he was elected to the Senate from Massachusetts and Quiggley control of New England was secured.

In the following thirteen years he consolidated his power over the eastern seaboard, gained backing of labor and management as far west as Kansas City, from Florida to New Orleans, and Texas oil interests were his and in a brilliant campaign that could not then have succeeded without his especial magnetism, style and destiny, Justin Freeman Quiggley turned out the rascals, fat and gouty with their war profits, and gave to the nation a springtime of the heart, a deep breath of youth, JFQ nailed to history, the golden lion, the beloved young king.

There were those who said he came of a corrupt house, and there was reason to think it so. But JFQ's magic was upon the land and its people in the palm of his hand. His power base secure, his word was law, and his young brother, Lash Quiggley, heading the Justice Department, was its enforcer. Justin and Lash whipped business interests in line with the President's enlightened view of the welfare of his people. In moments of remarkable feeling he spoke of them as, 'my children'.

As a campaign promise JFQ had forced a token defense budget cut which had brought a stabilization of warfare on the Eastern Front. Lash alone was privy to the burning intent in JFQ's heart to end war and transform the ravaged planet into the garden it once had been. The elder Quiggley, whose conception the king was, retiring into his dotage just before his son's election, would even now condemn such idealism, but Justin was not Matthew's, but Destiny's design which had placed him beyond considerations inferior to justice and peace.

And grumblings were heard in towers of commerce as the war effort was cut and profits cleaved away to budget social and welfare programs. When shown commodities distributed to the poor JFQ said, "Do you mean to tell me people eat this shit?"

In his first thousand days the mask of eastern respectability fell away and JFQ was revealed the mature father of the downtrodden and dispossessed; his carved jaw and tossled red hair, sleek as Jefferson, rugged as Jackson, Lincolnesque in the soft and wise words he spoke to the poor, as stunning in dialectic as the intellectual community might produce, and tall as a redwood.

Let us look into the Oval Office at the White House:

Fedder enters: "Sir, about the pair of workers to accompany you through Nuclear Strike Headquarters—"

"Don't speak to me again about the pair of workers, Fedder, I'll decide when the time comes."

"Yes sir, Mr. President." Fedder withdrew smartly from the presence.

It was no fearful lobbying union worker who had bought the tarnished American Dream who the President sought to speak for America, not the programmed American reduced to balancing taxes and writing checks. JFQ had a dream of what a free worker was: an itinerant who pursued quality. JFQ was trusting to his star to deliver such workers into his hand who would speak for the people at Nuclear Strike Headquarters. He would pick them off the road; he would know them when he saw them.

The President was gazing out the dreary window onto the Rose Garden. The President wanted to drive through the Rose Garden on a tractor pulling a harrow to cleave that symmetry into shiny black lumps awaiting new and vital growth. And, God save the nation from a missed heartbeat, there was that opportunist Harry Lynx Herod, the Vice President, entombed in baby fat at 62, conspiring with that idiot Ink, the gardening engineer. The President thought Ink should be on permanent exhibition in a modern art museum spinning geometric rose gardens on floor, walls and ceilings. The President felt that the custodian Ink family lived on a diet of pencil lead. The Ink family was like a creeping gray mold in the Executive Mansion, and most damnable was the gray fog in the glass of every window in the place.

The President hit a blue button which buzzed and beeped in the limousine, helicopter and pocket beeper of the Advisor for Nation Security Affairs: "Hank? The Boss. I want seven skylights in the roof of the White House, six by ten feet. I want this completed this week. I want light in this cave. Handle this personally, Hank, the Inks won't know until it's done."

"Is that all, Sir?"

"That's plenty."

The Vienna Summit Conference with Russian Premier Sonofavich, lay directly over the horizon. JFQ felt he could hold reins on American business, which holds reins on American foreign policy and so on the military, until world opinion could hail his policy as the salvation of the modern world and establish it in fact. No one was privy to this momentous plan but JFQ and Lash, and ICE.

Under the perennial gloom of the sky of Moscow Premier Sonofavich slapped his palms together and his laughter boomed across wide parquet floors of the Kremlin's Square Office and his florid cheeks jiggled.

"Does young American eagle come to my hand with innocence of dove?" asked Sonofavich, who anticipated no answer save his own, and therefore received none. "Then will I not bite off his head?" which amused Sonofavich so that his laughter shook the walls.

ICE was controlled by the apostate forces which would never enter into policies of light. Aware of the ultimate threat, JFQ's enemies would take steps to prevent his stride toward peace. Their bulldog was Chief of Staff, General Croesus LeMight, who had crushed the enemy on the Eastern Front, the Western Front, the Northern Front, and the Southern Front, who barked doggerel commands from a world of his own, whose cold shoulder several presidents had felt and whose surgically-cold, scalpel-sharp mind divided ligament and muscle of military might on a global corpus he considered his own to divide at will among whom he chose. ICE itself was powerless to kill General LeMight because he was the only man in the western world who knew what was happening militarily. General LeMight was sixty years old and looked forty, could kill a man half his age with one swing of his bearlike arm, he felt twenty and expected to command until he was one hundred which would allow him forty more years when the world would have forgotten the pink-tea and cookie ideals of that nit, JFQ.

It was JFQ's intention to put General LeMight out of work.

When intelligence reached General LeMight in Nuclear Strike Headquarters of JFQ's proposed Summit sellout LeMight had clambered into the cockpit of his X-666 supersonic jet interceptor fighter and flown into Andrews Air Force Base, commandeered a chopper and swooped onto the lawn of ICE Headquarters, stomped into the Director's office, took him by his arm from the presence of two Senators and marched the Director out under a cherry tree which the General's chopper had denuded, sat the Director in the blossoms and raising a finger drew it across his own great throat.

"I want the sonofabitch dead!" said General LeMight.

"Premier Sonofavich?" asked the Director with alarm.

"Not that sonofabitch, you dimwit, the other sonofabitch! The President! Kill him. That's an order!" General LeMight strode off toward his chopper baring his teeth at his chronometer. For a dollar he would strafe the Oval Office. Let JFQ make his publicized visit to Nuclear Strike Headquarters. No policy would be made by a dead man.

Meanwhile, Talldorf and Small, alive though reduced to nothing but the clothing they wore less underwear without which they felt they inhabited a free world of birds and wind and were not loath to sit in green grass when they tired of walking down chirruping gravel roads of Iowa between cornfields out under the blue sky, prospered in all that came to them. Each day took them further west.

They slept where they found themselves, at the roadside, with the warmth of the other beside him on a bed of leaves joyously surprised each morning by sun and bird song and life that blossomed in them after the dark night. They slept in fields and hay lofts and under trees beside streams, in cemeteries, and in feather beds when farmers hailed them from the road in twilight. No thought of war nor the great concerns of men troubled their minds. Rudolph said that it must have looked like this a thousand years ago under the morning sun. Never did they go longer than a day without a meal. And how good it was when the farmer's wife asked, "Three eggs? Four? Here is some bacon and ham. The coffee is ready. Could you eat some potatoes?" setting this before them in its rich aroma, and more, piles of toast, and cookies to brighten their eyes, and then they sat on the porch while the farmer smoked his pipe and talked.

The only baggage they carried was an old razor, a bar of soap, a toothbrush—which they shared after Small decided to use it one morning and after Rudolph recovered from his initial unbelief and revulsion; it was no worse he decided than sleeping side by side in a ditch, and rather brotherly—and a tobacco pouch given to them by an old farmer. So they walked down country roads west, waving to those they passed who waved again to Talldorf and Small.

"I never knew it felt so good to get out of a car, Tallie. May the old scarlet Studie rest in pieces."

"I like walking, Small. I could walk forever. I'm learning the names of all the crops. I didn't know what oatmeal was made out of before."

"I don't care what they look like before they're on my plate, Tallie. But I'm happy all this stuff is growing up around us, it's real comfortable."

They stopped in the afternoon for a smoke in the shade of a tree. "These roll-you-owns don't look like much," said Small, "but I like em better than Luckies and it's half the price. Even when I'm rich I'm gonna roll my own."

Small laid on his back with his ankles crossed and the plaid hat of the late Andrew Drew tipped over his eyes while he smoked and looked far into the blue sky and was content while Rudolph tasted stems and leaves of plants or studied the world of insects.

They chopped wood for farmers' wives and carried slop for hogs and corn for cows and shoveled grain from silos, not as irksome tasks but with joy in the vitality of their muscles.

"This is the life!" Talldorf often said, breathing deeply and stretching his arms to the sky. But Small's nose twitched and his green eyes narrowed when they neared a town. He was always looking over his shoulder and around at people and storefronts as though calculating.

Small would search out a cafe where they would take their ease over coffee and donuts. Invariably they fell to talking with townsmen or the waitress and Talldorf fell ever deeper in love with the common people. And yet he was not sorry to leave the towns behind and enter again the farmlands where the miracle of nature came to the roadside to greet them.

"In here," Small said one day and ducked into a hardware store where he talked the owner into exchanging two buckets and two squeegees of inferior quality for washing the windows.

"They ain't much, Tallie, but now we're back in business. I can't stay on vacation forever."

"I'd like to live in one of these little old frame houses out on the edge of town, Small, and belong to these good country people. They'd say, 'Look, it's Talldorf, our neighbor — Look, it's Small, the president of the window washing company.' We'd know everyone by their first names."

"Everybody knows your business in a small town, Talldorf. We're headin for Omaha, I need a little action."

"Small, I won't live in a city ever again."

"We'll just be passing through, Tallie. I ain't stopping till we get where we're goin."

"It would have to be Paradise to be better than Iowa."

"Then Paradise is our objective. Ain't my star led you into this wonderful poverty and anonymity where everything we need falls into our hands for free? But I'm too young to retire. We got buckets and squeegees again. Small is lookin to the heights, Talldorf."

Their first pay was a ten-dollar job at a roadside cafe with a gas pump out front. Small was jubilant. They were finishing up the two plate glass windows when sirens pierced the peaceful morning. Motorcycle cops skidded to a halt before the cafe followed by a sleek black limousine casting gravel, and a caravan of vehicles jamming up behind the limo. Rudolph, intent upon a perfect job, continued dusting a streak with his fingers. Small stood eyeing the lines of the sleek automobile with tinted windows, the exact type he had often imagined himself riding in. The owner and customers and a little yellow pup spilled from the cafe door.

Two impeccable young men with blond hair emerged from the limousine and surveyed the area, their eyes passing over Talldorf and Small and on toward the crowd at the cafe door. Other men, taut as whipcord, emerged from the other vehicles.

"Back off!" yelled a burly motorcycle cop, dismounting, and waving his black leather arms. "You guys! Out of that flower bed, back off from the limousine. Move, you rummies!"

Talldorf was stepping away but Small grabbed his arm.

"Talldorf! This is the biggest job of our lives! That's JFQ himself in there, the President of these United States!" and Small yelled, "Let's clean it up, Mr. President!" and slopped the windshield with his window brush as the motorcycle cop hit him in a flying tackle. The cop held Small down while Small pounded his helmet with his window brush. "You ape! Take off that tin badge I'll wipe up the county with you!" The wolf faces of Secret Service agents ringed the limousine and Small was lifted to his feet by one of the blond young men.

"Peace!" said JFQ himself, stepping from the phaeton. "Can't we even have peace in Iowa? Unhand this man. You are a window washer," charged the President. At the glance of those blue eyes Small saluted with his squeegees and stared fixedly at JFQ's golden eagle tie pin.

"A. Small, Your Excellency, President of Complicated Maintenance, and my lieutenant, R. Talldorf."

"Rudolph, Sir —" said Talldorf, awed by the man he would serve to the end.

"Itinerants, Your Excellency," continued Small holding his salute, "Fly-by-nights spreading light through the great garden of your peril-beset empire, at your service. Request permission to wash your windows, free of charge, Your Highness."

"Individuals! Casey Jones lives! Your country welcomes your services. Put some light in that black box I'm getting stiff in and wait for me here."

Bending to pat the yellow pup and greeting the open-mouthed owner at the door JFQ disappeared into the cafe.

"We're gonna wash the windows at the White House, Talldorf! We've reached the top! The President of the United States has seen the quality of our work."

"What a wonderful man, Small! Truly a great man! He *is* as tall as a redwood!"

"He ain't, Talldorf. He ain't as tall as you, I just seen him."

They washed and squeegeed, they ragged the edges and left not a streak while Secret Service agents peered over their shoulders, onto the roof and into the trees as if tomorrow might be discovered and disarmed. The President emerged from the cafe with a newspaper folded under his arm holding a cardboard tray of carry out coffee. "Talldorf and Small," he said.

Small snapped to attention.

"I need you men with me today. The windows are wonderful. Will you come?"

"Certainly, Your Highness!" snapped Small.

"Knock off that Your Highness business," said JFQ. "Let's move out!"

Climbing into the padded gloom after the President they met with the expressionless face of Lash Quiggley, the Attorney General, and beyond the separating glass forward the khaki hat of the colonel who was their driver and two sleek blond heads, the chosen knights of the king's service. The car roared ahead and Small was tumbled into the seat beside the President.

"You got your bucket, Talldorf?" and seeing he had, "These are rotten squeegees, Your Honor, but at the moment Talldorf and me are at the ebb, sir, of our worldly fortunes."

"Aren't we all," said JFQ, handing out the coffees. "But we will turn America around, Small. She will again lift her face to the sky. Colonel," said JFQ into a microphone, "Radio Omaha that we won't be stopping. The workers who will accompany me are with me now.. Also, I want two sets of professional window washing squeegees, best quality, two buckets and two window brushes delivered to us in transit," and turning to Talldorf and Small, "A worker must have his tools."

The President sat with one leg draped easily over the other, in contrast to Lash who sat with his elbows on his knees peering sharply ahead.

"You may recognize Lash, my brother."

"Talldorf and Small," said Lash extending his hand. His smile was dazzling. "My privilege." Immediately Lash peered again straight ahead with that sharpness in his eyes.

JFQ explained that two workers were to accompany him on a highly publicized inspection tour of Nuclear Strike Headquarters as representatives of America's work force, that every union had pressured for its representatives to be the chosen, but that he had hoped to find itinerants still roaming the back roads of America.

"That's us, Mr. President," affirmed Small.

"Call me Justin," said JFQ. "That's my name. Your self-reliance is priceless to me. Is it a good life you gentlemen lead?"

"It gets better and better, Your Honor—I mean, Justin. Not financially—Talldorf! We didn't get the ten bucks for the job we just did!"

Lash looked at them with wonder then again peered forward.

"Today you are on the government's payroll," said JFQ.

"Yes sir, Justin," said Small. "Me and Tallie don't need much, a place to sleep, a meal a day—we always work that up."

"You have no families?"

"Just each other, Justin. Tallie has been my partner so long we're brother's now."

"But we have many brothers, Mr. President," said Rudolph.

"Justin—" corrected JFQ kindly.

"Yes sir, Justin. All of the people we have known in our travels, these are our brothers and our family."

"All the peasants of your empire share with us," said Small. "They know everybody gets hungry."

I knew it was so!" JFQ exclaimed to Lash. "The heart of the people is sound. Now, tell me, how do you feel about nuclear warfare?"

"I'm against it, Justin," said Small.

"It is inconceivable that the mind of man should conceive such weapons of destruction, Sir Justin," said Rudolph. "It is shameful that my country tolerates tactics of terror."

"I keenly feel this shame, young Talldorf," said JFQ. "It is my wish that you voice your views of what we are about to witness at Nuclear Strike Headquarters to your countrymen. I urge you to be candid in your observations. If you have questions ask the generals. Remember, even General LeMight, the Chief of Staff, is not your superior but your servant and sworn protector."

Meanwhile, at Nuclear Strike Headquarters, somewhere under the innocent Nebraska wheat fields, preparations went apace for the President's visit. *MINE*, *DEATH* and *WINK* had positioned their celebrity reporters,

Tom, Dick and Harry, and TV networks had their mobile units and heavy-weight anchormen on the spot. The Special Security Police of FIB, in this instance commanded by Boris Dirk of ICE in direct command of General LeMight, outnumbered the media and the President's party thirteen to one. Boris Dirk was to walk on the President's left hand deferring only to General LeMight. When intelligence was received that Lash Quiggley was accompanying his brother, Boris Dirk suggested he break the Attorney General's legs and so remove him from the picture at which General LeMight laughed uproariously, spittle clinging to the shaggy ends of his mustache.

"No, no, Dirk, how tactless you Ivy Leaguers are. It is no doubt the anxiety of the bomb that stirs your brutish passions. Leave Lash to me! I will elbow him aside. There will be no doubt in the President's mind who commands here. I anticipate no trouble with the Bobsy Twins from the White House."

The motorcade sped through Omaha and west into open country and Talldorf and Small were presented from the hand of JFQ new buckets, window brushes and three each of the finest squeegees either had ever seen: arrow-straight black rubber blades in brass that gleamed like gold, the handles engraved with the Great Seal of the President.

Small settled easily in the seat. "Justin, I think you should sack General Mork on the Western Front. I seen the map in Mine Magazine and Mork had no business relying on cannon at Krinkle Pass. He should have been mobile but he sat down in his rocker."

JFQ's eyes brightened. "That is correct under the circumstances you project, Small, but Mine Magazine chooses its facts to serve the world of dark materialism. Mork failed to attack in the monsoon months and munitions sales fell thirty-four percent. Thus Mork lost his usefulness to the dark powers. Mork secured the pass with cannon while flourishing a light enticing action of cavalry to draw the enemy to the trap but they would not be deceived and Mork's troops were not firing a shot."

"Mork could have ferried troops by sea from Bezerum to rail terminals at Fabawh or Tesin," said Small, "and come onto the plateau from the north. They could have bottled the Third Tartar Division right through Krinkle Pass."

"Astute!" commented Lash peering straight ahead.

"Priceless," mused JFQ, "Exactly as I saw it, Small. How is it that a window washer has such a keen grasp of tactics?"

"Also I got a keen grasp of strategy. Now on the Northern Front you got General Mukluk—"

"Starbuck," corrected the President.

"The guy with the frosty beard and those boots. It must cost a million a month to supply that outfit on the ice."

"Two point eight million," said JFQ.

"Pull him out, sir, he's a publicity gimmick."

"When people are starving within a mile of the White House I do not miss the irony. He will go when I crack the back of the nuclear conglomerate. The Inks are great fans of General Starbuck—"

"Ach!" commented Lash, "The Inks!"

"The Inks are the White House window washers, aren't they, Justin?" asked Talldorf.

"Yes. Since 1840 the nation has been cursed with Inks. I gaze upon the world through the sloppy, degenerative work of the Ink family. That inky light obscures the great issues of the American people."

"Forgive me, Justin, but the Inks may not be bearers of light," suggested Talldorf.

"The Inks are not workers in clarity," said Small, "which is the first duty of the window washer, Justin."

"The Inks are morose, slow, and heavy of foot," said the President.

"A true window washer is light of foot, Justin. The very best can float. My own teacher, Short, floated a lot."

"Do you mean levitate?"

"Yes Sir," said Rudolph, "Snowball can fly, I think. he works in Wisconsin."

"I see by your eyes that you speak the truth, young Talldorf," said JFQ. "God willing, the day will arrive when such angels of noble crafts again adorn the White House and the stain upon us is removed. Look out your clean windows at the golden wheat fields. What irony that such glory conceals Nuclear Strike Headquarters."

Electric eyes, cameras, recording and warning devices had been winking, buzzing, blinking the tale of the motorcade's approach for the last twenty miles. General LeMight poured a trail of cigar smoke as he paced between columns of FIB Special Security Police standing with expressionless faces, and Boris Dirk sniffing the approach of the Presidential Party on the very ether was so intense a match might have ignited on his predatory flesh.

"You are certainly well-guarded, Justin," observed Rudolph as they watched black leather jackets of motorcycle squadrons flying before them.

"Ah no, young Talldorf," said JFQ. "If someone wishes to kill a man he will find the means. And yet it makes no difference. No mortal has power to end men's lives. Power resides in the impulse to virtue, there only is power to be found, to nourish the vine, the man with the watering can, the sower of seeds. That is why General LeMight and the force he represents will not prevail."

So when the limousine halted and JFQ stepped out under the blue Nebraska sky to perceive his doom in the eyes of General LeMight the young President smiled and went to shake the General's hand while cameras of the media fed the scene to the nation.

Small carried his empty bucket over his arm and Talldorf carried his in his hand and the new squeegees gleamed from Small's belt and Talldorf's pockets. As bands struck up 'Hail To the Chief' Small imagined the martial music played solely for himself and realized the great JFQ beside him with something like surprise.

General LeMight welcomed them as American workers to consider the technical excellence represented by Nuclear Strike Headquarters, and abruptly turned his broad back. Since the General stood on JFQ's left, Small moved to the President's right to stare up at the General who was astounded to see him in that proscribed location.

"Get out of there!" hissed Boris Dirk of ICE. "Nobody stands on the President's right!"

"Buzz off, Mac, I'm the President's advisor."

Noting the General's frown the President turned to see Small, and aware of the little man's unfamiliarity with protocol laid a kindly hand on Small's shoulder and turning gathered Talldorf in his left arm.

"We won't stand on ceremony here, General. What do you think of Nuclear Strike Headquarters, Small?"

"Not many windows," said Small.

General LeMight hated Small instinctively the second he saw him. He looked at the other — what the hell were they, window washers —? The President was standing for pictures with the two fools. The red-headed stringbean reeked of something like earth or wind and hung at the President's left as they moved between rank and file of military guards at attention allowing no room for Le Might, and the midget on the President's right – unheard of – strutting like a demented cock. Dirk looked like he could kill.

"Get hold of yourself," LeMight hissed, "The entire nation is watching your mug on TV. You can break their legs when this circus is over."

Small appeared to be on wheels, so swiftly did his short legs fly as he matched the swift strides of JFQ. Lash Quiggley strode on the left of Talldorf while General LeMight and Boris Dirk trailed ignominiously at their heels followed by rank and file of military brass and a gaggle of gray Senators.

Walter Smilerite's fatherly face and familiar mellow voice told the nation from their TV sets: "We have clarification on the names of the two the President has chosen to represent the workers of this nation whose labors have gone into this remarkable technical achievement of Nuclear Strike Headquarters that we are viewing today ... These are window washers, we are told. The tall young man who might be mistaken for a relative of the President is one Rudolph Victor Talldorf. The short fellow, walking against all protocol on the President's right hand – though this doesn't seem to disturb Mr. Quiggley – is – A. Small. I can't say at this point what A. stands for."

"AAAAIIIIEEE! – " howled Small's old nemesis, Bill, the Executioner who was standing in his black leather jacket before his TV set in the Windy City. "You are one of them, Alexander! AAAAIIIIEEE! Kill Kill Kill!" Bill snatched his Mauser automatic from the arsenal beneath his bed and shot Small off the TV screen.

Old Joe Talldorf walked up to the bar holding his pool cue. "He's a window washer just like you, Joe. Smilerite said his name's Rudolph Victor Talldorf." Joe sunk in a faint into the sawdust.

"Oh! Al! Al!" cried old Mrs. Deerly before her TV set in the Windy City. "It's Smally and Tallie walkin with the President. Bless their hearts!"

Across the Windy City in a highrise with a dazzling view Elvira emitted a choking sound and sank into a beanbag chair before her color TV.

The TV cameras panned fields of golden grain where only the curious windowless concrete structures showed the work of the hand of man. "Ah, if this were only smellevision," smiled Walter Smilerite. "What an aroma here in the midst of America's heartland. But now to the heart of the matter."

Steel doors closed across the camera view as the Presidential party descended into the bowels of the earth. No Mount Vernon this, airy on a hilltop, no palace of spires pointing to heaven but a subterranean bunker like children dig in vacant lots from which to spy on a scary world.

"I used to live in a basement, but I moved," commented Small in the silence of the elevator's plummeting descent.

"Concrete walls twenty feet thick sheeted in steel plating at intervals of thirteen inches. We can take a Richter reading of eight epicentered directly under foot and a direct hit above and still be in control," opined General LeMight over the President's shoulder.

"Of what?" asked Small.

General LeMight ignoring the question lifted his heavy jaw above the President's shoulder and scowled at the ceiling plates of the elevator.

"Answer the question, please," came the sharp voice of Lash Quiggley.

"Of *what?*" echoed JFQ himself, turning his head. "The workers of America ask you, General. What is your answer?"

"We will be in control...of the situation," said the General. The doors slid open.

The cameras received the Presidential party in sterile artificial light, and heels clicked down a glistening hall, at last a sharp turn, another, white-booted guards with white helmets, rifles at present-arms backing away, doors parting onto a gigantic balcony overlooking an amphitheater whose towering concave wall was a map of the globe glittering with colored lights. Men in military uniforms conducted frenzied activity below as if on the floor of a stock exchange under the light so bright it might be mistaken for the light of day. Though the arched ceiling was far above, Rudolph tended to duck as if intimidated by the amazing scene. But Small stood tall and his chest seemed to expand.

"We are to view for the first time ever on national television," smiled Walter Smilerite, "simulated nuclear warfare. Let us hope this is as near as we ever come to reality."

"I hope they don't get their wires crossed," many million Americans said simultaneously.

JFQ invited his fellow Americans to ponder well what they were about to witness.

The lights of the mezzanine dimmed and human faces darkened so that the global map might stand out in bright relief, a bizarre inverse conception of a world not unlike a pinball machine where cities, airdromes, submarine bases and fleets at sea were *US* or *THEM*, and every one was a target. Immediately swift trails of lights flew like medieval flights of arrows spanning oceans and Nebraska throbbed up with red light just as Blinz in eastern Asia erupted. On the great scoreboard under *US* and *THEM* target names lit up, *Dollar Cost,* and *Body Count* multiplying, parlaying by thousands and hundreds of thousands as Europe took fire from central Asia and the Middle East burned like a torch, and all of North America was ablaze, the yellow face of China flaring, Japan a red gash in the blue sea, the entire world a flashing blood-red glow lighting the chamber like the inside of Jack-the-Ripper's skull as the wisdom of General LeMight maintained *Dollar Cost* lower under *US* and drove Body Count higher under *THEM* until the lights of Asia flickered and died pestered only by gnat-like lights of our remaining fleets nibbling debris along the coast of the Eastern world and triumphantly,

VICTORY...VICTORY...VICTORY...

blinked above *US* with half the population of earth written off in the little lights of *Body Count*.

Light grew up in the War Room. General LeMight's face beamed like that of a child who has emulated adult behavior.

"Pitiless", spoke the resonant voice of JFQ into the silence wrapping the nation, that held even Walter Smilerite dumbfounded.

"General, turn off that ridiculous sign."

But General LeMight stood galvanized by the fantasy of his glory, uncaring even that the enemy had taped it and at this instant fell to analyzing the supposed errors that put out their lights.

"You see? Victory!" said the General, "Victory!"

"General!" smote the voice of JFQ. "Turn off the sign!"

An aide moved forward to the table of a console. The *VICTORY* sign went out.

"My opinion of what we have witnessed here will soon be known in clear and unmistakable detail," said JFQ to the television cameras, his face and voice resolute. "But now I defer to two of your fellow countrymen, window washers by trade, whose labors compliment our own for a better or worse

America. Mr. Small. Feel free to voice your thoughts on what we have seen here."

A. Small stepped out on his short legs, locked his hands behind his back and, looking up from the corner of his eyes at the indignant eagle face said, "General, give me one sane reason for maintaining nuclear strike capabilities."

Where the pride of General Croesus LeMight began in this life one might wonder. With his first victories on the battlefield? As he stood at the first of his class at West Point? Or perhaps the day when in short pants little Croesus took away the ice cream cone of tiny Timmy Weeker and pushed him into the sticker bush? And yet pride often seemed the very nature of A. Small. What match then was General Croesus LeMight for Small? What match down the ages is the pretender for the Commander history records. When, confronting Napoleon, the Admiral of the fleet dared lay his hand to his sword Napoleon stepped forward unarmed. Now, with all his might General LeMight blazed from his wide shoulders his ten silver stars and the flaming braid of his hat and the dazzling medals on his mighty breast and his looming powerful frame and his fierce visage with drooping mustaches like funeral wreaths for the world and his rapier black eyes at the little window washer who would not go up in smoke.

An icy finger of fear tickled the core of General LeMight as he read judgment in the green eyes.

"General, the man you must answer stands before you."

The open palm of the President indicated the abominable window washer. General LeMight grinned like a sickle.

"Victory!" he swore.

"How is it that you mistake victory for annihilation, General?" snapped Small. "How is it that an American general has risen so high on such faulty footing? If one bomb is fired it will bring ashes on our heads! So suicide is the sole use of the nuclear arsenal. Is this the way to run a war, General?" Small paced the mezzanine, his hands locked in the curious position behind his back. "Have you forgotten your predecessors, General, who paid with their heads for their failure of the people? You claim the honor of a soldier. How long General LeMight, since you marched with your troops? How long, General, since you kept your seat on horseback with smoke in your face and peered in the eyes of the enemy you slew? You are a soldier, General?"

General LeMight ground his molars and narrowed his eyes.

"Do uncallused fingers that play with plastic buttons presume to point the destinies of red-blooded men? Do you imagine that my countrymen with dirt beneath their nails care for the prattle of statistics from your stock exchanges of greed and death? Your policies, General, want not alone genius but sanity. Your tactics are ashes. Need I mention the Columbian Expedition? Or your disastrous strategy at Biarritz?"

The eyes of General LeMight closed to take comfort at the vision of the riderless black horse with empty boots backward in the stirrups and the mournful beat of the funeral drum which he could almost hear.

"The People's Advocate raises hard points for the General," whispered Walter Smilerite into his microphone," The Columbian Expedition, Biarritz, campaigns that were less than glorious for General LeMight. The President holds his peace. The General's demeanor is one of fortitude. I say, what is Lash Quiggley, the Attorney General doing there? It appears he is attempting to serve a subpoena on the unidentified man with the Presidential party..."

"Get away!" demanded Boris Dirk of ICE, backing away from the piece of paper.

"My," said Mrs. Deerly in the Windy City, "Isn't Smally telling that general some things, Al? I hope the boys don't get in trouble. Don't you think Rudolph is handsome, Al, just like a regular prince there beside the President."

"I mean we were going to be *married*, Windsor," cried Anne in Detroit. "And here he is with the President of the United States! I might have lived in the White House! No, Windsor, not the little ugly one, the tall handsome one beside the President!"

"That-a-way, Small! Tell the fat bastard where to get off!" yelled O'Toole at his color television set in a plush office looking as though Ricardo Ensardo's tailor had fitted his rich clothing.

"I was scarcely more than a boy," continued Small, "when I marveled at your charge of the Night Brigade in a sandstorm uphill on a moonless night, General. Your policies continue to display foolhardiness. Your policies are death in the mask of victory. They will not be tolerated by myself or by my countrymen . And if indeed soldier you are, I advise you to remember that you are merely an instrument of man's destiny, and not its arbiter."

General LeMight stood at rigid attention as he had been taught.

Small lifted his palm to the electrified map of the globe: "Unplug it, Mr. President, it profits us nothing."

"Is this then in reality the voice of the people?" asked judicious Walter Smilerite. "Surely we shall learn more of that in days to come. But we would seem to register one negative vote by this Mr. A. Small. Hark! The President turns to the tall window washer — bucket in hand — Mr. Rudolph Victor Talldorf."

"I wonder, Mr. President," said Rudolph Victor Talldorf, "if my humble opinion of such mighty doings can be of any consequence?" JFQ looked with kindly encouragement on this upright young man. "I defer to the judgments of Small on such matters as the direction of great events and which way to go and I believe he has spoken eloquently. But, Mr. President, I think one can't trust the light here. It feels like the inside of a mushroom. I am reminded of the morgue in Ford Hospital. It would clearly be shameful for us to cause such sorrow to befall our world." Talldorf swallowed, but his head was high.

"Terrible, it's a terrible business, Rudolph, dear — " said old Mrs. Deerly to her television set.

"Ooooh — " murmured Cynthia, the lab technician, who had melted at the sensitive face of Rudolph on her TV screen after the fire of Small had stirred her. I could never choose between them! She did not voice these feelings because of the young intern on the couch beside her with his hand on her thigh.

In Detroit, the wife of Rudolph's Uncle Adair cried: "He's famous!" Uncle Adair crushed his beer can: "He's a goddamned traitor!"

"Mr. Quiggley appears pleased with the two representatives of America's work force," explained Walter Smilerite, "And now the President of the United States places his hands on their shoulders posing for photographers. Hi, down there, Tom, Dick and Harry," said Walter in his downhome way. "Those are the well known reporters of Mine and Death and Wink of course. General LeMight appears grave. Lash Quiggley has pinned that paper to the suit of the unidentified man."

"It's on video tape, Dirk," said Lash Quiggley "I'll see you at the hearing."

Boris Dirk's expression nearly set even Lash Quiggley back on his heels. With his back to the cameras Dirk ripped the subpoena off his lapel and showed Lash where he stuck it, wadded into a ball inside his shoulder holster.

"That's ten more years," said Lash who was not to be trifled with.

I'll dance on your grave too, considered Boris Dirk of ICE who was also enraged at that midget strutting around shooting off his mouth at the General. Dirk wanted to hang the midget traitor in thumb screws. He would be on their heels the moment this was over.

General LeMight grinned like the grim reaper as he guided the Presidential party from station to station of death, the Retaliatory Strike Room, unmanned and dusty, and missile silos below golden grain fields. General LeMight was determined to preserve his image of magnanimity for the TV record in face of what would appear a direct attack from the Administration on national defense. And of course the President was as good as dead. Somehow, sometime he would see the vile midget who had dared to cross him throttled.

Premier Sonofavich was laughing joyfully as he gazed at the television monitor in the Kremlin's Square Office. "The General LeMight is a fool," commented Sonofavich to the assembled shadows in attendance upon him. "He allows us to tape his War Room. And the young President is the greater fool to imagine the might of my fist will not crush idealism like an egg."

JFQ strode through the subterranean halls past horrors he would defuse for the people of the world at the Summit Conference with Premier Sonofavich. To JFQ these diabolical instruments of destruction were fossils from some antediluvian age of mania more horrible than iron maidens because they were spawn of bloodless, heartless theoreticians, a race he foresaw doomed as the dinosaur, for it was his mission to lead his children toward light and in his heart was the deathless confidence that Good would prevail.

"Enough, General," said JFQ. "Take us topside, I will have the light."

Confident that the President's light would soon be extinguished General LeMight led them to the surface.

"What a snake!" yelled O'Toole at his color TV as General LeMight blinked reptilian in the sunlight. "Stomp him, Small!"

They breathed deeply the sweet aroma of the breadbasket of America. Flags whipped and drums rolled, bands played and JFQ strode with Talldorf on his left and Small on his right between honor guards. When the President turned to receive the salute of General LeMight he read again his doom in the General's eyes and JFQ smiled.

"I promise you, General, we shall meet again."

As the sun sinks into the west we bid goodbye to Nuclear Strike Headquarters. A ball of red fire sinks into fields of golden grain; it is an ocean of blood, it is an other-worldly radiance of golden light. The motorcade flew like a flight of arrows into the crown of oncoming night, into the rising star-studded sky of the east toward Omaha Air Force Base where awaited Air Force One.

"Do you fly directly to the Summit, Justin?" asked Rudolph.

"Directly," said JFQ, " after addressing the Teamster's convention in the Windy City."

Was it the chill of the Windy City that now touched Talldorf and Small to the bone or was it the dark road that lay before them?

"We'll leave you at the next highway north, Justin. Tallie and me figure to hitchhike into the Black Hills and the Badlands."

"The *Paka Sapa* and the *Maka Sica*, Small, as the Oglala named them. The Sioux have shared the beauty of their lands with me. Please bare to my red children the regard of my heart."

JFQ spoke into the microphone then jotted onto a card that bore the Great Seal a telephone number of thirteen digits and handed the card to Small.

"When I return from the Summit you can reach me by this direct line. I want you to clean the White House windows. The Inks must go. We will enjoy some fireside chats and you will tell me more of the hearts of my people. Ah—the red light, the Colonel slows, our parting is at hand. How dark is the night beyond these clear windows, but the stars shine brightly."

"If you gentlemen ever need a lawyer, feel free to call on me," said Lash Quiggley.

Talldorf and Small stepped into the night of a farmland crossroad where the winking lights of the motorcade glimmered feebly against the immense darkness.

"Examine your squeegees carefully," said JFQ. Small saluted, but JFQ reached out and took their hands in his own. "My friends," he said and then he was gone and with him the lights of the motorcade swallowed by the night as if they had never existed.

"May God guide that great man on his mission," said Talldorf.

Small lit a match. He was examining his squeegees.

"Holy smoke!" said Small. "There's a rolled up Grant in the handle of each of my squeegees. Check yours!"

They sat in gravel beside the pavement smoking roll-your-owns with $300 in their pockets.

"I'm going to like washing the windows at the White House, Tallie. We'll flood the nation with light, and I'll help JFQ revamp his global strategy in my spare time."

"Look, Small, headlights. Maybe this is our ride."

Talldorf and Small climbed to their feet, their buckets over their arms and stuck out their thumbs as the dancing headlights approached.

Chapter 28

THE RESERVATION

Meanwhile, back at Nuclear Strike Headquarters, General LeMight paced the flame-retardant carpet of his roomy bunker.

"Talldorf and Small will make good red herrings to feed the news-hounds," said Boris Dirk, cracking an ice cube between his teeth. "I can use those two window washers."

"I'm hunting bigger game than those lice, Dirk. After we take care of this little matter tomorrow, in which there will be no slip-ups—" Le Might sliced his index finger across his throat, "—the American public will know which side their bread is buttered on. Can I be blunt? Do the walls have ears? No slip-ups, Dirk. Someday they'll thank us. Someday the ungrateful bastards will hail us as the only Americans with the balls to do what has to be done to save our great country."

"Save it for the cameras, General."

LeMight sunk his great teeth into the butt of his Royal Guantanamo cigar. "Get Ames on the what-cha-ma-call-it. I know the men you have picked are raw specimens of steel American nerves, Dirk. They'd better be. Where are my gloves? Tell Ames to fire up the plane. We're due in Bermuda at 0 ten hundred. And cheer up, Borris. That is an order."

Talldorf and Small stood beneath the bowl of heaven.

"Stop waving your arms, Talldorf. This guy is gonna stop if you don't scare him off. I'm gonna exert the force of my personality."

Small furrowed his bushy eyebrows and centered his mind on the approaching headlights. The dark shadows of buttes moved in an eerie sweep of desolation as the rising roar of the engine changed to a screeching whine and the little fastback filled the night with sparks and the stench of burning rubber, flipped end to end twice, landed on its tires, turned and crept toward them from the opposite direction.

"Indians, Talldorf. I'll handle this. Howdy, Chief. That was some trick. Me and my partner need a lift. You braves probably seen us on television. Maybe you guys don't watch television. Me and Talldorf are personal representatives of the Great White Father in Washington. Get in, Talldorf!"

Not a muscle twitched or an eyelash flickered in the faces of Charlie Spotted Chicken and Leonard Hands In His Pockets. The Indians sat with their arms folded across their chests, their eyes glittered like arrowheads as Talldorf and Small scrambled into the back seat. Talldorf fastened his seat belt as the little fast-back sped across the moonless desert.

"Wanna beer?" asked Spotted Chicken.

"Now you're talkin, Chief," said Small exhilarated by the speed.

"Small!" hissed Talldorf. "You know what alcohol does to an Indian."

"Beer can't hurt us," allowed Spotted Chicken tearing off the bottle cap with his teeth.

"You guys spend the night on the res," said Hands In His Pockets.

"We accept your hospitality in the name of the President of the United States, Chief," said Small.

"I've always wanted to have a reservation on a reservation," said Talldorf.

The cluster of tarpaper shacks looked dour and poor. A few of the windows flickered blue with late-night TV. The bar sign flickered red. Talldorf and Small slept sweetly under government issue khaki blankets in Leonard Hands In His Pockets shack surrounded by a graveyard of Leonard's wrecked automobiles.

Leonard Hands In His Pockets had returned to the reservation after thirty-seven years of fighting off the advantages of the white man. White ways of thinking had been difficult to dislodge. Leonard had spent enough time in jails and insane asylums to discover the truth of his blood, but the tribe from which Leonard sprung rejected him as a pariah to whom they grudgingly threw a few bones. It was Nature's bond that healed Leonard's wounds. The bitterness, the hatred, drained slowly out of him. He became a vegetarian and ate only nuts and roots that he gathered himself, seeking his vision as his grandfathers had sought their visions. For this Leonard had been reviled, scorned by the squaws, gibed at by the wine bibbers, taunted by the children. Hands In His Pockets stood dumbly on the porch of the agency store and post office with his hands in his pockets. He went on forays into the bush for medicinal herbs.

The old blind medicine man, Coyote Tooth, who only spoke Hunkpa, was reticent and suspicious. Coyote Tooth sat in front of a tin stove in his tepee beneath the cottonwood that rasped the sorrows of a dying nation. Coyote Tooth was contemptuous of the tragedy of his people and of his own failure to live up to his vision. Conscious of Agency practices that swindled them Coyote Tooth had even outgrown the incredulousness and hate that had filled his heart with the extermination of his women and children. He waved off this *washichu* son, Leonard, who called himself an Indian, a lifetime better forgotten, mistakes uncorrected, vows taken and undone. Coyote Tooth folded his brittle arms stiffly to receive this false conjurer who was too eager to learn the secrets. The domestic misfortunes of city life were tatooed on Leonard's every expression of politeness and dissimulation. Old Coyote Tooth could feel the jitterings of Leonard's manic nerves from across the fire.

"Tell him he is too old, Spotted Chicken. Tell him his white brothers have contaminated him. Tell him he is welcome to raise his tepee on the res, but that if he starts snooping he's gonna wake the dogs."

Leonard had built his shack. Denied the teaching, he was caught between two worlds. He fasted and prayed to Wokan Tonka. He invented his own chants and rituals. He'd spent one moon wandering the hills day and night alone, living on nothing but wild honey and locust and was spotted luckily lying beside the highway half-starved and half-baked by an alert Western Trail's bus driver. Coyote Tooth himself had doctored Hands In His Pockets beside his smoldering fire.

Not long after Leonard's recovery Coyote Tooth had returned to the Happy Hunting Ground. The old man had come down suddenly with a high fever and gone into convulsions. Leonard had worked furiously through the night but Coyote Tooth was dead before dawn. The sun rose over the medicine man's corpse, his lips drawn back in a derisive rictus.

"Coyote Tooth was angry when he died," the squaws said. "Who could he be angry with? Not with us. Coyote Tooth was angry at Hands In His Pockets, that sham shaman, that sourpuss who calls himself a man."

"Nonsense," the braves said. "In his heart Coyote Tooth was angry with everybody. He made an angry face for us to remember him."

Leonard had sat in vigil at Coyote Tooth's scaffold for four days fasting and praying to the winds, the rocks and the four directions. He thought of his own seared flesh, his sacrifices and mortifications, offering to the Great Spirit who never answered.

"I am not worthy to speak Your name. I pray for rain in vain. The cows are dying of thirst. The corn is withered." Hands In His Pockets pulled himself to his feet, weak and dizzy, and headed wearily back toward his shack.

"If you are wakan then where is your magic?" the squaws questioned. "If you are wakan make lightning flash and rain come."

But the more Leonard prayed and fasted the more brilliant the sun became, the more parched the corn.

"Hi ya hey hey," chanted Hands In His Pockets pulling his hands out of his pockets and thrusting his palms toward the place where the sun went down. Some of the men felt sorry for him and occasionally brought him a half-dead chicken or calf to doctor. The Indian women still took their children a hundred miles to the white doctor in town.

Leonard's practice as medicine man was almost as insubstantial as his results in self-mastery. Nevertheless, Leonard was not melancholic as he once had been. The buzzard's feather plaited in his braid hung down his back as he went about the reservation cheerfully resigned to perfidious human misunderstandings.

Hands In His Pockets was up before the chickens, ceremonially laying the kindling as he had been doing since his return to the reservation. He broke off a piece of the dried cow pattie that had to serve for the buffalo chip used by shamen before him. Hands In His Pockets raised the pipe that Coyote Tooth had left him to the four directions and sang the Song of Thanksgiving high in his nostrils sending the Hunkpa words like arrows straight toward heaven as the east began to streak with the first light of dawn.

"Where's the coffee?" asked Small.

"I have great admiration for the dark knowledge of your people, Mr. Hands," said Talldorf as they sat around the rickity table in the kitchen. "I am ashamed of the broken treaties and the greed of white men."

"If it wasn't for the white man you wouldn't be sitting here today, Talldorf. The U.S. Cavalry paved the way for you. Don't tell me about no terrible deeds of the mounted men in blue. It's a God-given privilege to be a white man. Tell him, Leonard! We got to the South and I couldn't keep him out of the colored rest rooms. Remember, we've got an appointment at the White House, Talldorf."

"The Indian will have a voice in JFQ's government, Mr. Hands," Rudolph liberally assured Hands In His Pockets, who sat fingering a smooth piece of willow. "As Small's official secretary I will be happy to record your ideas for improvements. I will see to it that Small informs the President of every detail of your tribe's plight, and any complaint you have will be thoroughly investigated. By the way, what is the reason for the piece of wood you carry?"

"Five elements," said Hands In His Pockets holding up his palm. "Earth. Air. Fire. Water. Wood. In wood is the quintessence. The wood makes me remember to forget the past."

"Very interesting," said Talldorf jotting down the information.

Small felt triumphant. His abilities finally had been recognized. All roads led to Washington. He stuck his hand into his shirt front with the old Windy City confidence, taking his good fortune as further proof of his ability to navigate a shrewd course to the pot of gold. The wanderer's life had become the road to glory. Talldorf towered above Small as they strolled the hot dusty street past the shacks of the Indians.

Wrecked cars sat in the front yards like carcasses of rusting buffalo. The shacks were topped with TV aerials. Broken windows had been replaced with cardboard or ill-fitting sheets of plywood. Children played in the dirt around the useless machines which had been stripped of everything bolted down. Naked infants crawled through oil slicks, lean red girls jumped rope, barefoot boys stopped rolling hoops to stare at the strange pair of white men.

"The kids look like they're having fun, huh, Talldorf? Hi kids!" called Small. Talldorf shook his head sadly at the squalor. He took a dim view of the old people as they passed the brown paper sack, and made a note of the alcohol problem on the reservation. He and Small would do their small part in helping JFQ clean up the country, eliminate pockets of disease and poverty, bring hope where there was none.

"We've finished our inspection tour, Mr. Hands," said Talldorf enthusiastically. "You have a sanitation problem here that I'm sure you're aware of. It will require a team of government health experts. And the people need windows. Small and I intend to wash the few windows that are left."

"Wash the windows, but no improvements," said Hands In His Pockets. "Already they send too much spoiled food, too many used clothes, too many teachers and jungle jims. We do not want government interference. We wish to educate our children in our own way. We do not wish for more than we already have."

"The trouble with you, Leonard," said Small, "is you got an inferiority complex. Just like any American you're entitled to all you can get. You shouldn't settle for nothin less. I been fighting for what's comin to me since I was thirteen and I ain't got it yet. But I'm not gonna quit. What do Indians do for money, collect welfare checks?"

"Spotted Chicken works as a brakeman on the Mainline Trainline, don't you, cousin."

Spotted Chicken grunted his assent. "Hands In His Pockets is a medicine man," said Spotted Chicken. "He heals cows and chickens. Don't have much business."

"We have the sun and the heavens, the four-leggeds, the finned and winged creatures. The rocks and the streams are our own," continued Hands In His Pockets. "Our days are being fulfilled according to Hopi prophecies. Time will come when all men will be brothers. Now the white children grow their hair long and dance barefoot in the streets, but hard times are coming. Bad times."

Hands In His Pockets rubbed his thumb among the warm ashes and pressed it to his forehead. "I make the Ceremony of Ashes to mark your foreheads. In the name of the Holy One," he said pressing his thumb to Talldorf's forehead, and to Small's, who cocked one eye over his roll-your-own and regarded the Indian with suspicion.

"We must become brothers," said Hands In His Pockets. "Our blood will be mixed in your generations as it was spilled on the battlefield. We must conquer our hearts, not one another. I perform the rituals to restore the magic, I sing the sacred songs that Coyote Tooth taught me. The words are the same but the power is missing. The meat no longer has strength. The Great Spirit has turned his back on the Indian. This JFQ appears to be a shining example of honesty. He threatens the labor unions, the military and the corporations. I listen to the wind and hear nothing. The past was full of opportunity for living. Now there are no good deeds for an Indian, no honors to win. The Indian is finished but I do not choose to be an Indian. The white man too is finished. I do not choose to be a white man."

"Nonsense, Leonard," said Small. "The future never looked brighter. With JFQ in the White House even the Indians are gonna get rich."

The assasination of Justin Freeman Quiggley was broadcast to the nation by Walter Smilerite over the airwaves of the Cosmococcic Broadcasting System. The indefatigable Smilerite and his team of unflagging reporters were on the scene when the bullets ripped the roof off the President's head and remained on the scene four days, second by second, recreating the dastardly deed, piecing together the scanty information, following the dirge of the funeral cortege down Pennsylvania Avenue.

The people mourned his death.

Talldorf and Small were among the Americans glued to TV sets. When the FIB agents paraded the Executioner in front of the cameras Talldorf wept, and Small flung Andrew Drew's plaid hat across the room.

"The lying rats!" shouted Small, "I should have known it was gonna happen. I could smell the sulphur on LeMight's breath. I could have stopped it. That chicken-shit general is responsible for the great statesman's death and he ain't gonna get away with it!"

"You'd better not be talkin like that in public," said Leonard. "The wrong people hear you talk like that and they rub you out."

"You're right, Leonard. It's a miracle LeMight's agents haven't caught up to us yet. They must be combin the hills for us."

Small's nerves were on edge. Small felt like a victim. Justin Freeman Quiggley, his friend, was dead.

Talldorf attempted to express his misgivings and regrets in a rare letter to his grandparents:

> 'As window washers Small and I have done our best to light the lives of politicians, prostitutes and shopkeepers. We have tried to illuminate the dwellings of the working man as

well as the middle class. We have lent our talents to the rich to brighten their lives. Though we be hunted by darker forces we intend to survive. Long used to chicanery committed in the name of America the beautiful the Indians fear for our lives.

'The shadow of the President's death (he whom I counted among my dear personal friends) hangs over the reservation. Tonight the medicine man is taking us to the healing mud baths. The medicine man carries a piece of willow to remember to take his hands out of his pockets. He says he learned to put his hands in his pockets when he was among the white men.'

Talldorf dropped the stamped envelope, minus a return address, into the slot at the post office. Talldorf came out of the store after purchasing a hundred dollars worth of tools, toys and trinkets which Mr. Beesly, the Indian Agent, promised to distribute among the tribe in the name of the beloved dead President.

"Let's get back to Leonard's shack," said Small. "See that dust cloud? That's cars. It might be ICEmen."

Small sat at the kitchen table nibbling a tunafish sandwich and sprouting a beard which already hid his upper lip and made his cheeks bristle. Spotted Chicken and other friends came and went. Small drank beer with them while Talldorf sat cross-legged in the front room bagging herbs for Hands In His Pockets' medicine bundle. Talldorf continued to lament the President's death. Hands In His Pockets wisely kept him busy on missions into the desert: "Know without limit what it is possible to know," advised Hands In His Pockets, "Live on the edge. Make eyes and ears of every hair."

Talldorf knotted a red bandanna around his red head. The sky stretched forever as he strode the ties along the railroad embarkment. Living prehistoric rocks breathed their purple shapes and mist rose from the sage like steam from creation. The surveyor's glass eye had scanned the sweep of butte and mesa, the grandeur of that Rocky Mountain drainboard gerrymandered, parceled, sold, mortgaged, bought, stolen and traded by Talldorf's ancestors.

The children's limpid eyes and the women's dark beauty with their long midnight hair made Talldorf long to settle permanently on the reservation. He sniffed the wild sweet air scented with the sacred sage and doted on liquid notes of meadowlarks. He was impressed with Hands In His Pockets circumspection, the raw beauty of nature, the strength of the land. He brought colored stones, rodent skulls, feathers and plants back to the shack for Hands In His Pockets to identify. He listened intently to every word that Hands In His Pockets said.

"My grandfathers roamed freely over all this country but didn't own it," said Hands In His Pockets. "They knew better. My heritage has left me a witness to deceit and death. I do not grieve. The white man calls the extension of his civilization Manifest Destiny. I do not argue. I take what is given to me and give what I have."

Hands In His Pockets motioned toward rows of corn and beans, staked tomatoes, cucumber frames.

"We supply the tribe with fresh vegetables. These beehives provide us with honey all year. We have seeds of wild piñon and fruit trees. We keep chickens but do not kill the hen when she stops laying. I have heard of too much killing. Instead of killing we cooperate with Nature. The white man builds fences to pen up the Indian. The Indian builds fences to keep rabbits out. The white man murdered our greatest chiefs, Crazy Horse, Sitting Bull, many others. The same men who murdered your president slaughtered our old people, butchered our wives and children. They stripped the sacred trees, broke the hoop of the tribes and the hearts of the young. There are pockets of my people who have survived like I have. We are forgotten and wish to continue living in peace on the reservation."

"It's every man for himself now, Talldorf," said Small. "Our lives will be in constant jeopardy. The FIB and ICE will be turning over rocks looking for us. Those guys are cold-blooded killers so I don't blame ya if ya don't want to go. It makes me wonder, that the star of so great a human as JFQ goes out if maybe my star ain't going nova. But I ain't folding, Talldorf. I know where I'm goin. We might get caught in a few blizzards in the mountains so I can understand why ya got reservations. The biggest risk is always A. Small's policy, you know that. You racked your brain and come up with Indian blankets, feathers and war paint. So I racked my brain and come up with the only solution. If you want to become an Indian and rot on the reservation it's all right with me, but if not you gotta wear the dress." Small rubbed his palms together. "The elevator shoes will boost me up and the whiskers and the black suit will fool em. As Rhinchardt and Ruby Grueber, Amish gentlefolk, we can walk safely right under the ICEmen's noses. You got the complexion. We'll cover your peach fuzz with a little rouge. All you gotta do is swing it a little and pitch your voice an octave higher."

"I'll wear the dress, Small."

"No reservations, Talldorf?"

"I still have reservations, Small. I probably will always have reservations, but I'm going with you."

"No complaints when you gotta use the Ladies Room? Or that you gotta darn my socks and iron my clothes?"

"I never learned to darn or iron, Small."

"You're gonna have to play your part good enough to fool J. Lugar Edgar himself, Talldorf."

"I'll do my best, Small."

"I got the route laid out through the mountains, Tallie." Small traced the blue line on the map with his hairy index finger. "We gotta stay on country roads. We may have to do a lot of walking, but walkin's better than dying. We might head toward the salt flats and take refuge in the Holy City of The Greater Number of Brothers or aim at Nero, the Smallest Large City in the World. Bright lights, Talldorf. Plenty of broads. Interesting people and cheap food.

"No dumb mistakes, Talldorf, that's all I got to say. One dumb mistake and we end up like horsemeat."

Small's elevator shoes arrived from a Kansas City mail-order house. Spotted Chicken brought the clothes.

"We ran out the missionaries," said Hands In His Pockets, "but they'll love you out there."

Talldorf climbed into the petticoat and the long dress of gray muslin. Small put on the suit of black broadcloth and smoothed the wide brim of his black hat while Talldorf tied the strings to his bonnet.

"You carry the basket, honey," growled Small.

The furious evening star burned bright for sons and lovers as the curious couple stumbled out of the car.

"Thanks for everything, Leonard," said Small, pumping the medicine man's hand with affection.

Spotted Chicken squeeled the tires in a tight U-turn.

Talldorf and Small watched until there was nothing left of the Indians but a vanishing plume of silvery dust above the sagebrush.

Chapter 29

JUST PLAIN BILL

"Read not the *Times*. Read the Eternities." Thoreau

There are certain crumbs on the carpet of creation which we must sweep up before returning to the fate of our heroes.

The Summit Conference was scrapped. The new President, Harry Lynx Herod, announced this as an aside to more pressing business that would keep him at home in the White House. This was the result of a direct order from General Croesus LeMight, Chief of Staff, who breakfasted with the new President the morning after the assassination. President Harry Lynx Herod's baby-fat cheeks trembled as he received the iron gray stare of General LeMight over the wavering black mustaches beyond which a quarter pound of porkchop was being masticated.

"Do you know what your first official act is to be, Harry baby?"

"The Sum — Sum — Summit...?" stammered the President. The new President was wrong right off. His first act was to muzzle Lash Quiggley which order he received with relish.

"We are going to get along just fine, you and us," said the General. "We're going to get this country back on course." He aimed his cigar from his cleaver-like teeth at the President. The cigar looked like a cannon. "Give me a light, Harry," ordered the General from the side of his mouth.

Under the perennial gloom of the sky of Moscow Premiere Sonofavich wept when he heard the news that the young President was dead. He wept for a son of his spirit, he wept for the world, he wept for the future and he wept for himself.

Bill, the Executioner, wasn't having a real great time either. After being retrieved by Secret Service agents from the police and crazed mob that ripped off his black leather jacket—which was confiscated by three Windy City motorcycle cops who flipped coins for the souvenir—and indeed might have torn him to pieces, the Executioner was never maltreated by authorities who, rather in awe of the dimension of him judged so monstrous an assassin, preserved him for Justice like a trophy too rare, though he threw his tin plates of food in the faces of his jailers and bent the bars of his cell in paroxysms of rage.

It was impossible for anyone to interview the Executioner in his cell but bars must be between him and his interlocutor. They had taken away even his socks to prevent him from hanging himself in face of the evidence against him and given him a flour sack affair which he refused to wear, rather standing intimidatingly naked before his captors and drumming his hairy chest with great fists in electric rapidity bellowing curses on the heads of all.

The grieving American public was revolted at the incredible spectacle of the Executioner and condemned him unanimously.

As the dossier of the coordinated investigation on the Executioner grew, his name eluded them. A copy boy in the news room of *The Windy City Tribunal* gave to history and the press a name to clunk down the halls of infamy: Just Plain Bill.

Mine, Death, and *Wink* carried his rage-twisted face on their glossy covers and the face of Small's friend, the Executioner, was burned into the consciousness of America.

The Executioner refused to use speech, only bone-chilling growls and snarls, belligerent roars and blood-curdling howls in answer to the most inoffensive questions asked by the investigators. His history seemed one of back alleys and cheap rooms on the edge of the ghetto, the rent for which it was assumed he begged on the streets or, more likely, jackrolled from winos whom all agreed were luckier than poor JFQ, that shining being alas never more to be seen in this unhappy vale. But Just Plain Bill would pay, oh yes, just wait, the beast would pay, promised Boris Dirk, who headed up the investigation.

It was the incisive FIB investigation that revealed the Executioner had been frustrated with the modern world leading to paranoid envy directed with psychotic violence against the President who symbolized crushing authority and the hated father figure.

According to the M. Barris pole, this explanation was believed by 49% of all Americans with an IQ under 60.

As FIB agents sped to every end of the available net of information the surviving uncles of Rudolph Victor Talldorf were questioned about the history and whereabouts of this figure so prominent for an instant in national history and now vanished without a trace who was in some way connected with the accused killer in the JFQ assassination investigation.

The uncles of Talldorf pulled their caps over their eyes and muttered to one another, "I told you so."

The news of this connection was leaked to the press, and some were tasteless and brazen enough to suggest that the two workers who had spoken so irresponsibly at Nuclear Strike Headquarters were plants, and even then stalking the fallen leader.

"Now I'll just tell you, young man," said old Mrs. Deerly to two FIB agents wrinkling their noses at the dog stench of her musty quarters, "Tallie and Smally were two of the nicest boys. Now write that down on your paper. And they should get in touch with me if they need anything at all."

Two FIB agents and two ICEmen interviewed Elvira around her lacy sundeck table on the balcony over the park one morning and they all drank tea.

"He was very inventive," said Elvira of Small, "He was very obstinate. Gentlemen, more tea? Small not only had no political ambition, he had no ambition whatsoever, so I am certain he was not involved in any way with so tremendous a thing as the assassination. Why thank you, Mr. Murat, yes, I believe that I might be available for lunch."

Wolfie Vamp, the ambitious young FIB agent stationed in Nero, Nevada led an ICEman to O'Toole's private office in the Cruciform Casino.

"I used to watch him climb around on ladders. Him and Talldorf flew off in an airplane in a blizzard, that was before I went to Europe."

"Before you opened the whorehouse in Paris for Ensardo, O'Toole," corrected Wolfie Vamp.

"Come on, Wolfie, you know me, you're sworn to hold up free enterprise, I'm a businessman. I know nothing about either one of those guys. Now buzz off, I got business."

Matt Masterman, Director of the Desert District of FIB, had refused to accompany the ICEman to interview O'Toole, and had sent hyper Wolfie instead. Masterman just sat there with his Tony Lamas up on his desk beside his Stetson.

"You're barkin up the wrong tree, son," he said.

"You aren't interested, Masterman?" said the icy ICEman.

"Nope," said Matt.

The Windy City cops furnished the information that both Talldorf and Small had been at the death site of old Alphonse, the wino, found frozen in the alley beside their personal garbage can, and noted with invective the one hundred plus parking tickets unpaid by A. Small so many years before.

Sue O'Toole-Pool was livid with terror when the FIB agent interviewed her at the Pinchin & Penny Collection Agency Inc. in Ripple Forks, Wisconsin, and her husband, Mike, who insisted on sitting in on the conference spoke past her to the FIB agent as if she were demented and had no mind of her own. Mike Pool was aghast at this development lest his employer, the magnate, Sterling Penny, should get wind that his wife had been interrogated by the FIB. Sue O'Toole-Pool said she had neither seen nor heard of O'Toole since their divorce, that she had been a naive young girl when she met him and that she got rid of him just as fast as she could. She turned white when the FIB agent mentioned Talldorf and Small. She denied seeing them on TV and said she did not remember any of O'Toole's insane friends in those horrible Windy City days.

Not far away in another small Wisconsin town the three Smith sisters, Scarlet, Trudy, and Ella bowed their heads over the evening repast and were led in prayer by Ella for Papa Small and his handsome friend that no evil might befall them. And no investigative agents befell the three good sisters. Nor did an investigator set foot on the Indian reservation where not a word had stirred the air of Talldorf and Small since they had left.

"Unimpeachable," considered General LeMight summing up the investigative reports at Camp Saul, his shady vacation headquarters. "I could have the lice killed legally. But clamp a lid on their connection with Just Plain Bill, Dirk. Nobody rocks my boat. Those window washing freaks are enough to upset the applecart."

It was announced to the press that since no conspiracy had been discovered or considered likely that the two workers who had appeared on a certain TV news coverage were no longer being considered in the investigation. But Talldorf and Small were already on the road in disguise and unhappily this news did not reach them. Yet were there aficionados of crime detection who for years would consider them in elaborate conspiracy theories.

The evidence against Just Plain Bill, more green than ripe, was quickly harvested and slapped onto the table like a dead fish. The bizarre trial came immediately to the docket. The Executioner was handcuffed and wore leg irons in a sound proof, bulletproof glass box where spectators witnessed with horror the soundless grotesque contortions of his rage-maddened face and the ceaseless, manic struggle beneath his straight-jacket. There was none to speak in his defense. No, not one. But interminable was the list of experts from the technology of ballistics to the mystery of sanity in the modern world who testified against him, and astronomical the fees carried away for their services to the government prosecution. The plea of insanity was inadmissible because the defense lawyer had been unsuccessful in obtaining one decipherable word from the mouth of Just Plain Bill. He was found guilty of first degree murder and when queried by the judge if the prisoner had anything to say before sentence was pronounced upon him, his lips moved and his first words were heard electrified by the P.A. system:

"You can't electrocute me."

Although the Executioner had nothing more to say, the startled judge hastened to push the button that killed Just Plain Bill's microphone. He was condemned to death in the electric chair, which was the means of execution thought fitting by the particular state where the foul deed was done.

Let it not pass at this point that even JFQ had made mistakes: For a political favor, Amos Proot had been appointed warden of the prison where Just Plain Bill was to die.

Yes, even so, son to that same Reverend Proot who pontificated above the heads of Small and other orphans, and by far the more successful brother of him in rags and matted hair and flaming eyes with staff in hand who had accompanied Talldorf and Small through the horrors of the hurricane. Yes, Amos Proot, the very man whose Pea Ridge garage roof Talldorf and Small had dropped a tree limb through. Small world.

A hush most profound had fallen over the domestic life of Warden and Mrs. Proot since the Warden had announced his shocking decision which was the fruit of long and conscience searching rationality: "It is as if this beast, Just Plain Bill, has slain our own son," the childless Amos told his childless wife. "It was the wish of our late great President that my judgment should rule over the prison system of this state. The trust of our late great President was in me. I must not fail him now. I personally will throw the command switch at the execution of this killer most foul."

"Most foul—" echoed his wife, who had always been this law official's most profound critic.

There were many of more liberal persuasion, let it be said, who considered it wise to spare the life of Just Plain Bill so that the needles and minds of the scientific community might probe and prod for responses to the problem of homicidal violence which might profit society. Yet far more vast was the number applauding his swift demise, and countless again the inventive strategems proposed for novel deaths more fitting to the crime.

The swift days before the verdict was carried out left Just Plain Bill in comparative peace in the isolation of his death row cell. The days passed with a curious joy. He now took to a wild great rolling laughter in the face of all who came to him save the jailer who brought his food whom he contemplated with a stare of burning curiosity. But he spoke never a word.

When the chaplain came in the final hour the Executioner suffered them to drape his nakedness in a plain white chemise. He listened to the low voice of the chaplain with no indication that he comprehended the words of salvation and peace offered at this last hour and before his burning eyes, black as Bibles, the chaplain bowed his head.

The Executioner rose straight and huge before the corps of guards that came in the last minutes radiating a silence that rendered them mute. The prison physician succeeded in stabbing the hypodermic of phenobarbitol into the Executioner's triceps but he slapped it away as if it were a mosquito, breaking the needle off in his arm, and as the guards fell back he strode from his cell the few paces to the great iron door and stood waiting.

When the white-draped figure towered into the execution chamber a silence fell even on Tom, Dick, and Harry, the reporters for *Mine, Death* and *Wink* as they sat at the polished table behind the thick glass in the observation room. And yet, what had these cosmopolitans not witnessed? It was not the first execution for either of the three and their mockery would not be still.

"We got his ass now," said Tom.

"He came in his ghost suit," said Dick.

"The end of a perfect day," winked Harry.

One would have thought the Executioner had heard the joke, for as he stopped and faced the electric chair his laughter began, strange in the breathless room, rising up in thunder-like peals that boomed from wall to wall and addled the brains of Tom, Dick, and Harry, electrified as it was from the speaker above the witness table. With this his last word, the Executioner seated himself in the broad, stiff-backed electric chair which vastness seemed fitted to him. Not a guard in the band waiting attendance on Just Plain Bill who was not thankful he had seated himself so calmly, and two leaped forward to clamp the wrist and leg bands before he realized where he was and went berserk. They dreaded this moment; not the most hardened had stomach for a scene at the foot of the chair. They clamped the electrode dish to his skull and slipped the black bag over his head. So situated, he looked not unlike the pilot of a spaceship. A red light glowed on the wall and all present looked up to the white face of the wall clock where the small black hand stood at twelve and the large hand at one minute to. The red second hand was sweeping the last seconds to midnight and Friday and eternity.

Behind a one-way glass, opaque to the viewers in the execution chamber, but in all other respects identical to that through which Tom, Dick and Harry ogled, Warden Proot laid his soft hand to the cold steel of the switch he had sworn never to touch.

His milky eyes behind bifocals propped on the milky cheeks directed the young volunteers from the Rehabilitation Program on either hand to grasp their switches.

The thumb of Warden Proot depressed the button in the middle handle releasing blocks on the two accompanying switches. The eyes of the two volunteers from Rehabilitation were on the milk-white hand of Warden Proot. This service to the state meant $500 to each of them. They were going to join their girl friends afterward for a celebration at the new pizza place. The

Warden's eyes cast over his shoulder at the propitious calm and ready scene in the execution chamber. The narrow bones of the Warden's jaw were rigid as he watched the second hand slice through the seconds to midnight.

Behind the black hood the brain of Bill was spotlessly blank, and stainless, and still.

"Now!" ordered Warden Proot. Three hands plunged three switches.

The Executioner, offering no resistance whatsoever, an act with the simplicity of authentic genius, experienced an even greater clarity which seemed to widen his perspective to cosmic space. No lights dimmed above their heads. To the horror of Warden Proot the ohmmeter registered zero resistance. The body of Just Plain Bill sat unmoved.

"Again! Throw the switches again!" Proot ordered the two volunteers from Rehabilitation, "No money if you don't!"

"Warden, it's an act of God!" exclaimed the two in unison.

"Act of God be damned! The beast will not be spared! I order you: Throw the switches!"

The reptilian glint from the bifocals was too much for the volunteers from Rehabilitation who again threw their switches, dropped their sweating hands, and stared through the one-way glass where the ohmmeter again registered zero and Just Plain Bill sat with consciousness so expansive he might play with any of the worlds of creation.

"Again!" howled Warden Proot crazily, "Kill the killer!" but the volunteers from Rehabilitation shrunk back in horror from the awful switches.

Warden Proot jammed down three and held them down.

Such peace as the Executioner knew few men have known. Until his consciousness was attracted to a speck rising blue and green through velvet fields of clarity. There was recognition and an instant of sweet longing as he thought: 'You can't electrocute me,' in a white flash.

The corps of guards, and Tom, Dick and Harry saw the muscles of Just Plain Bill swell, shinning, bathed with his life juices, the great fists clench and wrist and leg clamps burst from their rivets as the body cast itself from the chair taking flight, a looming avenging angel filling the observation window, bursting through it, the black bag sheared from the roasted face where the white orbs of eyes smoked upward, turned rolling like a felled tree over the polished table amid arrows of splintered glass to crash into the laps of Tom, Dick, and Harry.

"Look, Small," said Talldorf as they stood at the side of a western road, "A falling star."

"It ain't mine," said Small.

Chapter 30

THE SPACEWAIF

It is well-known that the Shadow was Lamont Cranston, wealthy young man about town, that Superman was Clark Kent, that the Lone Ranger was a Texas cop, and even that Rhinehardt and Ruby Grueber were in reality Talldorf and Small.

But no man knew the identity of the Spacewaif.

It had not always been so. One moment he stood in the bosom of his average American family, its paragon and seeming source, when the bird of an idea flew through his head and he turned his mind unwaveringly to the curious mystery of his own existence, proceeding to unravel the tangled skein turn by turn every day and night and moment with every step and every breath. He released his hold on a world of anxiety and plunged toward his destiny. His beard grew, his hair went unkempt like a bird's nest, his eyes brightening in hollowing sockets and his fond family drawing back as if from too great heat, until they came no more.

He stood penniless in shabby rooms and then at roadsides staring, listening, with uncanny alertness for the next cue as each moment led him to his fate.

As Talldorf and Small had been flung from cities, so the Spacewaif was to be flung from earth. Already he was in virtual orbit, so far behind had he left all things which had been his own. Like dust from the careening boulder and spray from the wave, he was transmuting to finer stuff. A shadowy old white Pontiac station wagon, long and roomy and empty save for the Spacewaif carried him on the cosmic flow. The Spacewaif had nothing to sell. No business card confirmed his mission. He possessed only the clothing he wore: a T-shirt and baggy gray pants. He had no papers. His wallet was long gone. He had no toothbrush, he knew no fear. If he passed through fire or ice it was the same to him. A leaf blowing lightly on a breeze might point the Spacewaif's way. He asked for nothing and received manna from heaven. The Spacewaif was a man hot on the trail of home.

"Something's up to something up there," said Small squinting down the endless highway.

Small was of a firm purpose. They would follow his star. "I'm goin all the way, Talldorf."

Talldorf had stars in his eyes. "I'll see the mountains, Small. I never dreamed you'd take me to the mountains."

"Stick with me, Rudy baby," for Talldorf's muslin skirts brushed the ground. The blue eyes of Talldorf under his gray bonnet and Small's green ones beneath the broad black hat brim were wide open and still unprepared for what they would see.

They traveled back roads west under their alias. A picnic explained the great wicker basket the red-haired, flat-chested giant Mrs. Ruby Grueber carried over her aching arm while Rhinehardt strode ahead squat in black broadcloth burdened only by the Bible. The picnic basket contained not a crumb, but two buckets, six squeegees and a government surplus khaki blanket for cold nights they might encounter while crossing the high mountains and wide deserts of the West in search of a haven of peace and freedom.

"If I wasn't me," said Small from his bushy beard, "I'd say we ain't got a snowball's chance in hell. Thank God I ain't poor Rhinehardt Grueber but in reality I am A. Small, specially loved by the universe."

"And our red brothers have given us a wonderful new vision, Rhinehardt," said the spouse, sitting on the wicker basket at the roadside, legs spread wide, fanning his skirt for a breath of air. "If the evil government catches us and crucifies us like they did our great President our spirits will live on."

"You can call me Small when nobody but gophers are listenin, Talldorf. But stop doin that with your skirt, we're supposed to be one of them holy couples. Your red brothers think every day is a good day to die, but they ain't convinced this white brother. I won't have no holes poked in my skin. I ain't standin for no injustice to my person. It's shameful enough I got to wander my own country in disguise. Button your bodice."

"It's hot," pleaded Talldorf.

"That's the natural state of woman, Rudy, ha ha. I got to go around in this black suit like a cookie in an oven."

"I just want to find a nice quiet place where we can live in peace. There must be such a place in America."

"My star will lead us to Paradise, Talldorf." Small looked at the Bible. "How much do those guys make preachin on courthouse steps?"

"The Great Spirit would frown on that, Small," warned Talldorf. "And we must not attract crowds."

Oddly enough, the first person to give the Gruebers a ride was a Chinaman driving a limousine with a Florida license plate. He wore a blue cap with a shiny black brim.

"You honorable couple sit front by humble servant Yang Yin," he cried.

Talldorf stepped forward with his wide skirts and picnic basket so that her Rhinehardt might usher her into the limousine like a gentleman.

"Ruby!" yelled Small, "get out of the way. I'm the man, I get in first!" Talldorf backed out of Small's way.

"No fambly argue please I ride you China lots credit card Mr. Oglethorpee beeg bank man very rich boss no more no miss car till we get China you think?"

"You mean you stole this car?" asked Rhinehardt Grueber as they sped away.

"Introduce me, please, Rhinehardt dear," said Talldorf puckering his lips.

"This is my spouse, Mrs. Ruby Grueber. I'm Rhinehardt. Call me Rhiney."

"Ah so perty long Mrs. Ruby Goober my honor meet you."

"You may call me Ruby," said Talldorf.

"Is this car hot?" asked Small. The Chinaman hit a switch that nearly blew them from the front seat with a blast of icy air.

"Turn that thing off," Small said. "You're blowin up my wife's skirt. Look," said Small, the Bible in his lap, "we got to be safe, Yang Yin. If this car is hot the cops are gonna be right on top of us."

"Yes, Rhinehardt dear, we must get out right away if this is a stolen car."

"No cop on top Yang Yin car fast as airplane I fly 1000 miles hour." Yang Yin stomped the accelerator and they flew through the sagebrush on the black ribbon of road.

"Drive carefully," advised Ruby through tight lips.

"I bes driver America run over all America get free China I friend mountain in China they talk me moon shine in water for Yang Yin big America war there no care America not take mountain away here I get stuck in back with knife food taste like tin I weak in one hour he big America rice company steal Yang Yin in rice bag and brother send us leaky boat to little America Costa Rica take slave for banana farm put chain around Yang Yin neck like mean dog want throw us in sea we come moonlight in palm tree sell Yang Yin Mr. Oglethorpee no get good deal like he think Yang Yin no dumb Yankee but wise Chinaman big friend mountain and moon little Oglethorpee wind blow him away Yang Yin fly to freedom you come me China Rhiney Ruby in America all crazy."

"You said a mouthful," said Rhinehardt.

"Sma— I mean Rhinehardt," said Ruby, "This is Mr. Oglethorpe's limousine."

"Serves the old tyrant right, Tall—Ruby."

"Ruby tall some much," observed Yang Yin with agate eyes, "Perty hair red good luck China you lucky little man have fine big lady."

"She ain't all that great shakes," avowed Rhinehardt. "Yang Yin, we got to keep to backroads, there's a lot of heat from the Americans on me and Mrs. Grueber."

"America dragon eat you with fire?" asked Yang Yin swerving onto a dirt road and raising a funnel of yellow dust, "All road lead China."

"Just keep goin west," said Small, "If you're ridin this buggy to China you got to go through Alaska."

"East. I go east. Always east."

"You're goin *west*," corrected Rhinehardt Grueber, "you're drivin into the setting sun."

"I go from south west north to Alaska thank you all time east to China Yang Yin big mind see all this big drive much Oglethorpee credit card Yang Yin have big time Japan in big car drive down Ginza Tokyo give free ride Japan cousin good fellow know mountain moon talk but America cloud mind look all time Yankee dollar front nose Yang Yin slappim back say Hey, cousin, free ride lookee mountain moon water sing us they children no needy dollar cousin happy see Yang Yin say Oh you save us go crazy wise Manchu Yang Yin."

"Yes, yes—" breathed Mrs. Ruby Grueber.

"Ok! I'm with you, Yang Yin, in your flight to escape what looks to me like serious oppression," said Rhinehardt. "First, I must confess to you that I am not Mr. Rhinehardt Grueber, Amish gentlefolkman. In reality, I am A. Small!"

Small whipped off the black hat whose broad brim had been tormenting Yang Yin.

"Small, plain and simple," said Small staring into the impassive face of the Chinaman. "Probably you heard of me."

"No," said the Chinaman, glancing twice at Mrs. Ruby Grueber removing her gray bonnet.

"And I am Talldorf," smiled Rudolph at Yang Yin who nearly swerved off the road when Rudolph hiked up his skirts to expose a long hairy leg. It took an hour's further discussion to convince Yang Yin that Talldorf was a man.

Talldorf and Small impressed Yang Yin with their own great peril. Small had the road maps on his lap in the dash light.

"Where you turn north, Yang Yin," said Small, his finger on the map, "we got to go west. We ain't Chinamen."

"All men some Chinamen," affirmed Yang Yin.

"I know what you mean," said Small, "but me and Talldorf can't desert our country when it needs our light."

"Ah yes," grinned Yang Yin as he maneuvered the car at tremendous speeds on roads scarcely wide enough for it, "You Talldorf Small great warriors you Yankee Mandarin most noble save you nation Yang Yin humble man of mountain live rock and grass big sky cover Yang Yin stars sing me nights I bow you noble Yankee samurai America dragon run home fight you no chance you beat win great victory for all Chinamen I honor you noble brothers!"

"Don't bow," cautioned Small, "you're driving the car." But Talldorf was bowing his own head to his Chinese brother like a true Oriental.

They stopped at the Golden Flower Chinese Restaurant in a Wyoming town where Yang Yin's golden brothers switched license plates on Oglethorpe's limousine, slapped a Police Benevolent Association sticker onto the windshield, arranged papers to cross the border and alerted the yellow railroad to the north while Talldorf and Small enjoyed a banquet, although Small was suspicious of the fish dish.

They roared west through the night, or east, as Yang Yin maintained. "I'm hungry," said Talldorf. He was again crowned in his gray bonnet and sensed the altitude and heady, thin air.

"There's your road, Yang Yin," Small said. The car screeched to a halt.

"I go now," said Yang Yin, "save place for you beside me in mountains water sing I sink I hear it sweet night air."

"And we'll save a place for you in case they run you out," said Small.

"You so nice America holy couple warriors great samurai."

Talldorf thought Yang Yin might weep but Small saw a face ancient as stone at Yang Yin's parting words:

"We meet again."

They watched Mr. Oglethorpe's limousine disappear into the awakening day as the sun raised lofty mountains from the darkness to the west stretching from south to north as though they buttressed the great sky with their snow-rimmed peaks.

"Is this Paradise, Small?" asked Talldorf, who felt like an eagle, skirt-winged as he was, "I like it here, let's stay," though the mountains were yet a distance away.

They munched on fortune cookies, and in the heat of the day a semi-truck ground to a halt. He was going south, he told Rhinehardt Grueber, but promised he would go west in time. The driver treated the Gruebers to a donut and coffee in a roadside cafe when they arrived in a little town and asked if Rhinehardt would mind helping unload a little furniture. Rhinehardt puffed and panted as he and the driver unloaded fifteen sofas. They drove south. At the next town, where they must make another delivery, Rhinehardt said Ruby would help. The driver protested but Rhinehardt said, "She don't mind!"

"You got the right kind of woman, Mac," said the driver. "I think she's stronger than me."

"We try to help our fellow man," said Rhinehardt. "Too bad you'll have to do it all yourself next time. If I was you I'd quit." Small sat down in the shade and let Ruby and the driver continue.

"I can't say she's a beauty," said the driver, "but she sure is a prize."

"You got to know how to handle em," said Rhinehardt.

They unloaded the furniture van at its many stops throughout the day and made only twenty miles to the west. The mountains appeared no nearer.

The truck driver punched Rhinehardt in his weary arm with a great fist. "You must be some hell of a man, Shorty," and offered not a dollar for their labors as they dropped down from the cab where the westward highway crossed. The red tail lights of the old semi disappeared into the twilight of rolling open country toward the driver's home in some snug little town where his wife even now no doubt was preparing his supper.

But the evening air was pleasant and the grass by the roadside long enough for a soft bed. Small pondered why their labors had been required this day and freely given, yet here they stood little nearer their goal, supperless and pennyless.

And homeless, thought Talldorf, feeling adrift on the great ocean of America as darkness fell. Yang Yin might even now be in jeopardy at the border, and JFQ gone forever, and Hands In His Pockets too, but Talldorf took comfort in the small sturdy figure of Small and moved nearer in the darkness.

"Where are we, Small?"

"In the dark, ha ha," said Small just as two pinheads of light grew in the east.

A low car with a jacked-up rear end squealed to a halt. They clambered into the leather darkness.

"Hey, you two are some sight," said the traveling pool player on his way to a match. His black hair was slicked back and he had a big grin. "If I had smoked this first," he said raising a pipe in his hand, "I'd think I was seeing things. Farm folk are you? Got your skirts in, Mama?"

"One moment, dear," said Ruby flashing the driver a smile as he set the picnic basket on his lap and slammed the door. The hot little car shot into the night.

"Tell you what I thought. No offense intended. Looks like you hung Pa out to dry, Ma, and he shrunk, ha ha ha!"

Ruby chuckled with appreciation and the driver winked at her.

"What ya smokin in that pipe, young man?" said Rhinehardt.

"Now I see you two are them religious people. I don't know if I should tell you. I don't want to offend your simple sensitivities. I'm Jack Wheels, what do they call you folks?"

"Mr. and Mrs. Rhinehardt Grueber, Amish gentlefolk on our way to a picnic. She's my spouse."

"You lucky devil," winked Jack Wheels.

"Oh, stop it. And call me Ruby."

"Is that a hash pipe, young man?" asked Rhinehardt.

"That's what it is, Pa, and it ain't bad for you."

"I know it ain't," said Rhinehardt. "I smoke myself."

Jack Wheels expressed surprise. He lit the pipe and passed it. Rhinehardt offered it to the sky, the earth, and the four directions, took a hit and handed it to Ruby. "She smokes too," said Rhinehardt.

"Indeed I do," said Ruby inhaling the exotic smoke.

Ah, thought Small, picked out of the roadside weeds, flying west in the night toward his destiny, and stoned on good hash!

"Oh, surely we'll get to the mountains tonight, Rhinehardt," said Ruby.

"Sorry, Mama," said Jack Wheels, "I got a match tonight this side of the mountains. Load that pipe again, Pa," and he handed Small the makings. "That's where your picnic is, huh? You religious folk sure are a surprise to me. I never dreamed you were passing joints in those little black buggies on the back roads."

"They ain't all like us," admitted Rhinehardt.

"I see. You're the liberal wing of the church," estimated Jack Wheels.

"Liberal...liberated wings," mumbled Talldorf, quite stoned.

Jack Wheels perhaps took this as an invitation, for he reached across Small and patted Talldorf's skirted knee. "How liberated do you gentlefolk get?" asked Jack Wheels.

"That's as liberated as we folks get," said Small. "I don't mind ya pattin her knee, Jack, but don't try to raise her skirt."

"Certainly not!" exclaimed Talldorf.

"You're real lucky, you two, you don't know what a lonely life it is for a traveling gambler."

"You poor homeless thing," said Talldorf.

"Thank you, Mama," said Jack Wheels.

"I feel for you Jack," said Small, "but Ruby an me got our vows."

Jack Wheels would not think of coming between them. He said that he had the steadiest hand in the west this night, that he would dream the balls off the table, pick up a cool grand and head to California for some surfing. But don't think it's all gravy, he cautioned, they had each other while poor Jack Wheels ate in diners and slept with his pool cue. When the second bowl was finished Jack Wheels had come to his turn off and Talldorf and Small stepped under the stars into a new world.

"Now I know why we spent all day unloading that truck," said Small.

"So we could smoke hashish with Jack Wheels," said Talldorf.

"Exactly," said Small. Talldorf felt his high head mingle with the firmament, his nostrils resonate with nighttime odors of strange vegetation while time spiraled into a perfect moment.

"I like it here, Small." Talldorf trailed his skirts and danced around on the pavement like a great dark moth. "I almost feel like I could fly, Small."

"It's like the night I fell out of the sky in that airplane I stole when I escaped from the orphanage, Tallie."

"You never told me that story, Small."

"What a flight it was ! Nothin could compare with it. I was free at last, a bird escaped from the cage. I popped through the clouds. It was like I was sittin in glory all flooded with sunlight and fields of clouds throwing it back at me and the sky blue sweet as Abbie's eyes.

"The engine never missed a beat. I held the compass on N headin for the Windy City. But I had to play around bein just a kid. I took her down and skimmed along the clouds like a gull flyin through spray. There were maps in a pocket on the door and I spread em out and found where I wanted to go. I figured how long since I'd taken off and multiplied it times airspeed but winds were blowin too and I didn't know which way, and flyin a long time like I was it could amount to a distance. So I aimed west of north to make sure I wouldn't be blowin over the Atlantic Ocean.

"Cloud fields just covered me out of Florida and began to break up and I came down and skittered among em lookin down on patchy green and orange glad it wasn't the blue Atlantic and there was thunderstorms slantin down in gray sheets and there was rainbows all along my course. Then out of nowhere pops up this gigantic airfield.

"It was an abandoned naval air station way out in the boonies of Georgia. I'd never landed an airplane before but the runways were concrete and must have been a mile long. I pulled on the carburetor heat before I cut the throttle, I guess I did it all right because down I come and skimmed that concrete and set her down like apple pie.

"There wasn't a soul around. and there was gas in the pumps. There were forests all around, and moss hanging in the trees. I laid down in the grass on my blanket and slept all night and woke when the sun was high. I tied the stick back with the seat belt, cocked the throttle just a hair and went around in front to spin the propeller. I remembered the pictures in the comic book clear as if they was in front of my eyes. I grabbed hold, kicked my leg and spun her, jumpin back and she caught. I ran around the strut and she was already startin to roll. I ran alongside tryin to climb in, and she was pickin up speed when I got inside. I didn't think there was anything I couldn't do. It was a beautiful morning. I gunned her and up we went again but smoother than the day before cause no one was chasin me. I was on my way to the Windy City. The kids in the orphanage seemed a lifetime away.

"I saw Atlanta and hung away to the side in case they were lookin for my plane and I saw Chattanooga and followed highway 41 through the mountains toward Nashville where I was gonna have to come down for gas. That was rough goin cause there was thunderheads piled up and I got some rain on the windshield and it scared me, but I weaved in and out of the clouds and kept that highway in view and there lay Nashville and I come down and fortunately there was a kid not much older than me gasin at the pumps. He gased me right up. I told him I was a Scotch airforce cadet come for flight training in America, that I was 25 but we all looked a lot younger in Scotland and we was all short. He was so impressed he could hardly talk to me, told me he was 17 and only had 20 hours in a plane himself but that he wanted to be a pilot too. I told him there wasn't nothin to flying, which is the truth. He gave me a ticket and said I should pay inside and said he'd prop her for me when I come out.

"I walked into the terminal and went to the bathroom, and came back out. The kid asked me to send him a post card and tell him what neat kinds of planes I was flying for the air force and I said I'd try to remember. He propped her and I got out of there quick. I headed up toward Louisville and it was gettin late and soon I see I ain't goin to find a place to spend the night cause there wasn't nothin flat in all that Kentucky land, all hills and woods and those twisty dirt roads and then it all dissolved into night and I flew by the compass and air speed. It wasn't as bad as being in the clouds and by starlight I could keep her steady on the horizon. I could even see the Ohio River when I crossed her, long an twisty like a silver snake and lights of Louisville, then I just held her to N on the compass and I was over flat farmlands and that made me feel better cause I didn't want to try settin her down in those Kentucky hills, and by then I believed completely in my luck. I was too young to die. I didn't know how or where I'd come down, but I was sure everything would be all right. Well, it was a starry night just like this and the land was just as unfamiliar to me and I was kind of in a daze flyin so long and hoping the sun would come up before the gas ran out and the same thing happened as happened to you and me over Georgia. The engine quit. I knew it was all over. Dark as now, but I was wide awake and kept that air speed up so I wouldn't stall out and kept watchin the altitude, then when I was readin five hundred feet and couldn't see nothin I turned off the key so she wouldn't catch fire if we crashed, and sure enough we did. I felt a bash that drove my teeth together, I knew we'd hit and bounced and I was still trying to fly her though I couldn't see a thing then the wings sheared off between trees and me and the fuselage went through this woods like a bug ridin an arrow.

"I woke up layin in dewy grass and the sun was comin up. The plane had made a terrible wreck of that little woods but I was fine. I made tracks out of there across the farm fields and I'll tell you, Tallie, I was still headin north and right in my way was the farmhouse of Ma and Pa Sphincter, and that's how I came to belong to them."

Small had always thought his flight to freedom ended at the Sphincter's farmhouse. But that flight had never ended.

In the east, low under the bowl of stars, a glow manifested on the far horizon, steadily growing, seeming to float as it neared. "It's a car," said Small.

Talldorf straightened his skirts. "Who do you suppose it is, Small?"

From a mysterious interior light the car took the lines of a 1950s Pontiac station wagon scarcely bobbing on the roadway as it neared. An other-worldly sensation increased with its approach. Despite himself Small's thumb was out and the old white wagon halted, breathing resonantly beside them. Small opened the door and climbed in. "Howdy, neighbor," he said.

For a moment Small thought no one was there. But in a far corner of the driver's seat sat the Spacewaif.

"Welcome, I am anxious to hear what you have to tell me!"

His straw-colored hair looked still like a bird's nest, his stringy blond beard like Fu Manchu's, and blue eyes so large and clear that Rhinehardt and Ruby Grueber braced themselves from vertigo. The interior of the station wagon was vast and empty: not a suitcase, not a spare tire.

"Your overhead light is on," Small said.

"Isn't it wonderful? Everything works."

"You can see the road better if you turn if off," said Small.

Instantly the Spacewaif reached up and switched off the light. "It's true, I see better already. Thank you."

"You're welcome," said Small.

The Spacewaif gunned her up to-thirty mph and held her there.

"I'm Rhinehardt Grueber. Amish gentlefolkman on my way to a picnic. This is Mrs. Ruby Grueber, my honored spouse."

"I'm not surprised," said the Spacewaif.

"Pleased to meet you," said Talldorf.

"Pleased to meet you," echoed the Spacewaif.

"What, if I might inquire, is you name?" Small asked.

"I don't have a name."

There was a silence.

"Then you're the first person I ever met who didn't," replied Small.

"There are lots of us. I'm on my way to join them."

"Where?" said Small.

"I don't know."

Talldorf and Small looked glumly ahead at the empty road.

"Are you going across the mountains?" ventured Talldorf.

"All right. Which way are the mountains?"

Small whistled. "Straight in front of you."

"Wonderful, we're on our way! This car was given to me free in the last state. Which was that? They gased it up and the gas never goes down."

"The gas gauge is broke," explained Small.

"No, everything works. Listen how quietly this car runs."

"Maybe you're out of gas and we're coastin," said Small.

"Why no," said the Spacewaif. "We're going up hill. It really doesn't matter, because I'm leaving the world soon."

God, a suicide! thought Small. Talldorf gazed in alarm around his bonnet.

"Listen to me!" demanded Small, "I'm older than you—though it is true I have retained my youth admirably—so listen to a man who's seen real troubles. Me and Tallie—I mean me and the missus—we been broke and broken, homeless and chased, harassed and cheated and there's them that wants our heads this very minute if you can believe such a thing. But in here, young man," Small slapped his black broadcloth chest, "there is hope. What are you, a sniveling coward? I advise you not to kill yourself. You're sure to regret it. Especially don't kill yourself on these mountain roads."

"Even I, a gentlefolk lady, have sometimes felt the way you feel," piped Talldorf. "But where there is light there is hope! Where there is guilt there is redemption! Where there is—"

"I'm not going to kill myself, I'm going to live forever. I'm leaving the world in a spaceship."

"Ohhh—" said Talldorf and Small.

"I don't belong in this world. This is not my world. I'm going home to my own world, I'm going home!" said the Spacewaif ecstatically. Talldorf was touched, and Small scrunched beneath his black hat. "I'll find the spaceship because it is waiting for me and because I look so hard. I'm always looking, I've looked for so long!" He groaned. His head fell alarmingly onto his breast but he recovered himself in an instant. "There are many of us going."

"Not me," said Small.

"We'll all meet very soon," said the Spacewaif.

"Where?" scoffed Small.

"I don't know."

"I'm not surprised," said Small.

"It could be tonight. It could be tomorrow."

The three of them peered through the windshield in silence where the headlights illumined no spaceship, only deep dark pine forests lining the highway.

"The mountains would be the perfect place to find the spaceship," said the Spacewaif.

"So close to the sky, huh?" asked Small. "We ain't going to find a gas station up there either."

"This is all the money I have." The Spacewaif indicated three pennies lying in the ashtray.

"I hope you like the Rocky Mountains, Ruby," said Small, "cause maybe we're gonna stay here."

"You aren't Ruby," said the Spacewaif.

The eyes of Talldorf and Small shifted with alarm to the spacewaif. Small's voice spoke in a tone that chilled Talldorf: "Who is she if she ain't Rhinehardt Grueber's spouse?"

"She's Talldorf," said the Spacewaif. "And you are Small."

"Curses!" Small whipped off his broad-brimmed hat. "How did you know?"

"I saw you on television. Why are you dressed like that?"

"We're on the lam from villains who want to rub us out like they did to JFQ and Just Plain Bill," said Small.

"Because we spoke the truth," testified Talldorf.

"We ain't runnin scared," Small said, "this is a tactical maneuver. Our light will shine again all over our great land, Mr. Nameless."

"Yes, your light must shine," the Spacewaif said. "and fear not. I am your best friend because your best friend is the person next to you. He better be."

"Good point," Small observed.

"I have learned a great secret," said the Spacewaif: "There is no need to worry. Ha, ha, ha, everything is ok! EVERYTHING!"

"I ain't so sure," said Small and he warned the Spacewaif that he could not expect to survive in the manner he was employing because he had no logistical support. The Spacewaif answered that he had the support of the entire universe.

"You are my friend," said the Spacewaif. "So you are supporting me with great energy. The intention of the universe is that I reach my destination. My will is to rise to higher life. I am one with my will, so I will rise."

"You *will*!" said Talldorf.

"As soon as he finds his spaceship," said Small as the rocky walls of a canyon filed past in the headlights. "As your friend it is my responsibility to point out to you that you appear to me to be a bum and out of touch with reality."

"We lock ourselves up in our heads," said the Spacewaif as pine trees swept past, "That is the worst prison of all. We must give up everything, we must give up our prison walls. There is nothing beyond this moment on the way to the deliverance of the spaceship."

They peered out the windshield at the unwinding road which just then bridged a saddle that opened a field of stars spread over flatlands below.

"Anyone who wants can go on the spaceship."

"Thanks," said Small.

"You might want to if you see it," said the Spacewaif.

"Not me," said Small.

"You can change your mind."

"I might," said Talldorf.

"You're nuts, Talldorf. I don't see no spaceship in my star."

"Your star is within you," said the Spacewaif.

"Where do you think your spaceship is?" asked Small.

The sudden glow infused the forest ahead radiating whitely among the trees as if midday were being created among them.

"*Jesus* it's a train!" Small yelled as they rounded the wooded curve, "Brakes!" and was a hair from stomping the pedal already under the Spacewaif's foot as the car skidded to a halt in the illumined gravel at the roadside.

"The spaceship!" cried the Spacewaif who was out the door and hitching up his pants to be presentable. He extended his arms toward the towering ship, "I'm coming!"

For an instant the thought of his friends in the old white station wagon approached the horizon of consciousness like a feather's breath on the cheek but was lost amidst too great joy and he broke into a run. Talldorf and Small saw him running. He ran into the air. He rose across the meadow in silhouette, the sleeves of his T-shirt and his baggy pants flapping in the crisp night air to merge in the light of the ship which immediately rose steadily and surely radiating the great meadow, polishing the white hood of the station wagon, illuminating pinnacles of granite that soared into the black sky and forest tree tops stretching before them and gave back then shadow like a following sea to darkness returning softly and surely leaving the headlights on the gravel, the idling engine, the green light of the dash where the gas gauge read *Full*.

"Well, at least we don't have to walk," said Small sliding behind the wheel. Talldorf sat rigid, his mouth open, staring at where the ship had been.

"Snap out of it, Talldorf! Put your bonnet on before a cop comes by." Small shook Talldorf's arm. It felt like India rubber. "Talldorf! You got to learn to handle everyday life." Small jammed the bonnet onto Talldorf's head. "Everything's ok! We could have been kidnaped by space men but we're safe. I don't know who that guy was—"

"That," said Talldorf. "was the Spacewaif."

"Whoever he was the car is ours," said Small gunning the white station wagon onto the road.

Chapter 31

THE TEETH OF THE SIERRA

T he West was so huge it caused hallucinations, Small maintained, as they twisted down the western face of the Rocky Mountains in the old white Pontiac station wagon.

Talldorf smoothed his skirt and looked at Small from the corners of his eyes. "Obviously the spaceship was real, or where did the Spacewaif go?"

"What Spacewaif?"

"The one whose car you're driving."

"I guess you ain't figured it out, Talldorf, so I'll explain it to ya. That guy was an ICE agent sent by LeMight. That crazy trap backfired and blew em out of the universe and we got away with a free car."

The needle of the gas gauge pointed to *Full*, another sign designed to betray them.

"Won't we come to New Jerusalem soon?" asked Talldorf.

New Jerusalem, Holy City of the Number of Greater Brothers. Headquarters for the Greater Brothers Than Most Foundation For Philanthropic Distribution, economic capital of the new West on the alkali flats of dry Lake Pepper; sinks, hot springs, the desert where dinosaurs died.

"I don't want to worship gold, Talldorf, I want to spend it. We're among the number of lesser brothers. We wouldn't be welcome in New Jerusalem."

Small's star led them on: Land, always the land, ridge after ridge under the hammering sun as the white Pontiac carried them forward in the race of wits against the forces of evil while Talldorf sprawled in his seat like a wilted flower and Small squinted under his hat brim for the end. One evening, propped against a boulder on an arid rise Talldorf looked over the desert: "Let's stay," he said. It seemed to Small he had said, 'Sire, we have all of France.'

"Onward, Marshal," Small mumbled climbing into the driver's seat. "We're goin to Nero where Small takes em big."

They whizzed along at eighty-five miles an hour and saw the scarlet halo in the sky 100 miles away like the final smoldering twilight of man. "Get your bonnet straight, Tallie, we're headed for enemy territory and I expect you to act like a lady."

"I'm willing to try harder, Small. You didn't have to reveal our identities to Yang Yin, but you did. You couldn't keep your mouth shut."

"Don't be pointin fingers. If there's fingers to point the Commander'll point em. Small is givin orders and makin policy because I got better tactical brains, I care about stayin alive."

"Then we should stay out of cities, Small."

Cities is where they hide the money. Small fears nothin and no one, includin J. Lugar Edgar, his FIB, and the lice from ICE."

"We haven't had money up to now and we've done fine."

"We had money. You gave it away to your favorite charities."

"We don't even need gas."

"I don't want to hear about that, Talldorf." Small had crawled under the Pontiac and hammered on the gas tank with a rock. He concluded the carburetor was plugged so the fuel kept circulating and being reused. He said they didn't make cars like they used to.

"It ain't natural you not likin to gamble if your old man was a gambler, Talldorf. You never take chances because down deep you're afraid you got a real taste for runnin risks. Fools and children got angels to watch over em. Short said window washers have an Angel. But Short was senile. I got to take care of myself and you too. Don't worry, Small can handle it."

Kicking neon chorus legs flashed along the strip and a giant parrot winked a yellow eye at traffic. They squinted in the loveless light of Nero and Small's shoulders squared under his burying black coat. They parked in shadows and moved undistinguished among late-night freaks toward the cafe in the flatiron building. Green shades flapped on the second floor in the red brick building across the way. Plate glass, green-tinted with the late hour, curved around a triangular apex forming an island of light. The counter man in whites wore a paper cap. A narrow man in a hat and blue pinstripe suit sat on a counter stool beside a blonde in a red dress.

"Yes sir," said the counterman who was surprised at nothing.

"Coffee for my spouse and me and two chocolate donuts."

"One moment, young man," said Rudolph. "I would prefer the roast beef dinner, a side of sunny side up eggs with hash-browns, a piece of cherry pie and a chocolate milkshake."

The counter man cocked his head and slowly turned away. The man in blue pinstripes and his companion turned their sharp features to inspect the pigeons.

"Jeeze, Talldorf," hissed Small, "ya ever see a lady eat like that?"

"I can't afford to lose any more weight, Rhinehardt".

"Bring the roast beef, buddy! My wife don't want the eggs or potatoes or pie or milkshake. Coffee and donuts first! From now on," whispered Small, "I order for you. It's a religious tradition. The man talks, the woman keeps her mouth shut. That means you."

"Here ya go, Pops." The counter man slid donuts and coffee onto the counter.

"I'm usually addressed as Father."

"Sure—Father. We don't see many of your kind around here."

"There's no strength in meat, Rhinehardt. It'll make me sick. Tell the young man I want scrambled eggs and a chocolate milkshake."

"You tell him for Christ sake!"

"Young man, I can't eat roast beef because of my religious beliefs. You see my husband and I—"

"Make it eggs!" Small shouted. "She wants scrambled eggs and a chocolate milkshake."

"The giant's gonna drive the midget crazy," the counterman clued pinstripes.

Small sipped his coffee and ate some smoke. He felt the lure of great casinos looming like banks. They were surrounded by winners and losers, nighthawks and pigeons. Never before had he felt so acutely the drawn lines of battle nor so clearly perceived the enemy which was anyone between A. Small and the money. "We're here to make a killing," he growled. "When in Rome do as the Romans do. I been kiddin myself all this time. The only reason for wielding the squeegee is money and we gotta work fast."

"Paradise is our objective, Rhinehardt," Talldorf reminded Small.

"I want to take the money with me."

Rudolph stopped chewing to regard Small critically.

"Have I ever led you wrong?" said Small.

"Only at the Conservatory, dear."

"You'll never let me forget you took a fall, will ya, Ruby?"

The counter man laying out the victuals considered it just another family spat. Nor was he surprised that religious couples suffered like normal people. Sure as hell there was no god in this town, he'd make book on that.

Initiated once again into city life Talldorf and Small drove into the desert and parked under a cactus. They awoke long after one thousand soldiers awoke directly beneath them in caverns and tunnels burrowed into the desert earth by the busy military where humming computers sang the sinister song of the nuclear age.

"It looks like Paradise," yawned Talldorf.

"It ain't," said Small.

On the way into town Small outlined his plan: Talldorf was to solicit because people would take pity on a woman who looked like that.

"This town never heard of clean windows," Small observed. "They'll snap up your price without thinkin when they see you're a holy lady with no brains. Carry the Bible. We don't want em thinkin you're solicitin anything else. Now get out there and stick it to em."

Talldorf spotted the convex row of panes from the street and rushed up a dingy marble staircase of one of Nero's oldest buildings. His bladder had been full since Small had casually pissed in an alley while warning Talldorf not to squat behind an ash can. Talldorf hurtled past dark wainscotting and opaque glass doors to the ladies room at the end of the hall.

"My goodness, pardon me, Miss!"

"It's all right," said Purity Furbush. "Come in. I'm just freshening up. It gets so stuffy in the office with men smoking all the time and the windows are all stuck."

She looked at the passing figure of the pitifully tall bony creature in the shapeless dress and quaint gray bonnet.

"Oh—" sang Talldorf rushing through the door of the stall, "it must be awful."

Purity stood in front of the mirror brushing out her raven locks. She glowed with health and quivered with vitality. Her Miss America smile glittered from the tarnished glass. She kept trim skiing slopes of the high Sierra and doing half-gainers off high boards at casino pools. She was powdering her perfect nose when Talldorf hunched out of the stall.

"A thousand pardons. My name is Ruby — Ruby Grueber — Did I understand you to say the windows in your office are stuck, dear? I declare. My husband, Rhinehardt, and I have just arrived in this city of sin. You see I carry the Bible. Rhinehardt makes me. Poor Rhinehardt has run out of money. Rhinehardt is an expert at unsticking windows. We are Bible missionaries of the road. We wash windows and take donations for our important work of converting Christians into real Christians. We are a mom and pop team. We have no children. Lord knows I try, dear..."

"Oh, you poor thing. Here, sit down in the chair. Are you all right? Are you hungry? You look so pale."

Talldorf dropped onto the chair like a monstrous wounded partridge.

"Thankyou...I'm all right. I just get so nervous asking for charity. Lord knows Rhinehardt and I do good work."

"I'll run and ask Mr. Masterman to let you do the windows! You wait right here." She paused in the doorway. "I'm your friend, Ruby. Don't go away. I'll be right back."

Small grinned through his stove brush.

"I knew you could do it, Tallie!" he grabbed the buckets and bounded up the stairs. Purity welcomed them, standing curvaciously in the open door.

"You must be Purity." Small chuckled, swept off his hat and clicked his heels. "Allow me to introduce myself, Rhinehardt Grueber. I'm ready for anything, dear. Where's the sink? Me and the old lady'll fill our buckets."

"Excuse me, Mr. Grueber. I don't think your wife feels well."

"What are you talkin about?"

"I had one of my fainting spells, Rhinehardt".

"Everything's ok, Purity. She's always havin spells."

They filled their buckets in the alcove between offices.

"Coffee, Talldorf. Ya want a cup? Donations is a good idea. It was quick thinkin, but we'll probably get screwed. From the layout I'd say these guys are expensive divorce lawyers. Eyeballin it I'd call it twenty-five bucks. I'm gonna have to walk the ledge. Lucky I'm Small. They gotta consider the risk even though they don't. Besides which we gotta unstick the windows. What an angel Purity is! Whatever ya do, Talldorf, don't panic. Just back me up."

Small barged through an office door.

Wolford Vamp had been indefatigably pursuing his private investigation amid stacks of files cross referencing persons, places and facts relevant to the President's assassination.

"I'll get to the truth without computers and file cabinets too, Masterman," Wolford had growled more than once to Matt Masterman, Western Desert FIB Director. "You won't stop me and neither will they. I need space. I'm moving the furniture out of my office!"

Masterman and Purity Furbush had watched the piles of paper grow and cover the carpet as Wolfie grew haggard and leaner and meaner. Now Wolfie sprang from behind his desk.

"Watch out for those papers," he howled as Talldorf bumped into Small and dumped his bucket.

"I'm terribly sorry—" shrilled Talldorf as Wolfie dove to save soaked stacks of typescript: reports of agents on the scene, documents rife with manufactured incongruities, dossiers of unraveling complexities contradicting complexities, Wolfie's life's work set afloat on a soapy tide by some nincompoop.

"This is terrible," wailed Purity as she darted about retrieving soggy sheets.

"Who are these nincompoops? Why are they in my office?" howled Wolfie. He slapped his forehead: "You oughta be arrested as spies! You oughta be hanged! You've undone blood, sweat, and tears. Where have I seen you two before?" Wolfie pushed his face into Small's bristles and searched the jade eyes.

"These are the window washers, Wolford," said Purity wringing her hands. "It's all my fault. They mean no harm. They're missionaries— of the road."

"Missionaries? I won't have my window washed! Get them out of my office, Furbush!"

Matt Masterman stood in the doorway, his straight lips bent in amusement.

"How do," said Small, "I'm Rhinehardt Grueber, Amish gentlefolkman. This here is my spouse."

"Pleased to meet you, Mr. Grueber. And you—ah—Mrs. Grueber. They're going to wash the windows, Wolfie. You'll think better with more light in here."

Wolfie glared.

"I'm so sorry, Wolford," Purity said. "Really nothing is ruined. I'll dry out every one of your papers for you."

"Microdot! Microdot! I'm going over your head, Masterman. I'm putting in a requisition to J. Lugar Edgar himself. I'm going to lunch. Out of my way!" He elbowed Ruby aside in his rush to the door.

Small raised the windows with his muscles and a butter knife. He crawled out onto the ledge and closed the window. Fortunately he set down his bucket before noting the gold letters trimmed in black:

F I B

It was a silent bellow of betrayal, of outrage, the knife in the back, immediate and devastating reprisal condemning the Commander for delegating responsibility to a nincompoop. Small jammed his hat over his eyes and shrunk behind his beard. His very hands felt exposed as he plied brush and squeegee with the intensity prescribed by Count Squeegee for disarming a foe.

"Rhinehardt does the high work," Talldorf explained to Purity as he scrubbed the insides taking special care with the gold-leaf lettering. "We feel people will be better Christians with more light in their lives."

"But you have no home, no money?" asked Purity.

"We observe an unspoken vow of poverty."

Considering herself a Christian Purity felt obliged to invite Ruby and her little husband into her own home.

"You can sleep in my bed, Ruby."

"Oh, I mustn't consider it, Purity dear."

When Small crawled back inside he hissed: "You nincompoop! You've led us to the Gestapo! You've delivered your Commander into the hands of the enemy. We're washin the windows of FIB. *FIB*!" Talldorf's eyes bulged.

He grew deathly pale. "Never have I appreciated the immeasurable depth of your stupidity! If you ain't slew the Commander and yourself it ain't your fault. Let's get the money and get outta this den of vipers."

"Small—We've been invited for supper and the night to Miss Furbush's apartment—"

"You're *incompetent*, Talldorf."

But Small could not take his eyes from the curves of the despised female agent. The wild call of adventure would not let him go.

Masterman approached. The appraising brown eyes of the lawman gleamed under sagging lids. "What do we owe you, Mr. Grueber?"

"We work only for donation, sir," Small said. "Whatever you think it's worth."

"Make a paid-out to Mr. Grueber for twenty-five dollars, Purity. You do quality work, folks. Do you plan to stay awhile in our foul city?" Masterman chuckled dryly.

"We go where we're needed, sir," answered Small. "The Lord will inform us."

"Ruby and Mr. Grueber are going to stay with me for a few days, Matt."

"Splendid. I wish you a happy and safe stay." Masterman shook Small's hand and nodded to Ruby who bent in a woeful curtsy.

As they headed down the stairs Small said, "That Matt Masterman is a swell fella. He's sure we ain't us but he ain't sure who we are and he don't want to find out. But it ain't Masterman who worries me, it's that psycho, Wolfie."

Purity Furbush's admiration for Wolfie Vamp's intelligence had increased 200 percent and was going up.

"Masterman will be replaced by a computer," Wolfie told her. He tapped his forehead. "I'm going to sit at the big desk with my fingers on the strings of the network."

As he put calls through to Washington for imperative information Wolfie cursed Masterman for an old fashioned frontier lawman, cursed Masterman's boots and Masterman's string tie.

"They exiled me to this anus of the universe because they were afraid of my brains, Masterman," Wolfie barked. "I can smell a rat in the ink all the way from Washington. I didn't vote for the pinko sonofabitch but he was my Commander-In-Chief and somebody is pulling a cover-up. That *somebody* is big. The dogs on top are going to feel my heat. Big dogs, Masterman! Somebody up there is going to notice me. Someday you'll be working for me. I'll give you one more chance. What do you say, Matt. Put in Microdot. I'm begging you."

"Nope."

"The first bulletin alerted us to an extensive Marxist conspiracy. Then they tell us the assassin is a nobody. Just a nut. And who was he? — I got it right here. I can't find anything in this mess! This ain't it. This is Talldorf and Small, the window washers. Why don't they arrest them? They're the center of the conspiracy. Document 34956: Interview With Miss Deerly. The landlady. She said she'd seen Just Plain Bill at Small's apartment. Not once, *frequently*! Somebody in the Bureau is trying to cover for a lot of nobodies. I want to know why. I *will* know why!"

"Don't bet you life on it, son."

"Something came over the wire you didn't tell me about!"

"Nope."

"Visitors?"

"Yup."

"ICEmen!"

"Yup."

"Gee whiz, ICEmen! Something big is going on. Did you put it through to Washington?"

"Yup."

"And you haven't got an answer! With Microdot we'd have it: mug shots, fingerprints, morals check, license plates — Someone's in mortal danger."

"Yup."

"Let me handle the case, Matt. ICEmen, they're carnivores, those guys. They're here to ice a key witness. They've done it before, don't deny it! I have witnesses, don't think I haven't. I'm putting it together. I've got proof enough right now to hang a few rotten generals. There's the skinny cocktail waitress at the Gobi Club, what's her name. All she says is 'Fuck the President.' There's the fat bartender at the Pink Poodle. He was a rotten Commie sympathizer in the 30's. A thousand little details that add up to something *gigantic*! Waitresses, busboys, dishwashers, what a seedy sick poisonous sector of the population, Masterman. The poor, the insane, the dregs of this world. I'm not interested in having dregs for neighbors, but they know something, and they're not talking."

"Yup."

"I'll find out who ICE is tracking and get to them before those killers eliminate some vital source of information." Wolfie pulled his .38 Police Special out of his shoulder holster and pried it open. "No bullets, ha ha. Where does Purity keep the bullets? Point out the ICEmen, Matt. I'll tail them."

"Nope. And when you're outside the office I want you on double alert. ICEmen have been known to ice the wrong folk."

Small drummed his fingers on Purity's coffee table and sniffed the conditioned air. The carpet stretched like a trophy from wall to wall. There was only one door and they were on the third floor. It was suicidal to be here. But Small could not help himself. Small had designs on Purity in spite of Talldorf and Ruby both.

Purity Furbush was a wholesome American girl. Purity's mother had taught her how to cook and iron and darn her father's socks. Purity's father had worked for the post office for thirty years before dropping dead on his route. Elroy Furbush had carried doggie crumbs in his blue uniform pocket and kept a kennel of Boxers in the backyard of the modest Furbush home.

"I'm going to train them to eat people's heads off," he explained to his wife. "And I can do it, Mildred. Someday the police will see the value of vicious dogs for people control. I got a way with dogs and little girls."

Elroy Furbush had made a champion swimmer out of Purity when she was three years old. Purity's love of the pool exploded into a love for all sports and the out of doors. She had gone to secretarial school so she could earn money enough to enjoy nature.

Talldorf luxuriated in the long tub after locking the bathroom door against an unexpected intrusion by his new girl friend. The intimate inspection of Purity's life that was promised appealed to his prurience. At last he might find out what women really were. Small hammered on the bathroom door.

"Let me in, Ruby!" Small turned on both faucets. "For god's sake, Talldorf, watch yourself every minute. One slip and Furbush will know you ain't a woman. She'll scream for the Feds."

"I'm confident, Small. Tomorrow I'll dust and vacuum and clean the toilet bowl. Purity and I are friends already."

"Good, Talldorf. Very good. But don't like her because she's the enemy. Twenty cops will probably drop in here tonight just to say hello. Only you could get us into a mess like this. I'll distract her with some of my charm to take the heat off you and tomorrow I'll case Nero for what we're gonna knock over."

Small knew when a woman was attracted to him; Furbush couldn't hide it from Small. She dropped her dark eyes toward her wonderful breasts whenever Small winked at her.

"We ain't takin your bed, Purity, and that's final," Small said. "And quit callin me Mr. Grueber. Call me Rhiney, sweetie."

"Of course, Rhinehardt. Ruby, you can sleep on the couch, and, Rhiney, you can sleep on the floor."

In the morning Small slapped on his black hat. "I'm going out," he called as Talldorf pulled the plug on the vacuum cleaner. "Keep the home fires burnin, honey."

Talldorf watched Small's dark figure hunch away down the block and hurried to the kitchen to open Purity's well-stocked refrigerator. "I love to see men eat," Purity had said last night at supper as Ruby wiped up the last drop of tuna gravy on her plate and diligently abstained from more. "My father was a big eater. Please, Rhinehardt, help yourself."

It had been the same at breakfast. Full of french toast and sausage Small patted his black coat front and belched. With a breakfast like that he could race an ICE agent out of town and beat him over the mountains. Holding the Bible in front of him Small parted the sidewalk traffic like a little black boat. Small congratulated himself: nobody knows what to do about a religious nut like Rhinehardt Grueber, but avoid him. Nor did anyone fail to notice him, including Wolfie Vamp who was guzzling black coffee at the Straight Shooter Cafe as Small walked past. What ill did this bode for Small, whose green eyes had always been the sharpest, that the nail-hard ones of the FIBman saw him first?

Wolfie gulped his coffee and leaped out the door. Wolfie shadowed the little black figure straight down the middle of the walk. The midget was in disguise, any fool could see that. Wolfie racked his brains for notorious husband-wife teams as Small arrived at the Strip where glass casinos reflected arid Nevada. Small paused, ever curious who was riding while he walked, to witness a limousine pull to the curb. Out stepped a shoe like a mirror, a well-tailored gray suit, a smart fedora all on the unlikely person of O'Toole. Small struggled to believe his eyes. O'Toole strode toward him with his chin in the sky.

"O'Toole!" Small hissed. O'Toole didn't even look. Small trotted after him tugging at his coat tail.

"Leave go the threads little man before I hammer you into the sidewalk!"

"O'Toole, it's me, Small! Your old pal from the Windy City."

"Small!? Is it you?"

"Shhhhhh — I'm Rhinehardt Grueber. I'm in disguise."

"Small!" O'Toole opened his arms in welcome just as Wolfie Vamp emerged from behind a lamp post and came zeroing in.

"Who is this man!" demanded Wolfie. "What did you put this little freak up to, O'Toole? I'll find out. I have every Wanted poster since the beginning of time. I'll nail you as an accessory."

"To what?" said O'Toole.

"To the assassination of the President."

"I voted for him."

"Would you care for a Bible reading, sir?" Small inquired.

"I'll get you!" snarled Wolfie.

"Don't foam at the mouth, Wolfie," said O'Toole. "Rhinehardt Grueber's a harmless religious nut. See my boss if you got questions."

"Taborim begat Josephat," Small announced with the good book open, "And Josephat began Isamat and Goledon and —"

O'Toole jerked Small into the Quick Buck Lounge.

"Wonderful, Small," said O'Toole when they were seated in a rear booth. "The Feds never been onto me till you guys show up on television. Are you trying to get all your old friends killed? The Executioner, oh boy! ICE and the FIB were in my office as soon as it happened. I have no enemies, Small. I don't want enemies. You advise the President, they kill him the next day. Now you're a religious fanatic. You're trouble. What do you need, Small? Jesus, is Talldorf still around?"

"Wait till you see him, you'll never believe it."

"Why not? He's crazier than you. He follows you."

"How did you fall into the gold mine, O'Toole?"

O'Toole assured Small that everything was legitimate.

"I'm an executive at the Cruciform Casino, Small."

"You're in the rackets. Danger and death."

"Don't mention those words, Small. Bad luck."

O'Toole admitted his business had some wiggles to it but he had prospered because he could wiggle with it. The Big Man who moved into the Ensardo empire after that Wisconsin bloodbath that maybe Small had read about had legitimized the old rackets. The Big Man had called O'Toole from Paris where O'Toole had gone for a good time after the bad times of his marriage. In Paris O'Toole had found himself with a few girls and was running a profitable little business that turned exclusive when his girls attracted the diplomatic trade. Although O'Toole had never personally met him, the Big Man liked the way O'Toole had handled his girls, and had offered a position in Nero.

"You're a pimp," Small explained.

"No no no—" objected O'Toole . "I was having a good time. You don't understand subtleties, Small." O'Toole flicked a piece of lint from his immaculate cuff. "That's why I'm an executive."

"Danger and death," said Small.

"Please, Small. I'm riding high. I run a big piece of the action. The Big Man has vision but American business has no vision. There's no honor in American business, Small, but in our business there is honor. You're not required to kiss ass. I do my job and I'm well paid."

"How will you survive, O'Toole? You couldn't find a more honorable business than mine and they want me dead, like Bill."

"That maniac—" O'Toole belted down his scotch.

"He didn't do it, O'Toole. He was innocent as me and you."

"No wonder they fried him."

"For my years of quality service I end up a hunted man, O'Toole."

"No one's hunting you, Small. I saw Walter Smilerite on TV say you two were no longer being considered in the investigation."

"It's a trick to make me tip my hand. I tell you A. Small is the most wanted man in America. That dumb FIBman Vamp recognizes me already but he can't put it together. Because I told the truth at Nuclear Strike Headquarters I'm number one on the hit parade. I'm wanted. I'm desperate. But I'm gonna snatch a pile of cash right out from under their noses and head for paradise and you're gonna help me."

O'Toole and Small drove to the Cruciform Casino in the limo.

"How much do you want for the job, Small?"

"Two thousand bucks. Two hundred in advance."

"It's yours. Friendship is bigger than both of us. Small—keep a low profile."

"Thanks, O'Toole. Tomorrow morning Rhinehardt and Ruby Grueber will be washing your windows."

"Ruby?"

The brick-block apartment building in which Purity lived had the stolidity which made Talldorf feel at home. Chintz curtains turned gaily in the pleasant breeze coming through the open windows. It wasn't easy being a woman Talldorf reflected as he sliced another piece of ham and popped it into his mouth. He was reaching for the ice cream when a key turned in the lock and Purity waltzed through the door, her arms full of packages.

"Hello, Ruby," Purity said excitedly, "I've bought a few things I want you to try on." Purity's trim athletic figure swung the pleats in her skirt. Talldorf followed her into the bedroom, attempting to appear matronly.

Purity slipped out of her sweater and unhooked her brassiere. It was too late to turn away. When Talldorf had become a patriarch he would remember the lost moment of those full moons. She slipped into a T-shirt bearing the Olympic team logo.

"Take off your dress, Ruby. I bought you a new one."

"I can't! What would my husband say?"

"Ruby, don't be modest. It's just us girls. I bought these silk panties too."

"Oh, I couldn't—"

"I hope this fits. See, the cups are padded to give you more uplift."

"I mustn't, Purity. I could be excommunicated. Rhinehardt buys my underwear the same time he buys his. What's good enough for Rhinehardt is good enough for me is what Rhinehardt says."

"Ruby, believe me, trust me. I'm going to turn you into the beautiful woman you really are. Look through this copy of Wash That Man Out of Your Hair-Do Magazine. Here. Isn't she sexy? It will make your red curls blaze like a fire."

"I can't do it! Poor Rhinehardt. Right now he's trudging door to door trying to make a little money to further our good works. Rhinehardt is crazy about how I look. We can't offend Rhinehardt, Purity. He's easily offended as small men often are. He expects me to be modest and follow him to the ends of the earth. And I do my best. Why if I were to put on this little skirt — "

"You just mustn't let Rhinehardt rule your life, Ruby. My mother was loyal to my father and he gave it away in doggie crumbs. My father was a happy failure and my mother went down with him. Rhinehardt is not a failure yet but he seems well on his way. I think Rhinehardt has a lot of nerve treating a hard working woman like yourself like he does! Oh, Ruby, please don't look so sad. At least you have someone who loves you for who you are. I think you're lucky. I wish I could find someone but they're all so wishy-washy. Rhinehardt is so definite and manly. Actually I find him quite interesting and — attractive."

"You do?"

"Yes. I do. But don't worry. I was raised a Christian too, Ruby. I make it a policy to steer clear of married men."

Talldorf sat reluctantly in the kitchen draped in a towel as Purity sheared his rusty locks and goosebumps rippled as her bosom perfumed his brain. He protested the hair curlers that bent his hair; he enjoyed the manicure; he was aghast at the nail polish.

"I haven't had so much fun since I played with dolls," Purity beamed. "I just love this, Ruby, don't you? We'll put a little mascara on your pretty long lashes, and eyeliner to bring out your pretty blue eyes, and I've got a shade of lipstick just perfect for your coloring. I can't believe you've never put on lipstick. Ruby, oh please — "

"Lipstick is against every church rule, Purity. I can't! It would break Rhinehardt's heart."

"Ruby, it will make you look so sexy. I'll do it for you and the church can't say anything. Pucker — Now look in the mirror. Don't you feel a whole lot better already?"

A vulgar distortion of the photograph of his mother which he had so long cherished stared back at Talldorf.

"I feel disloyal. I should wash it off right away. My legs are ugly and hairy. Rhinehardt will laugh at me."

"I'll get my razor. Oh, this is so exciting, Ruby! Rhinehardt is a man. I guarantee you he's going to be pleased."

Talldorf met Small glumly at the door.

"What the hell happened to you?"

Rudolph held a painted finger to his painted lips. Small was grinning with glee.

"Where'd ya get the new duds, Ruby dear? You're so cute!"

"Doesn't she look nice, Rhinehardt?" Purity said.

"He's laughing at me!"

"I ain't laughing at ya, honey. I think ya look real sweet."

"You aren't angry about the make-up are you, Rhinehardt?" asked Purity.

"She turns me on," said Small, kissing Purity on the neck.

"Rhinehardt!" Ruby screamed.

"Just a friendly peck. Can't a married man have a female friend? I feel good, girls. I got us a big job and we're in the chips." Small flashed a wad of bills. "To celebrate my success I'm takin both you lovely things out for a steak dinner."

They dined at the *Inferno* in the Cruciform Casino. The dark paneled walls were covered with blazing oil paintings of nudes. Small sat with his back to the wall and his eye on the door.

"Don't ever say Rhinehardt Grueber don't know the in places," Small boasted, "Cause this is it and we're in. The three of us. You know what they say about threes, Ruby?"

"Three's a crowd," said Ruby.

"You got it, baby. What should I order for you? They got a weight watcher's plate: A peach and cottage cheese. I bet ya can get it in a doggie bag."

"Rhinehardt is always lighthearted and joking when we get a big job," Ruby explained to Purity. "I'll order what I want, Rhinehardt. I can make up my own mind."

"Since when?"

"Ruby and I had a little heart-to-heart about women's rights today, Rhinehardt," said Purity.

"Women ain't got rights. Especially married women. Especially my spouse."

Over dinner Small steered the conversation to Purity's job.

"Wolford is so dedicated to his work on the assassination," Purity said. "He works hard and I admire him so much. The facts he's uncovered are just horrifying. Wolford doesn't believe that horrible man committed the murder alone. I help him all I can. Mr. Masterman thinks it's silly but I think it's scary. Why the whole country is crawling with fugitives and Wolford is going to have them all arrested."

Small's skin crawled and Talldorf cringed involuntarily.

Coy looks had passed between Talldorf and Purity. Talldorf felt a compulsion to confess everything. Purity was so sweet and so generous. She was also a Fed, but what did that mean?

"The broad's got a crush on me but I ain't turnin a hair," whispered Small as Talldorf turned off the lamp. "And don't pull no long face, Talldorf. Ya sit right in there on her bed and watch her undress. She's naive I tell myself. Can any broad be so naive? How can she think Talldorf's a woman? You must be puttin on a terrific act. The company congratulates you. But don't get any ideas and don't show no sympathy. Whores got hearts of gold, Talldorf, but FIB agents got hearts of styrofoam."

"She's not an agent, Small. She's a secretary."

"She thinks Wolfie is a great American! See how attractive she is when you're rottin in the pen. She'd testify against ya and send ya postcards."

"She likes me for who I am, Small. Purity likes *me*.. And she trusts me."

"Get it straight, Ruby. She ain't never gonna know who you are because there's only one way to communicate that to a woman."

Chapter 32

SMALL FALLS

T he Cruciform Casino was a luxury hotel fifteen stories tall. The halls were arrow straight with small black worm designs in the red carpet, the walls a numbing beige, the low ceilings of acoustic tile so no footfall would distract a guest from the canned music washing the brain.

O'Toole laughed at Ruby Grueber: "I'm gonna put you in the movies, baby."

"Hey, nobody feels up Mrs. Grueber unless I say it's ok," Small said.

"O'Toole! Stop it!" Rudolph felt his dignity was being violated. O'Toole ordered coffee and Small sat at O'Toole's desk with his feet up.

"This is ridiculous," said O'Toole. "You can't put him on the ledges in those flying skirts, Small."

"Talldorf does the insides. Give him a pass key."

"Do you steal, Talldorf?"

"Talldorf's got the naive idea he don't need cash, O'Toole."

"And you're insured of course, Small."

"Small don't sue cause Small don't fall."

"Problems have arisen, Small. I remember the Gumm Tower and the Conservatory. You two were famous for disasters. For God's sake don't get anybody killed."

"You're still popping pills, O'Toole. What are you on now?"

"Vitamins, Small. I take care of myself."

"You still look like you're about to jump out of your skin. If you got no enemies how come you're a nervous wreck?"

"Executive pressures, Small."

"It ain't that I'm the most wanted man in America that's botherin you is it, O'Toole?"

"Nobody's after you guys."

"General LeMight and all kinds of federal agents are searching for Small and me, O'Toole."

"You're crazier than Small, Talldorf, which is proved by the skirt you're wearing. I never worried when you were with my ex, but I never suspected Small was kinky."

As his disguise relieved Talldorf of the strain of masculinity with Purity it now alleviated his old guilt toward O'Toole and supplied the temerity for him to con a friendly interest in O'Toole's former spouse. "How is Sue?" he asked tentatively.

"Don't mention that name!" O'Toole's sneer made Talldorf shrink. He'd made a mistake he had sworn he'd never make again. Deceit. Lies. Disguises. Sham.

"Danger and death," said Small as O'Toole popped another pill. "That's whats bad for your health, not a lack of vitamins. You're sittin on dynamite, O'Toole. Take the money and run before they rub you out."

"The risk I'm running is Small," O'Toole said with a wry look. He suggested they enjoy themselves and remember that they were in a vacation playground.

They began on the fifteenth floor.

Small planned to do a floor a day working his way along ornamental ledges that separated stories of the cross. The view was magnificent: sagebrush-covered desert swept to distant mountain peaks, but Small had no inclination for the view. He turned to the first grimy window and felt his helplessness. Nobody looked out the windows; no one came to Nero for the view. They watched their wallets and their chances.

"Death and destruction," muttered Small splashing the window with his brush. He cut the water with his gleaming squeegee, gift in faith from the second-to-last great martyr, fanned the window, let the edges drip and moved hurriedly on glancing down at the street. Just as he expected, Wolfie Vamp was spying at him from below. Yes, and several idlers gazed up to where he stood. None would lay a hand on A. Small. He would dance through their fingers.

Small found it difficult to keep his mind on his work. As the wind rose it annoyed him and when the sun came over the roof the glass streaked. Small ignored the streaks. In the afternoon he saw Wolfie again staring fixedly up. The lanky form of Matt Masterman ambled up the walk, glancing up from under his Stetson. He led Wolfie away by the sleeve and stuffed him into a government car which retreated toward town.

"I got you covered," Small boasted to the wind. "Nobody catches Small napping." Where was Talldorf? Lagging behind as usual.

Talldorf scrubbed the inner panes. A life of deception! It was too late; he was in too deep. How low. How cowardly to win the confidence of such an innocent creature with disguise and deceit! He was certain that Purity loved his true nature which he had not withheld from her. Would she not love him more when she knew it was Rudolph who understood with a delicacy she imagined capable only of woman?

Small glared through the window: "Hurry up!" He shot away on the ledge.

Rudolph felt a chill at the thought of a future without Small. But wouldn't it be paradise to have Purity for his own? Purity, Purity, Purity. Confusion so possessed him that he backed out of occupied rooms calling unwashed windows clean. His gangling feminine figure hunched down red tunnels of halls ducking nozzles of sprinklers from one door to the next with his pass key. He spoke falsetto to gamblers who pinched him while he longed only for the sweet murmur of Purity's confidence and the soft pillows of her tidy bed.

Coffee breaks were infrequent with Small on full alert.

"Have you got the makings, Small?" Talldorf whispered in a back booth of the *Inferno*. Since Talldorf had been wearing a dress it was Small's policy to roll the cigarettes. Male or female Talldorf was dependent on him.

"Roll your own, floozie, and don't forget to sweep up the crumbs."

The hurried pace of the job harried them both. Small was worse than a gadfly the way he worried about LeMight's agents behind every bush. But Talldorf did his best to remain cheerful.

"I'm sorry you're in such an evil humor, Rhinehardt. Things could be worse. We could be rotting in prison. You've outsmarted the Feds. We're seated comfortably in this fancy dining room drinking coffee out of the best china. Look at this perfect rosebud. The sun is shining. The sky is blue. We're breezing through the job."

It was why Small liked him. No matter how inept, clumsy or woebegone, Talldorf always did his best to cheer up Small.

"I'm ok, Ruby. Close the tobacco bag so it don't dry out."

Complaints, thought Small, why bother? I should forgive him his faults. He's come a long way since I took him in. I taught him all he knows. He fans a window with the best of em and he's stuck with my high standards. Talldorf's a loyal friend.

"Tallie, the Feds are runnin circles around our ankles but they can't even see us. We're gonna escape. We're gonna blow town with our pockets full of greenbacks. We're entitled to our share. I apologize for the way I been actin."

Back on the ledge Small's thoughts turned to Purity: A man pulling a big job like I am deserves some relaxation. Powder yourself up, Purity. Small ain't waitin. He turned a corner of the building into the wind, teetered, and hurried on. The sun angled deep and orange beyond the high Sierra when Small completed a slap-dash job on the last window. He retraced his steps along the ledge to find Talldorf, bonnet askew, squeegeeing far behind.

"Ruby," Small growled when Rudolph opened the windows. "You're way behind, like usual."

"A mom and pop team!" declared a man in a Hawaiian shirt. "That's what made America great, Myrtle. You two keep it up!"

"Up yours too," said Small crawling in the window. Myrtle shrunk behind Harry.

"Shake your tail, Ruby. *We* ain't on vacation."

"Rhinehardt dear, I was telling these nice people how we spread the good word."

"I'll be in the casino sloshin down a drink."

Small slammed the door and Myrtle took command.

"He certainly doesn't seem religious to me! You wretched thing," she said to Talldorf, "how do you put up with the beast?"

"I love him," said Talldorf squeegeeing the windows. "Poor Rhinehardt was an orphan. Please forgive him. He means no harm."

"Now if he beats you," offered Harry aiming his glass at Talldorf, "you get the law on him."

Small's brain turned green as he passed the payer's cage. He passed the travel agency in the lobby and wondered how much a ticket to Manchuria cost. A pretty blonde rested her breasts on a counter. He thought of Purity and his blood pounded in his veins. His progress through the casino, Bible in hand, scattered tourists like the advance of a black Bonaparte. He marched into a lounge.

"Whiskey on the rocks and fill it up with water."

He carried his poison to the gaming tables scanning faces for agents sent by LeMight. Small sat in a padded chair of the gallery with his drink and watched cards fly from the boot, hands reaching and pulling in the money. The action did not blind him to Wolfie Vamp, sniffing along the carpet past a roulette table, nor the two following Wolfie. With the Bible open Small watched them pass from beneath his hat brim. ICEmen stuck out on them like badges, their eyes like bullet holes; Wolfie was in real trouble. Small took a glug of whiskey feeling more invulnerable than ever.

No one had the brains to trap A. Small, and sharpies not so sharp as he were relieving suckers of their money. How tiresome that he would have to play their game before sticking the loot in his pocket. They would get a day flight. He wanted to see the America he had known sink into the sea. They would drink to the last sight of the continent, they would drink to freedom as the plane carried them away to paradise. When Talldorf laid his hand on Small's shoulder Small leaped to his feet spilling his drink.

"Don't do that!"

Talldorf stood with his hands in dishwater staring absently at his reflection in the louvered window above the sink. Purity was so appreciative, so pleased by his cheerful industry. Purity was so friendly. He began washing plates anxiously looking forward to another intimate chat in Purity's bedroom.

Purity was cheesecake. Small sat with a copy of *Mine Magazine* open on his lap oogling Purity, her white shirt stretched tightly across her luscious breasts and knotted above her naked mid-section. This ain't innocence, thought Small, it's seduction. The birds were few and far between but when they came they landed in Small's lap. Small probed his sensuous nether lip with a finger. The moment was not yet.

Purity sat on the bed hugging her knees. "I can't talk to anybody as freely as I talk to you, Ruby. Let's become truc friends! I don't really have any true friends. Wolford is so busy. Matt and I are friends but Matt is a man and so old fashioned." Purity sighed. "True men are so scarce, Ruby. Rhinehardt seems so learned. He knows so much about the Bible and he's going to stick by you. My mother always said never marry a handsome man. But then Rhinehardt isn't ugly. The more I see of Rhinehardt the more I like him. It's so cute the way he winks at me, te-he."

"Oh," lamented Ruby, "you don't have to tell me, Purity. Rhinehardt winks at all the girls. I used to be jealous but Rhinehardt can't help himself, poor thing."

"But you're loyal and true, Ruby."

"It can't be helped. Rhinehardt tells me that I am to remain true blue and I do my best, dear, putting up with what any sensible person like yourself sees as humiliation and mistreatment. Oh Purity—! If only I could tell you the whole truth my troubled mind might find some peace."

"Oh Ruby—please tell me."

"I need a true friend too, Purity. But I fear if I told you the whole truth our friendship would be dashed to smithereens."

"Ruby, tell me anything!"

"Can I trust you, Purity?"

"Oh yes, Ruby—!"

"I've got Rhinehardt by the thumbs. It may look like Rhinehardt Grueber is using me, but of course I'm really running the show. There's a woman behind every man, isn't there? And I'm it. But I fear Rhinehardt is about to go off his marbles. Since we first struck our partnership Rhinehardt has changed. Oh for the pastoral past on our little farm before we hit the road. Rhinehardt was always so dependable, always there walking just ahead of me down the primrose path."

"You make domestic life sound beautiful, Ruby."

"Married life is wonderful, my dear. It's hard, but worth it. If Rhinehardt is unfaithful—I might say as he has been in the past—far be it from me to interfere."

"Oh Ruby, I wasn't thinking of trying to seduce your husband."

"It might be good for Rhinehardt. All Rhinehardt has is me." Talldorf was anxious as a rat between two pieces of cheese. "Purity, your tenderness, your gentleness lead me to believe that you wouldn't betray me. Would your lips be sealed? Would Rhinehardt never know I told you what I am sworn never to tell?"

"Tell, Ruby—!"

Small pounded on the bedroom door. "What's goin on in there? Open up! I don't like ya bein in the bedroom with my wife, Purity. Why don't ya turn on some lights? Come outta there you two, I got a little item to show ya about that nut you work with, Purity."

Small read aloud:

" 'PIS, Nero: Agent Documents New Assassination Theory.

FIB Agent Wolford Vamp has put together an amazing string of coincidences which he claims will knock the government's assassination case into a cocked hat. According to Agent Vamp, Just Plain Bill was one member of a grand conspiracy designed to overthrow the United States government. Agent Vamp claims to be in possession of evidence that proves the murder of President Quiggley was ordered at the highest echelons of the U.S. military.' "

"Wolfie's famous!" cried Purity.

"Wolfie's rabid," said Small. "If Wolfie had his way most people would be in concentration camps."

"Matt says that Wolfie's mind is one in a million, Rhinehardt. I've typed so much for Wolford that I know his theory by heart but I never believed anyone believed it. Do you remember those window washers who were with the President on television? Well Wolford says they're in on it. I don't know what to think. What do you think, Rhinehardt? Wolford can't find them listed in the window washer's union."

"Wolfie couldn't find em if he was lookin at em," said Rhinehardt. "And ya oughta learn about unions too, Purity. Unions screw the worker."

"Absolutely!" avowed Ruby. "Rhinehardt is absolutely right about unions. They'll rob the working man blind. The mad and greedy-fisted money-sucking whore-mongers who run our government run the unions too, Purity dear."

"Gracious." Purity batted her lashes.

"You're young and you ain't seen much, Purity," Small assured her. "Rhinehardt Grueber has struggled for his bread with the sweat of his brow,

Genesis 7:11. I could show you a few things. Give Daddy Rhiney a little squeeze."

Opening his eyes on the sunlight of morning Talldorf was elated he had not betrayed Small and himself to Purity. If Purity were never to know him it was only a tragedy that other star-crossed lovers had known before them. This thought stole away the joy with which he awakened. He looked at Small sleeping in his blanket under the coffee table and was grateful his moral strength had preserved the gentle Small through another night. He thought of dear Purity sleeping beyond the bedroom door and a lump rose in his nightgown. He carefully unfolded his muslin dress and mournfully climbed into it, but felt much better as he straightened the skirts. They must carefully preserve their false identities with evil on every hand. Talldorf shuddered: He had almost spilled the beans. He was cheerful as they walked to the Cruciform but Small could not abide cheer in view of the danger in which they lived.

"Don't be cheerful! Be clear sighted like me. We gotta see em comin before they get us."

"Poor Small, it's been a terrible strain for you since we had to put on our disguises, but they're working well—"

"They better!"

"Purity hasn't suspected a thing. And I'll never tell her."

Small exploded. "Why would you tell her? Don't consider it one little bit. That broad is Wolfie's right hand man! She'd have us behind bars in a minute. You just might do something like that!"

"Never never, Small!" Talldorf suffered because he could not tell Small of last night and so prove his discretion.

Small glumly carried his bucket out a window on the fourteenth floor.

Maybe O'Toole would pay them before they finished. But then he would never finish. "Don't bother about streaks, Ruby. And don't drag your heels like yesterday. There's nothin but suspicious characters around here. Don't forget how hot we are."

He could have stood all day with one leg in the window and one out lecturing Talldorf because the work was odious. Small resented every move with brush or squeegee. The hell with streaks. His rags dangled unused. He accidentally cracked a pane with the handle of his window brush, which had never happened in all his career. He saw Wolfie pass on the walk below and the two who followed him; they entered the casino. Small hurried back along the ledge, found Talldorf three windows behind and upbraided him.

"You think they can't nail us anytime? Well they can! Damn your quality work. Stick close!"

But Wolfie did not appear. Each window was worse than the last. Small imagined himself climbing in windows, sacking bureau drawers, lifting pillows, withdrawing wallets. Everyone was sheep for the slaughter. Why should the casino get it all? Such thoughts put Small in even a fouler mood.

At a corner of the building he sat down wearily dangling his legs. Beyond the American flag, whipping at the end of the pole two stories below, he saw a suspicious car pull to the curb. Four men emerged, and one of them was a Chinaman. Small leaped to his feet and raced back along the ledge.

"The place is crawling with cops! Some of then got to be after Talldorf and Small. I think one of them's Yang Yin. I always suspected he was an agent of LeMight!"

"No!" said Talldorf.

"Yes!" insisted Small. "They're the slickest. Did you ever meet a Chinaman you could understand?"

Small hurried back to his bucket greatly excited. Why didn't the Feds make their move? They would never take Small alive. He peered cautiously into each window before touching it with his brush. He glared at the old couple from the edge of the window. She wore a gray bun on her head, and she was knitting. He was staring into space. On the table between them was a plate of cookies and two glasses of milk. Small squinted for ICEmen in disguise. He was braced to spring down the ledge in either direction. No one in the rooms appeared suspicious which confirmed Small's suspicions. There was no limit to which LeMight would not go to put out the lights of a dangerous man like Small.

Small pulled his hat brim low. Each moment that the four new agents, and one of them was a Chinaman, failed to reappear from the building Small's tension grew. None of them would have guts to step out on the ledge with him. Doubtless they would try to pounce from a window.

To calm himself Small thought of Purity's sleek form against the silk sheets. This made him twitch. If they made it back to the apartment Purity would be his. There was no other way. A wanted man can't live with danger and death every moment without distraction. That's why women were in the world. That's what Purity was for. It wasn't Talldorf, sitting all the time on Purity's bed, who needed distraction. Talldorf was distracted enough. Talldorf didn't take any of this seriously, Small suspected, which outraged him. He scrubbed viciously at the murky pane. Talldorf was a bag of rocks he had been dragging around for years. What good was he? Small leaned against the wall between windows and mopped sweat from his brow. He needed a cool shower. He needed to lie with Purity's soft flesh trembling in his hairy arms. Adultery will probably excite her, thought Small. He jerked upright and peered into the next window. The drapes were drawn.

"I know you niggers and redskins now. I'm the biggest redskin nigger of you all! Now they're after orphans. But watch out, Small's wide awake! Make a move. I'll wipe you out from LeMight down to Wolfie. They'll find Small's the nigger that invented peanuts, they'll think they got Sitting Bull by the tail when they close in on Small!"

Small jumped when the drapes leaped back.

"I've caught up with you, Rhiney!" sang Ruby.

"Damn your cheerfulness! Have you seen the four agents and one of em's a Chinaman?"

"No, Rhinehardt dear."

"Then you ain't lookin!"

"Are you sure they're agents, Rhinehardt?"

"I know a cop when I see one, Talldorf!"

"Shouldn't you call me Ruby on the job?"

"Yes! Ruby! It's good you're half awake, Talldorf. If we make it back to the apartment I got to relax. Any minute could be our last. Carry on!"

Not all afternoon did Small lay eyes on Wolfie or the two agents who followed him or the four and one of them was a Chinaman.

At day's end the fourteenth floor was finished.

"Are we stopping for coffee, Rhiney? I'm pooped."

"I got to hurry home and relax. You go out tonight. Enjoy a movie. Go window shop or somethin. You need a good time once in a while to take the pressure off all the lies you been tellin Purity."

"I'd enjoy just being at home, Small."

"Go out. I need peace and quiet."

"Purity and I can take a walk."

"Go alone. Here, we'll go in the drugstore for a quick coffee. Order me one. I'm going to the back of the store. Toothpaste."

Small crushed the cardboard box and flushed it down the toilet. He sighted the light fixture through one of the rubbers. Talldorf didn't know the score. Would Talldorf ever know the score? Small stepped into the shower. Talldorf had borne it well. Furbush had raised her eyebrows and offered to accompany Rhinehardt's luckless spouse, but Small had forbidden it. "She needs a little excitement," he had growled. Furbush had cocked her head listening for the worm. Small's eyes glittered as he scrubbed his pelt. Purity was interested but she didn't know it yet. Underneath her fancy clothes was a steaming wilderness. She didn't know that yet either. His skin tingled, his virility stirred. Small bounded from the shower and ripped Purity's comb through his matted locks before the mirror. He tucked the rubber into the towel flap, opened the door, and sank his toes into the shaggy carpet.

Small switched off the television and sat down on the couch beside Purity.

"Naked we come into the world and naked we go out: Exodus 13.3. Don't let nakedness offend ya, Purity. Take a good look. Women like men with hair on their chest. Don't look shocked."

"I—I'm not shocked, Rhinehardt—"

"I can see you ain't had much experience with men Purity. You're old enough. I got a personal interest in ya. I seen how ya look at me. You're curious. Ya reek of sex, Purity."

Small's nose twitched. Furbush's hair stood on end. He grabbed Purity's wrist and jerked her to her feet.

"I infatuate ya, Purity."

"I don't love you, Rhinehardt —! I—love someone else."

"Love don't have nothin to do with it. There ain't no need to put it off no longer."

Small put his arms around Purity's waist and waltzed her backward across the carpet.

"Please, Rhinehardt! Let me go. I—I love Wolford!"

Small let go and leaped back.

"That Gestapo bungler?"

"Wolford is very exceptional, Rhinehardt!"

"Oh dumb! Purity, you're so dumb! It ain't your fault. You was raised wrong. They gave you a bra when you was four years old. I shoulda known cause ya look like a woman don't mean ya are one. Ya think I don't belong in your nice civilized world. You ain't nothin but a high school broad. You bore me. Keep your Wolfies, your police, your fraud—"

"Please, Rhinehardt..."

"Don't Rhinehardt me! And don't prance in front of me with your tits hangin out. And I'm gonna tell ya something else, just cause I'm curious if an innocent child like you is a good American or a human being, the name ain't Rhinehardt. The name is Small, S-M-A-L-L. Did ya ever hear that name before? It's my name. Your boyfriend thinks I'm a great desperado. That's how smart he is. And Ruby Grueber, that flat-chested floozie ya feel so sorry for is, in reality, my lieutenant, Rudolph Victor Talldorf."

"Talldorf and Small—!"

"So, light shines through the cobwebs. How would ya like ta see a sweet guy like Ruby Grueber fry in the electric chair? Wolfie wants to burn us both. That's the kinda guy your Wolfie is. Dumb. Talldorf and Small standing right under his nose. You believe everything ya read in the papers. You believe in Mine and Death and Wink. You believe in moon and June. You believe everything but the truth.

"You won't wake up till your boyfriend's got you in the gas chamber. Now listen good, Purity," Small aimed his finger at her perfect nose. "I'm gonna educate ya about America. America is pretense. America is a con game of greed and you and all your respectable fellow citizens are gettin took. Your lives is hamburger for the profit machine. You're sellin your souls a dime a dozen. Run after your Wolfie, you pathetic lemming. He's leading ya straight ta hell but Small ain't losin no sleep over it." Small threw his towel on the coffee table and brasenly stalked to his blanket, rolled up and lay down.

"If ya want to see two innocent men burn in the chair pick up the phone and give your Nazi boyfriend a call."

When Small awoke in the morning Purity was gone.

Small shook Talldorf awake.

"Jump into your bloomers! Ain't no time to be hangin around crumbling middle class America."

Small didn't explain the need for such haste. He said it was Friday, the day for executions, that he felt them closing in, but that Talldorf shouldn't worry because Small was in command.

"Ha, Talldorf!" Small was looking in the window of the Straight Shooter Cafe. "Let's say hello to Wolfie."

"Rhinehardt—!" Talldorf hurried after, his heart skipping. Small tapped Wolfie on the shoulder.

"You're Wolfie Vamp, the FIBman."

"Why yes I am—" and seeing who addressed him Wolfie sneered.

"Yeah, it's just the humble Gruebers, spreaders of light. I seen ya sittin here dreamin, Wolfie, and since I ain't used up my good deed for the day I wanted to point out you been followed for the last two days by a couple of killers."

Wolfie's eyes grew round.

"The two cold fish in the second booth," said Small. "Eatin pancakes, eggs over easy, sausage, juice and coffee. ICEman expense accounts no doubt. One other thing: Purity Furbush is lookin for you with hot news. God bless America. She relies on smart cops like you. Me and my frau wish you a healthy and happy day."

The lobby of the Cruciform was abustle in the lovely morning hour. One-armed bandits glittered like mercenaries in rank and file before green felt pastures where the big boys played. Talldorf and Small passed through the crowd and up the wide staircase where brass rails gleamed. They went through the Private door into O'Toole's inner office. He was on the phone:

"Yes Sir, certainly Sir. I know Sir. No, no Sir, I'm not at all displeased — I'm grateful, you know that Sir—" O'Toole made a pained face. "My men will be watching Sir. On their toes. Yes. Thank you Sir. I'll be in touch."

"Small," O'Toole tossed a key. "Lock that door you guys came through. Foxy!" he said into the intercom. "I got the video eye on your office in case we get visitors. Coffee for three on the double, and buzz me the second anyone unfamiliar shows. Show em some leg, honey. Help is right around the corner. Get me Bix!"

"Bix? Loose the bloodhounds. Four squares and one's a Chinaman. A Chinaman. From China! How the hell do I know? Shake em down and bring em in. Stay on it!"

Foxy swayed in with a silver tray. Small snorted and ignored her.

"O'Toole, I seen those four."

"Where?" O'Toole sloshed coffee onto his desk.

"Yesterday. I saw em get out of this plain brown car. They're Feds. One of em's a Chinaman. LeMight sent em. They're after me and Talldorf."

"Jesus, what's next? The Big Man knows about em already. The Big Man thinks they got something on *me*."

"Relax, It's me and Talldorf they want. Those four and one of em's a Chinaman come straight from LeMight. They come to ice us."

"Nobody knows you guys are Talldorf and Small," said O'Toole.

"Rhinehardt, I mean Small, has been under a great strain," explained Talldorf who had lit up one of O'Toole's cigars. "I try to get him to relax."

"Crazy, am I? Talldorf, I'm tellin you we're in the biggest battle we ever been in! Keep your eyes open today or you'll be in LeMight's thumb screws tomorrow."

"Look, Small, my men will bring those four in and the Chinaman too. I"m going to pay you guys off right now. Nobody gives a damn if the windows are clean." O'Toole hit the intercom, "Foxy, get your finger out of your panties and bring two Gs in here."

O'Toole riffled the hundreds into a pile before Small. Small had thought if the money was in his hands he would leave in a minute and was surprised that it made no difference.

"I'm stickin this out to the last pane, O'Toole. Stick this in your bra, Talldorf. If they get me you escape to the ladies room. Get to the airport and buy a ticket to Manchuria, it's closer to Paradise. I'll be there some day."

Finally Rudolph was unnerved by Small's certainty that evils were about to overcome them.

"I'd never leave you, Small. I'll be right at your side. Do you think there's danger?"

"They don't have a chance against A. Small, Talldorf. Not all of LeMight's men. I welcome them. I hope they come right now!"

"There's a big mistake here," said O'Toole. "Nobody's after anybody."

Small stuck up a thumb as he climbed out the thirteenth floor window. And it was just as he had hoped. Wolfie was striding up the walk, and seeing Small he shook his fist. Small removed his black hat and sailed it into the morning sky. He made muscles and jumped up and down on the ledge. From a plain car that pulled up to the curb the two who had been shadowing Wolfie emerged, and behind them came the four, two by two, and one of them was a Chinaman.

"It's them, ha ha ha!" yelled Small through the window. "I'll meet you at the service stairs! Charge!"

Talldorf ran down the carpeted hall like a giant flushed turkey, water from his bucket splashing the walls. He terrorized a lady tourist whose husband blanched and froze against the wall as Talldorf thundered past.

Small raced along the ledge thirteen floors above the strolling tourists. Rubber peeled from his tennies as he skidded around a corner of the cross and raced with his beard flattened in the wind toward the service stairs. Who was the Chinaman? The Chinaman was the one! Get the Chinaman!

The Chinaman was rising to meet him.

When Wolfie had strode through the Cruciform's front doors O'Toole's men, who knew him, took note of his determined pace nor did they mistake the two who followed Wolfie and then their eyes fell on the four and one of them was a Chinaman, and Bix leading, O'Toole's men materialized from slot machine players in Hawaiian shirts, from the barber shop, from the nearest lounges and turned from behind potted plants to close on the four in a solid ring which unaccountably did not hold the Chinaman. Aware at last of thundering footsteps Wolfie had turned and was gathered into the chill arms of the two ICEmen. If he thought to reach for his .38 Police Special it was already, by a professional legerdemain not within his competence, in the pocket of the ICEman on his right and Wolfie said only, "What — ?" before the toxin from the needle jabbed into his breast froze his tongue and riveted his eyeballs nor did he know his feet had left the floor as the ICEmen whisked him out the service entrance. The plain brown car chauffeured by Private First Class Howard Spaff, Jr. stationed beneath the floor of the desert was waiting, and Wolfie was stuffed stiff as a dead man into the back seat, the door slammed and Pfc. Spaff stomped on the gas as ordered.

None resisted Bix and his men but implored in terror to be taken to Mr. O'Toole. "That's exactly where you're going," announced Bix. "Hey! Where's the Chinaman?"

The Chinaman was speeding toward the thirteenth floor in an elevator he alone commanded.

Small vaulted the railing onto the service porch as Talldorf arrived in a skid of swirling skirts. "Get them before they get us!" yelled Small not an instant before the Chinaman appeared flying along the hall toward them like a Peking duck right into the iron claw of Small who snagged him by his impeccable tie. This was a strange bird: this Chinaman was not Yang Yin.

"Who are you!" demanded Small.

"Yin Yang," chattered the Chinaman.

"LeMight sent you!" charged Small.

"Oh great warlord you something! Spare life of humble servant!"

"You're an ICEman!"

"Yin Yang less than nothing!"

"You're lying!"

"You mighty hairy man fire eyes of jade lord of creation allow humble Yin Yang poor insurance man sell you policy cheap!"

"Small's the one man in town who don't need insurance you devil! I'll make you talk English!" And with this he leaped.

What human commander does not arrive at his Waterloo? Small had long known the frontal assault was the most costly maneuver in battle. What madness then to fling himself into the face of the illusory Chinaman who stood in the door. It appeared to Talldorf that Small floated over the Chinaman who in his terror sought only to avoid the onslaught of this maddest of all Occidentals. Small sailed over the railing of the 13th floor like a man given wings.

The world was at his feet and Small knew terror, abandoned for the first time since the orphanage to an authority not his own.

Teetering at the railing Talldorf dropped his bucket in horror, his heart falling in a banshee wail: "*Small* —!" for the end of the world had come upon him.

Small glimpsed the gold ball of the flagpole a floor below and reached, his fingertips only grazing that cold gold grasped instead the red and white stripes which could not hold him as the flag sheared trailing like a banner and Small flew spread-eagled toward the concrete parking lot below.

Talldorf flung himself down the stairs a flight in two steps spiraling like a shot dove his one intent to catch his friend, even gaining, he thought, on the dark tumbling form trailing the red white and blue.

As stories of glass flashed past, Small saw the house of mirrors of years before — "*Short* —!" seeing not Short's ancient face but the loving eyes and golden ringlets of the Angel turning him in her arms as if to rest his wrinkled brow against her breasts and Small believed when *Dies Irae*! the end!

Small smashed at maximum velocity into the cosmic compost pile of a Nero City Disposal truck on the way to the dump. Talldorf saw him drop like a rock into a fetid swamp, lemon rinds rising in a golden mist scattering on the pavement, blown on the wind as the truck wheeled onto the Strip and sped away.

"*Madre de Dios*! Pedro, what de hell was dat!" said Jose in the cab.

"*Quien sabe*, Jose? Gringos loco don't you know? Trow a body in de truck probly, save de money for bury somebody. Trow away everyting here. Trow away de people. We jus haul it dump it. One more year we got de money go home to paradise. Let de gringo trow hemself away. Light de refer. I'm coming down, man, ha ha ha! Crazy country, eh Jose? *Ummmmm* — Primo Oaxaca! We flying home!"

The latest medical procedures and equipment were thrown into action as the attendants whisked Small out of the ambulance.

The emergency staff closed the tuna can wound in Small's forehead with 27 stitches, tweezed coffee grounds, glass, and toothpicks from his battered flesh and rushed him off to X-ray while Talldorf paced and smoked. The skull pictures came back negative. No bones were broken, no organs smashed. Dr. Fish was confident there was brain damage.

Talldorf signed Small's surrender papers.

"I'll put Small into your hands, Dr. Fish. What else can I do? I'm not a doctor. I'm not a woman either. Don't be fooled by these earrings or this dress. I can explain everything. You see my partner — Oh! Poor Small. Do whatever must be done to save Small's life. I don't know what I'll do without him. Just wander around I guess with no destination, no goal —"

"We'll just take a few cc's from this arm for a change," said the lab technician cheerfully as he uncorked his needle and plunged it into Small's vein.

They hauled Small off for an extensive series of tests while Talldorf sat in the chair beside the empty bed. When they brought Small back the nurse came in and sank a hollow steel shaft into his ass.

"For the pain," she explained.

They pasted electrodes to Small's temples, banged his knees with hammers, stuck a rubber tube up his anus and jammed him onto a bedpan.

Small lay silent, his green eyes flashing.

"Speak to me, Small," Talldorf pleaded.

Small said nothing. What could Small say?

"He's a lucky man," said Dr. Fish shining a penlight into Small's pupils. "No reaction. Blink your eyes, Mr. Small. Hmmmmm. Don't worry about a thing, Mrs. Small. There may be aphasia, loss of memory, even a fugue state — lucky devil! Tomorrow we'll get another picture of his brain. Nothing to it. I need the practice."

O'Toole paced the room.

"Small, why won't you speak to me? At least talk to Talldorf. Go on, Talldorf, get off your dead ass and try it again."

"Small," Talldorf said. "You're in Travelers Hospital. See, O'Toole? Small's eyes are wide open. Hi, Smally, it's me, Talldorf. How are you feeling? You fell thirteen stories, Small. Fortunately the garbage truck — "

"Hey, Small. It's O'Toole. The casino sent over these flowers. I got papers you gotta sign. We got good insurance. I bought a terrific policy from three guys and a Chinaman. Your bills are covered. It's on the house, enjoy yourself. If you need a surgeon or a shrink you got it. The only thing Cradle To The Grave Inc. don't pay for is keeping you on a backward of a mental hospital the rest of your life. Not funny, huh Small?"

Small stared past the faces of his two old friends. A slice of yellow mountain sunlight melted on the plaster wall. He felt perfectly relaxed. His body floated on the mattress. He was amazed that neither Talldorf nor O'Toole took notice of the beautiful diaphanous creature who hovered near. Small's eyes closed. Dying wasn't bad.

"Come back, Small!" shouted O'Toole. "You gotta sign these papers!'

"I think we should let Small rest, O'Toole. As Small's partner I'll be happy to fulfill any contractual obligations incurred by the company."

"Sign, Talldorf. This paper says Cradle To The Grave is responsible for Small's hospital bills. This one says Cradle To The Grave is responsible for his doctor bills. This one says Cradle To The Grave is not responsible. Don't worry about it. Here's a pen. It won't do any good to read the policy. I know how your mind works. Sign!"

Talldorf's grief was as cramped as his penmanship. He maintained an all night vigil in the chair beside the blanket-covered shape of his friend and mentor.

O'Toole gave him the long eye when he arrived with the morning paper. "You guys made the front page again, Talldorf. Congratulations. But you didn't get the headline."

'AGENT MURDERED

'The bullet-riddled body of Wolford Vamp, Deputy FIBAgent in Nero, was discovered today in the trunk of an abandoned car on a lonely stretch of Sulphur Ridge Road...'

"I bought you a shirt and pants, Talldorf. Take off the dress. How's the patient? Hey Small! Look at the front page. He don't even blink. What the hell's he staring at? Speak, Small! Nothin. You gotta snap out of it, Small. I got an appointment, Talldorf. I hate the smell of hospitals. Cheer up, Small. It's obvious he's deaf, Talldorf. Give me a ring the moment he starts talkin."

As he hurried away four men with cold eyes, and one of them was a Chinaman, made their way toward the Cruciform to meet with Mr. O'Toole.

When Talldorf returned from breakfast Small's catheter had been removed and his bloody bandage changed. He was propped on pillows. His face looked like ten pounds of hamburger. When Matt Masterman entered Talldorf leaped from his chair.

"I suppose you're here to see me, Mr. Masterman. My partner Alexander Small has suffered an unfortunate accident. I happen to be Rudolph Victor Talldorf. The disguise was Small's idea. I chose the blanket and feathers of our red brothers, but Small insisted on the dress. Are you going to arrest me?"

"Nope." Matt fingered the brim of his Stetson.

"That's a great relief, Mr. Masterman. Let me shake your hand. No doubt you've known all along that Small and I are patriots and were no more responsible for the President's death than any of our fellow Americans.'

"Yup."

"I admit I'm very confused, Mr. Masterman, but I'm not guilty. I am guilty by inference perhaps? Allow me to extend my heartfelt condolences for Agent Vamp. I think Wolfie was killed by two ICEmen. I'd recognize those killers anywhere. Small and I could stay in Nero to turn state's evidence."

Masterman offered a patient glance.

Dr. Fish skipped into the room.

"Good morning, Mr. Small," he called cheerily. "How's the patient? Fit as a fiddle and ready to travel?" Dr. Fish pinched Small's cheek. "See? He feels that. Bureau Chief Masterman tells me that Mr. Small will be healthier in some place other than Nero, Mr. Talldorf."

"Do you want us out of town by sundown, sir?" asked Talldorf.

"I can't guarantee the safety of my own agents, Mr. Talldorf."

"You're going to be all right, Mr. Small!" Dr. Fish shouted into Small's ear. "His hearing should improve. His mental outlook? Hard to say. It could go either way. If you'll just sign this release, Mr. Talldorf. Give him two of these pills if he complains of pain, though I don't expect Mr. Small will be doing much complaining."

Talldorf pushed Small in a wheelchair down the hall and out the front door to the station wagon. He picked up the uncomplaining Small and set him in the front seat like a doll, propped and covered him with the khaki blanket, climbed somberly into the driver's seat and pointed the Pontiac up the steep mountain grade.

It was crystal clear to Small: There was a greater tactician abroad than he. He would not duel with powers from another dimension. There were laws to be observed of which gravity was merely an indication. Short and Snowball put themselves in the hands of the Angel who raised them up. The Angel had taken away his fear and Small felt he flew; to awake to this.

"Don't worry about anything, Small. I'll take care of you. Breathe the mountain air. Winter's coming I know, but we're going to find a sunny place in the Golden State. California here we come!" sang Talldorf.

A freight train snaked its way down through the snow sheds and across the trestles of the steep Sierra. The endless string of boxcars wound through the pine trees braked by five diesel engines.

"Look, Small! There's a man and a dog in that boxcar. A fellow traveler, a free man, Small. God bless you stranger!" Talldorf honked the horn and waved.

Joseph Pipestems Talldorf had won big ducking beneath the twisted bougainvillea that clung to the stucco above the side entrance to the Three Palms Motel. With squeegees and bucket Joe and his handsome black labrador had hopped the freight before the San Joaquin County Sheriff had gotten wind of the game. Lady Luck had led him from Fairbanks to Sacramento and would guide him one more time south to Miami. The box car jolted merrily and sparks flew from the iron wheels. Joe Talldorf waved to his son and Eightball's tail thumped the cardboard.

Behind closed lids Small searched inner corridors for the one with golden ringlets who had held him in her arms. Where now, he who thought to bend the world to his will? What was to be won but surrender to the greater Commander? Was Small to give up all for a vision he might never see again? What might man build that was not ashes in his hands? How the centuries marched over the heads of the dead and the living. Why raise a finger, why speak a word? He would come inevitable as an arrow to the end. He had danced on the high ledges. His dance had been nothing. His head was due as the price of failure and he had been spared.

Night had fallen as Talldorf tooled the old white Pontiac wagon up the grade approaching Downer Pass where the Upper Party ate each other up early in the American adventure.

"I'll bring us through. We'll see golden fruit on the trees and the silver moon over the ocean like you always wanted to see, Smally. It isn't far, it can't be far.

"Small, when the sun rises on this new day I want you to speak again. I want you to tell me how you like it. I know you're excited too but don't tell me now. Just save it up and speak to me when you see how wonderful it is. I'll turn on the heater. Everything works on this car, doesn't it? We're getting high, Smally. Do you see those patches of snow that stretch into the trees? Brrrrr. What if we were lost in the High Sierras? There isn't a man I'd rather be lost with than you. I never worry when I'm with you, Small, even in your present silent state. I'd follow you through the woods because I know you'd lead me out. Do you hear? Rest up, Small. Old Rudolph's at the controls."

A black cascade flashed white in the headlights, leaping boulders in its haste to water the bitter desert below. A little tear popped from Small's eye. His blood felt broken and sang a mournful song.

"If I see a cafe at the summit old Talldorf'll pull her in. We'll get coffee and donuts, ok? And I'll roll you a bone."

Despite the heater Talldorf shivered beneath O'Toole's wool shirt in the chill of the high snow country that flashed in the headlights, the dark forests, the echoing absence of his friend. He tucked the blanket around Small and slapped at his own knees as the cold wind whistled past the window like a dirge.

"Downer Pass!" cried Talldorf. "Did you see the sign? No coffee shop. Sorry, Small. Look, a star! See it, Smally?

Small saw the star.